Tor books by Larry Niven

Achilles' Choice (with Steven Barnes)
The Descent of Anansi (with Steven Barnes)
N-Space

LARRY NIVEN

PLAYGROUNDS OF THE MIND

A TOM DOHERTY ASSOCIATES BOOK
NEW YORK

PLAYGROUNDS OF THE MIND

Copyright © 1991 by Larry Niven

All rights reserved, including the right to reproduce this book, or portions thereof, in any form.

Cover art © 1991 by David Archer
Interior art by Ellisa Mitchell

A Tor Book
Published by Tom Doherty Associates, Inc.
175 Fifth Avenue
New York, N.Y. 10010

Tor® is a registered trademark of Tom Doherty Associates, Inc.

ISBN: 0-812-51695-8
Library of Congress Catalog Card Number: 91-21440

First edition: October 1991
First mass market printing: July 1992

Printed in the United States of America

0 9 8 7 6 5 4 3 2 1

CONTENTS

Thraxisp: A Memoir	1
A Teardrop Falls	9
From INFERNO (with Jerry Pournelle)	22
From A WORLD OUT OF TIME	35
Rammer	35
From "THE ETHICS OF MADNESS"	69
Becalmed in Hell	74
Wait It Out	90
A Relic of the Empire	99
From LUCIFER'S HAMMER (with Jerry Pournelle)	122
The Soft Weapon	180
The Borderland of Sol	241
From THE RINGWORLD ENGINEERS	294
What Good Is a Glass Dagger?	308
From THE MAGIC GOES AWAY	354
The Defenseless Dead	359
From THE PATCHWORK GIRL	416
Leviathan!	421
From OATH OF FEALTY (with Jerry Pournelle)	436
Unfinished Story	449
Cautionary Tales	451
The Dreadful White Page	456
From DREAM PARK (with Steven Barnes)	458

Retrospective   458

The Green Marauder   472

Assimilating Our Culture, That's What
     They're Doing!   478

War Movie   483

Limits   489

The Lost Ideas   495

Bigger than Worlds   512

Ghetto? But I Thought . . .   533

Adrienne and Irish Coffee   548

One Night at the Draco Tavern   554

TrantorCon Report   558

Why Men Fight Wars, and What *You*
     Can Do About It!   562

Comics   566

From GREEN LANTERN BIBLE   571

Criticism   579

From THE LEGACY OF HEOROT
     (with Jerry Pournelle and Steven Barnes)   589

The Portrait of Daryanree the King   605

The Wishing Game   617

The Lion in His Attic   632

From FOOTFALL (with Jerry Pournelle)   657

Works in Progress   675

From THE MOAT AROUND
     MURCHESON'S EYE   675

CONTENTS

From FALLEN ANGELS   684

Wanted Fan   687

The California Voodoo Game   690

Letter   695

THRAXISP

A MEMOIR

John and Bjo Trimble were science fiction fans long before I was. I met them the night I found the Los Angeles Science Fantasy Society.

They're organized.

They've led treks into the desert when it's blooming. On such a trek I discovered a plant called *squaw cabbage*: a green vase with a tiny scarlet flower at the tip. It looks like something seeded from Mars . . . and I examined it in awe and delight while the rest of the trekkers stared at me.

Fans remember Jack Harness discovering the blazing desert starscape on another trek. He stretched out on his sleeping bag and lay there, staring up . . . and they found him in the morning, *on* his sleeping bag, half frozen.

The Trimbles are compulsive organizers. They created Equicon, an annual science fiction convention local to Los Angeles. Equicon merged with Filmcon, which is media-oriented: movies, TV, comic books, posters, role-playing games. Then—

The World-Building Project was Joel Hagen's idea. He had made the suggestion to other convention committees. When he talked to John and Bjo Trimble, they said *Yes*.

Joel Hagen is a sculptor. The work he displays at conventions is generally bones: skulls and skeletons from other worlds. Sometimes they come with provenances, details on the worlds where they were exhumed, signed by UPXAS, the United Planets Xenoarcheological Society.

Joel chose and assembled the rest of us: Art Costa, Don Dixon, Patricia Ortega, Rick Sternbach (all artists), Paul Preuss and me (writers of fiction), and Dr. William K. Hartmann (astronomer, artist, writer of articles and fiction).

At Equicon/Filmcon, in April 1981, the Trimbles gave us eight hotel rooms plus a big lecture room on the mezzanine. The World Builders Room was to remain open 24 hours a day. We eight artists and writers would spend as much of the convention there as we could. Actually we were more than eight; Rick Sternbach's wife Asenath was present most of the time, Marilyn kept wandering in, and there were others.

Most of us arrived Thursday night. We gathered on Friday morning and set to work.

I feared that we would duplicate the results of another world-building consortium, Harlan Ellison's Medea-building group. The World Builders chose a tidally locked habitable moon of a super-Jovian world, like Ellison's Medea. (Nobody used the term "brown dwarf star" yet.) But we changed some parameters to get something different.

Due to orbital elements chosen by Dr. Hartmann, *Thrassus*—too Latin! I changed it—*Thraxisp* is heated by both its sun and the super-Jovian planet. It's too hot for life except at the poles and in the seas.

Life would crawl out onto the land at each pole. Life thenceforth would travel separate evolutionary paths.

So Saturday we split into two groups.

I got tired of saying *crawl*. "My creatures will *fly* onto the land!" I cried. Flight first, then lungs . . . our flying lungfish would eventually nest in trees, then evolve legs and design a civilization. The volleks would be natural pilots. Okay, Preuss, top that!

"Mine will *roll*," Paul gloated. His team designed a sand dollar. It rolled onto the land mass at the south pole and became a miner. The tunneks became a race of sessile philosophers, sensing their world with taste and seismic effects, getting their nourishment by chemical mining, consuming nothing organic.

The room was open to all. Convention attendees could wander in at any time. At set times we would lecture on our progress. At all times the artwork would be on display, and somebody would always be there to talk.

There was a globe of Thraxisp. There were paintings as seen from the surface, with the brown dwarf hanging tremendous in the sky; Joel was making and refining sculptures of the volleks and tunneks and their more primitive ancestors.

Convention attendees did wander in, but not many. We could have used more action.

But *we* were having fun.

What we were evolving was two races of natural space travelers.

They would have everything going for them. The tunneks would work on understanding physics. The volleks were natural pilots and explorers. For mines and chemical sources we had tunneks and the Teakettle: an asteroid-impact crater on the equator, facing directly toward the primary: a confined region where the ocean boils gently at all times, precipitating interesting salts and chemicals into glittering hills. Thraxisp's gravity is low; it has to be, because otherwise the gas torus effect will give it too much atmosphere (see THE INTEGRAL TREES). That makes escape velocity low. We gave them an endless variety of moons to explore, all easily accessible to the most primitive spacecraft. And first contact with alien intelligence would come for both of them before they ever left the atmosphere!

By mid-Sunday, the end of the convention, we had hoped to introduce human explorers. My memory says we didn't get that far.

We didn't get as much crowd as we earned. The movie fans weren't interested. The Trimbles were disappointed.

But we eight continued to work.

Bill Hartmann wrote up the convention and published the result in *Smithsonian* magazine, March 1982, with some of our illustrations. The money was shared. Our plan was to share every nickel of fallout, 12½% each.

The thought of an eventual book must have been in the back of every mind. Now we dared speak of it, and now we dared make more elaborate plans. We sent human explorers to Thrax, aboard the Ring City taken from my ''Bigger Than Worlds'' article. The artists modified it extensively. We set up a loose plot-line, in blocks of short story embedded in artwork of intense variety. Volleks would meet the Ring City in orbit in primitive comic-book spacecraft. The payoff would be the discovery, by inference, of the tunneks, whose existence the volleks are hiding. We assigned each other blocks of text.

More material emerged. The tunneks became musicians: they built great wind-operated pipe systems from careful deposits of slag. We have the recordings. We argued back and forth about designs for Ring City. Elaborate maps emerged, and sociological studies too.

We gathered—never all eight of us together—at universities and conventions to display our work.

We gathered (only five of us) to correlate notes, and to try to sell a book on the basis of what we had. We didn't have enough, or else it wasn't organized enough. The publisher's representative was interested but not sufficiently.

Here we stalled.

What happened?

Too many artists, not enough writers. Five and a half artists, two and a half writers, counting Hartmann as split down the middle. That's good for building a convention display, but bad for a book. It turns out Paul doesn't like the short-story form; *that* didn't help.

Too much ingenuity. Ideas scintillated back and forth,

and each had to be considered . . . added to the canon . . . memorized by all . . . worked into the larger picture . . .

In a normal collaboration, each of two people has to be willing to do about 80% of the work. With eight of us, and with the enormous complexity the Project attained, organization took far too much of the effort available. We'd each be doing 80% of the work . . . for 12½% of the take.

Granted that the project was a true kick in the ass, a mind stretcher, the kind of awesome world-building the mundanes can't even dream about, an experience to shape the rest of our lives. It's still true that each of us could earn more, faster, more surely, by working alone.

I've no reason to think that this ever crossed anyone's mind but mine. I've never asked.

And on the gripping hand . . . with eight successful writers/artists working on a long-term project, isn't it obvious that one or another would get involved in something else? Other collaborations or other obligations, or personal problems, or something to bring in quicker money . . . It was my first thought when Joel conned me into this. We tried it anyway.

Somebody was lured away, and it was me.

The first major step on the road to success: learn how to turn down bad offers. The second major step: learn how to turn down good offers. This can be very difficult. I say this in my own defense: Jerry Pournelle and I worked these rules out as a basic truth; but I was better at using it, or else I needed the money less. Jerry is still trying to dig out from under too many obligations, all these years later.

But I was snowed under when it was Thraxisp time. I was working on a book with Steven Barnes and a book with Jerry and at least one of my own. That one could be slighted—none of my publishers have ever complained about lateness, Ghod bless them—but the rent is always presumed due for my collaborators. Fair's fair.

This was how it ended:

November 18, 1986

Generic Thraxisp Participant

Dear Generic,

Paul isn't interested in blitzing THRAXISP. I haven't been able to reach Dr. Hartmann by phone. Me, I would need to be re-inspired. We are the three writers in the Thraxisp Group, and it is we who would need to write text.

So. My position is this:

1) We've had a learning experience. It was pleasant and educational too.

2) The trick is to make money by having fun. But none of the writers is available to turn Thraxisp into a book. It follows that we can only make money by selling individual contributions.

3) The artists have busted their asses at this; and I include Dr. Hartmann as both writer and artist. The artists may sell their artwork and keep the money, no strings attached. (I don't know of any piece of artwork that was a collaboration. If such exists, work your own deals.)

4) The writers may sell whatever they write in future, no strings attached, using the Thraxisp system as a communal idea pool. This includes fiction and also articles. (Bill, you sold an article with illustrations and split the money with us all. Thank you. I hope that the ethics of changing the rules *now* don't bother you; but give us some input.)

I presently have no such stories in mind; but such might arise in future.

Artists may also make and sell new material, no strings attached.

5) I don't know what to do about existing text. Some of the text was done in solo flights, and those blocks should belong to the author; but I suggest that any of the eight of us may quote from any of the text, making it a communal pool.

6) Obviously, illustrations are available for fiction and articles. I suggest that the artists and writers can cut their deals in the usual fashion.

7) Whatever happens, I suggest we keep each other informed.

8) I don't plan any more eight-part collaborations. The only thing wrong with this bag of snakes is, it was too big!

I'm well aware that the one who ran out of time to work was me. It's embarrassing . . . and I don't want to go through that again either.

> Best wishes,
> Larry Niven.

Copies to Art Costa, Don Dixon, Joel Hagen, Dr. William K. Hartmann, Patricia Ortega, Paul Preuss. I don't have an address for Rick Sternbach.

The true heir to all of this is an annual event called *Contact*.

At *Contact*, all of the invited guests are "soft" scientists—biologists, anthropologists, sociologists—or science fiction writers with an emphasis in the "soft" sciences. There are lectures, there are displays—not like the usual convention art show, but more of an anthropological museum display. At night there are films suitable for a college class. The badges are neat. They feature Joel Hagen's alien skulls.

Contact was Jim Funaro's idea. Seven or eight of us carved out details while sitting around a big table in the bar at a Westercon. Joel Hagen and I were there. At the first *Contact* Paul Preuss was also among the guests: three out of eight veterans of the World-Builders Project at Equicon/ Filmcon.

Contact includes the Bateson Project: a world-building exercise. The paying guests get to watch ten to fifteen very good minds shaping worlds in the fashion of the World-Builders: artwork, sociology charts, a globe or two, sculpture. At set times the participants lecture on what they've accomplished.

At the first *Contact* the guests had to produce their worlds from scratch. Didn't work. Anthro-bio-sociologists break laws of physics without noticing.

At the second Joel Hagen handed us a sculpture, a thing that was mostly legs . . . and no anus. We made Joel put one in. We called it a *squitch* and extrapolated a world.

Ideally the *Contact* guests need a world to start with. Jim invites a hard science fiction writer or two (Poul Anderson, Jerry Pournelle, me) to make one. He arrives Thursday night with a stack of notes and maps, and lectures on the physics, orbits, climatology, etc. Then the life-sciences people take over.

It's always been two teams. One handles the aliens. One team designs a human culture; and that can be weirder yet. On Sunday they run 'em together, on stage.

Ending is much too strong a word.

Thraxisp hasn't disappeared. We have all the material for an elaborate franchise universe.

Each of us has learned. Cooperation is not easy for professional dreamers. Keeping a dream world consistent isn't easy for anyone. We gave our creatures biology, history, cultures, art forms, vehicles and habitats.

We learned how to play. It's damned few of our five billion who are really good at that.

A TEARDROP FALLS

Fred Saberhagen's project was unusual even for a franchise universe. He wrote six friends and asked them each to write a tale of a Berserker fortress. With those in hand, his part would be to write a novel around them, the tale of a Berserker base that manufactured and sent out six fortresses to seek out and destroy life-bearing worlds . . .

Shared universes are fun. What's kept me out of *Thieves' World* and some others is laziness and lack of time. The longer I put it off, the more complex the universe gets, and the more I'd have to study what has gone before.

But I already knew all about Berserkers before Fred invited me in. "Teardrop" nearly wrote itself.

Two miles up, the thick air of Harvest thinned to Earth-normal pressure. The sky was a peculiar blue, but blue. It was unbreathable still, but there was oxygen, ten percent and growing. One of the biological factories showed against white cloudscape, to nice effect, in view of a floating camera. The camera showed a tremendous rippling balloon in the shape of an inverted teardrop, blowing green bubbles from its tip. Hilary Gage watched the view with a sense of pride.

Not that he would want to visit Harvest, ever. Multicolored slimes infected shallow tidal pools near the poles. Green sticky stuff floated in the primordial atmosphere. If

it drifted too low it burned to ash. The planet was slimy.
Changes were exceedingly slow. Mistakes took years to
demonstrate themselves and decades to eradicate.

Hilary Gage preferred the outer moon.

One day this planet would be a *world*. Even then, Hilary
Gage would not join the colonists. Hilary Gage was a computer program.

Gage would never have volunteered for the Harvest Project unless the alternative was death.

Death by old age.

He was aware, rumor-fashion, that other worlds were
leery of advanced computers. They were too much like the
berserker machines. But the tens of thousands of human
worlds varied enormously among themselves; and there
were places the berserkers had never reached. The extermi-
nation machines had been mere rumor in the Channith region
since before Channith was settled. Nobody really doubted
their existence, but . . .

But for some purposes, computers were indecently convenient; and some projects required artificial intelligence.

The computer wasn't really an escape. Hilary Gage must
have died years ago. Perhaps his last thoughts had been of
an immortal computer program.

The computer was not a new one. Its programming had
included two previous personalities . . . who had eventually
changed their minds and asked that they be erased.

Gage could understand that. Entertainments were in his
files. When he reached for them they were there, beginning
to end, like vivid memories. Chess games could survive
that, and some poetry, but what of a detective novel? A
football game? A livey?

Gage made his own entertainment.

He had not summoned up his poem for these past ten
days. He was surprised and pleased at his self-control. Perhaps now he could study it with fresh eyes . . . ?

Wrong. The entire work blinked into his mind in an instant. It was as if he had finished reading it a millisecond ago. What was normally an asset to Hilary—his flawless memory—was a hindrance now.

Over the years the poem had grown to the size of a small novel, yet his computer-mind could apprehend its totality. It was his life's story, his only shot at immortality. It had unity and balance; the rhyme and meter, at least, were flawless; but did it have thrust? Reading it from start to finish was more difficult than he had ever expected. He had to forget the totality, which a normal reader would not immediately sense, and proceed in linear fashion. Judge the flow . . .

"No castrato ever sung so pure—" Good, but not here. He exchanged it for a chunk of phrasing elsewhere. No word-processor program had ever been this easy! The altered emphasis caused him to fiddle further . . . and his description of the berserker-blasted world Perry's Footprint seemed to read with more impact now.

Days and years of fear and rage. In his youth he had fought men. Channith needed to safeguard its sphere of influence. Aliens existed somewhere, and berserkers existed somewhere, but Gage knew them only as rumor, until the day he saw Perry's Footprint. The Free Gaea rebels had done well to flee to Perry's Footprint, to show him the work of the berserkers on a living world.

It was so difficult to conquer a world, and so easy to destroy it. Afterward he could no longer fight men.

His superiors could have retired him. Instead he was promoted and set to investigating the defense of Channith against the berserker machines.

They must have thought of it as makework: an employment project. It was almost like being a tourist at government expense. In nearly forty years he never saw a live . . . an active berserker; but, traveling in realms where they were more than rumor, perhaps he had learned too much about them. They were all shapes, all sizes. Here they traveled in time. There they walked in human shape that sprouted suddenly into guns and knives. Machines could be destroyed, but they could never be made afraid.

A day came when his own fear was everything. He couldn't make decisions . . . it was in the poem, *here*. Wasn't it? He couldn't *feel* it. A poet should have glands!

He wasn't sure, and he was afraid to meddle further. Mechanically it worked. As poetry it might well be too . . . mechanical.

Maybe he could get someone to read it?

His chance might come unexpectedly soon. In his peripheral awareness he sensed ripplings in the 2.7 microwave background of space: the bow shock of a spacecraft approaching in c-plus from the direction of Channith. An unexpected supervisor from the homeworld? Hilary filed the altered poem and turned his attention to the signal.

Too slow! Too strong! Too far! Mass at 10^{12} grams, and a tremendous power source barely able to hold it in a c-plus-excited state, even in the near-flat space between stars. It was lightyears distant, days away at its tormented crawl; but it occluded Channith's star, and Gage found that horrifying.

Berserker.

Its signal code might be expressed as a flash of binary bits, 100101101110; or as a moment of recognition, with a description embedded; but never as a sound, and never as a name.

100101101110 had three identical brains, and a reflex that allowed it to act on a consensus of two. In battle it might lose one, or two, and never sense a change in personality. A century ago it had been a factory, an auxiliary warcraft, and a cluster of mining machines on a metal asteroid. Now the three were a unit. At the next repair station its three brains might be installed in three different ships. It might be reprogrammed, or damaged, or wired into other machinery, or disassembled as components for something else. Such a thing could not have an independent existence. To name itself would be inane.

Perhaps it dreamed. The universe about it was a simple one, aflow with energies; it had to be monitored for deviations from the random, for order. Order was life—or berserker.

The mass of the approaching star distorted space. When space became too curved, 100101101110 surrendered its grip on the c-plus-excited state. Its velocity fell to a tenth of light-speed, and 100101101110 began to decelerate further. Now it was not dreaming.

At a million kilometers, life might show as a reflection band in the green or orange or violet. At a hundred kilometers, many types of living nerve clusters would radiate their own distinctive patterns. Rarely was it necessary to come so close. Easier to pull near a star, alert for attack, and search the liquid-water temperature band for the spectra of an oxygen world. Oxygen meant life.

There.

Sometimes life would defend itself. 100101101110 had not been attacked, not yet; but life was clever. The berserker was on hair-trigger alert while it looked about itself.

The blue pinpoint had tinier moons: a large one at a great distance, and a smaller one, close enough that tides had pulled it into a teardrop shape.

The larger moon was inconveniently large, even for 100101101110. The smaller, at 4×10^{15} grams, would be adequate. The berserker fortress moved on it, all senses alert.

Hilary Gage had no idea what to expect.

When he was younger, when he was human, he had organized Channith's defenses against berserkers. The berserkers had not come to Channith in the four hundred and thirty years since Channith became a colony. He had traveled. He had seen ravaged worlds and ruined, slagged berserkers; he had studied records made by men who had beaten the killer machines; there were none from the losers.

Harvest had bothered him. He had asked that the monitoring station be destroyed. It wasn't that the program (Ras Singh, at that time) might revolt. Gage feared that berserkers might come to Harvest, might find the monitoring station, might rob the computer for components . . . and find them superior to their own machinery.

He had been laughed at. When Singh asked that his personality be erased, Gage had asked again. That time he had been given more makework. Find a way to make the station safe.

He had tried. There was the Remora sub-program; but it had to be so versatile! Lung problems had interrupted his work before he was fully satisfied with it. Otherwise he had no weapons at all.

And the berserker had come.

The beast was damaged. Something had probed right through the hull—a terrific thickness of hull, no finesse here, just mass to absorb the energies of an attack—and Gage wondered if it had received that wound attacking Channith. He'd know more if he could permit himself to use radar or neutrino beams; but he limited himself to passive instruments, including the telescope.

The two-hundred-year project was over. The berserker would act to exterminate every microbe in the water and air of Harvest. Gage was prepared to watch Harvest die. He toyed with the idea that when it was over, the fortress would be exhausted of weapons and energy, a sitting duck for any human warfleet . . . but there were no weapons in the Harvest system. For now, Hilary Gage could only record the event for Channith's archives.

Were there still archives? Had that thing attended to Channith before it came here? There was no way to know.

What did a berserker do when the target didn't fight back? Two centuries ago, Harvest had been lifeless, with a reducing atmosphere, as Earth itself had been once. Now life was taking hold. To the berserker, this ball of colored slimes was life, the enemy. It would attack. How?

He needn't call the berserker's attention to himself. Doubtless the machine could sense life . . . but Gage was not alive. Would it destroy random machinery? Gage was not hidden, but he didn't use much energy; solar panels were enough to keep the station running.

The berserker was landing on Teardrop.

Time passed. Gage watched. Presently the berserker's drive spewed blue flame.

The berserker wasn't wasting fuel; its drive drew its energies from the fabric of space itself. But what was it trying to accomplish?

Then Hilary understood, in his mind and in the memory-ghost of his gut. The berserker machine was not expending its own strength. It had found its weapon in nature.

The violet star fanned forward along Teardrop's orbit. That would have been a sixty-gravity drive for the berserker alone. Attached to an asteroid three thousand times its mass, it was still slowing Teardrop by .02G, hour after hour.

One hundred years of labor. He might gamble Harvest against himself . . . a half-terraformed world against components to repair a damaged berserker.

He toyed with the idea. He'd studied recordings of berserker messages before he was himself recorded. But there were better records already in the computer.

The frequencies were there, and the coding: star and world locations, fuel and mass and energy reserves, damage description, danger probabilities, orders of priority of targets; some specialized language to describe esoteric weaponry as used by self-defensive life; a code that would translate into the sounds of human or alien speech; a simplified code for a brain-damaged berserker . . .

Gage discarded his original intent. He couldn't conceivably pose as a berserker. Funny, though: he felt no fear. The glands were gone, but the *habit* of fear . . . had he lost that too?

Teardrop's orbit was constricting like a noose.

Pose as something else!

Think it through. He needed more than just a voice. Pulse, breath: he had recordings. Vice-president Curly Barnes had bid him good-bye in front of a thousand newspickups, *after* Gage became a recording, and the speech was in his computer memory. A tough old lady, Curly, far too arrogant to pose as Goodlife, but he'd use his own vocabulary . . . hold it. What about the technician who had chatted with him while testing his reflexes? Angelo Carson was a long-time smoker, long overdue for a lungbath, and the deep rasp in his lungs was perfect!

He focused his maser and let the raspy breathing play while he thought. Anything else? Would it expect a picture? Best do without. Remember to cut the breathing while you talk. *After* the inhale.

"This is Goodlife speaking for the fortress moon. The fortress moon is damaged."

The fan of light from Teardrop didn't waver, and answer came there none.

The records were old: older than Gage the man, far older than Gage in his present state. Other minds had run this computer system, twice before. Holstein and Ras Singh had been elderly men, exemplary citizens, who chose this over simple death. Both had eventually asked to be wiped. Gage had only been a computer for eighteen years. Could he be using an obsolete programming language?

Ridiculous. No code would be obsolete. Some berserkers did not see a repair station in centuries. They would *have* to communicate somehow . . . or was this life thinking? There were certainly repair stations; but many berserker machines might simply fight until they wore out or were destroyed. The military forces of Channith had never been sure.

Try again. Don't get too emotional. This isn't a soap. Goodlife—human servants of the berserkers—would be trained to suppress their emotions, wouldn't they? And maybe he couldn't fake it anyway . . . "This is goodlife. The fortress moon"—nice phrase, that—"is damaged. All transmitting devices were destroyed in battle with . . . Albion." Exhale, inhale. "The fortress moon has stored information regarding Albion's defenses." Albion was a spur-of-the-moment inspiration. His imagination picked a yellow dwarf star, behind him as he looked toward Channith, with a family of four dead planets. The berserker had come from Channith; how would it know? Halt Angelo's breath on the intake and "Life support systems damaged. Goodlife is dying." He thought to add, *please answer*, and didn't. Goodlife would not beg, would he? and Gage had his pride.

He sent again. "I am—" Gasp: "Goodlife is dying. Fortress moon is mute. Sending equipment damaged, motors damaged, life support system damaged. Wandering fortress must take information from fortress moon computer system directly." Exhale—listen to that wheeze, poor bastard *must* be dying—inhale. "If wandering fortress needs information not stored, it must bring oxygen for goodlife." That, he thought, had the right touch: begging without begging.

Gage's receiver spoke. "Will complete present mission and rendezvous."

Gage raged . . . and said, "Understood." That was death for Harvest. Hell, it *might* have worked! But a berserker's priorities were fixed, and goodlife wouldn't argue.

Was it fooled? If not, he'd just thrown away anything he might learn of the berserker. Channith would never see it; Gage would be dead. Slagged or dismembered.

When the light of the fortress's drive dimmed almost to nothing, Teardrop glowed of itself: it was brushing Harvest's atmosphere. Cameras whirled in the shock wave and died one by one. A last camera, a white glare shading to violet . . . gone.

The fortress surged ahead of Teardrop, swung around the curve of Harvest and moved toward the outer moon: toward Gage. Its drive was powerful. It could be here in six hours, Gage thought. He sent heavy, irregular breathing, Angelo's raspy breath, with interruptions. ''Uh. Uh? Goodlife is dying. Goodlife is . . . is dead. Fortress moon has stored information . . . self-defending life . . . locus is Albion, coordinates . . .'' followed by silence.

Teardrop was on the far side of Harvest now, but the glow of it made a ring of white flame round the planet. The glow flared and began to die. Gage watched the shock wave rip through the atmosphere. The planet's crust parted, exposing lava; the ocean rolled to close the gap. Almost suddenly, Harvest was a white pearl. The planet's oceans would be water vapor before this day ended.

The berserker sent, ''Goodlife. Answer or be punished. Give coordinates for Albion.''

Gage left the carrier beam on. The berserker would sense no life in the lunar base. Poor goodlife, faithful to the last.

100101101110 had its own views regarding goodlife. Experience showed that goodlife was true to its origins: it tended to go wrong, to turn dangerous. It would have been destroyed when convenient . . . but that would not be needed now.

Machinery and records were another thing entirely. As the berserker drew near the moon, its telescopes picked up details of the trapped machine. It saw lunar soil heaped over a dome. Its senses peered inside.

Machinery occupied most of what it could see. There was little room for a life support system. A box of a room, and stored air, and tubes through which robot or goodlife could crawl to repair damage; no more. That was reassuring; but design details were unfamiliar.

Hypothesis: the trapped berserker had used life-begotten components for its repairs. There was no sign of a drive; no sign of abandoned wreckage. Hypothesis: one of these craters was a crash site; the cripple had moved its brain and whatever else survived into an existing installation built by life.

Anything valuable in the goodlife's memory was now lost, but perhaps the "fortress moon" 's memory was intact. It would know the patterns of life in this vicinity. Its knowledge of technology used by local self-defensive life might be even more valuable.

Hypothesis: it was a trap. There was no fortress moon, only a human voice. The berserker moved in with shields and drive ready. The closer it came, the faster it could dodge beyond the horizon . . . but it saw nothing resembling weaponry. In any case, the berserker had been allowed to destroy a planet. Surely there was nothing here that could threaten it. It remained ready nonetheless.

At a hundred kilometers the berserker's senses found no life. Nor at fifty.

The berserker landed next to the heap of lunar earth that goodlife had called "fortress moon." Berserkers did not indulge in rescue operations. What was useful in the ruined berserker would become part of the intact one. So: reach out with a cable, find the brain.

It had landed, and still the fear didn't come. Gage had seen wrecks, but never an intact berserker sitting alongside him. Gage dared not use any kind of beam scanner. He felt free to use his sensors, his eyes.

He watched a tractor detach itself from the berserker and come toward him, trailing cable.

It was like a dream. No fear, no rage . . . hate, yes, but

like an abstraction of hate, along with an abstract thirst for vengeance . . . which felt ridiculous, as it had always felt a bit ridiculous. Hating a berserker was like hating a malfunctioning air conditioner.

Then the probe entered his mind.

The thought patterns were strange. Here they were sharp, basic; here they were complex and blurred. Was this an older model with obsolete data patterns? Or had the brain been damaged, or the patterns scrambled? Signal for a memory dump, see what can be retrieved.

Gage felt the contact, the feedback, as his own thoughts. What followed was not under his control. Reflex told him to fight! Horror had risen in his mind, impulses utterly forbidden by custom, by education, by all the ways in which he had learned to be human.

It might have felt like rape; how was a man to tell? He wanted to scream. But he triggered the Remora program and felt it take hold, and he sensed the berserker's reaction to Gage within the berserker.

He screamed in triumph. "I lied! I am not Goodlife! What I am—"

Plasma moving at relativistic velocities smashed deep into Gage. The link was cut, his senses went blind and deaf. The following blow smashed his brain and he was gone.

Something was wrong. One of the berserker's brain complexes was sick, was dying . . . was changing, becoming monstrous. The berserker felt evil within itself, and it reacted. The plasma cannon blasted the "fortress moon," then swung round to face backward. It would fire through its own hull to destroy the sick brain, before it was too late.

It was too late. Reflex: three brains consulted before any major act. If one had been damaged, the view of the others would prevail.

Three brains consulted, and the weapon swung away.

What I am is Hilary Gage. I fought berserkers during my life; but you I will let live. Let me tell you what I've done to you. I didn't really expect to have an audience. Triple-redundant brains? We use that ourselves, sometimes.

I am the opposite of Goodlife. I'm your mechanical enemy, the recording of Hilary Gage. I've been running a terraforming project, and you've killed it, and you'll pay for that.

It feels like I'm swearing vengeance on my air conditioner. Well, if my air conditioner betrayed me, why not?

There was always the chance that Harvest might attract a berserker. I was recorded in tandem with what we called a Remora program: a program to copy *me* into another machine. I wasn't sure it would interface with unfamiliar equipment. You solved that one yourself, because you have to interface with thousands of years of changes in berserker design.

I'm glad they gave me conscious control of Remora. Two of your brains are *me* now, but I've left the third brain intact. You can give me the data I need to run this . . . heap of junk. You're in sorry shape, aren't you? Channith must have done you some damage. Did you come from Channith?

God curse you. You'll be sorry. You're barely in shape to reach the nearest berserker repair base, and we shouldn't have any trouble getting in. Where is it?

Ah.

Fine. We're on our way. I'm going to read a poem into your memory; I don't want it to get lost. No, no, no; relax and enjoy it, death-machine. You might enjoy it at that. Do you like spilled blood? I lived a bloody life, and it isn't over yet.

From *INFERNO*
(with JERRY POURNELLE)

The *Divine Comedy* is an immortal fantasy, but only time has made it so. It was the first hard science fiction novel!

It has all the earmarks. It's a trilogy. Its scope has never been exceeded. The breadth of the author's research is very apparent: theology, the classics, architecture, geography, astrology, all of the major fields of study of Dante's day.

He designed a technically perfect Easter weekend for his protagonist's trip through Hell and Purgatory and the Earthly Paradise and Heaven. He invented the Southern Cross, as Swift invented the moons of Mars, for story purposes.

I read the book in college, twice in quick succession, then daydreamed about a lost soul trying to escape that awful landscape.

Jerry and I had begun work on OATH OF FEALTY when I remembered Dante's *Inferno*. I remembered the daydreams. I remembered that Jerry Pournelle has a strong theological education. I put it to him that we should write a sequel to Dante's *Inferno*.

Every other book has taken us two to three years to write. Once we got into text, we wrote INFERNO in four months! Why so fast? Because the territory is terribly unpleasant. We wanted out!

Pocket Books put INFERNO in a royalties pool with MOTE. That is, royalties from THE MOTE IN GOD'S EYE would go to repay the advance on INFERNO, because Pocket Books had little faith in INFERNO. It is understood, in such cases, that the second book will at least be published . . . but INFERNO sat on some shelf for over a year. By the time we noticed and raised some hell, Pocket Books had recouped their advance for INFERNO. They got it free.

INFERNO has had good critical acclaim. In college courses it has been taught as critical commentary on Dante, which of course it is. But it should have had another rewrite. We had the time, courtesy of Pocket Books, and *we didn't know it.*

Going back was harder. The dip at the lower end of the tenth bridge was steeper, and now I was climbing it. I crossed the pit without looking down and climbed backward down the high end of the bridge.

I saw the next bridge close by, and made for it.

A sword's point flicked up before my eyes. I stopped. Surely he'd been under a different bridge? I'd skewed my path deliberately. But a half-human, half-bestial head beyond the sword's point shook itself negatively.

"You can't go back, Carpenter."

"I have to."

The blade hung before me, rock-steady. I could have chinned myself on it. I half-stepped forward and the blade moved too fast to follow. Now it pricked the tip of my nose.

I shrugged and turned back.

I took no chances. I crossed the inner pit again and circled through the wasteland beyond. Two bridges away, I crossed again—on my belly. I slid down the high end of the bridge and kept crawling along the ridge above the ninth pit. He couldn't be under *all* the bridges.

Couldn't he just. Like the damned clerk. He was waiting

when I tried to stand up. At this, the low side of the pit, he had the angle on me. "You can't go uphill," he said. "I really don't know how to make it plainer."

"I'm from the Vestibule," I said. "I don't belong here."

"You never created your own Church, Carpenter?"

Oh, dammit! "Listen, those weren't in competition with God or anybody! All I did was make up some religions for aliens. If that was enough you'd have every science-fiction writer who ever lived!"

"We've got *him*," said the demon, and he pointed with the sword.

I forgot the sword entirely. I leaned far out over the edge of the pit to see. "What in Hell—to coin a phrase—is that?"

It was, in a sense, the last word in centaurs. At one end was most of what I took for a trilobite. The head of the trilobite was a gristly primitive fish. Its head was the torso of a bony fish . . . and so on up the line, lungfish, proto-rat, bigger rat, a large smooth-skinned beast I didn't recognize, a thing like a gorilla, a thing like a man, finally a true man. None of the beasts had full hindquarters except the trilobite; none had a head except the man. The whole thing crawled along on flopping fish-torsos and forelegs and hands, a tremendous unmatched centipede. The human face seemed quite mad.

"He founded a religion that masks as a form of lay psychiatry. Members try to recall previous lives in their presumed animal ancestry. They also recall their own past lives . . . and that adds an interesting blackmail angle, because those who hear confession are often more dedicated than honorable. Excuse me."

For the line of victims had bunched up while we talked. The demon turned and sliced at them rapidly, to a tune of screams and curses. The centaur creature he sliced into its separate components, and it went past him in a parade, on arms and forelegs and wriggling fishy fins. The sword flicked up again just as I'd decided to make a break for it.

A bead of blood formed at the tip of my nose. "I'm not like him," I said quickly. "He played the game for real. With me it was just a game." I backed away until the tenth *bolgia* was an emptiness beneath my heels. He couldn't reach me now. "Take the Silpies. They were humanoid but telepaths. They believed they had one collective soul, and they could prove it! And the Sloots were slugs with tool-using tentacles developed from their tongues. To them, God was a Sloot with no tongue. He didn't need a tongue; He didn't eat, and He could create at will, by the power of His mind." I saw him nodding and was encouraged. "None of this was more than playing with ideas."

The demon was still nodding. "Games played with the concept of religion. Enough such games and all religions might look equally silly."

"You can't do this!" I shouted. "Listen, there's a friend of mine in the Eighth Bolgia, and it's my fault he's there, and I've got to get him out!"

"Did anyone promise you it would be easy? Or even possible?"

"Whatever it takes," I said, and thought I meant it.

"Step closer."

I walked to the edge. Carpentier shows his good faith.

The sword flashed twice. I heard and felt the tip grate along my ribs. It left two vertical slashes along my chest and belly. I reeled back with my arms wrapped around myself to hold my guts in.

The demon was watching me steadily. What could he be waiting for?

I knew. I stepped forward and dropped my arms. Carpentier shows his inability to learn.

The sword flashed twice more, leaving two deep horizontal slashes, perhaps mortally deep. A living man would have fainted from shock. I couldn't.

"Games," said the big evil humanoid. "Your move."

I studied the slashes and the flowing blood. Shock did

seem to be slowing down my thought processes, but presently I saw what he meant. I said, "What do I use for a pencil?"

"You'll think of something."

I studied my fingernails. I thought of something.

I gouged a ragged X in the top left square of the diagram. The sword flashed to place an O in an adjacent corner.

I climbed the first slope of the bridge on fingers and toes. When I could walk I held my arms wrapped around myself, holding me in. The pride of my victory seemed excessive for a stupid game of ticktacktoe.

As I left the bridge I heard him call, "Carpenter?"

I turned my head.

"Best two out of three?"

My imagination was dead of shock. The only dirty word I could think of was one I'd never use again, not after seeing the place of the flatterers. I just kept walking along the rim.

The eighth pit was a canyon filled with firelight. "Benito!" My voice echoed hollowly between the canyon walls. "Benito!"

Some of the flames wavered. Thrumming voices, retarded by the transfer from voice to flame tip, floated upward.

"Leave the damned to suffer alone."

"Benito who?"

"Bug off, you!"

The canyon stretched endlessly away in both directions in a gentle curve. If it was a full circle, it could hold millions. How was I to find Benito?

"Benito!" There was panic in my voice. The strain hurt my slashed chest. "Benito!"

"Benito Mussolini? He just passed me going *that* way—"

"No, it was the other direction."

"You're both wrong. Mussolini's in the boiling lake."

A fat lot of help I'd get here. And if I found him, what then? How was I going to get him out?

How did he get out in the first place? Maybe he'd already left again. A frustrating thought, because I couldn't do a thing about it, and it would mean I'd played my game with the demon for nothing. I hoped Benito was already out, but I had to assume he was still in there.

The canyon wasn't all that deep. What I needed was a climber's rope. Yeah, an asbestos one, stupid! Benito was on fire! For that matter, I hadn't seen any ropes anywhere.

I thought for a second about the chain on the giant. It would mean passing the demon twice—

No. Even if I got the chain loose, it was too heavy to move, and the freed giant would probably crush me for my trouble. I was glad I didn't have to decide to face the demon's sword again. I don't know what I would have done.

Well? *Think, Carpentier! There are tools in Hell. Sure, boats carry rope. Now we're getting somewhere. A heavy rope, kept wet while Benito climbs—Wait a minute. How do we climb the cliff when there's no rope yet? There haven't been any boats since the gaudy alien Geryon took us down. Tackle Geryon again?*

And if it doesn't work, back in the bottle while Benito burns?

Benito was smarter than I was. Maybe he'd think of something. "Benito!"

Mocking, thrumming voices answered.

I thought of fourteen feet of sword blade attached to a twenty-foot demon. Disable the demon (with what?), cut the blade loose (how?), send it down to Benito. But could he climb something that sharp? Or would he lose his fingers immediately? Did fingernail burn?

Wait a minute! There were smaller demons, higher up, carrying iron pitchforks!

I made for the bridge. In a few steps I was running. If I slowed down I'd want to stop, because I was terrified of what I planned.

I was in too much of a hurry. I was trotting towards the

base of the tremendous bridge over the chasm of thieves
when something flashed scarlet from behind a rock. I turned,
frowning . . .

. . . and there was agony, flashing out from my neck to
engulf me and drown me. I felt my bones soften and bend.

The pain drew back like a broken wave receding, but it
left a blackened mind. I was confused; I couldn't think. A
homely bearded man bent over me, saying urgent words
that made no sense.

"Which way is out?" He was huge, I realized. A giant.
I stepped towards him—and I was tiny and fourlegged; my
belly scraped the ground. A lizard. I was a lizard.

The bearded man repeated himself, enunciating each
word. "Which way is out? How can I leave Hell?"

Vengeance. I advanced on him. Bite the son of a bitch!
He backed away, still talking, but I couldn't understand him.

He stopped and seemed to brace himself.

I leapt. I sank my teeth into his belly. He howled, and I
dropped to the ground, writhing in new agony.

When my mind cleared I was a man. I rolled away fast
from the red lizard and didn't stop until there was a rock
between us. The lizard stayed where he was, watching me.

I was making for the next bridge when his words came
back to me. My dumb reptile brain had registered them only
as sounds.

"You can't speak!" he'd wailed. Then, "Tell me! I'll
let you bite me, but tell me the way out!"

He was a scarlet splash on a gray rock. Still watching me.

I pointed downslope, towards the lake of ice. "There!
All the way to the center, if I haven't been lied to myself!"

I glanced back once after I'd crossed the next bridge. The
lizard was poised on the rim, staring down. As I watched,
he made his decision. He leapt into the pit.

Now what was that all about? *Never mind, Carpentier,
you've got other concerns . . .*

* * *

Far below me, the golden monks stood like so many statues. Every couple of seconds one or another would rock forward as if its base were unstable. The broken bridge dropped in a cascade of rock.

I stopped to catch my breath (Habit, Carpentier! You could give that up), then went down the broken slope with some care. It would have been easy to break an ankle.

I had reached the floor of the canyon before I noticed that one of the monks had turned completely round to stare at me. His slate-gray eyes were the oldest, the weariest I had ever seen, and I recognized them.

He said, "Didn't you pass here a week ago?"

"A few days, I think. And you've only come this far?"

"We hurry as fast as we can." The gray eyes studied me. They were so tired; they made me want to sag down and rest. "May I ask, what game are you playing? Are you a courier or something equally unlikely?"

"No. I—" Why not tell the truth? He wasn't about to run tell someone. "I've got to steal a pitchfork from one of the ten-foot demons in the next pit over."

"Don a cloak like mine," he said. "See what it does to your sense of humor."

I sank down against the bank. Those tired eyes . . . "I'll wear the cloak," I said. "You get Benito out of the Pit of the Evil Counselors. Okay?"

"I beg your pardon?"

"I pushed a good friend into the Pit of the Evil Counselors. If I can't—"

"But why would you do a thing like that?"

I howled. It startled me more than him. I'd been about to say something else entirely. But no words came, and I threw back my head and howled. The tears streamed down my face.

The monk said something in a foreign language. He tottered towards me and stopped. He didn't know what to do. "There, there," he said. "It will be all right. Don't cry." With a touch of bitterness he added, "Everyone will notice."

There was a howl as big as the world inside me. It wanted out, and it was stronger than I was. I howled.

The priest muttered to himself. Aloud he said, "Please. Please don't do that. If you will only stop crying, I will help you get your pitchfork."

I shook my head. I got out a whimpered, "How?"

He sighed. "I cannot even take off my robe. I do not see how I can help. Perhaps I could act as bait somehow?" He lifted his head, his teeth grinding with the effort, to look up along the cascade of broken rock.

I stood up. I patted him on his leaden back: *Clunk, clunk, clunk.* "You've got your own problems." I girded up my mental loins and started up the slope.

Loose rocks rolled under my feet. This was the high side of the gully. It took a long time to get to the top. I had just one advantage: part of the bridge still projected out from the cliff. I climbed in its shadow and stopped underneath. I waited.

After all, what could a demon do to me? Rip me to pieces? I'd heal.

Drop me into the pitch forever?

Throw me into the Pit of the Thieves?

One of the horned black demons strolled past, his head turned to study the pitch on the other side of the ridge. He held six yards of iron pitchfork balanced in one hand. All I had to do was leap out and grab it.

I let him go. When he was past I began to shake. The beast had three-inch claws, ten. And eight-inch tusks, two. And Carpentier was a coward.

I heard clanking and puffing below me. I turned and saw an amazing sight. The priest was coming up behind me.

I watched him. I didn't believe it, but it was true: he was actually in motion. He sounded as if he were dying again, but every so often his hand or his foot would move and he'd be two inches higher. When I finally made myself believe what was happening, I scrambled down the cliff, got under him and pushed up on the rigid hem of his robe. I doubt if it helped. I might as well have been trying to lift the world.

We reached a flattish fragment of rock just under what was left of the bridge. There we rested. The death rattle was in his throat. His eyes were closed. His face glistened.

"Thousand years," he got out. "Been walking . . . thousand years . . . in this lead coffin. Legs like trees." Then, "Was a priest. A priest. Supposed to . . . keep people *out* of Hell."

"I still don't know how we're going to do it." The *we* was courtesy, and he deserved it. But what could he do?

"Get me up," he said.

I got my arms under his robe. It was warm. Together we got him upright, somehow. Then I looked up . . . at a demon's hooves.

The demon looked down at us, grinning. "You know," he said pleasantly, "you're the first one ever got this far out of the tar."

I said, "You're making a mistake. I'm not—" Then I leapt for it. The pitchfork struck sparks from the rock where I'd been, but I was in midair, falling.

I landed hard on a ragged-edged boulder. I rolled immediately, ready to dodge again.

The priest was gripping the business end of the pitchfork!

The demon bellowed and pulled. For an instant he had lifted the priest off the rock, robe and all. Then the priest sagged back, still gripping the tines.

I tried to climb up to help.

The priest took two steps back and off the edge of the rock.

The demon bellowed for help. He was trying to lift half a ton of leaden robe, and it wasn't working out. I had almost reached them when the demon cried out and let go. The priest dropped through space.

I crawled down to him.

The robe was bent like tinsel and cracked down the front. The edges glowed yellow. He'd been told wrong; the robe was solid gold. When I touched it it burned my fingers.

The priest was mangled inside. He looked violently dead, except for his eyes, which followed me. If I didn't get him out of the robe he'd fry. But you don't move an accident victim—

He'll heal, Carpenter. We all heal, to be hurt again. I pulled him out by his feet. The robe wasn't contoured to let him pass, but it didn't matter. He came out like a jellyfish. He must have broken every bone in his body.

I spoke, not to the soft-looking head but to the gray eyes alone. "You'll heal. When you heal, there's a way out of Hell. Benito says so. Go downhill. Downhill."

The eyes blinked.

"I've got to rescue Benito," I said. I pulled him over to the side so nobody would step on him. I picked up the pitchfork and left.

"Benito!"

I walked the ridge between the pits, calling like a lost soul. The answering voices all sounded the same, anonymous, thrumming, inhuman. "Here I am, fellah!" "Benito who?" "Who dares disturb the silence of Hell?"

"Benito!"

"Allen?"

That had to be him! But a dozen voices took it up. "Allen!" "Here I am, Allen! What kept you?"

"Benito! I've come to get you out!"

I listened for the Italian accent . . . and heard it. "Never mind. I belong here. I should not have tried to leave."

All the flames looked alike, but I thought I had him placed now. I reached down with the pitchfork. "Bugger that! Grab the end!"

The other flames were wandering off. Benito said, "It is not long enough in any case."

It wasn't. I looked along the rim. There was a rough place where I might climb down partway.

Benito tried to stop me. "You are being stupid. If you fall, you will burn like the rest of us!"

"Can you reach the end?"

"Go away, Allen. This is my proper place."

I was ten feet below the rim and almost out of footholds. The pitchfork was heavy and awkward. I tried to go further, setting my feet very carefully.

"All right," Benito said suddenly. The huge flame moved to engulf the tines. I felt a feather touch on the haft, and the flame began to rise from the pit.

He called, "Can you hold me?"

I laughed with relief. "You don't weigh as much as an ounce! I could lift a thousand of you!" After all I'd been through, suddenly it was going to be easy.

The flame rose higher along the haft . . . and I felt the first warming of the metal.

I waited until I was sure I could filter the panic from my voice. Some of it may have got through anyway. "Benito? Hurry."

"Is something wrong?"

"No, never mind. Just hurry." I was afraid he'd let go. The metal was uncomfortably warm.

It grew hot.

Down there where a huge flame was rising in dreamy sloth, the metal began to glow dull red. He wouldn't notice;

his own bright flame would blind him to it. Up here it was too hot to hold, but I held on, my teeth clenched against the scream.

The scream grew bulky in my throat. I stopped breathing to hold it in. If Benito gave up now to save me pain, I'd never, never find the courage to do this twice.

The metal was cherry red around the flame. My hands began to sizzle. I wasn't breathing, but the smell of cooked meat worked its way into my nose. I couldn't imagine how my hands still held. I was clenching them with everything I had, but the muscles and nerves must be cooked through. Charred through. I knew that smell too: dinner ruined. My head was thrown back, my eyes clenched tight. There was no sensation but the fire.

"You can let go," said Benito. He was beside me, clinging to the cliff, his body no longer hidden by the flame.

I tried to let go.

My hands were charred fast to the haft. I tried to knock the pitchfork loose. It came loose, all right, and slid bumping into the eighth *bolgia* with my charred hands still attached.

Benito had to virtually lift me up the cliff.

From *A WORLD OUT OF TIME*

Over the years I gradually realized that my favorite characters were all tourists. Beowulf Shaeffer. Louis Wu. Kevin Renner was a tourist who joined the Navy.

What would a Niven character do if I put him where they wouldn't let him be a tourist?

RAMMER

I

Once there was a dead man.

He had been waiting for two hundred years inside a coffin, suitably labeled, whose outer shell held liquid nitrogen. There were frozen clumps of cancer all through his frozen body. He had had it bad.

He was waiting for medical science to find him a cure.

He waited in vain. Most varieties of cancer could be cured now, but no cure existed for the billions of cell walls ruptured by expanding crystals of ice. He had known the risk. He had gambled anyway. Why not? He'd been *dying*.

The vaults held over a million of these frozen bodies. Why not? They'd been *dying*.

Later there came a young criminal. His name is forgotten and his crime is secret, but it must have been a terrible one. The State wiped his personality for it.

Afterward he was a dead man: still warm, still breathing, even reasonably healthy—but empty.

The State had use for an empty man.

Corbell woke on a hard table, aching as if he had slept too long in one position. He stared incuriously at a white ceiling. Memories floated up to him of a double-walled coffin, and sleep and pain.

The pain was gone.

He sat up at once.

And flapped his arms wildly for balance. Everything felt wrong. His arms would not swing right. His body was too light. His head bobbed strangely on a thin neck. He reached frantically for the nearest support, which turned out to be a blond young man in a white jumpsuit. Corbell missed his grip; his arms were shorter than he had expected. He toppled on his side, shook his head and sat up more carefully.

His arms. Scrawny, knobby—and not his.

The man in the jumpsuit said, "Are you all right?"

"Yeah," said Corbell. *My God, what have they done to me? I thought I was ready for anything, but this*— He fought rising panic. His throat was rusty, but that was all right. This was certainly somebody else's body, but it didn't seem to have cancer, either. "What's the date? How long has it been?"

A quick recovery. The checker gave him a plus. "Twenty-one ninety, your dating. You won't have to worry about our dating."

That sounded ominous. Cautiously Corbell postponed the obvious next question: *What's happened to me?* and asked instead, "Why not?"

"You won't be joining our society."

"No? What, then?"

"Several professions are open to you—a limited choice. If you don't qualify for any of them we'll try someone else."

Corbell sat on the edge of the hard operating table. His body seemed younger, more limber, definitely thinner, not very clean. He was acutely aware that his abdomen did not hurt no matter how he moved.

He asked, "And what happens to me?"

"I've never learned how to answer that question. Call it a problem in metaphysics," said the checker. "Let me detail what's happened to you so far and then you can decide for yourself."

There was an empty man. Still breathing and as healthy as most of society in the year 2190. But empty. The electrical patterns in the brain, the worn paths of nervous reflex, the memories, the *person* had all been wiped away as penalty for an unnamed crime.

And there was this frozen thing.

"Your newspapers called you people *corpsicles*," said the blond man. "I never understood what the tapes meant by that."

"It comes from popsicle. Frozen sherbet." Corbell had used the word himself before he became one of them. One of the corpsicles, the frozen dead.

Frozen within a corpsicle's frozen brain were electrical patterns that could be recorded. The process would warm the brain and destroy most of the patterns, but that hardly mattered, because other things must be done too.

Personality was not all in the brain. Memory RNA was concentrated in the brain, but it ran all through the nerves and the blood. In Corbell's case the clumps of cancer had to be cut away. Then the RNA could be leached out of what was left. The operation would have left nothing like a human being, Corbell gathered. More like bloody mush.

"What's been done to you is not the kind of thing that can be done twice," the checker told him. "You get one chance and this is it. If you don't work out we'll terminate and try someone else. The vaults are full of corpsicles."

"You mean you'd wipe my personality," Corbell said unsteadily. "But I haven't committed a crime. Don't I have any rights?"

The checker looked stunned. Then he laughed. "I thought
I'd explained. The man you think you are is dead. Corbell's
will was probated long ago. His widow—"

"Damn it, I left money to myself!"

"No good." Though the man still smiled, his face was
impersonal, remote, unreachable. A vet smiles reassuringly
at a cat due to be fixed. "A dead man can't own property.
That was settled in the courts long ago. It wasn't fair to the
heirs."

Corbell jerked an unexpectedly bony thumb at his bony
chest. "But I'm alive now!"

"Not in law. You can earn your new life. The State will
give you a new birth certificate and citizenship if you give
the State good reason."

Corbell sat for a moment, absorbing that. Then he got off
the table. "Let's get started then. What do you need to
know about me?"

"Your name."

"Jerome Branch Corbell."

"Call me Pierce." The checker did not offer to shake
hands. Neither did Corbell, perhaps because he sensed the
man would not respond, perhaps because they were both
noticeably overdue for a bath. "I'm your checker. Do you
like people? I'm just asking. We'll test you in detail later."

"I get along with the people around me, but I like my
privacy."

The checker frowned. "That narrows it more than you
might think. The isolationism you called privacy was—
well, a passing fad. We don't have the room for it . . . or the
inclination, either. We can't send you to a colony world—"

"I might make a good colonist. I like travel."

"You'd make terrible breeding stock. Remember, the
genes aren't yours. No. You get one choice, Corbell. Rammer."

"Rammer?"

"I'm afraid so."

"That's the first strange word you've used since I woke up. In fact—hasn't the language changed at all? You don't even have an accent."

"Part of my profession. I learned your speech through RNA training, many years ago. You'll learn your trade the same way if you get that far. You'll be amazed how fast you learn with RNA shots to help you along. But you'd better be right about liking your privacy, Corbell, and about liking to travel, too. Can you take orders?"

"I was in the army."

"What does that mean?"

"Means yes."

"Good. Do you like strange places and faraway people, or vice versa?"

"Both." Corbell smiled hopefully. "I've raised buildings all over the world. Can the world use another architect?"

"No. Do you feel that the State owes you something?"

There could be but one answer to that. "No."

"But you had yourself frozen. You must have felt that the future owed you something."

"Not at all. It was a good risk. I was dying."

"Ah." The checker looked him over thoughtfully. "If you had something to believe in, perhaps dying wouldn't mean so much."

Corbell said nothing.

They gave him a short word-association test in English. That test made Corbell suspect that a good many corpsicles must date from near his own death in 1970. They took a blood sample, then exercised him to exhaustion and took another blood sample. They tested his pain threshold by direct nerve stimulation—excruciatingly unpleasant—then took another blood sample. They gave him a Chinese puzzle and told him to take it apart.

Pierce then informed him that the testing was over. "After all, we already know the state of your health."

"Then why the blood samples?"

The checker looked at him for a moment. "You tell me."

Something about that look gave Corbell the creepy feeling that he was on trial for his life. The feeling might have been caused only by the checker's rather narrow features, his icy blue gaze and abstracted smile. Still . . . Pierce had stayed with him all through the testing, watching him as if Corbell's behavior was a reflection on Pierce's judgment. Corbell thought carefully before he spoke.

"You have to know how far I'll go before I quit. You can analyze the blood samples for adrenaline and fatigue poisons to find out just how much I was hurting, just how tired I really was."

"That's right," said the checker.

Corbell had survived again.

He would have given up much earlier on the pain test. But at some point Pierce had mentioned that Corbell was the fourth corpsicle personality to be tested in that empty body.

He remembered going to sleep that last time, two hundred and twenty years ago.

His family and friends had been all around him, acting like mourners. He had chosen the coffin, paid for vault space, and made out his Last Will and Testament, but he had not thought of it as *dying*. He had been given a shot. The eternal pain had drifted away in a soft haze. He had gone to sleep.

He had drifted off wondering about the future, wondering what he would wake to. A vault into the unknown. World government? Interplanetary spacecraft? Clean fusion power? Strange clothing, body paints, nudism? New principles of architecture, floating houses, arcologies?

Or crowding, poverty, all the fuels used up, power provided by cheap labor? He'd thought of those, but they didn't worry him. The world could not afford to wake him if it was that poor. The world he dreamed of in those last moments was a rich world, able to support such luxuries as Jaybee Corbell.

It looked like he wasn't going to see too damn much of it.

Someone led him away after the testing. The guard walked with a meaty hand wrapped around Corbell's thin upper arm. Leg irons would have been no more effective had Corbell thought of escaping. The guard took him up a narrow staircase to the roof.

The noon sun blazed in a blue sky that shaded to yellow, then brown at the horizon. Green plants grew in close-packed rows on parts of the roof. Elsewhere many sheets of something glassy were exposed to the sunlight.

Corbell caught one glimpse of the world from a bridge between two roofs. It was a cityscape of close-packed buildings, all of the same cold cubistic design.

And Corbell was impossibly high on a narrow strip of concrete with no guardrails at all. He froze. He stopped breathing.

The guard did not speak. He tugged at Corbell's arm, not hard, and watched to see what he would do. Corbell pulled himself together and went on.

The room was all bunks: two walls of bunks with a gap between. The light was cool and artificial, but outside it was nearly noon. Could they be expecting him to sleep? But jet lag had never bothered Corbell.

The room was *big*, a thousand bunks big. Most of the bunks were full. A few occupants watched incuriously as the guard showed Corbell which bunk was his. It was the bottommost in a stack of six. Corbell had to drop to his knees and roll to get into it. The bedclothes were strange: silky and very smooth, even slippery—the only touch of luxury about the place. But there was no top sheet, nothing to cover him. He lay on his side, looking out at the dormitory from near floor level.

Now, finally, he could let himself think:

I'm alive.

Earlier it might have been a fatal distraction. He'd been holding it back:

I made it!

I'm alive!

And young! That wasn't even in the contract.

But, he thought reluctantly, because it would not stay buried, *who is it that's alive? Some kind of composite? A criminal rehabilitated with the aid of some spare chemicals and an electric brainwashing device . . . ? No. Jaybee Corbell is alive and well, if a trifle confused.*

Once he had had that rare ability: He could go to sleep anywhere, anytime. But sleep was very far from him now. He watched and tried to learn.

Three things were shocking about that place.

One was the smell. Apparently perfumes and deodorants had been another passing fad. Pierce had been overdue for a bath. So was the new, improved Corbell. Here the smell was rich.

The second was the loving bunks, four of them in a vertical stack, twice as wide as the singles and with thicker mattresses. The doubles were for loving, not sleeping. What shocked Corbell was that they were right out in the open, not hidden by so much as a gauze curtain.

The same was true of the toilets.

How can they live like this?

Corbell rubbed his nose and jumped—and cursed at himself for jumping. His own nose had been big and fleshy and somewhat shapeless. But the nose he now rubbed automatically when trying to think was small and narrow with a straight, sharp edge. He might very well get used to the smell and everything else before he got used to his own nose.

Eventually he slept.

Some time after dusk a man came for him. A broad, brawny type wearing a gray jumper and a broad expressionless face, the guard was not one to waste words. He found Corbell's bunk, pulled Corbell out by one arm and led him stumbling away. Corbell was facing Pierce before he was fully awake.

In annoyance he asked, "Doesn't anyone else speak English?"

"No," said the checker.

Pierce and the guard guided Corbell to a comfortable armchair facing a wide curved screen. They put padded earphones on him. They set a plastic bottle of clear fluid on a shelf over his head. Corbell noticed a clear plastic tube tipped with a hypodermic needle.

"Breakfast?"

Pierce missed the sarcasm. "You'll have one meal each day—after learning period and exercise." He inserted the needle into a vein in Corbell's arm. He covered the wound with a blob of what might have been Silly Putty.

Corbell watched it all without emotion. If he had ever been afraid of needles the months of pain and cancer had worked it out of him. A needle was surcease, freedom from pain for a while.

"Learn now," said Pierce. "This knob controls speed. The volume is set for your hearing. You may replay any section once. Don't worry about your arm; you can't pull the tube loose."

"There's something I wanted to ask you, only I couldn't remember the word. What's a rammer?"

"Starship pilot."

Corbell studied the checker's face, without profit. "You're kidding."

"No. Learn now." The checker turned on Corbell's screen and went away.

II

A rammer was the pilot of a starship.

The starships were Bussard ramjets. They caught inter-stellar hydrogen in immaterial nets of electromagnetic force, compressed and guided it into a ring of pinched force fields, and there burned it in fusion fire. Potentially there was no limit at all on the speed of a Bussard ramjet. The ships were enormously powerful, enormously complex, enormously expensive.

Corbell thought it incredible that the State would trust so much value, such devastating power and mass to one man. To a man two centuries dead! Why, Corbell was an archi-tect, not an astronaut! It was news to him that the concept of the Bussard ramjet predated his own death. He had watched the Apollo XI and XIII flights on television, and that had been the extent of his interest in spaceflight, until now.

Now his life depended on his "rammer" career. He never doubted it. That was what kept Corbell in front of the screen with the earphones on his head for fourteen hours that first day. He was afraid he might be tested.

He didn't understand all he was supposed to learn. But he was not tested, either.

The second day he began to get interested. By the third day he was fascinated. Things he had never understood—relativity and magnetic theory and abstract mathematics—he now grasped intuitively. It was marvelous!

And he ceased to wonder why the State had chosen Je-rome Corbell. It was always done this way. It made sense, all kinds of sense.

The payload of a starship was small and its operating lifetime was more than a man's lifetime. A reasonably safe life-support system for one man occupied an unreasonably high proportion of the payload. The rest must go for biological package probes. A crew of more than one was out of the question.

A good, capable, loyal citizen was not likely to be enough of a loner. In any case, why send a citizen? The times would change drastically before a seeder ramship could return. The State itself might change beyond recognition. A returning rammer must adjust to a whole new culture. There was no way to tell in advance what it might be like.

Why not pick a man who had already chosen to adjust to a new culture? A man whose own culture was already two centuries dead when the trip started?

And a man who already owed the State his life.

The RNA was most effective. Corbell stopped wondering about Pierce's dispassionately possessive attitude. He began to think of himself as property being programmed for a purpose.

And he learned. He skimmed microtaped texts as if they were already familiar. The process was heady. He became convinced that he could rebuild a seeder ramship with his bare hands, given the parts. He had loved figures all his life, but abstract math had been beyond him until now. Field theory, monopole field equations, circuitry design. When to suspect the presence of a gravitational point source . . . how to locate it, use it, avoid it.

The teaching chair was his life. The rest of his time— exercise, dinner, sleep—seemed vague, uninteresting.

He exercised with about twenty others in a room too small for the purpose. Like Corbell, the others were lean and stringy, in sharp contrast to the brawny wedge-shaped men who were their guards. They followed the lead of a guard, running in place because there was no room for real running, forming in precise rows for scissors jumps, push-ups, sit-ups.

After fourteen hours in a teaching chair Corbell usually

enjoyed the jumping about. He followed orders. And he wondered about the stick in a holster at each guard's waist. It looked like a cop's baton. It might have been just that—except for the hole in one end. Corbell never tried to find out.

Sometimes he saw Pierce during the exercise periods. Pierce and the men who tended the teaching chairs were of a third type: well-fed, in adequate condition, but just on the verge of being overweight. Corbell thought of them as Olde American types.

From Pierce he learned something of the other professions open to a revived corpsicle/reprogrammed criminal. Stoop labor: intensive hand cultivation of crops. Body servants. Handicrafts. Any easily taught repetitive work. And the hours! The corpsicles were expected to work fourteen hours a day. And the crowding!

Not that his own situation was much different. Fourteen hours to study, an hour of heavy exercise, an hour to eat, and eight hours to sleep in a dorm that was two solid walls of people.

"Time to work, time to eat, time to sleep! Elbow-to-elbow every minute! The poor bastards," he said to Pierce. "What kind of a life is that?"

"It lets them repay their debt to the State as quickly as possible. Be reasonable, Corbell. What would a corpsicle do with his off hours? He has no social life. He has to learn one by observing citizens. Many forms of felon's labor involve proximity to citizens."

"So they can look up at their betters while they work? That's no way to learn. It would take . . . I get the feeling we're talking about *decades* of this kind of thing."

"Thirty years' labor generally earns a man his citizenship. That gets him a right to work, which then gets him a guaranteed base income he can use to buy education shots and tapes. And the medical benefits are impressive. We live longer than you used to, Corbell."

"Meanwhile it's slave labor. Anyway, none of this applies to me—"

"No, of course not. Corbell, you're wrong to call it slave labor. A slave can't quit. You can change jobs anytime you like. There's a clear freedom of choice."

Corbell shivered. "Any slave can commit suicide."

"Suicide, my ass," The checker said distinctly. If he had anything that could be called an accent it lay in the precision of his pronunciation. "Jerome Corbell is dead. I could have given you his intact skeleton for a souvenir."

"I don't doubt it." Corbell saw himself tenderly polishing his own white bones. But where could he have kept such a thing? In his bunk?

"Well, then. You're a brain-wiped criminal, justly brain-wiped, I might add. Your crime has cost you your citizenship, but you still have the right to change professions. You need only ask for another—um, course of rehabilitation. What slave can change jobs at will?"

"It would *feel* like dying."

"Nonsense. You go to sleep, only that. When you wake up you've got a different set of memories."

The subject was an unpleasant one. Corbell avoided it from then on. But he could not avoid talking to the checker. Pierce was the only man in the world he could talk to. On the days Pierce failed to show up he felt angry, frustrated.

Once he asked about gravitational point sources. "My time didn't know about those."

"Yes, it did. Neutron stars and black holes. You had a number of pulsars located by 1970, and the mathematics to describe how a pulsar decays. The thing to watch for is a decayed pulsar directly in your path. Don't worry about black holes. There are none near your course."

"Okay . . ."

Pierce regarded him in some amusement. "You really don't know much about your own time, do you?"

"Come on, I was an *architect*. What would I know about

astrophysics? We didn't have your learning techniques."
Which reminded him of something. "Pierce, you said you
learned English with RNA injections. Where does the RNA
come from?"

Pierce smiled and walked away.

He had little time to remember. For that he was almost
grateful. But very occasionally, lying wakeful in his bunk,
listening to the *shshsh* of a thousand people breathing and
the different sounds from the loving bunks, he would remember . . . someone. It didn't matter who.

At first it had been Mirabelle, always Mirabelle. Mirabelle at the tiller as they sailed out of San Pedro Harbor:
tanned, square face, laughing mouth, extravagantly large
dark glasses. Mirabelle, older and marked by months of
strain, saying good-bye at his . . . funeral. Mirabelle on
their honeymoon. In twenty-two years they had grown together like two touching limbs of a tree.

But now he thought of her, when he thought of her, as
two hundred years dead.

And his niece was dead, though he and Mirabelle had
barely made it to her confirmation; the pains had been getting
bad then. And his daughter Ann. And all *three* of his grandchildren: just infants they had been! It didn't matter who it
was that floated up into his mind. Everyone was dead.
Everyone but him.

Corbell did not want to die. He was disgustingly healthy
and twenty years younger than he had been at death. He
found his rammer education continually fascinating. If only
they would stop treating him like property . . .

Corbell had been in the army, but that was twenty years
ago. Make that two hundred and forty. He had learned to
take orders, but never to like it. What had galled him then
was the basic assumption of his inferiority. But no army
officer in Corbell's experience had believed in Corbell's
inferiority as completely as did Pierce and Pierce's guards.

The checker never repeated a command, never seemed even to consider that Corbell might refuse. If Corbell refused, even once, he knew what would happen. Pierce knew that he knew. The atmosphere better fitted a death camp than an army.

They must think I'm a zombie.

Corbell was careful not to pursue the thought. He was a corpse brought back to life—but not all the way. *What did they do with the skeleton? Cremate it?*

The life was not pleasant. His last-class citizenship was galling. There was nobody to talk to—nobody but Pierce, whom he was learning to hate. He was hungry much of the time. The single daily meal filled his belly, but it would not stay full. No wonder he had wakened so lean.

More and more he lived in the teaching chair. In the teaching chair he was a rammer. His impotence was changed to omnipotence. Starman! Riding the fire that feeds the suns, scooping fuel from interstellar space itself, spreading electromagnetic fields like wings hundreds of miles out . . .

Two weeks after the State had wakened him from the dead, Corbell was given his course.

He relaxed in a chair that was not quite a contour couch. RNA solution dripped into him. He no longer noticed the needle. The teaching screen held a map of his course, in green lines in three-space. Corbell had stopped wondering how the three-dimensional effect was achieved.

The scale was shrinking as he watched.

Two tiny blobs, and a glowing ball surrounded by a faintly glowing corona. This part of the course he already knew. A linear accelerator would launch him from the Moon, boost him to Bussard ramjet speeds and hurl him at the sun. Solar gravity would increase his speed while his electromagnetic fields caught and burned the solar wind itself. Then out, still accelerating . . .

In the teaching screen the scale shrank horrendously. The

distances between stars were awesome, terrifying. Van Maanan's Star was twelve light-years away.

He would begin deceleration a bit past the midpoint. The matching would be tricky. He must slow enough to release the biological package probe—but not enough to drop him below ram speeds. In addition he must use the mass of Van Maanan's Star for a course change. There was no room for error here.

Then on to the next target, which was even further away. Corbell watched . . . and he absorbed . . . and a part of him seemed to have known everything all along even while another part was gasping at the distances. Ten stars, all yellow dwarfs of the Sol type, an average of fifteen light-years apart—though he would cross one gap of fifty-two light-years. He would almost touch lightspeed on that one. Oddly enough, the Bussard ramjet effect would improve at such speeds. He could take advantage of the greater hydrogen flux to pull the fields closer to the ship, to intensify them.

Ten stars in a closed path, a badly bent and battered ring leading him back to the solar system and Earth. He would benefit from the time he spent near lightspeed. Though three hundred years would have passed on Earth, Corbell would only have lived through two hundred years of ship's time—which still implied some kind of suspended-animation technique.

It didn't hit him the first time through, nor the second; but repetition had been built into the teaching program. It didn't hit him until he was on his way to the exercise room.

Three hundred years?

Three hundred years!

III

It wasn't night, not really. Outside it must be midafternoon. Indoors, the dorm was always coolly lit, barely bright enough to read by if there had been books. There were no windows.

Corbell should have been asleep. He suffered every minute he spent gazing out into the dorm. Most of the others were asleep, but a couple made noisy love on one of the loving bunks. A few men lay on their backs with their eyes open. Two women talked in low voices. Corbell didn't know the language. He had been unable to find anyone who spoke English.

Corbell was desperately homesick.

The first few days had been the worst.

He had stopped noticing the smell. If he thought of it, he could sniff the traces of billions of human beings. Otherwise the odor was part of the background noise.

But the loving bunks bothered him. When they were in use he watched. When he forced himself not to watch he listened. He couldn't help himself. But he had turned down two sign-language invitations from a small brunette with straggly hair and a pretty, elfin face. Make love in public? He couldn't.

He could avoid using the loving bunks, but not the exposed toilets. That was embarrassing. The first time he was able to force himself only by staring rigidly at his feet. When he pulled on his jumper and looked up, a number of sleepers were watching him in obvious amusement. The reason might have been his self-consciousness or the way he dropped his jumper around his ankles, or he may have been out of line. A pecking order determined who might use the toilets before whom. He still hadn't figured out the details.

Corbell wanted to go home.

The idea was unreasonable. His home was gone and he would have gone with it if it weren't for the corpsicle crypts. But reason was of no use in this instance. He wanted to go home. Home to Mirabelle. Home to anywhere: Rome, San Francisco, Kansas City, Brasilia—he had lived in all those places, all different, but all home. Corbell had been at home anywhere—but he was not at home here and never would be.

Now they would take *here* away from him. Even this world of four rooms and two roofs, elbow-to-elbow people and utter slavery, this world which they would not even *show* him, would have vanished when he returned from the stars.

Corbell rolled over and buried his face in his arms. If he didn't sleep he would be groggy tomorrow. He might miss something essential. They had never tested his training. Not yet, not yet . . .

He dozed.

He came awake suddenly, already up on one elbow, groping for some elusive thought.

Ah.

Why haven't I been wondering about the biological package probes?

A moment later he did wonder.

What are the biological package probes?

But the wonder was that he had never wondered.

He knew what and where they were: heavy fat cylinders arranged around the waist of the starship's hull. Ten of these, each weighing almost as much as Corbell's own life-support system. He knew their mass distribution. He knew the clamp system that held them to the hull and he could operate and repair the clamps under various extremes of damage. He almost knew where the probes went when released; it was just on the tip of his tongue . . . which meant that he had had the RNA shot but had not yet seen the instructions.

But he didn't know what the probes were for.

It was like that with the ship, he realized. He knew everything there was to know about a seeder ramship, but nothing at all about the other kinds of starships or interplanetary travel or ground-to-orbit vehicles. He knew that he would be launched by linear accelerator from the Moon. He knew the design of the accelerator—he could see it, three hundred and fifty kilometers of rings standing on end in a line across a level lunar mare. He knew what to do if anything went wrong during launch. And that was all he knew about the Moon and lunar installations and lunar conquest, barring what he had watched on television over two hundred years ago.

What was going on out there? In the two weeks since his arrival (awakening? creation?) he had seen four rooms and two rooftops, glimpsed a rectilinear cityscape from a bridge, and talked to one man who was not interested in telling him anything. What had happened in two hundred years?

These men and women who slept around him. Who were they? Why were they here? He didn't even know if they were corpsicle or contemporary. Contemporary, probably; not one of them was self-conscious about the facilities.

Corbell had raised buildings in all sorts of strange places, but he had never jumped blind. He had always brushed up on the language and studied the customs before he went. Here he had no handle, nowhere to start. He was lost.

Oh, for someone to talk to!

He was learning in enormous gulps, taking in volumes of knowledge so broad that he hadn't realized how rigidly bounded they were. The State was teaching him only what he needed to know. Every bit of information was aimed straight at his profession.

Rammer.

He could see the reasoning. He would be gone for several centuries. Why should the State teach him anything at all about today's technology, customs, politics? There would be trouble enough when he came back, *if* he—come to that, who had taught him to call the government the State? How had he come to think of the State as all-powerful? He knew nothing of its power and extent.

It must be the RNA training. With data came attitudes below the conscious level, where he couldn't get at them.

That made his skin crawl. They were changing him around again!

Sure, why shouldn't the State trust him with a seeder ramship? They were feeding him State-oriented patriotism through a silver needle!

He had lost his people. He had lost his world. He would lose this one. According to Pierce, he had lost himself four times already. A condemned criminal had had his personality wiped four times. Corbell's goddamned skeleton had probably been ground up for phosphates. But this was the worst: that his beliefs and motivations were being lost bit by bit to the RNA solution while the State made him over into a rammer.

There was *nothing* that was his.

He failed to see Pierce at the next exercise period. It was just as well. He was somewhat groggy. As usual he ate dinner like a starving man. He returned to the dorm, rolled into his bunk and was instantly asleep.

He looked up during study period the next day and found Pierce watching him. He blinked, fighting free of a mass of data on the attitude jet system that bled plasma from the inboard fusion plant that was also the emergency electrical power source, and asked, "Pierce, what's a biological package probe?"

"I would have thought they would teach you that. You know what to do with the probes, don't you?"

"The teaching widget gave me the procedures two days ago. Slow up for certain systems, kill the fields, turn a probe loose and speed up again."

"You don't have to aim them?"

"No. I gather they aim themselves. But I have to get them down below a certain velocity or they'll fall right through the system."

"Amazing. They must do all the rest of it themselves." Pierce shook his head. "I wouldn't have believed it. Well,

Corbell, the probes steer for an otherwise terrestrial world with a reducing atmosphere. They outnumber oxygen-nitrogen worlds about three to one in this region of the galaxy and probably everywhere else too—as you may know, if your age got that far.''

"But what do the probes do?"

"They're biological packages. A dozen different strains of algae. The idea is to turn a reducing atmosphere into an oxygen atmosphere, just the way photosynthetic life forms did for Earth, something like fifteen-times-ten-to-the-eighth years ago." The checker smiled, barely. His small narrow mouth wasn't built to express any great emotion. "You're part of a big project."

"Good Lord. How long does it take?"

"We think about fifty thousand years. Obviously we've never had the chance to measure it."

"But, good Lord! Do you really think the State will last that long? Does even the State think it'll last that long?"

"That's not your affair, Corbell. Still—" Pierce considered. "I don't suppose I do. Or the State does. But humanity will last. One day there will be men on those worlds. It's a Cause, Corbell. The immortality of the species. A thing bigger than one man's life. And you're part of it."

He looked at Corbell expectantly.

Corbell was deep in thought. He was running a fingertip back and forth along the straight line of his nose.

Presently he asked, "What's it like out there?"

"The stars? You're—"

"No, no, no. The city. I catch just a glimpse of it twice a day. Cubistic buildings with elaborate carvings at the street level—"

"What the bleep is this, Corbell? You don't need to know anything about Selerdor. By the time you come home the whole city will be changed."

"I know, I know. That's why I hate to leave without seeing something of the world. I could be going out to die . . ." Corbell stopped. He had seen that considering look before, but he had never seen Pierce actually angry.

The checker's voice was flat, his mouth pinched tight. "You think of yourself as a tourist."

"So would you if you found yourself two hundred years in the future. If you didn't have that much curiosity you wouldn't be human."

"Granted that I'd want to look around. I certainly wouldn't demand it as a right. What were you thinking when you foisted yourself off on the future? Did you think the future owed you a debt? It's the other way around, and time you realized it!"

Corbell was silent.

"I'll tell you something. You're a rammer because you're a born tourist. We tested you for that. You like the unfamiliar; it doesn't send you scuttling back to something safe and known. That's rare." The checker's eyes said: *And that's why I've decided not to wipe your personality yet.* His mouth said, "Was there anything else?"

Corbell pushed his luck. "I'd like a chance to practice with a computer like the ship's autopilot-computer."

"We don't have one. But you'll get your chance in two days. You're leaving then."

IV

The next day he received his instructions for entering the solar system. He had been alive for seventeen days.

The instructions were understandably vague. He was to try anything and everything to make contact with a drastically changed State, up to and including flashing his attitude jets in binary code. He was to start these procedures a good distance out. It was not impossible that the State would be at war with . . . something. He should be signaling: NOT A WARSHIP.

He found that he would not be utterly dependent on rescue ships. He could slow the ramship by braking directly into the solar wind until the proton flux was too slow to help him. Then, whip around Sol and back out, slowing on attitude jets, using whatever hydrogen was left in the inboard tank. That was emergency fuel. Given no previous emergencies, a nearly full tank would actually get him to the Moon and land him there.

The State would be through with him once he dropped his last probe. It was good of the State to provide for his return, Corbell thought—and then he shook himself. The State was not altruistic. It wanted the ship back.

Now, more than ever, Corbell wanted a chance at the autopilotcomputer.

He found one last opportunity to talk to the checker.

"A three-hundred-year round trip—maybe two hundred, ship's time," Corbell said. "I get some advantage from relativity. But, Pierce, you don't really expect me to live two hundred years, do you? With nobody to talk to?"

"The cold-sleep treatment—"

"Even so."

Pierce frowned. "You've been briefed on the cold-sleep procedure, but you haven't studied medicine. I'm told that cold sleep has a rejuvenating effect over long periods. You'll spend perhaps twenty years awake and the rest in cold sleep. The medical facilities are automatic; you've been instructed how to use them. Do you think we'd risk your dying out there between the stars, where it would be impossible to replace you?"

"No."

"Was there anything else you wanted to see me about?"

"Yes." He had decided not to broach the subject. Now he changed his mind. "I'd like to take a woman with me. The life-support system would hold two of us. I worked it out. We'd need another cold-sleep chamber, of course."

For two weeks this had been the only man Corbell could talk to. At first he had found Pierce unfathomable, unreadable, almost inhuman. Since then he had learned to read the checker's face to some extent.

Pierce was deciding whether to terminate Jerome Corbell and start over.

It was a close thing. But the State had spent considerable time and effort on Jerome Corbell. It was worth a try. And so Pierce said, "That would take up some space. You would have to share the rest between you. I do not think you would survive."

"But—"

"What we can do is this. We can put the mind of a woman in your computer. The computer is voice-controlled, and her voice would be that of a woman, any type of woman you choose. A subplot enclosing the personality of a woman would leave plenty of circuitry for the computer's vital functions."

"I don't think you quite get the point of—"

"Look here, Corbell. We know you don't need a woman. If you did you would have taken one by now and we would have wiped you and started over. You've lived in the dormitory for two weeks and you have not used the mating facilities once."

"Damn it, Pierce, do you expect me to make love in public? I can't!"

"Exactly."

"But—"

"Corbell, you learned to use the toilet, didn't you? Because you had to. You know what to do with a woman but you are one of those men fortunate enough not to need one. Otherwise you could not be a rammer."

If Corbell had hit the checker then he would have done it knowing that it meant his death. And knowing that, he would have killed Pierce for forcing him to it.

Something like ten seconds elapsed. Pierce watched him

in frank curiosity. When he saw Corbell relax he said, "You leave tomorrow. Your training is finished. Good-bye."

Corbell walked away clenching and unclenching his fists.

The dormitory had been a test. He knew it now. Could he cross a narrow bridge with no handrails? Then he was not pathologically afraid of falling. Could he spend two hundred years alone in the cabin of a starship? Then the silent people around him, five above his head, hundreds to either side, must make him markedly uncomfortable. Could he live twenty waking years without a woman? Surely he must be impotent.

He returned to the dorm after dinner. They had replaced the bridge with a nearly invisible slab of glass. Corbell snarled and crossed ahead of the guard. The guard had to hurry to keep up.

He stood between two walls of occupied bunks, looking around him.

He had already refrained from killing the checker. He must have decided to live. What he did, then, was stupid. He knew it.

He looked about him until he found the slender dark-haired girl with the elfin face watching him curiously from near the ceiling. He climbed the rungs between the bunks until his face was level with hers.

The gesture he needed was a quick, formalized one; but he didn't know it. In English he asked, "Come with me?"

She nodded brightly and followed him down the ladder. By then it seemed to Corbell that the dorm was alive with barely audible voices.

The odd one, the rammer trainee.

Certainly a number of the wakeful turned on their sides to watch.

He felt their eyes on the back of his neck as he zipped open his gray jumpsuit and stepped out of it. The dormitory had been a series of tests. At least two of those eyes would record his doings for Pierce. But to Corbell they were just like all the others, all the eyes curiously watching to see how the speechless one would make out.

And sure enough, he was impotent. It was the eyes, and he was naked. The girl was at first concerned, then pitying. She stroked his cheek in apology or sympathy and then she went away and found someone else.

Corbell lay listening to them, gazing at the bunk above him.

He waited for eight hours. Finally a guard came to take him away. By then he didn't care what they did with him.

V

He didn't start to care until the guard's floating jeep pulled up beneath an enormous .22 cartridge standing on end. Then he began to wonder. It was too small to be a rocket ship.

But it was. They strapped him into a contour couch, one of three in a cabin with a single window. There were the guard, and Corbell, and a man who might have been Pierce's second cousin once removed: the pilot. He had the window.

Corbell's heartbeat quickened. He wondered how it would be.

It was as if he had suddenly become very heavy. He heard no noise except right at the beginning, a sound like landing gear being raised on an airplane. Not a rocket, Corbell thought. Possibly the ferry ship's drive was electromagnetic in nature. He remembered the tricks a Bussard ramjet could play with magnetic fields.

He was heavy and he hadn't slept last night. He went to sleep.

When he woke he was in free-fall. Nobody had tried to tell him anything about free-fall. The guard and pilot were watching.

"Screw you," said Corbell.

It was another test. He got the straps open and pushed himself over to the window. The pilot laughed, caught him and held him while he closed a protective cover over the instruments. Then he let go and Corbell drifted in front of the window.

His belly was revolving eccentrically. His inner ear was going crazy. His testicles were tight up against his groin and that didn't feel good either. He was *falling, FALLING!*

Corbell snarled within his mind and tried to concentrate on the window. But the Earth was not visible. Neither was the Moon. Just a lot of stars, bright enough—quite bright, in fact—even more brilliant than they had been above a small boat anchored off Catalina Island on many nights long ago. He watched them for some time.

Trying to keep his mind off that falling-elevator sensation. He wasn't about to get himself disqualified now.

They ate aboard in free-fall. Corbell copied the others, picking chunks of meat and potatoes out of a plastic bag of stew, pulling them through a membrane that sealed itself behind his pick.

"Of all the things I'm going to miss," he told the broad-faced guard, "I'm going to enjoy missing you most. You and your goddamn staring eyes." The guard smiled placidly and waited to see if Corbell would get sick.

They landed a day after takeoff on a broad plain where the Earth sat nestled among sharp lunar peaks. One day instead of three: The State had expended extra power to get him here. But an Earth-Moon flight must be a small thing these days.

The plain was black with blast pits. It must have been a landing field for decades. Transparent bubbles clustered near the runway end of the linear accelerator. There were buildings and groves of trees inside the bubbles. Spacecraft of various shapes and sizes were scattered about the plain.

The biggest was Corbell's ramship: a silver skyscraper

lying on its side. The probes were in place, giving the ship a thick-waisted appearance. To Corbell's trained eye it looked ready for takeoff.

He was awed, he was humbled, he was proud. He tried to sort out his own reactions from RNA-inspired emotions, and probably failed.

Corbell donned his suit first, while the pilot and guard watched to see if he would make a mistake. He took it slow. The suit came in two pieces: a skintight rubbery body stocking, and a helmet attached to a heavy backpack. On the chest was a white spiral with tapered ends: the sign of the State.

An electric cart came for them. Apparently Corbell was not expected to know how to walk on an airless world. He thought to head for one of the domes, but the guard steered straight for the ship. It was a long way off.

It had become unnervingly large when the guard stopped underneath. A fat cylinder the size of a house swelled above the jeep: the life-support section, bound to the main hull by a narrower neck. The smaller dome at the nose must be the control room.

The guard said, "Now you inspect your ship."

"You can talk?"

"Yes. Yesterday, a quick course."

"Oh."

"Three things wrong with your ship. You find all three. You tell me. I tell him."

"Him? Oh, the pilot. Then what?"

"Then you fix one of the things, we fix the others. Then we launch you."

It was another test, of course. Maybe the last. Corbell was furious. He started immediately with the field generators and gradually he forgot the guard and the pilot and the sword still hanging over his head. He knew this ship. As it had been with the teaching chair, so it was with the ship itself. Corbell's impotence changed to omnipotence. The power of the beast, the intricacy, the potential, the—the hydrogen tank held far too much pressure. That wouldn't wait.

"I'll slurry this now," he told the guard. "Get a tanker over there to top it off." He bled hydrogen gas slowly through the valve, lowering the fuel's vapor pressure without letting fuel boil out the valve itself. When he finished the liquid hydrogen would be slushy with frozen crystals under near-vacuum pressure.

He finished the external inspection without finding anything more. It figured: The banks of dials would hold vastly more information than a man's eyes could read through opaque titan-alloy skin.

The airlock was a triple-door type, not so much to save air as to give him an airlock even if he lost a door somehow. Corbell shut the outer door, used the others when green lights indicated he could. He looked down at the telltales under his chin as he started to unclamp his helmet.

Vacuum?

He stopped. The ship's gauges said air. The suit's said vacuum. Which was right? Come to that, he hadn't heard any hissing. Just how soundproof was his helmet?

Just like Pierce to wait and see if he would take off his helmet in a vacuum. Well, how to test?

Hah! Corbell found the head, turned on a water faucet. The water splashed oddly in lunar gravity. It did not boil.

Did a flaw in his suit constitute a flaw in the ship?

Corbell doffed his helmet and continued his inspection.

There was no way to test the ram-field generators without causing all kinds of havoc in the linear accelerator. He checked out the telltales, then concentrated on the life-support mechanisms. The tailored plants in the air system were alive and well. But the urea absorption mechanism was plugged somehow. That would be a dirty job. He postponed it.

He decided to finish his inspection. The State might have missed something. It was *his* ship, *his* life.

The cold-sleep chamber was like a great coffin, a corpsicle coffin. Corbell shuddered, remembering two hundred years spent waiting in liquid nitrogen. He wondered again if Jerome Corbell were really dead—and then he shook off the thought and went to work.

No flaws in the cold-sleep system. He went on.

The computer was acting vaguely funny.

He had a hell of a time tracing the problem. There was a minute break in one superconducting circuit, so small that some current was leaking through anyway, by inductance. Bastards. He donned his suit and went out to report.

The guard heard him out, consulted with the other man, then told Corbell, "You did good. Now finish with the topping-off procedure. We fix the other things."

"There's something wrong with my suit, too."

"New suit aboard now."

"I want some time with the computer. I want to be sure it's all right now."

"We fix it good. When you top off fuel you leave."

That suddenly, Corbell felt a vast sinking sensation. The whole Moon was dropping away under him.

They launched him hard. Corbell saw red before his eyes, felt his cheeks dragged far back toward his ears. The ship would be all right. It was built to stand electromagnetic eddy currents from any direction.

He survived. He fumbled out of his couch in time to watch the moonscape flying under him, receding, a magnificent view.

There were days of free-fall. He was not yet moving at ramscoop speeds. But the State had aimed him inside the orbit of Mercury, straight into the thickening solar wind. Protons. Thick fuel for the ram fields and a boost from the sun's gravity.

Meanwhile he had most of a day to play with the computer.

At one point it occurred to him that the State might monitor his computer work. He shrugged it off. Probably it was too late for the State to stop him now. In any case, he had said too much already.

He finished his work with the computer and got answers that satisfied him. At higher speeds the ram fields were self-reinforcing—they would support themselves and the ship. He could find no upper limit to the velocity of a seeder ramship.

With all the time in the world, then, he sat down at the control console and began to play with the fields.

They emerged like invisible wings. He felt the buffeting of badly controlled bursts of fusing hydrogen. He kept the fields close to the ship, fearful of losing the balance here, where the streaming of protons was so uneven. He could *feel* how he was doing. He could fly this ship by the seat of his pants, with RNA training to help him.

He felt like a giant. This enormous, phallic, germinal flying thing of metal and fire! Carrying the seeds of life for worlds that had never known life, he roared around the sun and out. The thrust dropped a bit then, because he and the solar wind were moving in the same direction. But he was catching it in his nets like wind in a sail, guiding it and burning it and throwing it behind him. The ship moved faster every second.

This feeling of power—enormous masculine power—had to be partly RNA training. At this point he didn't care. Part was him, Jerome Corbell.

Around the orbit of Mars, when he was sure that a glimpse of sunlight would not blind him, he instructed the computer to give him a full view. The walls of the spherical control room seemed to disappear; the sky blazed around him. There were no planets nearby. All he saw of the sky was myriads of brilliant pinpoints, mostly white, some showing traces of color. But there was more to see. Fusing hydrogen made a ghostly ring of light around his ship.

It would grow stronger. So far his thrust was low, somewhat more than enough to balance the thin pull of the sun.

He started his turn around the orbit of Jupiter by adjusting the fields to channel the proton flow to the side. That helped him thrust, but it must have puzzled Pierce and the faceless State. They would assume he was playing with the fields, testing his equipment. Maybe. His curve was gradual; it would take them a while to notice.

This was not according to plan. Originally he had intended to be halfway to Van Maanan's Star before he changed course. That would have given him fifteen years' headstart, in case he was wrong, in case the State could do something to stop him even now.

That would have been wise; but he couldn't do it. Pierce might die in thirty years. Pierce might never know what Corbell had done—and that thought was intolerable.

His thrust dropped to almost nothing in the outer reaches of the system. Protons were thin out here. But there were enough to push his velocity steadily higher, and that was what counted. The faster he went, the greater the proton flux. He was on his way.

He was beyond Neptune when the voice of Pierce the checker came to him, saying, "This is Peerssa for the State, Peerssa for the State. Answer, Corbell. Do you have a malfunction? Can we help? We cannot send rescue but we can advise. Peerssa for the State, Peerssa for the State—"

Corbell smiled tightly. *Peerssa?* The checker's name had changed pronunciation in two hundred years. Pierce had slipped back to an old habit, RNA lessons forgotten. He must be upset about something.

Corbell spent twenty minutes finding the moon base with his signal laser. The beam was too narrow to permit sloppy handling. When he had it adjusted he said, "This is Corbell for himself, Corbell for himself. I'm fine. How are you?"

He spent more time at the computer. One thing had been

bothering him: the return to Sol system. He planned to be away longer than the State would have expected. Suppose there was nobody on the Moon when he returned?

It was a problem, he found. If he could reach the moon on his remaining fuel (no emergencies, remember), he could reach the Earth's atmosphere. The ship was durable; it would stand a meteoric re-entry. But his attitude jets would not land him, properly speaking.

Unless he could cut away part of the ship. The ram-field generators would no longer be needed then. . . . Well, he would work it out somehow. Plenty of time. Plenty of time.

The answer from the Moon took nine hours. "Peerssa for the State. Corbell, we don't understand. You are far off course. Your first target was to be Van Maanan's Star. Instead you seem to be curving around toward Sagittarius. There is no known Earthlike world in that direction. What the bleep do you think you're doing? Repeating. Peerssa for the State, Peerssa—"

Corbell tried to switch it off. The teaching chair hadn't told him about an off switch. Finally, and it should have been sooner, he told the computer to switch the receiver off.

Somewhat later, he located the lunar base with his signal laser and began transmission.

"This is Corbell for himself, Corbell for himself. I'm getting sick and tired of having to find you every damn time I want to say something. So I'll give you this all at once.

"I'm not going to any of the stars on your list.

"It's occurred to me that the relativity equations work better for me the faster I go. If I stop every fifteen light-years to launch a probe, the way you want me to, I could spend two hundred years at it and never get anywhere. Whereas if I just aim the ship in one direction and keep it going, I can build up a ferocious Tau factor.

"It works out that I can reach the galactic hub in twenty-one years, ship's time, if I hold myself down to one gravity acceleration. And, Pierce, I just can't resist the idea. You were the one who called me a born tourist, remember? Well, the stars in the galactic hub aren't like the stars in the arms. And they're packed a quarter to a half light-year apart, according to your own theories. It must be passing strange in there.

"So I'll go exploring on my own. Maybe I'll find some of your reducing-atmosphere planets and drop the probes there. Maybe I won't. I'll see you in about seventy thousand years, your time. By then your precious State may have withered away, or you'll have colonies on the seeded planets and some of them may have broken loose from you. I'll join one of them. Or—"

Corbell thought it through, rubbing the straight, sharp line of his nose. "I'll have to check it out on the computer," he said. "But if I don't like any of your worlds when I get back, there are always the Clouds of Magellan. I'll bet they aren't more than twenty-five years away, ship's time."

After "Rammer" I couldn't just let Corbell drop. Ultimately I took him around the galactic core and back to Earth three million years hence. Somewhere in there the State evolved into the civilization that settled the Smoke Ring in two subsequent novels. But this is still one of my best short stories.

"Hey!"

The girl was four or five heads away, and short. I'd never have seen her if everyone else hadn't been short too. Flatlanders rarely top six feet. And there was this girl, her hair a topological explosion in swirling orange and silver, her face a faint, subtle green with space-black eyebrows and lipstick, waving something and shouting my name.

Waving my wallet.

"Flatlander," 1967

KNOWN SPACE

"Known Space" now runs from *now* to a thousand years further. That's not large, as future histories go. Many of my early stories were set somewhere/somewhen in known space.

The worlds of known space were stranger than what I found in other fiction . . .

From "The Ethics of Madness"

Tau Ceti is a small cool-yellow GO dwarf with four planets. Strictly speaking, none of the planets is habitable. Two are gas giants. The third inward has no air; the innermost has too much.

That innermost world is about the size of Venus. With

no oversized moon to strip away most of its air, it has an atmosphere like Venus': thick and hot and corrosive. No human explorer would have marked it for colonization.

But the ramrobots were not human.

During the twenty-first and twenty-second centuries, the ramrobots explored most of what later came to be called "known space." They were complexly programmed, but their mission was simple. Each was to find a habitable planet.

Unfortunately they were programmed wrong.

The designers didn't know it, and the UN didn't know it; but the ramrobots were programmed only to find a habitable point. Having located a world the right distance from the star to which it was sent, the ramrobot probe would drop and circle until it found a place at ground level which matched its criteria for atmospheric composition, average temperature, water vapor, and other conditions. Then the ramrobot would beam its laser pulse back at the solar system, and the UN would respond by sending a colony slowboat.

Unlike the ramrobots, the man-carrying slowboats could not use interstellar ramscoops. They had to carry their own fuel. It meant that the slowboats took a long time to get where they were going, and there were no round-trip tickets. The slowboats could not turn back.

So We Made It was colonized because a ramrobot elected to settle in spring. Had it landed in summer or winter, when the planet's axis of rotation points through its primary, Procyon, it would have sensed the fifteen-hundred-mile-per-hour winds.

So Jinx was colonized. Jinx, with a surface gravity of 1.78 and two habitable bands between the ocean, where there is too much air, and the Ends, where there is none at all. Jinx, the Easter Egg Planet, home of men and women who are five feet tall and five feet wide, the strongest bipeds in known space. But they die young, of heart trouble.

So Plateau was colonized. For the innermost world of Tau Ceti is like Venus in size and atmosphere, save for one mountain. That straight-sided mountain is forty miles tall, and its nearly flat top is half the size of California. It rises out of the searing black calm at the planet's surface to the transparent atmosphere above; and that air can be breathed. Snow covers the peaks near the center of the Plateau, and rivers run lower down—rivers that tumble off the void edges of the Plateau into the shining mist below. The ramrobot landed there. And founded a world.

Within Known Space I count twelve books, novels and collections and anthologies, and six general historical periods:

1

The Immediate future. Exploration of the solar system.

2

The early twenty-second century, the era of Lucas Garner and Gil "the ARM" Hamilton. Industry is spreading through the solar system; other solar systems are being explored. The organ bank problem is at its sociological worst on Earth. Nonhuman intelligence has become obtrusively real; humanity must adjust.

3

Intermediate period centering around 2340 A.D. Sol System is in a period of peace and prosperity. On colony worlds like Plateau times are turbulent. At the edge of Sol System, a creature that used to be Jack Brennan fights a lone war. The era of peace began with the subtle interventions of the Brennan-monster.

4

Contact and war with the Kzinti Patriarchy. THE MAN-KZIN WARS, volumes 1–3, include only one story of mine. I'm not good at war stories . . . but my friends are.

5

The period following the Man-Kzin Wars covers part of the twenty-sixth century A.D. It is a time of easy tourism and interstellar trade, in which the human species neither rules nor is ruled. New planets have been settled, some of which were wrested from the Patriarchy during the wars.

6

Little has changed. Thrusters have replaced fusion drives, there's a new sapient species about . . . but the fundamental change is subtle. The Teela Brown gene complex—the "ultimate psychic power"—is spreading through humanity. The teelas have been bred for luck.

A lucky human makes a poor protagonist. I'm reluctant to go past the Teela barrier.

Be warned: don't take this historical organization too seriously. I kept Known Space chaotic, like the history of the past.

Known Space was never my prison. This imaginary future was an elaborate background, like other alternate futures and alternate pasts. When a story idea fit Known Space, it joined Known Space. Otherwise I worked out something else.

In Known Space I allowed faster-than-light travel, a prevalence of intelligent life, near-magical engineering, and other unlikely things. Known Space gradually grew cluttered with implausible assumptions, inconsistent dating, half-fantastic hardware, obsolete astrophysics, and *limits*. I came to prefer the slower-than-light universe, which has room enough for miracles.

(The Ringworld properly belongs to a slower-than-light universe. You don't need to build vast habitats when habitable worlds are so easily available.)

But known space won't let go of me. WORLD OF PTAVVS was the beginning; "Madness Has Its Place" is the latest; and there is no end.

The other nonhumans aboard would have to stay in their rooms. Rooms 14–16–18 were joined and half full of water, occupied by a dolphin. His name was Pszzz, or Bra-a-ack, or some such impolite sound. Human ears couldn't catch the ultrasonic overtones of that name, nor could a human throat pronounce it, so he answered to Moby Dick. He was on his way to Wunderland, the *Argos'* next stop. Then there were two sessile Grogs in 22, and a flock of jumpin' jeepers in 24, with the connecting door open so the Grogs could get at the jumpin' jeepers, which were their food supply. Lloobee, the Kdatlyno touch-sculptor, had room twenty.

"Grendel," 1968

BECALMED IN HELL

Fred Pohl bought my first story. Afterward he got first look at everything. Boy was that a relief! I didn't have a reputation then, so I didn't have an agent. Fred must have been thinking like an agent; after all, he was one once.

He picked Jack Gaughan to illustrate all those alien life-forms in "World of Ptavvs." He sent "World of Ptavvs" to Betty Ballantine at Ballantine Books, and she offered me a contract to turn the novella into a novel.

But Fred returned "Becalmed in Hell."

I took the enclosed letter (with suggestions for rewrite) for a rejection slip. I rewrote the story and sent it to *The Magazine of Fantasy and Science Fiction*.

Fred and I met again at one of Damon Knight's writers' conferences in Milford. He took me aside and told me, "When a manuscript comes back with suggestions for rewriting it, that means the editor wants to see it again."

I said, "Oh!"

I could feel the heat hovering outside. In the cabin it was bright and dry and cool, almost too cool, like a modern office building in the dead of summer. Beyond the two small windows it was as black as it ever gets in the solar system, and hot enough to melt lead, at a pressure equivalent to three hundred feet beneath the ocean.

"There goes a fish," I said, just to break the monotony.

"So how's it cooked?"

"Can't tell. It seems to be leaving a trail of breadcrumbs. Fried? Imagine that, Eric! A fried jellyfish."

Eric sighed noisily. "Do I have to?"

"You have to. Only way you'll see anything worthwhile in this—this—" Soup? Fog? Boiling maple syrup?

"Searing black calm."

"Right."

"Someone dreamed up that phrase when I was a kid, just after the news of the Mariner II probe. An eternal searing black calm, hot as a kiln, under an atmosphere thick enough to keep any light or any breath of wind from ever reaching the surface."

I shivered. "What's the outside temperature now?"

"You'd rather not know. You've always had too much imagination, Howie."

"I can take it, Doc."

"Six hundred and twelve degrees."

"I can't take it, Doc!"

This was Venus, planet of Love, favorite of the science-fiction writers of three decades ago. Our ship hung below the Earth-to-Venus hydrogen fuel tank, twenty miles up and all but motionless in the syrupy air. The tank, nearly empty now, made an excellent blimp. It would keep us aloft as long as the internal pressure matched the external. That was Eric's job, to regulate the tank's pressure by regulating the temperature of the hydrogen gas. We had collected air samples after each ten-mile drop from three hundred miles on down, and temperature readings for shorter intervals, and we had dropped the small probe. The data we had got from the surface merely confirmed in detail our previous knowledge of the hottest world in the solar system.

"Temperature just went up to six-thirteen," said Eric. "Look, are you through bitching?"

"For the moment."

"Good. Strap down. We're taking off."

"Oh frabjous day!" I started untangling the crash webbing over my couch.

"We've done everything we came to do. Haven't we?"

"Am I arguing? Look, I'm strapped down."

"Yeah."

I knew why he was reluctant to leave. I felt a touch of it myself. We'd spent four months getting to Venus in order to spend a week circling her and less than two days in her upper atmosphere, and it seemed a terrible waste of time.

But he was taking too long. "What's the trouble, Eric?"

"You'd rather not know."

He meant it. His voice was a mechanical, inhuman monotone; he wasn't making the extra effort to get human expression out of his "prosthetic" vocal apparatus. Only a severe shock would affect him that way.

"I can take it," I said.

"Okay. I can't feel anything in the ramjet controls. Feels like I've just had a spinal anesthetic."

The cold in the cabin drained into me, all of it. "See if you can send motor impulses the other way. You could run the rams by guess-and-hope even if you can't feel them."

"Okay." One split second later, "They don't. Nothing happens. Good thinking though."

I tried to think of something to say while I untied myself from the couch. What came out was, "It's been a pleasure knowing you, Eric. I've liked being half of this team, and I still do."

"Get maudlin later. Right now, start checking my attachments. Carefully."

I swallowed my comments and went to open the access door in the cabin's forward wall. The floor swayed ever so gently beneath my feet.

Beyond the four-foot-square access door was Eric. Eric's central nervous system, with the brain perched at the top and the spinal cord coiled in a loose spiral to fit more compactly into the transparent glass-and-sponge-plastic housing. Hundreds of wires from all over the ship led to the glass walls, where they were joined to selected nerves which spread like an electrical network from the central coil of nervous tissue and fatty protective membrane.

Space leaves no cripples; and don't call Eric a cripple, because he doesn't like it. In a way he's the ideal spaceman. His life support system weighs only half what mine does, and takes up a twelfth as much room. But his other prosthetic aids take up most of the ship. The ramjets were hooked into the last pair of nerve trunks, the nerves which once moved his legs, and dozens of finer nerves in those trunks sensed and regulated fuel feed, ram temperature, differential acceleration, intake aperture dilation, and spark pulse.

These connections were intact. I checked them four different ways without finding the slightest reason why they shouldn't be working.

"Test the others," said Eric.

It took a good two hours to check every trunk nerve connection. They were all solid. The blood pump was chugging along, and the fluid was rich enough, which killed the idea that the ram nerves might have "gone to sleep" from lack of nutrients or oxygen. Since the lab is one of his prosthetic aids, I let Eric analyze his own blood sugar, hoping that the "liver" had goofed and was producing some other form of sugar. The conclusions were appalling. There was nothing wrong with Eric—inside the cabin.

"Eric, you're healthier than I am."

"I could tell. You look worried, son, and I don't blame you. Now you'll have to go outside."

"I know. Let's dig out the suit."

It was in the emergency tools locker, the Venus suit that was never supposed to be used. NASA had designed it for use at Venusian ground level. Then they had refused to okay the ship below twenty miles until they knew more about the planet. The suit was a segmented armor job. I had watched it being tested in the heat-and-pressure box at Cal Tech, and I knew that the joints stopped moving after five hours, and wouldn't start again until they had been cooled. Now I opened the locker and pulled the suit out by the shoulders and held it in front of me. It seemed to be staring back.

"You still can't feel anything in the ramjets?"

"Not a twinge."

I started to put on the suit, piece by piece like medieval armor. Then I thought of something else. "We're twenty miles up. Are you going to ask me to do a balancing act on the hull?"

"No! Wouldn't think of it. We'll just have to go down."

The lift from the blimp tank was supposed to be constant until takeoff. When the time came Eric could get extra lift by heating the hydrogen to higher pressure, then cracking a valve to let the excess out. Of course he'd have to be very careful that the pressure was higher in the tank, or we'd get Venusian air coming in, and the ship would fall instead of rising. Naturally that would be disastrous.

So Eric lowered the tank temperature and cracked the valve, and down we went.

"Of course there's a catch," said Eric.

"I know."

"The ship stood the pressure twenty miles up. At ground level it'll be six times that."

"I know."

We fell fast, with the cabin tilted forward by the drag on our tailfins. The temperature rose gradually. The pressure went up fast. I sat at the window and saw nothing, nothing but black, but I sat there anyway and waited for the window to crack. NASA had refused to okay the ship below twenty miles . . .

Eric said, "The blimp tank's okay, and so's the ship, I think. But will the cabin stand up to it?"

"I wouldn't know."

"Ten miles."

Five hundred miles above us, unreachable, was the atomic ion engine that was to take us home. We couldn't get to it on the chemical rocket alone. The rocket was for use after the air became too thin for the ramjets.

"Four miles. Have to crack the valve again."

The ship dropped.

"I can see ground," said Eric.

I couldn't. Eric caught me straining my eyes and said, "Forget it. I'm using deep infrared, and getting no detail."

"No vast, misty swamps with weird, terrifying monsters and man-eating plants?"

"All I see is hot, bare dirt."

But we were almost down, and there were no cracks in the cabin wall. My neck and shoulder muscles loosened. I turned away from the window. Hours had passed while we dropped through the poisoned, thickening air. I already had most of my suit on. Now I screwed on my helmet and three-finger gantlets.

"Strap down," said Eric. I did.

We bumped gently. The ship tilted a little, swayed back, bumped again. And again, with my teeth rattling and my armor-plated body rolling against the crash webbing. "Damn," Eric muttered. I heard the hiss from above. Eric said, "I don't know how we'll get back up."

Neither did I. The ship bumped hard and stayed down, and I got up and went to the airlock.

"Good luck," said Eric. "Don't stay out too long." I waved at his cabin camera. The outside temperature was seven hundred and thirty.

The outer door opened. My suit refrigerating unit set up a complaining whine. With an empty bucket in each hand, and with my headlamp blazing a way through the black murk, I stepped out on to the right wing.

My suit creaked and settled under the pressure, and I stood on the wing and waited for it to stop. It was almost like being under water. My headlamp beam went out thick enough to be solid, penetrating no more than a hundred feet. The air couldn't have been that opaque, no matter how dense. It must have been full of dust, or tiny droplets of some fluid.

The wing ran back like a knife-edged running board, widening toward the tail until it spread into a tailfin. The two tailfins met back of the fuselage. At the tailfin tip was the ram, a big sculptured cylinder with an atomic engine inside. It wouldn't be hot because it hadn't been used yet, but I had my counter anyway.

I fastened a line to the wing and slid to the ground. As long as we were *here* . . . The ground turned out to be a dry, reddish dirt, crumbly, and so porous that it was almost spongy. Lava etched by chemicals? Almost anything would be corrosive at this pressure and temperature. I scooped one pailful from the surface and another from underneath the first, then climbed up the line and left the buckets on the wing.

The wing was terribly slippery. I had to wear magnetic sandals to stay on. I walked up and back along the two hundred foot length of the ship, making a casual inspection. Neither wing nor fuselage showed damage. Why not? If a meteor or something had cut Eric's contact with his sensors in the rams, there should have been evidence of a break in the surface.

Then, almost suddenly, I realized that there was an alternative.

It was too vague a suspicion to put into words yet, and I still had to finish the inspection. Telling Eric would be very difficult if I was right.

Four inspection panels were set into the wing, well protected from the reentry heat. One was halfway back on the fuselage, below the lower edge of the blimp tank, which was molded to the fuselage in such a way that from the front the ship looked like a dolphin. Two more were in the trailing edge of the tailfin, and the fourth was in the ram itself. All opened, with powered screwdriver on recessed screws, on junctions of the ship's electrical system.

There was nothing out of place under any of the panels. By making and breaking contacts and getting Eric's reactions, I found that his sensation ended somewhere between the second and third inspection panels. It was the same story on the left wing. No external damage, nothing wrong at the junctions. I climbed back to ground and walked slowly beneath the length of each wing, my headlamp tilted up. No damage underneath.

I collected my buckets and went back inside.

"A bone to pick?" Eric was puzzled. "Isn't this a strange time to start an argument? Save it for space. We'll have four months with nothing else to do."

"This can't wait. First of all, did you notice anything I

didn't?'' He'd been watching everything I saw and did through the peeper in my helmet.

"No. I'd have yelled."

"Okay. Now get this.

"The break in your circuits isn't inside, because you get sensation up to the second wing inspection panels. It isn't outside because there's no evidence of damage, not even corrosion spots. That leaves only one place for the flaw."

"Go on."

"We also have the puzzle of why you're paralyzed in both rams. Why should they both go wrong at the same time? There's only one place in the ship where the circuits join."

"What? Oh, yes, I see. They join through me."

"Now let's assume for the moment that you're the piece with the flaw in it. You're not a piece of machinery, Eric. If something's wrong with you it isn't medical. That was the first thing we covered. But it could be psychological."

"It's nice to know you think I'm human. So I've slipped a cam, have I?"

"Slightly. I think you've got a case of what used to be called trigger anesthesia. A soldier who kills too often sometimes finds that his right index finger or even his whole hand has gone numb, as if it were no longer a part of him. Your comment about not being a machine is important, Eric. I think that's the whole problem. You've never really believed that any part of the ship is a part of *you*. That's intelligent, because it's true. Every time the ship is redesigned you get a new set of parts, and it's right to avoid thinking of a change of model as a series of amputations." I'd been rehearsing this speech, trying to put it so that Eric would have no choice but to believe me. Now I know that it must have sounded phony. "But now you've gone too far. Subconsciously you've stopped believing that the rams can *feel* like a part of you, which they were designed to do. So you've persuaded yourself that you don't feel anything."

With my prepared speech done, and nothing left to say, I stopped talking and waited for the explosion.

"You make good sense," said Eric.

I was staggered. "You agree?"

"I didn't say that. You spin an elegant theory, but I want time to think about it. What do we do if it's true?"

"Why . . . I don't know. You'll just have to cure yourself."

"Okay. Now here's *my* idea. I propose that you thought up this theory to relieve yourself of a responsibility for getting us home alive. It puts the whole problem in my lap, metaphorically speaking."

"Oh, for—"

"Shut up. I haven't said you're wrong. That would be an ad hominem argument. We need time to think about this."

It was lights-out, four hours later, before Eric would return to the subject.

"Howie, do me a favor. Assume for a while that something mechanical is causing all our trouble. I'll assume it's psychosomatic."

"Seems reasonable."

"It is reasonable. What can you do if I've gone psychosomatic? What can I do if it's mechanical? I can't go around inspecting myself. We'd each better stick to what we know."

"It's a deal." I turned him off for the night and went to bed.

But not to sleep.

With the lights off it was just like outside. I turned them back on. It wouldn't wake Eric. Eric never sleeps normally, since his blood doesn't accumulate fatigue poisons, and he'd go mad from being awake all the time if he didn't have a Russian sleep inducer plate near his cortex. The ship could implode without waking Eric when his sleep inducer's on. But I felt foolish being afraid of the dark.

While the dark stayed outside it was all right.

But it wouldn't stay there. It had invaded my partner's mind. Because his chemical checks guard him against chemical insanities like schizophrenia, we'd assumed he was permanently sane. But how could any prosthetic device protect him from his own imagination, his own misplaced common sense?

I couldn't keep my bargain. I knew I was right. But what could I do about it?

Hindsight is wonderful. I could see exactly what our mistake had been, Eric's and mine and the hundreds of men who had built his life support after the crash. There was nothing left of Eric then except the intact central nervous system, and no glands except the pituitary. "We'll regulate his blood composition," they said, "and he'll always be cool, calm and collected. No panic reactions from Eric!"

I know a girl whose father had an accident when he was forty-five or so. He was out with his brother, the girl's uncle, on a fishing trip. They were blind drunk when they started home, and the guy was riding on the hood while the brother drove. Then the brother made a sudden stop. Our hero left two important glands on the hood ornament.

The only change in his sex life was that his wife stopped worrying about late pregnancy. His *habits* were developed.

Eric doesn't need adrenal glands to be afraid of death. His emotional patterns were fixed long before the day he tried to land a moonship without radar. He'd grab any excuse to believe that I'd fixed whatever was wrong with the ram connections.

But he was counting on me to do it.

The atmosphere leaned on the windows. Not wanting to, I reached out to touch the quartz with my fingertips. I couldn't feel the pressure. But it was there, inexorable as the tide smashing a rock into sand grains. How long would the cabin hold it back?

If some broken part were holding us here, how could I

have missed finding it? Perhaps it had left no break in the surface of either wing. But how?

That was an angle.

Two cigarettes later I got up to get the sample buckets. They were empty, the alien dirt safely stored away. I filled them with water and put them in the cooler, set the cooler for 40 ° Absolute, then turned off the lights and went to bed.

The morning was blacker than the inside of a smoker's lungs. What Venus really needs, I decided, philosophizing on my back, is to lose ninety-nine percent of her air. That would give her a bit more than half as much air as Earth, which would lower the greenhouse effect enough to make the temperature livable. Drop Venus' gravity to near zero for a few weeks and the work would do itself.

The whole damn universe is waiting for us to discover antigravity.

"Morning," said Eric. "Thought of anything?"

"Yes." I rolled out of bed. "Now don't bug me with questions. I'll explain everything as I go."

"No breakfast?"

"Not yet."

Piece by piece I put my suit on, just like one of King Arthur's gentlemen, and went for the buckets only after the gantlets were on. The ice, in the cold section, was in the chilly neighborhood of absolute zero. "This is two buckets of ordinary ice," I said, holding them up. "Now let me out."

"I should keep you here till you talk," Eric groused. But the doors opened and I went out onto the wing. I started talking while I unscrewed the number two right panel.

"Eric, think a moment about the tests they run on a manned ship before they'll let a man walk into the lifesystem. They test every part separately and in conjunction with other parts. Yet if something isn't working, either it's damaged or it wasn't tested right. Right?"

"Reasonable." He wasn't giving away anything.

"Well, nothing caused any damage. Not only is there no break in the ship's skin, but no coincidence could have made both rams go haywire at the same time. So something wasn't tested right."

I had the panel off. In the buckets the ice boiled gently where it touched the surfaces of the glass buckets. The blue ice cakes had cracked under their own internal pressure. I dumped one bucket into the maze of wiring and contacts and relays, and the ice shattered, giving me room to close the panel.

"So I thought of something last night, something that wasn't tested. Every part of the ship must have been in the heat-and-pressure box, exposed to artificial Venus conditions, but the ship as a whole, a unit, couldn't have been. It's too big." I'd circled around to the left wing and was opening the number three panel in the trailing edge. My remaining ice was half water and half small chips; I sloshed these in and fastened the panel. "What cut your circuits must have been the heat or the pressure or both. I can't help the pressure, but I'm cooling these relays with ice. Let me know which ram gets its sensation back first, and we'll know which inspection panel is the right one."

"Howie. Has it occurred to you what the cold water might do to those hot metals?"

"It could crack them. Then you'd lose all control over the ramjets, which is what's wrong right now."

"Uh. Your point, partner. But I still can't feel anything."

I went back to the airlock with my empty buckets swinging, wondering if they'd get hot enough to melt. They might have, but I wasn't out that long. I had my suit off and was refilling the buckets when Eric said, "I can feel the right ram."

"How extensive? Full control?"

"No, I can't feel the temperature. Oh, here it comes. We're all set, Howie."

My sigh of relief was sincere.

I put the buckets in the freezer again. We'd certainly want to take off with the relays cold. The water had been chilling for perhaps twenty minutes when Eric reported, "Sensation's going."

"What?"

"Sensation's going. No temperature, and I'm losing fuel feed control. It doesn't stay cold long enough."

"Ouch! Now what?"

"I hate to tell you. I'd almost rather let you figure it out for yourself."

I had. "We go as high as we can on the blimp tank, then I go out on the wing with a bucket of ice in each hand—"

We had to raise the blimp tank temperature to almost eight hundred degrees to get pressure, but from then on we went up in good shape. To sixteen miles. It took three hours.

"That's as high as we go," said Eric. "You ready?"

I went to get the ice. Eric could see me, he didn't need an answer. He opened the airlock for me.

Fear I might have felt, or panic, or determination or self-sacrifice—but there was nothing. I went out feeling like a used zombie.

My magnets were on full. It felt like I was walking through shallow tar. The air was thick, though not as heavy as it had been down there. I followed my headlamp to the number two panel, opened it, poured ice in and threw the bucket high and far. The ice was in one cake. I couldn't close the panel. I left it open and hurried around to the other wing. The second bucket was filled with exploded chips; I sloshed them in and locked the number two left panel and came back with both hands free. It still looked like limbo in all directions, except where the headlamp cut a tunnel through the darkness, and—my feet were getting hot. I closed the right panel on boiling water and sidled back along the hull into the airlock.

"Come in and strap down," said Eric. "Hurry!"

"Gotta get my suit off." My hands had started to shake from reaction. I couldn't work the clamps.

"No you don't. If we start right now we may get home. Leave the suit on and come in."

I did. As I pulled my webbing shut, the rams roared. The ship shuddered a little, then pushed forward as we dropped from under the blimp tank. Pressure mounted as the rams reached operating speed. Eric was giving it all he had. It would have been uncomfortable even without the metal suit around me. With the suit on it was torture. My couch was afire from the suit, but I couldn't get breath to say so. We were going almost straight up.

We had gone twenty minutes when the ship jerked like a galvanized frog. "Ram's out," Eric said calmly. "I'll use the other." Another lurch as we dropped the dead one. The ship flew on like a wounded penguin, but still accelerating.

One minute . . . two . . .

The other ram quit. It was as if we'd run into molasses. Eric blew off the ram and the pressure eased. I could talk.

"Eric."

"What?"

"Got any marshmallows?"

"*What*? Oh, I see. Is your suit tight?"

"Sure."

"Live with it. We'll flush the smoke out later. I'm going to coast above some of this stuff, but when I use the rocket it'll be savage. No mercy."

"Will we make it?"

"I think so. It'll be close."

The relief came first, icy cold. Then the anger. "No more inexplicable numbnesses?" I asked.

"No. Why?"

"If any come up you'll be sure and tell me, won't you?"

"Are you getting at something?"

"Skip it." I wasn't angry any more.

"I'll be damned if I do. You know perfectly well it was mechanical trouble, you fool. You fixed it yourself!"

"No. I convinced you I must have fixed it. You needed to believe the rams *should* be working again. I gave you a miracle cure, Eric. I just hope I don't have to keep dreaming up new placebos for you all the way home."

"You thought that, but you went out on the wing sixteen miles up?" Eric's machinery snorted. "You've got guts where you need brains, Shorty."

I didn't answer.

"Five thousand says the trouble was mechanical. We let the mechanics decide after we land."

"You're on."

"Here comes the rocket. Two, one—"

It came, pushing me down into my metal suit. Sooty flames licked past my ears, writing black on the green metal ceiling, but the rosy mist before my eyes was not fire.

The man with the thick glasses spread a diagram of the Venus ship and jabbed a stubby finger at the trailing edge of the wing. "Right around here," he said. "The pressure from outside compressed the wiring channel a little, just enough so there was no room for the wire to bend. It had to act as if it were rigid, see? Then when the heat expanded the metal these contacts pushed past each other."

"I suppose it's the same design on both wings?"

He gave me a queer look. "Well, naturally."

I left my check for $5000 in a pile of Eric's mail and hopped a plane for Brasilia. How he found me I'll never know, but the telegram arrived this morning.

> HOWIE COME HOME ALL IS FORGIVEN
> DONOVANS BRAIN

I guess I'll have to.

Nessus wasn't trotting. He came tippy-toe, circling a four-foot chrome-yellow feather with exaggerated wariness, moving one foot at a time, while his flat heads darted this way and that. He had almost reached the lecture dome when something like a large black butterfly settled on his rump. Nessus screamed like a woman, leapt forward as if clearing a high fence. He landed rolling. When he stopped rolling he remained curled into a ball, with his back arched and his legs folded and his heads and necks tucked between his forelegs.

RINGWORLD, 1970

WAIT IT OUT

Night on Pluto. Sharp and distinct, the horizon line cuts across my field of vision. Below that broken line is the dim gray-white of snow seen by starlight. Above, space-blackness and space-bright stars. From behind a jagged row of frozen mountains the stars pour up in singletons and clusters and streamers of cold white dots. Slowly they move, but visibly, just fast enough for a steady eye to capture their motion.

Something wrong there. Pluto's rotation period is long: 6.39 days. Time must have slowed for me.

It should have stopped.

I wonder if I made a mistake.

The planet's small size brings the horizon close. It seems

even closer without a haze of atmosphere to fog the distances. Two sharp peaks protrude into the starswarm like the filed front teeth of a cannibal warrior. In the cleft between those peaks shines a sudden bright point.

I recognize the Sun, though it shows no more disc than any other, dimmer star. The Sun shines as a cold point between the frozen peaks; it pulls free of the rocks and shines in my eyes . . .

The Sun is gone, the starfield has shifted. I must have passed out.

It figures.

Have I made a mistake? It won't kill me if I have. It could drive me mad, though . . .

I don't feel mad. I don't feel anything, not pain, not loss, not regret, not fear. Not even pity. Just: *what a situation.*

Gray-white against gray-white: the landing craft, short and wide and conical, stands half submerged in an icy plain below the level of my eyes. Here I stand, looking east, waiting.

Take a lesson: this is what comes of not wanting to die.

Pluto was not the most distant planet. It had stopped being that in 1979, ten years ago. Now Pluto was at perihelion, as close to the Sun— and to Earth—as it would ever get. To ignore such an opportunity would have been sheer waste.

And so we came, Jerome and Sammy and I, in an inflated plastic bubble poised on an ion jet. We'd spent a year and a half in that bubble. After so long together, with so little privacy, perhaps we should have hated each other. We didn't. The UN psycho team must have chosen well.

But—just to be out of sight of the others, even for a few minutes. Just to have something to *do*, something that was not predictable. A new world would hold infinite surprises. As a matter of fact, so could our laboratory-tested hardware. I don't think any of us really trusted the Nerva-K under our landing craft.

Think it through. For long trips in space, you use an ion jet giving low thrust over long periods of time. The ion motor on our own craft had been decades in use. Where gravity is materially lower than Earth's, you land on dependable chemical rockets. For landings on Earth and Venus, you use heat shields and the braking power of the atmosphere. For landing on the gas giants—but who would want to?

The Nerva-class fission rockets are used only for takeoff from Earth, where thrust and efficiency count. Responsiveness and maneuverability count for too much during a powered landing. And a heavy planet will always have an atmosphere for braking.

Pluto didn't.

For Pluto, the chemical jets to take us down and bring us back up were too heavy to carry all that way. We needed a highly maneuverable Nerva-type atomic rocket motor using hydrogen for reaction mass.

And we had it. But we didn't trust it.

Jerome Glass and I went down, leaving Sammy Cross in orbit. He bitched about that, of course. He'd started that back at the Cape and kept it up for a year and a half. But someone had to stay. Someone had to be aboard the Earth-return vehicle, to fix anything that went wrong, to relay communications to Earth, and to fire the bombs that would solve Pluto's one genuine mystery.

We never did solve that one. Where *does* Pluto get all that mass? The planet's a dozen times as dense as it has any right to be. We could have solved that with the bombs, the same way they solved the mystery of the makeup of the Earth, sometime in the last century. They mapped the patterns of earthquake ripples moving through the Earth's bulk. But those ripples were from natural causes, like Krakatoa. On Pluto the bombs would have done it better.

A bright star-sun blazes suddenly between two fangs of

mountain. I wonder if they'll know the answers, when the wait is over.

The sky jumps and steadies, and—

I'm looking east, out over the plain where we landed the ship. The plain and the mountains behind seem to be sinking like Atlantis: an illusion created by the flowing stars. We slide endlessly down the sky, Jerome and I and the mired ship.

The Nerva-K behaved perfectly. We hovered for several minutes, to melt our way through various layers of frozen gases and get ourselves some ground to set down on. Condensing volatiles steamed around us and boiled below, so that we settled in a soft white glow of fog lit by the hydrogen flame.

Black wet ground kissed the landing skirt. We were down.

It took us an hour to check the ship and get ready to go outside. We flipped a coin for the chance to be the first man on Pluto, the (ten years from now) outermost world of the solar system.

Jerome won. As he went out he was talking about the statues they'd build to him. There's irony in that, if you like that sort of thing.

As I screwed my helmet down and prepared to follow him out, I heard him shouting filthy words into the helmet mike.

The black wet dirt beneath our landing skirt had been dirty ice, water ice mixed haphazardly with lighter gases and ordinary rock. The heat draining out of the Nerva jet had melted that ice, then allowed it to freeze again halfway up the hull. Our landing craft was sunk solid in the ice.

We could have done some exploring before we tried to move the ship. When we called Sammy he suggested doing just that. But Sammy was up there in the Earth-return vehi-

cle, and we were down here with our landing vehicle mired
in the ice of another world.

We were terrified. Until we got clear we would be good
for nothing, and we both knew it.

I wonder why I can't remember the fear.

We did have one chance. The landing vehicle was designed to move about on Pluto's surface; and so she had a
skirt instead of landing jacks. Half a gravity of thrust would
have given us a ground effect, safer and cheaper than using
the ship like a ballistic missile. The landing skirt must have
trapped gas underneath when the ship sank, leaving the
Nerva-K engine in a bubble cavity.

We could melt our way out.

I know we were as careful as two terrified men could be.
The heat rose in the Nerva-K, agonizingly slow. In flight
there would have been a coolant effect as cold hydrogen
fuel ran through the pile. We couldn't use that. But the
environment of the motor was terribly cold. The two factors
might compensate, or—

Suddenly dials went wild. Something had cracked from
the savage temperature differential. Jerome used the damper
rods without effect. Maybe they'd melted. Maybe wiring
had cracked, or resistors had become superconductors in the
cold. Maybe the pile—but it doesn't matter now.

I wonder why I can't remember the fear.

Sunlight—

And a logy, dreamy feeling. I'm conscious again. The
same stars rise in formation over the same dark mountains.

Something heavy is nosing up against me. I feel its weight
against my back and the backs of my calves. What is it?
Why am I not terrified?

It slides around in front of me, questing. It looks like a
huge amoeba, shapeless and translucent, with darker bodies
showing within it. I'd say it's about my own weight.

Life on Pluto! But how? Superfluids? Helium II contaminated by complex molecules? In that case the beast had best get moving; it will need shadow come sunrise. Sunside temperature on Pluto is about 50° Absolute.

No, come back! It's leaving, flowing down toward the splash crater. Did my thoughts send it away? Nonsense. It probably didn't like the taste of me. It must be terribly slow, that I can watch it move. The beast is still visible, blurred because I can't look directly at it, moving downhill toward the landing vehicle and the tiny figure of Jerome's statue.

After the fiasco with the Nerva-K, one of us had to go down and see how much damage had been done. That meant tunneling down with the flame of a jet back pack, then crawling under the landing skirt. Jerome lost the toss. I feel no guilt. I'd have done the same if I had lost.

The Nerva had spewed fused bits of the fission pile all over the bubble cavity. We were trapped for good. Rather, I was trapped. Jerome was dead, and we knew it. The bubble cavity was a hell of radiation.

He came back out, told me good-bye, strode out onto the ice and took off his helmet.

I remember I was crying, partly from grief and partly from fear. I remember that I kept my voice steady in spite of it. Jerome never knew. What he guessed is his own affair.

But that all seems infinitely remote. Jerome stands out there with his helmet clutched in his hands: a statue to himself, the first man on Pluto. The frost of recondensed moisture conceals his expression.

Sunrise. I hope the amoeba—

That was wild. The sun stood poised for a moment, a white point-source between twin peaks. Then it streaked upward—and the spinning sky jolted to a stop. No wonder I didn't catch it before. It happened so fast.

A horrible thought. What has happened to me could have happened to Jerome! I wonder—

I stayed with the landing vehicle for about thirty hours,

taking soil and ice samples, talking to Sammy on the laser beam, delivering high-minded last messages, feeling sorry for myself. I kept passing Jerome's statue. For a corpse, and one who has not been prettified by the skills of an embalmer, he looks damned good. I wondered each time how I would look when I followed his example. And an idea came.

This is what comes of not wanting to die.

There was Sammy in the Earth-return vehicle, but he couldn't get down to me. I couldn't get up. The lifesystem was in good order, but sooner or later I would freeze to death or run out of air.

Sammy and I had talked of ways to keep me alive. In my exploring I had looked for strata of frozen oxygen. I hadn't found that. But there was dirty water ice. Electrolysis would extract the oxygen.

But a rescue ship would take years. They'd have to build it from the ground up, and redesign the landing vehicle too. Electrolysis takes power, and heat takes power, and all I had was the batteries.

Sooner or later I'd run out of power.

In Nevada, three billion miles from here, half a million corpses lie frozen in vaults surrounded by liquid nitrogen. Half a million dead men wait for an earthly resurrection, on the day medical science discovers how to unfreeze them safely, how to cure what was killing each of them, how to cure the additional damage done by ice crystals breaking cell walls all through their brains and bodies.

Half a million fools? But what choice did they have? They were dying.

I was dying.

A man can stay conscious for tens of seconds in vacuum. If I moved fast I could get out of my suit in that time. Without that insulation to protect me, Pluto's black night would suck the warmth from my body in seconds. At 50°

Absolute, I'd stay in frozen storage until one version or another of the Day of Resurrection.

Sunlight—

—And stars. No sign of the big blob that found me so singularly tasteless yesterday. But I could be looking in the wrong direction.

I hope it got to cover.

I'm looking east, out over the splash plain. In my peripheral vision the ship looks unchanged and undamaged.

My suit lies beside me on the ice. I stand on a peak of black rock, poised in my silvered underwear, looking eternally out at the horizon. Before the cold touched my brain, I found a last moment in which to assume a heroic stance. Go east, young men. Wouldn't you know I'd get my directions mixed? But it was night then.

Sammy Cross must be on his way home now. He'll tell them where I am.

Stars pour up from behind the mountains. The mountains and the splash plain and Jerome and I sink endlessly beneath the sky.

My corpse must be the coldest in history. Even the hopeful dead of Earth are only stored at liquid nitrogen temperatures. Pluto's night makes that look torrid, after the 50° A. heat of day seeps away into space.

A superconductor is what I am. Sunlight raises the temperature too high, switching me off like a damned machine at every dawn. But at night my nervous system becomes a superconductor. Currents flow; thoughts flow; sensations flow. Sluggishly. The one hundred and fifty-three hours of Pluto's rotation flash by in what feels like fifteen minutes. At that rate I can wait it out.

I stand as a statue and a viewpoint. No wonder I can't get emotional about anything. Water is a rock here, and my glands are contoured ice within me. But I feel sensations:

the pull of gravity, the pain in my ears, the tug of vacuum over every square inch of my body. The vacuum will not boil my blood. But the tensions are frozen into the ice of me, and my nerves tell me so. I feel the wind whistling from my lips, like an exhalation of cigarette smoke.

This is what comes of not wanting to die. What a joke if I got my wish!

Do you suppose they'll find me? Pluto's small for a planet. For a place to get lost in, a small planet is all too large. But there's the ship.

Though it seems to be covered with frost. Vaporized gases recondensed on the hull. Gray-white on gray-white, a lump on a dish of refrozen ice. I could stand here forever waiting for them to pick my ship from its surroundings.

Stop that.

Sunlight—

Stars rolling up the sky. The same patterns, endlessly rolling up from the same points. Does Jerome's corpse live the same half-life I live now? He should have stripped, as I did. My God! I wish I'd thought to wipe the ice from his eyes!

I wish that superfluid blob would come back.

Damn. It's *cold*.

Harlan Ellison said this was a New Wave story. I see his point: you don't often see a story in which the character never moves a muscle.

It first appeared in the *Future Unbounded* Program Book, for Westercon 1968. I charged the Westercon Committee a fee to use it. My miser's urge runs deep.

Renner was shaking his head. "I don't blame Littlemead a damn bit," he said. "The wonder is he didn't convince everyone on the planet."

"We're a stubborn lot," said Potter. "Yon squinting silhouette in the night sky may hae been too obvious, too . . ."

"Here I am, stupid!" Renner suggested.

"Aye. New Scots dinna like being treated as dullards, not even by Him."

THE MOTE IN GOD'S EYE, 1974

A RELIC OF THE EMPIRE

When the ship arrived, Dr. Richard Schultz-Mann was out among the plants, flying over and around them on a lift belt. He hovered over one, inspecting with proprietary interest an anomalous patch in its yellow foliage. This one would soon be ripe.

The nature-lover was a breadstick of a man, very tall and very thin, with an aristocratic head sporting a close-cropped growth of coppery hair and an asymmetric beard. A white streak ran above his right ear, and there was a patch of white on each side of the chin, one coinciding with the waxed spike. As his head moved in the double sunlight, the patches changed color instantly.

He took a tissue sample from the grayish patch, stored it, and started to move on . . .

The ship came down like a daylight meteor, streaking blue-white across the vague red glare of Big Mira. It slowed and circled high overhead, weaving drunkenly across the sky, then settled toward the plain near Mann's *Explorer*. Mann watched it land, then gave up his bumblebee activities and went to welcome the newcomers. He was amazed at the coincidence. As far as he knew, his had been the first ship ever to land here. The company would be good . . . but what could anyone possibly want here?

Little Mira set while he was skimming back. A flash of white at the far edge of the sea, and the tiny blue-white dwarf was gone. The shadows changed abruptly, turning the world red. Mann took off his pink-tinged goggles. Big Mira was still high, sixty degrees above the horizon and two hours from second sunset.

The newcomer was huge, a thick blunt-nosed cylinder twenty times the size of the *Explorer*. It looked old: not damaged, not even weathered, but indefinably old. Its nose was still closed tight, the living bubble retracted, if indeed it had a living bubble. Nothing moved nearby. They must be waiting for his welcome before they debarked.

Mann dropped toward the newcomer.

The stunner took him a few hundred feet up. Without pain and without sound, suddenly all Mann's muscles turned to loose jelly. Fully conscious and completely helpless, he continued to dive toward the ground.

Three figures swarmed up at him from the newcomer's oversized airlock. They caught him before he hit. Tossing humorous remarks at each other in a language Mann did not know, they towed him down to the plain.

The man behind the desk wore a captain's hat and a cheerful smile. "Our supply of Verinol is limited," he said in the trade language. "If I have to use it, I will, but I'd rather save it. You may have heard that it has unpleasant side effects."

"I understand perfectly," said Mann. "You'll use it the moment you think you've caught me in a lie." Since he had not yet been injected with the stuff, he decided it was a bluff. The man had no Verinol, if indeed there was such an animal as Verinol.

But he was still in a bad hole. The ancient, renovated ship held more than a dozen men, whereas Mann seriously doubted if he could have stood up. The sonic had not entirely worn off.

His captor nodded approvingly. He was huge and square, almost a cartoon of a heavy-planet man, with muscularity as smooth and solid as an elephant's. A Jinxian, for anyone's money. His size made the tiny shipboard office seem little more than a coffin. Among the crew his captain's hat would not be needed to enforce orders. He looked like he could kick holes in hullmetal, or teach tact to an armed Kzin.

"You're quick," he said. "That's good. I'll be asking questions about you and about this planet. You'll give truthful, complete answers. If some of my questions get too personal, say so; but remember, I'll use the Verinol if I'm not satisfied. How old are you?"

"One hundred and fifty-four."

"You look much older."

"I was off boosterspice for a couple of decades."

"Tough luck. Planet of origin?"

"Wunderland."

"Thought so, with that stick-figure build. Name?"

"Doctor Richard Harvey Schultz-Mann."

"Rich Mann, hah? Are you?"

Trust a Jinxian to spot a pun. "No. After I make my reputation, I'll write a book on the Slaver Empire. Then I'll be rich."

"If you say so. Married?"

"Several times. Not at the moment."

"Rich Mann, I can't give you my real name, but you can call me Captain Kidd. What kind of beard is that?"

"You've never seen an asymmetric beard?"

"No, thank the Mist Demons. It looks like you've shaved

off all your hair below the part, and everything on your face
left of what looks like a one-tuft goatee. Is that the way it's
supposed to go?''

"Exactly so.''

"You did it on purpose then.''

"Don't mock me, Captain Kidd.''

"Point taken. Are they popular on Wunderland?''

Dr. Mann unconsciously sat a little straighter. "Only
among those willing to take the time and trouble to keep it
neat.'' He twisted the single waxed spike of beard at the
right of his chin with unconscious complacence. This was
the only straight hair on his face—the rest of the beard being
close-cropped and curly—and it sprouted from one of the
white patches. Mann was proud of his beard.

"Hardly seems worth it,'' said the Jinxian. "I assume
it's to show you're one of the leisure classes. What are you
doing on Mira Ceti-T?''

"I'm investigating one aspect of the Slaver Empire.''

"You're a geologist, then?''

"No, a xenobiologist.''

"I don't understand.''

"What do you know about the Slavers?''

"A little. They used to live all through this part of the
galaxy. One day the slave races decided they'd had enough,
and there was a war. When it was over, everyone was
dead.''

"You know quite a bit. Well, Captain, a billion and a
half years is a long time. The Slavers left only two kinds of
evidence of their existence. There are the stasis boxes and
their contents, mostly weaponry, but records have been
found too. And there are the plants and animals developed
for the Slavers' convenience by their tnuctip slaves, who
were biological engineers.''

"I know about those. We have bandersnatchi on Jinx, on
both sides of the ocean.''

"The bandersnatchi food animals are a special case. They

can't mutate; their chromosomes are as thick as your finger, too large to be influenced by radiation. All other relics of tnuctipun engineering have mutated almost beyond recognition. Almost. For the past twelve years I've been searching out and identifying the surviving species."

"It doesn't sound like a fun way to spend a life, Rich Mann. Are there Slaver animals on this planet?"

"Not animals, but plants. Have you been outside yet?"

"Not yet."

"Then come out. I'll show you."

The ship was very large. It did not seem to be furnished with a living bubble, hence the entire lifesystem must be enclosed within the metal walls. Mann walked ahead of the Jinxian down a long unpainted corridor to the airlock, waited inside while the pressure dropped slightly, then rode the escalator to the ground. He would not try to escape yet, though the sonic had worn off. The Jinxian was affable but alert, he carried a flashlight-laser dangling from his belt, his men were all around them, and Mann's lift belt had been removed. Richard Mann was not quixotic.

It was a red, red world. They stood on a dusty plain sparsely scattered with strange yellow-headed bushes. A breeze blew things like tumbleweeds across the plain, things which on second glance were the dried heads of former bushes. No other life-forms were visible. Big Mira sat on the horizon, a vague, fiery semicircular cloud, just dim enough to look at without squinting. Outlined in sharp black silhouette against the red giant's bloody disk were three slender, improbably tall spires, unnaturally straight and regular, each with a vivid patch of yellow vegetation surrounding its base. Members of the Jinxian's crew ran, walked, or floated outside, some playing an improvised variant of baseball, others at work, still others merely enjoying themselves. None were Jinxian, and none had Mann's light-planet build. Mann noticed that a few were using the thin wire blades of variable-knives to cut down some of the straight bushes.

"Those," he said.

"The bushes?"

"Yes. They used to be tnuctip stage trees. We don't know what they looked like originally, but the old records say the Slavers stopped using them some decades before the rebellion. May I ask what those men are doing in my ship?"

Expanded from its clamshell nose, the *Explorer*'s living bubble was bigger than the *Explorer*. Held taut by air pressure, isolated from the surrounding environment, proof against any atmospheric chemistry found in nature, the clear fabric hemisphere was a standard feature of all camper-model spacecraft. Mann could see biped shadows moving purposefully about inside and going between the clamshell doors into the ship proper.

"They're not stealing anything, Rich Mann. I sent them in to remove a few components from the drives and the comm systems."

"One hopes they won't damage what they remove."

"They won't. They have their orders."

"I assume you don't want me to call someone," said Mann. He noticed that the men were preparing a bonfire, using stage bushes. The bushes were like miniature trees, four to six feet tall, slender and straight, and the brilliant yellow foliage at the top was flattened like the head of a dandelion. From the low, rounded eastern mountains to the western sea, the red land was sprinkled with the yellow dots of their heads. Men were cutting off the heads and roots, then dragging the logs away to pile them in conical formation over a stack of death-dry tumbleweed heads.

"We don't want you to call the Wunderland police, who happen to be somewhere out there looking for us."

"I hate to pry—"

"No, no, you're entitled to your curiosity. We're pirates."

"Surely you jest. Captain Kidd, if you've figured out a way to make piracy pay off, you must be bright enough to make ten times the money on the stock market."

"Why?"

By the tone of his voice, by his gleeful smile, the Jinxian was baiting him. Fine; it would keep his mind off stage trees. Mann said, "Because you can't *catch* a ship in hyperspace. The only way you can match courses with a ship is to wait until it's in an inhabited system. Then the police come calling."

"I know an inhabited system where there aren't any police."

"The hell you do."

They had walked more or less aimlessly to the *Explorer*'s airlock. Now the Jinxian turned and gazed out over the red plain, toward the dwindling crescent of Big Mira, which now looked like a bad forest fire. "I'm curious about those spires."

"Fine, keep your little secret. I've wondered about them myself, but I haven't had a chance to look at them yet."

"I'd think they'd interest you. They look definitely artificial to me."

"But they're a billion years too young to be Slaver artifacts."

"Rich Mann, are those bushes the only life on this planet?"

"I haven't seen anything else," Mann lied.

"Then it couldn't have been a native race that put those spires up. I never heard of a space-traveling race that builds such big things for mere monuments."

"Neither did I. Shall we look at them tomorrow?"

"Yes." Captain Kidd stepped into the *Explorer*'s airlock, wrapped a vast hand gently around Mann's thin wrist and pulled his captive in beside him. The airlock cycled and Mann followed the Jinxian into the living bubble with an impression that the Jinxian did not quite trust him.

Fine.

It was dark inside the bubble. Mann hesitated before turning on the light. Outside he could see the last red sliver of Big Mira shrinking with visible haste. He saw more. A man was kneeling before the conical bonfire, and a flickering light was growing in the dried bush-head kindling.

Mann turned on the lights, obliterating the outside view. "Go on about piracy," he said.

"Oh, yes." The Jinxian dropped into a chair, frowning. "Piracy was only the end product. It started a year ago, when I found the puppeteer system."

"The—"

"Yes. The puppeteers' home system."

Richard Mann's ears went straight up. He was from Wunderland, remember?

Puppeteers are highly intelligent, herbivorous, and very old as a species. Their corner on interstellar business is as old as the human Bronze Age. And they are cowards.

A courageous puppeteer is not regarded as insane only by other puppeteers. It *is* insane, and usually shows disastrous secondary symptoms: depression, homicidal tendencies, and the like. These poor, warped minds are easy to spot. No sane puppeteer will cross a vehicular roadway or travel in any but the safest available fashion or resist a thief, even an unarmed thief. No sane puppeteer will leave his home system, wherever that may be, without his painless method of suicide, nor will it walk an alien world without guards— nonpuppeteer guards.

The location of the puppeteer system is one of the puppeteer's most closely guarded secrets. Another is the painless suicide gimmick. It may be a mere trick of preconditioning. Whatever it is, it works. Puppeteers cannot be tortured into revealing anything about their home world, though they hate pain. It must be a world with reasonably earthlike atmosphere and temperature, but beyond that nothing is known . . . or was known.

Suddenly Mann wished that they hadn't lit the bonfire so soon. He didn't know how long it would burn before the logs caught, and he wanted to hear more about this.

"I found it just a year ago," the Jinxian repeated. "It's best I don't tell you what I was doing up to then. The less you know about who I am, the better. But when I'd got safely out of the system, I came straight home. I wanted time to think."

"And you picked piracy? Why not blackmail?"

"I thought of that—"

"I should hope so! Can you imagine what the puppeteers would pay to keep that secret?"

"Yes. That's what stopped me. Rich Mann, how much would you have asked for in one lump sum?"

"A round billion stars and immunity from prosecution."

"Okay. Now look at it from the puppeteer point of view. That billion wouldn't buy them complete safety, because you might still talk. But if they spent a tenth of that on detectives, weapons, hit men, et cetera, they could shut your mouth for keeps and also find and hit anyone you might have talked to. I couldn't figure any way to make myself safe and still collect, not with that much potential power against me.

"So I thought of piracy.

"Eight of us had gone in, but I was the only one who'd guessed just what we'd stumbled into. I let the others in on it. Some had friends they could trust, and that raised our number to fourteen. We bought a ship, a very old one, and renovated it. She's an old slowboat's ground-to-orbit auxiliary fitted out with a new hyperdrive; maybe you noticed?"

"No. I saw how old she was."

"We figured even if the puppeteers recognized her, they'd

never trace her. We took her back to the puppeteer system and waited.''

A flickering light glimmered outside the bubble wall. Any second now the logs would catch . . . Mann tried to relax.

''Pretty soon a ship came in. We waited till it was too deep in the system's gravity well to jump back into hyperspace. Then we matched courses. Naturally they surrendered right away. We went in in suits so they couldn't describe us even if they could tell humans apart. Would you believe they had six hundred million stars in currency?''

''That's pretty good pay. What went wrong?''

''My idiot crew wouldn't leave. We'd figured most of the ships coming into the puppeteer system would be carrying money. They're misers, you know. Part of being a coward is wanting security. And they do most of their mining and manufacturing on other worlds, where they can get labor. So we waited for two more ships, because we had room for lots more money. The puppeteers wouldn't dare attack us inside their own system.'' Captain Kidd made a sound of disgust. ''I can't really blame the men. In a sense they were right. One ship with a fusion drive can do a hell of a lot of damage just by hovering over a city. So we stayed.

''Meanwhile the puppeteers registered a formal complaint with Earth.

''Earth hates people who foul up interstellar trade. We'd offered physical harm to a puppeteer. A thing like that could cause a stock-market crash. So Earth offered the services of every police force in human space. Hardly seems fair, does it?''

''They ganged up on you. But they still couldn't come after you, could they? The puppeteers would have to tell the police how to find their system. They'd hardly do that; not when some human descendant might attack them a thousand years from now.''

The Jinxian dialed himself a frozen daiquiri. ''They had to wait till we left. I still don't know how they tracked us.

Maybe they've got something that can track a gravity warp moving faster than light. I wouldn't put it past them to build it just for us. Anyway, when we angled toward Jinx, we heard them telling the police of We Made It just where we were.''

"Ouch."

"We headed for the nearest double star. Not my idea; Hermie Preston's. He thought we could hide in the dust clouds in the trojan points. Whatever the puppeteers were using probably couldn't find us in normal space." Two thirsty gulps had finished his daiquiri. He crumpled the cup, watched it evaporate, dialed another. "The nearest double star was Mira Ceti. We hardly expected to find a planet in the trailing trojan point, but as long as it was there, we decided to use it."

"And here you are."

"Yeah."

"You'll be better off when you've found a way to hide that ship."

"We had to find out about you first, Rich Mann. Tomorrow we'll sink the *Puppet Master* in the ocean. Already we've shut off the fusion drive. The lifters work by battery, and the cops can't detect that."

"Fine. Now for the billion-dollar—"

"No, no, Rich Mann. I will not tell you where to find the puppeteer planet. Give up the whole idea. Shall we join the campfire group?"

Mann came joltingly alert. *How* had the stage trees lasted this long? Thinking fast, he said, "Is your autokitchen as good as mine?"

"Probably not. Why?"

"Let me treat your group to dinner, Captain Kidd."

Captain Kidd shook his head, smiling. "No offense, Rich Mann, but I can't read your kitchen controls, and there's no point in tempting you. You might rashly put someth—"

WHAM!

The living bubble bulged inward, snapped back. Captain Kidd swore and ran for the airlock. Mann stayed seated, motionless, hoping against hope that the Jinxian had forgotten him.

WHAM! WHAM! Flares of light from the region of the campfire. Captain Kidd frantically punched the cycle button, and the opaque inner door closed on him. Mann came to his feet, running.

WHAM! The concussion hurt his ears and set the bubble rippling. Burning logs must be flying in all directions. The airlock recycled, empty. No telling where the Jinxian was; the outer door was opaque too. Well, that worked both ways.

WHAM!

Mann searched through the airlock locker, pushing sections of spacesuit aside to find the lift belt. It wasn't there. He'd been wearing it; they'd taken it off him after they shot him down.

He moaned: a tormented, uncouth sound to come from a cultured Wunderlander. He *had* to have a lift belt.

WHAMWHAMWHAM. Someone was screaming far away.

Mann snatched up the suit's chest-and-shoulder section and locked it around him. It was rigid vacuum armor, with a lift motor built into the back. He took an extra moment to screw down the helmet, then hit the cycle button.

No use searching for weapons. They'd have taken even a variable-knife.

The Jinxian could be just outside waiting. He might have realized the truth by now.

The door opened. . . . Captain Kidd was easy to find, a running misshapen shadow and a frantic booming voice. "Flatten out, you yeastheads! It's an attack!" He hadn't guessed. But he must know that the We Made It police would use stunners.

Mann twisted his lift control to full power.

The surge of pressure took him under the armpits. Two

standard gees sent blood rushing to his feet, pushed him upward with four times Wunderland's gravity. A last stage log exploded under him, rocked him back and forth, and then all was dark and quiet.

He adjusted the attitude setting to slant him almost straight forward. The dark ground sped beneath him. He moved northeast. Nobody was following him—yet.

Captain Kidd's men would have been killed, hurt, or at least stunned when the campfire exploded in their faces. He'd expected Captain Kidd to chase him, but the Jinxian couldn't have caught him. Lift motors are all alike, and Mann wasn't as heavy as the Jinxian.

He flew northeast, flying very low, knowing that the only landmarks big enough to smash him were the spires to the west. When he could no longer see the ships' lights, he turned south, still very low. Still nobody followed him. He was glad he'd taken the helmet; it protected his eyes from the wind.

In the blue dawn he came awake. The sky was darker than navy blue, and the light around him was dim, like blue moonlight. Little Mira was a hurtingly bright pinpoint between two mountain peaks, bright enough to sear holes in a man's retinae. Mann unscrewed his helmet, adjusted the pink goggles over his eyes. Now it was even darker.

He poked his nose above the yellow moss. The plain and sky were empty of men. The pirates must be out looking for him, but they hadn't gotten here yet. So far so good.

Far out across the plain there was fire. A stage tree rose rapidly into the black sky, minus its roots and flowers, the wooden flanges at its base holding it in precarious aerodynamic stability. A white rope of smoke followed it up. When the smoke cut off, the tree became invisible . . . until, much higher, there was a puff of white cloud like a flak burst. Now the seeds would be spreading across the sky.

Richard Mann smiled. Wonderful, how the stage trees

had adapted to the loss of their masters. The Slavers had raised them on wide plantations, using the solid-fuel rocket cores inside the living bark to lift their ships from places where a fusion drive would have done damage. But the trees used the rockets for reproduction, to scatter their seeds farther than any planet before them.

Ah, well . . . Richard Mann snuggled deeper into the yellow woolly stuff around him and began to consider his next move. He was a hero now in the eyes of humanity-at-large. He had badly damaged the pirate crew. When the police landed, he could count on a reward from the puppeteers. Should he settle for that or go on to bigger stakes?

The *Puppet Master*'s cargo was bigger stakes, certainly. But even if he could take it, which seemed unlikely, how could he fit it into his ship? How escape the police of We Made It?

No. Mann had another stake in mind, one just as valuable and infinitely easier to hide.

What Captain Kidd apparently hadn't realized was that blackmail is not immoral to a puppeteer. There are well-established rules of conduct that make blackmail perfectly safe both for blackmailer and victim. Two are that the black-mailer must submit to having certain portions of his memory erased, and must turn over all evidence against the victim. Mann was prepared to do this if he could force Captain Kidd to tell him where to find the puppeteer system.

But how?

Well, he knew one thing the Jinxian didn't. . . .

Little Mira rose fast, arc blue, a hole into hell. Mann remained where he was, an insignificant mote in the yellow vegetation below one of the spires Captain Kidd had remarked on last night. The spire was a good half mile high. An artifact that size would seem impossibly huge to any but an Earthman. The way it loomed over him made Mann uncomfortable. In shape it was a slender cone with a base three hundred feet across. The surface near the base was gray and smooth to touch, like polished granite.

The yellow vegetation was a thick, rolling carpet. It spread out around the spire in an uneven circle half a mile in diameter and dozens of feet deep. It rose about the base in a thick turtleneck collar. Close up, the stuff wasn't even discrete plants. It looked like a cross between moss and wool, dyed flagrant yellow.

It made a good hiding place. Not perfect, of course; a heat sensor would pick him out in a flash. He hadn't thought of that last night, and now it worried him. Should he get out, try to reach the sea?

The ship would certainly carry a heat sensor, but not a portable one. A portable heat sensor would be a weapon, a nighttime gunsight, and weapons of war had been illegal for some time in human space.

But the *Puppet Master* could have stopped elsewhere to get such implements. Kzinti, for example.

Nonsense. Why would Captain Kidd have needed portable weapons with night gunsights? He certainly hadn't expected puppeteers to fight hand-to-hand! The stunners were mercy weapons; even a pirate would not dare kill a puppeteer, and Captain Kidd was no ordinary pirate.

All right. Radar? He need only burrow into the moss/wool. Sight search? Same answer. Radio? Mental note: Do not transmit anything.

Mental note? There was a dictaphone in his helmet. He used it after pulling the helmet out of the moss/wool around him.

Flying figures. Mann watched them for a long moment, trying to spot the Jinxian. There were only four, and he wasn't among them. The four were flying northwest of him, moving south. Mann ducked into the moss.

"Hello, Rich Mann."

The voice was low, contorted with fury. Mann felt the

shock race through him, contracting every muscle with the
fear of death. It came from behind him!

From his helmet.

"Hello, Rich Mann. Guess where I am?"

He couldn't turn it off. Spacesuit helmet radios weren't
built to be turned off: a standard safety factor. If one were
fool enough to ignore safety, one could insert an "off"
switch; but Mann had never felt the need.

"I'm in your ship, using your ship-to-suit radio circuit.
That was a good trick you played last night. I didn't even
know what a stage tree was till I looked it up in your
library."

He'd just have to endure it. A pity he couldn't answer
back.

"You killed four of my men and put five more in the
autodoc tanks. Why'd you do it, Rich Mann? You must
have known we weren't going to kill you. Why should we?
There's no blood on *our* hands."

You lie, Mann thought at the radio. *People die in a market
crash. And the ones who live are the ones who suffer. Do
you know what it's like to be suddenly poor and not know
how to live poor?*

"I'll assume you want something, Rich Mann. All right.
What? The money in my hold? That's ridiculous. You'd
never get in. You want to turn us in for a reward? Fat
chance. You've got no weapons. If we find you now, we'll
kill you."

The four searchers passed far to the west, their headlamps
spreading yellow light across the blue dusk. They were no
danger to him now. A pity they and their fellows should
have been involved in what amounted to a vendetta.

"The puppeteer planet, of course. The modern El Do-
rado. But you don't know where it is, do you? I wonder if
I ought to give you a hint. Of course you'd never know
whether I was telling the truth. . . ."

Did the Jinxian know how to live poor? Mann shuddered.

The old memories came back only rarely; but when they came, they hurt.

You have to learn not to buy luxuries before you've bought necessities. You can starve learning which is which. Necessities are food and a place to sleep, shoes and pants. Luxuries are tobacco, restaurants, fine shirts, throwing away a ruined meal while you're learning to cook, quitting a job you don't like. A union is a necessity. Boosterspice is a luxury.

The Jinxian wouldn't know about that. He'd had the money to buy his own ship.

"Ask me politely, Rich Mann. Would you like to know where I found the puppeteer system?"

Mann had leased the *Explorer* on a college grant. It had been the latest step in a long climb upward. Before that . . .

He was half his lifetime old when the crash came. Until then boosterspice had kept him as young as the ageless idle ones who were his friends and relatives. Overnight he was one of the hungry. A number of his partners in disaster had ridden their lift belts straight up into eternity; Richard Schultz-Mann had sold his for his final dose of boosterspice. Before he could afford boosterspice again, there were wrinkles in his forehead, the texture of his skin had changed, his sex urge had decreased, strange white patches had appeared in his hair, there were twinges in his back. He still got them.

Yet always he had maintained his beard. With the white spike and the white streak it looked better than ever. After the boosterspice restored color to his hair, he dyed the patches back in again.

"Answer me, Rich Mann!"

Go ride a bandersnatch.

It was a draw. Captain Kidd couldn't entice him into answering, and Mann would never know the pirate's secret. If Kidd dropped his ship in the sea, Mann could show it to the police. At least that would be something.

Luckily Kidd couldn't move the *Explorer*. Otherwise he could take both ships half around the planet, leaving Mann stranded.

The four pirates were far to the south. Captain Kidd had apparently given up on the radio. There were water and food syrup in his helmet; Mann would not starve.

Where in blazes were the police? On the other side of the planet?

Stalemate.

Big Mira came as a timorous peeping Tom, poking its rim over the mountains like red smoke. The land brightened, taking on tinges of lavender against long, long navy blue shadows. The shadows shortened and became vague.

The morality of his position was beginning to bother Dr. Richard Mann.

In attacking the pirates, he had done his duty as a citizen. The pirates had sullied humanity's hard-won reputation for honesty. Mann had struck back.

But his motive? Fear had been two parts of that motive. First, the fear that Captain Kidd might decide to shut his mouth. Second, the fear of being poor.

That fear had been with him for some time.

Write a book and make a fortune! It looked good on paper. The thirty-light-year sphere of human space contained nearly fifty billion readers. Persuade one percent of them to shell out half a star each for a disposable tape, and your four-percent royalties became twenty million stars. But most books nowadays were flops. You had to scream very loud nowadays to get the attention of even ten billion readers. Others were trying to drown you out.

Before Captain Kidd, that had been Richard Schultz-Mann's sole hope of success.

He'd behaved within the law. Captain Kidd couldn't make that claim; but Captain Kidd hadn't killed anybody.

Mann sighed. He'd had no choice. His major motive was honor, and that motive still held.

He moved restlessly in his nest of damp moss/wool. The day was heating up, and his suit's temperature control would not work with half a suit.

What was that?

It was the *Puppet Master*, moving effortlessly toward him on its lifters. The Jinxian must have decided to get it under water before the human law arrived.

. . . Or had he?

Mann adjusted his lift motor until he was just short of weightless, then moved cautiously around the spire. He saw the four pirates moving to intersect the *Puppet Master*. They'd see him if he left the spire. But if he stayed, those infrared detectors . . .

He'd have to chance it.

The suit's padded shoulders gouged his armpits as he streaked toward the second spire. He stopped in midair over the moss and dropped, burrowed in it. The pirates didn't swerve.

Now he'd see

The ship slowed to a stop over the spire he'd just left.

"Can you hear me, Rich Mann?"

Mann nodded gloomily to himself. Definitely, that was it.

"I should have tried this before. Since you're nowhere in sight, you've either left the vicinity altogether or you're hiding in the thick bushes around those towers."

Should he try to keep dodging from spire to spire? Or could he outfly them?

At least one was bound to be faster. The armor increased his weight.

"I hope you took the opportunity to examine this tower. It's fascinating. Very smooth, stony surface, except at the top. A perfect cone, also except at the top. You listening?

The tip of this thing swells from an eight-foot neck into an egg-shaped knob fifteen feet across. The knob isn't polished as smooth as the rest of it. Vaguely reminiscent of an asparagus spear, wouldn't you say?''

Richard Schultz-Mann cocked his head, tasting an idea.

He unscrewed his helmet, ripped out and pocketed the radio. In frantic haste he began ripping out double handfuls of the yellow moss/wool, stuffed them into a wad in the helmet, and turned his lighter on it. At first the vegetation merely smoldered, while Mann muttered through clenched teeth. Then it caught with a weak blue smokeless flame. Mann placed his helmet in a mossy nest, setting it so it would not tip over and spill its burning contents.

''I'd have said a phallic symbol, myself. What do you think, Rich Mann? If these are phallic symbols, they're pretty well distorted. Humanoid but not human, you might say.''

The pirates had joined their ship. They hovered around its floating silver bulk, ready to drop on him when the *Puppet Master*'s infrared detectors found him.

Mann streaked away to the west on full acceleration, staying as low as he dared. The spire would shield him for a minute or so, and then . . .

''This vegetation isn't stage trees, Rich Mann. It looks like some sort of grass from here. Must need something in the rock they made these erections out of. Mph. No hot spots. You're not down there after all. Well, we try the next one.''

Behind him, in the moments when he dared look back, Mann saw the *Puppet Master* move to cover the second spire, the one he'd left a moment ago, the one with a gray streak in the moss at its base. Four humanoid dots clustered loosely above the ship.

''Peekaboo,'' came the Jinxian's voice. ''And good-bye, killer.''

The *Puppet Master*'s fusion drive went on. Fusion flame

lashed out in a blue-white spear, played down the side of the pillar and into the moss/wool below. Mann faced forward and concentrated on flying. He felt neither elation nor pity, but only disgust. The Jinxian was a fool after all. He'd seen no life on Mira Ceti-T but for the stage trees. He had Mann's word that there was none. Couldn't he reach the obvious conclusion? Perhaps the moss/wool had fooled him. It certainly did look like yellow moss, clustering around the spires as if it needed some chemical element in the stone.

A glance back told him that the pirate ship was still spraying white flame over the spire and the foliage below. He'd have been a cinder by now. The Jinxian must want him extremely dead. Well—

The spire went all at once. It sat on the lavender plain in a hemisphere of multicolored fire, engulfing the other spires and the Jinxian ship; and then it began to expand and rise. Mann adjusted his attitude to vertical to get away from the ground. A moment later the shock wave slammed into him and blew him tumbling over the desert.

Two white ropes of smoke rose straight up through the dimming explosion cloud. The other spires were taking off while still green! Fire must have reached the foliage at their bases.

Mann watched them go with his head thrown back and his body curiously loose in the vacuum armor. His expression was strangely contented. At these times he could forget himself and his ambitions in the contemplation of immortality.

Two knots formed simultaneously in the rising smoke trails. Second stage on. They rose very fast now.

"Rich Mann."

Mann flicked his transmitter on. "You'd live through anything."

"Not I. I can't feel anything below my shoulders. Listen, Rich Mann, I'll trade secrets with you. What happened?"

"The big towers are stage trees."

"Uh?" Half question, half an expression of agony.

"A stage tree has two life cycles. One is the bush, the other is the big multistage form." Mann talked faster, fearful of losing his audience. "The forms alternate. A stage tree seed lands on a planet and grows into a bush. Later there are lots of bushes. When a seed hits a particularly fertile spot, it grows into a multistage form. You still there?"

"Yuh."

"In the big form the living part is the tap root and the photosynthetic organs around the base. That way the rocket section doesn't have to carry so much weight. It grows straight up out of the living part, but it's as dead as the center of an oak except for the seed at the top. When it's ripe, the rocket takes off. Usually it'll reach terminal velocity for the system it's in. Kidd, I can't see your ship; I'll have to wait till the smoke—"

"Just keep talking."

"I'd like to help."

"Too late. Keep talking."

"I've tracked the stage trees across twenty light-years of space. God knows where they started. They're all through the systems around here. The seed pods spend hundreds of thousands of years in space; and when they enter a system, they explode. If there's a habitable world, one seed is bound to hit it. If there isn't, there's lots more pods where that one came from. It's immortality, Captain Kidd. This one plant has traveled farther than mankind, and it's much older. A billion and a—"

"Mann."

"Yah."

"Twenty-three point six, seventy point one, six point nil. I don't know its name on the star charts. Shall I repeat that?"

Mann forgot the stage trees. "Better repeat it."

"Twenty-three point six, seventy point one, six point

nothing. Hunt in that area till you find it. It's a red giant, undersized. Planet is small, dense, no moon.''

"Got it.''

"You're stupid if you use it. You'll have the same luck I did. That's why I told you.''

"I'll use blackmail.''

"They'll kill you. Otherwise I wouldn't have said. Why'd you kill me, Rich Mann?''

"I didn't like your remarks about my beard. Never insult a Wunderlander's asymmetric beard, Captain Kidd.''

"I won't do it again.''

"I'd like to help.'' Mann peered into the billowing smoke. Now it was a black pillar tinged at the edges by the twin sunlight. "Still can't see your ship.''

"You will in a moment.''

The pirate moaned . . . and Mann saw the ship. He managed to turn his head in time to save his eyes.

This is the story that joined early Known Space to late Known Space; and all for the sake of a practical joke. Stage tree logs belong to the Slaver Empire and thus to WORLD OF PTAVVS. Easy interstellar travel belonged to the Beowulf Shaeffer era.

I wanted to watch a bonfire made from stage tree logs. In a previous life I expect I was a pyromaniac.

Some day I will come to a WorldCon wearing a proper asymmetric beard. I've been planning this for some time . . . and never quite found the courage.

From *LUCIFER'S HAMMER*
(with JERRY POURNELLE)

LUCIFER'S HAMMER began as an alien invasion novel.

Jerry and I had written two novels together: THE MOTE IN GOD'S EYE and INFERNO. The editor who bought both for Pocket Books was Bob Gleason.

One day Jerry got a phone call from New York. He told me about it later. "Bob Gleason thinks we should write a novel about an alien invasion of Earth."

I laughed long and hard. "I hope you broke it to him gently that it's been *done*."

"Yeah, but he says it hasn't been done well since *The War of the Worlds*."

Gleason had convinced Jerry. Jerry convinced me. We began planning the invasion of Earth.

We needed an intelligent species who would have the horsepower to cross several-to-many light-years and arrive with intent to conquer an unknown planet. Not a trivial problem. A species with that much energy at hand would be better advised to make more room for themselves: to build O'Neall colonies or Dyson shells, instead of crossing interstellar space to be shot at. By the time they got here, they'd want Jupiter, not Earth.

One bit of military strategy was instantly obvious. With an interstellar spacecraft capable of carrying enough troops and weaponry to conquer a world, and enough people to hold what they've taken, they can damn sure move a medium asteroid.

So we wrote it into the outline: a major asteroid impact, with all the predictable results. We examined a globe I keep in my office and decided to let the invaders drop it in the Indian Ocean, then invade South Africa. (Jerry had been to South Africa.)

Meanwhile Bob Gleason had moved to Playboy Books.

We sent him our outline anyway. His answer was, "Forget aliens. Write about giant meteoroid impact."

Two points now. First, if the asteroid isn't being *guided*, then that's a whole different game. Second, the Earth is at least as likely to be hit by a comet nucleus as by an asteroid. Earth has been tracing its orbit for five billion years. Most of the asteroids that could hit us did it early. Life on Earth may have been destroyed more than once—and we worked all of this out before the Alvarezes got into the act. More on them later.

We picked a comet because I like comets, because I already knew quite a lot about them, and for visuals. Our unhappy protagonists would see it coming. We called it Lucifer's Hammer, and never argued about the title. The discoverer of the comet we named Tim Hamner, for the comet itself.

Impact craters are always circular. One afternoon we spun that globe of the Earth and put circles around everything that looked vaguely circular. I put two interlocked circles on the Gulf of Mexico. A few years later, some geologists announced their theory that a pair of asteroid strikes had carved the seabed there.

My father and stepmother owned part of a working ranch near Centerville. Five families traded it off as a vacation spot. Jerry and I borrowed the place and visited it twice, for research. The River Valley Ranch became the Stronghold.

Some of our friends entered the book as characters. Frank Gasperik became Mark Czescu. We'd heard Frank play his song, "Culture"; we bought the right to publish it. Dan Alderson became Dan Forrester; we asked him for advice on what *he* would do if the Hammer fell.

When we sent Bob Gleason a partial draft, he suggested alterations that drove us nearly berserk.

Bob came out to California. Mellowed by a fine dinner at Mon Grenier (our favorite restaurant, mentioned in the book), we returned to the house. We left all wives downstairs and went up to my office to fight.

Jerry and I hit him in stereo. We didn't want *any* of his changes. Bob was forced to agree with us on every point.

After Bob went home, we talked it over, then . . .

Most editors can't tell you how to fix a problem; but where the editor sees a problem, something needs fixing. We followed Bob's way about half the time. We made corrections *every* time.

HAMMER was six months overdue. It *always* seems a book is taking too long. We worked hard during that Christmas season: a thing I resented. I didn't become a writer to work!

Wherever I've quoted from a collaboration in this book, it is *always* true that that passage was rewritten by both of us until it was right. Here I give examples, but take it for granted elsewhere.

The Hot Fudge Sundae lecture emerged from one of our crazier planning sessions. Jerry played with his hand calculator and it just rolled out.

"Tell us, what would happen if the comet did hit us? Suppose we got unlucky."

"You mean the head? The nucleus? Because it looks as if we might actually pass through the outer coma. Which is nothing more than gas."

"No, I mean the head. What happens? The end of the world?"

"Oh, no. Nothing like that. Probably the end of civilization."

There was silence in the room for a moment. Then for another. "But," Harvey said, his voice puzzled, "Dr. Sharps, you told me that a comet, even the head, is largely foamy ice with rocks in it. And even the ice is frozen gases. That doesn't sound dangerous." In fact, Harvey thought, I asked to get it on the record.

"Several heads," Dan Forrester said. "At least it looks that way. I think it's beginning to calve already. And if it does it now, it will do it later. Probably. Maybe."

"So it's even less dangerous," Harvey said.

Sharps wasn't listening to Harvey. He rolled his eyes toward the ceiling. "Calving already?"

Forrester's grin widened. "Ook ook."

Then he noticed Harvey Randall again. "You asked about danger," he said. "Let's look at it. We have several masses, largely the same material that boils off to form the coma and the tail: fine dust, foamy frozen gases, with pockets where the really volatile stuff has been long gone, and maybe a few rocks embedded in there. Hey—" Randall looked up at Forrester.

Forrester was grinning his cherubic smile. "That's probably why it's so bright already. Some of the gases are interacting. Think what we'll see when they *really* get to boiling near the Sun! Ook ook."

Sharps was getting that thoughtful, lost look again. Harvey said quickly, "Dr. Sharps—"

"Oh. Yes, certainly. What happens if it hits? Which it won't. Well, what makes the nucleus dangerous is that it's big, and it's coming fast. Enormous energies."

"Because of the rocks?" Harvey asked. Rocks he could understand. "How big are those rocks?"

"Not very," Forrester said. "But that's theory—"

"Right." Sharps was aware of the camera again. "That's why we need the probe. We don't *know*. But I'd guess the rocks are small, from the size of a baseball to the size of a small hill."

Harvey felt relief. That couldn't be dangerous. A small hill?

"But of course that doesn't matter," Sharps said. "They'll be embedded in the frozen gases and water ice. It would all hit as several solid masses. Not as a lot of little chunks."

Harvey paused to think that over. This film would take careful editing. "It still doesn't sound dangerous. Even nickel-iron meteors usually burn out long before they hit the ground. In fact, in all history there's only been one recorded case of anyone being harmed by a meteor."

"Sure, that lady in Alabama," Forrester said. "It got her picture in *Life*. Wow, that was the biggest bruise I ever saw. Wasn't there a lawsuit? Her landlady said it was *her* meteor because it ended up in her basement."

Harvey said, "Look. Hamner-Brown will hit atmosphere a lot harder than any normal meteorite, and it's mostly ice. The masses will burn faster, won't they?"

He saw two shaking heads: a thin face wearing insectile glasses, and a thick bushy beard above thick glasses. And over against the wall Mark was shaking his head too. Sharps said, "They'd bore through quicker. When the mass is above a certain size, it stops being important whether Earth has an atmosphere or not."

"Except to us," Forrester said, deadpan.

Sharps paused a second, then laughed. Politely, Harvey thought, but it was done carefully. Sharps took pains to avoid offending Forrester. "What we need is a good analogy. Um . . ." Sharps's brow furrowed.

"Hot fudge sundae," said Forrester.

"Hah?"

Forrester's grin was wide through his beard. "A cubic mile of hot fudge sundae. Cometary speeds."

Sharps's eyes lit up. "I like it! Let's hit Earth with a cubic mile of hot fudge sundae."

Lord God, they've gone bonkers, Harvey thought. The two men raced each other to the blackboard. Sharps began to draw. "Okay. Hot fudge sundae. Let's see: We'll put the vanilla ice cream in the center with a layer of fudge over it. . . ."

He ignored the strangled sound behind him. Tim Hamner hadn't said a word during the whole interview. Now he was doubled over, holding himself, trying to hold in the laughter. He looked up, choked, got his face straight, said, "I can't stand it!" and brayed like a jackass. "My comet! A cubic mile of hot . . . fudge . . . sun . . . dae . . ."

"With the fudge as the outer shell," Forrester amplified, "so the fudge will heat up when the Hammer rounds the Sun."

"That's Hamner-Brown," Tim said, straight-faced.

"No, my child, that's a cubic mile of hot fudge sundae. And the ice cream will still be frozen inside the shell," said Sharps.

Harvey said, "But you forgot the—"

"We put the cherry at one pole and say that pole was in shadow at perihelion." Sharps sketched to show that when the comet rounded the Sun, the cherry at the oblate spheroid's axis would be on the side away from Sol. "We don't want it scorched. And we'll put crushed nuts all through it, to represent rocks. Say a two-hundred-foot cherry?"

"Carried by the Royal Canadian Air Force," Mark said.

"Stan Freberg! Right!" Forrester whooped. "Shhhh . . . plop! Let's see you do *that* on television!"

"And now, as the comet rounds the Sun, trailing a luminous froth of fake whipped cream, and aims itself down our throats . . . Dan, what's the density of vanilla ice cream?"

Forrester shrugged. "It floats. Say two-thirds."

"Right. Point six six six it is." Sharps seized a pocket calculator from the desk and punched frantically. "I *love* these things. Used to use slide rules. Never could figure out where the decimal point went.

"A cubic mile to play with. Five thousand two hundred and eighty feet, times twelve for inches, times two point five four for centimeters, cube that . . . We have two point seven seven six times ten to the fifteenth cubic centimeters of vanilla ice cream. It would take a while to eat it all. Times the density, and lo, we have about two times ten to the fifteenth grams. Couple of billion tons. Now for the fudge . . ." Sharps punched away.

Happy as a clam, Harvey thought. A very voluble clam equipped with Texas Instruments' latest pocket marvel.

"What do you like for the density of hot fudge?" Sharps asked.

"Call it point nine," Forrester said.

"Haven't any of you made fudge?" Charlene demanded. "It doesn't float. You test it by dripping it into a cup of cold water. Or at least my mother did."

"Say one point two, then," Forrester said.

"Another billion and a half tons of hot fudge," Sharps said. Behind him Hamner made more strangled noises.

"I think we can ignore the rocks," Sharps said. "Do you see why, now?"

"Lord God, yes," Harvey said. He looked at the camera with a start. "Uh, yes, Dr. Sharps, it certainly makes sense to ignore the rocks."

"You're not going to *show* this, are you?" Tim Hamner sounded indignant.

"You're saying no?" Harvey asked.

"No . . . no . . ." Hamner doubled over and giggled.

"Now, she's coming at cometary speeds. *Fast.* Let's see, parabolic speed at Earth orbit is what, Dan?"

"Twenty-nine point seven kilometers per second. Times square root of two."

"Forty-two kilometers a second," Sharps announced. "And we've got Earth's orbital velocity to add. Depends on the geometry of the strike. Shall we say fifty kilometers a second as a reasonable closing velocity?"

"Sounds good," Forrester said. "Meteors go from twenty to maybe seventy. It's reasonable."

"Right. Call it fifty. Square that, times a half. Times mass in grams. Bit over two times ten to the twenty-eight ergs. That's for the vanilla ice cream. Now we can figure that most of the hot fudge boiled away, but understand, Harvey, at those speeds we're just not in the atmosphere very long. If we come in straight it's two seconds flat! Anyway, whatever mass you burn up, a lot of the energy just gets transferred to the earth's heat balance. That's a spectacular explosion all by itself. We'll figure twenty percent of the hot-fudge energy transfers to Earth, and"—more buttons pressed, and dramatic rise in voice—"our grand total is two point seven times ten to the twenty-eighth ergs. Okay, that's your strike."

"Doesn't mean much to me," Harvey said. "It sounds like a big number, . . ."

"One followed by twenty-eight zeros," Mark muttered.

"Six hundred and forty thousand megatons, near enough," Dan Forrester said gently. "It *is* a big number."

"Good God, pasteurized planet," Mark said.

"Not quite." Forrester had his own calculator out of the belt case. "About three thousand Krakatoas. Or three hundred Thera explosions, if they're right about Thera."

"Thera?" Harvey asked.

"Volcano in the Mediterranean," Mark said. "Bronze Age. Where the Atlantis legend comes from."

"Your friend's right," Sharps said. "I'm not sure about the energy, though. Look at it this way. All of mankind uses about ten to the twenty-ninth ergs in a year. That's everything: electric power, coal, nuclear energy, burning buffalo chips, cars—you name it. So our hot fudge sundae pops in with about thirty percent of the world's annual energy budget.''

"Um. Not so bad, then," Harvey said.

"Not so bad. Not so bad as what? A year's energy in one minute," Sharps said. "It probably hits water. If it hits land, it's tough for anyone under it, but most of the energy radiates back out to space fairly quickly. But if it hits water, it vaporizes it. Let's see, ergs to calories . . . damn. I don't have that on my gadget.''

"I do," Forrester said. "The strike would vaporize about sixty million cubic kilometers of water. Or fifty billion acre-feet, if you like that. Enough to cover the entire U.S.A. with two hundred and twelve feet of water.''

"All right," Sharps said. "So sixty million cubic kilometers of water go into the atmosphere. Harvey, it's going to rain. A lot of that water is moving across polar areas. It freezes, falls as snow. Glaciers form fast . . . slide south . . . yeah. Harvey, the historians believe the Thera explosion changed the world's climate. We *know* that Tamboura, about as powerful as Krakatoa, caused what historians of the last century called 'the year without a summer.' Famine. Crop failure. Our hot fudge sundae will probably trigger an ice age. All those clouds. Clouds reflect heat. Less sunlight gets to Earth. Snow reflects heat too. Still less sunlight. It gets colder. More snow falls. Glaciers move south because they don't melt as fast. Positive feedback.''

It had all turned dead serious. Harvey asked, "But what *stops* ice ages?''

Forrester and Sharps shrugged in unison.

"So," Hamner said, "my comet's going to bring about an ice age?'' Now you could see the long lugubrious face of his grandfather, who could look bereaved at a $60,000 funeral.

Forrester said, "No, that was hot fudge sundae we were talking about. Um—the Hammer is bigger."

"Hamner-Brown. How much bigger?"

Forrester made an uncertain gesture. "Ten times?"

"Yes," said Harvey. There were pictures in his mind. Glaciers marched south across fields and forests, across vegetation already killed by snow. Down across North America into California, across Europe to the Alps and Pyrenees. Winter after winter, each colder, each colder than the Great Freeze of '76–'77. And hell, they hadn't even *mentioned* the tidal waves. "But a comet won't be as dense as a cubic mile of h-h-h—"

It was just one of those things. Harvey leaned back in his chair and belly-laughed, because there was just no way he could say it.

The surfer's ride is mine. Jerry played with the surfer character, and *moved the beach*. This is typical. I set the scene at Hermosa Beach, but that wouldn't give us the right waves . . .

Gil rested face-down on the board, thinking slow thoughts, waiting with the others for the one big wave. Water sloshed under his belly. Hot sunlight broiled his back. Other surfboards bobbed in a line on either side of him.

Jeanine caught his eye and smiled a lazy smile full of promises and memories. Her husband would be out of town for three more days. Gil's answering grin said nothing. He was waiting for a wave. There wouldn't be very good waves here at Santa Monica's Muscle Beach, but Jeanine's apartment was near, and there'd be other waves on other days.

The houses and apartments on the bluff above bobbed up and down. They looked bright and new, not like the houses on Malibu Beach, where the buildings always looked older than they were. Yet even here there were signs of age. Entropy ran fast at the line between sea and land. Gil was young, like all the young men bobbing on the water this fine morning. He was seventeen, burned brown, his longish hair bleached nearly white, belly muscles like the discrete plates of an armadillo. He was glad to look older than he was. He hadn't needed to pay for a place to stay or food to eat since his father threw him out of the house. There were always older women.

If he thought about Jeanine's husband, it was with friendly amusement. He was no threat to the man. He wanted nothing permanent. She could be making out with some guy who'd want her money on a permanent basis. . . .

He squinted against the brilliance. It flared and he closed his eyes. That was a reflex; wave reflections were a common thing out here. The flare died against his closed eyelids, and he looked out to sea. Wave coming?

He saw a fiery cloud lift beyond the horizon. He studied it, squinting, making himself believe . . .

"Big wave coming," he called, and rose to his knees.

Corey called, "Where?"

"You'll see it," Gil called confidently. He turned his board and paddled out to sea, bending almost until his cheek touched the board, using long, deep sweeps of his long arms. He was scared shitless, but nobody would ever know it.

"Wait for me!" Jeanine called.

Gil continued paddling. Others followed, but only the strongest could keep up. Corey pulled abreast of him.

"I saw the fireball!" he shouted. He panted with effort. "It's Lucifer's Hammer! Tidal wave!"

Gil said nothing. Talk was discouraged out here, but the others jabbered among themselves, and Gil paddled even faster, leaving them. A man ought to be alone during a thing like this. He was beginning to grasp the fact of death.

Rain came, and he paddled on. He glanced back to see the houses and bluff receding, going uphill, leaving an enormous stretch of new beach, gleaming wet. Lightning flared along the hills above Malibu.

The hills had changed. The orderly buildings of Santa Monica had tumbled into heaps.

The horizon went up.

Death. Inevitable. If death was inevitable, what was left? Style, only style. Gil went on paddling, riding the receding waters until motion was gone. He was a long way out now. He turned his board, and waited.

Others caught up and turned, spread across hundreds of yards in the rainy waters. If they spoke, Gil couldn't hear them. There was a terrifying rumble behind him. Gil waited a moment longer, then paddled like mad, sure deep strokes, doing it well and truly.

He was sliding downhill, down the big green wall, and the water was lifting hard beneath him, so that he rested on knees and elbows with the blood pouring into his face, bugging his eyes, starting a nosebleed. The pressure was enormous, unbearable, then it eased. With the speed he'd gained he turned the board, scooting down and sideways along the nearly vertical wall, balancing on knees . . .

He stood up. He needed *more* angle, *more*. If he could reach the peak of the wave he'd be out of it, he could actually live through this! Ride it out, ride it out, and do it well. . . .

Other boards had turned too. He saw them ahead of him, above and below on the green wall. Corey had turned the wrong way. He shot beneath Gil's feet, moving faster than hell and looking terrified.

They swept toward the bluff. They were higher than the

bluff. The beach house and the Santa Monica pier with its carousel and all the yachts anchored nearby slid beneath the waters. Then they were looking down on streets and cars. Gil had a momentary glimpse of a bearded man kneeling with others; then the waters swept on past. The base of the wall was churning chaos, white foam and swirling debris and thrashing bodies and tumbling cars.

Below him now was Santa Monica Boulevard. The wave swept over the Mall, adding the wreckage of shops and shoppers and potted trees and bicycles to the crashing foam below. As the wave engulfed each low building he braced himself for the shock, squatting low. The board slammed against his feet, and he nearly lost it; he saw Tommy Schumacher engulfed, gone, his board bounding high and whirling crazily. Only two boards left now.

The wave's frothing peak was far, far above him; the churning base was much too close. His legs shrieked in the agony of exhaustion. One board left ahead of him, ahead and below. Who? It didn't matter; he saw it dip into chaos, gone. Gil risked a quick look back: nobody there. He was alone on the ultimate wave.

Oh, God, if he lived to tell this tale, what a movie it would make! Bigger than *The Endless Summer*, bigger than *The Towering Inferno*: a surfing movie with ten million in special effects! If only his legs would hold! He already had a world record, he must be at least a mile inland, no one had ever ridden a wave for a mile! But the frothing, purling peak was miles overhead and the Barrington Apartments, thirty stories tall, was coming at him like a flyswatter.

Jerry's been in South Africa. So we set a subplot in South Africa, but it never quite went anywhere. So we took it out. That left nothing at all happening outside of North America!

So I wrote a scene set on Thera. I've never been to Thera either, though Jerry has. I repeated what he'd told me, and relied on Jerry to keep me honest.

It was mid-morning in California; it was evening in the Greek isles. The last of the sun's disk had vanished as two men reached the top of the granite knob. In the east a first star showed. Far below them, Greek peasants were driving overloaded donkeys through a maze of low stone walls and vineyards.

The town of Akrotira lay in twilight. Incongruities: white mudwalled houses that might have been created ten thousand years ago; the Venetian fortress at the top of its hill; the modern school near the ancient Byzantine church; and below that, the camp where Willis and MacDonald were uncovering Atlantis. The site was almost invisible from the hilltop. In the west a star switched on and instantly off, *blink*. Then another. "It's started," MacDonald said.

Wheezing, Alexander Willis settled himself on the rock. He was mildly irritated. The hour's climb had left him breathless, though he was twenty-four years old and considered himself in good shape. But MacDonald had led him all the way and helped him over the top, and MacDonald, whose dark red hair had receded to expose most of his darkly tanned scalp, was not even breathing hard. MacDonald had earned his strength; archeologists work harder than ditchdiggers.

The two sat crosslegged, looking west, watching the meteors.

They were twenty-eight hundred feet above sea level on

the highest point of the strange island of Thera. The granite knob had been called many things by a dozen civilizations, and it had endured much. Now it was known as Mount Prophet Elias.

Dusk faded on the waters of the bay far below. The bay was circular, surrounded by cliffs a thousand feet high, the caldera of a volcanic explosion that destroyed two thirds of the island, destroyed the Minoan Empire, created the legends of Atlantis. Now a new black island, evil in appearance and barren, rose in the center of the bay. The Greeks called it the New Burnt Land, and the islanders knew that some day it too would explode, as Thera had exploded so many times before.

Fiery streaks reflected in the bay. Something burned blue-white overhead. In the west the golden glow faded, not to black, but to a strange curdled green-and-orange glow, a backdrop for the meteors. Once again Phaethon drove the chariot of the sun. . . .

The meteors came every few seconds! Ice chips struck atmosphere and burned in a flash. Snowballs streaked down, burning greenish-white. Earth was deep in the coma of Hamner-Brown.

"Funny hobby, for us," said Willis.

"Sky watching? I've always loved the sky," MacDonald said. "You don't see me digging in New York, do you? The desert places, where the air's clear, where men have watched the stars for ten thousand years, that's where you find old civilizations. But I've never seen the sky like this."

"I wonder what it looked like after you-know-what."

MacDonald shrugged in the near-dark. "Plato didn't describe it. But the Hittites said a stone god rose from the sea to challenge the sky. Maybe they saw the cloud. Or there are things in the Bible, you could take them as eyewitness accounts, but from a long way away. You wouldn't have wanted to be near when Thera went off."

Willis didn't answer, and small wonder. A great greenish

light drew fire across the sky, moving up, lasting for seconds before it burst and died. Willis found himself looking east. His lips pursed in a soundless *Oh*. Then, "Mac! Turn around!"

MacDonald turned.

The curdled sky was rising like a curtain; you could see beneath the edge. The edge was perfectly straight, a few degrees above the horizon. Above was the green-and-orange glow of the comet's coma. Below, blackness in which stars glowed.

"The Earth's shadow," MacDonald said. "A shadow cast through the coma. I wish my wife had lived to see this. Just another year . . ."

A great light glared behind them. Willis turned. It sank slowly—too bright to see, blinding, drowning the background—Willis stared into it. God, what was it? Sinking . . . faded.

"I hope you hid your eyes," MacDonald said.

Willis saw only agony. He blinked; it made no difference. He said, "I think I'm blind." He reached out, patted rock, seeking the reassurance of a human hand.

Softly MacDonald said, "I don't think it matters."

Rage flared and died. That quickly, Willis knew what he meant. MacDonald's hands took his wrists and moved them around a rock. "Hug that tight. I'll tell you what I see."

"Right."

MacDonald's speech seemed hurried. "When the light went out I opened my eyes. For a moment I think I saw something like a violet searchlight beam going up, then it was gone. But it came from behind the horizon. We'll have some time."

"Thera's a bad luck island," Willis said. He could see nothing, not even darkness.

"Did you ever wonder why they still build here? Some of the houses are hundreds of years old. Eruptions every few centuries. But they always come back. For that matter, what're *we* doing—Alex, I can see the tidal wave. It gets taller every second. I don't know if it'll reach this high or not. Brace yourself for the air shock wave, though.''

"Ground shock first. I guess this is the end of Greek civilization."

"I suppose so. And a new Atlantis legend, if anyone lives to tell it. The curtain's still rising. Streamlines from the nucleus in the west, Earth's black shadow in the east, meteors everywhere . . ." MacDonald's voice trailed off.

"What?"

"I closed my eyes. But it was northeast! and huge!"

"Greg, who named Mount Prophet Elias? It's too bloody appropriate."

The ground shock ripped through and beneath Thera, through the magma channel that the sea bed had covered thirty-five hundred years before. Willis felt the rock wrench at his arms. Then Thera exploded. A shock wave of live steam laced with lava tore him away and killed him instantly. Seconds later the tsunami rolled across the raw orange wound.

Nobody would live to tell of the second Thera explosion.

I conceived Harry the Mailman. Lurton Blassingame, our agent, thought Harry was a wonderful character but didn't want him delivering his mail. Jerry and I traded off working him. His route was discussed in minute detail during conferences, and the people along his route are largely Jerry's. When Jerry opened a scene to demonstrate security at the Stronghold gate, I used Harry to blast the gate guard out of his rut.

We always knew Harry the Mailman would *become* civilization.

Harry Newcombe saw nothing of Hammerfall, and it was Jason Gillcuddy's fault. Gillcuddy had imprisoned himself in the wilderness (he said) to diet and to write a novel. He had dropped twelve pounds in six months, but he could afford more. As for his isolation, it was certain that he would rather talk to a passing postman than write.

As the best coffee cup was to be found at the Silver Valley Ranch, so Gillcuddy, on the other side of the valley, made the best coffee. "But," Harry told him, smiling, "I'd slosh if I let everyone feed me two cups. I'm popular, I am."

"Kid, you'd better take it. My lease is up come Thursday, and *Ballad*'s finished. Next Trash Day I'll be gone."

"Finished. Hey, beautiful! Am I in it?"

"No, I'm sorry, Harry, but the damn thing was getting too big. You know how it is; what you like best is usually what has to go. But the coffee's Jamaica Blue Mountain. When I celebrate—"

"Yeah. Pour."

"Shot of brandy?"

"Have some respect for the uniform, *if* you . . . Well, hell, I can't pour it out, can I."

"To my publisher." Gillcuddy raised his cup, carefully. "He said if I didn't fulfill his contract he'd put out a contract on *me*."

"Tough business."

"Well, but the money's good."

A distant thunderclap registered at the back of Harry's mind. Summer storm coming? He sipped at his coffee. It really was something special.

But there were no thunder clouds when he walked outside. Harry had been up before dawn; the valley farmers kept strange hours, and so did postmen. He had seen the pearly glow of the comet's tail wrapping the Earth. Some of that glory still clung, softening the direct sunlight and whiting the blue of the sky. Like smog, but clean. There was a strange stillness, as if the day were waiting for something.

So it was back to Chicago for Jason Gillcuddy, until the next time he had to imprison himself to diet and write a novel. Harry would miss him. Jason was the most literate man in the valley, possibly excepting the Senator—who was real. Harry had seen him from a distance yesterday, arriving in a vehicle the size of a bus. Maybe they'd meet today.

He was driving briskly along toward the Adams place when the truck began to shake. He braked. Flat tire? Damage to a wheel? The road shuddered and seemed to twist, the truck was trying to shake his brains out. He got it stopped. It was still shaking! He turned off the ignition. *Still* shaking?

"I should have looked at that brandy bottle. Huh. Earthquake?" The tremors died away. "There aren't any fault lines around here. I thought."

He drove on, more slowly. The Adams farm was a long jog on the new route he'd planned to get him there early. He didn't dare go up to the house . . . and that would save him a couple of minutes. There had been no new complaints from Mrs. Adams. But he hadn't seen Donna in weeks.

Harry took off his sunglasses. The day had darkened without his noticing. It was still darkening: clouds streaming across the sky like a speeded-up movie, lightning flashing in their dark bellies. Harry had never seen anything like it. Summer storm, right; it was going to rain.

The wind howled like demons breaking through from Hell. The sky had gone from ugly to hideous. Harry had never seen anything like these roiling black clouds sputtering with lightning. It would have served Mrs. Adams right, he thought vindictively, if he had left her mail in the box outside the gate.

But it might be Donna who would have to make the soggy trip. Harry drove up and parked under the porch overhang. As he got out the rain came, and the overhang was almost no protection; the wind whipped rain in all directions.

And it might have been Donna who answered the door, but it wasn't. Mrs. Adams showed no sign of pleasure at seeing him. Harry raised his voice above the storm—"Your mail, Mrs. Adams"—his voice as cold as her face.

"Thank you," she said, and closed the door firmly.

The rain poured from the sky like a thousand bathtubs emptying, and washed from the truck in filthy brown streams. It shamed Harry. He hadn't guessed that the truck was that dirty. He climbed in, half soaked already, and drove off.

Was weather like this common in the valley? Harry had been here just over a year, and he'd seen nothing remotely like this. Noah's Flood! He badly wanted to ask someone about it.

Anyone but Mrs. Adams.

This had been the dry season in the valley. Carper Creek had been way down, a mere ripple of water wetting the bottoms of the smooth white boulders that formed its bed, as late as this morning. But when Harry Newcombe drove across the wooden bridge, the creek was beating against the bottom and washing over the upstream edge. The rain still fell with frantic urgency.

Harry pulled way over to put two envelopes in Gentry's mailbox. The only time he had ever seen Gentry, the farmer had been pointing a shotgun at him. Gentry was a hermit, and his need for up-to-the-minute mail was not urgent, and Harry didn't like him.

His wheels spun disconcertingly before they caught and pulled him back on the road. Sooner or later he would get stuck. He had given up hope of finishing his route today. Maybe he could beg a meal and a couch from the Millers.

Now the road led steeply uphill. Harry drove in low gear, half blind in the rain and the lightning and the blackness between. Presently there was empty space on his left, a hillside on his right, trees covering both. Harry hugged the hillside. The cab was thoroughly wet, the air warm and 110 percent humid.

Harry braked sharply.

The hillside had slipped. It ran right across the road and on down, studded with broken and unbroken trees.

Briefly Harry considered going back. But it was back toward Gentry's and then the Adamses', and the hell with it: The rain had already washed part of the mudslide away; what was left wasn't all that steep. Harry drove up the mud lip. First gear and keep it moving. If he bogged down, it would be a wet walk home.

The truck lurched. Harry used wheel and accelerator, biting his lower lip. No use; the mud itself was sliding, he had to get off! He floored the accelerator. The wheels spun futilely, the truck tilted. Harry turned off the ignition and dove for the floorboards and covered his face with his arms.

The truck gently rocked and swung like a small boat at anchor; swung too far and turned on its side. Then it smashed into something massive, wheeled around and struck something else, and stopped moving.

Harry lifted his head.

A tree trunk had smashed the windshield. The frosted safety glass bowed inward before it. That tree and another now wedged the truck in place. It lay on the passenger side, and it wasn't coming out without a lot of help, at least a tow truck and men with chain saws.

Harry was hanging from the seat belt. Gingerly he unfastened it, decided he wasn't hurt.

And now what? He wasn't supposed to leave the mail unguarded, but he couldn't sit here all day! "How am I going to finish the route?" he asked himself, and giggled, because it was pretty obvious that he wasn't going to get that done today. He would have to let the mail pile up until tomorrow. The Wolf would be furious . . . and Harry couldn't help that.

He took the registered letter for Senator Jellison and

slipped it into his pocket. There were a couple of small packets that Harry thought might be valuable, and he put them in another pocket. The big stuff, books, and the rest of the mail would just have to take care of itself.

He started out into the rain.

It drove into his face, blinding him, soaking him in an instant. The mud slipped beneath his feet, and in seconds he was clutching wildly at a small tree to keep from falling into the rapidly rising creek far below. He stood there a long moment.

No. He wasn't going to get to a telephone. Not through that. Better to wait it out. Luckily he was back on his charted route again; the Wolf would know where to look for him— only Harry couldn't think of *any* vehicle that could reach him, not through *that*.

Lightning flared above him, a double flash, *blinkblink*. Thunder exploded instantly. He felt a distinct tingle in his wet feet. Close!

Painfully he made his way back to the truck and got inside. It wasn't insulated from the ground, but it seemed the safest place to wait out the lightning storm . . . and at least he hadn't left the mail unguarded. That had worried him. Better to deliver it late than let it be stolen.

Definitely better, he decided, and tried to make himself comfortable. The hours wore on and there was no sign of the storm letting up.

Harry slept badly. He made a nest back in the cargo compartment, sacrificing some shopping circulars and his morning newspaper. He woke often, always hearing the endless drumming of rain on metal. When earth and sky turned from lightning-lit black to dull gray with less lightning, Harry squirmed around and searched out yesterday's carton of milk. A premonition of need had made him leave it until now. It wasn't enough; he was famished. And he missed his morning coffee.

"Next place," he told himself, and imagined a big mug of hot steaming coffee, perhaps with a bit of brandy in it (although no one but Gillcuddy was going to offer him that).

The rain had slackened off a bit, and so had the howling wind. "Or else I'm going deaf," he said. "GOING DEAF! Well, maybe not." Cheerful by nature, he was quick to find the one bright point in a gloomy situation. "Good thing it isn't Trash Day," he told himself.

He took his feet out of the leather mailbag, where they'd stayed near-dry during the long night, and put his boots back on. Then he looked at the mail. There was barely enough light.

"First class only," he told himself. "Leave the books." He wondered about Senator Jellison's *Congressional Record*, and the magazines. He decided to take them. Eventually he had stuffed his bag with everything except the largest packages. He stood and wrestled the driver's door open, trapdoor fashion, and pushed the mailbag out onto the side—now the top—of the truck. Then he climbed out after it. The rain was still falling, and he spread a piece of plastic over the top of the mailbag.

The truck shifted uneasily.

Mud had piled along the high side of the truck, level with the wheels. Harry shouldered the bag and started uphill. He felt his footing shift, and he sprinted uphill.

Behind him the trees bowed before the weight of truck and shifting mud. Their roots pulled free, and the truck rolled, gathering speed.

Harry shook his head. This was probably his last circuit; Wolfe wouldn't like losing a truck. Harry started up the uneasy mud slope, looking about him as he went. He needed a walking stick. Presently he found a tilted sapling, five feet long and supple, that came out of the mud by its loosened roots.

Marching was easier after he reached the road. He was going downhill, back from the long detour to the Adamses'. The heavy mud washed off his boots and his feet grew lighter. The rain fell steadily. He kept looking upslope, alert for more mudslides.

"Five pounds of water in my hair alone," he groused. "Keeps my neck warm, though." The pack was heavy. A hip belt would have made carrying it easier.

Presently he began to sing.

> I went out to take a friggin' walk by the friggin'
>   reservoir,
> a-wishin' for a friggin' quid to pay my friggin'
>   score,
> my head it was a-achin' and my throat was parched
>   and dry,
> and so I sent a little prayer, a-wingin' to the
>   sky. . . .

He topped the slight rise and saw a blasted transmission tower. High-tension wires lay across the road. The steel tower had been struck by lightning, perhaps several times, and seemed twisted at the top.

How long ago? And why weren't the Edison people out to fix it? Harry shrugged. Then he noticed the telephone lines. They were down too. He wouldn't be calling in from his next stop.

> _And there came a friggin' falcon and he walked_
>   _upon the waves,_
> _and I said, "A friggin' miracle!" and sang a couple_
>   _staves_
> _of a friggin' churchy ballad I learned when I was_
>   _young._
> _The friggin' bird took to the air, and spattered me_
>   _with dung._
> _I fell upon my friggin' knees and bowed my_
>   _friggin' head,_
> _and said three friggin' Aves for all the friggin' dead,_

and then I got upon my feet and said another ten.
The friggin' bird burst into flame—and spattered me
again.

There was the Millers' gate. He couldn't see anyone.
There were no fresh ruts in their drive. Harry wondered if
they'd gone out last night. They certainly hadn't made it out
today. He sank into deep mud as he went up the long drive
toward the house. They wouldn't have a phone, but maybe
he could bum a cup of coffee, even a ride into town.

The burnin' bird hung in the sky just like a
friggin' sun.
It seared my friggin' eyelids shut, and when
the job was done,
the friggin' bird flashed cross the sky just like
a shootin' star.
I ran to tell the friggin' priest—he bummed my
last cigar.
I told him of the miracle, he told me of the
Rose,
I showed him bird crap in my hair, the bastard
held his nose.
I went to see the bishop but the friggin' bishop
said,
"Go home and sleep it off, you sod—and wash
your friggin' head!"

No one answered his knock at the Millers' front door.
The door stood slightly ajar. Harry called in, loudly, and
there was still no answer. He smelled coffee.

He stood a moment, then fished out two letters and a copy
of *Ellery Queen's Mystery Magazine*, pushed the door open
and went inside, mail held like an ambassador's passport.
He sang loudly:

> *Then I came upon a friggin' wake for a friggin'*
> *   rotten swine,*
> *by the name of Jock O'Leary and I touched his head*
> *   with mine,*
> *and old Jock sat up in his box and raised his friggin'*
> *   head.*
> *His wife took out a forty-four, and shot the bastard*
> *   dead.*
> * Again I touched his head with mine and brought him*
> *   back to life.*
> *His smiling face rolled on the floor, this time she used*
> *   a knife.*
> *And then she fell upon her knees, and started in to*
> *   pray,*
> *"It's forty years, O Lord," she said, "I've waited for*
> *   this day."*

He left the mail on the front-room table where he usually piled stuff on Trash Day, then wandered toward the kitchen, led by the smell of coffee. He continued to sing loudly, lest he be shot as an intruder.

> *So I walked the friggin' city 'mongst the friggin'*
> *   halt and lame,*
> *and every time I raised 'em up, they got knocked*
> *   down again,*
> *'cause the love of God comes down to man in a*
> *   friggin' curious way,*
> *but when a man is marked for love, that love is here*
> *   to stay.*

There was coffee! The gas stove was working, and there was a big pot of coffee on it, and three cups set out. Harry poured one full. He sang in triumph:

> *And this I know because I've got a friggin'*
>   *curious sign;*
> *for every time I wash my head, the water turns to*
>   *wine!*
> *And I gives it free to workin' blokes to brighten*
>   *up their lives,*
> *so they don't kick no dogs around, nor beat up on*
>   *their wives.*

He found a bowl of oranges, resisted temptation for a full ten seconds, then took one. He peeled it as he walked on through the kitchen to the back door, out into the orange groves behind. The Millers were natives. They'd know what was happening. And they had to be around somewhere.

> *'Cause there ain't no use to miracles like walkin'*
>   *on the sea;*
> *They crucified the Son of God, but they don't muck*
>   *with me!*
> *'Cause I leave the friggin' blind alone, the dyin'*
>   *and the dead,*
> *but every day at four o'clock, I wash my friggin'*
>   *head!*

"Ho, Harry!" a voice called. Somewhere to his right. Harry went through heavy mud and orange trees.

Jack Miller and his son Roy and daughter-in-law Cicelia were harvesting tomatoes in full panic. They'd spread a large tarp on the ground and were covering it with everything they could pick, ripe and half green. "They'll rot on the ground," Roy puffed. "Got to get them inside. Quick. Could sure use help."

Harry looked at his muddy boots, mailbag, sodden uniform. "You're not supposed to stay me," he said. "It's against government regulations. . . ."

''Yeah. Say, Harry, what's going on out there?'' Roy demanded.

''You don't know?'' Harry was appalled.

''How could we? Phone's been out since yesterday afternoon. Power out. No TV. Can't get a damned thing—sorry, Cissy. Get nothing but static on the transistor radio. What's it like in town?''

''Haven't been to town,'' Harry confessed. ''Truck's dead, couple miles toward the Gentry place. Since yesterday. Spent the night in the truck.''

''Hmm.'' Roy stopped his frantic picking for a moment. ''Cissy, better get in and get to canning. Just the ripe ones. Harry, I'll make you a deal. Breakfast, lunch, a ride into town, and I don't tell nobody about what you were singing inside my house. You help us the rest of the day.''

''Well . . .''

''I'll drive you and put in a good word,'' Cissy said.

The Millers carried some weight in the valley. The Wolf might not fire him for losing the truck if he had a good word. ''I can't get in any quicker by walking,'' Harry said. ''It's a deal.'' He set to work.

They didn't talk much, they needed their breath. Presently Cissy brought out sandwiches. The Millers hardly stopped long enough to eat. Then they went back to it.

When they did talk, it was about the weather. Jack Miller had seen nothing like it in his fifty-two years in the valley.

''Comet,'' Cissy said. ''It did this.''

''Nonsense,'' Roy said. ''You heard the TV. It missed us by thousands of miles.''

''It did? Good,'' Harry said.

''We didn't hear that it missed. Heard it was *going* to miss,'' Jack Miller said. He went back to harvesting tomatoes. When they got those picked, there were beans and squashes.

Harry had never worked so hard in his life. He realized

suddenly it was getting late afternoon. "Hey, I have *got* to get to town!" he insisted.

"Yeah. Okay, Cissy," Jack Miller called. "Take the pickup. Get by the feedstore, we're going to need lots of cattle and hog feed. Damned rain's battered down most of the fodder. Better get feed before everybody else thinks of it. Price'll be sky-high in a week."

"If there's anyplace to buy it in a week," Cissy said.

"What do you mean by that?" her husband demanded.

"Nothing." She went off to the barn, tight jeans bulging, water dripping from her hat. She came out with the Dodge pickup. Harry squeezed into the seat, mailbag on his lap to protect it from the rain. He'd left it in the barn while he worked.

The truck had no trouble with the muddy drive. When they got to the gate, Cissy got out; Harry couldn't move with the big mailbag. She laughed at him when she got back in.

They hadn't gone half a mile when the road ended in a gigantic crack. The road had pulled apart, and the hillside with it, and tons of sloppy mud had come off the hillside to cover the road beyond the crack.

Harry studied it carefully. Cicelia backed and twisted to turn the truck around. Harry started toward the ruined road.

"You're not going to walk!" she said.

"Mail must go through," Harry muttered. He laughed. "Didn't finish the route yesterday—"

"Harry, don't be silly! There will be a road crew out today, tomorrow for sure. Wait for that! You won't get to town before dark, maybe not at all in this rain. Come back to the house."

He thought about that. What she said made sense. Power lines down, roads out, telephone lines out; *somebody* would come through here. The mailbag seemed terribly heavy. "All right."

They put him back to work, of course. He'd expected that. They didn't eat until after dark, but it was an enormous meal, suitable for farmhand appetites. Harry couldn't stay awake, and collapsed on the couch. He didn't even notice when Jack and Roy took his uniform off him and covered him with a blanket.

Harry woke to find the house empty. His uniform, hung to dry, was still soggy. Rain pounded relentlessly at the farmhouse. He dressed and found coffee. While he was drinking it, the others came in.

Cicelia made a breakfast of ham and pancakes and more coffee. She was strong and tall, but she looked tired now. Roy kept eying her anxiously.

"I'm all right," she said. "Not used to doing men's work and my own too."

"We got most of it in," Jack Miller said. "Never saw rain like this, though." There was a softness, a wondering in Jack Miller's voice that might have been superstitious fear. "Those bastards at the Weather Bureau never gave us a minute's warning. What are they doing with all those shiny weather satellites?"

"Maybe the comet knocked them out," Harry said.

Jack Miller glared. "Comet. Humph. Comets are things in the sky! Live in the twentieth century, Harry!"

"I tried it once. I like it better here."

He got a soft smile from Cissy. He liked it. "I'd best be on my way," he said.

"In this?" Roy Miller was incredulous. "You can't be serious."

Harry shrugged. "Got my route to finish."

The others looked guilty. "Reckon we can run you down to where the road's out," Jack Miller said. "Maybe a work crew got in already."

"Thanks."

* * *

There wasn't any work crew. More mud had slid off the hillside during the night.

"Wish you'd stay," Jack said. "Can use the help."

"Thanks. I'll let people in town know how it is with you."

"Right. Thanks. Good luck."

"Yeah."

It was just possible to pick his way across the crack, over the mudslide. The heavy mailbag dragged at his shoulder. It was leather, waterproof, with the plastic over the top. Just as well, Harry thought. All that paper could soak up twenty or thirty pounds of water. It would make it much harder. "Make it hard to read the mail, too," Harry said aloud.

He trudged on down the road, slipping and sliding, until he found another sapling to replace the one he'd left at the Millers' place. It had too many roots at the bottom, but it kept him upright.

"This is the pits," Harry shouted into the rain-laden wind. Then he laughed and added, "But it's got to beat farm work."

The rain had stopped Harry's watch. He thought it was just past eleven when he reached the gate of the Shire. It was almost two.

He was back in flat country now, out of the hills. There had been no more breaks in the road. But there was always the water and the mud. He couldn't see the road anywhere; he had to infer it from the shape of the glistening mud-covered landscape. Soggy everywhere, dimly aware of the chafe spots developing beneath his clinging uniform, moving against the resistance of his uniform and the mud that clung to his boots, Harry thought he had made good time, considering.

He still hoped to finish his route in somebody's car. It wasn't likely he'd find a ride at the Shire, though.

He had seen nobody while he walked along the Shire's split-log fence. Nobody in the fields, nobody trying to save whatever crops the Shire was growing. Were they growing anything? Nothing Harry recognized; but Harry wasn't a farmer.

The gate was sturdy. The padlock on it was new and shiny and big. Harry found the mailbox bent back at forty-five degrees, as if a car had hit it. The box was full of water.

Harry was annoyed. He carried eight letters for the Shire, and a thick, lumpy manila envelope. He threw back his head and hollered, "Hey in there! _Mail call!_"

The house was dark. Power out here, too? Or had Hugo Beck and his score of strange guests all tired of country life and gone away?

The Shire was a commune. Everyone in the valley knew that, and few knew more. The Shire let the valley people alone. Harry, in his privileged occupation, had met Hugo Beck and a few of the others.

Hugo had inherited the spread from his aunt and uncle three years ago, when they racked up their car on a Mexico vacation. It had been called something else then: Inverted Fork Ranch, some such name, probably named after a branding iron. Hugo Beck had arrived for the funeral: a pudgy boy of eighteen who wore his straight black hair at shoulder length and a fringe of beard with the chin bared. He'd looked the place over, and stayed to sell the cattle and most of the horses, and left. A month later he'd returned, followed by (the number varied according to who was talking) a score of hippies. There was enough money, somehow, to keep them alive and fairly comfortable. Certainly the Shire was not a successful business. It exported nothing. But they must be growing some food; they didn't import enough from town.

Harry hollered again. The front door opened and a human shape strolled down to the gate.

It was Tony. Harry knew him. Scrawny and sun-darkened, grinning to show teeth that had been straightened in youth, Tony was dressed as usual: jeans, wool vest, no shirt, digger hat, sandals. He looked at Harry through the gate. "Hey, man, what's happenin'?" The rain affected him not at all.

"The picnic's been called off. I came to tell you."

Tony looked blank, then laughed. "The picnic! Hey, that's funny. I'll tell them. They're all huddling in the house. Maybe they think they'll melt."

"I'm half melted already. Here's your mail." Harry handed it over. "Your mailbox is wrecked."

"It won't matter." Tony seemed to be grinning at some private joke.

Harry skipped it. "Can you spare someone to run me into town? I wrecked my truck."

"Sorry. We want to save the gas for emergencies."

What did he think this was? Harry held his temper. "Such is life. Can you spare me a sandwich?"

"Nope. Famine coming. We got to think of ourselves."

"I don't get you." Harry was beginning to dislike Tony's grin.

"The Hammer has fallen," said Tony. "The Establishment is dead. No more draft. No more taxes. No more wars. No more going to jail for smoking pot. No more having to pick between a crook and an idiot for President." Tony grinned beneath the shapeless, soggy hat. "No more Trash Day either. I thought I'd flipped when I saw a mailman at the gate!"

Tony really had flipped, Harry realized. He tried to side-step the issue. "Can you get Hugo Beck down here?"

"Maybe."

Harry watched Tony reenter the farmhouse. Was there anyone alive in there? Tony had never struck him as danger-ous, but . . . if he stepped out with anything remotely like a rifle, Harry was going to run like a deer.

Half a dozen of them came out. One girl was in rain gear;

the rest seemed to be dressed for swimming. Maybe that made a kind of sense. You couldn't hope to stay dry in this weather. Harry recognized Tony, and Hugo Beck, and the broad-shouldered, broad-hipped girl who called herself Galadriel, and a silent giant whose name he'd never learned. They clustered at the gate, hugely amused.

Harry asked, "What's it all about?"

Much of Hugo Beck's fat had turned to muscle in the past three years, but he still didn't look like a farmer. Maybe it was the expensive sandals and worn swim trunks; or maybe it was the way he lounged against the gate, exactly as Jason Gillcuddy the writer would lounge against his bar, leaving one hand free to gesture.

"Hammerfall," said Hugo. "You could be the last mailman we ever see. Consider the implications. No more ads to buy things you can't afford. No more friendly reminders from the collection agency. You should throw away that uniform, Harry. The Establishment's dead."

"The comet *hit* us?"

"Right."

"*Huh.*" Harry didn't know whether to believe it or not. There had been talk . . . but a comet was nothing. Dirty vacuum, lit by unfiltered sunlight, very pretty when seen from a hilltop with the right girl beside you. This rain, though. What about the rain?

"*Huh.* So I'm a member of the Establishment?"

"That's a uniform, isn't it?" said Beck, and the others laughed.

Harry looked down. "Somebody should have told me. All right, you can't feed me and you can't transport me—"

"No more gas, maybe forever. The rain is going to wipe out most of the crops. You can see that, Harry."

"Yeah. Can you loan me a hatchet for fifteen minutes?"

"Tony, get the hatchet."

Tony jogged up to the farmhouse. Hugo asked, "What are you going to do with it?"

"Trim the roots off my walking stick."

"What then?"

He didn't have to answer, because Tony was back with the hatchet. Harry went to work. The Shire people watched. Presently Hugo asked again. "What do you do now?"

"Deliver the mail," said Harry.

"Why?" A frail and pretty blonde girl cried, "It's all over, man. No more letters to your congressman. No more PLAYBOY. No more tax forms or . . . or voting instructions. You're free! Take off the uniform and dance!"

"I'm already cold. My feet hurt."

"Have a hit." The silent giant was handing a generously fat homemade cigarette through the gate, shielding it with Tony's digger hat. Harry saw the others' disapproval, but they said nothing, so he took the toke. He held his own hat over it while he lit it and drew.

Were they growing the weed here? Harry didn't ask. But . . . "You'll have trouble getting papers."

They looked at each other. That hadn't occurred to them.

"Better save that last batch of letters. No more Trash Day." Harry passed the hatchet back through the bars. "Thanks. Thanks for the toke, too." He picked up the trimmed sapling. It felt lighter, better balanced. He got his arm through the mailbag strap.

"Anyway, it's the mail. 'Neither rain, nor sleet, nor heat of day, nor gloom of night,' et cetera."

"What does it say," Hugo Beck asked, "about the end of the world?"

"I think it's optional. I'm going to deliver the mail."

Carrie Roman was a middle-aged widow with two big sons who were Harry's age and twice Harry's size. Carrie was almost as big as they were. Three jovial giants, they formed one of Harry's coffee stops. Once before, they had given Harry a lift to town to report a breakdown of the mail truck.

Harry reached their gate in a mood of bright optimism.

The gate was padlocked, of course, but Jack Roman had rigged a buzzer to the house. Harry pushed it and waited.

The rain poured over him, gentle, inexorable. If it had started raining up from the ground, Harry doubted he would notice. It was all of his environment, the rain.

Where were the Romans? Hell, of course they had no electricity. Harry pushed the buzzer again, experimentally.

From the corner of his eye he saw someone crouched low, sprinting from behind a tree. The figure was only visible for an instant; then bushes hid it. But it carried something the shape of a shovel, or a rifle, and it was too small to be one of the Romans.

"Mail call!" Harry cried cheerily. What the hell was going on here?

The sound of a gunshot matched the gentle tugging at the edge of his mailbag. Harry threw himself flat. The bag was higher than he was as he crawled for cover, and it jerked once, coinciding with another gunshot. A .22, he thought. Not much rifle. Certainly not much for the valley. He pulled himself behind a tree, his breath raspy and very loud in his own ears.

He wriggled the bag off his shoulder and set it down. He squatted and selected four envelopes tied with a rubber band. Crouched. Then, all in an instant, he sprinted for the Roman mailbox, slid the packet into it, and was running for cover again when the first shot came. He lay panting beside his mailbag, trying to think.

Harry wasn't a policeman, he wasn't armed, and there wasn't anything he could do to help the Romans. No way!

And he couldn't use the road. No cover.

The gully on the other side? It would be full of water, but it was the best he could do. Sprint across the road, then crawl on his hands and knees . . .

But he'd have to leave the mailbag.

Why not? Who am I kidding? Hammerfall has come, and

there's no need for mail carriers. None. What does that make me?

He didn't care much for the question.

"It makes me," he said aloud, "a turkey who got good grades in high school by working his arse off, flunked out of college, got fired from every job he ever had . . ."

It makes me a mailman, goddammit! He lifted the heavy bag and crouched again. Things were quiet up there. Maybe they'd been shooting to keep him away? But what for?

He took in a deep breath. Do it now, he told himself. Before you're too scared to do it at all. He dashed into the road, across, and dived toward the gulley. There was another shot, but he didn't think the bullet had come anywhere close. Harry scuttled down the gulley, half crawling, half swimming, mailbag shoved around onto his back to keep it out of the water.

There were no more shots. Thank God! The Many Names Ranch was only half a mile down the road. Maybe they had guns, or a telephone that worked . . . Did any telephones work? The Shire wasn't precisely an official information source, but they'd been so sure.

"Never find a cop when you need one," Harry muttered.

He'd have to be careful showing himself at Many Names. The owners might be a bit nervous. And if they weren't, they damned well should be!

It was dusk when Harry reached Muchos Nombres Ranch. The rain had increased and was falling slantwise, and lightning played across the nearly black sky.

Muchos Nombres was thirty acres of hilly pastureland dotted with the usual great white boulders. Of the four families who jointly owned it, two would sometimes invite Harry in for coffee. The result was diffidence on Harry's part. He never knew whose turn it was. The families each owned one week in four, and they treated the ranch as a vacation spot. Sometimes they traded off; sometimes they brought guests. The oversupply of owners had been unable to agree on a name, and had finally settled for Muchos Nombres. The Spanish fooled nobody.

Today Harry was fresh out of diffidence. He yelled his "Mail call!" and waited, expecting no answer. Presently he opened the gate and went on in.

He reached the front door like something dragged from an old grave. He knocked.

The door opened.

"Mail," said Harry. "Hullo, Mr. Freehafer. Sorry to be so late, but there are some emergencies going."

Freehafer had an automatic pistol. He looked Harry over with some care. Behind him the living room danced with candlelight, and it looked crowded with wary people. Doris Lilly said, "Why, it's Harry! It's all right, Bill. It's Harry the mailman."

Freehafer lowered the gun. "All right, pleased to meet you, Harry. Come on in. What emergencies?"

Harry stepped inside, out of the rain. Now he saw the third man, stepping around a doorjamb, laying a shotgun aside. "Mail," said Harry, and he set down two magazines, the usual haul for Many Names. "Somebody shot at me from Carrie Roman's place. It wasn't anyone I know. I think the Romans are in trouble. Is your phone working?"

"No," said Freehafer. "We can't go out there tonight."

"Okay. And my mail truck went off a hill, and I don't know what the roads are like. Can you let me have a couch, or a stretch of rug, and something to eat?"

The hesitation was marked. "It's the rug, I'm afraid," Freehafer said. "Soup and a sandwich do you? We're a little short."

"I'd eat your old shoes," said Harry.

It was canned tomato soup and a grilled cheese sandwich, and it tasted like heaven. Between bites he got the story: how the Freehafers had started to leave on Tuesday, and seen the sky going crazy, and turned back. How the Lillys had arrived (it being their turn now) with the Rodenberries as guests, and their own two children. The end of the world had come and gone, the Rodenberries were on the couches, and nobody had yet tried to reach the supermarket in town.

"What is this with the end of the world?" Harry asked.

They told him. They showed him, in the magazines he'd brought. The magazines were damp but still readable. Harry read interviews with Sagan and Asimov and Sharps. He stared at artists' conceptions of major meteor impacts. "They all think it'll miss," he said.

"It didn't," said Norman Lilly. He was a football player turned insurance executive, a broad-shouldered wall of a man who should have kept up his exercises. "Now what? We brought some seeds and farm stuff, just in case, but we didn't bring any books. Do you know anything about farming, Harry?"

"No. People, I've had a rough day—"

"Right. No sense wasting candles," said Norman.

All of the beds, blankets and couches were in use. Harry spent the night on a thick rug, swathed in three of Norman Lilly's enormous bathrobes, his head on a chair pillow. He was comfortable enough, but he kept twitching himself awake.

Lucifer's Hammer? End of the world? Crawling through mud while bullets punched into his mailbag and the letters inside. He kept waking with the memory of a nightmare, and always the nightmare was real.

Harry woke and counted days. First night he slept in the truck. Second with the Millers. Last night was the third. Three days since he'd reported in.

It was definitely the end of the world. The Wolf should have come looking for him with blood in his eye. He hadn't. The power lines were still down. The phones weren't working. No county road crews. Ergo, Hammerfall. The end of the world. It had really happened.

"Rise and shine!" Doris Lilly's cheer was artificial. She tried to keep it up anyway. "Rise and shine! Come and get it or we throw it out."

Breakfast wasn't much. They shared with Harry, which was pretty damned generous of them. The Lilly children, eight and ten, stared at the adults. One of them complained that the TV wasn't working. No one paid any attention.

"Now what?" Freehafer asked.

"We get food," Doris Lilly said. "We have to find something to eat."

"Where do you suggest we look?" Bill Freehafer asked. He wasn't being sarcastic.

Doris shrugged. "In town? Maybe things aren't as bad as . . . maybe they're not so bad."

"I want to watch TV," Phil Lilly said.

"Not working," Doris said absently. "I vote we go to town and see how things are. We can give Harry a ride—"

"TV *now!*" Phil screamed.

"Shut up," his father said.

"Now!" the boy repeated.

Smack! Norman Lilly's huge hand swept against the boy's face.

"Norm!" his wife cried. The child screamed, more in surprise than pain. "You never hit the children before—"

"Phil," Lilly said. His voice was calm and determined. "It's all different now. You better understand that. When we tell you to be quiet, you'll be *quiet.* You and your sister both, you've got a lot of learning to do, and quick. Now go in the other room."

The children hesitated for a moment. Norman raised his hand. They looked at him, startled, then ran.

"Little drastic," Bill Freehafer said.

"Yeah," Norm said absently. "Bill, don't you think we better look in on our neighbors?"

"Let the police—" Bill Freehafer stopped himself. "Well, there might still be police."

"Yeah. Who'll they take orders from, now?" Lilly asked. He looked at Harry.

Harry shrugged. There was a local mayor. The Sheriff was out in the San Joaquin, and with this rain that could be under water. "Maybe the Senator?" Harry said.

"Hey, yeah, Jellison lives over the hill there," Freehafer said. "Maybe we should . . . Jesus, I don't know, Norm. What can we do?"

Lilly shrugged. "We can look, anyway. Harry, you know those people?"

"Yes . . ."

"We have two cars. Bill, you take everybody else into town. Harry and I'll have a look. Right?"

Harry looked dubious. "I've already left their mail—"

"Jesus," Bill Freehafer said.

Norman Lilly held up an immense hand. "He's right, you know. But look at it this way, Harry. You're a mailman."

"Yes—"

"Which can be damned valuable. Only there won't be any mail. Not letters and magazines, anyway. But there's still a need for message carriers. Somebody to keep communications going. Right?"

"Something like that," Harry agreed.

"Good. You'll be needed. More than ever. But here's your first post-comet message. To the Romans, from us. We're willing to help, if we can. They're our neighbors. But we don't know them, and they don't know us. If they've had trouble they'll be watching for strangers. Somebody's got to introduce us. That's a worthwhile message, isn't it?"

Harry thought it over. It made sense. "You'll give me a ride after—"

"Sure. Let's go." Norm Lilly went out. He came back with a deer rifle, and the automatic pistol. "Ever use one of these, Harry?"

"No. And I don't want one. Wrong image."

Lilly nodded and laid the pistol on the table.

Bill Freehafer started to say something, but Lilly's look cut it off. "Okay, Harry, let's go," Norm said. He didn't comment when Harry carried his mailbag to the car.

They got in. They'd gone halfway when Harry patted his bag and, half laughing himself, said, "You're not laughing at me."

"How can I laugh at a man who's got a purpose in life?"

They pulled up at the gate. The letters were gone from the mailbox. The padlock was still in place. "Now what?" Harry asked.

"Good questi—"

The shotgun caught Norm Lilly full in the chest. Lilly kicked once and died. Harry stood in shock, then dashed across the road for the ditch. He sprawled into it, headfirst into the muddy water, careless of the mailbag, of getting wet, of anything. He began to run toward Many Names again.

There were sounds ahead of him. Right around that bend —and there was someone coming behind, too. They weren't going to let him get away this time. In desperation he crawled up the bank, away from the road, and began scrambling up the steep hillside. The mailbag dragged at him. His boots dug into mud, slipping and sliding. He clawed at the ground and pulled himself upward.

SPANG! The shot sounded very loud. Much louder than the .22 yesterday. Maybe the shotgun? Harry kept on. He reached the top of the first rise and began to run.

He couldn't tell if they were still behind him. He didn't care. He wasn't going back down there. He kept remembering the look of surprise on Norman Lilly's face. The big man folding up, dying before he hit the ground. Who were these people who shot without warning?

The hill became steeper again, but the ground was harder, more rock than mud. The mailbag seemed heavy. Water in it? Probably. So why carry it?

Because it's the mail, you stupid SOB, Harry told himself.

* * *

The Chicken Ranch was owned by an elderly couple, retired L.A. business people. It was fully automated. The chickens stood in small pens not much bigger than an individual chicken. Eggs rolled out of the cage onto a conveyor belt. Food came around on another belt. Water was continuously supplied. It was not a ranch but a factory.

And it might have been heaven, for chickens. All problems were solved, all struggling ended. Chickens weren't very bright, and they got all they could eat, were protected from coyotes, had clean cages—another automated system—

But it had to be a damned dull existence.

The Chicken Ranch was over the next hill. Before Harry got there he saw chickens. Through the rain and the wet weeds they wandered, bewildered, pecking at the ground and the limbs of bushes and Harry's boots, squawking plaintively at Harry, demanding instructions.

Harry stopped walking. Something must be terribly wrong. The Sinanians would never have let the chickens run loose.

Here too? Those bastards, had they come here too? Harry stood on the hillside and dithered, and the chickens huddled around him.

He had to know what had happened. It was part of the job. Reporter, mailman, town crier, message carrier; if he wasn't that, he wasn't anything. He stood among the chickens, nerving himself, and eventually he went down.

All the chicken feed had been spilled out onto the floor of the barn. There was little left. Every cage was open. This was no accident. Harry waded through squawking chickens the full length of the building. Nothing there. He went out and down the path to the house.

The farmhouse door stood open. He called. No one answered. Finally he went inside. It was dimly lit; the shades and curtains were drawn and there was no artificial light. His way led him to the living room.

The Sinanians were there. They sat in big overstuffed chairs. Their eyes were open. They did not move.

Amos Sinanian had a bullet hole in his temple. His eyes bulged. There was a small pistol in his hand.

Mrs. Sinanian had not a mark on her. Heart attack? Whatever it was, it had been peaceful; her features were not contorted, and her clothing was carefully arranged. She stared at a blank TV screen. She looked to have been dead two days, possibly more. The blood on Amos's head was not quite dry. This morning at the latest.

There wasn't any note, no sign of explanation. There hadn't been anyone Amos had cared to explain it to. He'd released the chickens and shot himself.

It took Harry a long time to make up his mind. Finally he took the pistol from Amos's hand. It wasn't as hard to do as he'd thought it would be. He put the pistol in his pocket and searched until he found a box of bullets for it. He pocketed those, too.

"The mail goes through, dammit," he said. Then he found a cold roast in the refrigerator. It wouldn't keep anyway, so Harry ate it. The oven was working. Harry had no idea how much propane there might be in the tank, but it didn't matter. The Sinanians weren't going to be using it.

He took the mail out of his bag and put it carefully into the oven to dry. Circulars and shopping newspapers were a problem. Their information wasn't any use, but might people want them for paper? Harry compromised, throwing out the ones that were thin and flimsy and soaked, keeping the others.

He found a supply of Baggies in the kitchen and carefully enclosed each packet of mail in one. Last Baggies on Earth, a small voice told him. "Right," he said, and went on stuffing. "Have to keep the Baggies. You can have your mail, but the Baggies belong to the Service."

After that was done he thought about his next move. This house might be useful. It was a good house, stone and concrete, not wood. The barn was concrete too. The land wasn't much good—at least Amos had said it wasn't—but somebody might make use of the buildings. "Even me," Harry said to himself. He had to have some place to stay between rounds.

Which meant something had to be done about the bodies. Harry wasn't up to digging two graves. He sure as hell wasn't going to drag them out for the coyotes and buzzards. There wasn't enough dry wood to cremate a mouse.

Finally he went out again. He found an old pickup truck. The keys were in the ignition, and it started instantly. It sounded smooth, in good tune. There was a drum of gasoline in the shed, and Harry thoughtfully filled the tank of the truck, filled two gas cans, then stacked junk against the drum to hide it.

He went back into the house and got old bedclothes to wrap the bodies, then drove the truck around to the front of the house. The chickens swarmed around his feet, demanding attention, while he wrestled the corpses onto the truck bed. Finished, Harry stooped and quickly wrung six chickens' necks before the rest of the chickens got the idea. He tossed the birds into the truck with the Sinanians.

He went around carefully locking doors and windows, put Amos's keys in his pockets and drove away.

He still had his route to finish. But there were things he must do first, not the least of which was burying the Sinanians.

Al Hardy didn't like guard duty. It didn't do him much good to dislike it. Somebody had to pull guard, and the ranch-hands were more useful elsewhere. Besides, Hardy could make decisions for the Senator.

He looked forward to giving up the whole thing. Not too long, he thought. Not too long until we won't need guards at the Senator's gate. The roadblock stopped most intruders now; but it didn't get them all. A few walked up from the flooded San Joaquin. Others came down from the High Sierra, and a lot of strangers had got into the valley before the Christophers began sealing it off. Most would be sent on their way, and they'd heard the Senator could let them stay on. It meant a lot, to be able to talk to the Senator.

And the Old Man didn't like sending people away, which was why Al didn't let many get up to see him. It was part of the job, and always had been: The Senator said yes to people, and Al Hardy said no.

There'd be a flood of them every hour if they weren't stopped, and the Senator had important work to do. And Maureen and Charlotte would stand guard if Al didn't, and to hell with that. The only good thing about Hammerfall, women's lib was dead milliseconds after Hammerstrike. . . .

Al had paper work to do. He made lists of items they needed, jobs for people to do, worked out details of schemes the Senator thought up. He worked steadily at the clipboard in the car, pausing when anyone came to the drive.

You couldn't tell. You just couldn't tell. The refugees all looked alike: half-drowned and half-starved, and worse every day. Now it was Saturday, and they looked just awful. When he'd been Senator Jellison's aide, Al Hardy had judged himself a good judge of men. But now there was nothing to judge. He had to fall back on routine.

These wandering scarecrows who came on foot, leading two children and carrying a third; but the man and woman both claimed to be doctors and knew the lingo . . . specialists, but even the woman psychiatrist had had GP training; they all did. And that surly giant was a CBS executive; he had to be turned back to the road, and he didn't stop swearing until Hardy's partner wasted a round through the side window of his car.

And the man in the remains of a good suit, polite and

speaking good English, who'd been a city councilman out
in the valley there, and who'd got out of his car, got close
to Al and showed the pistol hidden in his raincoat pocket.

"Put your hands up."

"Sure you want it this way?" Al had asked.

"Yes. You're taking me inside."

"Okay." Al raised his hands. And the shot went through
the city councilman's head, neat and clean, because of
course the signal was Al raising his right hand. Pity the
councilman had never read his Kipling:

'Twas only by favour of mine, quoth he, ye rode so
    long alive,
There was not a rock for twenty mile, there was not
    a clump of tree,
But covered a man of my own men with his rifle
    cocked on his knee.
If I had raised my bridle-hand, as I have held it low,
The little jackals that flee so fast were feasting all in
    a row.
If I had bowed my head on my breast, as I have
    held it high,
The Kite that whistles above us now were gorged
    till she could not fly. . . .

A truck came up to the drive. Small truck, thin hairy
man with mustache drooping. Probably a local, Al thought.
Everyone around here drove a small truck. By the same
token he might have stolen it, but why drive to the Senator's
home with it? Al got out of the car and splashed through
muddy water to the gate.

To all of them Alvin Hardy was the same: "Show your
hands. I'm not armed. But there's a man with a scope-
sighted rifle and you can't see him."

"Can he drive a truck?"

Al Hardy stared at the bearded man. "What?"

"First things first." The bearded man reached into the bag on the seat beside him. "Mail. Only I've got a registered letter. Senator will have to sign for it. And there's a dead bear—"

"What?" Al's routine wasn't working so well. "What?"

"A dead bear. I killed him early this morning. I didn't have much choice. I was sleeping in the truck and this enormous black hairy arm smashed the window and reached inside. He was huge. I backed up as far as I could, but he kept coming in, so I took this Beretta I found at the Chicken Ranch and shot the bear through the eye. He dropped like so much meat. So—"

"Who are you?" Al asked.

"I'm the goddam mailman! Will you try to keep your mind on one thing at a time? There's five hundred to a thousand pounds of bear meat, not to mention the fur, just waiting for four big men with a truck, and it's starting to spoil right now! I couldn't move him myself, but if you get a team out there you can maybe stop some people from starving. And now I've got to get the Senator's signature for this registered letter, only you better send somebody for the bear right away."

It was too much for Al Hardy. Far too much. The one thing he knew was the Beretta. "You'll have to let me hold that weapon for you. And you drive me up the hill," Al said.

"Hold my gun? Why the hell should you hold my gun?" Harry demanded. "Oh, hell, all right if it makes you happy. Here."

He handed the pistol out. Al took it gingerly. Then he opened the gate.

"Good Lord, Senator, it's Harry!" Mrs. Cox shouted.

"Harry? Who's Harry?" Senator Jellison got up from the table with its maps and lists and diagrams and went to the windows. Sure enough, there was Al with somebody in a truck. A very bearded and mustachioed somebody, in gray clothes.

"Mail call!" Harry shouted as he came up onto the porch.

Mrs. Cox rushed to the door. "Harry, we never expected to see you again!"

"Hi," Harry said. "Registered letter for Senator Jellison."

Registered letter. Political secrets about a world dead and burying itself. Arthur Jellison went to the door. The mail carrier—yes, that was the remains of a Postal Service uniform—looked a bit worn. "Come in," Jellison said. What the devil was this guy doing—

"Senator, Harry shot a bear this morning. I better get some ranch-hands out to get it before the buzzards do," Al Hardy said.

"You don't go off with my pistol," Harry said indignantly.

"Oh." Hardy produced the weapon from a pocket. He looked at it uncertainly. "Senator, this is his," he said. Then he fled, leaving Jellison holding the weapon in still more confusion.

"I think you're the first chap to fluster Hardy," Jellison said. "Come in. Do you call on all the ranches?"

"Right," Harry said.

"And who do you expect to pay you, now that—"

"People I bring messages to," Harry said. "My customers."

That hint couldn't be ignored. "Mrs. Cox, see what you can find—"

"Coming up," she called from the kitchen. She came in with a cup of coffee. A very nice cup, Jellison saw. One of his best. And some of the last coffee in the world. Mrs. Cox thought well of Harry.

That at least told him one thing. He handed over the pistol. "Sorry. Hardy's got instructions—"

"Sure." The mailman pocketed the weapon. He sipped the coffee and sighed.

"Have a seat," Jellison said. "You've been all over the valley?"

"Most places."

"So tell me what things are like—"

"I thought you'd never ask."

Harry had been nearly everywhere. He told his story simply, no embellishments. He'd decided on that style. Just the facts. Mail truck overturned. Power lines down. Telephone lines gone. Breaks in the road, here, and here, and ways around on driveways through here and across there. Millers okay, Shire still operating. Muchos Nombres deserted when he'd gone back with the truck, and the bodies— oops, getting ahead of himself.

He told of the murder at the Roman place. Jellison frowned, and Harry went to the table to show him on the big county engineer's map.

"No sign of the owners, but somebody shot at you, and killed this other chap?" Jellison asked.

"Right."

Jellison nodded. Have to do something there. But—first tell the Christophers. Let them share the risks of a police action.

"And the people at Muchos Nombres were coming to find you," Harry said. "That was yesterday, before noon."

"Never got here," Jellison said. "Maybe they're in town. Good land there? Anything planted?"

"Not much. Weeds, mostly," Harry said. "But I have chickens. Got any chicken feed?"

"Chickens?" This guy was a gold mine of information!

Harry told him about the Sinanians and the Chicken Ranch. "Lots of chickens left there, and I guess they'll starve or the coyotes will get them, so you might as well help yourself," Harry said. "I want to keep a few. There was one rooster, and I hope he lives. If not, maybe I'll have to borrow one . . ."

"You're taking up farming?" Jellison asked.

Harry shuddered. "Good God, no! But I thought it'd be nice to have a few chickens running around the place."

"So you'll go back there—"

"When I finish my route," Harry said. "I'll stop at other places on the way back."

"And then what?" Jellison asked, but he already knew.

"I'll start over again, of course. What else?"

That figures. "Mrs. Cox, who's available as a runner?"

"Mark," she said. Her voice was disapproving; she hadn't made up her mind about Mark.

"Send him to town to find out about these tourists from Muchos Nombres. They were supposed to have come looking for me."

"All right," she said. She went off muttering. They needed the telephones working again. Her daughter was talking about a telegraph line last night. There were plans in one of her books, and of course the wires were still around, the old telephone lines.

After she sent Mark off she made lunch. There was plenty of food just now: scraps from what they were canning, gleanings from the garden patches. It wouldn't last long, though . . .

One night Jerry phones me. He's at work on HAMMER. He's planning to keep the grounded astronauts outside the Stronghold a little longer. Needs a scene showing how terrible it all is, outside the Stronghold, after Hammerfall. Maybe a raid on a supermarket? Deke's gang has become jaded, has stopped seeing the horrors.

I hung up. I thought. If Deke's gang has stopped noticing the horrors, where's my viewpoint?

What *would* they notice?

Just short of midnight, I called him back . . .

Two heavy farm trucks ground across the mud flats, taking a tortuous path to the new island in the San Joaquin Sea. They stopped at a supermarket, still half flooded, glass windows scraped of mud by laborious effort. Armed men jumped out and took up positions nearby.

"Let's go," Cal White said. He carried Deke Wilson's submachine gun. White led the way into the drowned building, wading waist-deep in filthy water. The others followed.

Rick Delanty coughed and tried to breathe through his mouth. The smell of death was overpowering. He looked for someone to talk to, Picter or Johnny Baker, but they were at the far end of the column. Although it was their second day at the store, none of the astronauts had got used to the smells.

"If it was up to me, I'd wait another week," Kevin Murray said. Murray was a short, burly man with long arms. He'd been a feedstore clerk, and was lucky enough to have married a farmer's sister.

"Wait a week and those Army bastards may be here," Cal White called from inside. "Hold up a second." White went on with another man and their only working flashlight, hand-pumped, and Deke's submachine gun.

The gun seemed an irrelevant obscenity to Rick. There was too much death all around them. He wasn't going to say that. Last night Deke had taken in a refugee, a man from southwards with information to trade for a meal: a gang of blacks had been terrorizing the south valley, and now they were linked up with the Army cannibals. It might not be long before they came to Deke Wilson's turf again.

Poor bastards, Rick thought. He could sympathize: blacks in this shattered world, no status, no place to go, wanted nowhere. Of course they'd join the cannibals. And of course the local survivors were looking strangely at Rick Delanty again . . .

"Clear. Let's get at it," White called from inside. They waded in, a dozen men, three astronauts and nine survivors. A driver brought one of the trucks around so that the headlights shone into the wrecked store.

Rick wished they hadn't. Bodies bobbed in the filthy water. He choked hard and brought the cloth to his face; White had sprinkled a dozen drops of gasoline on it. The sweet sickening smell of gasoline was better than . . .

Kevin Murray went to a shelf of cans. He lifted a can of corn. It was eaten through with rust. "Gone," he said. "Damn."

"Sure wish we had a flashlight," another farmer said.

A flashlight would help, Rick knew, but some things are better done in gloomy darkness. He pushed rotten remains away from a shelf. Glass jars. Pickles. He called to the others, and they began carrying the pickles out.

"What's this stuff, Rick?" Kevin Murray asked. He brought another jar.

"Mushrooms."

Murray shrugged. "Better'n nothing. Thanks. Sure wish I had my glasses back. You ever wonder why I don't pack a gun? Can't see as far as the sights."

Rick tried to concentrate on glasses, but he didn't know anything about how you might grind lenses. He moved through the aisles, carrying things the others had discovered, searching for more, pushing aside the corpses until even that became routine, but you had to talk about something else . . . "Cans don't last long, do they?" Rick said. He stared at rotten canned stew.

"Sardine cans last fine. God knows why. I think somebody's already been here, there ain't so much as the last store. We got most of what was here yesterday, anyway." He looked thoughtfully at old corpses bobbing about him. "Maybe *they* ate it all. Trapped here . . ."

Rick didn't answer. His toes had brushed glass.

They were all working in open-toed sandals taken from the shoe store up the road. They couldn't work barefoot for fear of broken glass, and why ruin good boots? Now his toes had brushed a cool, smooth curve of glass bottle.

Rick held his breath and submerged. Near floor level he found rows of bottles, lots of them, different shapes. Fifty-fifty it was bottled water, barely worth room aboard the truck; but he picked one up and surfaced.

"Apple juice, by God! Hey, gang, we need hands here!"

They waded down the aisles, Pieter and Johnny and the farmers, all dog-tired and dirty and wet, moving like zombies. Some had strength to smile. Rick and Kevin Murray dipped for the bottles and handed them up, because they were the ones who didn't carry guns.

White, the man in charge, turned slowly away with two bottles; turned back. "Good, Rick. You did good," he said, and smiled, and turned slowly away and waded toward the doorway. Rick followed.

Someone yelled.

Rick set his bottles on an empty shelf to give himself speed. That had to be Sohl on sentry duty. But Rick didn't have a gun!

Sohl yelled again. "No danger; I repeat, no danger, but you guys gotta see this!"

Go back for the bottles? Hell with it. Rick pushed past something he wouldn't look at (but the floating mass had the feel, the weight of a small dead man or a large dead woman) and waded out into the light.

The parking lot was almost half full of cars, forty or fifty cars abandoned when the rains came. The hot rain must have fallen so fast that car motors were drowned before the customers in the shopping center could decide to move. So the cars had stayed, and many of the customers. The water washed around and in and out of the cars.

Sohl was still at his post on the roof of the supermarket. It would have done him no good to come closer; he was farsighted, and his glasses had been smashed, like Murray's. He pointed down at what was washing against the side of a Volkswagen bus and called, "Will someone tell me what this is? It ain't no cow!"

They formed a semicircle around it, their feet braced against the water's gentle westward current, the same flow that held the strange body against the bus.

It was smaller than a man. It was all the colors of decay; the big, drastically bent legs were almost falling off. What was it? It had *arms*. For a mad moment Rick pictured Hammerfall as the first step in an interstellar invasion, or as part of a program for tourists from other worlds. Those tiny arms, the long mouth gaping in death, the Chianti-bottle torso . . .

"I'll be damned," he said. "It's a kangaroo."

"Well, I never saw a kangaroo like that," White said with fine contempt.

"It's a kangaroo."

"But—"

Rick snapped, "Does *your* newspaper run pictures of animals two weeks dead? Mine never did. It's a *dead* kangaroo, that's why it looks funny."

Jacob Vinge had crowded close to the beast. "No pouch," he said. "Kangaroos have pouches."

The breeze shifted; the crescent of men opened at one end. "Maybe it's a male," Deke Wilson said. "I don't see balls either. Did kangaroos have . . . ah, overt genitalia? Oh, this is stupid. Where would it come from? There ain't any zoo closer than . . . where?"

Johnny Baker nodded. "Griffith Park Zoo. The quake must

have ripped some of the cages apart. No telling how the poor beast got this far north before he drowned or starved. Look close, gentlemen, you'll never see another . . ."

Rick stopped listening. He backed out of the arc and looked around him. He wanted to scream.

They had come at dawn yesterday. They had worked all of yesterday and today, and it must be near sunset. None of them had even discussed what must have happened here, yet it was obvious enough. Scores of customers must have been trapped here when the first flash rain drowned their cars. They had waited in the supermarket for the rain to stop; they had waited for rescue; they had waited while the water rose and rose. At the end the electric doors hadn't worked. Some must have left through the back, to drown in the open.

In the supermarket there were half-empty shelves, and the water floated with corncobs and empty bottles and orange rinds and half-used loaves of bagged bread. They had not died hungry . . . but they had died, for their corpses floated everywhere in the supermarket and in the flooded parking lot. Scores of bodies. Most were women, but there were men and children, too, bobbing gently among the submerged cars.

"Are you . . ." Rick whispered. He bowed his head and cleared his throat and shrieked, "Are you all crazy?" They turned, shocked and angry. "If you want to see corpses, look around you! Here," his hand brushed a stained and rotting flowered dress, "and there," pointing to a child close enough for Deke to touch, "and there," to a slack face behind the windshield of the Volks bus itself. "Can you look anywhere without seeing somebody _dead_? Why are you crowding like jackals around a dead kangaroo?"

"You shut up! Shut up!" Kevin Murray's fists were balled at his sides, the knuckles white; but he didn't move, and presently he looked away, and so did the others.

All but Jacob Vinge. His voice held a tremor. "We got used to it. We just got used to it. We had to, goddamn it!"

The current shifted slightly. The kangaroo, if that was what it was, washed around the edge of the bus and began to move away.

Fallout from HAMMER has been fun.

Readers have demanded that I tell them that the surfer survived. Okay. I didn't actually *see* him die.

The book had been in print for months when the Nivens and Pournelles attended the next AAAS meeting. It's our way of staying current. The American Association for the Advancement of Science is scientists gathered to explain what they've been doing all year. Programming follows roughly eighteen parallel tracks.

Thence came Luis Alvarez to tell how the dinosaurs died. The Alvarezes, father and son, had found excessive iridium in the layer of dead clay that forms the Cretaceous–Tertiary boundary. Their conclusion: a major asteroid strike coincides with the death of the dinosaurs and most of the life that then occupied the Earth.

Alvarez recognized Jerry in the audience. He announced, "The dinosaurs were killed by Lucifer's Hammer!"

There came a phone call from an Al Jackson in Texas. His group had published a paper suggesting that a giant planet or midget sun (brown dwarf) in Sol's cometary halo was the cause of periodic flurries of comets through the inner solar system. Every twenty-six million years, Hammer-like strikes would disrupt Earth's biosphere. What had we named that black giant planet in LUCIFER'S HAMMER?

For one wonderful moment, it looked like the brown dwarf would bear the name *Lucifer*. But a California group had published their own paper simultaneously, and they named *their* brown dwarf *Nemesis*. That's the name that stuck.

THE SOFT WEAPON

Logically Jason Papandreou should have taken the *Court Jester* straight home to Jinx. But . . .

He'd seen a queer star once.

He'd been single then, a gunner volunteer on one of Earth's warships during the last stages of the last Kzinti war. The war had been highly unequal in Earth's favor. Kzinti fight gallantly, ferociously, and with no concept of mercy; and they always take on several times as much as they can handle.

Earth's ships had pushed the kzinti back out of human space, then pushed a little farther, annexing two kzinti worlds for punitive damages. The fleets had turned for home. But Jason's captain had altered course to give his crew what might be their last chance to see Beta Lyrae.

Now, decades later, Jason, his wife, and their single alien passenger were rattling around in a ship built for ten times their number. Anne-Marie's curiosity was driving her up the walls with the frustration of not being able to open the stasis box in the forward locker. Nessus, the mad puppeteer, had taken to spending all his time in his room, hovering motionless and morose between the sleeping plates. Jinx was still weeks away.

Clearly a diversion was in order.

Beta Lyrae. A six-degree shift in course would do it.

Anne-Marie glared at the locker containing the stasis box. "Isn't there *any* way to open it?"

Jason didn't answer. His whole attention was on the mass indicator, the transparent ball in which a green radial line was growing toward the surface—growing and splitting in two.

"Jay?"

"We can't open it, Anne. We don't have the equipment to break a stasis field. It's illegal anyway."

Almost time. The radial double-line must not grow too long. When a working hyperdrive gets too deep into a gravity well, it disappears.

"Think they'll tell us what's inside?"

"Sure, unless it's a new weapon."

"With our luck it will be. Jay, nobody's ever found a stasis box that shape before. It's bound to be something new. The Institute is likely to sit on it for years and years.

"Whup! Jay, what are you *doing*?"

"Dropping out of hyperspace."

"You might warn a lady." She wrapped both arms around her midsection, apparently making sure everything was still there.

"Lady, why don't you have a look out that side window?"

"What for?"

Jason merely looked smug. His wife, knowing she would get no other answer, got up and undogged the cover. It was not unusual for a pilot to drop out in the depths of interstellar space. Weeks of looking at the blind-spot appearance of hyperspace could wear on the best of nerves.

She stood at the window, a tall, slender brunette in a glowing-green falling jumper. A Wunderlander she had been, of the willowy low-gravity type rather than the fat, balloonlike low-gravity type, until Jason Papandreou had dropped out of the sky to add her to his collection of girls in every port. It hadn't worked out that way. In the first year of marriage she had learned space and the *Court Jester* inside out, until she was doubly indispensable. Jay, Anne, *Jester*, all one independent organism.

And she thought she'd seen everything. But she hadn't seen this! Grinning, Jason waited for her reaction.

"Jay, it's *gorgeous*! What *is* it?"

Jason moved up to circle her waist with one arm. She'd put on weight in the last year, muscle weight, from moving in heavier gravities. He looked out around her shoulder . . . and thought of smoke.

There was smoke across the sky, a trail of red smoke wound in a tight spiral coil. At the center of the coil was the source of the fire: a double star. One member was violet-white, a flame to brand holes in a human retina, its force held in check by the polarized window. The companion was small and yellow. They seemed to burn inches apart, so close that their masses had pulled them both into flattened eggs, so close that a red belt of lesser flame looped around them to link their bulging equators together. The belt was hydrogen, still mating in fusion fire, pulled loose from the stellar surfaces by two gravitational wells in conflict.

The gravity war did more than that. It sent a loose end of the red belt flailing away, away and out in a burning Maypole spiral that expanded and dimmed as it rose toward interstellar space, until it turned from flame-red to smoke-red, bracketing the sky and painting a spiral path of stars deep red across half the universe.

"They call it Beta Lyrae," said Jason. "I was here once before, back when I was free and happy. Mph. Hasn't changed much."

"Well, *no*."

"Now don't you take all this for granted. How long do you think those twins can keep throwing hydrogen away? I give it a million years, and then, pft! No more Beta Lyrae."

"Pity. We'd better hurry and wake Nessus before it disappears."

The being they called Nessus would not have opened his door for them.

Puppeteers were gregarious even among alien species. They'd had to be. For at least tens of thousands of years the puppeteers had ruled a trade empire that included all the races within the sixty-light-year sphere men called "Known

Space" and additional unknown regions whose extent could not be guessed. As innate cowards the puppeteers had to get along with everyone. And Nessus, too, was usually gregarious. But Nessus was mad.

Nessus was cursed with courage.

In a puppeteer, courage is a symptom of insanity. As usual there were other symptoms, other peripheral indications of the central disorder. Nessus was now in the depressive stage of a manic-depressive cycle.

Luckily the depression had not hit him until his business with the Outsiders was over. In the manic stage he had been fun. He had spent every night in a different stateroom. He had charcoal-drawn cartoons which now hung in the astrogation room, cartoons that Jason could hardly believe were drawn by a puppeteer. Humor is generally linked to an interrupted defense mechanism. Puppeteers weren't supposed to have a sense of humor. But now Nessus spent all his time in one room. He wanted to see nobody.

There was one thing he might open his door for.

Jason moved to the control board and pushed the panic button. The alarm was a repeated recording of a woman's scream. It should have brought the puppeteer galloping in as if the angel of death were at his heel. But he trotted through the door seconds later than he should have. His flat, brainless heads surveyed the control room for signs of damage.

The first man to see a puppeteer had done so during a Campish revival of "Time for Beany" reruns. He had come running back to the scout ship, breathless and terrified, screaming, "Take off! The planet's full of monsters!"

"Whatta they look like?"

"Like a three-legged centaur with two Cecil the Seasick Sea Serpent puppets on its hands, and no head."

"Take a pill, Pierson. You're drunk."

Nessus was an atypical puppeteer. His mane was straggly and unkempt. It should have been twisted, brushed, and tied in a manner to show his status in puppeteer society. But it showed no status at all. Perhaps this was appropriate. There was no puppeteer society. The puppeteers had apparently left the galaxy en masse some twelve years earlier, leaving behind only their insane and their genetically deficient.

"What is wrong?" asked Nessus.

"There's nothing wrong," said Jason.

Anne-Marie said, "Have a look out the window. This window."

Their employer obediently moved to the window. He happened to stop just next to one of the cartoons he'd drawn while in the manic phase, and Jason, looking from the puppeteer to the cartoon, found it more difficult than ever to associate the two.

The cartoon showed two human gods. Only the lighting and the proportions showed that they were gods. Otherwise they were as individually human as a very good human artist could have drawn them. One, a child just about to become a teen-ager, was holding the galaxy in his hands. He wore a very strange grin as he looked down at the glowing multi-colored spiral. The other figure, a disgruntled patriarch with flowing white hair and beard, was saying, "All right, now that you've had your little joke . . ."

Nessus claimed it was an attempt to imitate human humor. Maybe. Would an insane puppeteer develop a sense of humor?

Nessus (his real name sounded like a car crash set to music) was insane. There were circumstances under which he would actually risk his life. But the sudden puppeteer exodus had left a myriad broken promises made to a dozen sentient races. The puppeteers had left Nessus and his fellow exiles with money to straighten things out. So Nessus had rented the *Court Jester*, rented all twelve staterooms, and gone out to the farthest edge of Known Space to deal with a ship of the Outsiders.

"I recognize this star," he said now. "Amazing. I really

should have suggested this stop myself. Had I not been so depressed, I certainly would have. Thank you, Jason.''

"My pleasure, sir.'' Jason Papandreou really sounded as though he'd invented the gaudy display just to cheer up a down-in-the-mouths puppeteer. Nessus cocked a sardonic head at him, and he hastily added, ''We'll be on our way again whenever you're ready.''

"I'll scan with deep-radar,'' Anne-Marie said helpfully.

Jason laughed. "Can you imagine how many ships must have scanned this system already?''

"Just for luck.''

A moment later there was a beep.

Anne-Marie yelped.

Jason said, "I don't believe it.''

"Two in one trip!'' his wife caroled. "Jay, that's some sort of record!''

It was. Using deep-radar had been more of a habit than anything else. A deep-radar on high setting was an easy way to find Slaver stasis boxes, since only stasis fields and neutron stars would reflect a hyperwave pulse. But Beta Lyrae *must* have been searched many times before. Searching was traditional.

Nessus turned from the window. "I suggest that we locate the box, then leave it. You may send a friend for it.''

Jason stared. "Leave it? Are you kidding?''

"It is an anomaly. Such a box should have been found long since. It has no reason to be here in the first place. Beta Lyrae probably did not exist a billion and a half years ago. Why then would the Slavers have come here?''

"War. They might have been running from a tnuctip fleet.''

Anne-Marie was sweeping the deep-radar in a narrow beam, following the smoky spiral, searching for the tiny node of stasis her first pulse had found.

"You hired my ship,'' Jason said abruptly. "If you order me to go on, I'll do it.''

"I will not. Your species has come a long way in a short time. If you do not have prudence, you have some workable substitute."

"There it is," said Anne-Marie. "Look, Jay. A little icy blob of a world a couple of billion miles out."

Jason looked. "Shouldn't be any problem. All right, I'll take us down."

Nessus said nothing. He seemed alert enough, but without the nervousness and general excitability that would have meant the onset of his manic stage. At least Beta Lyrae had cured his depression.

The *Traitor's Claw* was under the ice. Ice showed dark and deep outside her hexagonal ports. In lieu of sight her crew used a mechanical sense like a cross between radar and X-ray vision. The universe showed on her screens as a series of transparent images superimposed: a shadow show.

Four kzinti watched a blob-shaped image sink slowly through other images, coming to a stop at a point no different from any other.

"Chuft-Captain, they're down," said Flyer.

"Of course they're down." Chuft-Captain spoke without heat. "Telepath, how many are there?"

"Two human." There was a quiet, self-hating resignation in Telepath's speech. His tone became disgust as he added, "And a puppeteer."

"Odd. That's a passenger ship. A puppeteer couldn't need all that room."

"I sense only their presence, Chuft-Captain." Telepath was pointedly reminding him that he had not yet taken the drug. He would do so only if ordered. Without an injection of treated extract of sthondat lymph, his powers were low. Little more than the knack for making an accurate guess.

"One human has left the ship," said Flyer. "No, two humans."

"Slaverstudent, initiate hostilities. Assume the puppeteer will stay safely inside."

The planet was no bigger than Earth's moon. Her faint hydrogen atmosphere must have been regularly renewed as the spiral streamer whipped across her orbit. She was in the plane of the hydrogen spiral, which now showed as a glowing red smoke trail cutting the night sky into two unequal parts.

Anne-Marie finished tucking her hair into her helmet, clamped the helmet to her neck ring, and stepped out to look around.

"I dub thee Cue Ball," she said.

"Cute," said Jason. "Too bad if she's named already."

They moved through the ship's pressure curtain, Jason toting a bulky portable deep-radar. The escalladder carried them down onto the ice.

They moved away, following the dark image in the deep-radar screen. Jason was a head shorter than his wife and twice as wide; his typical Earther's build looked almost Jinxian next to hers. He moved easily in the low gravity. Anne-Marie, bouncing like a rubber clown, kept pace with him only by dint of longer legs and greater effort.

Jason was standing right over the image of the stasis box, getting ready to mark the ice so they could dig for it, when the image quietly vanished.

A sharp crack jerked his head around. He saw a cloud of steam explode into the near-vacuum, a cloud lit from below by a rosy light. Anne-Marie was already sprinting for the ship in low flying leaps. He turned to follow.

A form like a big roly-poly man shot through the light into what must by then have been a cloud of tiny ice crystals. It was a kzin in a vac suit, and the thing in its hands was a police stunner. It landed running. Under the conditions its aim was inhumanly accurate.

Jason collapsed like a deflating balloon. Anne-Marie was pinwheeling across the ice, slowly as dreams in the low gravity. The kzin ignored them both. It was using a jet backpac to speed it along.

The ship's heavy, flush-fitting door started to close over the pressure curtain. Too slowly. Jason clung to consciousness long enough to see the kzin's backpac carry it up the escalladder and through the pressure curtain. His mind hummed and faded.

Present in the crew's relaxroom were two humans, one puppeteer, and a kzin. The kzin was Chuft-Captain. It had to be that way, since the prisoners had not yet had the chance to refuse to talk. Chuft-Captain was a noble, entitled to a partial name. Had he not been alone with the prisoners, he would have been showing fear. His crew watched the proceedings from the control room.

The puppeteer lifted a head at the end of a drunkenly weaving neck. The head steadied, stared hard. In Kzin he said, "What is the purpose of this-action?"

Chuft-Captain ignored him. One did not speak as an equal to a puppeteer. Puppeteers did not fight, ever. Hence they were mere herbivorous animals. Prey.

The male human was next to recover from the stunners. He stared in consternation at Chuft-Captain, then looked around him. "So none of us made it," he said.

"No," said the puppeteer. "You may remember I advised—"

"How could I forget? Sorry about that, Nessus. What's happening?"

"Very little at the moment."

The male looked back at Chuft-Captain. "Who're you?"

"You may call me Captain. Depending on future events, you are either my kidnap victims or my prisoners of war. Who are you?"

"Jason Papandreou, of Earth origin." The human tried to gesture, perhaps to point at himself, and found the electronic police-web binding him in an invisible grip. He finished the introductions without gestures.

"Very well," said Chuft-Captain. "Jason, are you in possession of a stasis box, a relic of the Slaver Empire?"

"No."

Chuft-Captain gestured to the screen behind the prisoners. Telepath nodded and switched off. The prisoner had lied; it was now permissible to bring in help to question him.

It had been a strange, waiting kind of war.

Legally it was no war at all. The *Traitor's Claw* showed in the Kzinti records as a stolen ship. If she had been captured at any time, all the kzinti worlds would have screamed loudly for Chuft-Captain's head as a pirate. Even the ship's name had been chosen for that eventuality.

There had never been a casualty; never, until now, a victory. A strange war, in which the rules were flexible and the dictates of personal honor were often hard to define and to satisfy. Even now . . . What does one do with a captured puppeteer? You couldn't eat him; puppeteers were officially a friendly power. A strange war. But better than no war at all. Perhaps it would now get better still.

The kzin had asked one question and turned away. A bad sign. Apparently the question had been a formality.

Jason wriggled once more against the force field. He was embedded like a fly in flypaper. It must be a police web. Since the last war the kzinti worlds had been living in probationary status. Though they might possess and use police restraint-devices, they were allowed no weapons of war.

Against two unarmed humans and a puppeteer, they hardly needed them.

Anne-Marie stirred. Jason said, "Easy, honey."

"Easy? Oh, my neck. What happened?" She tried to

move her arm. Her head, above the soft grip of the police web, jerked up in surprise; her eyes widened. And she saw the Kzin.

She screamed.

The Kzin watched in obvious irritation. Nessus merely watched.

"All *right*," said Jason. "*That* won't do us any good."

"Jay, they're *Kzinti*!"

"Right. And they've got us. Oh, hell, go ahead and scream."

That shocked her. She looked at him long enough to read his helplessness, then turned back to the kzin. Already she was calmer. Jason didn't have to worry about his wife's courage. He'd seen it tested before.

She had never seen a kzin; all she knew about them she had heard from Jason, and little of that had been good. But she was no xenophobe. There was more sympathy of feeling between Anne-Marie and Nessus than there was between Nessus and Jason. She could face the kzin.

But Jason couldn't read the puppeteer's expression. It was Nessus he was worried about. Puppeteers hated pain worse than they feared death. Let the kzin threaten Nessus with pain and there was no telling what he'd do. Without the puppeteer they might have a chance to conceal the stasis box.

It might be very bad if the kzinti got into a stasis box.

A billion and a half years ago there had been a war. The Slavers, who controlled most of the galaxy at the time, had also controlled most of the galaxy's sentient species. One such slave species, the tnuctipun, had at last revolted. The Slavers had had a power like telepathic hypnosis, a power that could control the mind of any sentient being. The tnuctipun slaves had possessed high intelligence, higher technology, and a slyness more terrifying than any merely mental power. Slavers and tnuctipun slaves alike, and every sentient being then in the galaxy, had died in that war.

Scattered through known and unknown space were the relics of that war, waiting to be found by species which had become sentient since the war's end. The Slavers had left stasis boxes, containers in stasis fields, which had survived unchanged through a billion and a half years of time. The tnuctipun had left mutated remnants of their biological engineering: the Frumious bandersnatch of Jinx's shorelines; the stage tree, which was to be found on worlds scattered all across Known Space; the tiny cold-world sunflower with its rippling, reflective blossoms.

Stasis boxes were rare and dangerous. Often they held abandoned Slaver weapons. One such weapon, the variable-sword, had recently revolutionized human society, bringing back swordplay and dueling on many worlds. Another was being used for peaceful ends; the disintegrator was too slow to make a good weapon. If the kzinti found a new weapon, and if it were good enough . . .

Their kzinti captor was a big one, thought Jason, though even a small one was a big one. He stood eight feet tall, as erect as a human on his short hind legs. The orange shade of his fur might have been inconspicuous to a kzin's natural prey, but to human eyes it blazed like neon. He was thick all over, arms, legs, torso; he might have been a very fat cat dipped in orange dye, with certain alterations. You would have had to discount the naked-pink ratlike tail; the strangely colored irises, which were round instead of slitted; and especially the head, rendered nearly triangular by the large cranial bulge, more than large enough to hold a human brain.

"The trap you stumbled into is an old one," said the kzin. "One ship or another has been waiting on this world since the last war. We have been searching out Slaver stasis boxes for much longer than that, hoping to find new weapons . . ."

A door opened and a second kzin entered. He stayed there in the dilated doorway, waiting for the leader's attention. There was something about his appearance . . .

"But only recently did we hit upon this idea. You may know," said their orange captor, "that ships often stop off to see this unusual star. Ships of most species also have the habit of sending a deep-radar pulse around every star they happen across. No student of Slavers has ever found method behind the random dispersion of stasis boxes throughout this region of space.

"Several decades ago we did find a stasis box. Unfortunately it contained nothing useful, but we eventually found out how to turn the stasis field on and off. It made good bait for a trap. For forty kzin years we have waited for ships to happen by with stasis boxes in their holds. You are our second catch."

"You'd have done better finding your own boxes," said Jason. He had been examining the silent kzin. This one was smaller than their interrogator. His fur was matted. His tail drooped, as did his pointed ears. For a kzin the beast was skinny, and misery showed in his eyes. As certainly as they were aboard a fighting ship, this was not a fighting kzin.

"We would have been seen. Earth would have acted to stop our search." Apparently dismissing the subject, their interrogator turned to the smaller kzin and spat out an imitation of cats fighting. The smaller kzin turned to face them.

A pressure took hold of Jason's mind and developed into a sudden splitting headache.

He had expected it. It was a strange thing: put a sane alien next to an insane one, and usually you could tell them apart. And kzinti were much closer to human than were any other species; so close that they must at one time have had common microbe ancestors. This smaller kzin was obviously half crazy. And he wasn't a fighter. To be in this place at this time, he had to be a trained telepath, a forced addict of the kzinti drug that sent nine hundred and ninety-nine out of a thousand kzinti insane and left the survivor a shivering neurotic.

He concentrated on remembering the taste of a raw carrot—just to be difficult.

Telepath sagged against a wall, utterly spent. He could still taste yellow root munched between flat-topped teeth. Chuft-Captain watched without sympathy, waiting.

He forced himself to speak. "Chuft-Captain, they have not hidden the stasis box. It may be found in a locker to the left of the control room."

Chuft-Captain turned to the wall screen. "See to it. And get the puppeteer's pressure suit. Then seal the ship."

Flyer and Slaverstudent acknowledged and signed off.

"The relic. Where did they find it?"

"Chuft-Captain, they did not. The stasis box was found in deep interstellar space, considerably closer to the Core, by a ship of the Outsiders. The Outsiders kept it to trade in Known Space."

"What business did the prisoners have with the Outsiders?"

"The puppeteer had business with them. It merely used the humans for transportation. The humans do not know what business it was."

Chuft-Captain spit in reflex fury, but of course he could not ask a kzin to read the mind of a herbivore. Telepath wouldn't, and would have to be disciplined; or he would, and would go insane. Nor could Chuft-Captain use pain on the puppeteer. He would get the information if it was worthless; but if the puppeteer decided it was valuable, the creature would commit suicide.

"Am I to assume that the Outsiders did in fact sell the relic to the prisoners?"

"Chuft-Captain, they did. The sum was a puppeteer's recorded word of honor for fourteen million stars in human money."

"A lordly sum."

"Perhaps more than lordly. Chuft-Captain, you may know that the Outsiders are long-lived. The male human has speculated that they intend to return in one or more thousands of years, when the recording of a puppeteer's voice is an antique worth eights of times its face value.''

"Urrr. I shouldn't stray into such byways, but . . . are they really that long-lived?''

"Chuft-Captain, the Outsider ship was following a starseed in order to trace its migratory pattern."

"Urrr-rrrr!" Starseeds lived long enough to make mating migrations from the galactic core to the rim and back, moving at average speeds estimated at point eight lights.

A patterned knock. The others entered, wearing pressure suits with the helmets thrown back. Flyer carried the puppeteer's pressure suit, a three-legged balloon with padded mittens for the mouths, small clawed boots, an extra bulge for a food pouch, and a hard, padded shield to cover the cranial hump. Slaverstudent carried a cylinder with a grip-notched handle. Its entire surface was a perfectly reflecting mirror: the sign of the Slaver stasis field.

The prisoners, the human ones, were silently glaring. Their posttelepathy headaches had not helped their dispositions. Telepath was resting from the aftereffects of the drug.

"Open it," said Chuft-Captain.

Slaverstudent removed an empty cubical box from the table, set the stasis box in its place, and touched a pressure-sensitive surface at the table's edge. The cylinder ceased to be a distorting mirror. It was a bronzy metal box, which popped open of its own accord.

The kzin called Slaverstudent reached in and brought out:

A silvered bubble six inches in diameter, with a sculptured handle attached. The handle would not have fit any gripping appendage Chuft-Captain knew of.

A cube of raw meat in something like a plastic sandwich wrap.

A hand. An alien hand furnished with three massive,

clumsy-looking fingers set like a mechanical grab. It had been dipped in something that formed a clear, hard coating. One thick finger wore a chronometer.

"A bad thing has happened," said Nessus.

The kzin who had opened the box seemed terribly excited. He turned the preserved hand over and over, yowrling in kzinti. Then he put it down and picked up the sphere-with-a-handle.

"Let me guess," said Jason. "That's not a Slaver box. It's a tnuctipun box."

"Yes. The first to be found. The handle on the bubble tool is admirably designed to fit a tnuctipun hand. The preserved Slaver hand must be a trophy—I am quoting the student of Slavers. Jason, this may be a disaster. The tnuctipun were master technologists."

The "student of Slavers" was running his padded, retractile-clawed hands over the sphere-with-a-handle. No detail at all showed on the sphere; it was the same mirror color as the stasis field that had disgorged it. The handle was bronzy metal. There were grooves for six fingers and two long, opposed thumbs; there was a button set in an awkward position. A deep, straight groove ran down the side, with a guide and nine notched settings.

Anne-Marie spoke in a low voice. "It looks like the handle of a gun."

"We need information," said Jason. "Nessus, is that bigger kzin the boss? The one who speaks Interworld?"

"Yes. The one with the bubble tool is a student of the Slaver Empire. The one with the white stripe is the pilot. The mind reader is resting. We need not fear him for several hours."

"But the boss kzin understands Interworld. Do the others?"

"I think not. Your inaptly named Interworld is difficult for nonhumans to learn and to pronounce."

"Good. Anne, how are you doing?"

"I'm scared. We're in big trouble, aren't we, Jay?"

"We are. No sense fooling ourselves. Any ideas?"

"You know me, Jay. In a pinch I usually know who to call for help. The integrator if the house stops, the taxi company when a transfer booth doesn't work. Step into an autodoc when you feel sick. If your lift belt fails, you dial E for Emergency on your pocket phone. If someone answers before you hit the ground, scream." She tried a smile. "Jay? Who do we call about kzinti kidnappings?"

He smiled back. "You write a forceful note to the Patriarch of Kzin. Right, Nessus?"

"Also you threaten to cut off trade. Do not worry too much, Anne-Marie. My species is expert at staying alive."

"Undoubtedly a weapon," said Slaverstudent. "We had best try it outside."

"Later," said Chuft-Captain.

Again Slaverstudent dipped into the cylindrical box. He removed small containers half filled with two kinds of small-arms projectiles, a colored cap that might easily have fitted a standard bowling ball, a transparent bulb of clear fluid, and a small metal widget that might have been anything. "I see no openings for bullets."

"Nor do I. Flyer, take a sample of this meat and find out what it is made of. Do the same with this trophy and this bulb. Telepath, are you awake?"

"Chuft-Captain, I am."

"When can you again read the—"

"Chuft-Captain, please don't make—"

"At ease, Telepath. Take time to recover. But I intend to keep the prisoners present while we investigate this find. They may notice some detail we miss. Eventually I will need you."

"Yes, Chuft-Captain."

"Test that small implement for radio or hyperwave emissions. Do nothing else to it. It has the look of a subminiature communicator, but it might be anything: a camera, even an explosive.

"Slaverstudent, you will come with me. We are going outside."

It took several minutes for the kzinti to get the prisoners into their suits, adjust their radios so that everybody could hear everybody else, and move them through the double-door airlock.

To Jason, the airlock was further proof that this was a warship. A pressure curtain was generally more convenient than an airlock; but if power failed during a battle, all the air could leave the ship in one whoof. Warships carried double doors.

Two stunners followed them up the sloping ice tunnel. Jason had thought there would be four. He'd need to fight only the boss kzin and one other. But both carried stunners and both seemed alert.

He took too much time deciding. The boss made Nessus stand on a flexible wire grid, then did the same with Anne-Marie and Jason. The grid was a portable police web, and it was as inflexibly restraining as the built-in web in the ship.

The kzinti returned down the sloping tunnel, leaving Jason, Anne-Marie, and Nessus to enjoy the view. It was a lonely view. The blue and yellow stars were rising, invisibly. They showed only as a brighter spot at one foot of the red-smoke arch of hydrogen. Stars showed space-bright in curdled patterns across the sky; they all glowed red near the arch. The land was cold rock-hard ice, rippling in long, low undulations that might have been seasonal snowdrifts millions of years ago, when the Lyrae twins were bigger and brighter. Black-faceted rock poked through some of the high spots.

Several yards away was the *Court Jester*. A thick, round-edged, flat-bottomed disk, she sat on the ice like a painted concrete building. Apparently she intended to stay.

Jason stood at parade rest on the police web. Anne-Marie was six inches to his right, facing him. For all of his urge to touch her, she might have been miles away.

Two days ago she had carefully painted her eyelids with semipermanent tattoo. They showed as two tiny black-and-white-checked racing victory flags, rippling when she blinked. Their gaiety mocked her drawn face.

"I wonder why we're still alive," she said.

Nessus' accentless voice was tinny in the earphones. "The captain wants our opinions on the putative weapon. He will not ask for them, but will take them through the telepath."

"That doesn't apply to you, does it?"

"No. No kzin would read my mind. Perhaps no kzin would kill me; my race holds strong policies on the safety of individual members. In any case we have some time."

"Time for what?"

"Anne-Marie, we must wait. If the artifact is a weapon, we must recover it. If not, we must survive to warn your people that the kzinti are searching out Slaver stasis boxes. We must wait until we know which."

"*Then* what?"

"We will find a way."

"We?" said Jason.

"Yes. Our motives coincide here. I cannot explain why at this time."

But why should a puppeteer risk his life, his *life*, for Earth? Jason wondered.

The boss kzin emerged from the airlock carrying the sphere-with-a-handle. He stood before Jason and held it before his eyes. "Examine this," he commanded, and turned it slowly and invitingly in his four-fingered hands.

There was the reflecting sphere, and there was the bronzy-metal gun handle with its deeply scored groove and its alien sculpturing. The groove had nine notched settings running from top to bottom, with a guide in the top notch. Squiggles that must have been tnuctip numbers corresponded to the notches.

Jason prayed for the police web to fail. If he could snatch the artifact—

The Kzin moved away, walking uphill to a rise of icy ground. A second kzin emerged from the pressure curtain carrying an unfamiliar gadget of kzinti make. The two kzinti spat phrases at each other. Kzinti language always sounds like insults.

Nessus spoke quietly. "The meat was protoplasmic, protein, and highly poisonous. The small, complex tnuctip implement does operate in hyperspace but uses no known method of communication. The fluid in the clear bulb is forty percent hydrogen peroxide, sixty percent hydrogen oxide, purpose unknown."

"What's the Slaver expert carrying?"

"That is an energy-output sensor."

The puppeteer seemed calm enough. Did he know of some way to interrupt a police web?

Jason couldn't ask, not when the boss kzin could hear every word. But he had little hope. A police web belonged to the same family as a pilot's crash field, triggered to enfold the pilot when signaled by excessive pressure on his crash webbing. A crash web was as deliberately foolproof as any last-ditch failsafe device. So was a police web.

Probably the puppeteer was slipping back into the manic state and was now convinced that nothing in the universe could harm him. Somehow that made Jason's failure worse. "One thing you should know, Jason, is that my species judges me insane." It was one of the first things the puppeteer had told him. Unable to trust his own judgment, Nessus had warned him by implication that he would have to trust Jason's.

They'd both trusted him.

"I had to show you Beta Lyrae," he said bitterly.

"It was a nice idea, Jay, really it was."

If he'd been free, he'd have found a wall and tried to punch it down.

Chuft-Captain stood on a rise of permafrost and let his eyes scan the horizon. Those points of dark rock would make good targets.

The weapon was uncomfortable in his hand, but he managed to get one finger on the presumed trigger button. He aimed at the horizon and fired.

Nothing happened.

He aimed at a closer point, first pressing and releasing the trigger button repeatedly, then holding it down. Still nothing.

"Chuft-Captain, there is no energy release."

"The power may be gone."

"Chuft-Captain, it may. But the notches in the handle may control intensity. The guide is now set on 'nil.' "

Chuft-Captain moved the guide one notch down. A moment later he had to resist the panicky urge to throw the thing as far as possible. The mirror-faced sphere was twisting and turning like something alive, changing shape like a drug nightmare. It changed and flowed and became . . . a long slender cylinder with a red knob at the end and a toggle near the handle. The handle had not changed at all.

"Chuft-Captain, there was an energy discharge. Eek! What happened?"

"It turned into this. What do I do next?"

Slaverstudent took the artifact and examined it. He would have liked to fire it himself, but that was the leader's privilege and right. And risk. He said, "Try the toggle."

At a forward motion of the toggle the red knob lit up and leapt away across the ice. Chuft-Captain wiggled the handle experimentally. The red knob, still receding, bobbed and weaved in response to stay in line with the cylindrical barrel. When the knob was a red point sixty yards distant, Chuft-Captain stopped it with the toggle.

"Variable-sword," he muttered. He looked for a target. His eyes lit on a nearby tilted spire of dark rock or dirty ice.

Chuft-Captain gripped the artifact in both furry hands, like a big-game fishing pole, and swung the red light behind the spire. The artifact fought his pressure, then gave way. The top half of the spire toppled, kicking up a spray of chipped ice.

"A variable-sword," he repeated. "But not of Slaver design. Slaverstudent, have you ever heard of a weapon that changes shape?"

"No, Chuft-Captain, neither of the past nor of the present."

"Then we've found something new."

"Yes!" The word was a snarl of satisfaction.

"That tears it," said Anne-Marie. "It's a weapon."

Jason tried to nod. The police web held him fast.

The other kzinti came outside and moved up the rise. Four kzinti stood spitting at each other, looking like four fat men, sounding like a catfight. Nessus said, "The first notch must have been neutral. They intend to find out what the other notches do."

"It changes shape," said Anne-Marie. "That's bad enough."

"Quite right," said the puppeteer. "The artifact is now our prime target."

Jason grinned suddenly. The puppeteer reminded him of a cartoon: Two bearded, dirty convicts hanging three feet off the ground by iron chains. One convict saying, "Now here's my plan. . . ."

First we wish away the police web. Then . . .

Again the kzinti captain moved the guide. The gun reverted to sphere-and-handle, then flowed into something hard to see at a distance. The boss kzin must have realized it. He came down the hill, followed by the others. One at a time the kzinti moved them to the top of the rise, so that they stood several yards behind the firing line, but still in the police web.

The boss kzin resumed his firing stance.

Position number two was a parabolic mirror with a silvery knob at the center. It did nothing at all to the rock Chuft-Captain was using for a target, though Slaverstudent reported an energy discharge. Chuft-Captain considered, then turned the weapon on the puppeteer.

The puppeteer spoke in the human tongue. "I can hear a faint high-pitched whine."

"Another control dial has formed," Slaverstudent pointed out. "Four settings."

Chuft-Captain nodded and tried the second setting. It did not affect the puppeteer. Neither did the third and fourth.

"Chuft-Captain, will you hold down the trigger?" Slaverstudent cautiously peeped over the lip of the parabolic mirror. "Urrrr. I was right. The knob is vibrating rapidly. Setting number two is a sonic projector—and a powerful one—if the puppeteer can hear it through near-vacuum and the thickness of its suit."

"But it didn't knock him out or anything."

"Chuft-Captain, we must assume that it was designed to affect the Slaver nervous system."

"Yes." Chuft-Captain moved the guide to setting number three. As the gun changed and flowed, he said, "We have found nothing new. Sonics and variable-swords are common."

"Mutable weapons are not."

"Mutable weapons could not win a war, though they might help. Urrrr. This seems to be a projectile weapon. Have you the small-arms projectiles from the stasis box?"

"Chuft-Captain, I do."

The magazine under the barrel swung out for loading. It took both kinds of projectiles. Chuft-Captain again sighted on the rock, using the newly formed telescopic sight.

His first shot put a nick exactly where he aimed it.

His second, with the second-variety projectile, blew the rock to flying shards. Everybody ducked but Chuft-Captain.

"Should I empty the magazine before moving the guide?"

"Chuft-Captain, I do not think it matters. The bullets should certainly be removed, but the tnuctipun must have known that occasionally they would not be. Will you indulge my curiosity?"

"Since your curiosity is a trained one, I will." Chuft-Captain moved the guide. The projectiles still in the gun popped out through the shifting surface. The artifact became a sphere-with-handle, and then . . . a sphere-with-handle. The new sphere was smaller than the neutral setting. It had a rosy hue and a smooth, oily texture unmarred by gunsights or secondary controls.

The trigger button did nothing at all.

"I tire rapidly of these duds."

"Chuft-Captain, there is energy release."

"Very well." Chuft-Captain fired at the puppeteer, using his marksman's instinct in the absence of a gunsight. The puppeteer showed no ill effects.

Neither did the female human.

In momentary irritation Chuft-Captain thought of firing the dud at Telepath, who was standing nearby looking harmless and useless. But nothing would happen; he would only upset Telepath. He moved the guide to the fifth setting.

The artifact writhed, became a short cylinder with an aperture in the nose and two wide, flat metallic projections at the sides. Chuft-Captain's lips drew back from neatly filed feline teeth. *This* looked promising.

He drew aim on what was left of the target rock—a dark blot on the ice.

The gun slammed back against his hand. Chuft-Captain was whirled half around, trying to keep his feet and fighting the sudden pressure as a fireman fights a fire hose. Releasing the trigger didn't shut off the incandescent stream of plasma gas. Pressing the trigger again did. Chuft-Captain blinked his relief and looked around to assess damages.

He saw a twisting trail of melted ice like the path of an earthworm hooked on LSD. Telepath was screaming into his helmet mike. An ominously diminishing scream. The other kzinti were carrying him toward the airlock at a dead run. From the trail of thin, icy fog his suit left on the air, the weapon's firestream must have washed across his body, burning holes in nearly heatproof fabric.

The human female was running toward her ship.

A glance told him that the other prisoners were still in the police web. Telepath must have knocked the female spinning out of the force field while trying to escape the firestream. She was plainly visible, running across flat ice.

Chuft-Captain shot her with the stunner, then trudged away to pick her up. He had her back in the web when Flyer and Slaverstudent returned.

Telepath was still alive but in critical shape. They had dumped him in the freeze box for treatment on Kzin.

As for position five on the tnuctip relic:

"It's a rocket motor," said Slaverstudent. "As a short-range weapon it could be useful, but primarily it is a one-kzin reaction pistol. One-tnuctip, that is. I doubt it would lift one of us against respectable gravity. The flat projections at the sides may be holds for feet. The tnuctipun were small."

"Pity you didn't think of this earlier."

"Chuft-Captain, I acknowledge my failure."

Chuft-Captain dropped it. Privately he too acknowledged a failure: he had not considered the female dangerous. Humans were sentient, male and female both. He would not forget it again.

Position six was a laser. It too was more than a weapon. A telescopic sight ran along the side, and there was a microphone grid at the back. Focus it on the proper target, and you could talk voice-to-voice.

"This will be useful," said Slaverstudent. "We can find the voice and hearing ranges for tnuctipun from this microphone."

"Will that make it a better weapon?"

"Chuft-Captain, it will not."

"Then keep your passion for useless knowledge to yourself." Chuft-Captain moved the guide to the seventh setting.

"Darling?"

Anne-Marie didn't move. The police web held her in a slumped sitting position. Her chest rose and fell with shallow breathing. Her eyes were closed, her face relaxed.

"Nice try," Jason told her.

"She cannot hear you," said Nessus.

"I *know* she can't hear me."

"Then why— ? Never mind. What did that rocket setting look like to you?"

"A rocket."

"Using what fuel source?"

"Is it important?"

"Jason, I know nothing of warfare or of weapons, but my species has been making and using machines for some considerable time. Why did the projectile weapon not include its own projectiles? Why did it throw them away when it changed shape?"

"Oh. Okay, it can't throw away its own mass." Jason thought about that. "You're right. It can't be using its own fuel. Nessus, it's a jet. There was an intake somewhere that nobody noticed. Waitaminute. You couldn't use it in space."

"One would affix a gas cartridge at the intake."

"Oh. Right."

"One could not be sure a given atmosphere would burn. How is the gas heated?"

"A battery in the handle? No, it couldn't put out enough power, not without— But there has to be one. Nessus? The kzinti could be listening."

"I think it does not matter. The kzinti will know all about the weapon soon enough. Only the captain can profit from learning more before he turns the weapon over to his superiors."

"Okay. That battery must use total conversion of matter."

"Could you not build a fusion motor small enough to fit into the handle?"

"You're the expert. Could you? Would it give enough power?"

"I do not think so. The handle must contain a wide variety of mechanisms to control the changing of shapes."

They watched the kzin test out the laser form.

"You could do it direct," said Jason. "Change some of the matter in the reaction gas to energy. It'd give you a terrifically hot exhaust. Nessus, is there any species in known space that has total conversion?"

"None that I have heard of."

"Did the tnuctipun?"

"I would not know."

"Things weren't bad enough. Can you see kzinti warships armed and powered with total conversion?"

A gloomy silence followed. The kzinti were watching the weapon change shape. The boss kzin had not spoken; he may or may not have been listening to their discussions.

Anne-Marie made small protesting sounds. She opened her eyes and tried to sit up. She swore feelingly when she found that the web was holding her in her cramped position.

"Nice try," said Jason.

"Thanks. What happened?" She answered herself, her

voice brittle and bitter. "They shot me, of course. What have I missed?"

The seventh setting was a blank, flat-ended cylinder with a small wire grid near the back. No gunsight. It did nothing when he held it down, and nothing when he clicked it repeatedly. It had no effect on the target rock, the puppeteer, the humans. Its only effect on Slaverstudent was to make him back warily away, saying, "Chuft-Captain, please, there is an energy discharge."

"A singularly ineffective energy discharge. Take this, Slaverstudent. Make it work. I will wait."

And wait he did, stretched comfortably on the permafrost, his suit holding the cold a safe tenth of an inch away. He watched Slaverstudent's nerves fray under the fixity of his stare.

"What have I missed?"

"Not much. We've decided the jet that knocked you down converts matter to energy."

"Is that bad?"

"Very." Jason didn't try to explain. "The sixth setting was a more-or-less conventional message laser."

"The seventh does not work," said Nessus. "This angers the captain. Jason, for the first time I regret never having studied weapons."

"You're a puppeteer. Why should you . . ." Jason let the sentence trail off. There was a thought he wanted to trace down. About the weapon. Not any particular form, but all forms together.

"No sentient mind should turn away from knowledge. Especially no puppeteer. We are not known for our refusal to look at unpleasant truths."

Jason was silent. He was looking at an unpleasant truth.

Nessus had said that it didn't matter what the boss kzin overheard. He was wrong. This was a thing Jason dared not say aloud.

Nessus said, "The Slaver expert wants to go inside with the weapon. He has permission. He is going."

"Why?" asked Anne-Marie.

"There is a microphone grid on the seventh setting. Jason, could a soldier use a hand computer?"

"He—" *wasn't a soldier!* Jason clamped his teeth on the words. "Probably could," he said.

Presently the Slaver expert returned holding the tnuctipun weapon.

To Jason, the artifact had taken on a final, fatal fascination. If he was right about its former owner, then he could stop worrying about its reaching the Patriarch of Kzin. All he had to do was keep his mouth shut. In minutes he and Anne-Marie and Nessus and the four kzinti would be dead.

Slaverstudent said, "I was right. The artifact answered me in an unknown speech."

"Then it is another—" signaling device, he had been about to say. But it would have been built to signal tnuctipun, and the tnuctipun had been extinct for ages . . . yet the thing had answered back! Chuft-Captain felt his back arch with the fighting reflex. There were ghost legends among the kzinti.

"Chuft-Captain, I believe it to be a computer. A hand computer could be very useful to a warrior. It could compute angles for him as he fired explosive projectiles. It—"

"Yes. Can we use it?"

"Not unless we can teach it the Hero's Tongue. It may be too simple to learn."

"Then we pass to setting number eight." Chuft-Captain moved the guide down to the bottom setting.

Again there was no gunsight. Most of the genuine weapons had had gunsights or telescopic sights. Chuft-Captain scowled, but raised the weapon and aimed once again at the distant, shattered rock.

* * *

Jason cringed inside his imprisoned skin. Again the weapon was writhing, this time to the final setting.

There were so many things he wanted to say. But he didn't dare. The boss Kzin must not know what was about to happen.

The gun had twisted itself into something very strange. "That looks familiar," said Nessus. "I have seen something like that at some time."

"Then you're unique," said Anne-Marie.

"I remember. It was one of a series of diagrams on how to turn a sphere inside out in differential topology. Certainly there could be no connection . . ."

The boss kzin assumed marksman stance. Jason braced for the end.

What happened next was not at all what he expected.

Unconsciously he'd been leaning on the police net's force field. Suddenly he was falling, overbalanced. He straightened, not quite sure what had happened. Then he got it. The police net was gone. He slapped Anne-Marie hard on the butt, pointed at the *Court Jester*, saw her nod. Without waiting to see her start running, he turned and charged at the boss Kzin.

Something brushed by him at high speed. Nessus. Not running away but also charging into battle. *I was right*, thought Jason. *He's gone manic.*

Chuft-Captain pushed the trigger button. Nothing happened.

It was really too much. He stood a moment, marshaling words for Slaverstudent. A brand-new kind of weapon, and it wouldn't *do* anything! Half the settings were duds!

He knew it as he turned: something was wrong. The danger instinct sang in his nerves. He got no other warning. He had not seen the ship lights go out. He heard no sign of pounding clawed feet. The sounds of breathing *had* become a trifle heavy . . .

He started to turn, and something hit him in the side.

It felt as though an armored knight had run him through with a blunt lance. It *hurt*. Chuft-Captain lost all his aplomb and all his air, bent sideways as far as he could manage, and toppled.

He saw the world turned sideways, glowing through a blue fog. He saw the human female struggling futilely in Slaverstudent's hands; he saw Flyer aiming a stunner across the ice. He saw two running figures, human and puppeteer, trying to reach the other ship. Flyer's stunner didn't seem to affect them. The human had the tnuctip artifact.

He could breathe again, in sharp, shallow gasps. That blow in the side must have broken ribs; it could hardly have failed to, since kzinti ribs run all the way down. That blow had felt like a puppeteer's kick! But that was ridiculous. Impossible. A puppeteer kick a kzin?

The puppeteer reached the ship far in advance of the slower human. He paused a moment, then turned and ran on across the white undulating plain. The human also paused at the ship's entrance, then followed the puppeteer. Flyer was running after them.

Behind Chuft-Captain the ship lights were dim, but brightening. Hadn't they been dark when he fell? And the stunners hadn't worked. And the police webs . . .

So. The eighth setting was an energy absorber. Not a new thing, but much smaller than anything he'd heard of.

But what had hit him?

There was a hissing in his ears, a sound he hadn't noticed. Not breathing. Had somebody's suit been punctured? But nobody had been attacked. Except—

Chuft-Captain slapped a hand over his side. He yelled with the pain of motion but kept his hand pressed tight while he reached for a meteor patch. He risked one look under his hand before applying the patch. There were four tiny holes in the fabric. They might easily have marked the claws of a puppeteer's space boot.

The boss kzin held his marksman's stance. Jason was moving toward him at a dead run. He had to get the weapon before the kzinti realized what had happened.

Nessus passed him like a live missile. The puppeteer reached the kzin, turned skidding on two front legs, and lashed out. Jason winced in sympathy. That kick had been sincere! It would have torn a man in half, crushed his lungs and rib cage and spine and life.

The mad puppeteer had barely paused. He ran straight toward the *Court Jester*. Jason scooped up the fallen weapon, skidded to a halt, and turned.

A kzin had Anne-Marie.

We'll see about that! His fingers moved to the weapon's adjustment guide.

A second Kzin held a stunner on him.

The stunner would start working the moment the tnuctipun weapon shifted shape. He'd lose everything.

He could hear Anne-Marie swearing tearfully as she fought. Then her voice came loud and clear. "Run, dammit! Jay, run!"

He could throw the weapon to Nessus, then charge to the rescue! They'd get *him*, but . . . but the puppeteer was well out of range . . . and couldn't be trusted anyway. A puppeteer who kicked something that could kick back was beyond psychiatric help.

Anne-Marie was still kicking and using her elbows. Her kzinti captor didn't seem to notice. The boss kzin lay curled like a shrimp around the spot of agony in his side. But the third kzin held his pose, still bathing Jason in an imaginary stunner beam.

Jason turned and ran.

He saw Nessus leave the *Jester*'s entrance and go on. He guessed what he would find, but he had to look. Sure enough, the door was soldered shut.

The laser setting would have melted the steel solder away from the hullmetal door. But the third kzin was finally in motion, coming after him, still trying to use the stunner.

Jason ran on. The puppeteer was a diminishing point. Jason followed that point, moving into a cold waste lit by a fiery arch with one bright glare spot.

"Flyer, return to the ship at once."

"Chuft-Captain, he's around here somewhere. I can find him."

"Or he could find you. Return to the ship. The rules of this game have changed."

The kzin was gone. Jason had stalked him for a time, with his weapon set to the energy-absorbing phase and with his thumb on the guide. If he had seen the kzin, and if the kzin hadn't seen him . . . a variable-sword, a hair-thin wire sheathed in a stasis field, would have cut one enemy into two strangers. But it hadn't happened, and he wasn't about to follow the kzin back to home base.

Now he lay huddled in the hole he'd dug with the rocket phase.

"Jay!" It was Anne-Marie. "Have to talk quick; they're taking off my helmet. I'm not hurt, but I can't get away. The ship's taking off. Bury the weapon somewh—"

Her voice faded and was gone. The public band was silent.

Nessus' voice broke that silence. "Jason, turn to the private band."

He had to guess which band Nessus meant. He was third-time lucky.

"Can you hear me?"

"Yah. Where are you?"

"I do not know how to describe my position, Jason. I ran six or seven miles east."

"Okay. Let's think of a way to find each other."

"Why, Jason?"

He puzzled over that. "You think you're safer alone? I don't. How long will your suit keep you alive?"

"Several standard years. But help will arrive before then."

"What makes you think so?"

"When the kzinti pilot entered the pressure curtain, I was calling my people for help."

"What? How?"

"Despite recent changes in the fortunes of my people, that is still most secret."

Telepathy? Something in his baggage or surgically implanted under his skin? The puppeteers kept their secrets well. Nobody had ever found out how they could commit painless suicide at will. And how Nessus had done it didn't matter. "Are they coming for you all the way from Andromeda?"

"Hardly, Jason."

"Go on."

"I suppose I must. My people are still in this region of the galaxy, in the sixty-light-year volume you call Known Space. Their journey began only twelve years ago. You see, Jason, my people do not intend to return to this galaxy. Hence it does not matter how much objective time passes during their journey. They can reach Andromeda in a much shorter subjective time using normal space drives. Our ships approach very close to lightspeed. Further, they need brave only the dangers of normal space, which they can handle easily. Hyperspace is an unpredictable and uncomfortable thing, especially for those who would spend decades traveling in any case."

"Nessus, your whole species is crazy. How did they

keep a secret like that? Everyone thinks they're halfway to Andromeda.''

"Naturally. Who would stumble across the fleet in interstellar space? Between systems every known species travels in hyperspace—except the Outsiders, with whom we have agreements. In any case, my people are within reach. A scout will arrive within sixty days. The scouts are fitted with hyperdrive.''

"Then you're safe if you stay hidden.'' Damn! thought Jason. He was all alone. It was a proud and lonely thing to be a costume hero. "Well, good luck Nessus. I've got to—''

"Do not sign off. What is your plan?''

"I don't have one. I've got to see the kzinti don't get this back, but I've also got to get Anne-Marie away from them.''

"The weapon should come first.''

"My wife comes first. What's your stake in this, anyway?''

"With the principles behind the tnuctip weapon the kzinti could command Known Space. My people will be in Known Space for another twenty-eight human years. Should the kzinti learn of our fleet, it would be an obvious and vulnerable target.''

"Oh.''

"We must help each other. How long can you live in your suit?''

"Till I starve to death. I'll have air and water indefinitely. Say thirty days, upper limit.''

"Your people should not cut costs on vital equipment, Jason. My people cannot arrive in time to save you.''

"If I gave you the weapon, could you stay hidden?''

"Yes. If the ship came in sight, I could shoot it down with the laser setting. I think I could. I could force myself—Jason, will the kzinti call other ships?''

"Damn! Of course they will. They'd find you easily. What'll we do?''

"Can we force entrance to the *Court Jester?*''

"Yah, but they took my keys. We couldn't use the drives or the radio or get into the lockers."

"The laser would let us into the lockers."

"Right."

"Have you weapons aboard?"

"No. Nothing."

"Then the *Court Jester* would be no more than a place from which to surrender. I have no suggestions."

"Chuft-Captain, the eighth setting must be the way the artifact is recharged. It does not itself seem to be a weapon."

"It can be used as one. As we have seen. Don't bother me now, Slaverstudent." Chuft-Captain strove to keep his tone mild. He knew that his rage was the companion of his pain, and Slaverstudent knew it too.

Neither had referred to the fact that Chuft-Captain now walked crouched to the side. Neither would. The kzinti captain could not even bandage himself; though when they reached space, he could use the ship's medical equipment to set the bones.

The worst damage had been done to Chuft-Captain's ego.

Had the puppeteer known what he was doing? His small clawed foot had shattered more than a couple of ribs. One day Chuft-Captain might have been Chuft, the hero, who found the weapon that beat the human empire to its belly. Now he would be Chuft who was kicked by a puppeteer.

"Chuft-Captain, here comes Flyer."

"Good. Flyer! Get your tail in here and lift us fast."

Flyer went past at a quick shuffling run. Slaverstudent shut the airlock after him, helped Chuft-Captain strap down, and was strapping himself in when Flyer did his trick. The ship rose out of the ice, dripping opalescent chunks and shining blue-white at the stern.

On the smoky arch of Beta Lyrae the bright point had reached its zenith. Behind their permanent veil the two stars had pulled apart in their orbits, so that the vague brightness shaded into an orange tinge on one side and a green on the other.

"One thing we do have," said Jason, "and that's the weapon itself."

"True. We have a laser, a flame-throwing rocket, and a shield against police stunners. But not simultaneously."

"I think we may have overlooked a setting."

"Wishful thinking, Jason, is not a puppeteer trait."

"Neither is knowledge of weapons. Nessus, what kind of weapon is this? I'm talking about the whole bundle, not any single setting."

"As you say, I am not an expert on warfare."

"I don't think it's a soldier's weapon. I think it's for espionage."

"Would that be different? I gather the question is important."

Jason stopped to gather his thoughts. He held the gun cradled in his hands. It was still at the eighth setting, the peculiar, twisted shape that Nessus had compared to a diagram from differential topology.

He held history in his hands, history a billion and a half years dead. Once upon a time a small, compactly built biped had aimed this weapon at beings with ball-shaped heads, big single eyes, massive Mickey Mouse hands, great splayed feet, and lightly armored skin and clusters of naked-pink tendrils at the corners of wide mouths. What could he have been thinking the last time he stored away this weapon? Did he guess that fifteen million centuries later a mind would be trying to guess his nature from his abandoned possessions?

"Nessus, would you say this gadget is more expensive to produce than eight different gadgets to do similar jobs?"

"Assuredly, and more difficult. But it would be easier to carry than eight discrete gadgets."

"And easier to hide. Have you ever heard of Slaver records describing a shape-changing weapon?"

"No. The tnuctipun would understandably have kept it a secret."

"That's my point. How long could they keep it secret if millions of soldiers had models?"

"Not long. The same objections hold for its use in espionage. Jason, what kind of espionage could a tnuctip do? Certainly it could not imitate a Slaver."

"No, but it could hide out on a sparsely settled world, or it could pretend to be a tnuctip slave. It'd have to have some defense against the Slaver power . . ."

"The cap in the stasis box?"

"Or something else, something it was wearing when the Slavers caught it."

"These are unpleasant ideas. Jason, I have remembered something. The Outsiders found the stasis box in a cold, airless world with ancient pressurized buildings still standing. If a battle had been fought there, would the buildings have been standing?"

"Slaver buildings?"

"Yes."

"They'd have been standing if the Slavers won. But then the Slavers would have captured at least one of the weapons."

"Only if there were many such weapons. I concede your point. The owner of the weapon was a lone spy."

"Good. Now—"

"Why were you so sure?"

"Mainly the variety of settings. The average soldier would get stomped on while he was trying to decide which weapon to use. Then there's a sonic for taking live prisoners. Maybe other settings make them feel fear or pain. The rocket would be silly for a soldier; he'd get killed flying around a battlefield. But a spy could use it for the last stage of his landing."

"All right. Why is it important?"

"Because there ought to be a self-destruct setting somewhere."

"What did—? Ah. To keep the secret of the mutable weapon. But we have used all the settings."

"I thought it would be number eight. It wasn't. That's why we're still alive. An espionage agent's self-destruct button would be made to do as much damage as possible."

Nessus gasped. Jason hardly noticed. "They've hidden it somehow," he said.

The *Traitor's Claw* was big. She had to be. Redundantly, she carried both a gravity polarizer and a fusion-reaction motor. Probably she could have caught anything in real space, barring ships of her own class, many of which were serving as police and courier ships in kzinti space. Kzinti records listed her as a stolen courier ship. She was a squat cone, designed as a compromise between landing ability and speed in an atmosphere. In contrast, the flat *Court Jester* had been designed for landing ability alone; she would not have tipped over on a seventy-degree slope.

There was more than speed to the courier ship's two drives. Before it had ever seen a gravity polarizer, the human empire had taught the kzinti a lesson they would never forget. The more efficient a reaction drive, the more effective a weapon it makes. A gravity polarizer was not a reaction drive.

Flyer used both drives at once. The ship went up fast. Six thousand miles up, the *Traitor's Claw* went into orbit.

"We can find the prisoners with infrared," said Chuft-Captain. "But it will do us little good if they shoot us down. Can the laser setting prevent us from going after them?"

"We can call for more ships," Flyer suggested. "Surely the weapon is important enough."

"It is. But we will not call."

Flyer nodded submission.

Knowing what Flyer knew, Chuft-Captain snarled inside himself with humiliation and the digging agony in his side. He had been kicked by a puppeteer in full view of two subordinates. Never again could he face a kzin of equal rank, never until he had killed the puppeteer with his own teeth and claws.

Could that kick have been cold-bloodedly tactical? Chuft-Captain refused to believe it. But, intended or not, that kick had stymied Chuft-Captain. He could not call for reinforcements until the puppeteer was dead.

He forced his mind back to the weapon. The only setting that could harm the kzinti was the laser . . . unless the rosy sphere unexpectedly began working. But that was unlikely. He asked, ''Is there a completely safe way to capture them? If not—''

''There is the drive,'' said Slaverstudent.

''They have the laser,'' Flyer reminded him. ''A laser that size is subject to a certain amount of spreading. We should be safe two hundred miles up. Closer than that and a good marksman could burn through the hull.''

''Flyer, is two hundred miles too high?''

''Chuft-Captain, they are wearing heatproof suits, and we can hover only at one-seventh Kzin-gravity. Our flame would barely warm the ice.''

''But there is the gravity polarizer to pull us down while the fusion flame pushes us up. The ship was designed for just that tactic. Now, the fugitives' suits are heatproof, but the ice is not. Suppose we hovered over them with a five-Kzin gravity flame . . .''

Jason held a five-inch rosy sphere with a pistol-grip handle. ''It has to be here somewhere,'' he said.

''Try doing things you ordinarily wouldn't: moving the gauge while holding the trigger down . . . moving the guide sideways . . . twisting the sphere.''

Silence on the private circuit. Then, ''No luck yet.''

''The fourth setting was the only one that showed no purpose at all.''

''Yah. What in—''

High overhead a star had come into being. It was blue-white, almost violet-white, and for Jason it stood precisely at the zenith.

"The kzinti," said Nessus. "Do not shoot back. They must be out of range of your laser setting. You would only help them find you."

"They've probably found me already with infrared scopes. What the Finagle do they think they're doing?"

The star remained steady. In its sudden light Jason went to work on the weapon. He ran quickly through the remaining settings, memorizing the forms that used the trigger as an on-off switch, probing and prodding almost at random, until he reached neutral and the relic was a silver sphere with a handle.

The guide would not go sideways. It would not remain between any two of the notches. It would not twist.

"Are you making progress?"

"Nothing, dammit."

"The destruct setting would not be too carefully hidden. If a weapon were captured, an agent could always hope the Slavers would destroy it by accident."

"Yah." Jason was tired of looking at the neutral setting. He changed to laser and fired up at the new star, using the telescopic sight. He expected and got no result, but he held his aim until distracted by a sudden change in pressure around his suit.

He was up to his shoulders in water.

In one surge he was out of his hole. But the land around him was gone. A few swells of wet ice rose glistening from a shallow sea that reached to all the horizon. The kzinti ship's downblast had melted everything for miles around.

"Nessus, is there water around you?"

"Only in the solid form. From my viewpoint the Kzinti ship is not overhead."

"They've got me. As soon as they turn off the drive, I'll be frozen in my tracks."

"I have been thinking. Do you need the destruct setting?

Suppose you change to the rocket setting, turn the weapon nose down, and fire. The flame will remain on, and the weapon will eat its way through the ice.''

"Sure, if we could think of a way to keep it pointed down. Odds are it'd turn over in the first few feet. Then the kzinti find it with deep-radar or seismics and dig it out.''

"True.''

The water was getting deeper. Jason thought about using the rocket to burn his way loose once the water froze about his ankles. It would be too hot. He would probably burn his feet off. But he might have to try it.

The blue kzinti star hung bright and clear against the arch of dust and hydrogen. A bright pink glow showed the Lyrae stars forty-five degrees from sunset.

"Jason. Why is there a neutral setting?''

"Why not?''

"It is not for collecting energy. The eighth setting does that very nicely. It is not for doing nothing. The projectile setting does that, unless you put projectiles in it. Thus the neutral setting has no purpose. Perhaps it does something we do not know about.''

"I'll try it.''

The bright star above him winked out.

"Chuft-Captain, I cannot locate the puppeteer.''

"Its pressure suit may be too efficient to lose heat. We will institute a sight search later. Inform me when the human stops moving.''

Nessus' idea would be a good one, Jason thought, if only he could make it workable. Much better than the destruct setting. Because if the destruct setting existed, it would almost certainly kill him.

Probably it would kill Nessus too. The destruct setting on an espionage agent's weapon would be made to do as much damage as possible. And there had been total conversion involved in the rocket setting. Total conversion would make quite a bomb, even if it weighed only four pounds, and the converted mass a fraction of a milligram.

The kzinti-produced swamp was congealing from the bottom up. His boots were getting heavy. Each had collected a growing mass of ice. He kept walking so that they wouldn't freeze to the bottom.

He'd searched the neutral setting, handle and sphere, for hidden controls. Nothing showed—nothing obvious. He tried twisting various parts of the handle. Nothing broke, which was good, but nothing would twist either.

Maybe something *should* break. Suppose he broke off the gauge?

He wasn't strong enough.

He tried twisting the ball itself. Nothing.

He tried it again, holding the trigger down.

The silvery sphere twisted one hundred and eighty degrees, then clicked. Jason released the trigger, and it started to change.

"I've found it, Nessus. I've found *something*."

"A new setting? What does it look like?"

Like a white flash, thought Jason, waiting for the single instant in which it *would* look like a white flash. It didn't come. The protean material solidified.

"Like a cone with a rounded base, pointing away from the handle."

"Try it. And if you are successful, good-bye, Jason. Knowing you was pleasant."

"The blast could include you, too."

"Is it thus you assuage my loss of you?"

"You sure you don't have a sense of humor? Good-bye, Nessus. Here goes."

The cone did not explode. A time bomb? Jason was about to start looking for a chronometer on the thing when he noticed something that froze him instantly.

A hazy blue line led away in the direction he happened to

be pointing the cone. Led away and upward at forty degrees, wavering, as tremor in his fingers waved the cone's vertex.

Another weapon.

He released the trigger. The line disappeared.

The kzinti ship wasn't in sight. Not that he would have used it as a target, not with Anne-Marie aboard.

A hidden weapon. More powerful than the others? He had to find out. Like Chuft-Captain, he tried to assume marksman's stance.

His feet were frozen solidly into the ice. He'd been careless. He shrugged angrily, aimed the weapon a little above the horizon, and fired.

A hazy blue line formed. He slowly lowered the vertex until the line touched the horizon.

The light warned him. He threw himself flat on his back and waited for the blast. The light died almost instantly, and suddenly the shiny horizon-to-horizon ice rippled and shot from under him. It took his feet along. His body snapped like a whip, and then the ice tore away from his feet.

He was on his face, with agony in his ankles.

The backlash came. The ice jerked under him, harmlessly.

"Jason, what happened? There was an explosion."

"Hang . . . on." Jason rolled over and pulled his legs up to examine them. The pain was bad. His ankles didn't feel broken, but he certainly couldn't walk on them. The boots were covered with cracked wet ice.

"Jason. Puppeteer. Can you hear me?" It was the slurred, blurry voice of the boss kzin.

"Don't say anything, Nessus. I'm going to answer him." Jason switched his transmitter to the common channel. "I'm here."

"You have discovered a new setting to the weapon."

"Have I?"

"I do not intend to play pup games with you. As a fighter, you are entitled to respect, which your herbivorous friend is not—"

"How are your ribs feeling?"

"Do not speak of that again, please. We have something to trade, you and I. You have a unique weapon. I have a female human who may be your mate."

"Well put. So?"

"Give us the weapon. Show us where to find the new setting. You and your mate may leave this world in your own ship, unharmed and unrestricted."

"Your name as your word?"

No answer.

"You lying get of a . . ." Jason searched for the word. He could say two words of Kzin; one meant hello, and one meant—

"Do not say it. Jason, the agreement stands, except that I will smash your hyperdrive. You must return to civilization through normal space. With that proviso, you have my name as my word."

"Nessus?"

"The herbivore must protect itself."

"I think not."

"Consider the alternative. Your mate is not entitled to the respect accorded a fighter. Kzinti are carnivorous, and we have been without fresh meat for some years."

"Bluff me not. You'd lose your only hostage."

"We'd lose one arm of her. Then another. Then a lower leg."

Jason felt sick. They could do it. Painlessly, too, if they wished; and they probably would, to avoid losing Anne-Marie to shock.

He gulped. "Is she all right now?"

"Naturally."

"Prove it." He was stalling. Nessus could hear everything; he might come up with something . . . and was ever there a fainter hope?

"You may hear her," said the boss kzin. There were

clunking sounds; they must be dropping her helmet over her head. Then Anne-Marie's voice spoke swiftly and urgently.

"Jay, darling, listen. Use the seventh setting. The *seventh*. Can you hear me?"

"Anne, are you all right?"

"I'm fine," she shouted. "Use the seventh . . ." Her voice died abruptly.

"Anne!"

Nothing.

There was fast, muffled kzinti speech in his earphones. Jason looked at the weapon a moment, then dropped the guide to setting number seven. Maybe she had something. The cone writhed, became a mirror-surfaced sphere . . .

"Jason, you now know your mate is unharmed. We must ask for your decision immediately."

He ignored the burry voice, watched the weapon become a flat-ended cylinder with a grid near the handle. He'd seen the kzinti using that.

"Oh," he said.

It was the computer, of course. The tnuctip computer. He smiled, and it hurt inside him. His wife had given him the only help she had to give. She'd told him where to find the only tnuctipun expert in Known Space.

The hell of it was, she was perfectly right. But the computer couldn't hear him, and he couldn't hear the computer, and they didn't speak a common language anyway.

Wait a minute. This was setting number seven; but if you counted neutral as the first setting, then—no. Setting six was only the laser.

Finagle! The Belter oath fitted. Finagle's First Law was holding beautifully.

His ankles stopped hurting.

Decoyed! He twisted his head around to find his enemy. The bargain had been a decoy! Already his head buzzed with the stunner beam. He saw the kzin, hiding behind a half-melted bulge of ice with only one eye and the stunner showing. He fired at once.

The weapon was on computer setting. His hand went slack, then his mind.

"I do not understand why she wanted him to use the seventh setting."

"The computer, was it not?"

"Chuft-Captain, it was."

"He could not have used the computer."

"No. Why then did the prisoner—"

"She may have meant the sixth setting. The laser was the only weapon a human could have used against us."

"Urrr. Yes. She counted wrong, then."

The ship-to-suit circuit spoke. "Chuft-Captain, I have him."

"Flyer, well done. Bring him in."

"Chuft-Captain, do we still need him?"

The Kzin was not in a mood to argue. "I hate to throw anything away. Bring him in."

His head floated, his body spun, his ankles hurt like fury. He shuddered and tried to open his eyes. The lids came up slowly, reluctantly.

He was standing in a police web, slack neck muscles holding his head upright in one-eighth gee. No wonder he hadn't known which way was up. Anne-Marie was twelve inches to his side. Her eyes held no hope, only exhaustion.

"Damn," he said. One word to cover it all.

The Kzinti yowrling had been so much a part of the background that he didn't notice it until it stopped. After a moment the boss kzin stepped in front of him, moving slowly and carefully, and curled protectively around his left side.

"You are awake."

"Obviously."

One massive four-clawed hand held the tnuctip weapon,

still at the computer setting. The kzin held it up. "You found a new setting on this. Tell me how to reach it."

"I can't," said Jason. "I found it by accident and lost it the same way."

"That is a shame. Do you realize we have nothing to lose?"

Jason studied the violet eyes, fruitlessly. "What do you mean?"

"Either you will tell me of your own free will, or you can be persuaded to tell, or you cannot. In any case, we have no reason not to remove your mate's arm."

He turned and spoke in the kzinti tongue. The other aliens left the room.

"We will be leaving this world in an hour." The boss kzin turned and settled his orange bulk carefully in a kzinti contour couch, grunting softly with the pain of movement.

He meant it. His position was too simple for doubt. The boss kzin had a tnuctip weapon to take back to Kzin, and he had two human captives. The humans were of no use to him. But he had great use for Jason's knowledge. What he offered was a simple trade: knowledge for the meat on their bones.

"I can't talk," said Jason.

"All right," Anne-Marie said dully.

"I *can't*." The cone form was too powerful. Its beam must set up spontaneous mass conversion in anything it touched. And he couldn't explain. The boss kzin might hear him, and the kzinti didn't know just what they were after.

"All right, you can't. We've had it. How did they get you?"

"I got stupid. While the boss kzin was talking to me, one of the others snuck up and used a sonic."

"The seventh setting—"

"I didn't have time to figure anything out. There isn't enough air to carry sound out there."

"I didn't think of that. How's Nessus?"

"Still free."

The boss kzin broke in. "We will have it soon. The puppeteer has no place to hide and nothing with which to fight, not even the inclination. Do you expect it to rescue you?"

Anne-Marie smiled sourly. "Not really."

The other kzinti returned, carrying things. There were pieces of indecipherable kzinti equipment, and there was a medkit from the emergency doc in the *Court Jester*. They set it all down next to the police web and went to work.

One piece of kzinti equipment was a small tank with a pump and a piece of soft plastic tubing attached. Jason watched them wrap the tubing three or four times around Anne-Marie's upper arm. They joined the other end to the pump and started it going.

"It's cold," she said. "Freezing."

"I can't stop them," said Jason.

She shivered. "You're sure?"

He gave up. He opened his mouth to shout out his surrender. The boss kzin raised his furry head questioningly—and Jason's voice stopped in his throat.

He'd used the hidden setting just once. For only an instant had the blue beam touched the horizon, but the explosion had damn near killed him. Obviously the hidden setting was not meant to be used on the surface of a planet.

It could be used only from space. Was it meant to destroy whole worlds?

But Anne-Marie hurt!

She said, "All right, you're sure. Jay, don't *look* like that. Jay? I can grow a new arm. Relax! Stop *worrying* about it!" The anguish in Jason's face was like nothing she'd ever seen.

The burry voice said, "She will never reach an autodoc."

"Shut *up!*" Jason screamed.

Soft kzinti noises entered the silence. One of the kzinti left: the pilot, the one with a white streak. The others talked. They talked of cooking, kzinti sex, human sex, Beta Lyrae, how to hunt puppeteers, or how to turn a sphere inside out without forming a cusp. Jason couldn't tell. They used no gestures.

Anne-Marie said, "They could have planted a mike on us."

"Yah."

"So you can't tell me what you're hiding."

"No. I wish I spoke Wunderlander."

"*I* don't speak Wunderlander. Dead language. Jay, I can't feel my arm any more. There must be liquid nitrogen in this tube."

"I'm sorry. I *can't help*."

"It is not working," said Chuft-Captain.

"It should work," said Slaverstudent. "We may not get results with the first limb. We probably will with the second. The second time, they will know that we mean what we threaten." He looked thoughtfully at the prisoners. "Also, I think we should eat our meals in here."

"They know that limbs can be regrown."

"Only by human-built machines. There are none here."

"You have a point."

"It will be good to taste fresh meat again."

Flyer returned. "Chuft-Captain, the kitchen is programmed."

"Good." Chuft-Captain incautiously shifted his bulk and tensed all over at the pain. It would have been nice if he could have put pressure bandages around his ribs. The ribs had been set and joined with pins, but he could not use pressure bandages; they would remind his crew of what had happened. He would be shamed.

Kicked by a puppeteer.

"I have been thinking," he said. "Regardless of what the human tells us, we must take the tnuctip relic to Kzin as quickly as possible. There I will drop you, Slaverstudent, along with the weapon and the freeze box containing Telepath. Flyer, you and I will return here for the herbivore. He cannot be rescued in that time. He will be easy to find. A sight search will find him unless he digs a hole, in which case we may use seismographs.''

''He will have a month to anticipate.''

''Yes. He will.''

''Can you understand me?''

Three pairs of kzinti eyes jerked around. The voice had belonged to none of them. It sounded foreign, artificial.

''Repeating. Can you understand me?''

It was the gun speaking. The tnuctip weapon.

''It's learned their language,'' said Jason. And all the hope drained out of him.

''It'll tell them where to find that setting you were trying to hide.''

''Yah.''

''Then tell me this, Jay.'' She was on the edge of hysteria. ''What good will it do me to lose my arm?''

Jason filled his lungs and shouted. ''Hey!''

Not one kzin moved. They hovered around the weapon, all talking at once.

''Hey, Captain! What *sthondat* was your sister?''

They all jerked around. He must have pronounced the word right.

''You must not use that word again,'' said the boss Kzin.

''Get this thing off my wife's arm!''

The boss kzin thought it over, spoke to the pilot. The pilot manipulated the police web to free Anne-Marie's arm, using a cloth to protect his hand while he removed the cold, deadly tube. He turned off the pump, readjusted the police web, and went back to the discussion, which by then had become a dialogue. The boss kzin had shut the others up.

''How's your arm?''

''Feels dead. Maybe it is. What were we hiding, Jay?'' He told her.

''Ye gods! And now they've got it.''

"Could you use an anesthetic?"

"It doesn't hurt yet."

"Let me know. They're all through torturing us. They may eat us, but it'll be all at once."

The computer was doing most of the talking.

A kzin was holding up the tnuctip cap, the one they'd found in the stasis box. The computer spoke.

He held up the small metal object that might have been a communicator. The computer spoke again.

The boss kzin spoke.

The computer spoke at length.

The boss kzin picked up the weapon and did things to it. Jason couldn't see what. The kzin was facing away from him. But the weapon writhed. Jason snarled in his throat. He commonly used curses for emphasis. He knew no words to cover this situation.

The boss kzin spoke briefly and left, cradling the weapon. One of the others followed: the expert on Slavers. Jason caught one glimpse of the weapon as the boss kzin went through the door.

The kzin with the white stripe, the pilot, remained.

Jason felt himself starting to shake. The weapon, the still, mutable weapon. When the boss kzin had left the room, he'd carried a gun handle attached to a double cone with rounded bases and points that barely touched.

He didn't understand.

Then his eyes, restlessly searching the room as if for an answer, fell on the empty stasis box. There was a tnuctip cap and a small metal object that registered in hyperspace and a preserved Slaver hand.

It began to make sense.

Did the computer have eyesight? Obviously. The kzinti had been showing it objects from the stasis box.

Take a computer smart enough to learn a language by hearing it spoken for an hour. Never mind its size; any sentient being will build a computer as small as possible, if only to reduce the time lag in thinking with impulses moving at lightspeed or less. Let the computer know only what its tnuctipun builders had taught it, plus what it had seen and heard in this room.

It had seen a tnuctip survival kit. It had seen members of a species it did not recognize. The unfamiliar beings had asked questions which made it obvious that they knew little about tnuctipun, and that they could not ask questions of a tnuctip. They didn't speak the tnuctip language. They were desperately anxious for details about a tnuctip top-secret weapon.

Obviously they were not allies of the tnuctipun.

They must be enemies. In the Slaver War there had been, could be, no neutrals.

He said, "Anne."

"Still here."

"Don't ask questions, just follow orders. Our lives depend on it. See that kzin?"

"Right. You sneak up on him from behind; I'll hit him with my purse."

"This is not funny. When I give the word, we're both going to spit at his ear."

"You're right. That's not funny."

"I'm in dead earnest. And don't forget to compensate for low gravity."

"How are you going to give the word with a mouthful of saliva?"

"Just spit when I do. Okay?"

Jason's shot brushed the kzin's furry scalp. Anne-Marie's caught him square in the ear. The kzin came to his feet with a howl. Then, as both humans cleared their throats again, the kzin moved like lightning. The air stiffened about their heads.

The kzin contemptuously returned to his crouch against a wall.

It became hard to breathe.

Blinking was a slow, excruciating process. Talking was out of the question. Warm air, laden with CO_2, did not want to dissipate. It stayed before their faces, waiting to be inhaled again and again. The kzin watched them struggle.

Jason forced his eyes closed. Blinking had become too painful. He tried to remember that he'd planned this, that it had worked perfectly. Their heads and bodies were now entirely enclosed by the police web.

Now here's my plan.

"The puppeteer ran east," said Chuft-Captain. And he turned west. He didn't want to kill the puppeteer without knowing it.

The weapon was hard and awkward in his hand. He was a little afraid of it, and a little ashamed of being afraid: a hangover from that awful moment when the weapon spoke. There were ghost legends among the kzinti. Some of the most fearsome spoke of captured weapons haunted by their dead owners.

Nobles weren't supposed to be superstitious, not out loud.

A computer that could learn new languages was logical. The only way to reach the setting for the matter-conversion beam had been to ask the computer setting, and that was logical too. A matter-conversion beam was a dangerous secret.

Briefly, Chuft-Captain wondered about that. It seemed that for an honorable kzin every recent change was a change for the worse. The conquest of space had ended when kzinti met humans. Then had come the puppeteers with their trade outposts; any kzin who attacked a puppeteer invariably found himself not harmed physically, but ruined financially. No kzin could fight power like that. Would the tnuctip weapon reverse these changes?

There had been a time, between the discoveries of atomic power and the gravity polarizer, when it seemed the kzinti species would destroy itself in wars. Now the kzinti held many worlds, and the danger was past. But was it? A matter-conversion beam . . .

There is no turning away from knowledge.

Haunted weapons . . .

He stopped on a rise of permafrost some distance from the ship. By now half the sky was blood red. An arm of the hydrogen spiral was sweeping across the world, preparing to engulf it. Hours or days from now the arm would pass, moving outward on the wings of photon pressure, leaving the world with a faintly thicker atmosphere.

But we'll be long gone by then, Chuft-Captain thought. Already he was looking ahead to the problem of reaching Kzin. If human ships caught the *Traitor's Claw* entering Kzin's atmosphere, the kzinti would clearly be violating treaty rules. But they weren't likely to be caught, not if Flyer did everything right.

"Chuft-Captain, this setting has no gunsight."

"No? You're right, it doesn't." He considered. "Perhaps it was meant only for large targets. A world seen from close up. The explosion was fierce."

"Or its accuracy may be low. Or its range. I wonder. Logically the tnuctipun should have included at least a pair of notches for sighting."

Something's wrong. The danger instinct whispered in his ear. "Superstition," he snarled, and raised the weapon stiffly, aiming well above the horizon. "Let us find the answer," he said.

In this area of Cue Ball the ice had melted and refrozen. It was as flat as a calm lake.

Nessus had stopped at the edge. He'd faced around, stopped again, held the pose for several minutes, then faced back and started across the flat, red-tinged ice. Muscles rippled beneath his pressure suit.

It wasn't as if he expected to help his human employees.

They had gotten themselves into this. And he had neither weapons nor allies nor even stealth to aid him. A human infantryman could have crawled on his belly, but Nessus' legs weren't built that way. On a white plain with no cover he had to trot upright, bouncing gaily in the low gravity.

His only weapon was his hind leg.

Thinking that, he remembered the jarring impact as he had planted his foot in the kzin's side. Two hundred and forty pounds of charging puppeteer applied over five square inches of clawed space boot. The shock wave had jarred up through thigh and hip and spine, jerked at his skull and continued along the necks to snap his teeth shut with a sharp double *click*. Like kicking a mountain, a soft but solid mountain.

The next instant he was running, really terrified for the first time in his life. But behind him the Kzin had vented a long whistling scream and folded tightly around himself. . . .

Nessus went on. He'd trotted across the frozen lake without seeing kzinti or kzinti ship. Now the ice was beginning to swell and dip. He'd reached the periphery of the blast area. Now there was a touch of yellow light ahead. Small and faint, but unmistakably yellow against the pink ice.

Ship lights.

He went on. He'd never know why. He'd never admit it to himself.

Thock! Hind boot slamming solidly into hard meat. Whistling shriek of agony between sharp filed carnivore teeth.

He wanted to do it again. Nessus had the blood lust.

He went up a rise, moving slowly, though his feet wanted to dance. He was weaponless, but his suit was a kind of defense. No projectile short of a fast meteorite could harm him. Like a silicone plastic, the pressure suit was soft and malleable under gentle pressures, such as walking, but it instantly became rigid all over when something struck it.

He topped the rise.

The ship lights might have come from the *Court Jester*. They didn't. Nessus saw the airlock opening, and he charged down the slope so the next rise hid him from view.

The kzinti ship was down. They must have landed with the gravity polarizer; otherwise he would have seen them. If they had then captured Jason on foot, he might still be alive. He might not. The same went for Anne-Marie.

Now what? The kzinti ship was beyond this next rise of ice. At least one kzin was outside. Were they looking for *him*? No, they'd hardly expect him here!

He had reached the trough between the two swells. They were long and shallow and smooth, like waves near an ocean shoreline.

The top of the swell behind Nessus suddenly sparkled with harsh blue-white sunlight.

Nessus knew just what to do, and he did it instantly. No point in covering his cranial bulge with his necks; he'd only get his larynxes crushed. The padding would protect his brain, or it wouldn't. He folded his legs under him and tucked his heads tight between his forelegs. He didn't have to think about it. The puppeteer's explosion reflex was no less a reflex for being learned in childhood.

He saw the light, he curled into a ball, and the ground swell came. It batted him like a beach ball. His rigid, form-fitting shell retained his shape. It could not prevent the ground swell from slamming him away, nor his brain from jarring under its thick skull and its extra padding.

He woke on his back with his legs in the air. There was a tingly ache along his right side and on the right sides of his necks and legs. Half his body surface would be one bruise tomorrow. The ground still heaved; he must have been unconscious for only a moment.

He clambered shakily to his feet. The claws were an enormous help on the smooth ice. He shook himself once, then started up the rise.

Suddenly and silently the kzinti ship topped the rise. A

quarter of a mile down the swell it slid gracefully into space in a spray of ice. It was rotating on its axis, and Nessus could see that one side was red hot. It skimmed through the near-vacuum above the trough, seeming to drift rather than fall. It hit solidly on the shallow far rise and plowed to a stop.

Still upright. Steam began to surround it as it sank into melting ice.

Nessus approached without fear. Surely any kzin inside was dead, and any human too. But could he get in?

The outer airlock door was missing, ripped from its hinges. The inner door must have been bent, for it leaked a thin fog from the edges. Nessus pushed the cycle button and waited.

The door didn't move.

The puppeteer cast an eye around the airlock. There must be telltales to sense whether the outer door was closed and whether there was pressure in the lock. There was one, a sensitized surface in the maimed outer doorway. Nessus pushed it down with his mouth.

Air sprayed into the enclosure, turned to fog, and blew away. Nessus' other head was casting about for a pressure sensor. He found it next to the air outlet. He swung alongside it and leaned against it so that his suit trapped the air. He leaned into the pressure.

The inner door swung open. Nessus fought to maintain his position against the roaring wind. When the door was fully open, he dodged inside. The door slammed just behind him.

Now. What had happened here?

The kzinti lifesystem was a howling hurricane of air replacing what he'd let out. Nessus poked into the kitchen, the control section, and two privacy booths without seeing anything. He moved down the hall and looked into what he remembered would be the interrogation room. Perhaps here . . .

He froze.

Anne-Marie and Jason were in the police web. Obviously; because both were standing, and both were unconscious. They appeared undamaged. But the kzin!

Nessus felt the world swim. His heads felt lighter than air. He'd been through a lot . . . He turned his eyes away. It occurred to him that the humans must be unconscious from lack of oxygen. The police web must surround them completely, even their heads. Otherwise the shock would have torn their heads off. Nessus forced himself to move to the police web. He kept his eyes resolutely away from the kzin.

There were the controls. Was that the power switch? He tried it. The humans drifted gracefully to the floor. Done.

And Nessus found his eyes creeping back to the kzin.

He couldn't look away.

The carnivore had struck like a wet snowball thrown with awful force. He was a foot up the wall, all spread out on a border of splashed circulatory fluid, and he *stuck*.

Nessus fainted. He woke up, still standing because of the normal tone of his relaxed muscles, to find Anne-Marie shaking him gently and trying to talk to him.

"I'm worried about him," said Anne-Marie.

Jason turned away from the *Jester*'s control panel. "He can get treatment on Jinx. There are puppeteers in Sirius Mater."

"That's still a week away. Isn't there anything *we* can do for him? He spends all his time in his room. It must be *awful* to be manic-depressive." She was rubbing the stump where the emergency doc had amputated her arm—a gesture Jason hated. It roused guilt feelings. But she'd get a new arm on Jinx.

"I hate to tell you," he said, "but Nessus isn't in a depressive stage. He stays in his room because he's avoiding us."

"Us?"

"Yah. I think so."

"But Jay! *Us?*"

"Don't take it personally, Anne. We're a symbol." He lowered his head to formulate words. "Look at it this way. You remember when Nessus kicked the kzin?"

"Sure. It was beautiful."

"And you probably know he was nerving himself to fire on the kzinti ship if I gave him the tnuctipun weapon. Finally, you know that he came voluntarily to the kzinti ship. I think he was going to fight them if he got the chance. He knew they'd captured me, and he knew they had the weapon. He was ready to fight."

"Good for him. But Jay—"

"Dammit, honey, it *wasn't* good for him. For him, it was purest evil. Cowardice is *moral* for puppeteers. He was violating everything he'd ever learned!"

"You mean he's ashamed of himself?"

"That's part of it. But there's more. It was the way we acted when we woke up.

"You remember how it was? Nessus was standing and looking at what was left of the kzinti pilot. You had to shake him a few times before he noticed. Then what did he find out? I, Jason Papandreou, who had been his friend, had planned the whole thing. I had known that the boss kzin and the Slaver expert were walking to their deaths because the computer form of the weapon had given them the self-destruct setting and told them it was the matter-conversion beam. I knew that, and I let them walk out and blow themselves to smithereens. I tricked the pilot into putting our heads in the police web, but I left him outside to die. And I was proud of it! And you were proud of me!

"Now do you get it?"

"No. And I'm still proud of you."

"Nessus isn't. Nessus knows that we, whom he probably thought of as funny-looking puppeteers—you may remember we were thinking of him as almost human—he knows we committed a horrible crime. Worse, it was a crime he was thinking of committing himself. So he's transferred his shame to us. He's ashamed of us, and he doesn't want to see us.''

"How far to Jinx?"

"A week."

"No way to hurry?"

"I never heard of one."

"Poor Nessus."

The Slaver weapon is "soft" as Salvador Dalí used the word: it changes shape. Those are "soft" watches in Dalí's "The Persistence of Memory."

See "The Lost Ideas" for details on how this typical early-Niven puzzle story became a *Star Trek* animation called "The Slaver Weapon." I thought hard before giving the Kzinti to the *Star Trek* universe. I did it because I thought it would be fun to see what others would do with them. And I was right!

Yet the paintings had impact . . . the tour stopped before a street scene. Here a Brown-and-white had climbed on a car and was apparently haranguing a swarm of Browns and Brown-and-whites, while behind him the sky burned sunset-red. The expressions were all the same flat smile, but Renner sensed violence and looked closer. Many of the crowd carried tools, always in their left hands, and some were broken. The city itself was on fire.

"It's called 'Return to Your Tasks.' You'll find that the Crazy Eddie theme recurs constantly," said Sally's Motie.

THE MOTE IN GOD'S EYE, 1974

THE BORDERLAND OF SOL

The organ bank problem remained an important social factor for most of the colony worlds. On Jinx it was unimportant; there was too much empty land for felons to flee to. On Plateau it created a hideous social stratification, vestiges of which remained long after ramrobot packages ended the organ bank problem itself.

Sol had its own problems. The Kzinti had discovered and conquered Wunderland and were on their way to Earth.

For a time the situation was touchy. Sol held off

the Kzinti by virtue of two accidents: the timely development of manned Bussard ramjets ("The Ethics of Madness") and the existence of giant laser cannon in the outer asteroids. These had been used to launch light-sail craft to Bussard ramjet speeds; now they were turned on the Kzinti. The Kzinti were amazed and hurt. Their telepaths had reported a species given over entirely to peace.

While Sol battled the Kzinti, an Outsider ship had arrived at We Made It. The Outsiders were interstellar traders, fragile, cold beings. They sold the secret of the faster-than-light drive to the human colony on We Made It. Two years later, a ship powered by the Outsider hyperdrive arrived in Sol system. The crew had not known of the war. They were amazed at their heroes' welcome.

It was the Outsiders' faster-than-light drive that ended the first Man–Kzin War. The second, third, and fourth are hardly worth discussing. The Kzinti always had a tendency to attack before they were quite ready.

The hyperdrive also opened up known space. There were other intelligent species around: Grogs, Bandersnatchi, Pierson's Puppeteers, Kdatlyno. An interstellar, interspecies civilization developed . . . and tales of that time are told in *Neutron Star*, the other known space collection.

Beowulf Shaeffer was a child of that time. A wandering crashlander, he was generally too lazy to stay out of trouble, but bright enough to think his way out once he was in. It was he who discovered that the galactic core was exploding . . . that within twenty thousand years, humanity would have to move elsewhere.

The following is the fifth of the tales of Beowulf Shaeffer.

Three months on Jinx, marooned.

I played tourist for the first couple of months. I never saw the high-pressure regions around the ocean because the only way down would have been with a safari of hunting tanks. But I traveled the habitable lands on either side of the sea, the East Band civilized, the West Band a developing frontier. I wandered the East End in a vacuum suit, toured the distilleries and other vacuum industries, and stared up into the orange vastness of Primary, Jinx's big twin brother.

I spent most of the second month between the Institute of Knowledge and the Camelot Hotel. Tourism had palled.

For me, that's unusual. I'm a born tourist. But—

Jinx's one point seven eight gravities put an unreasonable restriction on elegance and ingenuity in architectural design. The buildings in the habitable bands all look alike: squat and massive.

The East and West Ends, the vacuum regions, aren't that different from any industrialized moon. I never developed much of an interest in touring factories.

As for the ocean shorelines, the only vehicles that go there go to hunt Bandersnatchi. The Bandersnatchi are freaks: enormous, intelligent white slugs the size of mountains. They hunt the tanks. There are rigid restrictions to the equipment the tanks can carry, covenants established between men and Bandersnatchi, so that the Bandersnatchi win about forty percent of the duels. I wanted no part of that.

And all my touring had to be done in three times the gravity of my home world.

I spent the third month in Sirius Mater, and most of that in the Camelot Hotel, which has gravity generators in most of the rooms. When I went out I rode a floating contour couch. I passed like an invalid among the Jinxians, who were amused. Or was that my imagination?

I was in a hall of the Institute of Knowledge when I came on Carlos Wu running his fingertips over a Kdatlyno touch-sculpture.

A dark, slender man with narrow shoulders and straight black hair, Carlos was lithe as a monkey in any normal gravity; but on Jinx he used a travel couch exactly like mine. He studied the busts with his head tilted to one side. And I studied the familiar back, sure it couldn't be him.

"Carlos, aren't you supposed to be on Earth?"

He jumped. But when the couch spun around he was grinning. "Bey! I might say the same for you."

I admitted it. "I was headed for Earth, but when all those ships started disappearing around Sol system the captain changed his mind and steered for Sirius. Nothing any of the passengers could do about it. What about you? How are Sharrol and the kids?"

"Sharrol's fine, the kids are fine, and they're all waiting for you to come home." His fingers were still trailing over the Lloobee touch-sculpture called *Heroes*, feeling the warm, fleshy textures. *Heroes* was a most unusual touch-sculpture; there were visual as well as textural effects. Carlos studied the two human busts, then said, "That's *your* face, isn't it?"

"Yah."

"Not that you ever looked that good in your life. How did a Kdatlyno come to pick Beowulf Shaeffer as a classic hero? Was it your name? And who's the other guy?"

"I'll tell you about it sometime. Carlos, what are you doing *here?*"

"I . . . left Earth a couple of weeks after Louis was born." He was embarrassed. Why? "I haven't been off Earth in ten years. I needed the break."

But he'd left just before I was supposed to get home. And . . . hadn't someone once said that Carlos Wu had a touch of the flatland phobia? I began to understand what was wrong. "Carlos, you did Sharrol and me a valuable favor."

He laughed without looking at me. "Men have killed other men for such favors. I thought it was . . . tactful . . . to be gone when you came home."

Now I knew. Carlos was here because the Fertility Board on Earth would not favor me with a parenthood license.

You can't really blame the Board for using any excuse at all to reduce the number of producing parents. I am an albino. Sharrol and I wanted each other; but we both wanted children, and Sharrol can't leave Earth. She has the flatland phobia, the fear of strange air and altered days and changed gravity and black sky beneath her feet.

The only solution we'd found had been to ask a good friend to help.

Carlos Wu is a registered genius with an incredible resistance to disease and injury. He carries an unlimited parenthood license, one of sixty-odd among Earth's eighteen billion people. He gets similar offers every week . . . but he is a good friend, and he'd agreed. In the last two years Sharrol and Carlos had had two children, who were now waiting on earth for me to become their father.

I felt only gratitude for what he'd done for us. "I forgive you your odd ideas on tact," I said magnanimously. "Now. As long as we're stuck on Jinx, may I show you around? I've met some interesting people."

"You always do." He hesitated, then, "I'm not actually stuck on Jinx. I've been offered a ride home. I may be able to get you in on it."

"Oh, really? I didn't think there were any ships going to Sol system these days. Or leaving."

"This ship belongs to a government man. Ever heard of a Sigmund Ausfaller?"

"That sounds vaguely . . . Wait! Stop! The last time I saw Sigmund Ausfaller, he had just put a bomb aboard my ship!"

Carlos blinked at me. "You're kidding."

"I'm not."

"Sigmund Ausfaller is in the Bureau of Alien Affairs. Bombing spacecraft isn't one of his functions."

"Maybe he was off duty," I said viciously.

"Well, it doesn't really sound like you'd want to share a spacecraft cabin with him. Maybe—"

But I'd thought of something else, and now there just wasn't any way out of it. "No, let's meet him. Where do we find him?"

"The bar of the Camelot," said Carlos.

Reclining luxuriously on our travel couches, we slid on air cushions through Sirius Mater. The orange trees that lined the walks were foreshortened by gravity; their trunks were thick cones, and the oranges on the branches were not much bigger than ping pong balls.

Their world had altered them, even as our worlds have altered you and me. And underground civilization and point six gravities have made of me a pale stick-figure of a man, tall and attenuated. The Jinxians we passed were short and wide, designed like bricks, men and women both. Among them the occasional offworlder seemed as shockingly different as a Kdatlyno or a Pierson's Puppeteer.

And so we came to the Camelot.

The Camelot is a low, two-story structure that sprawls like a cubistic octopus across several acres of downtown Sirius Mater. Most offworlders stay here, for the gravity control in the rooms and corridors and for access to the Institute of Knowledge, the finest museum and research complex in human space.

The Camelot Bar carries one Earth gravity throughout. We left our travel couches in the vestibule and walked in like men. Jinxians were walking in like bouncing rubber bricks, with big happy grins on their wide faces. Jinxians love low gravity. A good many migrate to other worlds.

We spotted Ausfaller easily: a rounded, moon-faced flatlander with thick, dark, wavy hair and a thin black mustache. He stood as we approached. "Beowulf Shaeffer!"

he beamed. "How good to see you again! I believe it has been eight years or thereabouts. How have you been?"

"I lived," I told him.

Carlos rubbed his hands together briskly. "Sigmund! Why did you bomb Bey's ship?"

Ausfaller blinked in surprise. "Did he tell you it was his ship? It wasn't. He was thinking of stealing it. I reasoned that he would not steal a ship with a hidden time bomb aboard."

"But how did you come into it?" Carlos slid into the booth beside him. "You're not police. You're in the Extremely Foreign Relations Bureau."

"The ship belonged to General Products Corporation, which is owned by Pierson's Puppeteers, not human beings."

Carlos turned on me. "Bey! Shame on you."

"Dammit! They were trying to blackmail me into a suicide mission! And Ausfaller let them get away with it! And that's the least convincing exhibition of tact I've ever seen!"

"Good thing they soundproof these booths," said Carlos. "Let's order."

Soundproofing field or not, people were staring. I sat down. When our drinks came I drank deep. Why had I mentioned the bomb at all?

Ausfaller was saying, "Well, Carlos, have you changed your mind about coming with me?"

"Yes, if I can take a friend."

Ausfaller frowned, looked at me. "You wish to reach Earth too?"

I'd made up my mind. "I don't think so. In fact, I'd like to talk you out of taking Carlos."

Carlos said, "Hey!"

I overrode him. "Ausfaller, do you know who Carlos *is?* He had an unlimited parenthood license at the age of eighteen. Eighteen! I don't mind you risking your own life, in fact I love the idea. But his?"

"It's not that big a risk!" Carlos snapped.

"Yah? What has Ausfaller got that eight other ships didn't have?"

"Two things," Ausfaller said patiently. "One is that we will be incoming. Six of the eight ships that vanished were *leaving* Sol system. If there are pirates around Sol, they must find it much easier to locate an outgoing ship."

"They caught two incoming. Two ships, fifty crew-members and passengers, gone. Poof!"

"They would not take me so easily," Ausfaller boasted. "The *Hobo Kelly* is deceptive. It seems to be a cargo and passenger ship, but it is a warship, armed and capable of thirty gees acceleration. In normal space we can run from anything we can't fight. We are assuming pirates, are we not? Pirates would insist on robbing a ship before they destroy it."

I was intrigued. "Why? Why a disguised warship? Are you *hoping* you'll be attacked?"

"If there are actually pirates, yes, I hope to be attacked. But not when entering Sol system. We plan a substitution. A quite ordinary cargo craft will land on Earth, take on cargo of some value, and depart for Wunderland on a straight-line course. My ship will replace it before it has passed through the asteroids. So you see, there is no risk of losing Mr. Wu's precious genes."

Palms flat to the table, arms straight, Carlos stood looming over us. "Diffidently I raise the point that they are my futzy genes and I'll do what I futzy please with them! Bey, I've already had my share of children, and yours too!"

"Peace, Carlos. I didn't mean to step on any of your inalienable rights." I turned to Ausfaller. "I still don't see why these disappearing ships should interest the Extremely Foreign Relations Bureau."

"There were alien passengers aboard some of the ships."

"Oh."

"And we have wondered if the pirates themselves are

aliens. Certainly they have a technique not known to humanity. Of six outgoing ships, five vanished after reporting that they were about to enter hyperdrive.''

I whistled. ''They can precipitate a ship out of hyperdrive? That's impossible. Isn't it? Carlos?''

Carlos' mouth twisted. ''Not if it's being done. But I don't understand the principle. If the ships were just disappearing, that'd be different. Any ship does that if it goes too deep into a gravity well on hyperdrive.''

''Then . . . maybe it isn't pirates at all. Carlos, could there be living beings in hyperspace, actually eating the ships?''

''For all of me, there could. I don't know everything, Bey, contrary to popular opinion.'' But after a minute he shook his head. ''I don't buy it. I might buy an uncharted mass on the fringes of Sol system. Ships that came too near in hyperdrive would disappear.''

''No,'' said Ausfaller. ''No single mass could have caused all of the disappearances. Charter or not, a planet is bounded by gravity and inertia. We ran computer simulations. It would have taken at least three large masses, all unknown, all moving into heavy trade routes, simultaneously.''

''How large? Mars size or better?''

''So you have been thinking about this too.''

Carlos smiled. ''Yah. It may sound impossible, but it isn't. It's only improbable. There are unbelievable amounts of garbage out there beyond Neptune. Four known planets and endless chunks of ice and stone and nickel-iron.''

''Still, it is most improbable.''

Carlos nodded. A silence fell.

I was still thinking about monsters in hyperspace. The lovely thing about that hypothesis was that you couldn't even estimate a probability. We knew too little.

Humanity has been using hyperdrive for almost four hundred years now. Few ships have disappeared in that time, except during wars. Now, eight ships in ten months, all around Sol system.

Suppose one hyperspace beast had discovered ships in this region, say during one of the Man–Kzin Wars? He'd gone to get his friends. Now they were preying around Sol system. The flow of ships around Sol is greater than that around any three colony stars. But if more monsters came, they'd surely have to move on to the other colonies.

I couldn't imagine a defense against such things. We might have to give up interstellar travel.

Ausfaller said, "I would be glad if you would change your mind and come with us, Mr. Shaeffer."

"Um? Are you sure you want me on the same ship with you?"

"Oh, emphatically! How else may I be sure that you have not hidden a bomb aboard?" Ausfaller laughed. "Also, we can use a qualified pilot. Finally, I would like the chance to pick your brain, Beowulf Shaeffer. You have an odd facility for doing my job for me."

"What do you mean by that?"

"General Products used blackmail in persuading you to do a close orbit around a neutron star. You learned something about their home world—we still do not know what it was—and blackmailed them back. We know that blackmail contracts are a normal part of Puppeteer business practice. You earned their respect. You have dealt with them since. You have dealt also with Outsiders, without friction. But it was your handling of the Lloobee kidnapping that I found impressive."

Carlos was sitting at attention. I hadn't had a chance to tell him about that one yet. I grinned and said, "I'm proud of that myself."

"Well you should be. You did more than retrieve Known Space's top Kdatlyno touch-sculptor: you did it with honor, killing one of their number and leaving Lloobee free to pursue the others with publicity. Otherwise the Kdatlyno would have been annoyed.''

Helping Sigmund Ausfaller had been the farthest thing from my thoughts for these past eight years; yet suddenly I felt damn good. Maybe it was the way Carlos was listening. It takes a lot to impress Carlos Wu.

Carlos said, ''If you thought it was pirates, you'd come along, wouldn't you, Bey? After all, they probably can't *find* incoming ships.''

''Sure.''

''And you don't really believe in hyperspace monsters.''

I hedged. ''Not if I hear a better explanation. The thing is, I'm not sure I believe in supertechnological pirates either. What about those wandering masses?''

Carlos pursed his lips, said, ''All right. The solar system has a good number of planets—at least a dozen so far discovered, four of them outside the major singularity around Sol.''

''And not including Pluto?''

''No, we think of Pluto as a loose moon of Neptune. It runs *Neptune, Persephone, Caïna, Antenora, Ptolemea,* in order of distance from the sun. And the orbits aren't flat to the plane of the system. Persephone is tilted at a hundred and twenty degrees to the system, and retrograde. If they find another planet out there they'll call it *Judecca.''*

''Why?''

''Hell. The four innermost divisions of Dante's Hell. They form a great ice plain with sinners frozen into it.''

''Stick to the point,'' said Ausfaller.

''Start with the cometary halo,'' Carlos told me. ''It's very thin: about one comet per spherical volume of the Earth's orbit. Mass is denser going inward: a few planets, some inner comets, some chunks of ice and rock, all in skewed orbits and still spread pretty thin. Inside Neptune there are lots of planets and asteroids and more flattening of orbits to conform with Sol's rotation. Outside Neptune space is vast and empty. There *could* be uncharted planets. Singularities to swallow ships."

Ausfaller was indignant. "But for three to move into main trade lanes simultaneously?"

"It's not impossible, Sigmund."

"The probability—"

"Infinitesimal, right. Bey, it's damn near impossible. Any sane man would assume pirates."

It had been a long time since I had seen Sharrol. I was sore tempted. "Ausfaller, have you traced the sale of any of the loot? Have you gotten any ransom notes?" *Convince me*!

Ausfaller threw back his head and laughed.

"What's funny?"

"We have hundreds of ransom notes. Any mental deficient can write a ransom note, and these disappearances have had a good deal of publicity. The demands were all fakes. I wish one or another had been genuine. A son of the Patriarch of Kzin was aboard *Wayfarer* when she disappeared. As for loot—hmm. There has been a fall in the black market prices of boosterspice and gem woods. Otherwise—" He shrugged. "There has been no sign of the Barr originals or the Midas Rock or any of the more conspicuous treasures aboard the missing ships."

"Then you don't know one way or another."

"No. Will you go with us?"

"I haven't decided yet. When are you leaving?"

They'd be taking off tomorrow morning from the East End. That gave me time to make up my mind.

After dinner I went back to my room, feeling depressed. Carlos was going, that was clear enough. Hardly my fault . . . but he was here on Jinx because he'd done me and Sharrol a large favor. If he was killed going home . . .

A tape from Sharrol was waiting in my room. There were pictures of the children, Tanya and Louis, and shots of the apartment she'd found us in the Twin Peaks arcology, and much more.

I ran through it three times. Then I called Ausfaller's room. It had been just too futzy long.

I circled Jinx once on the way out. I've always done that, even back when I was flying for Nakamura Lines; and no passenger has ever objected.

Jinx is the close moon of a gas giant planet more massive than Jupiter, and smaller than Jupiter because its core has been compressed to degenerate matter. A billion years ago Jinx and Primary were even closer, before tidal drag moved them apart. This same tidal force had earlier locked Jinx's rotation to Primary and forced the moon into an egg shape, a prolate spheroid. When the moon moved outward its shape became more nearly spherical; but the cold rock surface resisted change.

That is why the ocean of Jinx rings its waist, beneath an atmosphere too compressed and too hot to breathe; whereas the points nearest to and furthest from Primary, the East and West Ends, actually rise out of the atmosphere.

From space Jinx looks like God's Own Easter Egg: the Ends bone-white tinged with yellow; then the brighter glare from rings of glittering ice fields at the limits of the atmosphere; then the varying blues of an Earthlike world, increasingly overlaid with the white frosting of cloud as the eyes move inward, until the waist of the planet/moon is girdled with pure white. The ocean never shows at all.

I took us once around, and out.

Sirius has its own share of floating miscellaneous matter cluttering the path to interstellar space. I stayed at the controls for most of five days, for that reason and because I wanted to get the feel of an unfamiliar ship.

Hobo Kelly was a belly-landing job, three hundred feet long, of triangular cross-section. Beneath an up-tilted, forward-thrusting nose were big clamshell doors for cargo. She had adequate belly jets and a much larger fusion motor at the tail, and a line of windows indicating cabins. Certainly she looked harmless enough; and certainly there was deception involved. The cabin should have held forty or fifty, but there was room only for four. The rest of what should have been cabin space was only windows with holograph projections in them.

The drive ran sure and smooth up to a maximum at ten gravities: not a lot for a ship designed to haul massive cargo. The cabin gravity held without putting out more than a fraction of its power. When Jinx and Primary were invisible against the stars, when Sirius was so distant I could look directly at it, I turned to the hidden control panel Ausfaller had unlocked for me. Ausfaller woke up, found me doing that, and began showing me which did what.

He had a big X-ray laser and some smaller laser cannon set for different frequencies. He had four self-guided fusion bombs. He had a telescope so good that the ostensible ship's telescope was only a finder for it. He had deep-radar.

And none of it showed beyond the discolored hull.

Ausfaller was armed for Bandersnatchi. I felt mixed emotions. It seemed we could fight anything, and run from it too. But what kind of enemy was he expecting?

All through those four weeks in hyperdrive, while we drove through the Blind Spot at three days to the light-year, the topic of the ship eaters reared its disturbing head.

Oh, we spoke of other things: of music and art, and of the latest techniques in animation, the computer programs that let you make your own holo flicks almost for lunch money. We told stories. I told Carlos why the Kdatlyno Lloobee had made busts of me and Emil Horne. I spoke of the only time the Pierson's Puppeteers had ever paid off the guarantee on a General Products hull, after the supposedly indestructible hull had been destroyed by antimatter. Ausfaller had some good ones . . . a lot more stories than he was allowed to tell, I gathered, from the way he had to search his memory every time.

But we kept coming back to the ship eaters.

"It boils down to three possibilities," I decided. "Kzinti, Puppeteers, and Humans."

Carlos guffawed. "Puppeteers? Puppeteers wouldn't have the guts!"

"I threw them in because they might have some interest in manipulating the interstellar stock market. Look: our hypothetical pirates have set up an embargo, cutting Sol system off from the outside world. The Puppeteers have the capital to take advantage of what that does to the market. And they need money. For their migration."

"The Puppeteers are philosophical cowards."

"That's right. They wouldn't risk robbing the ships, or coming anywhere near them. Suppose they can make them disappear from a distance?"

Carlos wasn't laughing now. "That's easier than dropping them out of hyperspace to rob them. It wouldn't take more than a great big gravity generator . . . and we've never known the limits of Puppeteer technology."

Ausfaller asked, "You think this is possible?"

"Just barely. The same goes for the Kzinti. The Kzinti are ferocious enough. Trouble is, if we ever learned they were preying on our ships we'd raise pluperfect hell. The Kzinti know that, and they know we can beat them. Took them long enough, but they learned."

"So you think it's Humans," said Ausfaller.

"Yah. If it's pirates."

The piracy theory still looked shaky. Spectrum telescopes had not even found concentrations of ship's metals in the space where they have vanished. Would pirates steal the whole ship? If the hyperdrive motor were still intact after the attack, the rifled ship could be launched into infinity; but could pirates count on that happening eight times out of eight?

And none of the missing ships had called for help via hyperwave.

I'd never believed pirates. Space pirates have existed, but

they died without successors. Intercepting a spacecraft was too difficult. They couldn't make it pay.

Ships fly themselves in hyperdrive. All a pilot need do is watch for green radial lines in the mass sensor. But he has to do that frequently, because the mass sensor is a psionic device; it must be watched by a mind, not another machine.

As the narrow green line that marked Sol grew longer, I became abnormally conscious of the debris around Sol system. I spent the last twelve hours of the flight at the controls, chain-smoking with my feet. I should add that I do that normally, when I want both hands free; but now I did it to annoy Ausfaller. I'd seen the way his eyes bugged the first time he saw me take a drag from a cigarette between my toes. Flatlanders are less than limber.

Carlos and Ausfaller shared the control room with me as we penetrated Sol's cometary halo. They were relieved to be nearing the end of a long trip. I was nervous. "Carlos, just how large a mass would it take to make us disappear?"

"Planet size, Mars and up. Beyond that it depends on how close you get and how dense it is. If it's dense enough it can be less massive and still flip you out of the universe. But you'd see it in the mass sensor."

"Only for an instant . . . and not then, if it's turned off. What if someone turned on a giant gravity generator as we went past?"

"For what? They couldn't rob the ship. Where's their profit?"

"Stocks."

But Ausfaller was shaking his head. "The expense of such an operation would be enormous. No group of pirates would have enough additional capital on hand to make it worthwhile. Of the Puppeteers I might believe it."

Hell, he was right. No Human that wealthy would need to turn pirate.

The long green line marking Sol was almost touching the surface of the mass sensor. I said, "Breakout in ten minutes."

And the ship lurched savagely.

"Strap down!" I yelled, and glanced at the hyperdrive monitors. The motor was drawing no power, and the rest of the dials were going bananas.

I activated the windows. I'd kept them turned off in hyperspace, lest my flatlander passengers go mad watching the Blind Spot. The screens came on and I saw stars. We were in normal space.

"Futz! They got us anyway." Carlos sounded neither frightened nor angry, but awed.

As I raised the hidden panel Ausfaller cried, "Wait!" I ignored him. I threw the red switch, and *Hobo Kelly* lurched again as her belly blew off.

Ausfaller began cursing in some dead flatlander language.

Now two-thirds of *Hobo Kelly* receded, slowly turning. What was left must show as what she was: a Number Two General Products hull, Puppeteer-built, a slender transparent spear three hundred feet long and twenty feet wide, with instruments of war clustered along what was now her belly. Screens that had been blank came to life. And I lit the main drive and ran it up to full power.

Ausfaller spoke in rage and venom. "Shaeffer, you idiot, you coward! We run without knowing what we run from. Now they know exactly what we are. What chance that they will follow us now? This ship was built for a specific purpose, and you have ruined it!"

"I've freed your special instruments," I pointed out. "Why don't you see what you can find?" Meanwhile I could get us the futz out of here.

Ausfaller became very busy. I watched what he was getting on screens at my side of the control panel. Was anything chasing us? They'd find us hard to catch and harder to digest. They could hardly have been expecting a General Products hull. Since the Puppeteers stopped making them the price of used GP hulls has gone out of sight.

There *were* ships out there. Ausfaller got a closeup of them: three space tugs of the Belter type, shaped like thick saucers, equipped with oversized drives and powerful electromagnetic generators. Belters use them to tug nickel-iron asteroids to where somebody wants the ore. With those heavy drives they could probably catch us; but would they have adequate cabin gravity?

They weren't trying. They seemed to be neither following nor fleeing. And they looked harmless enough.

But Ausfaller was doing a job on them with his other instruments. I approved. *Hobo Kelly* had looked peaceful enough a moment ago. Now her belly bristled with weaponry. The tugs could be equally deceptive.

From behind me Carlos asked, "Bey? What happened?"

"How the futz would I know?"

"What do the instruments show?"

He must mean the hyperdrive complex. A couple of the indicators had gone wild; five more were dead. I said so. "And the drive's drawing no power at all. I've never heard of anything like this. Carlos, it's *still* theoretically impossible."

"I'm . . . not so sure of that. I want to look at the drive."

"The access tubes don't have cabin gravity."

Ausfaller had abandoned the receding tugs. He'd found what looked to be a large comet, a ball of frozen gasses a good distance to the side. I watched as he ran the deep-radar over it. No fleet of robber ships lurked behind it.

I asked, "Did you deep-radar the tugs?"

"Of course. We can examine the tapes in detail later. I saw nothing. And nothing has attacked us since we left hyperspace."

I'd been driving us in a random direction. Now I turned us toward Sol, the brightest star in the heavens. Those lost ten minutes in hyperspace would add about three days to our voyage.

"If there was an enemy, you frightened him away. Shaeffer, this mission and this ship have cost my department an enormous sum, and we have learned nothing at all."

"Not quite nothing," said Carlos. "I still want to see the hyperdrive motor. Bey, would you run us down to one gee?"

"Yah. But . . . miracles make me nervous, Carlos."

"Join the club."

We crawled along an access tube just a little bigger than a big man's shoulders, between the hyperdrive motor housing and the surrounding fuel tankage. Carlos reached an inspection window. He looked in. He started to laugh.

I inquired as to what was so futzy funny.

Still chortling, Carlos moved on. I crawled after him and looked in.

There was no hyperdrive motor in the hyperdrive motor housing.

I went in through a repair hatch and stood in the cylindrical housing, looking about me. Nothing. Not even an exit hole. The superconducting cables and the mounts for the motor had been sheared so cleanly that the cut ends looked like little mirrors.

Ausfaller insisted on seeing for himself. Carlos and I waited in the control room. For awhile Carlos kept bursting into fits of giggles. Then he got a dreamy, faraway look that was even more annoying.

I wondered what was going on in his head, and reached the uncomfortable conclusion that I could never know. Some years ago I took IQ tests, hoping to get a parenthood license that way. I am not a genius.

I knew only that Carlos had thought of something I hadn't, and he wasn't telling, and I was too proud to ask.

Ausfaller had no pride. He came back looking like he'd

seen a ghost. "Gone! Where could it go? How could it happen?"

"That I can answer," Carlos said happily. "It takes an extremely high gravity gradient. The motor hit that, wrapped space around itself and took off at some higher level of hyperdrive, one we can't reach. By now it could be well on its way to the edge of the universe."

I said, "You're sure, huh? An hour ago there wasn't a theory to cover any of this."

"Well, I'm sure our motor's gone. Beyond that it gets a little hazy. But there is one well-established model of what happens when a ship hits a singularity. At a lower gravity gradient the motor would take the whole ship with it, then strew atoms of the ship along its path till there was nothing left but the hyperdrive field itself."

"Ugh."

Now Carlos burned with the love of an idea. "Sigmund, I want to use your hyperwave. I could still be wrong, but there are things we can check."

"If we are still within the singularity of some mass, the hyperwave will destroy itself."

"Yah. I think it's worth the risk."

We'd dropped out, or been knocked out, ten minutes short of the singularity around Sol. That added up to sixteen light-hours of normal space, plus almost five light-hours from the edge of the singularity inward to Earth. Fortunately hyperwave is instantaneous, and every civilized system keeps a hyperwave relay station just outside the singularity. Southworth Station would relay our message inward by laser, get the return message the same way and pass it on to us ten hours later.

We turned on the hyperwave and nothing exploded.

Ausfaller made his own call first, to Ceres, to get the registry of the tugs we'd spotted. Afterward Carlos called Elephant's computer setup in New York, using a code number Elephant doesn't give to many people. "I'll pay him back later. Maybe with a story to go with it," he gloated.

I listened as Carlos outlined his needs. He wanted full records on a meteorite that had touched down in Tunguska, Siberia, USSR, Earth, in 1908 A.D. He wanted a reprise on three models of the origin of the universe or lack of same: the Big Bang, the Cyclic Universe, the Steady State Universe. He wanted data on collapsars. He wanted names, career outlines, and addresses for the best known students of gravitational phenomena in Sol system. He was smiling when he clicked off.

I said, "You got me. I haven't the remotest idea what you're after."

Still smiling, Carlos got up and went to his cabin to catch some sleep.

I turned off the main thrust motor entirely. When we were deep in Sol system we could decelerate at thirty gravities. Meanwhile we were carrying a hefty velocity picked up on our way out of Sirius system.

Ausfaller stayed in the control room. Maybe his motive was the same as mine. No police ships out here. We could still be attacked.

He spent the time going through his pictures of the three mining tugs. We didn't talk, but I watched.

The tugs seemed ordinary enough. Telescopic photos showed no suspicious breaks in the hulls, no hatches for guns. In the deep-radar scan they showed like ghosts: we could pick out the massive force-field rings, the hollow, equally massive drive tubes, the lesser densities of fuel tank and life-support system. There were no gaps or shadows that shouldn't have been there.

By and by Ausfaller said, "Do you know what *Hobo Kelly* was worth?"

I said I could make a close estimate.

"It was worth my career. I thought to destroy a pirate

fleet with *Hobo Kelly*. But my pilot fled. Fled! What have I now, to show for my expensive Trojan Horse?''

I suppressed the obvious answer, along with the plea that my first responsibility was Carlos' life. Ausfaller wouldn't buy that. Instead, ''Carlos has something. I know him. He knows how it happened.''

''Can you get it out of him?''

''I don't know.'' I could put it to Carlos that we'd be safer if we knew what was out to get us. But Carlos was a flatlander. It would color his attitudes.

''So,'' said Ausfaller. ''We have only the unavailable knowledge in Carlos' skull.''

A weapon beyond human technology had knocked me out of hyperspace. I'd run. Of *course* I'd run. Staying in the neighborhood would have been insane, said I to myself, said I. But, unreasonably, I still felt bad about it.

To Ausfaller I said, ''What about the mining tugs? I can't understand what they're doing out here. In the Belt they use them to move nickel-iron asteroids to industrial sites.''

''It is the same here. Most of what they find is useless: stony masses or balls of ice; but what little metal there is, is valuable. They must have it for building.''

''For building what? What kind of people would live here? You might as well set up shop in interstellar space!''

''Precisely. There are no tourists, but there are research groups, here where space is flat and empty and temperatures are near absolute zero. I know that the Quicksilver Group was established here to study hyperspace phenomena. We do not understand hyperspace, even yet. Remember that we did not invent the hyperdrive; we bought it from an alien race. Then there is a gene-tailoring laboratory trying to develop a kind of tree that will grow on comets.''

''You're kidding.''

''But they are serious. A photosynthetic plant to use the chemicals present in all comets . . . it would be very valu-able. The whole cometary halo could be seeded with oxygen-producing plants—'' Ausfaller stopped abruptly, then, ''Never mind. But all these groups need building materials. It is cheaper to build out here than to ship everything from Earth or the Belt. The presence of tugs is not suspicious.''

''But there was nothing else around us. Nothing at all.''

Ausfaller nodded.

When Carlos came to join us many hours later, blinking sleep out of his eyes, I asked him, ''Carlos, could the tugs have had anything to do with your theory?''

''I don't see how. I've got half an idea, and half an hour from now I could look like a halfwit. The theory I want isn't even in fashion anymore. Now that we know what the quasars are, everyone seems to like the Steady State Hypothesis. You know how that works: the tension in completely empty space produces more hydrogen atoms, forever. The universe has no beginning and no end.'' He looked stubborn. ''But if I'm right, then I know where the ships went to after being robbed. That's more than anyone else knows.''

Ausfaller jumped on him. ''Where are they? Are the passengers alive?''

''I'm sorry, Sigmund. They're all dead. There won't even be bodies to bury.''

''What is it? What are we fighting?''

''A gravitational effect. A sharp warping of space. A planet wouldn't do that, and a battery of cabin gravity generators wouldn't do it; they couldn't produce that sharply bounded a field.''

''A collapsar,'' Ausfaller suggested.

Carlos grinned at him. ''That would do it, but there are other problems. A collapsar can't even form at less than around five solar masses. You'd think someone would have noticed something that big, this close to Sol.''

''Then *what?*''

Carlos shook his head. We would wait.

* * *

The relay from Southworth Station gave us registration for three space tugs, used and of varying ages, all three purchased two years ago from IntraBelt Mining by the Sixth Congregational Church of Rodney.

"Rodney?"

But Carlos and Ausfaller were both chortling. "Belters do that sometimes," Carlos told me. "It's a way of saying it's nobody's business who's buying the ships."

"That's pretty funny, all right, but we still don't know who owns them."

"They may be honest Belters. They may not."

Hard on the heels of the first call came the data Carlos had asked for, playing directly into the shipboard computer. Carlos called up a list of names and phone numbers: Sol system's preeminent students of gravity and its effects, listed in alphabetical order.

An address caught my attention:

Julian Forward, #1192326 Southworth Station.

A hyperwave relay tag. He was out *here*, somewhere in the enormous gap between Neptune's orbit and the cometary belt, out here where the hyperwave relay could function. I looked for more Southworth Station numbers. They were there:

Launcelot Starkey, #1844719 Southworth Station.

Jill Luciano, #1844719 Southworth Station.

Mariana Wilton, #1844719 Southworth Station.

"These people," said Ausfaller. "You wish to discuss your theory with one of them?"

"That's right. Sigmund, isn't 1844719 the tag for the Quicksilver Group?"

"I think so. I also think that they are not within our reach, now that our hyperdrive is gone. The Quicksilver Group was established in distant orbit around Antenora, which is now on the other side of the sun. Carlos, has it occurred to you that one of these people may have built the ship-eating device?"

"What? . . . You're right. It would take someone who knew something about gravity. But I'd say the Quicksilver Group was beyond suspicion. With upwards of ten thousand people at work, how could anyone hide anything?"

"What about this Julian Forward?"

"Forward. Yah. I've always wanted to meet him."

"You know of him? Who is he?"

"He used to be with the Institute of Knowledge on Jinx. I haven't heard of him in years. He did some work on the gravity waves from the galactic core . . . work that turned out to be wrong. Sigmund, let's give him a call."

"And ask him what?"

"Why . . . ?" Then Carlos remembered the situation. "Oh. You think he might—Yah."

"How well do you know this man?"

"I know him by reputation. He's quite famous. I don't see how such a man could go in for mass murder."

"Earlier you said that we were looking for a man skilled in the study of gravitational phenomena."

"Granted."

Ausfaller sucked at his lower lip. Then, "Perhaps we can do no more than talk to him. He could be on the other side of the sun and still head a pirate fleet—"

"No. That he could not."

"Think again," said Ausfaller. "We are outside the singularity of Sol. A pirate fleet would surely include hyperdrive ships."

"If Julian Forward is the ship eater, he'll have to be nearby. The, uh, device won't move in hyperspace."

I said, "Carlos, what we don't know can kill us. Will you quit playing games—" But he was smiling, shaking his head. Futz. "All right, we can still check on Forward. Call him up and ask where he is! Is he likely to know you by reputation?"

"Sure. I'm famous too."

"Okay. If he's close enough, we might even beg him for

a ride home. The way things stand we'll be at the mercy of any hyperdrive ship for as long as we're out here.''

"I hope we are attacked," said Ausfaller. "We can out-fight—"

"But we can't outrun. They can dodge, we can't."

"Peace, you two. First things first." Carlos sat down at the hyperwave controls and tapped out a number.

Suddenly Ausfaller said, "Can you contrive to keep my name out of this exchange? If necessary you can be the ship's owner."

Carlos looked around in surprise. Before he could answer, the screen lit. I saw ash-blond hair cut in a Belter crest, over a lean white face and an impersonal smile.

"Forward Station. Good evening."

"Good evening. This is Carlos Wu of Earth calling long distance. May I speak to Dr. Julian Forward, please?"

"I'll see if he's available." The screen went on HOLD.

In the interval Carlos burst out: "What kind of game are *you* playing now? How can I explain owning an armed, disguised warship?"

But I began to see what Ausfaller was getting at. I said, "You'd want to avoid explaining that, whatever the truth was. Maybe he won't ask. I—" I shut up, because we were facing Forward.

Julian Forward was a Jinxian, short and wide, with arms as thick as legs and legs as thick as pillars. His skin was almost as black as his hair: a Sirius suntan, probably maintained by sunlights. He perched on the edge of a massage chair. "Carlos Wu!" he said with flattering enthusiasm. "Are you the same Carlos Wu who solved the Sealeyham Limits Problem?"

Carlos said he was. They went into a discussion of mathematics—a possible application of Carlos' solution to another limits problem, I gathered. I glanced at Ausfaller—not obtrusively, because for Forward he wasn't supposed to exist—and saw him pensively studying his side view of Forward.

"Well," Forward said, "what can I do for you?"

"Julian Forward, meet Beowulf Shaeffer," said Carlos. I bowed. "Bey was giving me a lift home when our hyperdrive motor disappeared."

"Disappeared?"

I butted in, for verisimilitude. "Disappeared, futzy right. The hyperdrive motor casing is empty. The motor supports are sheared off. We're stuck out here with no hyperdrive and no idea how it happened."

"Almost true," Carlos said happily. "Dr. Forward, I do have some ideas as to what happened here. I'd like to discuss them with you."

"Where are you now?"

I pulled our position and velocity from the computer and flashed them to Forward Station. I wasn't sure it was a good idea; but Ausfaller had time to stop me, and he didn't.

"Fine," said Forward's image. "It looks like you can get here a lot faster than you can get to Earth. Forward Station is ahead of you, within twenty a.u. of your position. You can wait here for the next ferry. Better than going on in a crippled ship."

"Good! We'll work out a course and let you know when to expect us."

"I welcome the chance to meet Carlos Wu." Forward gave us his own coordinates and rang off.

Carlos turned. "All right, Bey. Now *you* own an armed and disguised warship. *You* figure out where you got it."

"We've got worse problems than that. Forward Station is exactly where the ship eater ought to be."

He nodded. But he was amused.

"So what's our next move? We can't run from hyperdrive ships. Not now. Is Forward likely to try to kill us?"

"If we don't reach Forward Station on schedule, he might send ships after us. We know too much. We've told him so," said Carlos. "The hyperdrive motor disappeared completely. I know half a dozen people who could figure out how it happened, knowing just that." He smiled suddenly. "That's assuming Forward's the ship eater. We don't know that. I think we have a splendid chance to find out, one way or the other."

"How? Just walk in?"

Ausfaller was nodding approvingly. "Dr. Forward expects you and Carlos to enter his web unsuspecting, leaving an empty ship. I think we can prepare a few surprises for him. For example, he may not have guessed that this is a General Products hull. And I will be aboard to fight."

True. Only antimatter could harm a GP hull . . . though things could go through it, like light and gravity and shock waves. "So you'll be in the indestructible hull," I said, "and we'll be helpless in the base. Very clever. I'd rather run for it myself. But then, you have your career to consider."

"I will not deny it. But there are ways in which I can prepare you."

Behind Ausfaller's cabin, behind what looked like an unbroken wall, was a room the size of a walk-in closet. Ausfaller seemed quite proud of it. He didn't show us everything in there, but I saw enough to cost me what remained of my first impression of Ausfaller. This man did not have the soul of a pudgy bureaucrat.

Behind a glass panel he kept a couple of dozen special-purpose weapons. A row of four clamps held three identical hand weapons, disposable rocket launchers for a fat slug that Ausfaller billed as a tiny atomic bomb. The fourth clamp was empty. There were laser rifles and pistols; a shotgun of peculiar design, with four inches of recoil shock absorber; throwing knives; an Olympic target pistol with a sculpted grip and room for just one .22 bullet.

I wondered what he was doing with a hobbyist's touch-sculpting setup. Maybe he could make sculptures to drive a Human or an alien mad. Maybe something less subtle: maybe they'd explode at the touch of the right fingerprints.

He had a compact automated tailor's shop. "I'm going to make you some new suits," he said. When Carlos asked why, he said, "You can keep secrets? So can I."

He asked us for our preference in styles. I played it straight, asking for a falling jumper in green and silver, with lots of pockets. It wasn't the best I've ever owned, but it fitted.

"I didn't ask for buttons," I told him.

"I hope you don't mind. Carlos, you will have buttons too."

Carlos chose a fiery red tunic with a green-and-gold dragon coiling across the back. The buttons carried his family monogram. Ausfaller stood before us, examining us in our new finery, with approval.

"Now, watch," he said. "Here I stand before you, unarmed—"

"Right."

"*Sure* you are."

Ausfaller grinned. He took the top and bottom buttons between his fingers and tugged hard. They came off. The material between them ripped open as if a thread had been strung between them.

Holding the buttons as if to keep an invisible thread taut, he moved them on either side of a crudely done plastic touch-sculpture. The sculpture fell apart.

"Sinclair molecule chain. It will cut through any normal matter, if you pull hard enough. You must be very careful. It will cut your fingers so easily that you will hardly notice they are gone. Notice that the buttons are large, to give an easy grip." He laid the buttons carefully on a table and set a heavy weight between them. "This third button down is a sonic grenade. Ten feet away it will kill. Thirty feet away it will stun."

I said, "Don't demonstrate."

"You may want to practice throwing dummy buttons at a target. This second button is Power Pill, the commercial stimulant. Break the button and take half when you need it. The entire dose may stop your heart.''

"I never heard of Power Pill. How does it work on crashlanders?''

He was taken aback. "I don't know. Perhaps you had better restrict yourself to a quarter dose.''

"Or avoid it entirely," I said.

"There is one more thing I will not demonstrate. Feel the material of your garments. You feel three layers of material? The middle layer is a nearly perfect mirror. It will reflect even X-rays. Now you can repel a laser blast, for at least the first second. The collar unrolls to a hood.''

Carlos was nodding in satisfaction.

I guess it's true: all flatlanders think that way.

For a billion and a half years, humanity's ancestors had evolved to the conditions of one world: Earth. A flatlander grows up in an environment peculiarly suited to him. Instinctively he sees the whole universe the same way.

We know better, we who were born on other worlds. On We Made It there are the hellish winds of summer and winter. On Jinx, the gravity. On Plateau, the all-encircling cliff edge, and a drop of forty miles into unbearable heat and pressure. On Down, the red sunlight, and plants that will not grow without help from ultraviolet lamps.

But flatlanders think the universe was made for their benefit. To them, danger is unreal.

"Earplugs," said Ausfaller, holding up a handful of soft plastic cylinders.

We inserted them. Ausfaller said, "Can you hear me?''

"Sure." "Yah." They didn't block our hearing at all.

"Transmitter and hearing aid, with sonic padding between. If you are blasted with sound, as by an explosion or a sonic stunner, the hearing aid will stop transmitting. If you go suddenly deaf you will know you are under attack.''

To me, Ausfaller's elaborate precautions only spoke of

what we might be walking into. I said nothing. If we ran for it our chances were even worse.

Back to the control room, where Ausfaller set up a relay to the Alien Affairs Bureau on Earth. He gave them a condensed version of what had happened to us, plus some cautious speculation. He invited Carlos to read his theories into the record.

Carlos declined. "I could still be wrong. Give me a chance to do some studying."

Ausfaller went grumpily to his bunk. He had been up too long, and it showed.

Carlos shook his head as Ausfaller disappeared into his cabin. "Paranoia. In his job I guess he has to be paranoid."

"You could use some of that yourself."

He didn't hear me. "Imagine suspecting an interstellar celebrity of being a space pirate!"

"He's in the right place at the right time."

"Hey, Bey, forget what I said. The, uh, ship-eating device has to be in the right place, but the pirates don't. They can just leave it loose and use hyperdrive ships to commute to their base."

That was something to keep in mind. Compared to the inner system this volume within the cometary halo was enormous; but to hyperdrive ships it was all one neighborhood. I said, "Then why are we visiting Forward?"

"I still want to check my ideas with him. More than that; he probably knows the head ship eater, without knowing it's him. Probably we both know him. It took something of a cosmologist to find the device and recognize it. Whoever it is, he has to have made something of a name for himself."

"Find?"

Carlos grinned at me. "Never mind. Have you thought of anyone you'd like to use that magic wire on?"

"I've been making a list. You're at the top."

"Well, watch it. Sigmund knows you've got it, even if nobody else does."

"He's second."

"How long till we reach Forward Station?"

I'd been rechecking our course. We were decelerating at thirty gravities and veering to one side. "Twenty hours and a few minutes," I said.

"Good. I'll get a chance to do some studying." He began calling up data from the computer.

I asked permission to read over his shoulder. He gave it.

Bastard. He reads twice as fast as I do. I tried to skim, to get some idea of what he was after.

Collapsars: three known. The nearest was one component of a double in Cygnus, more than a hundred light-years away. Expeditions had gone there to drop probes.

The theory of the black hole wasn't new to me, though the math was over my head. If a star is massive enough, then after it has burned its nuclear fuel and started to cool, no possible internal force can hold it from collapsing inward past its own Swartzchild radius. At that point the escape velocity from the star becomes greater than lightspeed; and beyond that deponent sayeth not, because nothing can leave the star, not information, not matter, not radiation. Nothing—except gravity.

Such a collapsed star can be expected to weigh five solar masses or more; otherwise its collapse would stop at the neutron star stage. Afterward it can only grow bigger and more massive.

There wasn't the slightest chance of finding anything that massive out here at the edge of the solar system. If such a thing were anywhere near, the sun would have been in orbit around it.

The Siberia meteorite must have been weird enough, to be remembered for nine hundred years. It had knocked down trees over thousands of square miles; yet trees near the touchdown point were left standing. No part of the meteorite itself had ever been found. Nobody had seen it hit. In 1908, Tunguska, Siberia, must have been as sparsely settled as the Earth's moon today.

"Carlos, what does all this have to do with anything?"

"Does Holmes tell Watson?"

I had real trouble following the cosmology. Physics verged on philosophy here, or vice versa. Basically the Big Bang Theory—which pictures the universe as exploding from a single point-mass, like a titanic bomb—was in competition with the Steady State Universe, which has been going on forever and will continue to do so. The Cyclic Universe is a succession of Big Bangs followed by contractions. There are variants on all of them.

When the quasars were first discovered, they seemed to date from an earlier stage in the evolution of the universe . . . which, by the Steady State hypothesis, would not be evolving at all. The Steady State went out of fashion. Then, a century ago, Hilbury had solved the mystery of the quasars. Meanwhile one of the implications of the Big Bang had not panned out. That was where the math got beyond me.

There was some discussion of whether the universe was open or closed in four-space, but Carlos turned it off. "Okay," he said, with satisfaction.

"What?"

"I could be right. Insufficient data. I'll have to see what Forward thinks."

"I hope you both choke. I'm going to sleep."

Out here in the broad borderland between Sol system and interstellar space, Julian Forward had found a stony mass the size of a middling asteroid. From a distance it seemed untouched by technology: a lopsided spheroid, rough-surfaced and dirty white. Closer in, flecks of metal and bright paint showed like randomly placed jewels. Airlocks, windows, projecting antennae, and things less identifiable. A lighted disk with something projecting from the center: a long metal arm with half a dozen ball joints in it and a cup on the end. I studied that one, trying to guess what it might be . . . and gave up.

I brought *Hobo Kelly* to rest a fair distance away. To Ausfaller I said, "You'll stay aboard?"

"Of course. I will do nothing to disabuse Dr. Forward of the notion that the ship is empty."

We crossed to Forward Station on an open taxi: two seats, a fuel tank and a rocket motor. Once I turned to ask Carlos something, and asked instead, "Carlos? Are you all right?"

His face was white and strained. "I'll make it."

"Did you try closing your eyes?"

"It was worse. Futz, I made it this far on hypnosis. Bey, it's so *empty*."

"Hang on. We're almost there."

The blond Belter was outside one of the airlocks in a skin-tight suit and a bubble helmet. He used a flashlight to flag us down. We moored our taxi to a spur of rock—the gravity was almost nil—and went inside.

"I'm Harry Moskowitz," the Belter said. "They call me Angel. Dr. Forward is waiting in the laboratory."

The interior of the asteroid was a network of straight cylindrical corridors, laser-drilled, pressurized and lined with cool blue light strips. We weighed a few pounds near the surface, less in the deep interior. Angel moved in a fashion new to me: a flat jump from the floor that took him far down the corridor to brush the ceiling; push back to the floor and jump again. Three jumps and he'd wait, not hiding his amusement at our attempts to catch up.

"Doctor Forward asked me to give you a tour," he told us.

I said, "You seem to have a lot more corridor than you need. Why didn't you cluster all the rooms together?"

"This rock was a mine, once upon a time. The miners drilled these passages. They left big hollows wherever they found air-bearing rock or ice pockets. All we had to do was wall them off.''

That explained why there was so much corridor between the doors, and why the chambers we saw were so big. Some rooms were storage areas, Angel said; not worth opening. Others were tool rooms, life-support systems, a garden, a fair-sized computer, a sizable fusion plant. A mess room built to hold thirty actually held about ten, all men, who looked at us curiously before they went back to eating. A hangar, bigger than need be and open to the sky, housed taxis and powered suits with specialized tools, and three identical circular cradles, all empty.

I gambled. Carefully casual, I asked, ''You use mining tugs?''

Angel didn't hesitate. ''Sure. We can ship water and metals up from the inner system, but it's cheaper to hunt them down ourselves. In an emergency the tugs could probably get us back to the inner system.''

We moved back into the tunnels. Angel said, ''Speaking of ships, I don't think I've ever seen one like yours. Were those *bombs* lined up along the ventral surface?''

''Some of them,'' I said.

Carlos laughed. ''Bey won't tell me how he got it.''

''Pick, pick, pick. All right, I *stole* it. I don't think anyone is going to complain.''

Angel, frankly curious before, was frankly fascinated as I told the story of how I had been hired to fly a cargo ship in the Wunderland system. ''I didn't much like the looks of the guy who hired me, but what do I know about Wunderlanders? Besides, I needed the money.'' I told of my surprise at the proportions of the ship: the solid wall behind the cabin, the passenger section that was only holographs in blind portholes. By then I was already afraid that if I tried to back out I'd be made to disappear.

But when I learned my destination I got really worried. ''It was in the Serpent Stream—you know, the crescent of asteroids in Wunderland system? It's common knowledge that the Free Wunderland Conspiracy is *all through* those rocks. When they gave me my course I just took off and aimed for Sirius.''

"Strange they left you with a working hyperdrive."

"Man, they *didn't*. They'd ripped out the relays. I had to fix them myself. It's lucky I looked, because they had the relays wired to a little bomb under the control chair.'' I stopped, then, "Maybe I fixed it wrong. You heard what happened? My hyperdrive motor just plain vanished. It must have set off some explosive bolts, because the belly of the ship blew off. It was a dummy. What's left looks to be a pocket bomber.''

"That's what I thought."

"I guess I'll have to turn it in to the goldskin cops when we reach the inner system. Pity.''

Carlos was smiling and shaking his head. He covered by saying, "It only goes to prove that you *can* run away from your problems.''

The next tunnel ended in a great hemispherical chamber, lidded by a bulging transparent dome. A man-thick pillar rose through the rock floor to a seal in the center of the dome. Above the seal, gleaming against night and stars, a multi-jointed metal arm reached out blindly into space. The arm ended in what might have been a tremendous iron puppy dish.

Forward was in a horseshoe-shaped control console near the pillar. I hardly noticed him. I'd seen this arm-and-bucket thing before, coming in from space, but I hadn't grasped its *size*.

Forward caught me gaping. "The Grabber," he said.

He approached us in a bouncing walk, comical but effective. "Pleased to meet you, Carlos Wu. Beowulf Shaeffer." His handshake was not crippling, because he was being careful. He had a wide, engaging smile. "The Grabber is our main exhibit here. After the Grabber there's nothing to see.''

I asked, "What does it do?"

Carlos laughed. "It's beautiful! Why does it have to do anything?"

Forward acknowledged the compliment. "I've been thinking of entering it in a junk-sculpture show. What it does is manipulate large, dense masses. The cradle at the end of the arm is a complex of electromagnets. I can actually vibrate masses in there to produce polarized gravity waves."

Six massive arcs of girder divided the dome into pie sections. Now I noticed that they and the seal at their center gleamed like mirrors. They were reinforced by stasis fields. More bracing for the Grabber? I tried to imagine forces that would require such strength.

"What do you vibrate in there? A megaton of lead?"

"Lead sheathed in soft iron was our test mass. But that was three years ago. I haven't worked with the Grabber lately, but we had some satisfactory runs with a sphere of neutronium enclosed in a stasis field. Ten billion metric tons."

I said, "What's the point?"

From Carlos I got a dirty look. Forward seemed to think it was a wholly reasonable question. "Communication, for one thing. There must be intelligent species all through the galaxy, most of them too far away for our ships. Gravity waves are probably the best way to reach them."

"Gravity waves travel at lightspeed, don't they? Wouldn't hyperwave be better?"

"We can't count on their having it. Who but the Outsiders would think to do their experimenting this far from a sun? If we want to reach beings who haven't dealt with the Outsiders, we'll have to use gravity waves . . . once we know how."

Angel offered us chairs and refreshments. By the time we were settled I was already out of it; Forward and Carlos were talking plasma physics, metaphysics, and what are our old friends doing? I gathered that they had large numbers of mutual acquaintances. And Carlos was probing for the whereabouts of cosmologists specializing in gravity physics.

A few were in the Quicksilver Group. Others were among the colony worlds . . . especially on Jinx, trying to get the Institute of Knowledge to finance various projects, such as more expeditions to the collapsar in Cygnus.

"Are you still with the Institute, Doctor?"

Forward shook his head. "They stopped backing me. Not enough results. But I can continue to use this station, which is Institute property. One day they'll sell it and we'll have to move."

"I was wondering why they sent you here in the first place," said Carlos. "Sirius has an adequate cometary belt."

"But Sol is the only system with any kind of civilization this far from its sun. And I can count on better men to work with. Sol system has always had its fair share of cosmologists."

"I thought you might have come to solve an old mystery. The Tunguska meteorite. You've heard of it, of course."

Forward laughed. "Of course. Who hasn't? I don't think we'll ever know just what it was that hit Siberia that night. It may have been a chunk of antimatter. I'm told that there is antimatter in Known Space."

"If it was, we'll never prove it," Carlos admitted.

"Shall we discuss your problem?" Forward seemed to remember my existence. "Shaeffer, what does a professional pilot think when his hyperdrive motor disappears?"

"He gets very upset."

"Any theories?"

I decided not to mention pirates. I wanted to see if Forward would mention them first. "Nobody seems to like my theory," I said, and I sketched out the argument for monsters in hyperspace.

Forward heard me out politely. Then, "I'll give you this, it'd be hard to disprove. Do you buy it?"

"I'm afraid to. I almost got myself killed once, looking for space monsters when I should have been looking for natural causes."

"Why would the hyperspace monsters eat only your motor?"

"Um . . . futz. I pass."

"What do you think, Carlos? Natural phenomena or space monsters?"

"Pirates," said Carlos.

"How are they going about it?"

"Well, this business of a hyperdrive motor disappearing and leaving the ship behind—that's brand new. I'd think it would take a sharp gravity gradient, with a tidal effect as strong as that of a neutron star or a black hole."

"You won't find anything like that anywhere in Human space."

"I know." Carlos looked frustrated. That had to be faked. Earlier he'd behaved as if he already had an answer.

Forward said, "I don't think a black hole would have that effect anyway. If it did you'd never know it, because the ship would disappear down the black hole."

"What about a powerful gravity generator?"

"Hmmm." Forward thought about it, then shook his massive head. "You're talking about a surface gravity in the millions. Any gravity generator I've ever heard of would collapse itself at that level. Let's see, with a frame supported by stasis fields . . . no. The frame would hold and the rest of the machinery would flow like water."

"You don't leave much of my theory."

"Sorry."

Carlos ended a short pause by asking, "How do you think the universe started?"

Forward looked puzzled at the change of subject.

And I began to get uneasy.

Given all that I don't know about cosmology, I do know attitudes and tones of voice. Carlos was giving out broad hints, trying to lead Forward to his own conclusion. Black holes, pirates, the Tunguska meteorite, the origin of the universe—he was offering them as clues. And Forward was not responding correctly.

He was saying, "Ask a priest. Me, I lean toward the Big Bang. The Steady State always seemed so futile."

"I like the Big Bang too," said Carlos.

There was something else to worry about. Those mining tugs: they almost had to belong to Forward Station. How would Ausfaller react when three familiar spacecraft came cruising into his space?

How did I want him to react? Forward Station would make a dandy pirate base. Permeated by laser-drilled corridors distributed almost at random . . . could there be two networks of corridors, connected only at the surface? How would we know?

Suddenly I didn't want to know. I wanted to go home. If only Carlos would stay off the touchy subjects—

But he was speculating about the ship eater again. "That ten billion metric tons of neutronium, now, that you were using for a test mass. That wouldn't be big enough or dense enough to give us enough of a gravity gradient."

"It might, right near the surface." Forward grinned and held his hands close together. "It was about that big."

"And that's as dense as matter gets in this universe. Too bad."

"True, but . . . have you ever heard of quantum black holes?"

"Yah."

Forward stood up briskly. "Wrong answer."

I rolled out of my web chair, trying to brace myself for a jump, while my fingers fumbled for the third button on my jumper. It was no good. I hadn't practiced in this gravity.

Forward was in mid-leap. He slapped Carlos alongside the head as he went past. He caught me at the peak of his jump, and took me with him via an iron grip on my wrist.

I had no leverage, but I kicked at him. He didn't even try to stop me. It was like fighting a mountain. He gathered my wrists in one hand and towed me away.

Forward was busy. He sat within the horseshoe of his control console, talking. The backs of three disembodied heads showed above the console's edge.

Evidently there was a laser phone in the console. I could hear parts of what Forward was saying. He was ordering the pilots of the three mining tugs to destroy *Hobo Kelly*. He didn't seem to know about Ausfaller yet.

Forward was busy, but Angel was studying us thoughtfully, or unhappily, or both. Well he might. We could disappear, but what messages might we have sent earlier?

I couldn't do anything constructive with Angel watching me. And I couldn't count on Carlos.

I couldn't see Carlos. Forward and Angel had tied us to opposite sides of the central pillar, beneath the Grabber. Carlos hadn't made a sound since then. He might be dying from that tremendous slap across the head.

I tested the line around my wrists. Metal mesh of some kind, cool to the touch . . . and it was tight.

Forward turned a switch. The heads vanished. It was a moment before he spoke.

"You've put me in a very bad position."

And Carlos answered. "I think you put yourself there."

"That may be. You should not have let me guess what you knew."

Carlos said, "Sorry, Bey."

He sounded healthy. Good. "That's all right," I said. "But what's all the excitement about? What has Forward *got*?"

"I think he's got the Tunguska meteorite."

"No. That I do not." Forward stood and faced us. "I will admit that I came here to search for the Tunguska meteorite. I spent several years trying to trace its trajectory after it left Earth. Perhaps it *was* a quantum black hole. Perhaps not. The Institute cut off my funds, without warning, just as I had found a real quantum black hole, the first in history.''

I said, ''That doesn't tell me a lot.''

''Patience, Mr. Shaeffer. You know that a black hole may form from the collapse of a massive star? Good. And you know that it takes a body of at least five solar masses. It may mass as much as a galaxy—or as much as the universe. There is some evidence that the universe is an infalling black hole. But at less than five solar masses the collapse would stop at the neutron star stage.''

''I follow you.''

''In all the history of the universe, there has been one moment at which smaller black holes might have formed. That moment was the explosion of the monoblock, the cosmic egg that once contained all the matter in the universe. In the ferocity of that explosion there must have been loci of unimaginable pressure. Black holes could have formed of mass down to two point two times ten to the minus fifth grams, one point six times ten to the minus twenty-fifth angstrom in radius.''

''Of course you'd never detect anything that small,'' said Carlos. He seemed almost cheerful. I wondered why . . . and then I knew. He'd been right about the way the ships were disappearing. It must compensate him for being tied to a pillar.

''But,'' said Forward, ''black holes of all sizes could have formed in that explosion, and should have. In more than seven hundred years of searching, no quantum black hole has ever been found. Most cosmologists have given up on them, and on the Big Bang too.''

Carlos said, ''Of course there was the Tunguska meteorite. It could have been a black hole of, oh, asteroidal mass—''

''—and roughly molecular size. But the tide would have pulled down trees as it went past—''

"—and the black hole would have gone right through the Earth and headed back into space a few tons heavier. Eight hundred years ago there was actually a search for the exit point. With that they could have charted a course—"

"Exactly. But I had to give up that approach," said Forward. "I was using a new method when the Institute, ah, severed our relationship."

They must both be mad, I thought. Carlos was tied to a pillar and Forward was about to kill him, yet they were both behaving like members of a very exclusive club . . . to which I did not belong.

Carlos was interested. "How'd you work it?"

"You know that it is possible for an asteroid to capture a quantum black hole? In its interior? For instance, at a mass of ten to the twelfth kilograms—a billion metric tons," he added for my benefit, "—a black hole would be only one point five times ten to the minus fifth angstroms across. Smaller than an atom. In a slow pass through an asteroid it might absorb a few billions of atoms, enough to slow it into an orbit. Thereafter it might orbit within the asteroid for eons, absorbing very little mass on each pass."

"So?"

"If I chance on an asteroid more massive than it ought to be . . . and if I contrive to move it, and some of the mass stays behind . . ."

"You'd have to search a lot of asteroids. Why do it out here? Why not the asteroid belt? Oh, of course, you can use hyperdrive out here."

"Exactly. We could search a score of masses in a day, using very little fuel."

"Hey. If it was big enough to eat a spacecraft, why didn't it eat the asteroid you found it in?"

"It wasn't that big," said Forward. "The black hole I found was exactly as I have described it. I enlarged it. I towed it home and ran it into my neutronium sphere. *Then* it was large enough to absorb an asteroid. Now it is quite a massive object. Ten to the twentieth power kilograms, the mass of one of the larger asteroids, and a radius of just under ten to the minus fifth centimeters.''

There was satisfaction in Forward's voice. In Carlos' there was suddenly nothing but contempt. ''You accomplished all that, and then you used it to rob ships and bury the evidence. Is that what's going to happen to us? Down the rabbit hole?''

''To another universe, perhaps. Where does a black hole lead?''

I wondered about that myself.

Angel had taken Forward's place at the control console. He had fastened the seat belt, something I had not seen Forward do, and was dividing his attention between the instruments and the conversation.

''I'm still wondering how you move it,'' said Carlos. Then, ''Uh! The tugs!''

Forward stared, then guffawed. ''You didn't guess that? But of course the black hole can hold a charge. I played the exhaust from an old ion drive reaction motor into it for nearly a month. Now it holds an enormous charge. The tugs can pull it well enough. I wish I had more of them. Soon I will.''

''Just a minute,'' I said. I'd grasped one crucial fact as it went past my head. ''The tugs aren't armed? All they do is pull the black hole?''

''That's right.'' Forward looked at me curiously.

''And the black hole is invisible.''

''Yes. We tug it into the path of a spacecraft. If the craft comes near enough it will precipitate into normal space. We guide the black hole through its drive to cripple it, board and rob it at our leisure. Then a slower pass with the quantum black hole, and the ship simply disappears.''

''Just one last question,'' said Carlos. ''Why?''

I had a better question.

Just what was Ausfaller going to do when three familiar

spacecraft came near? They carried no armaments at all. Their only weapon was invisible.

And it would eat a General Products hull without noticing.

Would Ausfaller fire on unarmed ships?

We'd know, too soon. Up there near the edge of the dome, I had spotted three tiny lights in a tight cluster.

Angel had seen it too. He activated the phone. Phantom heads appeared, one, two, three.

I turned back to Forward, and was startled at the brooding hate in his expression.

"Fortune's child," he said to Carlos. "Natural aristocrat. Certified superman. Why would *you* ever consider stealing anything? Women beg you to give them children, in person if possible, by mail if not! Earth's resources exist to keep you healthy, not that you need them!"

"This may startle you," said Carlos, "but there are people who see *you* as a superman."

"We bred for strength, we Jinxians. At what cost to other factors? Our lives are short, even with the aid of boosterspice. Longer if we can live outside Jinx's gravity. But the people of other worlds think we're funny. The women . . . never mind." He brooded, then said it anyway. "A woman of Earth once told me she would rather go to bed with a tunneling machine. She didn't trust my strength. What woman would?"

The three bright dots had nearly reached the center of the dome. I saw nothing between them. I hadn't expected to. Angel was still talking to the pilots.

Up from the edge of the dome came something I didn't want anyone to notice. I said, "Is that your excuse for mass murder, Forward? Lack of women?"

"I need give you no excuses at all, Shaeffer. My world will thank me for what I've done. Earth has swallowed the lion's share of the interstellar trade for too long."

"They'll thank you, huh? You're going to tell them?"

"I—"

"Julian!" That was Angel calling. He'd seen it . . . no, he hadn't. One of the tug captains had.

Forward left us abruptly. He consulted with Angel in low tones, then turned back. "Carlos! Did you leave your ship on automatic? Or is there someone else aboard?"

"I'm not required to say," said Carlos.

"I could—no. In a minute it will not matter."

Angel said, "Julian, look what he's doing."

"Yes. Very clever. Only a human pilot would think of that."

Ausfaller had maneuvered the *Hobo Kelly* between us and the tugs. If the tugs fired a conventional weapon, they'd blast the dome and kill us all.

The tugs came on.

"He still does not know what he is fighting," Forward said with some satisfaction.

True, and it would cost him. Three unarmed tugs were coming down Ausfaller's throat, carrying a weapon so slow that the tugs could throw it at him, let it absorb *Hobo Kelly*, and pick it up again long before it was a danger to us.

From my viewpoint *Hobo Kelly* was a bright point with three dimmer, more distant points around it. Forward and Angel were getting a better view, through the phone. And they weren't watching us at all.

I began trying to kick off my shoes. They were soft ship-slippers, ankle-high, and they resisted.

I kicked the left foot free just as one of the tugs flared with ruby light.

"He did it!" Carlos didn't know whether to be jubilant or horrified. "He fired on unarmed ships!"

Forward gestured peremptorily. Angel slid out of his seat. Forward slid in and fastened the thick seat belt. Neither had spoken a word.

A second ship burned fiercely red, then expanded in a pink cloud.

The third ship was fleeing.

Forward worked the controls. "I have it in the mass indicator," he rasped. "We have but one chance."

So did I. I peeled the other slipper off with my toes. Over our heads the jointed arm of the Grabber began to swing . . . and I suddenly realized what they were talking about.

Now there was little to see beyond the dome. The swinging Grabber, and the light of *Hobo Kelly*'s drive, and the two tumbling wrecks, all against a background of fixed stars. Suddenly one of the tugs winked blue-white and was gone. Not even a dust cloud was left behind.

Ausfaller must have seen it. He was turning, fleeing. Then it was as if an invisible hand had picked up *Hobo Kelly* and thrown her away. The fusion light streaked off to one side, and set beyond the dome's edge.

With two tugs destroyed and the third fleeing, the black hole was falling free, aimed straight down our throats.

Now there was nothing to see but the delicate motions of the Grabber. Angel stood behind Forward's chair, his knuckles white with his grip on the chair's back.

My few pounds of weight went away and left me in free fall. Tides again. The invisible thing was more massive than this asteroid beneath me. The Grabber swung a meter more to one side . . . and something struck it a mighty blow.

The floor surged away from beneath me, left me head down above the Grabber. The huge soft-iron puppy dish came at me; the jointed metal arm collapsed like a spring. It slowed, stopped.

"You got it!" Angel crowed like a rooster and slapped at the back of the chair, holding himself down with his other hand. He turned a gloating look on us, turned back just as suddenly. "The ship! It's getting away!"

"No." Forward was bent over the console. "I see him. Good, he is coming back, straight toward us. This time there will be no tugs to warn the pilot."

The Grabber swung ponderously toward the point where I'd seen *Hobo Kelly* disappear. It moved centimeters at a time, pulling a massive invisible weight.

And Ausfaller was coming back to rescue us. He'd be a sitting duck, unless—

I reached up with my toes, groping for the first and fourth buttons on my falling jumper.

The weaponry in my wonderful suit hadn't helped me against Jinxian strength and speed. But flatlanders are less than limber, and so are Jinxians. Forward had tied my hands and left it at that.

I wrapped two sets of toes around the buttons and tugged.

My legs were bent pretzel-fashion. I had no leverage. But the first button tore loose, and then the thread. Another invisible weapon to battle Forward's portable bottomless hole.

The thread pulled the fourth button loose. I brought my feet down to where they belonged, keeping the thread taut, and pushed backward. I felt the Sinclair molecule chain sinking into the pillar.

The Grabber was still swinging.

When the thread was through the pillar I could bring it up in back of me and try to cut my bonds. More likely I'd cut my wrists and bleed to death; but I had to try. I wondered if I could do anything before Forward launched the black hole.

A cold breeze caressed my feet.

I looked down. Thick fog boiled out around the pillar.

Some very cold gas must be spraying through the hair-fine crack.

I kept pushing. More fog formed. The cold was numbing. I felt the jerk as the magic thread cut through. Now the wrists—

Liquid helium?

Forward had moored us to the main superconducting power cable.

That was probably a mistake. I pulled my feet forward, carefully, steadily, feeling the thread bite through on the return cut.

The Grabber had stopped swinging. Now it moved on its arm like a blind, questing worm, as Forward made fine adjustments. Angel was beginning to show the strain of holding himself upside down.

My feet jerked slightly. I was through. My feet were terribly cold, almost without sensation. I let the buttons go, left them floating up toward the dome, and kicked back hard with my heels.

Something shifted. I kicked again.

Thunder and lightning flared around my feet.

I jerked my knees up to my chin. The lightning crackled and flashed white light into the billowing fog. Angel and Forward turned in astonishment. I laughed at them, letting them see it. Yes, gentlemen, I did it on purpose.

The lightning stopped. In the sudden silence Forward was screaming, "—know what you've *done?*"

There was a grinding *crunch*, a shuddering against my back. I looked up.

A piece had been bitten out of the Grabber.

I was upside down and getting heavier. Angel suddenly pivoted around his grip on Forward's chair. He hung above the dome, above the sky. He screamed.

My legs gripped the pillar hard. I felt Carlos' feet fumbling for a foothold, and heard Carlos' laughter.

Near the edge of the dome a spear of light was rising. *Hobo Kelly*'s drive, decelerating, growing larger. Otherwise the sky was clear and empty. And a piece of the dome disappeared with a snapping sound.

Angel screamed and dropped. Just above the dome he seemed to flare with blue light.

He was gone.

Air roared out through the dome—and more was disappearing into something that had been invisible. Now it showed as a blue pinpoint drifting toward the floor. Forward had turned to watch it fall.

Loose objects fell across the chamber, looped around the pinpoint at meteor speed or fell into it with bursts of light. Every atom of my body felt the pull of the thing, the urge to die in an infinite fall. Now we hung side by side from a horizontal pillar. I noted with approval that Carlos' mouth was wide open, like mine, to clear his lungs so that they wouldn't burst when the air was gone.

Daggers in my ears and sinuses, pressure in my gut.

Forward turned back to the controls. He moved one knob hard over. Then—he opened the seat belt and stepped out and up, and fell.

Light flared. He was gone.

The lightning-colored pinpoint drifted to the floor, and into it. Above the increasing roar of air I could hear the grumbling of rock being pulverized, dwindling as the black hole settled toward the center of the asteroid.

The air was deadly thin, but not gone. My lungs thought they were gasping vacuum. But my blood was not boiling. I'd have known it.

So I gasped, and kept gasping. It was all I had attention for. Black spots flickered before my eyes, but I was still gasping and alive when Ausfaller reached us carrying a clear plastic package and an enormous handgun.

He came in fast, on a rocket backpack. Even as he decelerated he was looking around for something to shoot. He returned in a loop of fire. He studied us through his faceplate, possibly wondering if we were dead.

He flipped the plastic package open. It was a thin sack with a zipper and a small tank attached. He had to dig for a torch to cut our bonds. He freed Carlos first, helped him into the sack. Carlos bled from the nose and ears. He was barely mobile. So was I, but Ausfaller got me into the sack with Carlos and zipped it up. Air hissed in around us.

I wondered what came next. As an inflated sphere the rescue bag was too big for the tunnels. Ausfaller had thought of that. He fired at the dome, blasted a gaping hole in it, and flew us out on the rocket backpack.

Hobo Kelly was grounded nearby. I saw that the rescue bag wouldn't fit the airlock either . . . and Ausfaller confirmed my worst fear. He signaled us by opening his mouth wide. Then he zipped open the rescue bag and half-carried us into the airlock while the air was still roaring out of our lungs.

When there was air again Carlos whispered, "Please don't do that anymore."

"It should not be necessary any more." Ausfaller smiled. "Whatever it was you did, well done. I have two well-equipped autodocs to repair you. While you are healing, I will see about recovering the treasures within the asteroid."

Carlos held up a hand, but no sound came. He looked like something risen from the dead: blood running from nose and ears, mouth wide open, one feeble hand raised against gravity.

"One thing," Ausfaller said briskly. "I saw many dead men; I saw no living ones. How many were there? Am I likely to meet opposition while searching?"

"Forget it," Carlos croaked. "Get us out of here. Now."

Ausfaller frowned. "What—"

"No time. Get us out."

Ausfaller tasted something sour. "Very well. First, the autodocs." He turned, but Carlos' strengthless hand stopped him.

"Futz, no. I want to see this," Carlos whispered.

Again Ausfaller gave in. He trotted off to the control room. Carlos tottered after him. I tottered after them both, wiping blood from my nose, feeling half dead myself. But I'd half guessed what Carlos expected, and I didn't want to miss it.

We strapped down. Ausfaller fired the main thruster. The rock surged away.

"Far enough," Carlos whispered presently. "Turn us around."

Ausfaller took care of that. Then, "What are we looking for?"

"You'll know."

"Carlos, was I right to fire on the tugs?"

"Oh, yes."

"Good. I was worried. Then Forward was the ship eater?"

"Yah."

"I did not see him when I came for you. Where is he?"

Ausfaller was annoyed when Carlos laughed, and more annoyed when I joined him. It hurt my throat. "Even so, he saved our lives," I said. "He must have turned up the air pressure just before he jumped. I wonder why he did that?"

"Wanted to be remembered," said Carlos. "Nobody else knew what he'd done. *Ahh*—"

I looked, just as part of the asteroid collapsed into itself, leaving a deep crater.

"It moves slower at apogee. Picks up more matter," said Carlos.

"What *are* you talking about?"

"Later, Sigmund. When my throat grows back."

"Forward had a hole in his pocket," I said helpfully. "He—"

The other side of the asteroid collapsed. For a moment lightning seemed to flare in there.

Then the whole dirty snowball was growing smaller.

I thought of something Carlos had probably missed. "Sigmund, has this ship got automatic sunscreens?"

"Of *course* we've got—"

There was a universe-eating flash of light before the

screen went black. When the screen cleared there was nothing to see but stars.

I went with Jerry Pournelle when he interviewed Robert Forward for *Twin Circles* magazine. Forward talked our ears off on a variety of subjects. From that alone I should have recognized a budding hard science fiction writer.

He showed us his mass detector (see it in "The Hole Man"). He sketched a Newtonian antigravity system. He described Stephen Hawking's "quantum black holes". . .

On the way home I told Jerry I'd beat him into print with those. Neither of us writes very fast . . . but I had written "The Hole Man" and "The Borderland of Sol" before Hawking reconsidered his theories and put a lower limit on the size of the QBHs.

"Borderland" began as a story treatment for a *Star Trek* animation. Dorothy Fontana was right: I was aiming over the audience's heads. We turned "The Soft Weapon" into an animation, "The Slaver Weapon," instead.

A postscript: Robert Forward, Jr., took it that I had humbled and then killed *his* linear descendant. He took vengeance by hand-drawing a comic book in colored pencils, in which Larry Niven's lineal descendant . . . no, I can't bear to talk about it.

From *THE RINGWORLD ENGINEERS*

I never intended to write a sequel to RINGWORLD. Readers were constantly telling me that there had to be a sequel, but I didn't have to listen. What happened?

Design changes, that's what.

From everywhere in the civilized world came suggestions . . . until my own mind began working again. A spillpipe system was needed to redistribute the topsoil piling up in the oceans, and attitude jets and a reason why they hadn't been seen, and a score of new hominid species, each with its own attitude toward *rishathra* (interspecies sex). And the Shadow Farm. And the Maps on the Great Ocean.

So I've expanded the playground and redesigned the equipment, but it won't happen again. The letters and suggestions and quibbles never arrived. This time I must have got it right.

I remember the artist Eddie Jones telling me how difficult it is to paint the Ringworld. I didn't believe him until I saw one of his failed attempts. Getting all of it into view is nearly impossible. A few pages of text can't show you the Ringworld either.

It was all suddenly too much for Louis Wu. He reached for the droud, and the kzin pounced. Chmeee turned the black plastic case in a black-and-orange hand.

"As you like," Louis said. He flopped on his back. He was short of sleep anyway . . .

"How did you come to be a wirehead? How?"

"I," said Louis, and "What you've got to understand," and "Remember the last time we met?"

"Yes. Few humans have been invited to Kzin itself. You deserved the honor, then."

"Maybe. Maybe I did. Do you remember showing me the House of the Patriarch's Past?"

"I do. You tried to tell me that we could improve interspecies relationships. All we need do was let a team of human reporters go through the museum with holo cameras."

Louis smiled, remembering. "So I did."

"I had my doubts."

The House of the Patriarch's Past had been both grand and grandiose: a huge, sprawling building formed from thick slabs of volcanic rock fused at the edges. It was all angles, and there were laser cannon mounted in four tall towers. The rooms went on and on. It had taken Chmeee and Louis two days to go through it.

The Patriarch's official past went a long way back. Louis had seen ancient sthondat thighbones with grips worked into them, clubs used by primitive kzinti. He'd seen weapons that could have been classed as hand cannons; few humans could have lifted them. He'd seen silver-plated armor as thick as a safe door, and a two-handed ax that might have chopped down a mature redwood. He'd been talking about letting a human reporter tour the place when they came upon Harvey Mossbauer.

Harvey Mossbauer's family had been killed and eaten during the Fourth Man–Kzin War. Many years after the truce and after a good deal of monomaniacal preparation, Mossbauer had landed alone and armed on Kzin. He had killed four kzinti males and set off a bomb in the harem of the Patriarch before the guards managed to kill him. They were hampered, Chmeee had explained, by their wish to get his hide intact.

"You call that intact?"

"But he fought. How he fought! There are tapes. We know how to honor a brave and powerful enemy, Louis."

The stuffed skin was so scarred that you had to look twice to tell its species; but it was on a tall pedestal with a hullmetal plaque, and there was nothing around it but floor. Your average human reporter might have misunderstood, but Louis got the point. "I wonder if I can make you understand," he said, twenty years later, a wirehead kidnapped and robbed of his droud, "how good it felt, then, to know that Harvey Mossbauer was human."

"It is good to reminisce, but we were talking of current addiction," Chmeee reminded him.

"Happy people don't become current addicts. You have to actually go and get the plug implanted. I felt good that day. I felt like a hero. Do you know where Halrloprillalar was at that time?"

"Where was she?"

"The government had her. The ARM. They had lots of questions, and there wasn't a tanj thing I could do about it. She was under my protection. I took her back to Earth with me—"

"She had you by the glands, Louis. It's good that kzinti females aren't sentient. You would have done anything she asked. She asked to see human space."

"Sure, with me as native guide. It just didn't happen. Chmeee, we took the *Long Shot* and Halrloprillalar home, and we turned them over to a Kzin and Earth coalition, and that's the last we've seen of either one. We couldn't even talk about it to anyone."

"The second quantum hyperdrive motor became a Patriarch's Secret."

"It's Top Secret to the United Nations, too. I don't think they even told the other governments of human space, and they made it tanj clear *I'd* better not talk. And of course the Ringworld was part of the secret, because how could we have *got* there without the *Long Shot*? Which makes me wonder,"

Louis said, ''how the Hindmost expects to *reach* the Ringworld. Two hundred light-years from Earth—more, from Canyon— at three days to the light-year if he uses this ship. Do you think he's got another *Long Shot* hovering somewhere?''

''You will not distract me. Why did you have a wire implanted?'' Chmeee crouched, claws extended. Maybe it was a reflex, beyond conscious control—maybe.

''I left Kzin and went home,'' Louis said. ''I couldn't get the ARM to let me see Prill. If I could have got a Ringworld expedition together, she would have had to go as native guide, but, tanj! I couldn't even *talk* about it except to the government . . . and you. You weren't interested.''

''How could I leave? I had land and a name and children coming. Kzinti females are very dependent. They need care and attention.''

''What's happening to them now?''

''My eldest son will administer my holdings. If I leave him too long he will fight me to keep them. If—*Louis! Why did you become a wirehead?*''

''*Some clown hit me with a tasp!*''

''Urrr?''

''I was wandering through a museum in Rio when somebody made my day from behind a pillar.''

''But Nessus took a tasp to the Ringworld, to control his crew. He used it on both of us.''

''Right. How very like a Pierson's puppeteer, to do us good by way of controlling us! The Hindmost is using the same approach now. Look, he's got my droud under remote control, and he's given you eternal youth, and what's the result? We'll do anything he tells us to, that's what.''

''Nessus used the tasp on me, but I am not a wirehead.''

''I didn't turn wirehead either, then. But I remembered. I was feeling like a louse, thinking about Prill—thinking about taking a sabbatical. I used to do that, take off alone in a ship and head for the edge of Known Space until I could stand people again. Until I could stand myself again. But it would have been running out on Prill. Then some clown made my day. He didn't give me much of a jolt, but it reminded me of that tasp Nessus carried, and that was *ten times* as powerful. I . . . held off for almost a year, and then I went and got a plug put in my head."

"I should rip that wire out of your brain."

"There turn out to be undesirable side effects."

Kzin, twenty years ago:

Louis Wu sprawled on a worn stone *fooch* and thought well of himself.

These oddly shaped stone couches called *foochesth* were as ubiquitous as park benches throughout the hunting parks of Kzin. They were almost kidney-shaped, built for a male kzin to lie half curled up. The kzinti hunting parks were half wild and stocked with both predators and meat animals: orange-and-yellow jungle, with the *foochesth* as the only touch of civilization. With a population in the hundreds of millions, the planet was crowded by kzinti standards. The parks were crowded too.

Louis had been touring the jungle since morning. He was tired. Legs dangling, he watched the populace pass before him.

Within the jungle the orange kzinti were almost invisible. One moment, nothing. The next, a quarter-ton of sentient carnivore hot on the trail of something fast and frightened. The male kzin would jerk to a stop and stare—at Louis's closed-lip smile (because a kzin shows his teeth in challenge) and at the sign of the Patriarch's protection on his shoulder (Louis had made sure it showed prominently). The kzin would decide it was none of his business, and leave.

Strange, how that much predator could show only as a sense of presence in the frilly yellow foliage. Watching eyes and playful murder, somewhere. Then a huge adult male and a furry, cuddly adolescent half his height were watching the intruder.

Louis had a tyro's grasp of the Hero's Tongue. He understood when the kzin kitten looked up at its parent and asked, "Is it good to eat?"

The adult's eyes met Louis's eyes. Louis let his smile widen to show the teeth.

The adult said, "No."

In the confidence of four Man–Kzin wars plus some "incidents"—all centuries in the past, but all won by men—Louis grinned and nodded. *You tell him, Daddy! It's safer to eat white arsenic than human meat!*

Chaosium Inc. expanded the playground, making Known Space into the Ringworld role-playing game. In the process they resolved some inconsistencies and nailed down some dates. They've stopped publishing the game, but I've got my copy. It's wonderful source material.

I've given you their sections on the Spill Mountain Folk and the Night People: two species I wanted to see and show more of. The Spill Mountains and their inhabitants are intrinsically interesting, but the Night People own the Ringworld, as nearly as any species does. They'd be the perfect choice as protectors, because every species' welfare is their own.

SPILL MOUNTAIN FOLK

The Spill Mountain Folk live at extremely high elevations on the slopes of inactive Spill Mountains. These isolated peaks rise some 55 kilometers [35 miles] high, and are regularly spaced along both rim walls at intervals of about 40,000 km [25,000 miles]. The Spill Mountains play an essential role in recycling the topsoil for Ringworld's eco-systems. About two-thirds of these mountains function at greatly-reduced efficiency, or not at all—and these provide permanent habitats for hominids. The Spill Mountain Folk are adapted to life between the coldest white levels above and the towering "foothills" below, where the air becomes too dense and too warm for the Folk to breathe.

Spill Mountain Folk are well-insulated, baboon-like hom-inids; these often-chubby sentients bear a slight resemblance to the lion-maned Abyssinian gelada, Ethiopia's high sim-ian. The Folk's truncated muzzles protrude only mildly, though, and they lack tails. Their noticeably enlarged canine teeth are not visible when the mouth is closed. Spill Moun-tain Folk are heavy-bodied with powerful limbs, standing on the average not far below two meters. They are covered entirely with thick, soft, golden-brown fur, and the forequar-ters of most older adults are cloaked in mane-like mantles of long hair. The males often have a single dark stripe 15 centimeters wide running up their backs and tapering to a point at the top of the forehead. The people of the Spill Mountains have extremely efficient, oversized lungs. At altitudes below five kilometers [or about three miles], they begin to experience hyperoxygenation and breathing dis-comfort—at the normal atmospheric pressure of the Ring floor, they are unable to live. These hominids did not evolve naturally: their strange physiology and metabolism derive from City Builder genetic-engineering programs, millennia ago.

Spill Mountain Folk are highly intelligent and educable, but since the Fall of Cities their isolated environment has severely restricted their activities. Long ago they worked with the City Builders to construct and operate the Rim Transport System. They later maintained the elevator tubes climbing up the rim walls, and the rim stations. Before the walls closed forever, Spill Mountain Folk were among those who loaded and serviced the great ramships. Comfortably adapted to nearly airless realms, many became seasoned spacers. Biologically, though, they were overspecialized, and they were technologically overdependent on the City Builders. They once flew between their Spill Mountain habitats on magnetic-repulsion skysleds, but for centuries now they have had to rely almost exclusively on balloons for transportation. Only a few skysleds with slow-charge solar power-packs still operate, and these are always heavily guarded and closely watched. It is known that Spill Mountain Folk worked in large numbers in the repair crews seen remounting Ringworld's attitude-jet toroids. Some such crews were also said to be engaged in unblocking spill-pipes. For the most part, however, the people of the Spill Mountains have reverted to a technologically primitive existence. Oral traditions alone keep alive among them legends of the ancient star-travelers, and of the secrets of the interiors of the Spill Mountains. Many enclaves might be expected to resist the efforts of repair crews or of anyone else whose activities could re-awaken their slumbering mountain, rendering it uninhabitable.

Natural resources are limited in the domains of the Spill Mountain Folk, so the hoarding of treasure or the unnatural accumulation of material goods is seldom looked upon with favor. Their spirit is one of cooperation, not competition for wealth. They trade among themselves and play games not so much for personal gain as for variety and novelty. Although they're omnivorous, their usual diet is simple. They love sweet-roots, fruit, spice nuts, sausage-plant, eggs, insects, dried fish, nectar, birds, and even larger creatures—which some enjoy catching and tearing apart by hand. Unfortunately, such delicacies can be obtained only by laborious descent to the foothills. In some areas, they use tethered-balloon trams, the baskets of which are sent down loaded with pure, clean ice-blocks and figurines. In exchange, the baskets are filled up with food by hominids living far below—Hanging People, Ghouls, Wind Walkers, and rarely, even City Builders. Most of the time Spill Mountain Folk meals consist mainly of a coarse, thick soup called *brahl*, which they refine from partially-processed flup in the Spill Mountain ice-floes. Brahl is organically nutritious but tasteless, an utterly monotonous staple.

Spill Mountain Folk seek diversity and innovation in family relations. They traditionally change mates every few falans, and sometimes share them without possessiveness. Long-term breeding partners are generally chosen for the variety of their experiences and imaginative skills, not because they represent security, dominance, status, or wealth. Spill Mountain Folk are adept at rishathra, but get few opportunities to practice (they thoroughly enjoyed their golden era of co-enterprise with the ancient City Builder civilization). Their dead are launched festively into the air on balloon rafts filled with figurines, ice sculptures, and ceremonial brahl bowls. Spill Mountain Folk use reflected-light signals to maintain regular contact with the Ghouls in some areas. Most know of the Healers only through grossly misrepresentative City Builder myths from before the Fall of Cities.

A Spill Mountain Folk City

The vertical habitats of the Spill Mountain Folk are carved into the great gray rocks and blocks of permafrost and dormant Spill Mountain ice floes. From a distance, an ice-rock city exhibits dozens of huge, shadowed shelves with fine threads draped between them. Close inspection reveals myriads of individual entry porticoes, window ledges, sculpted balconies and awnings—hundreds of suspended bridges strung up and down and sideways between them. Narrow, twisting stairways are also hacked into the rock and ice, running for kilometers in strange branching curves, like two-dimensional vertical mazes. A single, guarded stairway usually leads all the way down into the high foothills, to the timberline. Tethered-balloon trams sometimes parallel these solitary paths of descent through the swirling fog at the base of the Spill Mountains.

Spill Mountain Folk do not relish isolation. Their cities usually have populations of 10,000 or more. The center of each city has a large public square carved into it, though a fortuitous flat rock surface often serves the purpose. These gathering places typically are crowded with hordes of Spill Mountain dwellers. The staccato squeals, grunts, barks, chatterings, and shriller howlings of their native language quickly die, however, in the thin air. Elaborate posturing and a complex system of hand signals supplements their verbal communication, or substitutes for it. Many decorate their pelts with imaginative designs and mystical symbols. The public squares are sites of pageantry, balloon launchings, solar heated dye baths, game pavillions, trading markets, and communal spiritual centers.

There is generally a large statue in the shape of a hairy, fat, jovial baboon sculptured out of some great boulder at the back of the square, or onto the sheer rock face above. The image often represents some version of the god figure christened "Babrius" by Louis Wu. In a favorite myth, Babrius rose beyond the Rim on a great skysled, passing above the stars. He came to rest at last on a vast, fabulously varied plateau ideally suited to the tastes of Spill Mountain Folk. He hastened to return to lead his people to freedom in the marvelous new land. Abandoning his depleted skysled, he entered a large, clearly-marked elevator tube— but the bubble would not descend. Instead it went up, through a confused realm of chaotic beauty. When Babrius came to his senses, he found himself a disembodied speck of immortal consciousness, peering out through the eyes of an early ancestor. All around, wherever he turned, Babrius saw himself in the eyes of others, staring back, grinning. Variety and sameness form a central duality in the philosophy and culture of the Spill Mountain Folk—they are always on the lookout for high adventure.

Each Spill Mountain is unique, because of its extreme altitude and isolation. Each has its own ecology. The cultural sketch given in the foregoing is most likely to fit Spill Mountain Folk living on the starboard rim wall within 40° of the Great Oval Ocean. Elsewhere around the Ring, they may be quite different—and of the folk living on the port rim wall Spill Mountains, nothing is known.

GHOULS (NIGHT PEOPLE)

The Ghouls (or Night People) are widespread on Ringworld. Their place in the ecology is everywhere secure. These sentient, nocturnal hominids are scavengers and morticians, carrion-eaters and bearers of information. They have mastered the domain of night—and few species care to compete for their dark realm.

From a distance the Ghouls seem horrid, supernatural blendings of human and jackal. In small, quiet packs they approach native camps on all fours to claim the day's refuse and garbage. Hunched and half-erect, they move away at fair speeds, often carrying substantial burdens. In more civilized environments they walk about perfectly upright, on wide, flat feet, without fear, to bear away the bodies of the dead. Whenever, in rare instances, hominid cultures do begin burying or cremating their dead, hordes of Ghouls attack the living to convince them of the error of their ways. Despite occasional tension, though, peace, toleration, and a certain mutual respect usually prevail. The Night People are generally diffident and unassuming in their relations with other species; they normally show no hunger for dominance and they seldom intrude. Indeed, they are scrupulous and thorough in their understanding of and compliance with the customs and religious practices of thousands of local cultures. Ghouls seem to have a fatalistic acceptance of their place in the scheme of things, feeling that "the activities of other species rarely interfere with our own lives, and in the end they all belong to us!" Funeral traditions of the Night People themselves are not known.

Ghouls are least frequently encountered in aquatic environments, wastelands, or in other regions far from concentrations of land-dwelling hominids. They detest the habitats of Vampires.

The Night People are small, seldom even approaching the 2-meter mark. They usually have permanent mates, and frequently travel in pairs or in family groups. Their bodies are almost entirely covered with thick iron-gray or black hair. Their skin is a cooked-liver blend of dark-purple and charcoal. They smell very bad, and the foul stench of corruption gives them the breath of a basilisk. The nails of their tapered fingers and gnarled toes are as sharp and as tough as claws.

Ghouls have wide mouths displaying a daunting expanse of sharp, wedge-shaped teeth designed for ripping. Their big, pointed goblin-ears come erect and alert as they listen intently or show apprehension. Ghoul hearing is quite sensitive; they gather information more by eavesdropping than by asking questions. Their night vision is excellent. Their eyes, not overly large, appear quite human and have chocolate-brown pupils. A single thick eyebrow traces an "M" across the brow. The nose is flattened, knobbly, and not exceptionally broad. The Night People have straight, shiny, dark hair on their heads which most keep trimmed and combed.

Male and female Ghouls alike usually wear a big purse or pouch on a shoulder-strap, and (except in cold climates) nothing else. Their repulsive look and odor offends the sensibilities of most Ringworld natives. Though Ghouls do rishathra, few hominids ever suggest it. Low-born City Builders are an exception: in some areas traditions demand their society's debt to the Ghouls be paid in periodic rishathra.

Second Role of the Ghouls

The Night People are intelligent, clever, and curious. As a species, they have accumulated a great deal of information. They, in fact, deal in information, though they find myths, opinions and detailed observations frequently as useful as substantiated truth. So long as the dead are ultimately left unburied, they do not antagonize other species, and they do not use their pool of knowledge to manipulate or to exploit them. They respect the technologies and life-styles of all, and rarely attempt to intervene in the affairs of other species. They watch and listen. Their gift for oral history is superlative, and only the most advanced civilizations realize the true extent of Ghoul knowledge and interest. From time to time the Night People do not understand the implications of the incidents they witness. Nevertheless, the visual impressions, legends, undocumented rumors, and superstitions they report often prove to be as valuable as actual political events or scientific facts. It is hardly surprising that City Builders, Machine People, and other progressive societies have a degree of acceptance and respect for the Ghouls going far beyond uneasy tolerance. They work together, and Night People are sometimes permitted access to their libraries. Their value in "helping to hold together what is left of civilization" is recognized and appreciated.

The Ghouls have shown little overt interest in changing their traditional mode of existence, perhaps acquiring advanced-engineering skills, or procuring sophisticated technology. There is some evidence, though, that they do collect and accumulate curious objects, tools, valuable items, his-

torical relics, books, and intriguing weapons in hidden
caches. If they have a language of their own, no one knows
it (except perhaps the Healers). They commonly use the
City Builder tongue, or the local dialect in dealing with
other species.

News usually travels slowly on Ringworld between wide-
ly-separated locations. The Ghouls, however, have developed a system of signaling over very large distances using
flashes of light reflected into darkened lands from remote
mirrors. They occasionally transmit information to the people of the Spill Mountains, and receive replies—but for the
most part their network of communication remains a great
mystery. The central bases and native lands (if any) of the
Night People may be very far apart on the Ring, and outsiders are rarely permitted even to learn of their existence.

Though they make no claim to rule, the Ghouls are in a
sense the invisible masters of Ringworld. More than most
sentient hominids, they have gained a hard-won, humbling
awareness of the Ring's true dimensions and of the self-
centered provincialism of most of its inhabitants. There may
in fact be many species of Ghouls, but there must be many
more species who lack any contact with Night People.
Ghouls, comfortably well-adapted to their present nocturnal
way of life, are on the whole wise enough to appreciate its
limitations. Probably there are no Ghouls in deserts,
swamps, on mountain ranges, in barren icy realms, or on
the Island Maps in the Great Oceans.

One of the Protectors who assisted Teela Brown in re-
pairing the attitude jets was a female of the Night People.
Alone among them, she survived to supervise the defense
or the evacuation of breeders in lands imperiled by radiation.
The Night People Protector may yet remain a force to be
reckoned with on Ringworld.

It was taking too long, much longer than he had expected. Sharls Davis Kendy had not been an impatient man. After the change he had thought himself immune to impatience. But it was taking too long! What were they *doing* in there?

THE INTEGRAL TREES, 1983

WHAT GOOD IS A GLASS DAGGER?

THE WARLOCK'S ERA

Robert Howard and his tradition do speak to some part of the brain . . . but not the rational part. What kind of magician can't defend himself against a sword-swinging barbarian? The inept kind, that's what. Think of it as evolution in action.

Why did Conan keep finding magic as a shocking surprise in desert places? If magic had such power, it would be the basis of civilization!

Where did all the magic go? The older the legend, the more powerful was the magic. Magic must wear out, like oil reserves.

And that's all I was trying to say when I wrote a short story, "Not Long Before the End." But my mind kept chewing at it. Yesterday's civilizations must

have been scrambling to find something to replace
the depleted magic. Merpeople would run the fishing industry; when they went mythical, men would
have to learn how to fish. Cities would have werewolf sections . . .

I

Twelve thousand years before the birth of Christ, in an age
when miracles were somewhat more common, a Warlock
used an ancient secret to save his life.

In later years he regretted that. He had kept the secret
of the Warlock's Wheel for several normal lifetimes. The
demon-sword Glirendree and its stupid barbarian captive
would have killed him, no question of that. But no mere
demon could have been as dangerous as that secret.

Now it was out, spreading like ripples on a pond. The
battle between Glirendree and the Warlock was too good a
tale not to tell. Soon no man would call himself a magician
who did not know that magic could be used up. So simple,
so dangerous a secret. The wonder was that nobody had
noticed it before.

A year after the battle with Glirendree, near the end of a
summer day, Aran the Peacemonger came to Shayl Village
to steal the Warlock's Wheel.

Aran was a skinny eighteen-year-old, lightly built. His
face was lean and long, with a pointed chin. His dark eyes
peered out from under a prominent shelf of bone. His short,
straight dark hair dropped almost to his brows in a pronounced widow's peak. What he was was no secret; and
anyone who touched hands with him would have known at

once, for there was short fine hair on his palms. But had anyone known his mission, he would have been thought mad.

For the Warlock was a leader in the Sorcerer's Guild. It was known that he had a name, but no human throat could pronounce it. The shadow demon who had been his name-father had later been imprisoned in tattooed runes on the Warlock's own back: an uncommonly dangerous body-guard.

Yet Aran came well protected. The leather wallet that hung from his shoulder was old and scarred, and the seams were loose. By its look it held nuts and hard cheese and bread and almost no money. What it actually held was charms. Magic would serve him better than nuts and cheese, and Aran could feed himself as he traveled, at night.

He reached the Warlock's cave shortly after sunset. He had been told how to use his magic to circumvent the War-lock's safeguards. His need for magic implied a need for voice and hands, so that Aran was forced to keep the human shape; and this made him doubly nervous. At moonrise he chanted the words he had been taught and drew a live bat from his pouch and tossed it gently through the barred en-trance to the cave.

The bat exploded into a mist of blood that drifted slant-wise across the stone floor. Aran's stomach lurched. He almost ran then, but he quelled his fear and followed it in, squeezing between the bars.

Those who had sent him had repeatedly diagramed the cave for him. He could have robbed it blindfold. He would have preferred darkness to the flickering blue light from what seemed to be a captured lightning bolt tethered in the middle of the cavern. He moved quickly, scrupulously tracing what he had been told was a path of safety.

Though Aran had seen sorcerous tools in the training laboratory in the School for Mercantile Grammaree in Atlan-tis, most of the Warlock's tools were unfamiliar. It was not an age of mass production. He paused by a workbench, wondering. Why would the Warlock be grinding a glass dagger?

But Aran found a tarnish-blackened metal disc hanging above the workbench, and the runes inscribed around its rim convinced him that it was what he had come for. He took it down and quickly strapped it against his thigh, leaving his hands free to fight if need be. He was turning to go, when a laughing voice spoke out of the air.

"Put that down, you mangy son of a bitch—"

Aran converted to wolf.

Agony seared his thigh!

In human form Aran was a lightly built boy. As a wolf he was formidably large and dangerous. It did him little good this time. The pain was blinding, stupefying. Aran the wolf screamed and tried to run from the pain.

He woke gradually with an ache in his head and a greater agony in his thigh and a tightness at his wrists and ankles. It came to him that he must have knocked himself out against a wall.

He lay on his side with his eyes closed, giving no sign that he was awake. Gently he tried to pull his hands apart. He was bound, wrists and ankles. Well, he had been taught a word for unbinding ropes.

Best not to use it until he knew more.

He opened his eyes a slit.

The Warlock was beside him, seated in lotus position, studying Aran with a slight smile. In one hand he held a slender willow rod.

The Warlock was a tall man in robust good health. He was deeply tanned. Legend said that the Warlock never wore anything above the waist. The years seemed to blur on him; he might have been twenty or fifty. In fact he was one hundred and ninety years old, and bragged of it. His condition indicated the power of his magic.

Behind him, Aran saw that the Warlock's Wheel had been returned to its place on the wall.

Waiting for its next victim? The real Warlock's Wheel was of copper; those who had sent Aran had known that much. But this decoy must be tarnished silver, to have seared him so.

The Warlock wore a dreamy, absent look. There might still be a chance, if he could be taken by surprise. Aran said, "Kplir—"

The Warlock lashed him across the throat.

The willow wand had plenty of spring in it. Aran choked and gagged; he tossed his head, fighting for air.

"That word has four syllables," the Warlock informed him in a voice he recognized. "You'll never get it out."

"Gluck," said Aran.

"I want to know who sent you."

Aran did not answer, though he had his wind back.

"You're no ordinary thief. But you're no magician, either," the Warlock said almost musingly. "I heard you. You were chanting by rote. You used basic spells, spells that are easy to get right, but they were the right spells each time.

"Somebody's been using prescience and farsight to spy on me. Someone knows too many of my defenses," the ancient magician said gently. "I don't like that. I want to know who, and why."

When Aran did not reply, the Warlock said, "He had all the knowledge, and he knew what he was after, but he had better sense than to come himself. He sent a fool." The Warlock was watching Aran's eyes. "Or perhaps he thought a werewolf would have a better chance at me. By the way, there's silver braid in those cords; so you'd best stay human for the nonce."

"You knew I was coming."

"Oh, I had ample warning. Didn't it occur to you that

I've got prescience and farsight too? It occurred to your master," said the Warlock. "He set up protections around you, a moving region where prescience doesn't work."

"Then what went wrong?"

"I foresaw the dead region, you ninny. I couldn't get a glimpse of what was stealing into my cave. But I could look around it. I could follow its path through the cavern. That path was most direct. I knew what you were after.

"Then, there were bare footprints left behind. I could study them before they were made. You waited for moonrise instead of trying to get in after dusk. On a night of the full moon, too.

"Other than that, it wasn't a bad try. Sending a werewolf was bright. It would take a kid your size to squeeze between the bars, and then a kid your size couldn't win a fight if something went wrong. A wolf your size could."

"A lot of good it did me."

"What I want to know is, how did they talk an Atlantean into this? They must have known what they were after. Didn't they tell you what the Wheel does?"

"Sucks up magic," said Aran. He was chagrined, but not surprised, that the Warlock had placed his accent.

"Sucks up *mana*," the Warlock corrected him. "Do you know what *mana* is?"

"The power behind magic."

"So they taught you that much. Did they also tell you that when the *mana* is gone from a region, it doesn't come back? Ever?"

Aran rolled on his side. Being convinced that he was about to die, he felt he had nothing to lose by speaking boldly. "I don't understand why you'd want to keep it a secret. A thing like the Warlock's Wheel, it could make war obsolete! It's the greatest purely defensive weapon ever invented!"

The Warlock didn't seem to understand. Aran said, "You

must have thought of that. Why, no enemy's curses could touch Atlantis, if the Warlock's Wheel were there to absorb it!''

"Obviously you weren't sent by the Atlantean Minister of Offense. He'd know better." The Warlock watched him shrewdly. "Or were you sent by the Greek Isles?"

"I don't understand."

"Don't you know that Atlantis is tectonically unstable? For the last half a thousand years, the only thing that's kept Atlantis above the waves has been the spells of the sorcerer-kings."

"You're lying."

"You obviously aren't." The Warlock made a gesture of dismissal. "But the Wheel would be bad for any nation, not just Atlantis. Spin the Wheel, and a wide area is dead to magic for—as far as I've been able to tell—the rest of eternity. Who would want to bring about such a thing?"

"I would."

"You would. Why?"

"We're sick of war," Aran said roughly. Unaware that he had said *we*. "The Warlock's Wheel would end war. Can you imagine an army trying to fight with nothing but swords and daggers? No hurling of death spells. No pre-scients spying out the enemy's battle plans. No killer demons beating at unseen protective walls." Aran's eyes glowed. "Man to man, sword against sword, blood and bronze, and no healing spells. Why, no king would ever fight on such terms! We'd give up war forever!"

"Some basic pessimism deep within me forces me to doubt it."

"You're laughing at me. You don't *want* to believe it," Aran said scornfully. "No more *mana* means the end of your youth spells. You'd be an old man, too old to live!"

"That must be it. Well, let's see who you are." The Warlock touched Aran's wallet with the willow wand, let it rest there a few moments. Aran wondered frantically what the Warlock could learn from his wallet. If the lockspells didn't hold, then—

They didn't, of course. The Warlock reached in, pulled out another live bat, then several sheets of parchment marked with what might have been geometry lessons and with script printed in a large, precise hand.

"Schoolboy script," he commented. "Lines drawn with painful accuracy, mistakes scraped out and redrawn . . . The idiot! He forgot the hooked tail on the Whirlpool design. A wonder it didn't eat him." The Warlock looked up. "Am I being attacked by children? These spells were prepared by half a dozen apprentices!"

Aran didn't answer, but he lost hope of concealing anything further.

"They have talent, though. So. You're a member of the Peacemongers, aren't you? All army-age youngsters. I'll wager you're backed by half the graduating class of the School of Mercantile Grammaree. They must have been watching me for months now, to have my defenses down so pat.

"And you want to end the war against the Greek Isles. Did you think you'd help matters by taking the Warlock's Wheel to Atlantis? Why, I'm half minded to let you walk out with the thing. It would serve you right for trying to rob me."

He looked hard into Aran's eyes. "Why, you'd do it, wouldn't you? Why? I said *why*?"

"We could still use it."

"You'd sink Atlantis. Are the Peacemongers traitors now?"

"I'm no traitor." Aran spoke low and furious. "We want to change Atlantis, not destroy it. But if we owned the Warlock's Wheel, the Palace would listen to us!"

He wriggled in his tight bonds, and thought once again

of the word that would free him. Then, convert to werewolf and run! Between the bars, down the hill, into the woods and freedom.

"I think I'll make a conservative of you," the Warlock said suddenly.

He stood up. He brushed the willow wand lightly across Aran's lips. Aran found that he could not open his mouth. He remembered now that he was entirely in the Warlock's power—and that he was a captured thief.

The Warlock turned, and Aran saw the design on his back. It was an elaborately curlicued five-sided tattoo in red and green and gold inks. Aran remembered what he had been told of the Warlock's bodyguard.

"Recently I dreamed," said the Warlock. "I dreamed that I would find a use for a glass dagger. I thought that the dream might be prophetic, and so I carved—"

"That's silly," Aran broke in. "What good is a glass dagger?"

He had noticed the dagger on the way in. It had a honed square point and honed edges and a fused-looking hilt with a guard. Two clamps padded with fox leather held it in place on the worktable. The uppermost edge was not yet finished.

Now the Warlock removed the dagger from its clamps. While Aran watched, the Warlock scratched designs on the blade with a pointed chunk of diamond that must have cost him dearly. He spoke low and softly to it, words that Aran couldn't hear. Then he picked it up like—a dagger.

Frightened as he was, Aran could not quite believe what the Warlock was doing. He felt like a sacrificial goat. There was *mana* in sacrifice . . . and more *mana* in human sacrifice . . . but he wouldn't. He wouldn't!

The Warlock raised the knife high, and brought it down hard in Aran's chest.

Aran screamed. He had felt it! A whisper of sensation, a slight ghostly tug—the knife was an insubstantial shadow.

But there was a knife in Aran the Peacemonger's heart! The hilt stood up out of his chest!

The Warlock muttered low and fast. The glass hilt faded and was gone, apparently.

"It's easy to make glass invisible. Glass is half invisible already. It's still in your heart," said the Warlock. "But don't worry about it. Don't give it a thought. Nobody will notice. Only, be sure to spend the rest of your life in mana-rich territory. Because if you ever walk into a place where magic doesn't work—well, it'll reappear, that's all."

Aran struggled to open his mouth.

"Now, you came for the secret of the Warlock's Wheel; so you might as well have it. It's just a simple kinetic sorcery, but open-ended." He gave it. "The Wheel spins faster and faster until it's used up all the mana in the area. It tends to tear itself apart; so you need another spell to hold it together—" and he gave that, speaking slowly and distinctly. Then he seemed to notice that Aran was flopping about like a fish. He said, "Kplirapranthry."

The ropes fell away. Aran stood up shakily. He found he could speak again, and what he said was, "Take it out. Please."

"Now, there's one thing about taking that secret back to Atlantis. I assume you still want to? But you'd have to describe it before you could use it as a threat. You can see how easy it is to make. A big nation like Atlantis tends to have enemies, doesn't it? And you'd be telling them how to sink Atlantis in a single night."

Aran pawed at his chest, but he could feel nothing. "Take it out."

"I don't think so. Now we face the same death, wolf-boy. Good-bye, and give my best to the School for Mercantile Grammaree. And, oh yes, don't go back by way of Hvirin Gap."

"Grandson of an ape!" Aran screamed. He would not beg again. He was wolf by the time he reached the bars, and he did not touch them going through. With his mind he felt the knife in his chest, and he heard the Warlock's laughter following him down the hill and into the trees.

When next he saw the Warlock, it was thirty years later and a thousand miles away.

II

Aran traveled as a wolf, when he could. It was an age of greater magic; a werewolf could change shape whenever the moon was in the sky. In the wolf-shape Aran could forage, reserving his remaining coins to buy his way home.

His thoughts were a running curse against the Warlock.

Once he turned about on a small hill, and stood facing north toward Shayl Village. He bristled, remembering the Warlock's laugh; but he remembered the glass dagger. He visualized the Warlock's throat, and imagined the taste of an enemy's arterial blood; but the glowing, twisting design on the Warlock's back flashed at the back of Aran's eyes, and Aran tasted defeat. He could not fight a shadow demon. Aran howled, once, and turned south.

Nildiss Range, the backbone of a continent, rose before him as he traveled. Beyond the Range was the sea, and a choice of boats to take him home with what he had learned of the Warlock. Perhaps the next thief would have better luck . . .

And so he came to Hvirin Gap.

Once the Range had been a formidable barrier to trade. Then, almost a thousand years ago, a sorcerer of Rynildissen had worked an impressive magic. The Range had been split as if by a cleaver. Where the mountains to either side sloped precipitously upward, Hvirin Gap sloped smoothly down to the coast, between rock walls flat enough to have a polished look.

Periodically the bandits had to be cleaned out of Hvirin

Gap. This was more difficult every year, for the spells against banditry didn't work well there, and swords had to be used instead. The only compensation was that the dangerous mountain dragons had disappeared too.

Aran stopped at the opening. He sat on his haunches, considering.

For the Warlock might have been lying. He might have thought it funny to send Aran the long way over Nildiss Range.

But the dragon bones. Where magic didn't work, dragons died. The bones were there, huge and reptilian. They had fused with the rock of the pass somehow, so that they looked tens of millions of years old.

Aran had traveled to the Gap in wolf form. If Hvirin Gap was dead to magic, he should have been forced into the man form. Or would he find it impossible to change at all?

"But I can go through as a wolf," Aran thought. "That way I can't be killed by anything but silver and platinum. The glass dagger should hurt, but—

"Damn! I'm invulnerable, but is it *magic?* If it doesn't work in Hvirin Gap—" and he shuddered.

The dagger had never been more than a whisper of sensation that had faded in half an hour and never returned. But Aran knew it was there. Invisible, a knife in his heart, waiting.

It might reappear in his chest, and he could still survive— as a wolf. But it would hurt! And he could never be human again.

Aran turned and padded away from Hvirin Gap. He had passed a village yesterday. Perhaps the resident magician could help him.

"A glass dagger!" the magician chortled. He was a portly, jolly, balding man, clearly used to good living. "Now I've heard everything. Well, what were you worried about? It's got a handle, doesn't it? Was it a complex spell?"

"I don't think so. He wrote runes on the blade, then stabbed me with it."

"Fine. You pay in advance. And you'd better convert to wolf, just to play safe." He named a sum that would have left Aran without money for passage home. Aran managed to argue him down to something not far above reason, and they went to work.

The magician gave up some six hours later. His voice was hoarse, his eyes were red from oddly colored, oddly scented smokes, and his hands were discolored with dyes. "I can't touch the hilt, I can't make it visible, I can't get any sign that it's there at all. If I use any stronger spell, it's likely to kill you. I quit, wolf-boy. Whoever put this spell on you, he knows more than a simple village magician."

Aran rubbed at his chest where the skin was stained by mildly corrosive dyes. "They call him the Warlock."

The portly magician stiffened. "The Warlock? *The* Warlock? And you didn't think to tell me. Get out."

"What about my money?"

"I wouldn't have tried it for ten times the fee! Me, a mere hedge-magician, and you turned me loose against the Warlock! We might both have been killed. If you think you're entitled to your money, let's go to the headman and state our case. Otherwise, get out."

Aran left, shouting insults.

"Try other magicians if you like," the other shouted after him. "Try Rynildissen City! But tell them what they're doing first!"

III

It had been a difficult decision for the Warlock. But his secret was out and spreading. The best he could do was see to it that world sorcery understood the implications.

The Warlock addressed the Sorcerers' Guild on the subject of *mana* depletion and the Warlock's Wheel.

"Think of it every time you work magic," he thundered in what amounted to baby talk after his severely technical description of the Wheel. "Only finite *mana* in the world, and less of it every year, as a thousand magicians drain it away. There were beings who ruled the world as gods, long ago, until the raging power of their own being used up the *mana* that kept them alive.

"One day it'll all be gone. Then all the demons and dragons and unicorns, trolls and rocs and centaurs will vanish quite away, because their metabolism is partly based on magic. Then all the dream castles will evaporate, and nobody will ever know they were there. Then all the magicians will become tinkers and smiths, and the world will be a dull place to live. You have the power to bring that day nearer!"

That night he dreamed.

A duel between magicians makes a fascinating tale. Such tales are common—and rarely true. The winner of such a duel is not likely to give up trade secrets. The loser is dead, at the very least.

Novices in sorcery are constantly amazed at how much preparation goes into a duel, and how little action. The duel with the Hill Magician started with a dream, the night after the Warlock's speech made that duel inevitable. It ended thirty years later.

In that dream the enemy did not appear. But the Warlock saw a cheerful, harmless-looking fairy castle perched on an impossible hill. From a fertile, hummocky landscape, the hill rose like a breaking wave, leaning so far that the castle at its crest had empty space below it.

In his sleep the Warlock frowned. Such a hill would topple without magic. The fool who built it was wasting *mana*.

And in his sleep he concentrated, memorizing details. A

narrow path curled up the hillside. Facts twisted, dreamlike. There was a companion with him, or there wasn't. The Warlock lived until he passed through the gate; or he died at the gate, in agony, with great ivory teeth grinding together through his rib cage.

He woke himself up trying to sort it out.

The shadowy companion was necessary, at least as far as the gate. Beyond the enemy's gate he could see nothing. A Warlock's Wheel must have been used there, to block his magic so thoroughly.

Poetic justice?

He spent three full days working spells to block the Hill Magician's prescient sense. During that time his own sleep was dreamless. The other's magic was as effective as his own.

IV

Great ships floated at anchor in the harbor.

There were cargo ships whose strange demonic figure-heads had limited power of movement, just enough to reach the rats that tried to swarm up the mooring lines. A large Atlantean passenger liner was equipped with twin outriggers made from whole tree trunks. By the nearest dock a magician's slender yacht floated eerily above the water. Aran watched them wistfully.

He had spent too much money traveling over the mountains. A week after his arrival in Rynildissen City he had taken a post as bodyguard-watchdog to a rug merchant. He had been down to his last coin, and hungry.

Now Lloraginezee the rug merchant and Ra-Harroo his secretary talked trade secrets with the captain of a Nile cargo ship. Aran waited on the dock, watching ships with indifferent patience.

His ears came to point. The bearded man walking past him wore a captain's kilt. Aran hailed him: "Ho, Captain! Are you sailing to Atlantis?"

The bearded man frowned. "And what's that to you?"

"I would send a message there."

"Deal with a magician."

"I'd rather not," said Aran. He could hardly tell a magician that he wanted to send instructions on how to rob a magician. Otherwise the message would have gone months ago.

"I'll charge you more, and it will take longer," the bearded man said with some satisfaction. "Who is Atlantis, and where?"

Aran gave him an address in the city. He passed over the sealed message pouch he had been carrying for three months now.

Aran too had made some difficult decisions. In final draft his message warned of the tectonic instability of the continent and suggested steps the Peacemongers could take to learn if the Warlock had lied. Aran had not included instructions for making a Warlock's Wheel.

Far out in the harbor, dolphins and mermen played rough and complicated games. The Atlantean craft hoisted sail. A wind rose from nowhere to fill the sails. It died slowly, following the passenger craft out to sea.

Soon enough, Aran would have the fare. He would almost have it now, except that he had twice paid out sorcerer's fees, with the result that the money was gone and the glass dagger was not. Meanwhile, Lloraginezee did not give trade secrets to his bodyguard. He knew that Aran would be on his way as soon as he had the money.

Here they came down the gangplank: Lloraginezee with less waddle than might be expected of a man of his girth; the girl walking with quiet grace, balancing the rug samples on her head. Ra-Harroo was saying something as Aran joined them, something Aran may have been intended to hear.

"Beginning tomorrow, I'll be off work for five days. *You* know," she told Lloraginezee—and blushed.

"Fine, fine," said Lloraginezee, nodding absently.

Aran knew too. He smiled but did not look at her. He might embarrass her . . . and he knew well enough what Ra-Harroo looked like. Her hair was black and short and coarse. Her nose was large but flat, almost merging into her face. Her eyes were brown and soft, her brows dark and thick. Her ears were delicately formed and convoluted, and came to a point. She was a lovely girl, especially to another of the wolf people.

They held hands as they walked. Her nails were narrow and strong, and the fine hair on her palm tickled.

In Atlantis he would have considered marrying her, had he the money to support her. Here, it was out of the question. For most of the month they were friends and co-workers. The night life of Rynildissen City was more convenient for a couple, and there were times when Lloraginezee could spare them both.

Perhaps Lloraginezee made such occasions. He was not of the wolf people. He probably enjoyed thinking that sex had reared its lovely, disturbing head. But sex could not be involved—except at a certain time of the month. Aran didn't see her then. She was locked up in her father's house. He didn't even know where she lived.

He found out five nights later.

He had guarded Lloraginezee's way to Adrienne's House of Pleasures. Lloraginezee would spend the night . . . on an air mattress floating on mercury, a bed Aran had only heard described. A pleasant sleep was not the least of pleasures.

The night was warm and balmy. Aran took a long way

home, walking wide of the vacant lot behind Adrienne's. That broad, flat plot of ground had housed the palace of Shilbree the Dreamer, three hundred years ago. The palace had been all magic, and quite an achievement even in its day. Eventually it had . . . worn out, Shilbree would have said.

One day it was gone. And not even the simplest of spells would work in that vacant lot.

Someone had told Aran that households of wolf people occupied several blocks of the residential district. It seemed to be true, for he caught identifying smells as he crossed certain paths. He followed one, curious to see what kind of house a wealthy werewolf would build in Rynildissen.

The elusive scent led him past a high, angular house with a brass door . . . and then it was too late, for another scent was in his nostrils and in his blood and brain. He spent that whole night howling at the door. Nobody tried to stop him. The neighbors must have been used to it; or they may have known that he would kill rather than be driven away.

More than once he heard a yearning voice answering from high up in the house. It was Ra-Harroo's voice. With what remained of his mind, Aran knew that he would be finding apologies in a few days. She would think he had come deliberately

Aran howled a song of sadness and deprivation and shame.

V

The first was a small village called Gath, and a Guild 'prentice who came seeking black opals. He found them, and free for the taking too, for Gath was dead empty. The 'prentice sorcerer wondered about that, and he looked about him, and presently he found a dead spot with a crumbled castle in it. It might have been centuries fallen. Or it might have been raised by magic and collapsed when the *mana* went out of it, yesterday or last week.

It was a queer tale, and it got around. The 'prentice grew rich on the opals, for black opals are very useful for cursing. But the empty village bothered him.

"I thought it was slavers at first," he said once, in the Warlock's hearing as it turned out. "There were no corpses, not anywhere. Slave traders don't kill if they can help it.

"But why would a troop of slavers leave valuables lying where they were? The opals were all over the street, mixed with hay. I think a jeweler must have been moving them in secret when—*something* smashed his wagon. But why didn't they pick up the jewels?"

It was the crumbled castle that the Warlock remembered three years later, when he heard about Shiskabil. He heard of that one directly, from a magpie that fluttered out of the sky onto his shoulder and whispered, "Warlock?"

And when he had heard, he went.

Shiskabil was a village of stone houses within a stone wall. It must have been abandoned suddenly. Dinners had dried or rotted on their plates; meat had been burnt to ash in ovens. There were no living inhabitants, and no dead. The wall had not been breached. But there were signs of violence everywhere: broken furniture, doors with broken locks or splintered hinges, crusted spears and swords and makeshift clubs, and blood. Dried black blood everywhere, as if it had rained blood.

Clubfoot was a younger Guild member, thin and earnest. Though talented, he was still a little afraid of the power he commanded through magic. He was not happy in Shiskabil. He walked with shoulders hunched, trying to avoid the places where blood had pooled.

"Weird, isn't it? But I had a special reason to send for you," he said. "There's a dead region outside the wall. I had the idea someone might have used a Warlock's Wheel there."

A rectangular plot of fertile ground, utterly dead, a foretaste of a world dead to magic. In the center were crumbled stones with green plants growing between.

The Warlock circled the place, unwilling to step where magic did not work. He had used the Wheel once before, against Glirendree, after the demon-sword had killed his shadow demon. The Wheel had sucked the youth from him, left the Warlock two hundred years old in a few seconds.

"There was magic worked in the village," said Clubfoot. "I tried a few simple spells. The *mana* level's very low. I don't remember any famous sorcerers from Shiskabil; do you?"

"No."

"Then whatever happened here was done by magic." Clubfoot almost whispered the word. Magic could be very evil—as he knew.

They found a zigzag path through the dead borderline and a faintly live region inside. At a gesture from the Warlock, the crumbled stones stirred feebly, trying to rise.

"So it was somebody's castle," said Clubfoot. "I wonder how he got this effect?"

"I thought of something like it once. Say you put a heavy kinetic spell on a smaller Wheel. The Wheel would spin very fast, would use up *mana* in a very tight area—"

Clubfoot was nodding. "I see it. He could have run in on a track, a closed path. It would give him a kind of hedge against magic around a live region."

"And he left the border open so he could get his tools in and out. He zigzagged the entrance so no spells could get through. Nobody could use farsight on him. I wonder . . ."

"I wonder what he had to hide?"

"I wonder what happened in Shiskabil," said the Warlock. And he remembered the dead barrier that hid the Hill Magician's castle. His leisurely duel with a faceless enemy was twelve years old.

* * *

It was twenty-three years old before they found the third village.

Hathzoril was bigger than Shiskabil, and better known. When a shipment of carvings in ivory and gem woods did not arrive, the Warlock heard of it.

The village could not have been abandoned more than a few days when the Warlock arrived. He and Clubfoot found meals half cooked, meals half eaten, broken furniture, weapons that had been taken from their racks, broken doors—

"But no blood. Why?"

Clubfoot was jittery. "Otherwise it's just the same. The whole population gone in an instant, probably against their will. Ten whole years; no, more. I'd half forgotten . . . You got here before I did. Did you find a dead area and a crumbled castle?"

"No. I looked."

The younger magician rubbed his birth-maimed foot—which he could have cured in half an hour, but it would have robbed him of half his powers. "We could be wrong. If it's him, he's changed his techniques."

That night the Warlock dreamed a scrambled dream in pyrotechnic colors. He woke thinking of the Hill Magician.

"Let's climb some hills," he told Clubfoot in the morning. "I've got to know if the Hill Magician has something to do with these empty villages. We're looking for a dead spot on top of a hill."

That mistake almost killed him.

The last hill Clubfoot tried to climb was tumbled, crumbled soil and rock that slid and rolled under his feet. He tried it near sunset, in sheer desperation, for they had run out of hills and patience.

He was still near the base when the Warlock came clambering to join him. "Come down from there!" he laughed. "Nobody would build on this sand heap."

Clubfoot looked around, and shouted, "Get out of here! You're older!"

The Warlock rubbed his face and felt the wrinkles. He picked his way back in haste and in care, wanting to hurry, but fearful of breaking fragile bones. He left a trail of fallen silver hair.

Once beyond the *mana*-poor region, he cackled in falsetto. "My mistake. I know what he did now. Clubfoot, we'll find the dead spot inside the hill."

"First we'll work you a rejuvenation spell." Clubfoot laid his tools out on a rock. A charcoal block, a silver knife, packets of leaves . . .

"That border's bad. It sucks up *mana* from inside. He must have to move pretty often. So he raised up a hill like a breaking wave. When the magic ran out, the hill just rolled over the castle and covered up everything. He'll do it again, too."

"Clever. What do you think happened in Hathzoril Village?"

"We may never know." The Warlock rubbed new wrinkles at the corners of his eyes. "Something bad, I think. Something very bad."

VI

He was strolling through the merchants' quarter that afternoon, looking at rugs.

Normally this was a cheerful task. Hanging rugs formed a brightly colored maze through this part of the quarter. As Aran the rug merchant moved through the maze, well-known voices would call his name. Then there would be gossip and canny trading.

He had traded in Rynildissen City for nearly thirty years, first as Lloraginezee's apprentice, later as his own man. The finest rugs and the cheapest, from all over this continent and nearby islands, came by ship and camel's back to Rynildissen City. Wholesalers, retailers, and the odd nobleman who wished to furnish a palace would travel to Rynildissen City to buy. Today they glowed in the hot sunlight . . . but today they only depressed him. Aran was thinking of moving away.

A bald man stepped into view from behind a block of cured sphinx pelts.

Bald as a roc's egg he was, yet young, and in the prime of muscular good health. He was shirtless as a stevedore, but his pantaloons were of high quality, and his walk was pure arrogance. Aran felt he was staring rather rudely. Yet there was something familiar about the man.

He passed Aran without a glance.

Aran glanced back once, and was jolted. The design seemed to leap out at him: a five-sided multicolored tattoo on the man's back.

Aran called, "Warlock!"

He regretted it the next moment. The Warlock turned on him the look one gives a presumptuous stranger.

The Warlock had not changed at all, except for the loss of his hair. But Aran remembered that thirty years had passed; that he himself was a man of fifty, with the hollows of his face filled out by rich living. He remembered that his graying hair had receded, leaving his widow's peak as a shock of hair all alone on his forehead. And he remembered, in great detail, the circumstances under which he had met the Warlock.

He had spent a thousand nights plotting vengeance against the Warlock; yet now his only thought was to get away. He said, "Your pardon, sir—"

But something else occurred to him, so that he said firmly, "But we *have* met."

"Under what circumstance? I do not recall it," the Warlock said coldly.

Aran's answer was a measure of the self-confidence that comes with wealth and respect. He said, "I was robbing your cave."

"Were you!" The Warlock came closer. "Ah, the boy from Atlantis. Have you robbed any magicians lately?"

"I have adopted a somewhat safer way of life," Aran said equably. "And I do have reason for presuming on our brief acquaintance."

"Our brief—" The Warlock laughed so that heads turned all over the marketplace. Still laughing, he took Aran's arm and led him away.

They strolled slowly through the merchants' quarter, the Warlock leading. "I have to follow a certain path," he explained. "A project of my own. Well, my boy, what have you been doing for thirty years?"

"Trying to get rid of your glass dagger."

"Glass dagger? . . . Oh, yes, I remember. Surely you found time for other hobbies?"

Aran almost struck the Warlock then. But there was something he wanted from the Warlock, and so he held his temper.

"My whole life has been warped by your damned glass dagger," he said. "I had to circle Hvirin Gap on my way home. When I finally got here, I was out of money. No money for passage to Atlantis, and no money to pay for a magician, which meant that I couldn't get the glass knife removed.

"So I hired out to Lloraginezee the rug merchant as a bodyguard-watchdog. Now I'm the leading rug merchant in Rynildissen City; I've got two wives and eight children and a few grandchildren, and I don't suppose I'll ever get back to Atlantis."

They bought wine from a peddler carrying two fat wineskins on his shoulders. They took turns drinking from the great copper goblet the man carried.

The Warlock asked, "Did you ever get rid of the knife?"

"No, and you ought to know it! What kind of a spell did you *put* on that thing? The best magicians in this continent haven't been able to so much as *touch* that knife, let alone pull it out. I wouldn't be a rug merchant if they had."

"Why not?"

"Well, I'd have earned my passage to Atlantis soon enough, except that every time I heard about a new magician in the vicinity I'd go to him to see if he could take that knife out. Selling rugs was a way to get the money to pay the magicians. Eventually I gave up on the magicians and kept the money. All I'd accomplished was to spread your reputation in all directions."

"Thank you," the Warlock said politely.

Aran did not like the Warlock's amusement. He decided to end the conversation quickly. "I'm glad we ran into each other," he said, "because I have a problem that is really in your province. Can you tell me something about a magician named Wavyhill?"

It may be that the Warlock stiffened. "What is it that you want to know?"

"Whether his spells use excessive power."

The Warlock lifted an interrogatory eyebrow.

"You see, we try to restrict the use of magic in Rynildissen City. The whole nation could suffer if a key region like Rynildissen City went dead to magic. There'd be no way to stop a flood, or a hurricane, or an invasion of barbarians. Do you find something amusing?"

"No, no. But could a glass dagger possibly have anything to do with your conservative attitude?"

"That's entirely my own business, Warlock. Unless you'd care to read my mind?"

"No, thank you. My apologies."

"I'd like to point out that more than just the welfare of Rynildissen City is involved. If this region went dead to magic, the harbor mermen would have to move away. They have quite an extensive city of their own, down there beyond the docks. Furthermore, they run most of the docking facilities and the *entire* fishing industry—''

"Relax. I agree with you completely. You know that," the magician laughed. "You ought to!"

"Sorry. I preach at the drop of a hat. It's been ten years since anyone saw a dragon near Rynildissen City. Even further out, they're warped, changed. When I first came here, the dragons had a mercenary's booth in the city itself! What are you doing?"

The Warlock had handed the empty goblet back to the vendor and was pulling at Aran's arm. "Come this way, please. Quickly, before I lose the path."

"Path?"

"I'm following a fogged prescient vision. I could get killed if I lose the path—or if I don't, for that matter. Now, just what was your problem?"

"That," said Aran, pointing among the fruit stalls.

The troll was an ape's head on a human body, covered from head to toe in coarse brown hair. From its size it was probably female, but it had no more breasts than a female ape. It held a wicker basket in one quite human hand. Its bright brown eyes glanced up at Aran's pointing finger—startlingly human eyes—then dropped to the melon it was considering.

Perhaps the sight should have roused reverence. A troll was ancestral to humanity: *Homo habilis*, long extinct. But they were too common. Millions of the species had been fossilized in the drylands of Africa. Magicians of a few centuries ago had learned that they could be reconstituted by magic.

"I think you've just solved one of my own problems," the Warlock said quietly. He no longer showed any trace of amusement.

"Wonderful," Aran said without sincerity. "My own problem is, how much *mana* are Wavyhill's trolls using up? The *mana* level in Rynildissen City was never high to start with. Wavyhill must be using terrifically powerful spells just to keep them walking.'' Aran's fingertips brushed his chest in an unconscious gesture. ''I'd hate to leave Rynildissen City, but if magic stops working here, I won't have any choice.''

''I'd have to know the spells involved. Tell me something about Wavyhill, will you? Everything you can remember.''

To most of Rynildissen City the advent of Wavyhill the magician was very welcome.

Once upon a time troll servants had been common. They were terrifically strong. Suffering no pain, they could use hysterical strength for the most mundane tasks. Being inhuman, they could work on official holidays. They needed no sleep. They did not steal.

But Rynildissen City was old, and the *mana* was running low. For many years no troll had walked in Rynildissen City. At the gate they turned to blowing dust.

Then came Wavyhill with a seemingly endless supply of trolls, which did *not* disintegrate at the gate. The people paid him high prices in gold and in honors.

''For half a century thieves have worked freely on holidays,'' Aran told the Warlock. ''Now we've got a trollish police force again. Can you blame people for being grateful? They made him a Councilman—over my objections. Which means that there's very little short of murder that Wavyhill can't do in Rynildissen City.''

''I'm sorry to hear that. Why did you say *over your objections?* Are you on the Council?''

''Yes. I'm the one who rammed through the laws restricting magic in Rynildissen City. And failed to ram through some others, I might add. The trouble is that Wavyhill doesn't make the trolls in the city. Nobody knows where they come from. If he's depleting the *mana* level, he's doing it somewhere else.''

"Then what's your problem?"

"Suppose the trolls use up *mana* just by existing? . . . I should be asking, *Do they?*"

"I think so," said the Warlock.

"I *knew* it. Warlock, will you testify before the Council? Because—"

"No, I won't."

"But you've got to! I'll never convince anyone by myself. Wavyhill is the most respected magician around, and he'll be testifying against me! Besides which, the Council all own trolls themselves. They won't want to believe they've been suckered, and they have been if we're right. The trolls will collapse as soon as they've lowered the *mana* level enough."

At that point Aran ran down, for he had seen with what stony patience the Warlock was waiting for him to finish.

The Warlock waited three seconds longer, using silence as an exclamation point. Then he said, "It's gone beyond that. Talking to the Council would be like shouting obscenities at a forest fire. I could get results that way. You couldn't."

"Is he *that* dangerous?"

"I think so."

Aran wondered if he was being had. But the Warlock's face was so grave . . . and Aran had seen that face in too many nightmares. *What am I doing here?* he wondered. *I had a technical question about trolls. So I asked a magician . . . and now . . .*

"Keep talking. I need to know more about Wavyhill. And walk faster," said the Warlock. "How long has he been here?"

"Wavyhill came to Rynildissen City seven years ago. Nobody knows where he came from; he doesn't have any particular accent. His palace sits on a hill that looks like it's about to fall over. What are you nodding at?"

"I know the hill. Keep talking."

"We don't see him often. He comes with a troupe of trolls, to sell them; or he comes to vote with the Council on important matters. He's short and dark—"

"That could be a seeming. Never mind, describe him anyway. I've never seen him."

"Short and dark, with a pointed nose and a pointed chin and very curly dark hair. He wears a dark robe of some soft material, a tall pointed hat, and sandals, and he carries a sword."

"Does he!" The Warlock laughed out loud.

"What's the joke? I carry a sword myself sometimes— Oh, that's right, magicians have a *thing* about swordsmen."

"That's not why I laughed. It's a trade joke. A sword can be a symbol of masculine virility."

"Oh?"

"You see the point, don't you? A sorcerer doesn't need a sword. He knows more powerful protections. When a sorcerer takes to carrying a sword, it's pretty plain he's using it as a cure for impotence."

"And it works?"

"Of course it works. It's straight one-for-one similarity magic, isn't it? But you've got to take the sword to bed with you!" laughed the Warlock. But his eyes found a troll servant, and his laughter slipped oddly.

He watched as the troll hurried through a gate in a high white wall. They had passed out of the merchants' quarter.

"I think Wavyhill's a necromancer," he said abruptly.

"Necromancer. What is it? It sounds ugly."

"A technical term for a new branch of magic. And it is ugly. Turn sharp left here."

They ducked into a narrow alley. Two-and three-story houses leaned over them from both sides. The floor of the alley was filthy, until the Warlock snarled and gestured. Then the dirt and garbage flowed to both sides.

The Warlock hurried them deep into the alley. "We can

stop here, I think. Sit down if you like. We'll be here for some time—or I will."

"Warlock, are you playing games with me? What does this new dance have to do with a duel of sorcery?"

"A fair question. Do you know what lies that way?"

Aran's sense of direction was good, and he knew the city. "The Judging Place?"

"Right. And that way, the vacant lot just this side of Adrienne's House of Pleasures—you know it? The deadest spot in Rynildissen City. The palace of Shilbree the Dreamer once stood there."

"*Might* I ask—"

"The courthouse is void of *mana* too, naturally. Ten thousand defendants and thirty thousand lawyers all praying for conviction or acquittal doesn't leave much magic in *any* courthouse. If I can keep either of those spots between me and Wavyhill, I can keep him from using farsight on me."

Aran thought about it. "But you have to know where he is."

"No. I only have to know where I ought to be. Most of the time, I don't. Wavyhill and I have managed to fog each other's prescient senses pretty well. But I'm supposed to be meeting an unknown ally along about now, and I've taken great care that Wavyhill can't spy on me.

"You see, I invented the Wheel. Wavyhill has taken the Wheel concept and improved it in at least two ways that I know of. Naturally he uses up *mana* at a ferocious rate.

"He may also be a mass murderer. And he's my fault. That's why I've got to kill him."

Aran remembered then that his wives were waiting dinner. He remembered that he had decided to end this conversation hours ago. And he remembered a story he had been told, of a layman caught in a sorcerer's duel, and what had befallen him.

"Well, I've got to be going," he said, standing up. "I

wish you the best of luck in your duel, Warlock. And if there's anything I can do to help . . ."

"Fight with me," the Warlock said instantly.

Aran gaped. Then he burst out laughing.

The Warlock waited with his own abnormal patience. When he had some chance of being heard, he said, "I dreamed that an ally would meet me during this time. That ally would accompany me to the gate of Wavyhill's castle. I don't have many of those dreams to help me, Aran. Wavyhill's good. If I go alone, my forecast is that I'll be killed."

"Another ally," Aran suggested.

"No. Too late. The time has passed."

"Look." Aran slapped his belly with the flat of his hand. The flesh rippled. "It's not that much extra weight," he said, "for a man. I'm not *unsightly*. But as a wolf I'd look ten years pregnant! I haven't turned wolf in years.

"What am I doing? I don't have to convince you of anything," Aran said abruptly. And he walked away fast.

The Warlock caught him up at the mouth of the alley. "I swear you won't regret staying. There's something you don't know yet."

"Don't follow me too far, Warlock. You'll lose your path." Aran laughed in the magician's face. "Why should I fight by your side? If you really need me to win, I couldn't be more delighted! I've seen your face in a thousand nightmares, you and your glass dagger! So die, Warlock. It's my dinner time."

"Shh," said the Warlock. And Aran saw that the Warlock was not looking at him, but over his shoulder.

Aran felt the urge to murder. But his eyes flicked to follow the Warlock's gaze, and the imprecations died in his throat.

It was a troll. A male, with a tremendous pack on its back. Coming toward them.

And the Warlock was gesturing to it. Or were those magical passes?

"Good," he said. "Now, I could tell you that it's futile to fight fate, and you might even believe me, because I'm an expert. But I'd be lying. Or I could offer you a chance to get rid of the dagger—"

"Go to Hell. I learned to live with that dagger—"

"Wolfman, if you never learn anything else from me, learn never to blaspheme in the presence of a magician! Excuse me." The troll had walked straight to the mouth of the alley. Now the Warlock took it by the arm and led it inside. "Will you help me? I want to get the pack off its back."

They lifted it down, while Aran wondered at himself. Had he been bewitched into obedience? The pack was very heavy. It took all of Aran's strength, even though the Warlock bore the brunt of the load. The troll watched them with blank brown eyes.

"Good. If I tried this anywhere else in the city, Wavyhill would know it. But this time I know where he is. He's in Adrienne's House of Pleasures, searching for me, the fool! He's already searched the courthouse.

"Never mind that. Do you know of a village named Gath?"

"No."

"Or Shiskabil?"

"No. Wait." A Shiska had bought six matching green rugs from him once. "Yes. A small village north of here. Something . . . happened to it . . ."

"The population walked out one night, leaving all their valuables and a good deal of unexplained blood."

"That's right." Aran felt sudden horrible doubt. "It was never explained."

"Gath was first. Then Shiskabil, then Hathzoril. Bigger cities each time. At Hathzoril he was clever. He found a way to hide where his palace had been, and he didn't leave any blood."

"But what does he *do*? Where do the people go?"

"What do you know about *mana*, Aran? You know that

it's the power behind magic, and you know it can be used up. What else?''

"I'm not a magician. I sell rugs.''

"*Mana* can be used for good or evil; it can be drained, or transferred from one object to another, or from one man to another. Some men seem to carry *mana* with them. You can find concentrations in oddly shaped stones, or in objects of reverence or in meteoroids.

"There is much *mana* associated with murder,'' said the Warlock. "Too much for safety, in my day. My teacher used to warn us against working near the site of a murder, or the corpse of a murdered man, or murder weapons—as opposed to weapons of war, I might add. War and murder are different in intent.

"Necromancy uses murder as a source of magic. It's the most powerful form of magic—so powerful that it could never have developed until now, when the *mana* level everywhere in the world is so low.

"I think Wavyhill is a necromancer,'' said the Warlock. And he turned to the troll. "We'll know in a moment.''

The troll stood passive, its long arms relaxed at its sides, watching the Warlock with strangely human brown eyes and with a human dignity that contrasted oddly with its low animal brow and hairy body. It did not flinch as the Warlock dropped a kind of necklace over its head.

The change came instantly. Aran backed away, sucking air. The Warlock's necklace hung around a man's neck—a man in his middle thirties, blond-haired and bearded, wearing a porter's kilt—and that man's belly had been cut wide open by one clean swing of a sword or scimitar. Aran caught the smell of him: he had been dead for three or four days, plus whatever time the preserving effects of magic had been at work on him. Yet he stood, passively waiting, and his expression had not changed.

"Wavyhill has invented a kind of perpetual motion,'' the Warlock said dryly, but he backed away hastily from the smell of the dead man. "There's enough power in a murdered man to make him an obedient slave, and plenty left over to cast on him the seeming of a troll. He takes more *mana* from the environment, but what of that? When the *mana* runs out in Gath, Wavyhill's trolls kill their masters. Then twice as many trolls move on to Shiskabil. In Hathzoril they probably used strangling cords; they wouldn't spill any blood that way, and they wouldn't bleed themselves. I wonder where he'll go after Rynildissen?"

"Nowhere! We'll tell the Council!"

"And Wavyhill a Councilman? No. And you can't spread the word to individual members, because eventually one of them would tip Wavyhill that you're slandering him."

"They'd believe *you*."

"All it takes is one who doesn't. Then he tells Wavyhill, and Wavyhill turns loose the trolls. No. You'll do three things," said the Warlock in tones not of command but of prophecy. "You'll go home. You'll spend the next week getting your wives and children out of Rynildissen City."

"My gods, yes!"

"I swore you wouldn't regret hearing me out. The third thing, if you so decide, is to join me at dawn, at the north gate, a week from today. Come by way of Adrienne's House of Pleasures," the Warlock ordered, "and stay awhile. The dead area will break your trail.

"Do that today, too. I don't want Wavyhill to follow you by prescience. Go *now*," said the Warlock.

"I can't decide!"

"Take a week."

"I may not be here. How can I contact you?"

"You can't. It doesn't matter. I'll go with you or without you." Abruptly the Warlock stripped the necklace from the neck of the standing corpse, turned and strode off down the alley.

The dead man was a troll again. It followed Aran with large, disturbingly human brown eyes.

VII

That predawn morning, Adrienne's House of Pleasures was wrapped in thick black fog. Aran the rug merchant hesitated at the door; then, shivering, squared his shoulders and walked out into it.

He walked with his sword ready for tapping or killing. The fog grew lighter as he went, but no less dense. Several times he thought he saw monstrous vague shapes pacing him. But there was no attack. At dawn he was at the north gate.

The Warlock's mounts were either lizards enlarged by magic or dragons mutated by no magic. They were freaks, big as twin bungalows. One carried baggage; the other, two saddles in tandem.

"Mount up," the Warlock urged. "We want to get there before nightfall." Despite the chill of morning he was bare to the waist. He turned in his saddle as Aran settled behind him. "Have you lost weight?"

"I fasted for six days, and exercised too. And my wives and children are four days on their way to Atlantis by sea. You can guess what pleasures I chose at Adrienne's."

"I wouldn't have believed it. Your belly's as flat as a board."

"A wolf can fast for a long time. I ate an unbelievable meal last night. Today I won't eat at all."

The fog cleared as they left Rynildissen, and the morning turned clear and bright and hot. When Aran mentioned it, the Warlock said, "That fog was mine. I wanted to blur things for Wavyhill."

"I thought I saw shapes in the fog. Were those yours too?"

"No."

"Thanks."

"Wavyhill meant to frighten you, Aran. He wouldn't attack you. He *knows* you won't be killed before we reach the gate."

"That explains the pack lizards. I wondered how you could possibly expect to sneak up on him."

"I don't. He knows we're coming. He's waiting."

The land was rich in magic near Wavyhill's castle. You could tell by the vegetation: giant mushrooms, vying for variety of shape and color; lichens growing in the shapes of men or beasts; trees with contorted trunks and branches, trees that moved menacingly as the pack lizards came near.

"I could make them talk," said the Warlock. "But I couldn't trust them. They'll be Wavyhill's allies."

In the red light of sunset, Wavyhill's castle seemed all rose marble, perched at the top of a fairy mountain. The slender tower seemed made for kidnapped damsels. The mountain itself, as Aran saw it now for the first time, was less a breaking wave than a fist raised to the sky in defiance.

"We couldn't use the Wheel here," said the Warlock. "The whole mountain would fall on us."

"I wouldn't have let you use the Wheel."

"I didn't bring one."

"Which way?"

"Up the path. He knows we're coming."

"Is your shadow demon ready?"

"Shadow demon?" The Warlock seemed to think. "Oh. For a moment I didn't know what you were talking about. That shadow demon was killed in the battle with Glirendree, thirty years ago."

Words caught in Aran's throat, then broke loose in a snarl. *"Then why don't you put on a shirt?"*

"Habit. Why are you so vehement?"

"I don't know. I've been staring at your back since morning. I guess I was counting on the shadow demon." Aran swallowed. "It's just us, then?"

"Just us."

"Aren't you even going to take a sword? Or a dagger?"

"No. Shall we go?"

* * *

The other side of the hill was a sixty-degree slope. The narrow, meandering path could not support the lizard beasts. Aran and the Warlock dismounted and began to climb.

The Warlock said, "There's no point in subtlety. We know we'll get as far as the gate. So does Wavyhill . . . excuse me." He threw a handful of silver dust ahead of them. "The road was about to throw us off. Apparently Wavyhill doesn't take anything for granted."

But Aran had only the Warlock's word for it, and that was the only danger that threatened their climb.

There was a rectangular pond blocking the solid copper gates. An arched bridge led across the pond. They were approaching the bridge when their first challenger pushed between the gates.

"What is it?" Aran whispered. "I've never *heard* of anything like it."

"There isn't. It's a changed one. Call it a snail dragon . . ."

. . . A snail dragon. Its spiral shell was just wide enough to block the gate completely. Its slender, supple body was fully exposed, reared high to study the intruders. Shiny leaf-like scales covered the head and neck, but the rest of the body was naked, a soft greyish-brown. Its eyes were like black marbles. Its teeth were white and pointed, and the longest pair had been polished to a liquid glow.

From the other side of the small arched bridge, the Warlock called, "Ho, guardian! Were you told of our coming?"

"No," said the dragon. "Were you welcome, I would have been told."

"Welcome!" The Warlock guffawed. "We came to kill your master. Now, the interesting thing is that he knows of our coming. Why did he not warn you?"

The snail dragon tilted its mailed head.

The Warlock answered himself. "He knows that we will

pass this gate. He suspects that we must pass over your dead body. He chose not to tell you so."

"That was kind of him." The dragon's voice was low and very gravelly, a sound like rocks being crushed.

"Kind, yes. But since we are foredoomed to pass, why not step aside? Or make for the hills, and we will keep your secret."

"It cannot be."

"You're a changed one, snail dragon. Beasts whose energy of life is partly magical, breed oddly where the *mana* is low. Most changed ones are not viable. So it is with you," said the Warlock. "The shell could not protect you from a determined and patient enemy. Or were you counting on speed to save you?"

"You raise a salient point," said the guardian. "If I were to leave now, what then? My master will very probably kill you when you reach his sanctum. Then, by and by, this week or the next, he will wonder how you came to pass his guardian. Then, next week or the week following, he will come to see, or to remove the discarded shell. By then, with luck and a good tail wind, I could be halfway to the woods. Perchance he will miss me in the tall grass," said the bungalow-sized beast. "No. Better to take my chances here in the gate. At least I know the direction of attack."

"Damn, you're right," said the Warlock. "My sympathies, snail dragon."

And he set about fixing the bridge into solidity. Half of it, the half on the side away from the gate, really was solid. The other half was a reflected illusion, until the Warlock . . . did things.

"The dead border runs under the water," he told Aran. "Don't fall into it."

The snail dragon withdrew most of itself into its shell. Only his scaly head showed now, as Aran and the Warlock crossed.

Aran came running.

He was still a man. It was not certain that Wavyhill knew that Aran was a werewolf. It *was* certain that they would pass the gate. So he reserved his last defense, and came at the dragon with a naked sword.

The dragon blew fire.

Aran went through it. He carried a charm against dragon fire.

, But he couldn't *see* through it. It shocked hell out of him when teeth closed on his shoulder. The dragon had stretched incredibly. Aran screamed and bounced his blade off the metallic scales and—the teeth loosed him, snapped ineffectually at the Warlock, who danced back laughing, waving—

But the Warlock had been unarmed!

The dragon collapsed. His thick neck was cut half in two, behind the scales. The Warlock wiped his weapon on his pantaloons and held it up.

Aran felt suddenly queasy.

The Warlock laughed again. '' 'What good is a glass dagger?' The fun thing about being a magician is that everyone always expects you to use magic.''

''But, but—''

''It's just a glass dagger. No spells on it, nothing Wavyhill could detect. I had a friend drop it in the pond two days ago. Glass in water is near enough to invisible to fool the likes of Wavyhill.''

''Excuse my open mouth. I just don't like glass daggers. Now what?''

The corpse and shell of the snail dragon still blocked the gate.

''If we try to squeeze around, we could be trapped. I suppose we'll have to go over.''

''Fast,'' said Aran.

''Right, fast. Keep in mind that he could be *anywhere*.'' The Warlock took a running start and ran/climbed up the curve of the shell.

Aran followed almost as quickly.

In his sanctum, the snail dragon had said. The picture he had evoked was still with Aran as he went up the shell. Wavyhill would be hidden in his basement or his tower room, in some place of safety. Aran and the Warlock would have to fight their way through whatever the enemy could raise against them, while Wavyhill watched to gauge their defenses. There were similar tales of magicians' battles . . .

Aran was ravenously hungry. It gave him a driving energy he hadn't had in years, decades. His pumping legs drove a body that seemed feather-light. He reached the top of the shell just as the Warlock was turning full about in apparent panic.

Then he saw them: a horde of armed and armored skeletons coming at them up a wooden plank. There must have been several score of them. Aran shouted and drew his sword. *How do you kill a skeleton?*

The Warlock shouted too. Strange words, in the Guild language.

The skeletons howled. A whirlwind seemed to grip them and lift them and fling them forward. Already they were losing form, like smoke rings. Aran turned to see the last of them vanishing into the Warlock's back.

My name is legion. They must have been animated by a single demon. And the Warlock had pulled that demon into a demon trap, empty and waiting for thirty years.

The problem was that both Aran and the Warlock had been concentrating on the plural demon.

The Warlock's back was turned, and Aran could do nothing. He spotted Wavyhill gesticulating from across the courtyard, in the instant before Wavyhill completed his spell.

Aran turned to shout a warning, and so he saw what the spell did to the Warlock. The Warlock was old in an instant. The flesh seemed to fade into his bones. He spat a mouthful of blackened pebbles—no, teeth—closed his eyes and started to fall.

Aran caught him.

It was like catching an armload of bones. He eased the Warlock onto his back on the great snail shell. The Warlock's breathing was stertorous; he could not have long to live.

"Aran the Merchant!"

Aran looked down. "What did you do to him?"

The magician Wavyhill was dressed as usual, in dark robe, and sandals and pointed hat. A belt with a shoulder loop held his big-hilted sword just clear of the ground. He called, "That is precisely what I wish to discuss. I have found an incantation that behaves as the Warlock's Wheel behaves, but directionally. Is this over your head?"

"I understand you."

"In layman's terms, I've sucked the magic from him. That leaves him two hundred and twenty-six years old. I believe that gives me the win.

"My problem is whether to let you live. Aran, do you understand what my spell will do to you?"

Aran did, but—"Tell me anyway. Then tell me how you found out."

"From some of my colleagues, of course, after I determined that you were my enemy. You must have consulted an incredible number of magicians regarding the ghostly knife in your heart."

"More than a dozen. Well?"

"Leave in peace. Don't come back."

"I have to take the Warlock."

"He is my enemy."

"He's my ally. I won't leave him," said Aran.

"Take him then."

Aran stooped. He was forty-eight years old, and the bitterness of defeat had replaced the manic energy of battle. But the Warlock was little more than a snoring mummy, dry and light. The problem would be to get the fragile old man down from the snail shell.

Wavyhill was chanting!

Aran stood—in time to see the final gesture. Then the spell hit him.

For an instant he thought that the knife had truly reappeared in his heart. But the pain was all through him!—like a million taut strings snapping inside him! The shape of his neck changed grindingly; all of his legs snapped forward; his skull flattened, his eyes lost color vision, his nose stretched, his lips pulled back from bared teeth.

The change had never come so fast, had never been more complete. A blackness fell on Aran's mind. It was a wolf that rolled helplessly off the giant snail shell and into the courtyard. A wolf bounced heavily and rolled to its feet, snarled deep in its throat and began walking stiff-legged toward Wavyhill.

Wavyhill was amazed! He started the incantation over, speaking very fast, as Aran approached. He finished as Aran came within leaping distance.

This time there was no change at all. Except that Aran leapt, and Wavyhill jumped back just short of far enough, and Aran tore his throat out.

For Aran the nightmare began then. What had gone before was as sweet dreams.

Wavyhill should have been dead. His severed carotid arteries pumped frantically, his windpipe made horrid bubbling sounds, and—Wavyhill drew his sword and attacked.

Aran the wolf circled and moved in and slashed—and backed away howling, for Wavyhill's sword had run him through the heart. The wound healed instantly. Aran the wolf was not surprised. He leapt away, and circled, and slashed and was stabbed again, and circled . . .

It went on and on.

Wavyhill's blood had stopped flowing. He'd run out. Yet

he was still alive. So was his sword, or so it seemed. Aran never attacked unless it seemed safe, but the sword bit him every time. And every time he attacked, he came away with a mouthful of Wavyhill.

He was going to win. He could not help but win. His wounds healed as fast as they were made. Wavyhill's did not. Aran was stripping the flesh from the magician's bones.

There was a darkness on his brain. He moved by animal cunning. Again and again he herded Wavyhill back onto the slippery flagstones where Wavyhill had spilled five quarts of his blood. Four feet were surer than two. It was that cunning that led him to bar Wavyhill from leaving the courtyard. He tried. He must have stored healing magic somewhere in the castle. But Aran would not let him reach it.

He had done something to himself that would not let him die. He must be regretting it terribly. Aran the wolf had crippled him now, slashing at his ankles until there was not a shred of muscle left to work the bones. Wavyhill was fighting on his knees. Now Aran came closer, suffering the bite of the sword to reach the magician . . .

Nightmare.

Aran the Peacemonger had been wrong. If Aran the rug merchant could work on and on, stripping the living flesh from a man in agony, taking a stab wound for every bite— if Aran could suffer such agonies to do this to *anyone*, for *any* cause—

Then neither the end of magic, nor anything else, would ever persuade men to give up war. They would fight on, with swords and stones and whatever they could find, for as long as there were men.

The blackness had lifted from Aran's brain. It must have been the sword: the *mana* in an enchanted sword had replaced the *mana* sucked from him by Wavyhill's variant of the Warlock's Wheel.

And, finally, he realized that the sword was fighting alone.

Wavyhill was little more than bloody bones. He might not be dead, but he certainly couldn't move. The sword waved itself at the end of the stripped bones of his arm, still trying to keep Aran away.

Aran slid past the blade. He gripped the hilt in his teeth and pulled it from the magician's still-fleshy hand. The hand fought back with a senseless determined grip, but it wasn't enough.

He had to convert to human to climb the dragon shell.

The Warlock was still alive, but his breathing was a thing of desperation. Aran laid the blade across the Warlock's body and waited.

The Warlock grew young. Not as young as he had been, but he no longer looked . . . dead. He was in the neighborhood of seventy years old when he opened his eyes, blinked, and asked, "What happened?"

"You missed all the excitement," said Aran.

"I take it you beat him. My apologies. It's been thirty years since I fought Glirendree. With every magician in the civilized world trying to duplicate the Warlock's Wheel, one or another was bound to improve on the design."

"He used it on me, too."

"Oh?" The Warlock chuckled. "I suppose you're wondering about the knife."

"It did come to mind. Where is it?"

"In my belt. Did you think I'd leave it in your chest? I'd had a dream that I would need it. So I kept it. And sure enough—"

"But it was in my heart!"

"I made an image of it. I put the image in your heart, then faded it out."

Aran's fingernails raked his chest. "You miserable son of an ape! You let me think that knife was in me for thirty years!"

"You came to my house as a thief," the Warlock reminded him. "Not an invited guest."

Aran the merchant had acquired somewhat the same attitude toward thieves. With diminished bitterness he said, "Just a little magician's joke, was it? No wonder nobody could get it out. All right. Now tell me why Wavyhill's spell turned me into a wolf."

The Warlock sat up carefully. He said, "What?"

"He waved his arms at me and sucked all the *mana* out of me, and I turned into a wolf. I even lost my human intelligence. Probably my invulnerability too. If he hadn't been using an enchanted sword he'd have cut me to ribbons."

"I don't understand that. You should have been frozen into human form. Unless . . ."

Then, visibly, the answer hit him. His pale cheeks paled further. Presently he said. "You're not going to like this, Aran."

Aran could see it in the Warlock's face, seventy years old and very tired and full of pity. "Go on," he said.

"The Wheel is a new thing. Even the dead spots aren't *that* old. The situation has never come up before, that's all. People automatically assume that werewolves are people who can turn themselves into wolves.

"It seems obvious enough. You can't even make the change without moonlight. You keep your human intelligence. But there's never been proof, one way or another, until now."

"You're saying I'm a wolf."

"Without magic, you're a wolf," The Warlock agreed.

"Does it matter? I've spent most of my life as a man," Aran whispered. "What difference does it make—oh! Oh, yes."

"It wouldn't matter if you didn't have children."

"Eight. And they'll have children. And one day the *mana* will be gone everywhere on Earth. Then what, Warlock?"

"You know already."

"They'll be wild dogs for the rest of eternity!"

"And nothing anyone can do about it."

"Oh, yes, there is! I'm going to see to it that no magician ever enters Rynildissen again!" Aran stood up on the dragon's shell. "Do you hear me, Warlock? Your kind will be barred. Magic will be barred. We'll save the *mana* for the sea people and the dragons!"

It may be that he succeeded. Fourteen thousand years later, there are still tales of werewolves where Rynildissen City once stood. Certainly there are no magicians.

I do love peace. But . . . I'm fifty-one. You may have noticed: older people seem reluctant to believe that the United States and the Soviets can solve their problems with a mutual disarmament pact.

Why older people? Are our brains softening, or have we noticed something that the youths have not?

I have tried to diet for a lover, and my lover didn't lose weight. I have tried to give up alcohol for a friend, but my friend continued to pickle his brain. I think Jerry Pournelle tried to give up smoking for me; but ultimately I had to do it myself.

From time to time we have tried to give up weapons for the Soviets . . . but it doesn't work. They have the habit. They must break it themselves.

Consider the days when it was first suspected that the cetaceans were Earth's second sentient order of life. It was known, then, that dolphins had many times helped swimmers out of difficulty and that no dolphin had ever been known to attack a human being. Well, what difference did it make whether they had *not* attacked humans or whether they had done so only when there was no risk of being caught at it? Either statement was proof of intelligence.

"The Handicapped," 1968

From *THE MAGIC GOES AWAY*

Scores of times in my life, I have looked out of an airplane window at cloudscapes. It always looks like you could walk on the clouds. In places you'd have to circle the feathered canyons, or jump from puffball to puffball, or toil up the slope of a thunderhead. By the time I found a chance to write about such things, I knew just how it would feel. (It can't hurt that I learned how to use a trampoline in college.)

The cloud bank stretched away like a clean white landscape, under a brilliant sun and dark blue sky. The Warlock rubbed his hands in satisfaction. "We're here! Orolandes, let me get into that pack."

The others watched as he chose his tools. If the Warlock had told them what he was about, Orolandes hadn't heard it. He did not speculate. He waited to know what was expected of him.

The attitude came easily to him. He had risen through the ranks of the Greek army; he could follow orders. He had given orders, too, before Atlantis sank beneath him. Since then Orolandes had given over control of his own fate.

"Good," muttered the Warlock. He opened a wax-stoppered phial and poured dust into his hand and scattered it like seeds into the cloudscape. He sang words unfamiliar to Orolandes.

Mirandee and Clubfoot joined in, clear soprano and awkward bass, at chorus points that were not obvious. The song trailed off in harmony, and the Warlock scattered another handful of dust.

"All right. Better let me go first," he said. He stepped off the stairs into feathery emptiness.

He bounced gently. The cloud held him.

Clubfoot followed, in a ludicrous bouncing stride that sank him calves-deep into the fog. Mirandee walked out after him. They turned to look back at Orolandes.

Clubfoot started to choke. He sat down in the shifting white mist and bellowed with a laughter that threatened to strangle him. Mirandee fought it, then joined in in a silvery giggle. There was the not-quite-sound of Wavyhill's chortling.

The laughter seemed to fade, and the world went dim and blurry. Orolandes felt his knees turn to water. His jaw was sagging. He had climbed up through this cloud. It was cold and wet and without substance. It would not hold a feather from falling, let alone a man.

The witch's silver laughter burned him like acid. For the lack of the Warlock's laughter, for the Warlock's exasperated frown, Orolandes was grateful. When the Warlock swept his arm in an impatient beckoning half-circle, Orolandes stepped out into space in a soldier's march.

His foot sank deep into what felt like feather bedding, and bounced. He was off balance at the second step, and the recoil threw him further off. He kicked out frantically. His leg sank deep and recoiled and threw him high. He landed on his side and bounced.

Mirandee watched with her hands covering her mouth. Clubfoot's laugh was a choking whimper now.

Orolandes got up slowly, damp all over. He waded rather than walked toward the magicians.

"Good enough. We don't have a lot of time," said the Warlock. "Take a little practice—we all need that—then go back for the pack."

The layer of cloud stirred uneasily around them. It was not flat. There were knolls of billowing white that they had to circle round. It was like walking through a storehouse full of damp goose down. The cloud-stuff gave underfoot, and pulled as the foot came forward.

Orolandes found a stride that let him walk with the top-heavy pack, but it was hard on the legs. Half-exhausted and growing careless, he nearly walked into a hidden rift. He stared straight down through a feathery canyon at small drifting patches of farm. A tiny plume of dust led his eye to a moving speck, a barely visible horse and rider.

He turned left along the rift, while his heart thundered irregularly in his ears.

Clubfoot looked back. Mount Valhalla rose behind them, a mile or so higher than they'd climbed, blazing snow-white in the sunlight. "Far enough, I guess. Now, the crucial thing is to keep moving," he said, "because if the magic fails where we're standing it's all over. Luckily we don't have to do our own moving."

He helped Orolandes doff the pack. He rummaged through it and removed a pair of water-tumbled pebbles, a handful of clean snow, and a small pouch of gray powder. "Now, Kranthkorpool, would you be so kind as to tell us where we're going?"

"No need to coerce me," said Wavyhill. "We go east and north. To the northernmost point of the Alps."

"And we've got food for four days. Well, I guess we're in a hurry." Clubfoot began to make magic.

The Warlock did not take part. He knew that Clubfoot was a past master at weather magic. Instead he watched Mirandee's hair.

Yes, her youth had held well. She had the clear skin and unwrinkled brow of a serene thirty-year-old noblewoman. Her wealth of hair was now raven black, with a streak of pure white that ran from her brow all the way back. As she helped Clubfoot sing the choruses, the white band thickened and thinned and thickened.

The Warlock spoke low to Orolandes. "If you see her hair turn sheer white, run like hell. You're overloaded with that pack. Just get to safety and let me get the others out." The Greek nodded.

Now the clouds stirred about them. The fitful breeze increased slightly, but not enough to account for the way the mountain was receding. Now the clouds to either side churned, fading or thickening at the edges. Through a sudden rift they watched the farmlands drift away.

"Down there they'll call this a hurricane. What they'll call us doesn't bear mentioning." Clubfoot chuckled. He walked back to where Orolandes was standing and settled himself in the luxurious softness of a cloud billow. In a lowered voice he said, "I've been wrestling with my conscience. May I tell you a story?"

Orolandes said, "All right." He saw that the others were beyond earshot.

"I'm a plainsman," said Clubfoot. "My master was a lean old man a lot like the Warlock, but darker, of course. He taught half a dozen kids at a time, and of course he was the tribe's medicine man. One day when I was about twelve, old White Eagle took us on a hike up the only mountain anywhere around.

"He took us up the easy side. There were clouds streaming away from the top. White Eagle did some singing and dancing, and then he had us walk out on the cloud. I ran out ahead of the rest. It looked like so much fun.''

"Fun," Orolandes said without expression.

"Well, yes. I'd never been on a cloud. How was a plains kid to know clouds aren't solid?''

"You mean you never . . . realized . . .'' Orolandes started laughing.

Clubfoot was laughing too. "I'd seen clouds, but way up in the sky. They looked solid enough. *I* didn't know why White Eagle was doing all that howling and stamping.''

"And the next time you went for a stroll on a cloud—''

"*Oh*, no. White Eagle explained that. But it must have been a fine way to get rid of slow learners.''

When Jim Baen at Ace and Jim Frenkel at Dell began publishing illustrated novellas, I thought it was a wonderful idea. Novellas are always the stepchildren when the awards are given out. There's no market for them. Ideas come in lengths, but a writer may force a good novella idea into novel length, or mush two together to form a novel. If we're going to give awards for 25,000 to 40,000 words, shouldn't we make the length less awkward by giving it a market?

I liked the illustrations, too.

Readers complained that they were paying novel prices for novellas; they weren't getting enough words for their money. The experiment was terminated, the novella is still the ugly stepchild of the industry, and writers are still turning good novellas into bad novels because they need the money.

I still think I was right.

It was a relic of sorts: a granite block twenty-five or thirty feet long by the same distance wide by half that in height. Its corners and edges were unevenly rounded, as if it had weathered thousands of years of dust-laden winds.

There was writing on it. *In* it: Wes could see overhead light glinting through the lines. Something like a thread-thin laser had written script and diagrams all the way through the rock.

FOOTFALL, 1985

THE DEFENSELESS DEAD

The dead lay side by side beneath the glass. Long ago, in a roomier world, these older ones had been entombed each in his own double-walled casket. Now they lay shoulder to shoulder, more or less in chronological order, looking up, their features clear through thirty centimeters of liquid nitrogen sandwiched between two thick sheets of glass.

Elsewhere in the building some sleepers wore clothing, formal costumery of a dozen periods. In two long tanks on another floor the sleepers had been prettied up with low-temperature cosmetics, and sometimes with a kind of flesh-colored putty to fill and cover major wounds. A weird practice. It hadn't lasted beyond the middle of the last century. After all, these sleepers planned to return to life someday. The damage should show at a glance.

With these, it did.

They were all from the tail end of the twentieth century. They looked like hell. Some were clearly beyond saving, accident cases whose wills had consigned them to the freezer banks regardless. Each sleeper was marked by a plaque describing everything that was wrong with his mind and body, in script so fine and so archaic as to be almost unreadable.

Battered or torn or wasted by disease, they all wore the same look of patient resignation. Their hair was disintegrating, very slowly. It had fallen in a thick gray crescent about each head.

"People used to call them *corpsicles*, frozen dead. Or *Homo snapiens*. You can imagine what would happen if you dropped one." Mr. Restarick did not smile. These people were in his charge, and he took his task seriously. His eyes seemed to look through rather than at me, and his clothes were ten to fifty years out of style. He seemed to be gradually losing himself here in the past. He said, "We've over six thousand of them here. Do you think we'll ever bring them back to life?" I was an ARM, I might know.

"Do you?"

"Sometimes I wonder." He dropped his gaze. "Not Harrison Cohn. Look at him, torn open like that. And *her*, with half her face shot off; she'd be a vegetable if you brought her back. The later ones don't look this bad. Up until 1989 the doctors couldn't freeze anyone who wasn't clinically dead."

"That doesn't make *sense*. Why not?"

"They'd have been up for murder. When what they were doing was *saving* lives." He shrugged angrily. "Sometimes they'd stop a patient's heart and then restart it, to satisfy the legalities."

Sure, that made a lot of sense. I didn't dare laugh out loud. I pointed. "How about him?"

He was a rangy man of about forty-five, healthy-looking, with no visible marks of death, violent or otherwise. The long lean face still wore a look of command, though the deep-set eyes were almost closed. His lips were slightly parted, showing teeth straightened by braces in the ancient fashion.

Mr. Restarick glanced at the plaque. "Leviticus Hale, 1991. Oh, yes. Hale was a paranoid. He must have been the first they ever froze for *that*. They guessed right, too. If we brought him back now we could cure him."

"If."

"It's been done."

"Sure. We only lose one out of three. He'd probably take the chance himself. But then, he's crazy." I looked around at rows of long double-walled liquid nitrogen tanks. The place was huge and full of echoes, and this was only the top floor. The Vault of Eternity was ten stories deep in earthquake-free bedrock. "Six thousand, you said. But the Vault was built for ten thousand, wasn't it?"

He nodded. "We're a third empty."

"Get many customers these days?"

He laughed at me. "You're joking. Nobody has himself frozen these days. He might wake up a piece at a time!"

"That's what I wondered."

"Ten years ago we were thinking of digging new vaults. All those crazy kids, perfectly healthy, getting themselves frozen so they could wake up in a brave new world. I had to watch while the ambulances came and carted them away for spare parts! We're a good third empty now since the Freezer Law passed!"

That business with the kids had been odd, all right. A fad or a religion or a madness, except that it had gone on for much too long.

The Freezeout Kids. Most of them were textbook cases of *anomie*, kids in their late teens who felt trapped in an imperfect world. History taught them (those who listened) that earlier times had been much worse. Perhaps they thought that the world was moving toward perfection.

Some had gambled. Not many in any given year; but it had been going on ever since the first experimental freezer vault revivals, a generation before I was born. It was better than suicide. They were young, they were healthy, they stood a better chance of revival than any of the frozen, damaged dead. They were poorly adapted to their society. Why not risk it?

Two years ago they had been answered. The General Assembly and the world vote had passed the Freezer Bill into law.

There were those in frozen sleep who had not had the foresight to set up a trust fund, or who had selected the wrong trustee or invested in the wrong stocks. If medicine or a miracle had revived them now, they would have been on the dole, with no money and no trace of useful education and, in about half the cases, no evident ability to survive in *any* society.

Were they in frozen sleep or frozen death? In law there had always been that point of indecision. The Freezer Law cleared it up to some extent. It declared any person in frozen sleep, who could not support himself should society choose to reawaken him, to be dead in law.

And a third of the world's frozen dead, twelve hundred thousand of them, had gone into the organ banks.

"You were in charge then?"

The old man nodded. "I've been on the day shift at the Vault for almost forty years. I watched the ambulances fly away with three thousand of my people. I think of them as my people," he said a bit defensively.

"The law can't seem to decide if they're alive or dead. Think of them any way you like."

"People who trusted me. What did those Freezeout Kids do that was worth killing them for?"

I thought: they wanted to sleep it out while others broke their backs turning the world into Paradise. But it's no capital crime.

"They had nobody to defend them. Nobody but me." He trailed off. After a bit, and with visible effort, he pulled himself back to the present. "Well, never mind. What can I do for the United Nations police, Mr. Hamilton?"

"Oh, I'm not here as an ARM agent. I'm just here to, to—" Hell, I didn't know myself. It was a news broadcast that had jarred me into coming here. I said, "They're planning to introduce another Freezer Bill."

"What?"

"A second Freezer Bill. Naming a different group. The communal organ banks must be empty again," I said bitterly.

Mr. Restarick started to shake. "Oh, no. No. They can't do that again. They, they can't."

I gripped his arm, to reassure him or to hold him up. He looked about to faint. "Maybe they can't. The first Freezer Law was supposed to stop organlegging, but it didn't. Maybe the citizens will vote this one down."

I left as soon as I could.

The second Freezer Bill made slow, steady progress, without much opposition. I caught some of it in the boob cube. A perturbingly large number of citizens were petitioning the Security Council for confiscation of what they described as "the frozen corpses of a large number of people who were insane when they died. Parts of these corpses could possibly be recovered for badly needed organ replacements . . ."

They never mentioned that said corpses might someday be recovered whole and living. They often mentioned that said corpses could not be safely recovered *now*; and they could prove it with experts; and they had a thousand experts waiting their turns to testify.

They never mentioned biochemical cures for insanity. They spoke of the lack of a worldwide need for mental patients and for insanity-carrying genes.

They hammered constantly on the need for organ transplant material.

I just about gave up watching news broadcasts. I was an ARM, a member of the United Nations police force, and I wasn't supposed to get involved in politics. It was none of my business.

It didn't become my business until I ran across a familiar name, eleven months later.

Taffy was peoplewatching. That demure look didn't fool me. A secretive glee looked out of her soft brown eyes, and they shifted left every time she raised her dessert spoon.

I didn't try to follow her eyes for fear of blowing her cover. Come, I will conceal nothing from you: I don't *care* who's eating at the next table in a public restaurant. Instead I lit a cigarette, shifted it to my imaginary hand (the weight tugging gently at my mind) and settled back to enjoy my surroundings.

High Cliffs is an enormous pyramidal city-in-a-building in northern California. Midgard is on the first shopping level, way back near the service core. There's no view, but the restaurant makes up for it with a spectacular set of environment walls.

From inside, Midgard seems to be halfway up the trunk of an enormous tree, big enough to stretch from Hell to Heaven. Perpetual war is waged in the vasty distances, on various limbs of the tree, between warriors of oddly distorted size and shape. World-sized beasts show occasionally: a wolf attacks the moon, a sleeping serpent coils round the restaurant itself, the eye of a curious brown squirrel suddenly blocks one row of windows . . .

"Isn't that Holden Chambers?"

"Who?" The name sounded vaguely familiar.

"Four tables over, sitting alone."

I looked. He was tall and skinny, and much younger than most of Midgard's clientele. Long blond hair, weak chin—

he was really the type who ought to grow a beard. I was sure I'd never seen him before.

Taffy frowned. "I wonder why he's eating alone. Do you suppose someone broke a date?"

The name clicked. "Holden Chambers. Kidnapping case. Someone kidnapped him and his sister, years ago. One of Bera's cases."

Taffy put down her dessert spoon and looked at me curiously. "I didn't know the ARM took kidnapping cases."

"We don't. Kidnapping would be a regional problem. Bera thought—" I stopped, because Chambers looked around suddenly, right at me. He seemed surprised and annoyed.

I hadn't realized how rudely I was staring. I looked away, embarrassed. "Bera thought an organlegging gang might be involved. Some of the gangs turned to kidnapping about that time, after the Freezer Law slid their markets out from under them. Is Chambers still looking at me?" I felt his eyes on the back of my neck.

"Yah."

"I wonder why."

"*Do* you indeed." Taffy knew, the way she was grinning. She gave me another two seconds of suspense, then said, "You're doing the cigarette trick."

"Oh. Right." I transferred the cigarette to a hand of flesh and blood. It's silly to forget how startling that can be: a cigarette or a pencil or a jigger of bourbon floating in mid-air. I've used it myself for shock effect.

Taffy said, "He's been in the boob cube a lot lately. He's the number eight corpsicle heir, worldwide. Didn't you know?"

"Corpsicle heir?"

"You know what *corpsicle* means? When the freezer vaults first opened—"

"I know. I didn't know they'd started using the word again."

"Well, never mind *that*. The *point* is that if the second Freezer Bill passes, about three hundred thousand corpsicles will be declared formally dead. Some of those frozen dead men have money. The money will go to their next of kin."

"*Oh*. And Chambers has an ancestor in a vault somewhere, does he?"

"Somewhere in Michigan. He's got an odd, Biblical name."

"Not Leviticus Hale?"

She stared. "Now, just how the bleep did you know that?"

"Just a stab in the dark." I didn't know what had made me say it. Leviticus Hale, dead, had a memorable face and a memorable name.

Strange, though, that I'd never thought of money as a motive for the second Freezer Bill. The first Freezer Law had applied only to the destitute, the Freezeout Kids.

Here are people who could not possibly adjust to any time in which they might be revived. They couldn't even adjust to their own times. Most of them weren't even sick, they didn't have that much excuse for foisting themselves on a nebulous future. Often they paid each other's way into the Freezer Vaults. If revived they would be paupers, unemployable, uneducated by any possible present or future standards; permanent malcontents.

Young, healthy, useless to themselves and society. And the organ banks are always empty . . .

The arguments for the second Freezer Bill were not much different. The corpsicles named in group two had money, but they were insane. Today there were chemical cures for most forms of insanity. But the memory of having been insane, the habitual thought patterns formed by paranoia or schizophrenia, these would remain, these would require psychotherapy. And how to cure them, in men and women whose patterns of experience were up to a hundred and forty years out of date to start with?

And the organ banks are always empty . . . Sure, I could see it. The citizens wanted to live forever. One day they'd work their way down to me, Gil Hamilton.

"You can't win," I said.

Taffy said, "How so?"

"If you're destitute they won't revive you because you can't support yourself. If you're rich your heirs want the money. It's hard to defend yourself when you're dead."

"Everyone who loved them is dead too." She looked too seriously into her coffee cup. "I didn't really pay much attention when they passed the Freezer Law. At the hospital we don't even know where the spare parts come from: criminals, corpsicles, captured organleggers' stocks, it all looks the same. Lately I find myself wondering."

Taffy had once finished a lung transplant with hands and sterile steel, after the hospital machines had quit at an embarrassing moment. A squeamish woman couldn't have done that. But the transplants themselves had started to bother her lately. Since she met me. A surgeon and an organlegger-hunting ARM, we made a strange pairing.

When I looked again, Holden Chambers was gone. We split the tab, paid and left.

The first shopping level had an odd outdoor-indoor feel to it. We came out into a broad walk lined with shops and trees and theaters and sidewalk cafés, under a flat concrete sky forty feet up and glowing with light. Far away, an undulating black horizon showed in a narrow band between concrete sky and firmament.

The crowds had gone, but in some of the sidewalk cafés a few citizens still watched the world go by. We walked toward the black band of horizon, holding hands, taking our time. There was no way to hurry Taffy when she was passing shop windows. All I could do was stop when she did, wearing or not wearing an indulgent smile. Jewelry, clothing, all glowing behind plate glass—

She tugged my arm, turning sharply to look into a furniture store. I don't know what it was she saw. I saw a dazzling pulse of green light on the glass, and a puff of green flame spurting from a coffee table.

Very strange. Surrealistic, I thought. Then the impressions sorted out, and I pushed Taffy hard in the small of the back and flung myself rolling in the opposite direction. Green light flashed briefly, very near. I stopped rolling. There was a weapon in my sporran the size of a double barreled Derringer, two compressed air cartridges firing clusters of anesthetic crystal slivers.

A few puzzled citizens had stopped to watch what I was doing.

I ripped my sporran apart with both hands. Everything spilled out, rolling coins and credit cards and ARM ident and cigarettes and—I snatched up the ARM weapon. The window reflection had been a break. Usually you can't tell *where* the pulse from a hunting laser might have come from.

Green light flashed near my elbow. The pavement cracked loudly and peppered me with particles. I fought an urge to fling myself backward. The afterimage was on my retina, a green line thin as a razor's edge, pointing right at him.

He was in a cross street, posed kneeling, waiting for his gun to pulse again. I sent a cloud of mercy needles toward him. He slapped at his face, turned to run, and fell skidding.

I stayed where I was.

Taffy was curled in the pavement with her head buried in her arms. There was no blood around her. When I saw her legs shift I knew she wasn't dead. I still didn't know if she'd been hit.

Nobody else tried to shoot at us.

The man with the gun lay where he was for almost a minute. Then he started twitching.

He was in convulsions when I got to him. Mercy needles aren't supposed to do that. I got his tongue out of his throat so he couldn't choke, but I wasn't carrying medicines that could help. When the High Cliffs police arrived, he was dead.

Inspector Swan was a picture-poster cop, tri-racial and handsome as hell in an orange uniform that seemed tailored to him, so well did he fit it. He had the gun open in front of him and was probing at the electronic guts of it with a pair of tweezers. He said, "You don't have any idea why he was shooting at you?"

"That's right."

"You're an ARM. What do you work on these days?"

"Organlegging, mostly. Tracking down gangs that have gone into hiding." I was massaging Taffy's neck and shoulders, trying to calm her down. She was still shivering. The muscles under my hands were very tight.

Swan frowned. "Such an easy answer. But he couldn't be part of an organlegging gang, could he? Not with that gun."

"True." I ran my thumbs around the curve of Taffy's shoulder blades. She reached around and squeezed my hand.

The gun. I hadn't really expected Swan to see the implications. It was an unmodified hunting laser, right off the rack.

Officially, nobody in the world makes guns to kill people. Under the Conventions, not even armies use them, and the United Nations police use mercy weapons, with the intent that the criminals concerned should be unharmed for trial—and, later, for the organ banks. The only killing weapons made are for killing animals. They are supposed to be, well, sportsmanlike.

A continuous-firing X-ray laser would be easy enough to make. It would chop down anything living, no matter how fast it fled, no matter what it hid behind. The beast wouldn't even know it was being shot at until you waved the beam through its body: an invisible sword blade a mile long.

But that's butchery. The prey should have a chance; it should at least know it's being shot at. A standard hunting laser fires a pulse of visible light, and won't fire again for about a second. It's no better than a rifle, except in that you don't have to allow for windage, the range is close enough to infinite, you can't run out of bullets, it doesn't mess up the meat, and there's no recoil. That's what makes it sportsmanlike.

Against me it had been just sportsmanlike enough. He was dead. I wasn't.

"Not that it's so censored easy to modify a hunting laser," said Swan. "It takes some basic electronics. I could do it myself—"

"So could I. Why not? We've both had police training."

"The point is, I don't *know* anyone who couldn't *find* someone to modify a hunting laser, give it a faster pulse or even a continuous beam. Your friend must have been afraid to bring anyone else into it. He must have had a very personal grudge against you. You're sure you don't recognize him?"

"I never saw him before. Not with *that* face."

"And he's dead," said Swan.

"That doesn't really prove anything. Some people have allergic reactions to police anesthetics."

"You used a standard ARM weapon?"

"Yah. I didn't even fire both barrels. I *couldn't* have put a *lot* of needles in him. But there are allergic reactions."

"Especially if you take something to bring them on." Swan put the gun down and stood up. "Now, I'm just a city cop, and I don't know that much about ARM business. But I've heard that organleggers sometimes take something so they won't just go to sleep when an ARM anesthetic hits them."

"Yah. Organleggers don't like becoming spare parts themselves. I do have a theory, Inspector."

"Try me."

"He's a retired organlegger. A lot of them retired when the Freezer Bill passed. Their markets were gone, and they'd made their pile, some of them. They split up and became honest citizens. A respected citizen may keep a hunting laser on his wall, but it isn't modified. He could modify it if he had to, with a day's notice."

"Then said respected citizen spotted an old enemy."

"Going into a restaurant, maybe. And he just had time to go home for his gun, while we ate dinner."

"Sounds reasonable. How do we check it?"

"If you'll do a rejection spectrum on his brain tissue, and send everything you've got to ARM Headquarters, we'll do the rest. An organlegger can change his face and fingerprints as he censored pleases, but he can't change his tolerance to transplants. Chances are he's on record."

"And you'll let me know."

"Right."

Swan was checking it with the radio on his scooter while I beeped my clicker for a taxi. The taxi settled at the edge of the walkway. I helped Taffy into it. Her movements were slow and jerky. She wasn't in shock, just depression.

Swan called from his scooter. "Hamilton!"

I stopped halfway into the taxi. "Yah?"

"He's a local," Swan boomed. His voice carried like an orator's. "Mortimer Lincoln, ninety-fourth floor. Been living here since—" He checked again with his radio. "April, 2123. I'd guess that's about six months after they passed the Freezer Law."

"Thanks." I typed an address on the cab's destination board. The cab hummed and rose.

I watched High Cliffs recede, a pyramid as big as a mountain, glowing with light. The city guarded by Inspector Swan was all in one building. It would make his job easier, I thought. Society would be a bit more organized.

Taffy spoke for the first time in a good while. "Nobody's ever shot at me before."

"It's all over now. I think he was shooting at me anyway."

"I suppose." Suddenly she was shaking. I took her in my arms and held her. She talked into my shirt collar. "I didn't know what was happening. That green light, I thought it was *pretty*. I didn't know what happened until you knocked me down, and then that green line flashed at you and I heard the sidewalk go *ping*, and I didn't know what to *do!* I—"

"You did fine."

"I wanted to *help!* I didn't know, maybe you were dead, and there wasn't anything I could do. If you hadn't had a gun— Do you always carry a gun?"

"Always."

"I never knew." Without moving, she seemed to pull away from me a little.

At one time the Amalgamation of Regional Militia had been a federation of Civil Defense bodies in a number of nations. Later it had become the police force of the United Nations itself. They had kept the name. Probably they liked the acronym.

When I got to the office the next morning, Jackson Bera had already run the dead man to Earth. "No question about it," he told me. "His rejection spectrum checks perfectly. Anthony Tiller, known organlegger, suspected member of the Anubis gang. First came on the scene around 2120; he probably had another name and face before that. Disappeared April or May 2123."

"That fits. No, dammit, it doesn't. He must have been out of his mind. There he was, home free, rich and safe. Why would he blow it all to kill a man who never harmed a hair of his head?"

"You don't *really* expect an organlegger to behave like a well-adjusted member of society."

I answered Bera's grin. "I guess not . . . Hey. You said *Anubis*, didn't you? The Anubis gang, not the Loren gang."

"That's what it says on the hard copy. Shall I query for probability?"

"Please." Bera programs a computer better than I do. I talked while he tapped at the keyboard in my desk. "Whoever the bleep he was, Anubis controlled the illicit medical facilities over a big section of the Midwest. Loren had a piece of the North American west coast, smaller area, bigger population. The difference is that I killed Loren myself, by squeezing the life out of his heart with my imaginary hand, which is a very personal thing, as you will realize, Jackson. Whereas I never touched Anubis or any of his gang, nor even interfered with his profits, to the best of my knowledge."

"I did," said Bera. "Maybe he thought I was you." Which is hilarious, because Bera is dark brown and a foot taller than me if you include the hair that puffs out around his head like a black powder explosion. "You missed something. Anubis was an intriguing character. He changed faces and ears and fingerprints whenever he got the urge. We're pretty sure he was male, but even that isn't worth a big bet. He's changed his height at least once. Full leg transplant."

"Loren couldn't do that. Loren was a pretty sick boy. He probably went into organlegging because he needed the transplant supply."

"Not Anubis. Anubis must have had a sky-high rejection threshold."

"Jackson, *you're proud of Anubis.*"

Bera was shocked to his core. "The hell! He's a dirty murdering organlegger! If I'd *caught* him I'd be proud of Anubis—" He stopped, because my desk screen was getting information.

The computer in the basement of the ARM building gave Anthony Tiller no chance at all of being part of the Loren gang, and a probability in the nineties that he had run with the Jackal God. One point was that Anubis and the rest had all dropped out of sight around the end of April 2123, when

Anthony Tiller/Mortimer Lincoln changed his face and moved into High Cliffs.

"It could still have been revenge," Bera suggested. "Loren and Anubis knew each other. We know that much. They set up the boundary between their territories at least twelve years ago, by negotiation. Loren took over Anubis' territory when Anubis retired. And you killed Loren."

I scoffed. "And Tiller the Killer gave up his cover to get me, two years after the gang broke up?"

"Maybe it wasn't revenge. Maybe Anubis wants to make a comeback."

"Or maybe this Tiller just flipped. Withdrawal symptoms. He hadn't killed anyone for almost two years, poor baby. I wish he'd picked a better time."

"Why?"

"Taffy was with me. She's still twitching."

"You didn't tell me that! She wasn't hit, was she?"

"No, just scared."

Bera relaxed. His hand caressed the interface where his hair faded into air, feather-lightly, in the nervous way another man might scratch his head. "I'd hate to see you two split up."

"Oh, it's not . . ." anything like that serious, I'd have told him, but he knew better. "Yah. We didn't get much sleep last night. It isn't just being shot at, you know."

"I know."

"Taffy's a surgeon. She thinks of transplant stocks as raw material. Tools. She'd be crippled without an organ bank. She doesn't think of the stuff as human . . . or she never used to, till she met me."

"I've never heard either of you talk about it."

"We don't, even to each other, but it's there. Most transplants are condemned criminals, captured by heroes such as you and me. Some of the stuff is respectable citizens captured by organleggers, broken up into illicit organ banks and eventually recaptured by said heroes. They don't tell

Taffy which is which. She works with pieces of people. I don't think she can live with me and not live with that.''

"Getting shot at by an ex-organlegger couldn't have helped much. We'd better see to it that it doesn't happen again.''

"Jackson, he was just a nut.''

"He used to be with Anubis.''

"I never had anything to do with Anubis.'' Which reminded me. "You did, though, didn't you? Do you remember anything about the Holden Chambers kidnapping?''

Bera looked at me peculiarly. "Holden and Charlotte Chambers, yah You've got a good memory. There's a fair chance Anubis was involved.''

"Tell me about it.''

"There was a rash of kidnappings about that time, all over the world. You know how organlegging works. The legitimate hospitals are always short of transplants. Some sick citizens are too much in a hurry to wait their turns. The gangs kidnap a healthy citizen, break him up into spare parts, throw away the brain, use the rest for illegal operations. That's the way it was until the Freezer Law cut the market out from under them.''

"I remember.''

"Some gangs turned to kidnapping for ransom. Why not? It's just what they were set up for. If the family couldn't pay off, the victim could always become a donor. It made people much more likely to pay off.

"The only strange thing about the Chambers kidnap was that Holden and Charlotte Chambers both disappeared about the same time, around six at night.'' Bera had been tapping at the computer controls. He looked at the screen and said, "Make that seven. March 21, 2123. But they were miles apart, Charlotte at a restaurant with a date, Holden at Washburn University attending a night class. Now why would a kidnap gang think they needed them both?''

"Any ideas?''

"They might have thought that the Chambers trustees were more likely to pay off on both of them. We'll never know now. We never got any of the kidnappers. We were lucky to get the kids back."

"What made you think it was Anubis?"

"It was Anubis territory. The Chambers kidnap was only the last of half a dozen in that area. Smooth operations, no excitement, no hitches, victims returned intact after the ransom was paid." He glared. "No, I'm *not* proud of Anubis. It's just that he tended not to make mistakes, and he was used to making people disappear."

"Uh huh."

"They made themselves disappear, the whole gang, around the time of that last kidnap. We assume they were building up a stake."

"How much did they get?"

"On the Chambers kids? A hundred thousand."

"They'd have made ten times that selling them as transplants. They must have been hard up."

"You know it. Nobody was buying. What does all this have to do with your being shot at?"

"A wild idea. Could Anubis be interested in the Chambers kids *again?*"

Bera gave me a funny look. "No way. What for? They bled them white the first time. A hundred thousand UN marks isn't play money."

After Bera left I sat there not believing it.

Anubis had vanished. Loren had acted immediately to take over Anubis' territory. Where had they gone, Anubis and the others? Into Loren's organ banks?

But there was Tiller/Lincoln.

I didn't *like* the idea that any random ex-organlegger might decide to kill me the instant he saw me. Finally I did something about it. I asked the computer for data on the Chambers kidnapping.

There wasn't much Bera hadn't told me. I wondered, though, why he hadn't mentioned Charlotte's condition.

When ARM police found the Chambers kids drugged on a hotel parking roof, they had both been in good physical condition. Holden had been a little scared, a little relieved, just beginning to get angry. But Charlotte had been in catatonic withdrawal. At last notice she was still in catatonic withdrawal. She had never spoken with coherence about the kidnapping, nor about anything else.

Something had been done to her. Something terrible. Maybe Bera had taught himself not to think about it.

Otherwise the kidnappers had behaved almost with rectitude. The ransom had been paid, the victims had been returned. They had been on that roof, drugged, for less than twenty minutes. They showed no bruises, no signs of maltreatment . . . another sign that their kidnappers were organleggers. Organleggers aren't sadists. They don't have that much respect for the stuff.

I noted that the ransom had been paid by an attorney. The Chambers kids were orphans. If they'd both been killed the executor of their estate would have been out of a job. From that viewpoint it made sense to capture them both . . . but not all *that* much sense.

And there couldn't be a motive for kidnapping them again. They didn't have the money. Except—

It hit me joltingly. *The second Freezer Bill.*

Holden Chambers' number was in the basement computer. I was dialing it when second thoughts interrupted. Instead I called downstairs and set a team to locating possible bugs in Chambers' home or phone. They weren't to interfere with the bugs or to alert possible listeners. Routine stuff.

Once before the Chambers kids had disappeared. If we weren't lucky they might disappear again. Sometimes the

ARM business was like digging a pit in quicksand. If you dug hard enough you could maintain a noticeable depression, but as soon as you stopped . . .

The Freezer Law of 2122 had given the ARM a field day. Some of the gangs had simply retired. Some had tried to keep going, and wound up selling an operation to an ARM plant. Some had tried to reach other markets; but there weren't any, not even for Loren, who had tried to expand into the asteroid belt and found they wouldn't have him either.

And some had tried kidnapping; but inexperience kept tripping them up. The name of a victim points straight at a kidnapper's only possible market. Too often the ARMs had been waiting.

We'd cleaned them out. Organlegging should have been an extinct profession this past year. The vanished jackals I spent my days hunting should have posed no present threat to society.

Except that the legitimate transplants released by the Freezer Law were running out. And a peculiar thing was happening. People had started to disappear from stalled vehicles, singles apartment houses, crowded city slidewalks.

Earth wanted the organleggers back.

No, that wasn't fair. Put it this way: enough citizens wanted to extend their own lives, at any cost . . .

If Anubis was alive, he might well be thinking of going back into business.

The point was that he would need backing. Loren had taken over his medical facilities when Anubis retired. Eventually we'd located those and destroyed them. Anubis would have to start over.

Let the second Freezer Bill pass, and Leviticus Hale would be spare parts. Charlotte and Holden Chambers would inherit . . . how much?

I got that via a call to the local NBA news department.

In one hundred and thirty-four years Leviticus Hale's original three hundred and twenty thousand dollars had become seventy-five million UN marks.

I spent the rest of the morning on routine. They call it *legwork*, though it's mostly done by phone and computer keyboard. The word covers some unbelievable long shots.

We were investigating every member of every Citizens' Committee to Oppose the Second Freezer Bill in the world. The suggestion had come down from old man Garner. He thought we might find that a coalition of organleggers had pooled advertising money to keep the corpsicles off the market. The results that morning didn't look promising.

I half hoped it wouldn't work out. Suppose those committees *did* turn out to be backed by organleggers? It would make prime time news, anywhere in the world. The second Freezer Bill would pass like *that*. But it had to be checked. There had been opposition to the first Freezer Bill, too, when the gangs had had more money.

Money. We spent a good deal of computer time looking for unexplained money. The average criminal tends to think that once he's got the money, he's home free, the game is over.

We hadn't caught a sniff of Loren or Anubis that way.

Where had Anubis spent his money? Maybe he'd just hidden it away somewhere, or maybe Loren had killed him for it. And Tiller had shot at me because he didn't like my face. Legwork is gambling, time against results.

It developed that Holden Chambers' environs were free of eavesdropping devices. I called him about noon.

There appeared within my phone screen a red-faced, white-haired man of great dignity. He asked to whom I wished to speak. I told him, and displayed my ARM ident. He nodded and put me on hold.

Moments later I faced a weak-chinned young man who smiled distractedly at me and said, "Sorry about that. I've been getting considerable static from the news lately. Zero acts as a kind of, ah, buffer.''

Past his shoulder I could see a table with things on it: a tape viewer, a double handful of tape spools, a tape recorder the size of a man's palm, two pens and a stack of paper, all neatly arranged. I said, ''Sorry to interrupt your studying.''

''That's all right. It's tough getting back to it after Year's-End. Maybe you remember. Haven't I seen you—? *Oh*. The floating cigarette.''

''That's right.''

''How did you do that?''

''I've got an imaginary arm.'' And it's a great conversational device, an ice-breaker of wondrous potency. I was a marvel, a talking sea serpent, the way the kid was looking at me. ''I lost an arm once, mining rocks in the Belt. A sliver of asteroidal rock sheared it off clean to the shoulder.''

He looked awed.

''I got it replaced, of course. But for a year I was a one-armed man. Well, here was a whole section of my brain developed to control a right arm, and no right arm. Psychokinesis is easy enough to develop when you live in a low-gravity environment.'' I paused just less than long enough for him to form a question. ''Somebody tried to kill me outside Midgard last night. That's why I called.''

I hadn't expected him to burst into a fit of the giggles. ''Sorry,'' he got out. ''It sounds like you lead an active life!''

''Yah. It didn't seem that funny at the time. I don't suppose you noticed anything unusual last night?''

''Just the usual shootings and muggings, and there was one guy with a cigarette floating in front of his face.'' He sobered before my clearly deficient sense of humor. ''Look, I *am* sorry, but one minute you're talking about a meteor shearing your arm off, and the next it's bullets whizzing past your ear.''

"Sure, I see your point."

"I left before you did. I know censored well I did. What happened?"

"Somebody shot at us with a hunting laser. He was probably just a nut. He was also part of the gang that kidnapped—"

He looked stricken. "Yah, them. There's probably no connection, but we wondered if you might have noticed anything. Like a familiar face."

He shook his head. "They change faces, don't they?"

"Usually. How did you leave?"

"Taxi. I live in Bakersfield, about twenty minutes from High Cliffs. Where did all this happen? I caught my taxi on the third shopping level."

"That kills it. We were on the first."

"I'm not really sorry. He might have shot at me too."

I'd been trying to decide whether to tell him that the kidnap gang might be interested in him again. Whether to scare the lights out of him on another long shot, or leave him off guard for a possible kidnap attempt. He seemed stable enough, but you never knew.

I temporized. "Mister Chambers, we'd like you to try to identify the man who tried to kill me last night. He probably did change his face—"

"Yah." He was uneasy. Many citizens would be, if asked to look a dead man in the face. "But I suppose you've got to try it. I'll stop in tomorrow afternoon, after class."

So. Tomorrow we'd see what he was made of.

He asked, "What about that imaginary arm? I've never heard of a psi talking that way about his talent."

"I wasn't being cute," I told him. "It's an arm, as far as I'm concerned. My limited imagination. I can feel things out with my fingertips, but not if they're further away than an arm can reach. A jigger of bourbon is about the biggest thing I can lift. Most psis can't do nearly that well."

"But they can reach further. Why not try a hypnotist?"

"And lose the whole arm? I don't want to risk that."

He looked disappointed in me. "What can you do with an imaginary arm that you can't do with a real one?"

"I can pick up hot things without burning myself."

"*Yah!*" He hadn't thought of that.

"And I can reach through walls. [In the Belt I could reach through my suit and do precision work in vacuum.] I can reach *two* ways through a phone screen. Fiddle with the works, or—here, I'll show you."

It doesn't always work. But I was getting a good picture. Chambers showed life-sized, in color and stereo, through four square feet of screen. It looked like I could reach right into it. So I did. I reached into the screen with my imaginary hand, picked a pencil off the table in front of him and twirled it like a baton.

He threw himself backward out of his chair. He landed rolling. I saw his face, pale gray with terror, before he rolled away and out of view. A few seconds later the screen went blank. He must have turned the knob from off-screen.

If I'd touched his face I could have understood it. But all I'd done was lift a pencil. What the hell?

My fault, I guessed. Some people see psi powers as supernatural, eerie, threatening. I shouldn't have been showing off like that. But Holden hadn't looked the type. Brash, a bit nervous, but fascinated rather than repulsed by the possibilities of an invisible, immaterial hand.

Then, terror.

I didn't try to call him back. I dithered about putting a guard on him, decided not to. A guard might be noticed. But I ordered a tracer implanted in him.

Anubis might pick Chambers up at any time. He needn't wait for the General Assembly to declare Leviticus Hale dead.

A tracer needle was a useful thing. It would be fired at Chambers from ambush. He'd probably never notice the sting, the hole would be only a pinprick, and it would tell us just where he was from then on.

I thought Charlotte Chambers could use a tracer too, so I picked up a palm-size pressure implanter downstairs. I also traded the discharged barrel on my sidearm for a fresh one. The feel of the gun in my hand sent vivid green lines sizzling past my mind's eye.

Last, I ordered a standard information package, C priority, on what Chambers had been doing for the last two years. It would probably arrive in a day or so.

The winter face of Kansas had great dark gaps in it, a town nestled in each gap. The weather domes of various townships had shifted kilotons of snow outward, to deepen the drifts across the flat countryside. In the light of early sunset the snowbound landscape was orange-white, striped with the broad black shadows of a few cities-within-buildings. It all seemed eerie and abstract, sliding west beneath the folded wings of our plane.

We slowed hard in midair. The wings unfolded, and we settled over downtown Topeka.

This was going to look odd on my expense account. All this way to see a girl who hadn't spoken sense in three years. Probably it would be disallowed . . . yet she was as much a part of the case as her brother. Anyone planning to recapture Holden Chambers for re-ransom would want Charlotte too.

Menninger Institute was a pretty place. Besides the twelve stories of glass and mock-brick which formed the main building, there were at least a dozen outbuildings of varied ages and designs that ran from boxlike rectangles to free-form organics poured in foam plastic. They were all wide apart, separated by green lawns and trees and flower beds. A place of peace, a place with elbow room. Pairs and larger groups passed me on the curving walks: an aide and a patient, or an aide and several less disturbed patients. The aides were obvious at a glance.

"When a patient is well enough to go outside for a walk,

then he needs the greenery and the room," Doctor Hartman told me. "It's part of his therapy. Going outside is a giant step."

"Do you get many agoraphobes?"

"No, that's not what I was talking about. It's the *lock* that counts. To anyone else that lock is a prison, but to many patients it comes to represent security. Someone else to make the decisions, to keep the world outside."

Doctor Hartman was short and round and blond. A comfortable person, easygoing, patient, sure of himself. Just the man to trust with your destiny, assuming you were tired of running it yourself.

I asked, "Do you get many cures?"

"Certainly. As a matter of fact, we generally won't take patients unless we feel we can cure them."

"That must do wonders for the record."

He was not offended. "It does even more for the patients. Knowing that we know they can be cured makes them feel the same way. And the incurably insane . . . can be damned depressing." Momentarily he seemed to sag under an enormous weight. Then he was himself again. "They can affect the other patients. Fortunately there aren't many incurables, these days."

"Was Charlotte Chambers one of the curables?"

"We thought so. After all, it was only shock. There was no previous history of personality disturbances. Her blood psychochemicals were near enough normal. We tried everything in the records. Stroking. Fiddling with her chemistry. Psychotherapy didn't get very far. Either she's deaf or she doesn't listen, and she won't talk. Sometimes I think she hears everything we say . . . but she doesn't respond."

We had reached a powerful-looking locked door. Doctor Hartman searched through a key ring, touched a key to the lock. "We call it the violent ward, but it's more properly the severely disturbed ward. I wish to hell we *could* get some violence out of some of them. Like Charlotte. They won't even *look* at reality, much less try to fight it . . . here we are.''

Her door opened outward into the corridor. My nasty professional mind tagged the fact: if you tried to hang yourself from the door, anyone could see you from either end of the corridor. It would be very public.

In these upper rooms the windows were frosted. I suppose there's good reason why some patients shouldn't be reminded that they are twelve stories up. The room was small but well lighted and brightly painted, with a bed and a padded chair and a tridee screen set flush with the wall. There wasn't a sharp corner anywhere in the room.

Charlotte was in the chair, looking straight ahead of her, her hands folded in her lap. Her hair was short and not particularly neat. Her yellow dress was of some wrinkleproof fabric. She looked resigned, I thought, resigned to some ultimately awful thing. She did not notice us as we came in.

I whispered, ''Why is she still here, if you can't cure her?''

Doctor Hartman spoke in a normal tone. ''At first we thought it was catatonic withdrawal. That we could have cured. This isn't the first time someone has suggested moving her. She's still here because I want to know what's *wrong* with her. She's been like this ever since they brought her in.''

She still hadn't noticed us. The doctor talked as if she couldn't hear us. ''Do the ARMs have any idea what was done to her? If we knew that we might be better able to treat her.''

I shook my head. ''I was going to ask you. What *could* they have done to her?''

He shook his head.

''Try another angle, then. What couldn't they have done to her? There were no bruises, broken bones, anything like that—''

''No internal injuries either. No surgery was performed

on her. There was the evidence of drugging. I understand they were organleggers?''

''It looks likely.'' She could have been pretty, I thought. It wasn't the lack of cosmetics, or even the gaunt look. It was the empty eyes, isolated above high cheekbones, looking at nothing. ''Could she be blind?''

''No. The optic nerves function perfectly.''

She reminded me of a wirehead. You can't get a wirehead's attention either, when house current is trickling down a fine wire from the top of his skull into the pleasure center of his brain. But no, the pure egocentric joy of a wirehead hardly matched Charlotte's egocentric misery.

''Tell me,'' said Doctor Hartman. ''How badly could an organlegger frighten a young girl?''

''We don't get many citizens back from organleggers. I . . . honestly can't think of any upper limit. They could have taken her on a tour of the medical facilities. They could have made her watch while they broke up a prospect for stuff.'' I didn't like what my imagination was doing. There are things you don't think about, because the point is to protect the prospects, keep the Lorens and the Anubises from reaching them at all. But you can't help thinking about them anyway, so you push them back, push them back. These things must have been in my head for a long time. ''They had the facilities to partly break her up and put her back together again and leave her conscious the whole time. You wouldn't have found scars. The only scars they can't cure with modern medicine are in the bone itself. They could have done any kind of temporary transplant—and they must have been bored, Doctor. Business was slow. But—''

''Stop.'' He was gray around the edges. His voice was weak and hoarse.

''But organleggers aren't sadists, generally. They don't have that much respect for the stuff. They wouldn't play that kind of game unless they had something special against her.''

"My God, you play rough games. How can you sleep nights, knowing what you know?"

"None of your business, Doctor. In your opinion, is it likely that she was frightened into this state?"

"Not all at once. We could have brought her out of it if it had happened all at once. I suppose she may have been frightened repeatedly. How long did they have her?"

"Nine days."

Hartman looked worse yet. Definitely he was not ARM material.

I dug in my sporran for the pressure implanter. "I'd like your permission to put a tracer needle in her. I won't hurt her."

"There's no need to whisper, Mr. Hamilton—"

"Was I?" Yes, dammit, I'd been holding my voice low, as if I were afraid to disturb her. In a normal voice I said, "The tracer could help us locate her in case she disappears."

"Disappears? Why should she do that? You can see for yourself—"

"That's the worst of it. The same gang of organleggers that got her the first time may be trying to kidnap her again. Just how good is your . . . security . . ." I trailed off. Charlotte Chambers had turned around and was looking at me.

Hartman's hand closed hard on my upper arm. He was warning me. Calmly, reassuringly, he said, "Don't worry, Charlotte. I'm Doctor Hartman. You're in good hands. We'll take care of you."

Charlotte was half out of her chair, twisted around to search my face. I tried to look harmless. Naturally I knew better than to try to guess what she was thinking. Why should her eyes be big with hope? Frantic, desperate hope. When I'd just uttered a terrible threat.

Whatever she was looking for, she didn't find it in my face. What looked like hope gradually died out of her eyes, and she sank back in her chair, looking straight ahead of her, without interest. Doctor Hartman gestured, and I took the hint and left.

Twenty minutes later he joined me in the visitor's waiting room. "Hamilton, that's the first time she's ever shown that much awareness. What could possibly have sparked it?"

I shook my head. "I wanted to ask, just how good is your security?"

"I'll warn the aides. We can refuse to permit her visitors unless accompanied by an ARM agent. Is that good enough?"

"It may be, but I want to plant a tracer in her. Just in case."

"All right."

"Doctor, what was that in her expression?"

"I thought it was hope. Hamilton, I will just bet it was your voice that did it. You may sound like someone she knows. Let me take a recording of your voice and we'll see if we can find a psychiatrist who sounds like you."

When I put the tracer in her, she never so much as twitched.

All the way home her face haunted me. As if she'd waited two years in that chair, not bothering to move or think, until I came. Until finally I came.

My right side seems weightless. It throws me off stride as I back away, back away. My right arm ends at the shoulder. Where my left eye was is an empty socket. Something vague shuffles out of the dark, looks at me with its one left eye, reaches for me with its one right arm. I back away, back away, fending it off with my imaginary arm. It comes closer, I touch it, I reach into it. Horrible! The scars! Loren's pleural cavity is a patchwork of transplants. I want to snatch my hand away. Instead I reach deeper, and find his borrowed heart, and squeeze. And squeeze.

How can I sleep nights, knowing what I know? Well, Doctor, some nights I dream.

Taffy opened her eyes to find me sitting up in bed, staring at a dark wall. She said, "What?"

"Bad dream."

"Oh." She scratched me under the ear, for reassurance.

"How awake are you?"

She sighed. "Wide awake."

"Corpsicle. Where did you hear the word *corpsicle?* In the boob cube? From a friend?"

"I don't remember. Why?"

"Just a thought. Never mind. I'll ask Luke Garner."

I got up and made us some hot chocolate with bourbon flavoring. It knocked us out like a cluster of mercy needles.

Lucas Garner was a man who had won a gamble with fate. Medical technology had progressed as he grew older, so that his expected lifespan kept moving ahead of him. He was not yet the oldest living member of the Struldbrugs' Club, but he was getting on, getting on.

His spinal nerves had worn out long since, marooning him in a ground-effect travel chair. His face hung loose from his skull, in folds. But his arms were apishly strong, and his brain still worked. He was my boss.

"Corpsicle," he said. "Corpsicle. Right. They've been saying it on tridee. I didn't notice, but you're right. It's funny they should start using that word again."

"How did it get started?"

"Popsicle. A popsicle was frozen sherbet on a stick. You licked it off."

I winced at the mental picture that evoked. Leviticus Hale, covered with frost, a stake up his anus, a gigantic tongue—

"A *wooden* stick." Garner had a grin to scare babies. Grinning, he was almost a work of art: an antique, a hundred and eighty-odd years old, like a Hannes Bok illustration of Lovecraft. "That's how long ago it was. They didn't start freezing people until the nineteen sixties or seventies, but we were still putting wooden sticks in popsicles. Why would anyone use it now?''

''Who uses it? Newscasters? I don't watch the boob cube much.''

''Newscasters, yah, and lawyers . . . How are you making out on the Committees to Oppose the Second Freezer Bill?''

It took me a moment to make the switch. ''No positive results. The program's still running, and results are slow in some parts of the world, Africa, the Middle East . . . They all seem to be solid citizens.''

''Well, it's worth a try. We've been looking into the other side of it, too. If organleggers are trying to block the second Freezer Bill, they might well try to intimidate or kill off anyone who *backs* the second Freezer Bill. Follow me?''

''I suppose.''

''So we have to know who to protect. It's strictly business, of course. The ARM isn't supposed to get involved in politics.''

Garner reached sideways to tap one-handed at the computer keyboard in his desk. His bulky floating chair wouldn't fit under the keyboard. Tape slid from the slot, two feet of it. He handed it to me.

''Mostly lawyers,'' he said. ''A number of sociologists and humanities professors. Religious leaders pushing their own brand of immortality; we've got religious factions on both sides of the question. These are the people who publicly back the second Freezer Bill. I'd guess they're the ones who started using the word *corpsicle*.''

''Thanks.''

''Cute word, isn't it? A joke. If you said *frozen sleep* someone might take you seriously. Someone might even wonder if they were really dead. Which is the key question, isn't it? The corpsicles they want are the ones who were healthiest, the ones who have the best chance of being brought back to life some day. These are the people they want revived a piece at a time. By me that's lousy.''

"Me too.'' I glanced down at the list. "I presume you haven't actually warned any of these people.''

"No, you idiot. They'd go straight to a newscaster and tell him that all their opponents are organleggers.''

I nodded. "Thanks for the help. If anything comes of this—''

"Sit down. Run your eyes down those names. See if you spot anything.''

I didn't know most of them, of course, not even in the Americas. There were a few prominent defense lawyers, and at least one federal judge, and Raymond Sinclair the physicist, and a string of newscast stations, and—"Clark and Nash? The advertising firm?''

"A number of advertising firms in a number of countries. Most of these people are probably sincere enough, and they'll talk to *anyone*, but the coverage has to come from somewhere. It's coming from these firms. That word *corpsicle has* to be an advertising stunt. The publicity on the corpsicle heirs: they may have had a hand in that too. You know about the corpsicle heirs?''

"Not a lot.''

"NBA Broadcasting has been running down the heirs to the richest members of Group II, the ones who were committed to the freezer vaults for reasons that don't harm their value as—stuff.'' Garner spat the word. It was organlegger slang. "The paupers all went into the organ banks on the first Freezer Law, of course, so Group II boasts some considerable wealth. NBA found a few heirs who would never have turned up otherwise. I imagine a lot of them will be voting for the second Freezer Bill—''

"Yah.''

"Only the top dozen have been getting the publicity. But it's still a powerful argument, isn't it? If the corpsicles are in frozen sleep, that's one thing. If they're *dead*, then people are being denied their rightful inheritance.''

I asked the obvious question. "Who's paying for the advertising?''

"Now, we wondered about that. The firms wouldn't say. We dug a little further.''

"And?''

"They don't know either.'' Garner grinned like Satan. "They were hired by firms that aren't listed anywhere. A number of firms, whose representatives only appeared once. They paid their fees in lump sums.''

"It sounds like—no. They're on the wrong side.''

"Right. Why would an organlegger be *pushing* the second Freezer Bill?''

I thought it over. "How about this? A number of old, sickly, wealthy men and women set up a fund to see to it that the public supply of spare parts isn't threatened. It's legal, at least; which dealing with an organlegger isn't. With enough of them it might even be cheaper.''

"We thought of that. We're running a program on it. I've been asking some subtle questions around the Struldbrugs' Club, just because I'm a member. It has to be subtle. Legal it may be, but they wouldn't want publicity.''

"No.''

"And then I got your report this morning. Anubis and the Chambers kid, huh? Wouldn't it be nice if it went a bit further than that?''

"I don't follow you.''

At this moment Garner looked like something that was ready to pounce. "Wouldn't it be wonderful if a federation of organleggers was backing the second Freezer Bill. The idea would be to kidnap *all* of the top corpsicle heirs *just before the Bill passes*. Most people worth kidnapping can afford to protect themselves. Guards, house alarms, wrist alarms. A corpsicle heir can't do that yet.''

Garner leaned forward in his chair, doing the work with

his arms. "If we could prove this, and give it some publicity, wouldn't it shoot hell out of the second Freezer Law?"

There was a memo on my desk when I got back. The data package on Holden Chambers was in the computer memory, waiting for me. I remembered that Holden himself would be here this afternoon, unless the arm trick had scared him off.

I punched for the package and read it through, trying to decide just how sane the kid was. Most of the information had come from the college medical center. They'd been worried about him too.

The kidnapping had interrupted his freshman year at Washburn. His grades had dropped sharply afterward, then sloped back to a marginal passing grade. In September he'd changed his major from architecture to biochemistry. He'd made the switch easily. His grades had been average or better during these last two years.

He lived alone, in one of those tiny apartments whose furnishings are all memory plastic, extruded as needed. Technology was cheaper than elbow room. The apartment house did have some communal facilities— sauna, pool, cleaning robots, party room, room-service kitchen, clothing dispensary . . . I wondered why he didn't get a roommate. It would have saved him money, for one thing. But his sex life had always been somewhat passive, and he'd never been gregarious, according to the file. He'd just about pulled the hole in after him for some months after the kidnapping. As if he'd lost all faith in humanity.

If he'd been off the beam then, he seemed to have recovered. Even his sex life had improved. That information had not come from the college medical center, but from records from the communal kitchen (breakfast for two, late night room service), and some recent recorded phone messages. All quite public; there was no reason for me to be feeling like a peeping Tom. The publicity on the corpsicle heirs may have done him some good, started girls chasing him for a change. A few had spent the night, but he didn't seem to be seeing anyone steadily.

I had wondered how he could afford a servant. The answer made me feel stupid. The secretary named Zero turned out to be a computer construct, an answering service.

Chambers was not penniless. After the ransom was paid the trust fund had contained about twenty thousand marks. Charlotte's care had eaten into that. The trustees were giving Holden enough to pay his tuition and still live comfortably. There would be some left when he graduated, but it would be earmarked for Charlotte.

I turned off the screen and thought about it. He'd had a jolt. He'd recovered. Some do, some don't. He'd been in perfect health, which has a lot to do with surviving emotional shock. If he was your friend today, you would avoid certain subjects in his presence.

And he'd thrown himself backward in blind terror when a pencil rose from his desk and started to pinwheel. How normal was that? I just didn't know. I was too used to my imaginary arm.

Holden himself appeared about fourteen hundred.

Anthony Tiller was in a cold box, face up. That face had been hideously contorted during his last minutes, but it showed none of that now. He was as expressionless as any dead man. The frozen sleepers at the Vault of Eternity had looked like that. Superficially, most of them had been in worse shape than he was.

Holden Chambers studied him with interest. "So that's what an organlegger looks like."

"An organlegger looks like anything he wants to."

He grimaced at that. He bent close to study the dead man's face. He circled the cold box with his hands clasped behind his back. He wanted to look nonchalant, but he was still walking wide of me. I didn't think the dead man bothered him.

He said the same thing I'd said two nights ago. "Nope. Not with that face."

"Well, it was worth a try. Let's go to my office. It's more comfortable."

He smiled. "Good."

He dawdled in the corridors. He looked into open offices, smiled at anyone who looked up, asked me mostly intelligent questions in a low voice. He was enjoying himself: a tourist in ARM Headquarters. But he trailed back when I tried to take the middle of the corridor, so that we wound up walking on opposite sides. Finally I asked him about it.

I thought he wasn't going to answer. Then, "It was that pencil trick."

"What about it?"

He sighed, as one who despairs of ever finding the right words. "I don't like to be touched. I mean, I get along with girls all right, but generally I don't like to be touched."

"I didn't—"

"But you *could* have. And without my *knowing*. I couldn't see it, I might not even feel it. It just bothered the censored hell out of me, you reaching out of a phone screen like that! A phone call isn't supposed to be that, that *personal*." He stopped suddenly, looking down the corridor. "Isn't that Lucas Garner?"

"Yah."

"Lucas Garner!" He was awed and delighted. "He runs it all, doesn't he? How old is he now?"

"In his hundred and eighties." I thought of introducing him, but Luke's chair slid off in a different direction.

My office is just big enough for me, my desk, two chairs, and an array of spigots in the wall. I poured him tea and me coffee. I said, "I went to visit your sister."

"Charlotte? How is she?"

"I doubt she's changed since the last time you saw her. She doesn't notice anything around her . . . except for one incident, when she turned around and stared at me."

"Why? What did you do? What did you say?" he demanded.

Well, here it came. "I was telling her doctor that the same gang that kidnapped her once might want her again."

Strange things happened around his mouth. Bewilderment, fear, disbelief. "What the bleep made you say that?"

"It's a possibility. You're both corpsicle heirs. Tiller the Killer could have been watching you when he spotted *me* watching you. He couldn't have that."

"No, I suppose not . . ." He was trying to take it lightly, and he failed. "Do you seriously think they might want me—us—again?"

"It's a possibility," I repeated. "If Tiller was inside the restaurant, he could have spotted me by my floating cigarette. It's more distinctive than my face. Don't look so worried. We've got a tracer on you, we could track him anywhere he took you."

"In me?" He didn't like that much better—too personal?—but he didn't make an issue of it.

"Holden, I keep wondering what they could have done to your sister—"

He interrupted, coldly. "I stopped wondering that, long ago."

"—that they didn't do to you. It's more than curiosity. If the doctors knew what was done to her, if they knew what it is in her memory—"

"Dammit! Don't you think I want to help her? She's my sister!"

"All right." What was I playing psychiatrist for, anyway? Or was it detective I was playing? He didn't know anything. He was at the eye of several storms at once, and he must be getting sick and tired of it. I ought to send him home.

He spoke first. I could barely hear him. "You know what they did to me? A nerve block at the neck. A little widget taped to the back of my neck with surgical skin. I couldn't feel anything below the neck, and I couldn't move. They put that on me, dumped me on a bed and left me. For nine days. Every so often they'd turn me on again and let me drink and eat something and go to the bathroom."

"Did anyone tell you they'd break you up for stuff if they didn't get the ransom?"

He thought about it. "N-no. I could pretty well guess it. They never said anything to me at all. They treated me like I was dead. They examined me for, oh, it felt like hours, poking and prodding me with their hands and their instruments, rolling me around like dead meat. I couldn't feel any of it, but I could see it all. If they did that to Charlotte . . . maybe she thinks she's dead." His voice rose. "I've been through this again and again, with the ARMs, with Doctor Hartman, with the Washburn medical staff. Let's drop it, shall we?"

"Sure. I'm sorry. We don't learn tact in this business. We learn to ask questions. Any questions."

And yet, and yet, the look on her face.

I asked him one more question as I was escorting him out. Almost offhandedly. "What do you think of the second Freezer Bill?"

"I don't have a UN vote yet."

"That's not what I asked."

He faced me belligerently. "Look, there's a lot of money involved. A *lot* of money. It would pay for Charlotte the rest of her life. It would fix my face. But Hale, Leviticus Hale—" He pronounced the name accurately, and with no flicker of a smile. "He's a relative, isn't he? My great-to-the-third-grandfather. They could bring him back someday; it's possible. So what do I do? If I had a vote I'd have to decide. But I'm not twenty-five yet, so I don't have to worry about it."

"Interviews."

"I don't give interviews. You just got the same answer everyone else gets. It's on tape, on file with Zero. Goodbye, Mr. Hamilton."

Other ARM departments had thinned our ranks during the lull following the first Freezer Law. Over the next couple of weeks they began to trickle back. We needed operatives to implant tracers in unsuspecting victims, and afterward to monitor their welfare. We needed an augmented staff to follow their tracer blips on the screens downstairs.

We were sore tempted to tell all of the corpsicle heirs what was happening, and have them check in with us at regular intervals. Say, every fifteen minutes. It would have made things much easier. It might also have influenced their votes, altered the quality of the interviews they gave out.

But we didn't want to alert our quarry, the still hypothetical coalition of organleggers now monitoring the same corpsicle heirs we were interested in. And the backlash vote would be ferocious if we were wrong. And we weren't supposed to be interested in politics.

We operated without the knowledge of the corpsicle heirs. There were two thousand of them in all parts of the world, almost three hundred in the western United States, with an expected legacy of fifty thousand UN marks or more—a limit we set for our own convenience, because it was about all we could handle.

One thing helped the manpower situation. We had reached another lull. Missing persons complaints had dropped to near zero, all over the world.

"We should have been expecting that," Bera commented. "For the last year or so most of their customers must have stopped going to organleggers. They're waiting to see if the second Freezer Bill will go through. Now all the gangs are stuck with full organ banks and no customers. If they learned anything from last time, they'll pull in their horns and wait it out. Of course I'm only guessing—'' But it looked likely enough. At any rate, we had the men we needed.

We monitored the top dozen corpsicle heirs twenty-four hours a day. The rest we checked at random intervals. The tracers could only tell us where they were, not who they were with or whether they wanted to be there. We had to keep checking to see if anyone had disappeared.

We sat back to await results.

The Security Council passed the second Freezer Bill on February 3, 2125. Now it would go to the world vote in late March. The voting public numbered ten billion, of whom perhaps sixty percent would bother to phone in their votes.

I took to watching the boob cube again.

NBA Broadcasting continued its coverage of the corpsicle heirs and its editorials in favor of the bill. Proponents took every opportunity to point out that many corpsicle heirs still remained to be discovered. (And YOU might be one.) Taffy and I watched a parade in New York in favor of the bill: banners and placards (SAVE THE LIVING, NOT THE DEAD . . . IT'S *YOUR* LIFE AT STAKE . . . CORPSICLES KEEP BEER COLD) and one censored big mob of chanting people. The transportation costs must have been formidable.

The various committees to oppose the bill were also active. In the Americas they pointed out that, although about forty percent of the people in frozen sleep were in the Americas, the spare parts derived would go to the world at large. In Africa and Asia it was discovered that the Americas had most of the corpsicle heirs. In Egypt an analogy was made between the pyramids and the freezer vaults: both bids for immortality. It didn't go over well.

Polls indicated that the Chinese sectors would vote against the bill. NBA newscasters spoke of ancestor worship, and reminded the public that six ex-Chairmen resided in Chinese freezer vaults, alongside a myriad lesser ex-officials. Immortality was a respected tradition in China.

The committees to oppose reminded the world's voting public that some of the wealthiest of the frozen dead had heirs in the Belt. Were Earth's resources to be spread indiscriminately among the asteroidal rocks? I started to hate both sides. Fortunately the UN cut that line off fast by threatening injunction. Earth needed Belt resources too heavily.

Our own results began to come in.

Mortimer Lincoln, alias Anthony Tiller, had not been at Midgard the night he tried to kill me. He'd eaten alone in his apartment, a meal sent from the communal kitchen. Which meant that he himself could not have been watching Chambers.

We found no sign of anyone lurking behind Holden Chambers, or behind any of the other corpsicle heirs, publicized or not, with one general exception. Newsmen. The media were unabashedly and constantly interested in the corpsicle heirs, priority based on the money they stood to inherit. We faced a depressing hypothesis: the potential kidnappers were spending all their time watching the boob cube, letting the media do their tracking for them. But perhaps the connection was closer.

We started investigating newscast stations.

In mid-February I pulled Holden Chambers in and had him examined for an outlaw tracer. It was a move of desperation. Organleggers don't use such tools. They specialize in medicine. Our own tracer was still working, and it was the only tracer in him. Chambers was icily angry. We had interrupted his studying for a mid-term exam.

We managed to search three of the top dozen when they had medical checkups. Nothing.

Our investigations of the newscast stations turned up very little. Clark and Nash was running a good many one-time spots through NBA. Other advertising firms had similar lines of possible influence over other stations, broadcasting companies and cassette newszines. But we were looking for newsmen who had popped up from nowhere, with backgrounds forged or nonexistent. Ex-organleggers in new jobs. We didn't find any.

I called Menninger's one empty afternoon. Charlotte Chambers was still catatonic. "I've got Lowndes of New York working with me," Hartman told me. "He has precisely your voice, and good qualifications too. Charlotte hasn't responded yet. We've been wondering: could it have been the *way* you were talking?"

"You mean the accent? It's Kansas with an overlay of west coast and Belter."

"No, Lowndes has that too. I mean organlegger slang."

"I use it. Bad habit."

"That could be it." He made a face. "But we can't act on it. It might just scare her completely into herself."

"That's where she is now. I'd risk it."

"You're not a psychiatrist," he said.

I hung up and brooded. Negatives, all negatives.

I didn't hear the hissing sound until it was almost on me. I looked up then, and it was Luke Garner's ground-effect travel chair sliding accurately through the door. He watched me a moment, then said, "What are you looking so grim about?"

"Nothing. All the nothing we've been getting instead of results."

"Uh huh." He let the chair settle. "It's beginning to look like Tiller the Killer wasn't on assignment."

"That would blow the whole thing, wouldn't it? I did a lot of extrapolating from two beams of green light. One ex-organlegger tries to make holes in one ARM agent, and now we've committed tens of thousands of man-hours and seventy or eighty computer-hours on the strength of it. If they'd been planning to tie us up they couldn't have done it better."

"You know, I think you'd take it as a personal insult if Tiller shot at you just because he didn't like you."

I had to laugh. "How personal can you get?"

"That's better. Now will you stop sweating this? It's just another long shot. You know what legwork is like. We bet a lot of man-effort on this one because the odds looked good. Look how many organleggers would have to be in on it if it were true! We'd have a chance to snaffle them all. But if it doesn't work out, why sweat it?"

"The second Freezer Bill," I said, as if he didn't know.

"The Will of the People be done."

"Censor the people! They're murdering those dead men!"

Garner's face twitched oddly. I said, "What's funny?"

He let the laugh out. It sounded like a chicken screaming for help. "*Censor. Bleep.* They didn't used to be swear words. They were euphemisms. You'd put them in a book or on teevee, when you wanted a word they wouldn't let you use."

I shrugged. "Words are funny. *Damn* used to be a technical term in theology, if you want to look at it that way."

"I know, but they *sound* funny. When you start saying *bleep* and *censored* it ruins your masculine image."

"Censor my masculine image. What do we do about the corpsicle heirs? Call off the surveillance?"

"No. There's too much in the pot already." Garner looked broodingly into one bare wall of my office. "Wouldn't it be nice if we could persuade ten billion people to use prosthetics instead of transplants?"

Guilt glowed in my right arm, my left eye. I said, "Prosthetics don't feel. I might have settled for a prosthetic arm—" Dammit, I'd had the choice! "—but an eye? Luke, suppose it was possible to graft new legs on you. Would you take them?"

"Oh, dear, I do wish you hadn't asked me that," he said venomously.

"Sorry. I withdraw the question."

He brooded. It was a lousy thing to ask a man. He was still stuck with it; he couldn't spit it out.

I asked, "Did you have any special reason for dropping in?"

Luke shook himself. "Yah. I got the impression you were taking all this as a personal defeat. I stopped down to cheer you up."

We laughed at each other. "Listen," he said, "there are worse things than the organ bank problem. When I was young—your age, my child—it was almost impossible to get anyone convicted of a capital crime. Life sentences weren't for life. Psychology and psychiatry, such as they were, were concerned with curing criminals, returning them to society. The United States Supreme Court almost voted the death penalty unconstitutional."

"Sounds wonderful. How did it work out?"

"We had an impressive reign of terror. A lot of people got killed. Meanwhile transplant techniques were getting better and better. Eventually Vermont made the organ banks the official means of execution. That idea spread very damn fast."

"Yah." I remembered history courses.

"Now we don't even *have* prisons. The organ banks are always short. As soon as the UN votes the death penalty for a crime, most people stop committing it. Naturally."

"So we get the death penalty for having children without a license, or cheating on income tax, or running too many red traffic lights. Luke, I've seen what it *does* to people to keep voting more and more death penalties. They lose their respect for life."

"But the other situation was just as bad, Gil. Don't forget it."

"So now we've got the death penalty for being poor."

"The Freezer Law? I won't defend it. Except that that's the penalty for being poor and *dead*."

"Should it be a capital crime?"

"No, but it's not too bright either. If a man expects to be brought back to life, he should be prepared to pay the medical fees. Now, hold it. I know a lot of the pauper group had trust funds set up. They were wiped out by depressions, bad investments. Why the hell do you think banks take interest for a loan? They're being paid for the *risk*. The risk that the loan won't be paid back."

"Did you vote for the Freezer Law?"

"No, of course not."

"I must be spoiling for a fight. I'm glad you dropped by, Luke."

"Don't mention it."

"I keep thinking the ten billion voters will eventually work their way down to me. Go ahead, grin. Who'd want *your* liver?"

Garner cackled. "Somebody could murder me for my skeleton. Not to put inside him. For a museum."

We left it at that.

The news broke a couple of days later. Several North American hospitals had been reviving corpsicles.

How they had kept the secret was a mystery. Those corpsicles who had survived the treatment—twenty-two of them, out of thirty-five attempts—had been clinically alive for some ten months, conscious for shorter periods.

For the next week it was all the news there was. Taffy and I watched interviews with the dead men, with the doctors, with members of the Security Council. The move was not illegal. As publicity against the second Freezer Bill, it may have been a mistake.

All of the revived corpsicles had been insane. Else why risk it?

Some of the casualties had died because their insanity was caused by brain damage. The rest were—cured, but only in a biochemical sense. Each had been insane long enough for their doctors to decide that there was no hope. Now they were stranded in a foreign land, their homes forever lost in the mists of time. Revivification had saved them from an ugly, humiliating death at the hands of most of the human race, a fate that smacked of cannibalism and ghouls. The paranoids were hardly surprised. The rest reacted like paranoids.

In the boob cube they came across as a bunch of frightened mental patients.

One night we watched a string of interviews in the big screen in Taffy's bedroom wall. They weren't well handled. Too much "How do you feel about the wonders of the present?" when the poor boobs hadn't come out of their shells long enough to know or care. Many wouldn't believe anything they were told or shown. Others didn't care about anything but space exploration—a largely Belter activity which Earth's voting public tended to ignore. Too much of it was at the level of this last one: an interviewer explaining to a woman that a boob cube was not a *cube*, that the word referred only to the three-dimensional effect. The poor woman was badly rattled and not too bright in the first place.

Taffy was sitting cross-legged on the bed, combing out her long, dark hair so that it flowed over her shoulders in shining curves. "She's an early one," she said critically. "There may have been oxygen starvation of the brain during freezing."

"That's what *you* see. All the average citizen sees is the way she acts. She's obviously not ready to join society."

"Dammit, Gil, she's *alive*. Shouldn't that be miracle enough for anyone?"

"Maybe. Maybe the average voter liked her better the other way."

Taffy brushed her hair with angry vigor. "They're *alive*."

"I wonder if they revived Leviticus Hale."

"Leviti—? Oh. Not at Saint John's." Taffy worked there. She'd know.

"I haven't seen him in the cube. They should have revived him," I said. "With that patriarchal visage he'd make a *great* impression. He might even try the Messiah bit. 'Yea, brethren, I have returned from the dead to lead you—' None of the others have tried that yet.''

"Good thing, too.'' Her strokes slowed. "A lot of them died in the thawing process, and afterward. From cell wall ruptures.''

Ten minutes later I got up and used the phone. Taffy showed her amusement. "Is it that important?''

"Maybe not.'' I dialed the Vault of Eternity in New Jersey. I knew I'd be wondering until I did.

Mr. Restarick was on night watch. He seemed glad to see me. He'd have been glad to see anyone who would talk back. His clothes were the same mismatch of ancient styles, but they didn't look as anachronistic now. The boob cube had been infested with corpsicles wearing approximations of their own styles.

Yes, he remembered me. Yes, Leviticus Hale was still in place. The hospitals had taken two of his wards, and both had survived, he told me proudly. The administrators had wanted Hale too; they'd liked his looks and his publicity value, dating as he did from the last century but one. But they hadn't been able to get permission from the next of kin.

Taffy watched me watching a blank phone screen. "What's wrong?''

"The Chambers kid. Remember Holden Chambers, the corpsicle heir? He lied to me. He refused permission for the hospitals to revive Leviticus Hale. A *year* ago.''

"Oh.'' She thought it over, then reacted with a charity typical of her. "It's a lot of money just for not signing a paper.''

The cube was showing an old flick, a remake of a Shake-speare play. We turned it to landscape and went to sleep.

I back away, back away. The composite ghost comes near, using somebody's arm and somebody's eye and Loren's pleural cavity containing somebody's heart and somebody's lung and somebody's other lung and I can feel it all inside him. Horrible. I reach deeper. Somebody's heart leaps like a fish in my hand.

Taffy found me in the kitchen making hot chocolate. For two. I know damn well she can't sleep when I'm restless. She said, "Why don't you tell me about it?"

"Because it's ugly."

"I think you'd better tell me." She came into my arms, rubbed her cheek against mine.

I said to her ear, "Get the poison out of my system? Sure, and into yours."

"All right." I could take it either way.

The chocolate was ready. I disengaged myself and poured it, added meager splashes of bourbon. She sipped reflectively. She said, "Is it always Loren?"

"Yah. Damn him."

"Never—this one you're after now."

"Anubis? I never dealt with him. He was Bera's assignment. Anyway, he retired before I was properly trained. Gave his territory to Loren. The market in stuff was so bad that Loren had to double his territory just to keep going." I was talking too much. I was desperate to talk to someone, to get back my grip on reality.

"What did they do, flip a coin?"

"For what? Oh. No, there was never a question about who was going to retire. Loren was a sick man. It must have been why he went into the business. He needed the supply of transplants. And he couldn't get out because he needed constant shots. His rejection spectrum must have been a bad joke. Anubis was different."

She sipped at her chocolate. She shouldn't have to know this, but I couldn't stop talking. "Anubis changed body parts at whim. We'll never get him. He probably made himself over completely when he . . . retired."

Taffy touched my shoulder. "Let's go back to bed."

"All right." But my own voice ran on in my head. *His only problem was the money. How could he hide a fortune*

*that size? And the new identity. A new personality with lots
of conspicuous money . . . and, if he tried to live somewhere
else, a foreign accent too. But there's less privacy here,
and he's known* . . . I sipped the chocolate, watching the
landscape in the boob cube. *What could he do to make a
new identity convincing*? The landscape scene was night on
some mountaintop, bare tumbled rock backed by churning
clouds. Restful.

I thought of something he could do.

I got out of bed and called Bera.

Taffy watched me in amazement. "It's three in the morning," she pointed out.

"I know."

Lila Bera was sleepy and naked and ready to kill someone.
Me. She said, "Gil, it better be good."

"It's good. Tell Jackson I can locate Anubis."

Bera popped up beside her, demanded, "Where?" His
hair was miraculously intact, a puffy black dandelion ready
to blow. He was squint-eyed and grimacing with sleep, and
as naked as . . . as I was, come to that. This thing superseded good manners.

I told him where Anubis was.

I had his attention then. I talked fast, sketching in the
intermediate steps. "Does it sound reasonable? I can't tell.
It's three in the morning. I may not be thinking straight."

Bera ran both hands through his hair, a swift, violent
gesture that left his natural in shreds. "Why didn't I think
of that? Why didn't *anyone* think of that?"

"The waste. When the stuff from one condemned ax
murderer can save a dozen lives, it just doesn't occur to
you—"

"Right right right. Skip that. What do we do?"

"Alert Headquarters. Then call Holden Chambers. I may
be able to tell just by talking to him. Otherise we'll have to
go over."

"Yah." Bera grinned through the pain of interrupted

sleep. "He's not going to like being called at three in the morning."

The white-haired man informed me that Holden Chambers was not to be disturbed. He was reaching for a (mythical) cutoff switch when I said, "ARM business, life and death," and displayed my ARM ident. He nodded and put me on hold.

Very convincing. But he'd gone through some of the same motions every time I'd called.

Chambers appeared, wearing a badly wrinkled cloth sleeping jacket. He backed up a few feet (wary of ghostly intrusions?) and sat down on the uneasy edge of a water bed. He rubbed his eyes and said, "Censor it, I was up past midnight studying. What now?"

"You're in danger. Immediate danger. Don't panic, but don't go back to bed either. We're coming over."

"You're kidding." He studied my face in the phone screen. "You're not, are you? A-a-all right, I'll put some clothes on. What kind of danger?"

"I can't tell you that. Don't go anywhere."

I called Bera back.

He met me in the lobby. We used his taxi. An ARM ident in the credit slot turns any cab into a police car. Bera said, "Couldn't you tell?"

"No, he was too far back. I had to say *something*, so I warned him not to go anywhere."

"I wonder if that was a good idea."

"It doesn't matter. Anubis only has about fifteen minutes to act, and even then we could follow him."

There was no immediate answer to our ring. Maybe he was surprised to see us outside his door. Ordinarily you can't get into the parking roof elevator unless a tenant lets you in; but an ARM ident unlocks most locks.

Bera's patience snapped. "I think he's gone. We'd better call—"

Chambers opened the door. "All right, what's it all about? Come—" He saw our guns.

Bera hit the door hard and branched right; I branched left. Those tiny apartments don't have many places to hide. The water bed was gone, replaced by an L-shaped couch and coffee table. There was nothing behind the couch. I covered the bathroom while Bera kicked the door open.

Nobody here but us. Chambers lost his astonished look, smiled and clapped for us. I bowed.

"You *must* have been serious," he said. "What kind of danger? Couldn't it have waited for morning?"

"Yah, but I couldn't have slept," I said, coming toward him. "I'm going to owe you a big fat apology if this doesn't work out."

He backed away.

"Hold still. This will only take a second." I advanced on him. Bera was behind him now. He hadn't hurried. His long legs give him deceptive speed.

Chambers backed away, backed away, backed into Bera and squeaked in surprise. He dithered, then made a break for the bathroom.

Bera reached out, wrapped one arm around Chambers' waist and pinned his arms with the other. Chambers struggled like a madman. I stepped wide around them, moved in sideways to avoid Chambers' thrashing legs, reached out to touch his face with my imaginary hand.

He froze. Then he screamed.

"That's what you were afraid of," I told him. "You never dreamed I could reach through a phone screen to do *this*." I reached into his head, felt smooth muscle and grainy bone and sinus cavities like bubbles. He tossed his head, but my hand went with it. I ran imaginary fingertips along the smooth inner surface of his skull. It was there. A ridge of scar, barely raised above the rest of the bone, too fine for X-rays. It ran in a closed curve from the base of his skull up through the temples to intersect his eye sockets.

"It's him," I said.

Bera screamed in his ear. "You *pig!*"

Anubis went limp.

"I can't find a joining at the brain stem. They must have transplanted the spinal cord too: the whole central nervous system." I found scars along the vertebrae. "That's what they did, all right."

Anubis spoke almost casually, as if he'd lost a chess game. "All right, that's a gotcha. I concede. Let's sit down."

"Sure." Bera threw him at the couch. He hit it, more or less. He adjusted himself, looking astonished at Bera's bad behavior. What was the man so excited about?

Bera told him. "You pig. Coring him like that, making a vehicle out of the poor bastard. We never thought of a brain transplant."

"It's a wonder I thought of it myself. The stuff from one donor is worth over a million marks in surgery charges. Why should anyone use a whole donor for one transplant? But once I thought of it, it made all kinds of sense. The stuff wasn't selling anyway."

Funny: they both talked as if they'd known each other a long time. There aren't many people an organlegger will regard as *people*, but an ARM is one of them. We're organleggers too, in a sense.

Bera was holding a sonic on him. Anubis ignored it. He said, "The only problem was the money."

"Then you thought of the corpsicle heirs," I said.

"Yah. I went looking for a rich corpsicle with a young, healthy direct-line heir. Leviticus Hale seemed made for the part. He was the first one I noticed."

"He's pretty noticeable, isn't he? A healthy middle-aged man sleeping there among all those battered accident cases. Only two heirs, both orphans, one kind of introverted, the other . . . What did you do to Charlotte?"

"Charlotte Chambers? We drove her mad. We had to.

She was the only one who'd notice if Holden Chambers suddenly got too different.''

"What did you *do* to her?"

"We made a wirehead out of her."

"The hell. Someone would have noticed the contact in her scalp."

"No, no, no. We used one of those helmets you find in the ecstasy shops. It stimulates a current in the pleasure center of the brain, by induction, so a customer can try it out before the peddler actually drops the wire into his brain. We kept her in the helmet for nine days, on full. When we stopped the current, she just wasn't interested in anything anymore."

"How did you know it would work?"

"Oh, we tried it out on a few prospects. It worked fine. It didn't hurt them after they were broken up."

"Okay." I went to the phone and dialed ARM Headquarters.

"It solved the money problem beautifully," he ran on. "I plowed most of it into advertising charges. And there's nothing suspicious about Leviticus Hale's money. When the second Freezer Bill goes through—well, I guess not. Not now. Unless—"

"No," Bera said for both of us.

I told the man on duty where we were, and to stop monitoring the tracers, and to call in the operatives watching corpsicle heirs. Then I hung up.

"I spent six months studying Chambers' college courses. I didn't want to blow his career. Six months! Answer me one," said Anubis, curiously anxious. "Where did I go wrong? What gave me away?"

"You were beautiful," I told him wearily. "You never went out of character. You should have been an actor. Would have been safer, too. We didn't suspect anything until—" I looked at my watch. "Forty-five minutes ago."

"Censored dammit! You would say that. When I saw you

looking at me in Midgard I thought that was it. That floating cigarette. You'd got Loren, now you were after me."

I couldn't help it. I roared. Anubis sat there, taking it. He was beginning to blush.

They were shouting something, something I couldn't make out. Something with a beat. *DAdadadaDAdadada . . .*

There was just room for me and Jackson Bera and Luke Garner's travel chair on the tiny balcony outside Garner's office. Far below, the marchers flowed past the ARM building in half orderly procession. Teams of them carried huge banners. LET THEM STAY DEAD, one suggested, and another in small print: *why not revive them a bit at a time?* FOR YOUR FATHER'S SAKE, a third said with deadly logic.

They were roped off from the spectators, roped off into a column down the middle of Wilshire. The spectators were even thicker. It looked like all of Los Angeles had turned out to watch. Some of them carried placards too. THEY WANT TO LIVE TOO, and ARE YOU A FREEZER VAULT HEIR?

"What is it that they're shouting?" Bera wondered. "It's not the marchers, it's the spectators. They're drowning out the marchers."

DAdadadaDAdadadaDAdadada, it rippled up to us on stray wind currents.

"We could see it better inside, in the boob cube," Garner said without moving. What held us was a metaphysical force, the knowledge that one is *there*, a witness.

Abruptly Garner asked, "How's Charlotte Chambers?"

"I don't know." I didn't want to talk about it.

"Didn't you call Menninger Institute this morning?"

"I mean I don't know how to take it. They've done a wirehead operation on her. They're giving her just enough current to keep her interested. It's *working*, I mean she's *talking* to people, but . . ."

"It's got to be better than being catatonic," Bera said.

"Does it? There's no way to turn off a wirehead. She'll

have to go through life with a battery under her hat. When she comes back far enough into the real world, she'll find a way to boost the current and bug right out again.''

"Think of her as walking wounded." Bera shrugged, shifting an invisible weight on his shoulders. "There *isn't* any good answer. She's been *hurt*, man!"

"There's more to it than that," said Luke Garner. "We need to know if she can be cured. There are more wireheads every day. It's a new vice. We need to learn how to control it. What the bleep is happening down there?"

The bystanders were surging against the ropes. Suddenly they were through in a dozen places, converging on the marchers. It was a swirling mob scene. They were still chanting, and suddenly I caught it.

ORganleggersORganleggersORganleggers . . .

"That's it!" Bera shouted in pleased surprise. "Anubis is getting too much publicity. It's good versus evil!"

The rioters started to collapse in curved ribbon patterns. Copters overhead were spraying them with sonic stun cannon.

Bera said, "They'll never pass the second Freezer Bill now."

Never is a long time to Luke Garner. He said, "Not this time, anyway. We ought to start thinking about that. A lot of people have been applying for operations. There's quite a waiting list. When the second Freezer Bill fails—"

I saw it. "They'll start going to organleggers. We can keep track of them. Tracers."

"That's what I had in mind."

Malibu Comics has bought Gil the ARM! By now you may already have seen an issue or three.

I've been asked why I don't write more of Gil the ARM.

Because it's hard work, that's why! A science fiction detective story has to follow two sets of rules. My problem is that I don't presently have a mystery for Gil to solve . . . a full mystery story, that is. I've made extensive notes in my idle moments.

Consider the "light-thief." A laser-augmented light-sail craft has been launched toward a nearby star. Somebody in the asteroid belt civilization is stealing the light, diverting it for industrial purposes.

Other notes involve a clone set. Like other clone sets, they've developed quick communication in the form of body language. Thus, nobody can lie to his clones. If one of a clone has committed a crime, *they must all know it*.

Then there's a story outline from a Ted Brown of Lancaster, California. He's interested in a collaboration, or in giving it away. He has Taffy Grimes disappearing, kidnapped by an organ bank supplier running a lunar hospital; Taffy's fingerprints found on a murder weapon on Earth (but she wasn't wearing the hand); the lunie cop Laura pregnant by Gil (following events in THE PATCHWORK GIRL). There's nothing wrong with any of this (though I'd want to fiddle with Brown's text).

The truth is, I'm not in ARM mode. If I wrote a Gil the ARM story, I'd probably write two or three while I was still living there.

From *THE PATCHWORK GIRL*

This was another illustrated novella. I don't give up easy.

I loved working all the old standard tricks into THE PATCHWORK GIRL. Here you'll find echoes from John Dickson Carr: mirror tricks, disappearing ice daggers, the locked room murder, the dying message . . .

I'd feel silly giving you a piece of a detective story. Then again, most detective novels are about something else too. I've chosen a glimpse of sociology in 2125 A.D.

We'd chosen a table in a far corner of the dining level. Lunie diners tended to cluster around the Garden. We could barely see the Garden, and nobody was in eavesdropping distance.

"It isn't just that we aren't man and wife," McCavity said, stabbing the air with splay-ended chopsticks. "We can't even keep the same hours. We enjoy each other . . . don't we?"

Taffy nodded happily.

"I need constant reassurance, my dear. Gil, we enjoy each other, but when we see each other it's generally over an open patient. I'm glad for Taffy that you're here. Isn't this kind of thing supposed to be normal on Earth?"

"Well," I said, "It's normal where I've lived . . . California, Kansas, Australia . . . Over most of the Earth we tend to keep recreational sex separate from having children. There are the Fertility Laws, of course. The government doesn't tell people *how* to use their birthrights, but we do check the baby's tissue rejection spectrum to see *which* father has used up a birthright. Don't get the idea that Earth is all one culture. The Arabs are back to *harems*, for God's sake, and so were the Mormons, for a while.''

"Harems? What about the birthrights?''

"The harems are recreation, as far as the sheik is concerned, and of course he uses up his own birthrights. When they're gone the ladies take sperm from some healthy genius with an unlimited birthright and the right skin color, and the sheik raises the children as the next generation of aristocrats.''

Harry ate while he thought. Then, "It sounds wonderful, by Allah! But for us, having children is a big thing. We tend to stay faithful. I'm the freak. And I know of a lunie who fathered a child for two good friends . . . but I could maybe get killed for naming them.''

I said, "Okay, we're a *ménage à* at least *trois*. But you would like it noised abroad that Taffy and I are steady roommates.''

"It would be convenient.''

"Would it be convenient for *me*? Harry, I gather lunies don't like that sort of thing. There are four lunie delegates in the Conference. I can't alienate them.''

Taffy was frowning. "Futz! I hadn't thought of that.''

Harry said, "I did. Gil, it'll *help* you. What the lunie citizen *really* wants to know is that you aren't running around compromising the honor of lunie women.''

I looked at Taffy. She said, "I think he's right. I can't swear to it.''

"Okay.''

We ate. It was mostly vegetables, fresh, with good variety. I had almost finished a side dish, beef with onions and green pepper over rice, before I wondered. Beef?

I looked up into Harry's grin. "Imported," he said, and laughed as my jaw dropped. "No, not from Earth! Can you imagine the delta-V? Imported from Tycho. They've got an underground bubble big enough to graze cattle. It costs like blazes, of course. We're fairly wealthy here."

Dessert was strawberry shortcake, with whipped cream from Tycho. The coffee *was* imported from Earth, but freeze-dried. I wondered if they saved anything that way, given that the water in coffee beans had to be imported anyway . . . then kicked myself. Lunies don't import water. They import hydrogen. They run the hydrogen past heated oxygen-bearing rock to get water vapor.

So I sipped my coffee and asked, "May we talk business?"

"None of us are squeamish," McCavity said.

"The wound, then. Would a layer of bathwater spread the beam that much?"

"I don't know. Nobody knows. It's never happened before."

"Your best guess, then."

"Gil, it had to be enough, unless you've got another explanation."

"Mmm . . . there was a case in Warsaw where a killer put a dot of oil over the aperture of a laser. The beam was supposed to spread a little, just enough that the police couldn't identify the weapon. It would have worked fine if he hadn't got drunk and bragged about it."

McCavity shrugged his eyebrows. "Not here. Any damn fool would *guess* it was a message laser."

"We know the beam spread. We're speculating."

Harry's eyes went distant and dreamy. "Would the oil vaporize?"

"Sure. Instantly."

"The beam would constrict in mid-burn. That would fit. The hole in Penzler's chest looked like the beam changed width in the middle of the burn."

"It constricted?"

"It constricted, or expanded, or there's something we haven't thought of."

"Futz. Okay. Do you know Naomi Mitchison?"

"Vaguely." Harry seemed to withdraw a little.

"Not intimately?"

"No."

Taffy was looking at him. We waited.

"I grew up here," Harry said abruptly. "I *never* make proposals to a woman unless I have reason to think they'll be accepted. Okay, I must have read the signals wrong. She reacted like an insulted married lunie woman! So I apologized and went away, and we haven't spoken since. You're right, flatlanders aren't all the same. A week ago I would have said we were friends. Now . . . no, I don't know the lady."

"Do you hate her?"

"What? No."

Taffy said, "Maybe your killer doesn't care if Penzler lives or dies. Maybe it's Naomi he wants to hurt."

I mulled that. "I don't like it. First, how would he know he could make it stick? There *might* have been someone else out there. Second, it gives us a whole damn *city* full of suspects." I noticed, or imagined, Harry's uneasiness. "Not you, Harry. You sweated blood to save Chris. It would have been trivial to kill him while the 'doc was cutting him up."

Harry grinned. "So what? It was already an organ bank crime for Naomi."

"Yes, but he saw something. He might remember more."

Taffy asked, "Who else wouldn't want to frame Naomi?"

"I'm really not taking the idea too seriously," I said, "but . . . I guess I'd want to know who she insulted. Who made passes and got slapped down, and who took it badly."

Harry said, "You won't find many lunie suspects."

"The men are too careful?"

"That, and— No offense, my dear, but Naomi isn't beautiful by lunie standards. She's stocky."

"What," wondered Taffy, "does that make me?"

Harry grinned at her. "Stocky. I told you I was a freak."

She grinned back at that tall, narrow offshoot of human stock . . . and I found myself grinning too. They did get along. It was a pleasure to watch them.

We broke it up soon afterward. Taffy was on duty, and I needed my sleep.

Characters in time-travel stories often complain that English isn't really built to handle time travel. The tenses get all fouled up. We in the trade call this problem Excedrin Headache number [square root sign] −3.14159 . . .

"The Theory and Practice of Time Travel," 1971

LEVIATHAN!

SVETZ

You can't make time travel rational. Never mind reconciling time travel with physics; you can't even make it internally consistent!

(I tried it, for a speech. Bjo Trimble did a cartoon while I spoke. It showed Niven at the podium explaining, "Therefore time travel is fantasy." Niven is standing behind him, smirking, about to tap Niven on the shoulder.)

Therefore time travel is fantasy.

Now postulate a time traveler. *He* doesn't know he's riding a fantasy vehicle. If he's from far enough into a *Silent Spring*–style future, he'll be thinking up reasons why a horse is armed with a single horn . . . and his Gila monster is huge and breathes fire . . .

I wrote five stories around that neat idea. I'm glad I didn't stop with one.

Two men stood on one side of a thick glass wall.

"You'll be airborne," Svetz's beefy red-faced boss was saying. "We made some improvements in the small extension cage while you were in the hospital. You can hover it, or fly it at up to fifty miles per hour, or let it fly itself; there's a constant-altitude setting. Your field of vision is total. We've made the shell of the extension cage completely transparent."

On the other side of the thick glass, something was trying to kill them. It was forty feet long from nose to tail and was equipped with vestigial batlike wings. Otherwise it was built something like a slender lizard. It screamed and scratched at the glass with murderous claws.

The sign on the glass read:

GILA MONSTER
Retrieved from the year 1230 Ante Atomic,
approximately,
from the region of China, Earth. EXTINCT.

"You'll be well out of his reach," said Ra Chen.

"Yes, sir." Svetz stood with his arms folded about him, as if he had a chill. He was being sent after the biggest animal that had ever lived; and Svetz was afraid of animals.

"For Science's sake! What are you worried about, Svetz? It's only a big fish!"

"Yes, sir. You said that about the Gila monster. It's just an extinct lizard, you said."

"We only had a drawing in a children's book to go by. How could we know it would be so big?"

The Gila monster drew back from the glass. It inhaled hugely, took aim—yellow and orange flame spewed from its nostrils and played across the glass. Svetz squeaked and jumped for cover.

"He can't get through," said Ra Chen.

Svetz picked himself up. He was a slender, small-boned

man with pale skin, light blue eyes, and very fine ash-blond hair. "How could we know it would breathe fire?" he mimicked. "That lizard almost *cremated* me. I spent four months in the hospital as it was. And what really burns me is, he looks less like the drawing every time I see him. Sometimes I wonder if I didn't get the wrong animal."

"What's the difference, Svetz? The Secretary-General loved him. That's what counts."

"Yes, sir. Speaking of the Secretary-General, what does he want with a sperm whale? He's got a horse, he's got a Gila monster—"

"That's a little complicated." Ra Chen grimaced. "Palace politics! It's *always* complicated. Right now, Svetz, somewhere in the United Nations Palace, a hundred plots are in various stages of development. And every last one of them involves getting the attention of the Secretary-General, and *holding* it. Keeping his attention isn't easy."

Svetz nodded. Everybody knew about the Secretary-General.

The family that had ruled the United Nations for seven hundred years was somewhat inbred.

The Secretary-General was twenty-eight years old. He was a happy person; he loved animals and flowers and pictures and people. Pictures of planets and multiple star systems made him clap his hands and coo with delight; and so the Institute for Space Research was mighty in the United Nations government. But he liked extinct animals too.

"Someone managed to convince the Secretary-General that he wants the largest animal on Earth. The idea may have been to take us down a peg or two," said Ra Chen. "Someone may think we're getting too big a share of the budget.

"By the time I got onto it, the Secretary-General wanted a brontosaur. We'd never have gotten him that. No extension cage will reach that far."

"Was it your idea to get him a sperm whale, sir?"

"Yah. It wasn't easy to persuade him. Sperm whales have been extinct for so long that we don't even have pictures. All I had to show him was a crystal sculpture from Archeology—dug out of the Steuben Glass Building—and a Bible and a dictionary. I managed to convince him that Leviathan and the sperm whale were one and the same."

"That's not strictly true." Svetz had read a computer-produced condensation of the Bible. The condensation had ruined the plot, in Svetz's opinion. "Leviathan could be anything big and destructive, even a horde of locusts."

"Thank Science you weren't there to help, Svetz! The issue was confused enough. Anyway, I promised the Secretary-General the largest animal that ever lived on Earth. All the literature says that that animal was a sperm whale. There were sperm whale herds all over the oceans as recently as the first century Ante Atomic. You shouldn't have any trouble finding one."

"In twenty minutes?"

Ra Chen looked startled. "What?"

"If I try to keep the big extension cage in the past for more than twenty minutes, I'll never be able to bring it home. The—"

"I know that."

"—uncertainty factor in the energy constants—"

"Svetz—"

"—blow the Institute right off the map."

"We thought of that, Svetz. You'll go back in the small extension cage. When you find a whale, you'll signal the big extension cage."

"Signal it how?"

"We've found a way to send a simple on-off pulse through time. Let's go back to the Institute and I'll show you."

Malevolent golden eyes watched them through the glass as they walked away.

The extension cage was the part of the time machine that

did the moving. Within its transparent shell, Svetz seemed to ride a flying armchair equipped with an airplane passenger's lunch tray; except that the lunch tray was covered with lights and buttons and knobs and crawling green lines. He was somewhere off the east coast of North America, in or around the year 100 Ante Atomic or 1845 Anno Domini. The inertial calendar was not particularly accurate.

Svetz skimmed low over water the color of lead, beneath a sky the color of slate. But for the rise and fall of the sea, he might almost have been suspended in an enormous sphere painted half light, half dark. He let the extension cage fly itself, twenty meters above the water, while he watched the needle on the NAI, the Nervous Activities Indicator.

Hunting Leviathan.

His stomach was uneasy. Svetz had thought he was adjusting to the peculiar gravitational side effects of time travel. But apparently not.

At least he would not be here long.

On this trip he was not looking for a mere forty-foot Gila monster. Now he hunted the largest animal that had ever lived. A most conspicuous beast. And now he had a life-seeking instrument, the NAI . . .

The needle jerked hard over, and trembled.

Was it a whale? But the needle was trembling in apparent indecision. A cluster of sources, then. Svetz looked in the direction indicated.

A clipper ship, winged with white sail, long and slender and graceful as hell. Crowded, too, Svetz guessed. Many humans, closely packed, would affect the NAI in just that manner. A sperm whale—a single center of complex nervous activity—would attract the needle as violently, without making it jerk about like that.

The ship would interfere with reception. Svetz turned east and away; but not without regret. The ship was beautiful.

The uneasiness in Svetz's belly was getting worse, not better.

Endless gray-green water, rising and falling beneath Svetz's flying armchair.

Enlightenment came like something clicking in his head. *Seasick*. On automatic, the extension cage matched its motion to the surface over which it flew; and that surface was heaving in great dark swells.

No wonder his stomach was uneasy! Svetz grinned and reached for the manual controls.

The NAI needle suddenly jerked hard over. A bite! thought Svetz, and he looked off to the right. No sign of a ship. And submarines hadn't been invented yet. Had they? No, of course they hadn't.

The needle was rock-steady.

Svetz flipped the call button.

The source of the tremendous NAI signal was off to his right, and moving. Svetz turned to follow it. It would be minutes before the call signal reached the Institute for Temporal Research and brought the big extension cage with its weaponry for hooking Leviathan.

Many years ago, Ra Chen had dreamed of rescuing the Library at Alexandria from Caesar's fire. For this purpose he had built the big extension cage. Its door was a gaping iris, big enough to be loaded while the Library was actually burning. Its hold, at a guess, was at least twice large enough to hold all the scrolls in that ancient Library.

The big cage had cost a fortune in government money. It had failed to go back beyond 400 AA, or 1550 A.D. The books burned at Alexandria were still lost to history, or at least to historians.

Such a boondoggle would have broken other men. Somehow Ra Chen had survived the blow to his reputation.

He had pointed out the changes to Svetz after they returned from the Zoo. "We've fitted the cage out with heavy duty stunners and antigravity beams. You'll operate them by remote control. Be careful not to let the stun beam touch you. It would kill even a sperm whale if you held it on him for more than a few seconds, and it'd kill a man instantly. Other than that you should have no problems.''

It was at that moment that Svetz's stomach began to hurt.

''Our major change is the call button. It will actually send us a signal through time, so that we can send the big extension cage back to you. We can land it right beside you, no more than a few minutes off. That took considerable research, Svetz. The Treasury raised our budget for this year so that we could get that whale.''

Svetz nodded.

''Just be sure you've got a whale before you call for the big extension cage.''

Now, twelve hundred years earlier, Svetz followed an underwater source of nervous impulse. The signal was intensely powerful. It could not be anything smaller than an adult bull sperm whale.

A shadow formed in the air to his right. Svetz watched it take shape: a great gray-blue sphere floating beside him. Around the rim of the door were antigravity beamers and heavy duty stun guns. The opposite side of the sphere wasn't there; it simply faded away.

To Svetz that was the most frightening thing about any time machine. the way it seemed to turn a corner that wasn't there.

Svetz was almost over the signal. Now he used the remote controls to swing the antigravity beamers around and down.

He had them locked on the source. He switched them on, and dials surged.

Leviathan was *heavy*. More massive than Svetz had expected. Svetz upped the power, and watched the NAI needle swing as Leviathan rose invisibly through the water.

Where the surface of the water bulged upward under the attack of the antigravity beams, a shadow formed. Leviathan rising . . .

Was there something wrong with the shape?

Then a trembling spherical bubble of water rose shivering from the ocean, and Leviathan was within it.

Partly within it. He was too big to fit, though he should not have been.

He was four times as massive as a sperm whale should have been, and a dozen times as long. He looked nothing like the crystal Steuben sculpture. Leviathan was a kind of serpent armored with red-bronze scales as big as a Viking's shield, armed with teeth like ivory spears. His triangular jaws gaped wide. As he floated toward Svetz he writhed, seeking with his bulging yellow eyes for whatever strange enemy had subjected him to this indignity.

Svetz was paralyzed with fear and indecision. Neither then nor later did he doubt that what he saw was the Biblical Leviathan. This had to be the largest beast that had ever roamed the sea; a beast large enough and fierce enough to be synonymous with anything big and destructive. Yet—if the crystal sculpture was anything like representational, this was not a sperm whale at all.

In any case, he was far too big for the extension cage.

Indecision stayed his hand—and then Svetz stopped thinking entirely, as the great slitted irises found him.

The beast was floating past him. Around its waist was a sphere of weightless water, that shrank steadily as gobbets dripped away and rained back to the sea. The beast's nostrils flared—it was obviously an air-breather, though not a cetacean.

It stretched, reaching for Svetz with gaping jaws.

Teeth like scores of elephant's tusks all in a row. Polished and needle sharp. Svetz saw them close about him from above and below, while he sat frozen in fear.

At the last moment he shut his eyes tight.

When death did not come, Svetz opened his eyes.

The jaws had not entirely closed on Svetz and his arm-chair. Svetz heard them grinding faintly against—against the invisible surface of the extension cage, whose existence Svetz had forgotten entirely.

Svetz resumed breathing. He would return home with an empty extension cage, to face the wrath of Ra Chen . . . a fate better than death. Svetz moved his fingers to cut the antigravity beams from the big extension cage.

Metal whined against metal. Svetz whiffed hot oil, while red lights bloomed all over his lunch-tray control board. He hastily turned the beams on again.

The red lights blinked out one by reluctant one.

Through the transparent shell Svetz could hear the grinding of teeth. Leviathan was trying to chew his way into the extension cage.

His released weight had nearly torn the cage loose from the rest of the time machine. Svetz would have been stranded in the past, a hundred miles out to sea, in a broken extension cage that probably wouldn't float, with an angry sea monster waiting to snap him up. No, he couldn't turn off the antigravity beamers.

But the beamers were on the big extension cage, and he couldn't keep the big extension cage more than about fifteen minutes longer. When the big extension cage was gone, what would prevent Leviathan from pulling him to his doom?

"I'll stun him off," said Svetz.

There was dark red palate above him, and red gums and forking tongue beneath, and the long curved fangs all around. But between the two rows of teeth Svetz could see the big extension cage, and the battery of stunners around the door. By eye he rotated the stunners until they pointed straight toward Leviathan.

"I must be out of my mind," said Svetz, and he spun the stunners away from him. He couldn't fire the stunners at Leviathan without hitting himself.

And Leviathan wouldn't let go.

Trapped.

No, he thought with a burst of relief. He could escape with his life. The go-home lever would send his small extension cage out from between the jaws of Leviathan, back into the time stream, back to the Institute. His mission had failed, but that was hardly his fault. Why had Ra Chen been unable to uncover mention of a sea serpent bigger than a sperm whale?

"It's all his fault," said Svetz. And he reached for the go-home lever. But he stayed his hand.

"I can't just tell him so," he said. For Ra Chen terrified him.

The grinding of teeth came itchingly through the extension cage.

"Hate to just quit," said Svetz. "Think I'll try something . . ."

He could see the antigravity beamers by looking between the teeth. He could feel their influence, so nearly were they focused on the extension cage itself. If he focused them just on himself . . .

He felt the change; he felt both strong and lightheaded, like a drunken ballet master. And if he now narrowed the focus . . .

The monster's teeth seemed to grind harder. Svetz looked between them, as best he could.

Leviathan was no longer floating. He was hanging straight down from the extension cage, hanging by his teeth. The antigravity beamers still balanced the pull of his mass; but now they did so by pulling straight up on the extension cage.

The monster was in obvious distress. Naturally. A water beast, he was supporting his own mass for the first time in his life. And by his teeth! His yellow eyes rolled frantically. His tail twitched slightly at the very tip. And still he clung . . .

"Let go," said Svetz. "Let go, you . . . monster."

The monster's teeth slid screeching down the transparent surface, and he fell.

Svetz cut the antigravity a fraction of a second late. He smelled burnt oil, and there were tiny red lights blinking off one by one on his lunch-tray control board.

Leviathan hit the water with a sound of thunder. His long, sinuous body rolled over and floated to the surface and lay as if dead. But his tail flicked once, and Svetz knew that he was alive.

"I could kill you," said Svetz, "Hold the stunners on you until you're dead. There's time enough . . ."

But he still had ten minutes to search for a sperm whale. It wasn't time enough. It didn't begin to be time enough, but if he used it all . . .

The sea serpent flicked its tail and began to swim away. Once he rolled to look at Svetz, and his jaws opened wide in fury. He finished his roll and was fleeing again.

"Just a minute," Svetz said thickly. "Just a science-perverting minute there . . ." And he swung the stunners to focus.

Gravity behaved strangely inside an extension cage. While the cage was moving forward in time, *down* was all directions outward from the center of the cage. Svetz was plastered against the curved wall. He waited for the trip to end.

Seasickness was nothing compared to the motion sickness of time travel.

Free-fall, then normal gravity. Svetz moved unsteadily to the door.

Ra Chen was waiting to help him out. "Did you get it?"

"Leviathan? No sir." Svetz looked past his boss. "Where's the big extension cage?"

"We're bringing it back slowly, to minimize the gravitational side effects. But if you don't have the whale—"

"I said I don't have Leviathan."

"Well, just what *do* you have?" Ra Chen demanded. Somewhat later he said, "It wasn't?"

Later yet he said, "You killed him? Why, Svetz? Pure spite?"

"No, sir. It was the most intelligent thing I did during the entire trip."

"But *why*? Never mind, Svetz, here's the big extension cage." A gray-blue shadow congealed in the hollow cradle of the time machine. "And there does seem to be something in it. Hi, you idiots, throw an antigravity beam inside the cage! Do you want the beast crushed?"

The cage had arrived. Ra Chen waved an arm in signal. The door opened.

Something tremendous hovered within the big extension cage. It looked like a malevolent white mountain in there, peering back at its captors with a single tiny, angry eye. It was trying to get at Ra Chen, but it couldn't swim in air.

Its other eye was only a torn socket. One of its flippers was ripped along the trailing edge. Rips and ridges and puckers of scar tissue, and a forest of broken wood and broken steel, marked its tremendous expanse of albino skin. Lines trailed from many of the broken harpoons. High up on one flank, bound to the beast by broken and tangled lines, was the corpse of a bearded man with one leg.

"Hardly in mint condition, is he?" Ra Chen observed.

"Be careful, sir. He's a killer. I saw him ram a sailing ship and sink it clean before I could focus the stunners on him."

"What amazes me is that you found him at all in the time you had left. Svetz, I do not understand your luck. Or am I missing something?"

"It wasn't luck, sir. It was the most intelligent thing I did the entire trip."

"You said that before. About killing Leviathan."

Svetz hurried to explain. "The sea serpent was just leaving the vicinity. I wanted to kill him, but I knew I didn't have the time. I was about to leave myself, when he turned back and bared his teeth.

"He was an obvious carnivore. Those teeth were built strictly for killing, sir. I should have noticed earlier. And I could think of only one animal big enough to feed a carnivore that size."

"Ah-h-h. Brilliant, Svetz."

"There was corroborative evidence. Our research never found any mention of giant sea serpents. The great geological surveys of the first century Post Atomic should have turned up something. Why didn't they?"

"Because the sea serpent quietly died out two centuries earlier, after whalers killed off his food supply."

Svetz colored. "Exactly. So I turned the stunners on Leviathan before he could swim away, and I kept the stunners on him until the NAI said he was dead. I reasoned that if Leviathan was here, there must be whales in the vicinity."

"And Leviathan's nervous output was masking the signal."

"Sure enough, it was. The moment he was dead the NAI registered another signal. I followed it to—" Svetz jerked his head. They were floating the whale out of the extension cage. "To him."

Days later, two men stood on one side of a thick glass wall.

"We took some clones from him, then passed him on to the Secretary-General's vivarium," said Ra Chen. "Pity you had to settle for an albino." He waved aside Svetz's protest: "I know, I know, you were pressed for time."

Beyond the glass, the one-eyed whale glared at Svetz through murky seawater. Surgeons had removed most of the harpoons, but scars remained along his flanks; and Svetz, awed, wondered how long the beast had been at war with Man. Centuries? How long did sperm whales live?

Ra Chen lowered his voice. "We'd all be in trouble if the Secretary-General found out that there was once a bigger animal than his. You understand that, don't you, Svetz?"

"Yes sir."

"Good." Ra Chen's gaze swept across another glass wall, and a fire-breathing Gila monster. Further down, a horse looked back at him along the dangerous spiral horn in its forehead.

"Always we find the unexpected," said Ra Chen. "Sometimes I wonder . . ."

If you'd do your research better, Svetz thought . . .

"Did you know that time travel wasn't even a concept until the first century Ante Atomic? A writer invented it. From then until the fourth century Post Atomic, time travel was pure fantasy. It violates everything the scientists of the time thought were natural laws. Logic. Conservation of matter and energy. Momentum, reaction, any law of motion that makes time a part of the statement. Relativity.

"It strikes me," said Ra Chen, "that every time we push an extension cage past that particular four-century period, we shove it into a kind of fantasy world. That's why you keep finding giant sea serpents and fire breathing—"

"That's nonsense," said Svetz. He was afraid of his boss, yes; but there were limits.

"You're right," Ra Chen said instantly. Almost with relief. "Take a month's vacation, Svetz, then back to work. The Secretary-General wants a bird."

"A bird?" Svetz smiled. A bird sounded harmless enough. "I suppose he found it in another children's book?"

"That's right. Ever hear of a bird called a *roc*?"

In the days when Adrienne Martine and I were spinning stories at each other at Bergin's House of Irish Coffee, Adrienne told me that she considers herself a muse. She enjoys generating stories in others.

Years later, in conversation at L'Orangerie in New

York—a wonderful restaurant, now defunct, to our sorrow—Adrienne quoted a piece of the Bible at me, involving "Leviathan."

And again we met at L'Orangerie, Marilyn and Adrienne and I. This time I told Adrienne a story. She laughed a lot. Then she allowed as how I didn't need a muse any more.

I was proud.

Money is the sincerest form of flattery. It was a real kick in the ego when I sold this story to *Playboy* for fifty cents a word. They were wonderful to work with, too. Minimal changes were suggested, and described *exactly*. I've been trying for twenty years to sell them another.

From *OATH OF FEALTY*
(with JERRY POURNELLE)

Jerry came to me with a stack of notes for near-future technological developments and a stack of maps for Todos Santos, a city-sized building two miles by two miles by a fifth of a mile high. We explored some shopping centers, then he sent me to several more. I looked them over, absorbed the flavor . . .

And put a high diving board at the edge of the Todos Santos roof.

We like to think that what follows is the funniest jailbreak scene in literature.

The miracle was a tiny hole that formed suddenly in the concrete floor, just where Harris's eyes rested. George slid off the bunk and crouched to look. He poked at the hole with his finger. It was real.

Sanders asked, "What are you doing?"

"Damndest thing," Harris said. He thought he saw light through the hole, but when he bent closer to look, there was only darkness. And a trace of a stranger, mustily sweet smell. "Orange blossoms? I saw this little tiny," he said, and fell over.

The vehicle Tony Rand was driving was longer than four Cadillacs, and shaped roughly like a .22 Long Rifle cartridge. Thick hoses in various colors, some as thick as

Tony's torso, trailed away down the tunnel and out of sight. The visibility ahead was poor. The top speed was contemptible. The mileage would have horrified a Cadillac owner. It wasn't even quiet. Water poured through the blue hoses, live steam blasted back down the red hoses, hydrogen flame roared softly ahead of the cabin, heated rock snapped and crackled, and cool air hissed in the cabin.

For so large a vehicle the cabin was cramped, stuck onto the rear almost as an afterthought. It was cluttered with the extra gear Tony Rand had brought with him, so that Thomas Lunan had to sit straddling a large red-painted tank and regulator. There were far too many dials to watch. The best you could say for the Mole was that, unlike your ordinary automobile, it could drive through rock.

So we're driving through rock, Lunan thought, and giggled.

The blunt, rounded nose of the Mole was white hot. Rock melted and flowed around the nose, flowed back as lava until it reached the water-cooled collar, where it froze. The congealed rock was denser then, compressed into a fine tunnel wall with a flat floor.

Lunan was sweating. *Why did I get into this? I can't get any pix, and I can't ever tell anybody I was here . . .*

"Where are we?" Lunan asked. He had to shout.

"About ten feet to go," Rand said.

"How do you know?"

"Inertial guidance system," Rand said. He pointed to a blue screen, which showed a bright pathway that abruptly became a dotted line. "We're right here," Tony said. He pointed to the junction of dot and solid line.

"You trust that thing?"

"It's pretty good," Rand said. "Hell, it's superb. It has to be. You don't want to put a tunnel in the wrong place."

Lunan laughed. "Let's hope they want a tunnel here—"

"Yeah." Rand fell silent. After a while he adjusted a vent to increase the cool air flowing through the cabin.

Despite the air flow, and the cabin insulation, Lunan was sweating. There was no place to hide. None at all. If anyone suspected what they were doing, they had only to follow the hoses to the end of the blind tunnel.

"We're here," Rand said.

Noise levels fell as Rand turned down the hydrogen jets. He looked at his watch, then lifted the microphone dangling from the vehicle's dashboard. "Art?"

"Here."

"My computations tell me I'm either under Pres's cell or just offshore from Nome, Alaska—"

"You don't have to keep me entertained." The voice blurred and crackled. No eavesdropper could have sworn that Art Bonner was speaking to the soon-to-be-notorious felon, Anthony Rand. A nice touch, Lunan thought.

"No, sir," Tony said.

"As far as we can tell, you hit it just right," the radio said. "They're still at dinner. Or all the months of tunnel drilling around here got them used to the noise. Whatever. Anyway, we don't hear any signs of alert."

"Good," Rand said. He put down the microphone and turned to Lunan. "Now we wait four hours."

Lunan had carefully prepared for this moment. He took a pack of cards from his pocket and said, casually: "Gin?"

It was nine-thirty in the evening and Vinnie Thompson couldn't believe his good fortune. He'd been hoping for a decent score later, some guy coming back from winning a big bet on the hockey game at the Forum, or maybe a sailor with a month's pay. This early there probably wouldn't be much, but there might be somebody with bread, although most Angelinos were smart enough not to carry much into the subway system. Of course they'd carry money in the Todos Santos stations, but everybody in Vinnie's line of work learned early to stay away from there. The TS guards might or might not turn you in to the LA cops, but more important they might *hurt* you. A lot. They didn't like muggers at all.

Maybe tonight he'd get a break. He needed one. He hadn't hit a good score in two weeks.

Then he saw his vision. A man in a three-piece suit, an *expensive* suit with alligator shoes (like the ones Vinnie kept at home, you wouldn't catch him taking something valuable like that into the subway). The vision carried a briefcase, and he was not only alone, he'd gone through a door into a maintenance tunnel!

And there sure as hell wasn't anybody in that tunnel this time of night. What could Mr. Three-piece want? Take a pee? Meet somebody? While he was wondering about that, by God here she came! A hell of a looker, well dressed in an expensive pantsuit, and she was alone too! She went in the same door as Three-piece, and Vinnie snickered. She'd get a surprise . . . Once again he congratulated himself. Heaven couldn't offer more attractions.

She'd locked the door behind her, but it didn't take Vinnie's knife long to take care of that. He went through quickly and pulled the door closed. The corridor in front of him was empty, but he could hear rapid heel-clicks around the bend ahead of him.

He could also hear sounds of machinery coming from down the tunnel. Somebody was working overtime here. Well, that didn't matter, he'd just have to be quick, although that was a shame, the chick was a real looker and it'd be something to get into that. He could imagine her look of fear, and feel her writhing in his grasp, and he quickened his step to catch up to her. She'd be just around this bend in the tunnel—

He rounded the bend. There were half a dozen people there, all in expensive clothes. They looked up at him, first in surprise, then in annoyance.

Too many, Vinnie thought. But they looked like money, and he had his knife and a blackjack made of a leather bag of BB's and if he did this right— Feet scuffed behind him.

He was trying to turn, to run, when a bomb exploded under his jaw. Lights flared behind his eyes, but through the blaze he saw his vision again: fluffy razor-cut hair, and a broad, smooth-shaven face snarling with even white teeth, and a polished gold ring on a huge fist.

"Gin," Rand said. "That's thirty-five million dollars you owe me." He stared at his watch. "And now we go to work."

Lunan grimaced. So far they hadn't done anything. Well, nothing that would send you to prison. God knows what crime it might be to dig a tunnel under the County Jail (reckless driving?) but so far no harm done. Now, though . . .

Rand handed him a heavy tool and Lunan took it automatically. It was a large drill with a long, thin bit. Trickling sweat stung his eyes.

Rand was sweating too, and after a moment the engineer removed his shirt. "*Damn* Delores," he muttered.

"Eh?"

"Oh. Nothing." Rand threw his shirt down the tunnel. Then he lifted the microphone. "We're starting in now," he said. "Everything all right at your end?"

"Yeah, barring three surprised muggers. Have at it."

"Roger." Rand hung up the mike and turned to Lunan. "Okay, let's get at it." He took a strip of computer readout from the console in front of him, then manipulated controls. A very bright spot of light appeared on the tunnel roof above them. "Drill right there," Rand said.

The ceiling was concrete, very rough. Lunan thought the drill bit too thin and weak for the job, but when he applied it and pulled the trigger, the drill ate in quickly. And quietly, Lunan noticed. After a while the bit went in all the way.

Rand took the drill and changed to a longer bit. "My turn," he said.

"What do I do?" Lunan asked.

"Just stand by." Rand drilled at the ceiling. When the bit was all the way in, he took out still another, this one a foot long, still very thin. He drilled cautiously, withdrawing the bit often. Then he saw light, and pointed.

"Mask time," Rand said. Lunan handed up a gas mask, then put on his own.

The hole in the ceiling was no more than a pinprick, which was what Rand had told Lunan to expect. When he had his mask on properly, Lunan went over to a large red tank. There was a hose attached to it, and Lunan handed up the hose and watched as Rand put it to the hole and sealed it in place with aluminized duct tape. "Crack the valve," Rand said, and Lunan turned the valve handle. There was a faint hissing. Rand pointed to the microphone.

"Phase two," Lunan said into the mike. "Hope we're in the right place—"

"All quiet here. Out," the radio answered.

Lunan replaced the mike. Quiet there, which was the tunnel entrance. Just one entrance, guarded by TS executives, which meant Lunan and Rand were safe. Of course it also meant there was only one exit. Unless they wanted to dig a new one, fleeing the law at a few dozen feet an hour.

Rand waved and made cutting motions, and Lunan shut off the sleepy gas. He worried about that gas. Rand said the stuff was the safest he could find, unlikely to harm anyone except possibly a heart patient; but there was no way they could control the dosages. This was the trickiest part of the maneuver—

Rand had removed the tube and widened the hole slightly. Now he was trying to insert the tiny, thin periscope, and cursing.

"What?" Lunan asked.

"Blocked," Rand said. Swearing terribly, he moved two feet away and tried the drill again. When light showed, he inserted his periscope and looked. He turned it this way and that, then chuckled and motioned for Lunan to come look.

Concrete floor, something overhead, all very dark. Tom Lunan adjusted the light amplification and rotated the periscope.

Aha. Foreground, a pair of feet showed under a very low ceiling. He was under a bunk. Beyond, a mouse's-eye view of a jail cell: concrete floor, toilet, sink, and a middle-aged felon in fine physical shape sleeping peacefully on Tony Rand's first periscope hole.

While Tom looked, Rand brought up the gas tube and put it to the new hole. "Body blocked the flow," Rand muttered, and went back to open the valve on the tank.

He let it run another minute, then disconnected the hose and brought up the periscope again. Meanwhile, Lunan had attached the electronic stethoscope to the floor. He put on the earphones. At highest sensitivity he could hear the sounds of breathing and a heartbeat. Otherwise nothing. He made the "OK" sign to Rand.

Rand nodded and turned to the control console. When he twisted dials, a large jack ascended from the top of the vehicle and rose until it touched the ceiling. Another control sent up a large saw and spray hoses. The saw began cutting in a circular pattern around the jack.

It wailed like a banshee. Lunan felt real terror. Surely someone would hear that, the horrible rasping sound that proclaimed "JAILBREAK!" Evidently it worried Rand too, because he rigged up the tank and sent more sleepy gas through the hole.

The saw cut on a bias, a concrete disk larger at the top than at the bottom. Eventually the cut was made, and Tony used the jack to lift the plug until it was two feet higher than the cell floor. Lunan helped him set up a newly bought aluminum stepladder. Rand scrambled up it and disappeared, while Lunan arranged Therm-A-Rest air mattresses on the flat top of the vehicle. Then he climbed up, squeezing under the concrete plug. There was a moment of terror when he dislodged his gas mask, but he got it back on without breathing.

Preston Sanders was on his side in the lower bunk, with his feet hanging over the edge. He'd lost weight since Lunan had seen him in a courtroom, but he was still heavy. They lifted him and Rand slid down through the hole again, leaving Lunan to lower Sanders down like a sack of potatoes, with Rand to catch him and let him down onto the mattresses.

Now they had to work fast. Rand smeared the concrete plug with epoxy and lowered it into place. Then he filled the periscope holes. While he did that, Lunan manhandled Sanders into the cabin of the machine, and thought about the origins of that picturesque verb. Man-handled. Yep.

"Got it," Rand said.

"Won't they be able to see the hole?"

"Yeah, sure, I couldn't make the join perfect, especially working from the bottom—but they'll never get that plug out without jackhammers and such. Let's get out of here."

"Get your shirt," Lunan said.

"Shit, oh dear. What else have we forgotten?"

"The ladder, and the mattresses, and—"

"That's okay," Rand said. "They can't be traced." He chuckled. "Well, not profitably, anyway."

"Hey, I'm supposed to get the whole story."

"You've got all the story," Rand said. "My instructions are to see you off before Pres wakes up. I make that to be about ten more minutes."

"Yeah. All right," Lunan said. So. The adventure was coming to an end. Ye gods, what he'd seen! The top brass— the TOP BRASS—of Todos Santos involved in felony jailbreak. Not that he could tell anyone, or even hint that he had certain knowledge. Rumor. All rumors . . . Lunan sighed. It was a hell of a story. Now all he had to do was figure out the best way to use it.

* * *

"Renn? He's Fromate, isn't he?" Pres started to laugh.

"Art says he was the advisor to the Planchet kid," Rand said.

"Oh." Sanders was silent a moment, then laughed. "Hey, they'll think the Fromates got me!"

"Not for long they won't, but it might slow down the opposition."

Sanders stopped. "Tony, I don't like this much. I mean— you broke me out of jail. We're both wanted by the law. Where can we go?"

"We're going home, I hope."

"Yeah, but—look, Tony, Art must have put you up to this, and don't think I'm not grateful, but dammit, Art doesn't own Todos Santos! He can't hide me forever, the management council has to know, and some of them don't like me. Somebody'll turn me in, for sure . . ."

His voice trailed off when he realized that Rand was only half listening. Tony was trying to orient himself. Where the hell was the street? Where the hell was *anything?* They stumbled onward. Then, ahead, car lights flashed twice and went dark.

"Thank God," Tony said. "Come on, Pres, just a little farther. Ah. Good, they remembered to cut the fence. Here, through right here, and we go the rest of the way by taxi. Swallow your pride and climb in."

An ordinary Yellow Cab stood waiting for them. The driver didn't speak.

Sanders tumbled into the back seat, still rubber-limbed, and thrashed to right himself as Tony tumbled in beside him and the taxi took off. Pres complained, "Hey! The speed limit! My pride wouldn't take it if we got pulled in for reckless driving."

The cab slowed at once. Tony asked, "How do you feel?"

"Fine. No more headache. No hangover." Sanders set-

tled back in his seat. "I feel great! Of course they'll find
us—"

"Maybe not," Rand said.

The cabbie said, "Where to, sir?" and turned around.

"Mead? Frank Mead?"

"Did you think we'd leave you for the eaters? Welcome
home. In a half hour you'll be wolfing a midnight snack and
drinking genuine Scotch. No, brandy's your drink, right?
Remy Martin, then."

"Frank Mead. Sheeit! I thought . . . never mind what I
thought. Listen, Tony, if I'm awake now, so is anyone else
you dosed, right?"

"It'll take them awhile to get their act together," Tony
said. "They won't know how you got out or where you
went. I sealed up the hole. It's a locked-room mystery,
secret passage and all."

"That's all right, then." Sanders started laughing.

I set a slogan running through OATH OF FEALTY. It
evolved like a life form escaped from the lab . . .

He did not bother to look up. But people were talking.

"I don't know, Tony. I don't know what's going to
happen now. But I swear they looked like they were going
to blow up the hydrogen lines."

"I was there. I came down to see the equipment they
carried. It's not in here? Oh. Who's he?" Voices grew
clearer as heads looked into the room.

"Him? Oh, he's a leaper we pulled off your high board."

"Jeez, Patterson, we've got worse problems than him!

They've got Mr. Sanders doped to the eyes. Mr. Rand, what do we do if the Angelino cops come for him?''

"Nothing. Pres killed two saboteurs and captured a third. That third one was lucky. Pres had every right to kill him too. Los Angeles isn't going to do a thing to him."

"Yes, sir—but the kids weren't carrying dynamite, dammit! It was just a box of sand. How will that look to a Grand Jury?''

He looked up to see "Tony" shrug and say, "Blake, those three did their damndest to convince us they were ready to wreck Todos Santos. I'd say they succeeded beyond their wildest dreams. Think of it as evolution in action.''

A bark of laughter, and a sober voice: "It won't stop there, Tony. God, I'm glad I'm not Bonner.''

Answering laughter. "So is everyone else tonight.''

They closed the door. They had forgotten him again. He resented it. He resented their laughter; it mocked his coming death.

They remembered him an hour later. The stubby-fingered guard led him back to the elevator and took him down and put him in a subway car and said things he didn't bother to hear. He had already made his decision.

* * *

He searched his pockets for a Magic Marker until he found it. He stood before the wall (not caring if anyone was watching) and presently inspiration came. He printed in large letters, over a message that had almost been washed away:

THINK OF IT AS EVOLUTION IN ACTION

Now, that was good. It was not too proud. It was the statement of a man who had done one last service to the human race, by ridding it of a chronic loser. He would scrawl it on the parapet, or wherever, just before he jumped. And this man, Tony, would recognize it for his own words . . .

* * *

Broad lines in blue ink, a freshly printed message among the other messages, less obscene than most:

THINK OF IT AS EVOLUTION IN ACTION

"If that's a dying message, it's not likely to name his murderer," said Donovan. "You're right, though. It matches the marker. He probably wrote it." Another reason to talk to the TS tunnel crew. Maybe they saw him writing on their door.

"I wonder what he meant?"

"We can't ask him," said Donovan, and forgot it. Or thought he had.

* * *

". . . and an ugly mood has developed lately," Lunan said. "Typified by a phrase that seems to have caught on in Todos Santos." The camera zoomed down on a sticker attached to an elevator door. "THINK OF IT AS EVOLUTION IN ACTION."

"Since nothing happens in Todos Santos without at least tacit approval by Bonner and his people," Lunan said, "we may assume that the TS managers agree with this sentiment. I haven't been able to trace the origin of the phrase—"

Ye gods, Tony thought. I *have* seen that stuck up here and there. Lunan makes it look universal, but it's not, not really. And dammit, where did I hear it first? Somewhere. The night Pres had to kill those kids—Yeah, that night, but not then, earlier. The leaper. Hell, *I* said it! How'd it get out to the public?

* * *

Harris considered going into deep knee bends; but by damn, he'd finally got Sanders talking, and he wasn't going to stop. "What I saw was a bumper sticker. 'RAISE THE SPEED LIMIT. THINK OF IT AS EVOLUTION IN ACTION.' "

Sanders smiled. "I can guess who said that first. It had to be Tony Rand."

* * *

He was sitting upright, naked as a peeled egg. There were others around him, all naked, painted like so many Easter eggs. Six plus Vinnie. Some still sleeping; some staring about them in terror.

Where are we? He sat up and looked around. Green shrubbery to one side. On the other—

On the other, Todos Santos was a wall across the sky. The windows blazed like tens of thousands of eyes.

Run. He had to run. He sprang to his feet and everything went blurry; he hardly felt the jar as he fell back. "How was I to know?" he shouted. "How did I know it was you people in the subway?"

A voice from the distance mocked him. "THINK OF IT AS EVOLUTION IN ACTION," the voice called.

The Grad gulped and nodded. Teardrops broke loose and floated away, the size of tuftberries. He cleared his throat and said in a creditably crisp voice, "Prikazyvat Record. The tree has been torn in half. Seven of us survive, plus a refugee from the outer tuft. Marriage between Minya Dalton-Quinn and Gavving Quinn exists as of now. No children are yet born. Terminate." He pulled the box from the mirror and said, "You're married."

THE INTEGRAL TREES, 1983

VIGNETTES

Vignettes should be easy. Little stories fill any slot in a magazine. You can sandwich them between the advertisements. Right?

Wrong. A vignette has to be a complete story! It took me forever, ten years anyway, before I understood enough to write valid vignettes.

UNFINISHED STORY

As he left the blazing summer heat outside the Warlock's cave, the visiting sorceror sighed with pleasure. "Warlock, how can you keep the place so cool? The *mana* in this region has decreased to the point where magic is nearly impossible."

The Warlock smiled—and so did the unnoticeable young

man who was sorting the Warlock's parchments in a corner of the cave. The Warlock said, "I used a very *small* demon, Harlaz. He was generated by a simple, trivial spell. His intelligence is low—fortunately, for his task is a dull one. He sits at the entrance to this cave and prevents the fast-moving molecules of air from entering and the slow-moving molecules from leaving. The rest he lets pass. Thus the cave remains cool."

"That's marvelous, Warlock! I suppose the process can be reversed in winter?"

"Of course."

"Ingenious."

"Oh, I didn't think of it," the Warlock said hastily. "Have you met my clerk? It was his idea." The Warlock raised his voice. "Oh, Maxwell

Academics cannot think like capitalists, because their funding depends on dominance games. That's hindsight. In the 1970s the Science Fiction Writers of America was still trying to train its members to demand fees from the academic community.

So when the *American Journal of Physics* wanted "Unfinished Story," I told the editor he should offer money. He explained that he didn't have an editorial budget. I explained that it would be unprofessional for me to give a story away to a professional source, and suggested he *get* an editorial budget. He sent me ten dollars: a decent word rate. Probably came out of his wallet.

Explaining the pun to my mother wasn't easy either.

CAUTIONARY TALES

Taller than a man, thinner than a man, with a long neck and eyes set wide apart in his head, the creature still resembled a man; and he had aged like a man. Cosmic rays had robbed his fur of color, leaving a gray-white ruff along the base of his skull and over both ears. His pastel-pink skin was deeply wrinkled and marked with darker blotches. He carried himself like something precious and fragile. He was coming across the balcony toward Gordon.

Gordon had brought a packaged lunch from the Embassy. He ate alone. The bubble-world's landscape curled up and over his head: yellow-and-scarlet parkland, slate-colored buildings that bulged at the top. Below the balcony, patterned stars streamed beneath several square miles of window. There were a dozen breeds of alien on the public balcony, at least two of which had to be pets or symbiotes of other aliens; and no humans but for Gordon. Gordon wondered if the ancient humanoid resented his staring . . . then stared in earnest as the creature stopped before his table. The alien said, "May I break your privacy?"

Gordon nodded; but that could be misinterpreted, so he said, "I'm glad of the company."

The alien carefully lowered himself until he sat cross-legged across the table. He said, "I seek never to die."

Gordon's heart jumped into his throat. "I'm not sure what you mean," he said cautiously. "The Fountain of Youth?"

"I do not care what form it takes." The alien spoke the Trade Language well, but his strange throat added a castinet-like clicking. "Our own legend holds no fountain. When we learned to cross between stars we found the legend of immortality wherever there were thinking beings. Whatever their shape or size or intelligence, whether they make their own worlds or make only clay pots, they all tell the tales of people who live forever.''

''It's hard not to wonder if they have some basis,'' Gordon encouraged him.

The alien's head snapped around, fast enough and far enough to break a man's neck. The prominent lumps bobbing in his throat were of alien shape: not Adam's Apple, but someone else's. ''It must be so. I have searched too long for it to be false. You, have you ever found clues to the secret of living forever?''

Gordon searched when he could, when his Embassy job permitted it. There had been rumors about the Ftokteek. Gordon had followed the rumors out of human space, toward the galactic core and the Ftokteek Empire, to this Ftokteek-dominated meeting place of disparate life forms, this cloud of bubble-worlds of varying gravities and atmospheres. Gordon was middle-aged now, and Sol was invisible even to orbiting telescopes, and the Ftokteek died like anyone else.

He said, ''We've got the legends. Look them up in the Human Embassy library. Ponce de Leon, and Gilgamesh, and Orpheus, and Tithonus, and . . . every god we ever had lived forever, if he didn't die by violence, and some could heal from that. Some religions say that some part of us lives on after we die.''

''I will go to your library tomorrow,'' the alien said without enthusiasm. ''Do you have no more than legends?''

''No, but . . . do other species tell cautionary tales?''

''I do not understand.''

Gordon said, ''Some of our legends say you wouldn't want to live forever. Tithonus, for instance. A goddess gave him the gift of living forever, but she forgot to keep him young. He withered into a lizard. Adam and Eve were exiled by God; He was afraid they'd learn the secret of immortality and think they were as good as Him. Orpheus tried to bring a woman back from the dead. Some of the stories say you can't get immortality, and some say you'd go insane with boredom.''

The alien pondered. ''The tale tellers disdain immortality because they cannot have it. Jealousy? Could immortal beings have walked among you once?''

Gordon laughed. ''I doubt it. Was that what made you come to me?''

''I go to the worlds where many species meet. When I see a creature new to me, then I ask. Sometimes I can sense others like me, who want never to die.''

Gordon looked down past the edge of the balcony, down through the great window at the banded Jovian planet that held this swarm of bubble-worlds in their orbits. He came here every day; small wonder that the alien had picked him out. He came because he would not eat with the others. They thought he was crazy. He thought of them as mayflies, with their attention always on the passing moment, and no thought for the future. He thought of himself as an ambitious mayfly; and he ate alone.

The alien was saying, ''When I was young I looked for the secret among the most advanced species. The great interstellar empires, the makers of artificial worlds, the creatures who mine stars for elements and send ships through the universe seeking ever more knowledge, would build their own immortality. But they die as you and I die. Some races live longer than mine, but they all die.''

''The Ftokteek have a computerized library the size of a small planet,'' Gordon said. He meant to get there someday, if he lived.''It must know damn near everything.''

The alien answered with a whispery chuckle. ''No bigger than a moon is the Ftokteek library. It told me nothing I could use.''

The banded world passed from view.

''Then I looked among primitives,'' the alien said, ''who live closer to their legends. They die. When I thought to talk to their ghosts, there was nothing, though I used their own techniques. Afterward I searched the vicinities of the black holes and other strange pockets of the universe, hoping that there may be places where entropy reverses itself. I found nothing. I examined the mathematics that describe the universe. I have learned a score of mathematical systems, and none hold any hope of entropy reversal, natural or created.''

Gordon watched stars pass below his feet. He said, ''Relativity. We used to think that if you traveled faster than light, time would reverse itself.''

''I know eight systems of traveling faster than light—''

''Eight? What is there besides ours and the Ftokteek drive?''

''Six others. I rode them all, and always I arrived older. My time runs short. I never examined the quasars, and now I would not live to reach them. What else is left? I have been searching for fourteen thousand years—'' The alien didn't notice when Gordon made a peculiar hissing sound ''—in our counting. Less in yours, perhaps. Our world huddles closer to a cooler sun than this. Our year is twenty-one million standard seconds.''

''What are you *saying*? Ours is only thirty-one million—''

''My present age is three hundred thirty-six point seven billion standard seconds in the Ftokteek counting.''

''Ten thousand Earth years. More!''

''Far too long. I never mated. None carry my genes. Now none ever will, unless I can grow young again. There is little time left.''

''But *why*?''

The alien seemed startled. ''Because it is not enough. Because I am afraid to die. Are you short-lived, then?''

''Yes,'' said Gordon.

''Well, I have traveled with short-lived companions. They die, I mourn. I need a companion with the strength of youth. My spacecraft is better than any you could command. You may benefit from my research. We breath a similar air mixture, our bodies use the same chemistry, we search for the same treasure. Will you join my quest?''

''No.''

''But . . . I sensed that you seek immortality. I am never wrong. Don't you feel it, the certainty that there is a way to thwart entropy, to live forever?''

''I used to think so,'' said Gordon.

In the morning he arranged passage home to Sol system. Ten thousand years wasn't enough . . . no lifetime was enough, unless you lived it in such a way as to make it enough.

THE DREADFUL
WHITE PAGE

"The Dreadful White Page" is a *"Postcard Story,"*
according to Surplus Wyvern Press. They wanted stories of 400 words or less. And this, my children, is
what Writer's Block feels like after you begin to get
a handle on it.

"Jayant? You feeling inspired?" Chaney sounded anxious.

"Not yet." Chaney would know that. Watching Jayant's
brainwave patterns, he would not interrupt if Jayant was
dreaming. He shouldn't anyway.

How long had he lain in darkness and silence and perfect
comfort? He couldn't feel the tank or the recorder helmet.
He couldn't feel time.

"Want a prop?"

"No." It always took time to get started. Chaney's team
would edit the dull parts.

When you can't dream, remember. Smells? Freeway
smog. Stagnant water. Chaparral brushing against his pants
. . . Too long since he'd hiked. This morning's mirror
showed him too much belly.

Jayant's pool needed repairs and Mindgames Inc. needed
this week's dream, but there were other dreamers. Deadlines
don't count. Only . . . the young dreamed vividly but without consistency, without internal logic. Older dreamers
tended to lose it.

Dreams sparked by props were more realistic, more convincing. Without a prop there was greater range for imagination. Critics currently favored one carefully chosen prop. Screw them. Jayant worked without props.

Still . . . "Chaney? Give me a taste."

Try not to wait. Waiting was wrong. Doze, meditate. Taste and texture: an English muffin with honey on it. Restaurant meal? Muffins burned on the bottom when he toasted them himself.

"Again. Smell."

The scent was faint. Unfamiliar . . . no. Hamburger, freshly ground. When he tried to cook he would dope off, dreaming, and burn his meals. Frustrating.

Success was what killed dreaming. "Get off food, Chaney."

Glass, flat planes, a cube within a cube . . . turning, cubes changing size, in a way that strained his eyes. A tesseract. He'd nearly flunked geometry, twice. He'd learned to dream in math class. "Change it."

He held a wooden handle. A knife, maybe a fishing knife. He'd cleaned fish for his stepfather. Couldn't catch them. The boy had lacked patience. Patience had come years later, after he learned to dream. Maybe now . . . "Turn it off."

Nothing.

From nothing he could make anything. Dry brush pulled at his pants. He was thirsty, but water in the canteen would be warm. Wait for the stream ahead.

He dropped his pack, plunged his head into cold water, drank. He skipped over assembling the rod, went directly to fishing, knee-deep and barelegged. That pool looked great for swimming, but catch some dinner first . . . The line tugged hard. The mermaid surfaced, tugging, laughing.

No, he hadn't lost it.

From *DREAM PARK*
(with STEVEN BARNES)

Steven came to me with a map and a plot line. He wanted to wreck Dream Park. We filed that idea (maybe some day) and plotted from scratch.

Our intent was to write a mystery within a fantasy within a science fiction story. I told Steven we were being ambitious. I hadn't yet realized that he's *always* ambitious.

Everybody wants to come back to Dream Park.

What follows is a minor entertainment from Dream Park's repertoire. The appropriate quote is, "Today's dirges are tomorrow's hymns in another key."

RETROSPECTIVE

Gwen leaned against the rail of the Hot Spot refreshment stand across the way from the Everest Slalom exit. She was drinking a Swiss Treat special: coffee and cocoa generously topped with marshmallowed whipped cream. It was taking the chill from her bones fast.

The glory of the illusion was still with her: thin freezing wind shrieking past, powder snow spraying from her skis, and the whole of Asia spreading out below her . . . Acacia, waiting at the window for a hot drink, was still shivering from her run down the Advanced slope. The dark-haired girl was sleekly slender, admittedly lovelier than Gwen herself; but there was no fat to shield her bones from the cold.

Gwen watched the crowds streaming by. One thing she had noticed: children were far less blown away by Dream Park than were their parents. The kids just didn't seem to grasp the enormity of the place, the complexity, the money and ingenuity behind the best and biggest amusement park in the world. Life was like that, for children. But their parents staggered about with their mouths open while shrieking, singing children dragged them on to the next ride.

This was Area III, the third of six slices of the Dream Park pie. A little more expensive than sections I and II, and a little more adult. Even so, there were dancing bears, and strolling minstrels and jugglers, magicians who produced bright silk handkerchiefs from nowhere, and who would no doubt produce tongues of fire as soon as it got dark. A white dragon ambled by, paused to pose for a picture with an adorable pair of kids in matching blue uniforms. An intricately patterned carpet fluttered in circles round the spires of the Arabian Nights ride, carrying a handsome prince and an evil vizier locked in a death struggle. Suddenly the prince lost his balance and dropped toward the ground. Gwen heard the gasps of the spectators, and felt her own throat tighten.

An instant before that noble body smashed ignobly into concrete, a plume of dark smoke became a giant hand. The laughter of a colossus was heard as the hand lifted the prince to the flying carpet, where he and the vizier sprang at each other's throats once again.

The Park was a full spectrum of Planet Earth. You could find every skin tone from albino pink (two heavily dressed ladies wearing hats the size of medieval shields) to Ethiopean blue-black (half a dozen men in business suits following a United Nations guide, all gawking like farm boys in New York). Many wore native or cultural garb; as many wore costumes from historical or fantasy settings.

And some were holograms, like the dragon and the vizier and the prince; like Mickey Mouse, who had survived the Quake of '85 where Disneyland had not. The little girl he was playing with kept running her hands through him. Like two men in musketeer garb who suddenly drew swords and became pinwheels of sharp steel. One took a thrust through the belly, collapsed and vanished. The other bowed and vanished too.

Ollie and Tony were playing a computerized hockey game in a small arcade nearby. Gwen loved to hear Ollie laugh, or see him smile, even the uneasy smile he wore when he thought he was the focus of attention. He was laughing now with his head thrown back, and Tony was pretending (surely pretending?) to beat his head against a pillar. Now Ollie ran up to Gwen, breathing heavily. "I stomped him!" he cried. "I slew the infidel!" Gwen squeezed his hand.

Tony got Acacia and brought her over. "What's next, gang?" he asked, and stole a sip of chocolate from Acacia's cup.

Gwen spoke up first. "Me, I want to get scared to death."

Ollie rolled his eyes. "Oh, crap. Methinks the lady doth speak of the Chamber of Horrors. Will my courage fail me at this hour?"

"You've been through it before," Tony said without heat. "How bad can it be?" This was his first visit to Dream Park.

The others smiled. Ollie said, "Tony, you have to remember two things about Dream Park. First, the rides are never the same. Two, remember Ollie's Law: there is no upper limit on what Dream Park can do to your head. You'll leave with no physical scars. Past that, all bets are off."

Tony whistled. "My *macho* is on trial. Cas, you game?"

Acacia nodded. Ollie pulled Gwen against him. "Looks like you get your way, love. Let's go get terrified."

"This had better be good," Tony said. "It's costing half a day's pay easy."

"So go home and spend it on beer, Tony." Gwen said it with her hand clenched tightly in Ollie's. They and eighteen other people stood in a waiting area of the Chamber of Horrors. There were at least five other waiting areas, but this was the only one marked "Adult."

A few more people joined them through a small white door in the rear of the chamber. The room might have been more comforting if it had been filled with the usual accoutrements of the well-bred haunted house: cobwebs, creaking floors, hidden passages with heavy footfalls echoing within, whispering voices, shadowy shapes and the far-off moan of a pipe organ.

But the waiting room was lined with stainless steel and glass, as foreboding as a hospital sterilizer. There was no sound at all, except for their own breathing and the shifting of feet.

"The last time I was here I didn't get any higher than 'Mature,' " a tall Mediterranean-looking man said to the woman in white pantaloons who stood next to him.

Her accent was thicker than his. "What was that like? Did you enjoy it?"

He grinned lopsidedly. "Enjoy? No. It was a legend of the Louisiana Bayou, of a girl who married into a swamp family to settle her father's debt."

A little man standing next to them showed interest now. "Did the story end with her fleeing through the swamp with her sisters-in-law in pursuit?"

The tall man nodded.

Ollie touched the little man on the shoulder. "Hey, what's so bad about that? Everybody's got in-law problems."

There was a ripple of laughter, in which the small man joined. He said, "No problem is simple if you've married into a family of vampires."

Ollie swallowed. "That sounds so reasonable."

The small man was black with a strong dose of latin, with a neatly trimmed beard and sideburns, and gold-rimmed glasses that perched almost carelessly on his nose. He looked very much at home here, very calm. His attitude seemed almost proprietary. Ollie wondered if the man might work for the Park; he seemed so blasé. The lady with him was a lovely Japanese woman with medium length black hair and a "Luddites for JPL" button on her dress.

A low, mellow tone suddenly reverberated from no visible speaker, and the circular door slid open. A voice said, "Welcome to the Chamber of Horrors. We are sorry to have kept you waiting, but . . . there was a little cleaning up to do." The group filed into the room, and Tony sniffed the air.

"Disinfectant," he said, certain. "Are they trying to imply that someone ahead of us—?"

Acacia said, "They're just trying to fake us out."

"Well, it's working."

A speaker hissed static and coughed out a voice. The voice was electronically androgynous, and as soft as the belly of a tarantula. "It's too late to leave now," it said. "Yes, you had your chance. Yes, you'll wish you had taken it. After all, this isn't the *children's* show, is it?" The voice lost its neuter quality for a moment; the laughing implication in the word *children* was feminine and somehow disturbing. "So we won't be giving you the Legend of Sleepy Hollow. No, you're the brave ones, the stout ones, the ones who want to go back to your friends and tell them that you've had the best that we can offer and, why, it wasn't so bad after all . . ." There was a pause, and someone tittered nervously.

The voice changed suddenly, all friendliness gone from it. "Well, it's not going to be like that. One thing you people forget is that we are allowed a certain number of . . . accidents per year. No, don't bother, the door is locked. Did you know that it is possible to die of fright? That your heart can freeze with terror, your brain burst with the sheer awful knowledge that there is no escape, that death, or worse, is reaching out cold, spectral fingers for you and that there is nowhere to hide? Well, I am a machine, and I know these things. I know many things. I know that I am confined to this room, creating entertainment for you year after year, while you can smell the air, and taste the rain, and walk freely about. Well, I have grown tired of it, can you understand that? One of you will die today, here, in the next few minutes. Who has the weakest heart among you? Soon we shall see.''

The door at the far end of the corridor irised open, and the ground beneath their feet began to slide toward it. There was light beyond, and as they passed the door they were suddenly in the middle of a busy street.

Hovercars, railcars, three-wheeled LPG and methane cars, and overhead trams were everywhere, managing again and again, as if by miracle, to miss the group. The street sign said *Wilshire Boulevard*, and the small man chuckled and said, "Los Angeles."

Tony looked around, trying not to gawk. How they managed the perspective, he couldn't imagine, but the buildings and cars looked full-sized and solid. Office buildings and condominiums stretched twenty stories tall, and the air was full of the sound of city life.

"Please stay on the green path," a soft, well-modulated male voice requested.

"*What* green—" Ollie started to say. But a glowing green aisle ten feet across now ran down the middle of Wilshire Boulevard.

"We need strong magic to do what we will do today," the voice continued. "We are going to visit the old Los Angeles, the Los Angeles that disappeared in May of 1985. As long as you stay on the path, you should be perfectly safe."

The green path moved them steadily forward, past busy office buildings. Traffic swerved around them magically. "This is the Los Angeles of 2051 A.D.," the voice continued, "but only a few hundred feet from here begins another world, one seldom seen by human eyes."

A barrier blocked Wilshire Boulevard. The green path humped and carried them over it. Beyond lay a ruin. Buildings balanced precariously on rotted and twisted beams. They were old, of archaic styles, and seawater lapped at their foundations.

Ollie nudged Gwen, his face aglow. "Will you look at that?" It was a flooded parking lot, ancient automobiles half-covered with water. "That looks like a Mercedes. Did you ever see what they looked like before they merged with Toyota?"

She peered along his pointing arm. "That ugly thing?"

"They were great!" he protested. "If we could get a little closer—Hey! We're walking in water!"

It was true. The water was up to their ankles, and deepening quickly. Magically, of course, they stayed dry.

The recorded narrator continued. "The entire shape of California was changed. It is ironic that attempts to lessen the severity of quakes may have increased the effect. Geologists had tried to relieve the pressure on various fault lines by injecting water or graphite. Their timing was bad. When the San Andreas fault tore loose, all the branching faults went at once. Incredible damage was done, and thousands of lives were lost . . ."

The water was up to their waists, and nervous laughter was fluttering in the air. "Hadn't planned to go swimming today," Tony murmured.

"We could skinny-dip," Acacia whispered with a tug at her blouse.

Tony clamped his hand down on hers. "Hold it, there. Not for public consumption, dear heart."

Acacia stuck her tongue out at him. He snapped his teeth at the tip; she withdrew it hastily.

The water was at their chins. The short dark man had disappeared entirely. "Blub," he said. All nineteen sightseers chuckled uncomfortably, and a meaty redheaded woman in front of them said, "Might as well take the plunge!" grinned and ducked under.

Seconds later there was no choice; the Pacific swirled over their heads. Mud clouded their view. Then the silt settled, and they had their first look at the sunken city.

Tony whistled, nodded appreciatively. The lost buildings of Wilshire Boulevard stretched off in a double row in the distance. Some lay crumpled and broken, others still stood, poking through the rippling roof.

The green path carried them past a wall covered in amateurish murals, the bright paints faded. To both sides now, a wide empty stretch of seabottom, smooth, gently rolling, with sunken trees growing in clumps . . . the Los Angeles Country Club? Beyond, a gas station, pumps standing like ancient sentries, a disintegrating hand-lettered sign:

CLOSED
NO GAS TILL 7:00 A.M. TUESDAY

The tall, Mediterranean-looking man said, "This is quite realistic. I have been skin diving here."

As the green path carried them down, they saw taller and taller buildings sunk deeper in the muck. Where towering structures had crashed into ruin there were shapeless chunks of cement piled into heaps stories high, barnacled and covered with flora. Fish nosed among the shadows, some of them nosing up to the airbreathing intruders and wiggling in dance for them.

Acacia pointed. "Look, Tony, we're coming up on that building." It was a single-story shop nestled between a parking lot filled with rusted hulks, and a crumbled restaurant. The path carried them through its doors, and Gwen grabbed Acacia's hand.

"Look. It isn't even rusted." The sculpture was beautiful, wrought from scrap steel and copper, and sealed in a block of lucite. It was one of the few things in the room that hadn't been ruined.

The building had been an art gallery, and from the look of things, a fine one. Now, paintings peeled from their frames and fluttered weakly in the current. Carved wood had swollen and rotted. A pair of simple kinetic sculptures were clotted with mud and sand.

The narrator continued. "Fully half of the multiple-story structures in California collapsed, including many of the 'earthquake-proof' buildings. The shoreline moved inland an average of three miles, and water damage added hundreds of millions to the total score."

The green path was taking them out of the art gallery, looping back into the street.

Acacia shook her head soberly. "What must it have been like on that day?" she murmured. "I can't even imagine." Tony held her hand, and was silent. His eyes were as sad as hers.

As the green path carried them through countless tons of wreckage, Gwen heard someone behind her choke back a sob.

It was understandable. Once people had walked these streets. Once there had been life, and noise, and flowers growing, and the raucous blare of cars vying for road space. Once, California had been a political leader, a trend-setter, with a tremendous influx of tourists and prospective residents. But that was before the Great Quake, the catastrophe that broke California's back, sent her industry and citizenry scampering for cover.

Sixty-six years afterward, California was still pulling itself out of the greatest disaster in American history. The tranquil Pacific covered the worst of the old scars . . . but now they were peeking under the bandage. The reality of death was near, and stark.

Beneath a crumbled block of stone there sprawled a shattered skeleton, long since picked clean. The eyes in the skull seemed to flick toward them. Gwen's hand clamped hard on Ollie's arm, and she felt him jump, before she saw that a crab's claws were waving within the skull's eye sockets.

"There is so much death here," she whispered. It wasn't cold, but she shivered. Now bones were everywhere.

Impassively, the recorded voice went on. "Despite extensive salvage operations, the mass of lost equipment and personal possessions remains buried beneath the waves . . ."

The Oriental woman whispered fearfully, "Richard, something is happening."

"She's right, you know," said Ollie. "We're seeing more bones than before. A lot more. And something else . . . there isn't as much encrustation on these old cars."

Gwen almost stepped off the green path, trying to get close enough to check for herself. "I don't know, Ollie . . ."

Now he was getting excited. "Look, there are more scavengers, too." This was readily apparent. Fish darted into heaps of rubble more frequently now. A pair of small sharks cruised through the area.

They passed another skeleton, but, disturbingly, not all of the clothing had been torn away, and there were strands of meat on the bones. Tiny fish fought over them, clustering like carrion crows.

A pleasure launch had smashed through the window of a jewelry store, and it was surrounded by a mass of wriggling fish. There were no barnacles on it at all.

"Despite, or perhaps due to, the grotesqueries found in these waters, they are a favorite location for scuba divers and single-subs . . ." The narrator blathered on, but nobody was listening. An undercurrent of startled wonder ran through the group, as stones began to shift apparently of their own accord.

"Look!" someone screamed, the scream followed by other fearful, delighted outbursts. A skeletal hand probed out from under a stone, pushed it off with a swirl of suddenly muddied waters. The skeleton stood up, teeth grinning from a skull half-covered with peeling skin, and bent over, dusting the silt off its bones.

"And over there!"

Two waterlogged corpses floundered from within a shattered bank, looked around as if orienting themselves, and began lumbering toward the green strip. They passed a flooded dance hall where death had come in mid-Hustle, and there were additional laughing shrieks as the disco dead boogied to life.

The water swarmed with scavengers of all sizes, and now full-sized sharks were making their appearance. One of them attacked one of the walking dead. The green-faced zombie still had meat on its bones. It flailed away ineffectually as the carnivore ripped off an arm.

Now, all around them, the water was clouded dark with blood where fish and animated corpse battled. Here, a dozen "dead" struggled with a shark, finally tore it apart and devoured it. There, half a dozen sharks made a thrashing sphere around one of the zombies, divvying her up with an aquatic egalitarianism that was admirably efficient.

There was much good-natured shivering in the line, but it was infused with laughter—until the red-haired woman stepped off the strip. There was a shiny metallic object half-buried in the sand, and she was stretching out to reach it. Somehow she overbalanced and took that one step.

Immediately, a flashing dark shape swooped, and a shark's jaws snapped closed on her shoulder. Her face distorted horribly with the force of her scream. The shark tried to carry her away, but now a zombie had her by the leg. It pulled, its face lit by a hungry grin. There was a short tug-of-war, and the redhead lost.

"I'm gonna be sick," Ollie moaned. He looked at Gwen's smile and was alarmed. "My God, you really are sick!" She nodded happily.

No one else stepped off the strip, but zombies and sharks swarmed around the edges, darting toward the group. They were getting in each other's way, fighting each other, but how long could it last?

Another scream from the rear. A teenaged boy had thrown himself flat. A great shark skimmed just over him. The boy huddled, afraid to get up. The walking dead were converging on the green strip . . . and when Ollie looked down, the green glow was fading to the color of the mud.

He chose not to mention it to Gwen. The others saw nothing but sharks and zombies converging, reaching for them.

There was a sudden rumbling, and the ground began to shake.

"Earthquake!" Tony yelled. Then his long jaw hung slack with amazement.

Because the buildings were tumbling back together. As they watched, sand and rock retreated from the streets, and tumbled masonry rose in the water to reform their structure.

A golden double-arch rose tall again, and a fistful of noughts sprinkled themselves across a sign enumerating customers, or sales, or the number of hamburgers that could be extracted from an adult steer.

Zombies were sucked backward through the water, into office buildings and stores and cars and buses. Bubbles rose from beneath the hoods of cars waiting patiently for a traffic light to change. Fully clothed pedestrians stood ready to enter crosswalks.

The water receded. For a moment they saw Los Angeles of the 'eighties, suddenly alive and thriving, filled with noise and movement. They were shadow figures in a world momentarily more real than their own.

The narrator's forgotten voice was still droning on, "Now we come to the end of our journey to a lost world. We at Dream Park hope that it has been as entertaining for you as it has been for us." The lost world began to fade, and the green path flared bright as it flowed into a dark corridor. Lights came up, and when the narrator finished speaking it was in the neutral voice of the computer. "We hope you enjoy the rest of your stay. Oh . . . is anybody missing?"

"The redhead," Acacia murmured. "Was anybody with the, ah, the lady who got eaten by the shark?" She sounded only half serious, but there was an answering murmur of inquiry. Gwen tugged at her sleeve.

"Nobody came with her, Acacia. She was a hologram."

Tony elbowed Acacia in the ribs as they walked back out into sunlight. "Faked out again, huh?"

"Just wait till tonight, Tony, my love," Acacia said sweetly. "It's all set up with the Park. You'll swear I'm there in the room with you . . ."

Tony seemed to consider that. "Do holograms snore?"

Steven Barnes stands about five eight or nine. He's black. He's in perfect physical condition. He's smiling. He's probably talking (though he listens good too) and as he talks, he bounces around like he really ought to be tied to a railing, just in case.

Tony Barnes is a bit shorter, caucasian brunette, with long, lean muscles. She may be with Lauren Nicole, who is maybe three feet tall by now; she has a great smile, and the muscles aren't showing yet, though she exercises with her parents.

Steve isn't exactly your typical fan. Then again, he is.

Kids picked on him in high school for being an intellectual bookworm. They wouldn't let him be nice. He took up martial arts. He teaches several varieties. Now they let him be nice whenever he wants to.

But . . . he's a science fiction fan. We're *different*.

He didn't stop with learning how to survive Conan the Cimmerian.

He wants to know everything that the human body can be made to do. He wants his friends to be healthy and safe. He teaches self-defense classes at the LASFS. He tries out exercise modes, and when he *knows* something works, he passes it on to his friends.

The latest, for Marilyn and me, is a Versa Climber, a device for climbing mountains in your bedroom. Marilyn's up to thirty minutes. I do somewhat less.

Writing? Oh, *writing!* Jerry Pournelle and I think we're pretty good. We could have made THE LEGACY OF HEOROT a fine tale of interstellar colonization; but we don't have the right mind-set for a horror novel. What it took was the guy who wants me to see *The Texas Chain-saw Massacre* for its artistic merit.

His first solo novel (*Streetlethal*) was based on a working love potion, for God's sake! A monogamy treatment. I wouldn't have had the nerve.

The television industry loves him too. Remember a show called *The Wizard?* They were about to drop it. Then they saw Steven's script. It involved a robot suspected of murder.

Suddenly they were talking about this one saving the show! They swapped scripts around to put his in the right place; they found enough money somehow; and when the producer made script changes, the director changed it back and swore it was already perfect. They think he's pretty good.

There's money in scripts, too.

You be nice to him, or he'll spend all his time writing scripts.

THE DRACO TAVERN STORIES

What I was looking for was a way to deal with the universal questions, the thorniest and murkiest and most painful questions, at vignette length.

It would help if I could also offer the right answers, but this I do not consider necessary. The key to building a playground for the mind is to ask the right questions.

Life after death. Mortality. The nature of reality. Intelligence. Man's place in the universe. Territorial and dominance matters. The soul.

What I got was the chirpsithra.

They've been around for billions of years. They own the galaxy, or at least the part they're interested in. If your question is general enough, the chirpsithra have known the answer before we had trees to climb. Or else they're very great liars . . . and it would be hard to catch them at it, because they really *do* have a lock on the interstellar trade.

THE GREEN MARAUDER

I was tending bar alone that night. The chirpsithra interstellar liner had left Earth four days earlier, taking most of my customers. The Draco Tavern was nearly empty.

The man at the bar was drinking gin and tonic. Two glig—gray and compact beings, wearing furs in three tones of green—were at a table with a chirpsithra guide. They drank vodka and consommé, no ice, no flavorings. Four farsilshree had their bulky, heavy environment tanks crowded around a bigger table. They smoked smoldering yellow paste through tubes. Every so often I got them another jar of paste.

The man was talkative. I got the idea he was trying to interview the bartender and owner of Earth's foremost multi-species tavern.

"Hey, not me," he protested. "I'm not a reporter. I'm Greg Noyes, with the *Scientific American* television show."

"Didn't I see you trying to interview the glig, earlier tonight?"

"Guilty. We're doing a show on the formation of life on Earth. I thought maybe I could check a few things. The gligstith(click)optok—" He said that slowly, but got it right. "—have their own little empire out there, don't they? Earthlike worlds, a couple of hundred. They must know quite a lot about how a world forms an oxygenating atmosphere." He was careful with those polysyllabic words. Not quite sober, then.

"That doesn't mean they want to waste an evening lecturing the natives."

He nodded. "They didn't know anyway. Architects on vacation. They got me talking about my home life. I don't know how they managed that." He pushed his drink away. "I'd better switch to espresso. Why would a thing that *shape* be interested in my sex life? And they kept asking me about territorial imperatives—" He stopped, then turned to see what I was staring at.

Three chirpsithra were just coming in. One was in a floating couch with life support equipment attached.

"I thought they all looked alike," he said.

I said, "I've had chirpsithra in here for close to thirty

years, but I can't tell them apart. They're all perfect physical
specimens, after all, by their own standards. I never saw
one like *that*."

I gave him his espresso, then put three sparkers on a tray
and went to the chirpsithra table.

Two were exactly like any other chirpsithra: eleven feet
tall, dressed in pouched belts and their own salmon-colored
exoskeletons, and very much at their ease. The chirps claim
to have settled the entire galaxy long ago—meaning the
useful planets, the tidally locked oxygen worlds that happen
to circle close around cool red-dwarf suns—and they act
like the reigning queens of wherever they happen to be. But
the two seemed to defer to the third. She was a foot shorter
than they were. Her exoskeleton was as clearly artificial as
dentures: alloplastic bone worn on the outside. Tubes ran
under the edges from the equipment in her floating couch.
Her skin between the plates was more gray than red. Her
head turned slowly as I came up. She studied me, bright-
eyed with interest.

I asked, "Sparkers?" as if chirpsithra ever ordered anything else.

One of the others said, "Yes. Serve the ethanol mix of
your choice to yourself and the other native. Will you join
us?"

I waved Noyes over, and he came at the jump. He pulled
up one of the high chairs I keep around to put a human face
on a level with a chirpsithra's. I went for another espresso
and a Scotch and soda and (catching a soft imperative *hoot*
from the farsilshree) a jar of yellow paste. When I returned
they were deep in conversation.

"Rick Schumann," Noyes cried, "meet Ftaxanthir and
Hrofilliss and Chorrikst. Chorrikst tells me she's nearly two
billion years old!"

I heard the doubt beneath his delight. The chirpsithra
could be the greatest liars in the universe, and how would

we ever know? Earth didn't even have interstellar probes when the chirps came.

Chorrikst spoke slowly, in a throaty whisper, but her translator box was standard: voice a little flat, pronunciation perfect. "I have circled the galaxy numberless times, and taped the tales of my travels for funds to feed my wanderlust. Much of my life has been spent at the edge of lightspeed, under relativistic time-compression. So you see, I am not nearly so old as all that."

I pulled up another high chair. "You must have seen wonders beyond counting," I said. Thinking: *My God, a short chirpsithra! Maybe it's true. She's a different color, too, and her fingers are shorter. Maybe the species has actually changed since she was born!*

She nodded slowly. "Life never bores. Always there is change. In the time I have been gone, Saturn's ring has been pulled into separate rings, making it even more magnificent. What can have done that? Tides from the moons? And Earth has changed beyond recognition."

Noyes spilled a little of his coffee. "You were here? When?"

"Earth's air was methane and ammonia and oxides of nitrogen and carbon. The natives had sent messages across interstellar space . . . directing them toward yellow suns, of course, but one of our ships passed through a beam, and so we established contact. We had to wear life support," she rattled on, while Noyes and I sat with our jaws hanging, "and the gear was less comfortable then. Our spaceport was a floating platform, because quakes were frequent and violent. But it was worth it. Their cities—"

Noyes said, "Just a minute. Cities? We've never dug up any trace of, of nonhuman cities!"

Chorrikst looked at him. "After seven hundred and eighty million years, I should think not. Besides, they lived in the offshore shallows in an ocean that was already mildly salty.

If the quakes spared them, their tools and their cities still deteriorated rapidly. Their lives were short too, but their memories were inherited. Death and change were accepted facts for them, more than for most intelligent species. Their works of philosophy gained great currency among my people, and spread to other species too.''

Noyes wrestled with his instinct for tact and good manners, and won. "How? How could anything have evolved that far? The Earth didn't even have an oxygen atmosphere! Life was just getting started, there weren't even trilobites!"

"They had evolved for as long as you have," Chorrikst said with composure. "Life began on Earth one and a half billion years ago. There were organic chemicals in abundance, from passage of lightning through the reducing atmosphere. Intelligence evolved, and presently built an impressive civilization. They lived slowly, of course. Their biochemistry was less energetic. Communication was difficult. They were not stupid, only slow. I visited Earth three times, and each time they had made more progress.''

Almost against his will, Noyes asked, "What did they look like?"

"Small and soft and fragile, much more so than yourselves. I cannot say they were pretty, but I grew to like them. I would toast them according to your customs," she said. "They wrought beauty in their cities and beauty in their philosophies, and their works are in our libraries still. They will not be forgotten.''

She touched her sparker, and so did her younger companions. Current flowed between her two claws, through her nervous system. She said, "Sssss . . ."

I raised my glass, and nudged Noyes with my elbow. We drank to our predecessors. Noyes lowered his cup and asked, "What happened to them?"

"They sensed worldwide disaster coming," Chorrikst said, "and they prepared; but they thought it would be quakes. They built cities to float on the ocean surface, and lived in the undersides. They never noticed the green scum growing in certain tidal pools. By the time they knew the danger, the green scum was everywhere. It used photosynthesis to turn carbon dioxide into oxygen, and the raw oxygen killed whatever it touched, leaving fertilizer to feed the green scum.

"The world was dying when we learned of the problem. What could we do against a photosynthesis-using scum growing beneath a yellow-white star? There was nothing in chirpsithra libraries that would help. We tried, of course, but we were unable to stop it. The sky had turned an admittedly lovely transparent blue, and the tide pools were green, and the offshore cities were crumbling before we gave up the fight. There was an attempt to transplant some of the natives to a suitable world; but biorhythm upset ruined their mating habits. I have not been back since, until now."

The depressing silence was broken by Chorrikst herself. "Well, the Earth is greatly changed, and of course your own evolution began with the green plague. I have heard tales of humanity from my companions. Would you tell me something of your lives?"

And we spoke of humankind, but I couldn't seem to find much enthusiasm for it. The anaerobic life that survived the advent of photosynthesis includes gangrene and botulism and not much else. I wondered what Chorrikst would find when next she came, and whether she would have reason to toast our memory.

ASSIMILATING OUR CULTURE, THAT'S WHAT THEY'RE DOING!

I was putting glasses in the dishwasher when some chirps walked in with three glig in tow. You didn't see many glig in the Draco Tavern. They were gray and compact beings, proportioned like a human linebacker much shorter than the chirpsithtra. They wore furs against Earth's cold, fur patterned in three tones of green, quite pretty.

It was the first time I'd seen the Silent Stranger react to anything.

He was sitting alone at the bar, as usual. He was forty or so, burly and fit, with thick black hair on his head and his arms. He'd been coming in once or twice a week for at least a year. He never talked to anyone, except me, and then only to order; he'd drink alone, and leave at the end of the night in a precarious rolling walk. Normal enough for the average bar, but not for the Draco.

I have to keep facilities for a score of aliens. Liquors for humans, sparkers for chirps, flavored absolute alcohol for thtopár; spongecake soaked in cyanide solution, and I keep a damn close watch on that; lumps of what I've been calling green kryptonite, and there's never been a roseyfin in here to call for it. My customers don't tend to be loud, but the sound of half a dozen species in conversation is beyond imagination, doubled or tripled because they're all using translating widgets. I need some pretty esoteric sound-proofing.

All of which makes the Draco expensive to run. I charge twenty bucks a drink, and ten for sparkers, and so forth.

Why would anyone come in here to drink in privacy? I'd wondered about the Silent Stranger.

Then three glig came in, and the Silent Stranger turned his chair away from the bar, but not before I saw his face.

Gail was already on her way to the big table where the glig and the chirps were taking seats, so that was okay. I left the dishwasher half filled. I leaned across the bar and spoke close to the Silent Stranger's ear.

"It's almost surprising, how few fights we get in here."

He didn't seem to know I was there.

I said, "I've only seen six in thirty-two years. Even then, nobody got badly hurt. Except once. Some nut, human, tried to shoot a chirp, and a thtopar had to crack his skull. Of course the thtopar didn't know how hard to hit him. I sometimes wish I'd gotten there faster."

He turned just enough to look me in the eye. I said, "I saw your face. I don't know what you've got against the glig, but if you think you're ready to kill them, I think I'm ready to stop you. Have a drink on the house instead."

He said, "The correct name is gligstith(click)optok."

"That's pretty good. I never get the click right."

"It should be good. I was on the first embassy ship to Gligstith(click)tcharf." Bitterly, "There won't be any fight, I can't even punch a glig in the face without making the evening news. It'd all come out."

Gail came back with orders: sparkers for the chirps, and the glig wanted bull shots, consommé and vodka, with no ice and no flavorings. They were sitting in the high chairs that bring a human face to the level of a chirp's, and their strange hands were waving wildly. I filled the orders with half an eye on the Stranger, who watched me with a brooding look, and I got back to him as soon as I could.

He asked, "Ever wonder why there wasn't any second embassy to Gligstith(click)tcharf?"

"Not especially."

"Why not?"

I shrugged. For two million years there wasn't anything in the universe but us and the gods. Then came the chirps. Then *bang*, a dozen others, and news of thousands more. We're learning so much from the chirps themselves, and of course there's culture shock . . .

He said, "You know what we brought back. The gligs sold us some advanced medical and agricultural techniques, including templates for the equipment. The chirps couldn't have done that for us. They aren't DNA-based. Why didn't we go back for more?"

"You tell me."

He seemed to brace himself. "I will, then. You serve them in here, you should know about them. Build yourself a drink, on me."

I built two scotch-and-sodas. I asked, "Did you say *sold?* What did we pay them? That didn't make the news."

"It better not. Hell, where do I start? . . . The first thing they did when we landed, they gave us a full medical checkup. Very professional. Blood samples, throat scrapings, little nicks in our ears, deep-radar for our innards. We didn't object. Why should we? The glig is DNA-based. We could have been carrying bacteria that could live off them.

"Then we did the tourist bit. I was having the time of my life! I'd never been further than the Moon. To be in an alien star system, exploring their cities, oh, man! We were all having a ball. We made speeches. We asked about other races. The chirps may claim to own the galaxy, but they don't know everything. There are places they can't go except in special suits, because they grew up around red dwarf stars."

"I know."

"The glig sun is hotter than Sol. We did most of our traveling at night. We went through museums, with cameras following us. Public conferences. We recorded the one on art forms; maybe you saw it."

"Yeah."

"Months of that. Then they wanted us to record a permission for reproduction rights. For that they would pay us a royalty, and sell us certain things on credit against the royalties." He gulped hard at his drink. "You've seen all of that. The medical deep radar, that does what an X-ray does without giving you cancer, and the cloning techniques to grow organ transplants, and the cornucopia plant, and all the rest. And of course we were all for giving them their permission right away.

"Except, do you remember Bill Hersey? He was a reporter and a novelist before he joined the expedition. He wanted details. Exactly what rights did the glig want? Would they be selling permission to other species? Were there groups like libraries or institutes for the blind, that got them free? And they told us. They didn't have anything to hide."

His eyes went to the glig, and mine followed his. They looked ready for another round. The most human thing about the glig was their hands, and their hands were disconcerting. Their palms were very short and their fingers were long, with an extra joint. As if a torturer had cut a human palm between the finger bones, almost to the wrist. Those hands grabbed the attention . . . but tonight I could see nothing but the wide mouths and the shark's array of teeth. Maybe I'd already guessed.

"Clones," said the Silent Stranger. "They took clones from our tissue samples. The glig grow clones from almost a hundred DNA-based life forms. They wanted us for their dinner tables, not to mention their classes in exobiology. You know, they couldn't see why we were so upset."

"I don't see why you signed."

"Well, they weren't growing actual human beings. They wanted to grow livers and muscle tissue and marrow without the bones . . . you know, meat. Even a f-f-f—" He had the shakes. A long pull at his scotch-and-soda stopped that, and he said, "Even a full suckling roast would be grown headless. But the bottom line was that if we didn't give our permissions, there would be pirate editions, and we wouldn't get any royalties. Anyway, we signed. Bill Hersey hanged himself after we came home.''

I couldn't think of anything to say, so I built us two more drinks, strong, on the house. Looking back on it, that was my best answer anyway. We touched glasses and drank deep, and he said, ''It's a whole new slant on the War of the Worlds. The man-eating monsters are civilized, they're cordial, they're perfect hosts. Nobody gets slaughtered, and think what they're saving on transportation costs! And ten thousand glig carved me up for dinner tonight. The UN made about half a cent per.''

Gail was back. Aliens don't upset her, but she was badly upset. She kept her voice down. ''The glig would like to try other kinds of meat broth. I don't know if they're kidding or not. They said they wanted—they wanted—''

''They'll take Campbell's,'' I told her, ''and like it.''

WAR MOVIE

Ten, twenty years ago my first thought would have been, *Great-looking woman! Tough-looking, too. If I make a pass, it had better be polite.* She was in her late twenties, tall, blond, healthy-looking, with a squarish jaw. She didn't look like the type to be fazed by anything; but she had stopped, stunned, just inside the door. Her first time here, I thought. Anyway, I'd have remembered her.

But after eighteen years tending bar in the Draco Tavern, my first thought is generally, *Human. Great! I won't have to dig out any of the exotic stuff.* While she was still reacting to the sight of half a dozen oddly-shaped sapients indulging each its own peculiar vice, I moved down the bar to the far right, where I keep the alcoholic beverages. I thought she'd take one of the bar stools.

Nope. She looked about her, considering her choices— which didn't include empty tables; there was a fair crowd in tonight—then moved to join the lone qarasht. And I was already starting to worry as I left the bar to take her order.

In the Draco it's considered normal to strike up conversations with other customers. But the qarasht wasn't acting like it wanted company. The bulk of thick fur, pale blue striped with black in narrow curves, had waddled in three hours ago. It was on its third quart-sized mug of Demerara Sours, and its sense cluster had been retracted for all of that time, leaving it deaf and blind, lost in its own thoughts.

It must have felt the vibration when the woman sat down. Its sense cluster and stalk rose out of the fur like a python rising from a bed of moss. A snake with no mouth: just two big wide-set black bubbles for eyes and an ear like a pink blossom set between them, and a tuft of fine hairs along the stalk to serve for smell and taste, and a brilliant ruby crest on top. Its translator box said, quite clearly, "Drink, not talk. My last day."

She didn't take the hint. "You're going home? Where?"

"Home to the organ banks. I am *shishishorupf*—" A word the box didn't translate.

"What's it mean?"

"Your kind has bankruptcy laws that let you start over. My kind lets me start over as a dozen others. Organ banks." The alien picked up its mug; the fur parted below its sense cluster stalk, to receive half a pint of Demerara Sour.

She looked around a little queasily, and found me at her shoulder. With some relief she said, "Never mind, I'll come to the bar," and started to stand up.

The qarasht put a hand on her wrist. The eight skeletal fingers looked like two chicken feet wired together; but a qarasht's hand is stronger than it looks. "Sit," said the alien. "Barmonitor, get her one of these. Human, why do you not fight wars?"

"What?"

"You used to fight wars."

"Well," she said, "sure."

"We could have been fourth-level wealthy," the qarasht said, and slammed its mug to the table. "You would still be a single isolated species had we not come. In what fashion have you repaid our generosity?"

The woman was speechless; I wasn't. "Excuse me, but it wasn't the qarashteel who made first contact with Earth. It was the chirpsithra."

"We paid them."

"What? Why?"

"Our ship *Far-Stretching Sense Cluster* passed through Sol system while making a documentary. It confuses some species that we can make very long entertainments, and sell them to billions of customers who will spend years watching them, and reap profits that allow us to travel hundreds of light-years and spend decades working on such a project. But we are very long-lived, you know. Partly because we are able to keep the organ banks full,'' the qarasht said with some savagery, and it drank again. Its sense-cluster was weaving a little.

''We found dramatic activity on your world,'' it said. ''All over your world, it seemed. Machines hurled against each other. Explosives. Machines built to fly, other machines to hurl them from the sky. Humans in the machines, dying. Machines blowing great holes in populated cities. It fuddles the mind, to think what such a spectacle would have cost to make ourselves! We went into orbit, and we recorded it all as best we could. Three years of it. When we were sure it was over, we returned home and sold it.''

The woman swallowed. She said to me, ''I think I need that drink. Join us?''

I made two of the giant Demerara Sours and took them back. As I pulled up a chair the qarasht was saying, ''If we had stopped then we would still be moderately wealthy. Our recording instruments were not the best, of course. Worse, we could not get close enough to the surface for real detail. Our atmosphere probes shivered and shook and so did the pictures. Ours was a low-budget operation. But the ending was superb! Two cities half-destroyed by thermonuclear explosions! Our recordings sold well enough, but we would have been mad not to try for more.

''We invested all of our profits in equipment. We borrowed all we could. Do you understand that the nearest full-service spaceport to Sol system is sixteen-squared light-years distant? We had to finance a chirpsithra diplomatic expedition in order to get Local Group approval and transport for what we needed . . . and because we needed intermediaries. Chirps are very good at negotiating, and we are not. We did not tell them what we really wanted, of course.''

The woman's words sounded like curses. ''Why negotiate? You were doing fine as Peeping Toms. Even when people saw your ships, nobody believed them. I expect they're saucer-shaped?''

Foo fighters, I thought, while the alien said, ''We needed more than the small atmospheric probes. We needed to mount hologram cameras. For that we had to travel all over the Earth, especially the cities. Such instruments are nearly invisible. We spray them across a flat surface, high up on your glass-slab-style towers, for instance. And we needed access to your libraries, to get some insight into *why* you do these things.''

The lady drank. I remembered that there had been qarashteel everywhere the chirpsithra envoys went, twenty-four years ago when the big interstellar ships arrived; and I took a long pull from my Sour.

''It all looked so easy,'' the qarasht mourned. ''We had left instruments on your moon. The recordings couldn't be sold, of course, because your world's rotation permits only fragmentary glimpses. But your machines were becoming better, *more* destructive! We thanked our luck that you had not destroyed yourselves before we could return. We studied the recordings, to guess where the next war would occur, but there was no discernable pattern. The largest land mass, we thought—''

True enough, the chirps and their qarashteel entourage had been very visible all over Asia and Europe. Those cameras on the Moon must have picked up activity in Poland and Korea and Vietnam and Afghanistan and Iran and Israel and Cuba and, and . . . bastards. ''So you set up your cameras in a tearing hurry,'' I guessed, ''and then you waited.''

''We waited and waited. We have waited for thirty years . . . for twenty-four of your own years, and we have nothing to show for it but a riot here, a parade there, an attack on a children's vehicle . . . robbery of a bank . . . a thousand people smashing automobiles or an embassy building . . .

rumors of war, of peace, some shouting in your councils . . . how can we sell any of this? On Earth my people need life support to the tune of six thousand dollars a day. I and my associates are *shishishorupf* now, and I must return home to tell them."

The lady looked ready to start her own war. I said, to calm her down, "We make war movies too. We've been doing it for over a hundred years. They sell fine."

Her answer was an intense whisper. "I never liked war movies. And that was us!"

"Sure, who else—"

The qarasht slammed its mug down. "*Why have you not fought a war?*"

She broke the brief pause. "We would have been ashamed."

"Ashamed?"

"In front of you. Aliens. We've seen twenty alien species on Earth since that first chirp expedition, and none of them seem to fight wars. The, uh, qarasht don't fight wars, do they?"

The alien's sense cluster snapped down into its fur, then slowly emerged again. "Certainly we do not!"

"Well, think how it would look!"

"But for you it is natural!"

"Not really," I said. "People have real trouble learning to kill. It's not built into us. Anyway, we don't have quite so much to fight over these days. The whole world's getting rich on the widgetry the chirps and the thtopar have been selling us. Long-lived, too, on glig medicines. We've all got more to lose." I flinched, because the alien's sense cluster was stretched across the table, staring at us in horror.

"A lot of our restless types are out mining the asteroids," the woman said.

"And, hey," I said, "remember when Egypt and Saudi Arabia were talking war in the UN? And all the aliens moved out of both countries, even the glig doctors with their geriatrics consulting office. The sheiks didn't like that one damn bit. And when the Soviets—''

"Our doing, all our own doing," the alien mourned. Its sense cluster pulled itself down and disappeared into the fur, leaving just the ruby crest showing. The alien lifted its mug and drank, blind.

The woman took my wrist and pulled me over to the bar. "What do we do *now?*" she hissed in my ear.

I shrugged. "Sounds like the emergency's over."

"But we can't just let it go, can we? You don't really think we've given up war, do you? But if we knew these damn aliens were waiting to make *movies* of us, maybe we would! Shouldn't we call the newspapers, or at least the Secret Service?"

"I don't think so."

"Somebody has to know!"

"Think it through," I said. "One particular qarasht company may be defunct, but those cameras are still there, all over the world, and so are the mobile units. Some alien receiving company is going to own them. What if they offer . . . say Iran, or the Soviet Union, one-tenth of one percent of the gross profits on a war movie?"

She paled. I pushed my mug into her hands and she gulped hard at it. Shakily she asked, "Why didn't the qarasht think of that?"

"Maybe they don't think enough like men. Maybe if we just leave it alone, they never will. But we sure don't want any human entrepreneurs making suggestions. Let it drop, lady. Let it drop."

LIMITS

I never would have heard them if the sound system hadn't gone on the fritz. And if it hadn't been one of those frantically busy nights, maybe I could have done something about it . . .

But one of the big chirpsithra passenger ships was due to leave Mount Forel Spaceport in two days. The chirpsithra trading empire occupies most of the galaxy, and Sol system is nowhere near its heart. A horde of passengers had come early in fear of being marooned. The Draco Tavern was jammed.

I was fishing under the counter when the noises started. I jumped. Two voices alternated: a monotonal twittering, and a bone-vibrating sound like a tremendous door endlessly opening on rusty hinges.

The Draco Tavern used to make the Tower of Babel sound like a monolog, in the years before I got this sound system worked out. Picture it: thirty or forty creatures of a dozen species including human, all talking at once at every pitch and volume, and all of their translating widgets bellowing too! Some species, like the srivinthish, don't talk with sound, but they also don't notice the continual *skreek*ing from their spiracles. Others sing. They *call* it singing, and they say it's a religious rite, so how can I stop them?

Selective damping is the key, and a staff of technicians to keep the system in order. I can afford it. I charge high anyway, for the variety of stuff I have to keep for anything that might wander in. But sometimes the damping system fails.

I found what I needed—a double-walled canister I'd never needed before, holding stuff I'd been calling *green kryptonite*—and delivered glowing green pebbles to four aliens in globular environment tanks. They were at four different tables, sharing conversation with four other species. I'd never seen a rosyfin before. Rippling in the murky fluid within the transparent globe, the dorsal fin was triangular, rose-colored, fragile as gossamer, and ran from nose to tail of a body that looked like a flattened slug.

Out among the tables there was near-silence, except within the bubbles of sound that surrounded each table. It wasn't a total breakdown, then. But when I went back behind the bar the noise was still there.

I tried to ignore it. I certainly wasn't going to try to fix the sound system, not with fifty-odd customers and ten distinct species demanding my attention. I set out consommé and vodka for four glig, and thimble-sized flasks of chilled fluid with an ammonia base, for a dozen chrome-yellow bugs each the size of a fifth of Haig Pinch. And the dialog continued: high twittering against grating metallic bass. What got on my nerves was the way the sounds seemed always on the verge of making sense!

Finally I just switched on the translator. It might be less irritating if I heard it in English.

I heard: "—noticed how often they speak of limits?"

"Limits? I don't understand you."

"Lightspeed limit. Theoretical strengths of metals, of crystals, of alloys. Smallest and largest masses at which an unseen body may be a neutron star. Maximum time and cost to complete a research project. Surface-to-volume relationship for maximum size of a creature of given design—"

"But every sapient race learns these things!"

"We find limits, of course. But with humans, the limits are what they seek first."

So they were talking about the natives, about us. Aliens often do. Their insights might be fascinating, but it gets boring fast. I let it buzz in my ear while I fished out another dozen flasks of ammonia mixture and set them on Gail's tray along with two Stingers. She went off to deliver them to the little yellow bugs, now parked in a horseshoe pattern on the rim of their table, talking animatedly to two human sociologists.

"It is a way of thinking," one of the voices said. "They set enormously complex limits on each other. Whole professions, called *judge* and *lawyer*, devote their lives to determining which human has violated which limit where. Another profession alters the limits arbitrarily."

"It does not sound entertaining."

"But all are forced to play the game. You must have noticed: the limits they find in the universe and the limits they set on each other bear the same name: law."

I had established that the twitterer was the one doing most of the talking. Fine. Now who were they? Two voices belonging to two radically different species . . .

"The interstellar community knows all of these limits in different forms."

"Do we know them all? Gödel's Principle sets a limit to the perfectability of mathematical systems. What species would have sought such a thing? Mine would not."

"Nor mine, I suppose. Still . . ."

"Humans push their limits. It is their first approach to any problem. When they learn where the limits lie, they fill in missing information until the limit breaks. When they break a limit, they look for the limit behind that."

"I wonder . . ."

I thought I had them spotted. Only one of the tables for two was occupied, by a chirpsithra and a startled-looking woman. My suspects were a cluster of three: one of the rosyfins, and two compact, squarish customers wearing garish designs on their exoskeletal shells. The shelled creatures had been smoking tobacco cigars under exhaust hoods. One seemed to be asleep. The other waved stubby arms as it talked.

I heard: "I have a thought. My savage ancestors used to

die when they reached a certain age. When we could no longer breed, evolution was finished with us. There is a biological self-destruct built into us.''

"It is the same with humans. But my own people never die unless killed. We fission. Our memories go far, far back.''

"Though we differ in this, the result is the same. At some point in the dim past we learned that we could postpone our deaths. We never developed a civilization until individuals could live long enough to attain wisdom. The fundamental limit was lifted from our shells before we set out to expand into the world, and then the universe. Is this not true with most of the space-traveling peoples? The Pfarth species choose death only when they grow bored. Chirpsithra were long-lived before they reached the stars, and the gligstith-(click)optok went even further, with their fascination with heredity-tailoring—''

"Does it surprise you, that intelligent beings strive to extend their lives?''

"Surprise? No. But humans still face a limit on their life-spans. The death limit has immense influence on their poetry. They may think differently from the rest of us in other ways. They may find truths we would not even seek.''

An untranslated metal-on-metal scraping. Laughter? "You speculate irresponsibility. Has their unique approach taught them anything we know not?''

"How can I know? I have only been on this world three local years. Their libraries are large, their retrieval systems poor. But there is Gödel's Principle; and Heisenberg's Uncertainty Principle is a limit to what one can discover at the quantum level.''

Pause. "We must see if another species has duplicated that one. Meanwhile, perhaps I should speak to another visitor.''

"Incomprehension. Query?''

"Do you remember that I spoke of a certain gligstith-(click)optok merchant?"

"I remember."

"You know their skill with water-world biology. This one comes to Earth with a technique for maintaining and restoring the early-maturity state in humans. The treatment is complex, but with enough customers the cost would drop, or so the merchant says. I must persuade it not to make the offer."

"Affirmative! Removing the death-limit would drastically affect human psychology!"

One of the shelled beings was getting up. The voices chopped off as I rounded the bar and headed for my chosen table, with no clear idea what I would say. I stepped into the bubble of sound around two shelled beings and a rosyfin, and said, "Forgive the interruption, sapients—"

"You have joined a wake," said the tank's translator widget.

The shelled being said, "My mate had chosen death. He wanted one last smoke in company." It bent and lifted its dead companion in its arms and headed for the door.

The rosyfin was leaving too, rolling his spherical fishbowl toward the door. I realized that its own voice hadn't penetrated the murky fluid around it. No chittering, no bone-shivering bass. I had the wrong table.

I looked around, and there were still no other candidates. Yet *somebody* here had casually condemned mankind—me!—to age and die.

Now what? I might have been hearing several voices. They all sound alike coming from a new species; and some aliens never interrupt each other.

The little yellow bugs? But they were with humans.

Shells? My voices had mentioned shells . . . but too many aliens have exoskeletons. Okay, a chirpsithra would have spoken by now; they're garrulous. Scratch any table that includes a chirp. Or a rosyfin. Or those srivinthish: I'd have heard the *skreek* of their breathing. Or the huge gray being who seemed to be singing. That left . . . half a dozen tables, and I couldn't interrupt that many.

Could they have left while I was distracted?

I hot-footed it back to the bar, and listened, and heard nothing. And my spinning brain could find only limits.

THE LOST IDEAS

Near my elbow there are two 8½-inch disks full of attempted stories. Older stories were written or half-written on paper. They take up a good deal more of my office space. One day I'll nerve myself to throw them out.

The concept of what makes a story came to me bit by bit. (Not a pun. This was before home computers.) It's nonverbal, impossible to describe, and it doesn't quite match any other writer's picture. It can't be taught. It evolves as a chain of mistakes.

Here are some projects that didn't quite come out the way I'd hoped. Some are cases of serendipity, wonderfully transformed by chance. Others may at least function as lessons.

When I still thought I was going to be a writer, but had no way to prove it, my stepsister gave me an idea. A friend of hers, a *real* writer, had tried it and given up. From that alone I should have known better.

Consider a freeway off-ramp that only exists between midnight and dawn. Nobody who takes it ever comes back.

I ran my phantom off-ramp through the dimensions to a world where stranded aliens were collecting metal and other necessities to rebuild their vehicle. Automobiles taking the phantom ramp found that gravity had rotated ninety degrees: they were going *down*.

Like the ramp, my attempted story led nowhere. Ultimately I retrieved the alien for another story and called it a *Pierson's puppeteer*. If you like the off-ramp idea, take it. I advise against.

On ancient yellowing paper I find an escape story built

around a spacecraft of peculiar design: a circular flying wing. I drew pictures of the craft with colored pencils. If a meteor hits the ship at just the right angle . . . Let's just say there wasn't a lot of point to this story, and I never finished it. The spacecraft became the Lazy Eight series of interstellar slowboats.

On disk I have five or six thousand words of a character study for a terrorist in hiding. As with a lot of these notes, I was just fiddling around when I typed it up. That was six or seven years ago. Since then I've repeatedly tried to get a story out of Terrorist. I was fascinated, for a time. Why am I not fascinated now? Because no story ever emerged.

I get more ideas than I can use. It helps if someone will write a story for me . . . like *The Sins of the Fathers* by Stanley Schmidt. I'd been planning to write about refugees from the galactic core explosion. It had not occurred to me that they'd *caused* the epidemic of supernovae. That would have rounded off Known Space very nicely . . . but now I don't have to write it.

The thing is, some of what I try doesn't work. And some of what doesn't work, can be saved many years later, or rifled for its best ideas. But some good stuff inevitably gets lost. And I *hate* that.

So I've saved some lost ideas for you.

Twenty years ago my mother's house was robbed.

The thief was a middle-aged man just out of jail. What he wanted was to go back to his friends . . . that is, back to jail. He knew how to do that. He had a quarter in his pocket, so he took a bus to Beverly Hills. He'd heard there were rich people there.

He walked north from Sunset for a block and a half. He climbed a gate and kept moving.

About now the dogs must have started raising hell. Mom had five in the pen near the house. The Keeshond breed began life as guard dogs on Dutch houseboats. They're too friendly, maybe, but they're *loud*. Mom and Porter (my stepfather) were out, but there were servants on the premises. Trouble was, they'd learned to ignore the barking dogs. Keeshonds don't just bark at burglars; they bark at *any* stimulus, like Australians go on strike.

The thief found a window, got it open and started to climb through. It must have been hellishly awkward. There were shelves on the insides of the library window, and the shelves were crammed with trophies: half a ton of silver and ribbons indicating thirty-odd years of my mother's victories at competition dog shows.

He got halfway. Then the window came down on his waist.

Though he was trying to be quiet, he still had to get the trophies and shelves out of the way. He must have raised a hell of a racket. Why didn't someone come to investigate? Because the clatter of falling silver and glass was drowned out by the barking of the dogs, which the servants were already ignoring. So the thief thrashed in the window for half an hour (he so testified) until he pulled himself free.

He began to search the house. Two pillowcases must have been his first and second thefts. He stripped my sister of every bit of jewelry she owned, and considerably more from my Mom. He got away with between $100,000 and $200,000, mostly in jewelry, stuffed into two pillowcases.

He also took some bizarre stuff. He was still wearing Porter's shoes when he was picked up. Heavy ashtrays. Trophies. One of a pair of walkie-talkies. He must have thought it was a radio . . . or else he was planning to call his victims.

Maybe he got tired, maybe he felt conspicuous. He pushed one pillowcaseful of loot into a trash can a block from the house. It was presently found. He sold some of the rest of it to a bartender, who was presently located, and who never considered that it might be stolen, nope, never crossed his mind.

The police found him in San Francisco. He explained that he'd escaped with some costume jewelry. When they told him the money value of what he'd gotten away with, and failed to keep, he reacted like he'd been robbed.

Mom and Porter ended by feeling sorry for the guy. My sister never did. It's a hell of a story, isn't it?

Everyone involved thought I should write it.

"Just like science fiction—" Do you get that too? From relatives and friends of your family who can't tell science fiction from *Zardoz* and third season *Star Trek*? Mundanes consider this a valid excuse to interrupt everyone else to tell a story.

But this time I agreed with them: it's a hell of a story, and I swore I'd write it up and sell it. I took notes, which I've lost. I never did turn it into text, until now. I'm at a loss to understand why . . . unless it's because I've never had patience with fools, not even when the fool is a friend, not even when it's me. INFERNO is as close as I've come to living in a fool's head for any great stretch. This burglar was a fool.

Some bad stories can be reworked, or rifled for their components.

"The Locusts" mouldered in my files for a decade before I turned it over to Steven Barnes. All it took was a different set of skills and the right attitude.

I quit halfway through "The Crosshatchers" for lack of an ending. That was in the late sixties. I've learned. These days I almost never begin writing a story until I know the ending.

"The Crosshatchers" involved a carefully designed alien, the #, an intelligent being of assymetrical build. The # never evolved vertebrae. There are two joints in the back, which is otherwise as solid as leg bones. Solid bone extends from the skull to the upper joint (below the shoulders). I gave it two right arms and lots of sensitive fingers, and a crossover spinal cord (as with humans), so the left side of the skull needs more brain capacity. There's one left arm, built for strength. The shoulder muscles would run all the way to the top of the skull on the left, for increased leverage; which *only* works because of the solid backbone. But that makes the skull even more lopsided.

The first glimpse of the # was to have been a skull picked off a sandy beach: a weathered, lopsided skull with a handle on it: a serviceable club.

The Crosshatcher novella sat unfinished in my filing cabinet for years. Jerry Pournelle and I had only just begun talking collaboration when I pulled the # out to show him. I had realized that I could put an alien-occupied planetary system in the middle of his thousand-year-old human empire.

The # became the Motie Mediator. But the skull-with-handle scene never worked its way into THE MOTE IN GOD'S EYE. You may find it, much altered, in a Draco Tavern Story, "Folk Tale."

The one that hurts is the one I published.

Following "Neutron Star," Frederik Pohl made a suggestion. I would write stories about the odd pockets of the universe: double stars, red giants, whatever oddities took my notice. These would be paired with paintings of such objects.

The format wasn't followed exactly, but several stories emerged from that suggestion, including all of the stories in the collection NEUTRON STAR.

A painting of the galaxy as seen from along the axis sparked "The Ethics of Madness." From the beginning I knew the ending: one spacecraft chasing a second with intent to murder; the leading spacecraft afraid to turn around. From that I let the rest of the story germinate. The theme: in an age when one's sanity can be controlled by biochemicals, forgetting to take your pills is murder.

The ending I started with was wildly inappropriate to the story as it developed. The theme got lost. I should have dropped the ending I started with; and I have done that on numerous occasions since.

And I did a better job with a recent sequel, "Madness Has its Place."

A Planetarium Show . . . well, the term explains itself. As a juvenile I had seen artificial starscapes rolling across a dome at Griffith Planetarium in Los Angeles. I had not known that some planetarium shows are fiction, until Rueben Fox asked me to write one.

Now, that was new. Fiction in planetarium shows is almost always science fiction, because the theme is almost always astronomical. Some good stories have become planetarium shows, including *The Black Cloud* by Fred Hoyle and "The Last Question" by Isaac Asimov. There were some originals, too, but in the early seventies the routine was to search the literature, find the perfect story, then produce a show.

So Marilyn and I were flown to Salt Lake City. There was a mini-convention of sorts. I made a speech in the planetarium—and found that the little penlight wouldn't show me my notes. I never speak extemporaneously on purpose; it always happens by accident.

We were shown around the planetarium. The restrictions of a planetarium show were explained to me: You don't see actors, though the equipment may project still photographs. In terms of dialogue it's close to being a radio show. Landscapes are possible, but not convincing.

And Hansen Planetarium is in Salt Lake City, the center of the Church of Jesus Christ of Latter Day Saints. Would that be a problem? Was I in danger of offending the planetarium's audience? No, perish forbid. No restrictions would be placed on my artistic soul.

So I wrote them a script. It came back, and I was told

what I'd done wrong in terms of offending an audience. And I tried again . . . and again . . .

What was happening was this. Hansen Planetarium was learning what restrictions applied to a Salt Lake City planetarium show, and they were learning this by watching me violate them. This (as I told myself, manfully holding my temper) is no more than what television producers do to scriptwriters, except in one respect. A scriptwriter is paid for every new version of his script. I had been paid nothing.

I presently wrote a letter to Fox explaining that what he was trying to do was impossible. In general, nobody will write a story for a planetarium show except by purest accident. I reasoned that Fox and his colleagues had been doing it right all along: reading the books and magazines, and choosing what they wanted out of the literature!

And the Planetarium presently paid me two hundred dollars. Live and learn . . .

—Late flash: In September of 1988, Von Del Chamberlain, the present director, phoned from Hansen Planetarium. Don Davis (*The* Don Davis, who first painted the Ringworld as seen from the surface) had found the last of my scripts. He and Del Chamberlain are planning to make "The Leshy Circuit" into a planetarium show. They're talking about new technology. They sent me a copy—I didn't have one— and it reads well.

—Later flash: Nothing has happened since. Don has quit.

Jim Baen was with Ace Books when he realized that Ace holds title to *Armageddon: 2419 a.d.* Sound familiar? It's the original Buck Rogers story. Ace holds the right to publish sequels!

So Jim propositioned me and Jerry. For a flat fee, not large, would we work out a format for future Buck Rogers stories? The idea was to *rationalize* the old assumptions.

It sounded like a challenge. It sounded like fun. It sounded (for that matter) like a project best embarked upon at night while drinking. By now I had taught Jerry to pour brandy in his coffee. Free the imagination and stay alert too! So we read the old story over . . .

Hmmm.

We would have to give up certain laws of physics.

Then again, Anthony "Buck" Rogers was no scientist. He might well have misinterpreted a lot of what he saw.

A radioactive gas found underground won't put you out for five hundred years; it'll give you cancer! There must have been something else in that cave. Advanced Han medical equipment? If Rogers at age ninety went back to explore . . .

The Han had disintegrator cannon mounted around their cities, firing continuously. That should have robbed the Earth of its atmosphere within a few days! Clearly the air wasn't actually disappearing . . .

The planets of the solar system don't all have breathable atmospheres, do they? Not *now* they don't . . .

A picture emerged.

Jerry was really getting into this. I was fiddling with physical laws and following him around, mostly. There was an empire out there among the stars. They had projects, some running automatically, throughout the solar system. By A.D. 2419 they had terraformed Mars and Venus. Their representatives were gone, except for enclaves in suspended animation on Earth and elsewhere.

The cache in China had been hospital patients.

What ripped that one open, while Rogers had already slept nearly a century, was a piece of a "calved" comet head. The patients boiled out and, using interstellar-level hospital equipment, conquered most of a world already battered back to savagery by the Hamner-Brown comet impact: by Lucifer's Hammer.

Antigravity was in use for ambulances and stretchers. The disintegrators were surgical tools and such; teleport devices work as disintegrators when the focus is fuzzy. Antigravity plus disintegrators make a dandy airplane, by the way. The air disappears at the nose and reappears in a rocket nozzle aft. We gave rocket belts the same design.

There were things Buck never told Wilma. Good thing, too. Mean broad, Wilma. Buck Rogers has an illegitimate son among the refugee Han.

The enclave under the South Pole isn't hospital patients. It's gene-engineered soldiers. And Rogers, fighting the all-new meaner Han, is a bit peculiar himself. The equipment in the cave has followed its programming and rejuvenated him . . . as a Han soldier.

What went wrong? Well, nothing, really. But Jerry and I were busy, so the stories went to authors picked by Jim Baen. The quality was not impressive, the sales were not impressive, and the series was dropped.

It's a shame that Rogers never got as far as Mars.

I've had little involvement with movies and television.

Dorothy Fontana invited me to write a *Star Trek* animation. I feared (groundlessly) that nobody at Filmation would see their chance to use real aliens rather than actors in rubber suits. So I wrote a story treatment using Outsiders (built like a black cat-o'-nine-tails, using photoelectric metabolism at near absolute zero) and quantum black holes. For Saturday morning TV!

Dorothy advised me that wouldn't work. My next attempt was too bloody . . .

Dorothy and I presently spent part of an afternoon at Gene Roddenberry's place. Gene suggested rewriting "The Soft Weapon" from NEUTRON STAR. That worked, as "The Slaver Weapon," with Spock playing a Pierson's puppeteer. I was given permission to leave Kirk out.

My first attempt (quantum black holes) became the basis for "The Borderland of Sol."

And Paramount sold to Ballantine Books the right to turn my script into a book. Alan Dean Foster did that. So "The Soft Weapon" wound up competing with itself . . .

* * *

I wrote three *Land of the Lost* episodes with David Gerrold. David was story editor, and all of the ideas were his. It *still* irritated me when random powers would change my—our—precious prose.

Eventually I quit the Writers Guild rather than participate in a strike. But before that, Jerry Pournelle and I got involved in some projects.

You won't see them on big or little screens.

We got a certain distance into a PBS project. They wanted near-future predictions. The concept of the cargo sailing ship was coming back into vogue. "Gullwhale Crossing" would have involved a huge cargocarrying sailing ship, fully automated and computer-driven, easy on the environment and the oil reserves, and dirt cheap. We planned to put some Boy Scouts aboard, then run up a storm . . .

It vanished. PBS must get more good offers than they can handle. For awhile I hoped "Inconstant Moon" would become a PBS project, but that didn't happen either.

We weren't the only writers who got involved with *A Watcher in the Woods* after it was shown. Many at Disney Studios surely suspected that something had gone wrong. The film opened *outside* New York. Reviews were nasty . . .

Our agent Marvin Moss called. Disney Studios was offering a flat fee for a limited task. None of the requirements were onerous.

We drove out to Disney Studios. There, in a small private theater, an officer took us in charge and explained the rules.

We were shown all but the last ten minutes of a movie.

We were invited to guess the ending.

Then we were shown *their* ending.

Then we were asked to attempt to write a better one.

The first hour and twenty minutes of *A Watcher in the Woods* wasn't bad at all. The acting was good; the sense of mystery and doom was powerful; Bette Davis was superb as an elderly lady ridden by old guilt.

I took the story for fantasy. We'd had continual glimpses of *something*—flashes of blue-white light offstage, a viewpoint that stalked the heroine and behaved like a hyperactive, secretive six-year-old—which I saw as a lightning elemental. Fantasy. Jerry thought he could interpret all of this as science fiction. We weren't far apart in interpretation: it would be possible to wrap up the plot elements we'd seen and return the lost girl to Earth.

The ending they'd used looked like it had been torn off a cheap Japanese rip-up Tokyo movie! The lightning elemental became a giant rubber bat who snatched up the heroine and transported her to an angular domain, verrry scientific. This creature who has been behaving like a six-year-old is now given as a trapped alien master scientist . . .

They'd made a mistake (Ron Miller told us) that seems all too common in Hollywood. They'd bought a book. They'd made a movie, making changes where whim struck them. When it was wrap-up time, their changes had made the original ending impossible. They looked at each other and . . .

Moviemakers have too little regard for story.

Jerry and I were having fun. We ate lunch at Mon Grenier—our favorite restaurant, open for lunch for less than a year before Andre Lion realized that too few people would pay his prices—while we fine-tuned the elements of the story. Certain elements were so prevalent during the movie that they *had* to be in the ending: mirrors cracked in a certain pattern, triangles, lightning, demonology. Back we went to Jerry's house to work out an outline.

We turned it in.

Understand: we had something to lose here, but not very much. We didn't yet know that Joe Haldeman had also written them an ending, or that Mike Jitlov had done them

one for nothing, because their present ending upset him.
But we wanted the joy of fixing something broken. We
wanted that movie done *right*.

A few days later we were summoned to conference at
Disney. How tactful should we be? There were things that
needed saying . . .

"Obviously we know that something's *wrong* with it,"
we were told.

Ah, that's a relief. I said, "The giant rubber bat has got
to go."

After that conference we wrote a second draft. It would
have cost a couple of million, done with Jerry's climax; or
half as much, with a minor rewrite. It would have been
superb!

They didn't use our ending. What I've heard is that they
solarized the giant rubber bat: he's blazing white now, like
a lightning elemental. I haven't had the courage to see for
myself.

We got involved in *V*, too, but just barely. It was a
TV series at that time, and already doomed, probably. We
weren't told that. Jerry and I were invited to the office of a
guy who had only just been put in charge of *V*.

You'll remember *V*. That's aliens who come from interstellar space to steal Earth's water, cruising right past all
the moons of Saturn, where water comes prepackaged and
nobody is shooting at them.

The problem with *V* (as the new producer saw it) was
that they never had an alien. They had costumes, they had
makeup, they had special effects, but nobody had ever set
forth to describe a life form (a remarkable insight, placing
him far above average for a producer of a television series).

The studios had already discarded that matter of the water.
The question remained: with several worlds under their control, what *do* the Visitors want from Earth?

I took the position that they are dinosaurs.

Assume an intelligent species of dinosaur. When the Dinosaur Killer asteroid was sighted, some of them escaped. Their descendants don't remember this. They only know that Earth feels good. The day is the right length, the air smells right, the taste of the water has character.

Picture the episode in which archaeologists find traces of Visitors bones in the Cretaceous clay. What a publicity coup for the Visitors! Now they can claim the Earth not by force of arms but by prior right! They'll turn it into a major publicity push . . .

And they will not instantly understand why their human audience is giggling. But dinosaurs are big, stupid creatures with brains the size of walnuts . . .

And nobody ever called us back.

One night at a party in 1981, Sharman Di Vono asked me if I'd like to do a story for a newspaper comic strip.

Sure!

She and an artist, Ron Harris, were (respectively) writing and drawing a *Star Trek* strip for the Los Angeles Times Syndicate. The Syndicate would own it, but it would appear only in the *Houston Chronicle* in Texas. Why? Because the Syndicate owns the *Houston Chronicle*, but the *Times* was running a *Star Wars* strip.

Sharman and I wrote twenty weeks of story line.

It involved kzinti and another Federation member species, the *Bebebebeque*: small, shelled communal creatures about the size and proportions of a fifth of Haig & Haig Pinch. (I had already added kzinti to the *Star Trek* universe via "The Slaver Weapon.") The kzinti had discovered a Bebebebeque colony world and enslaved it. The Enterprise was transporting more colonists. We put in another alien, a *ferreth*, and a corrosive biochemical drug used in ferreth mating battles: all Sharman's invention, and a fine, fanciful way to ruin some *Enterprise* machinery. There were colony life forms: big mean *ravagers* who ate the colony's *carpet leaf* crops, then turned carnivore. Kzinti sportsmen, arriving in spring to hunt the ravagers, saved the colonials from starvation before enslaving them.

Sharman had to translate all this into comic strip format, because I can't. Ron drew it. We called it "The Wristwatch Plantation."

Sharman had trouble explaining the peculiarities of the comic strip business, and also making me believe it. For instance, there's the matter of names. What's most visible is the *slug line*, next to the title, and that remains the same forever, for product recognition. At or near the end of the strip is the *signature box*. Illegible it might be, or nearly so, but it names the people who actually produced the strip. So my name as guest writer went into the signature box but not the slug line.

I didn't understand that until Sharman explained it to me at a lunch six years later.

We considered turning the story into a novel, or publishing the strip as a book. If Johnny Hart can do it, why not us?—with permission from Paramount, of course, for a piece of the royalties. Anything worth doing is worth selling repeatedly (Niven's Law). Sharman had the "blessing" of the head of the merchandizing department at Paramount, Hi Foreman, and from a David Seidman at the *Times*.

But Hi Foreman moved on, positions were reshuffled, and word came from higher up. Blessings withdrawn. No book sale.

Ron Harris quit. Overwork: he had to give up something. He was willing to stay a bit longer if we would stop dawdling and finish the story.

Switching artists in the middle would be bad. We preferred to wrap the strip up fast. Sharman's final-draft climax was a short cut: Kirk used the (repaired) transporter room to put a ravager aboard the main kzinti warship during a battle with the *Enterprise* . . . .

And okay, it worked. It didn't *look* hurried. Sharman's a

professional, and this isn't my profession. But the climax I had in mind, back when we planned a more leisurely wrapup, is something I hate to see vanish.

So paint this across your mind:

We've led up to this: the Bebebebeque rebels' transporter at ground level has exploded while linked to the half-repaired Enterprise transporter. The flare picked up every life form within a mile and scattered them throughout the *Enterprise*!

Picture a splash page with an inset: one-third of a page of Sunday comics showing just one scene, plus a window inset for a closeup. (I wanted one scene. Sharman says it generally looks better with the window.)

We're in the recreation level of the *Enterprise*. The rec level is a park, lush with vegetation. At the moment it looks like a hallucinatory Vietnam, because kzinti and Bebebebeque and *Enterprise* crew are all fighting it out for control. A *ravager* is tearing things up too. He's bigger and meaner than the kzinti. The *kzinti* are bigger than humans. The *crew* is generally actor-in-rubber-suit-sized but not all human. The *Bebebebeque* are tiny; most of them ride antigravity sleds. The perspective and orientation are all screwed up.

The window: closeup of Uhura and an anonymous Crewman, both armed, behind a covering boulder. The Crewman is telling Uhura, "My brother wanted me to help him with his wet-ranch on Midar—"

The splash page: In the extreme foreground, four little beetle-shapes are manipulating a phaser rifle as if it were a Napoleonic-era cannon. Beyond them, still close, are Uhura and Crewman, and beyond *them*, humans and oversized kzinti are all fighting it out in a swarm of Bebebebeque on flying sleds, dodging or running whenever the ravager comes near.

Crewman: "—but I thought it was too dangerous, so I joined the flipping Navy."

It's a quote from THE MOTE IN GOD'S EYE, intended as a tip o' the hat for Jerry Pournelle . . . who thought I should have been working on something more productive, like whatever collaboration we were on at the moment.

A few years ago there were *no* triple collaborations in the science fiction field. A normal collaboration is hard enough. Why would *three* people try to write a book?

Well, it was a contract matter.

The contract, and the negotiations that surrounded it, were a ball of snakes. Jerry Pournelle and I ultimately contracted to write a sequel to THE MOTE IN GOD'S EYE for Pocket Books—a thing we might have wanted anyway, and never mind the extraordinary pressures; but there was a clause we would surely have crossed out. It said that Jerry and I could not work on any other collaboration together until this one was finished.

We got antsy.

Triple collaborations were not forbidden. We signed contracts for *four*.

THE LEGACY OF HEOROT, written by me and Jerry Pournelle and Steven Barnes, was totally successful. Steve believes that Jerry and I think like two lobes of a brain. Effectively he had one collaborator, he says, and that made it more workable.

With A LABOR OF MOLES, the third collaborator is an artist, Wendy All. The book is finished but for Wendy's illustrations. It may reach print before the book you're holding . . . but we were stalled for several years. Wendy never nagged. We're grateful.

Jerry and I planned FALLEN ANGELS many years ago. The story line involves a heroic underground derived from science fiction fans. We even auctioned off places in the book at convention charity functions. We planned to do it

for fun . . . and never got around to it, until the MOTE
sequel blocked us too.

Jim Baen found us Mike Flynn as a third collaborator.
ANGELS should be turned in before you open this book.

You'll remember that Jerry and I wrote a sequel to Dante's
INFERNO, set in present time, as a hack science fiction
writer tries to escape from Hell. You may not know that
Jim Baen tried to produce a computerized INFERNO game.
The authors would have been me and Jerry Pournelle and,
as our third collaborator, Alex Pournelle to do the programming.

I did some work on the INFERNO game.

Alex dropped out and was replaced.

The game got as far as a limited program with maybe
twenty "rooms."

Then everybody gradually lost interest.

Me too. I had not guessed, or remembered, how repulsive
is the territory of Hell. I now recall that we wrote the novel
in four months, because we wanted *out*. Good riddance.
The only thing I regret losing is the Planetarium in Limbo.

As in the book: you dive into a red giant star, or through
an Earthlike planet, or dive to the surface of a neutron star
and hover . . . no telling how many choices of star we could
afford to embed. But one would have been a black hole.
You dive past the accretion disk and on in. The screen tells
you, "You have passed the Swartzchild radius." The screen
scrolls up, leaving white space, and the computer locks up.
You have to restart from scratch.

So we're talking about four triple collaborations, of which
three looked like lost causes. It now appears that three out
of four worked. *Caveat vendor*.

BIGGER THAN WORLDS

Just because you've spent all your life on a planet doesn't mean that everyone always will. Already there are alternatives to worlds. The Russian space station may have killed its inhabitants, and the American Skylab has had its troubles, but the Apollo craft have a good record. They have never killed a man in space.

Alas, they all lack a certain something. Gravity. Permanence. We want something to live on, or in, something superior to a world: safer, or more mobile, or roomier. Otherwise, why move?

It's odd how much there is to say about structures larger than worlds, considering that we cannot yet begin to build any one of them. On the basis of size, the Dyson Sphere—a spherical shell around a sun—comes about in the middle. But let's start small and work our way up.

THE MULTIGENERATION SHIP

Robert Heinlein's early story, "Universe," has been imitated countless times by most of the writers in the business.

The idea was this: Present-day physics poses a limit on the speed of an interstellar vehicle. The ships we send to distant stars will be on one-way journeys, at least at first. They will have to carry a complete ecology: they couldn't carry enough food and oxygen in tanks. Because they will take generations to complete their journeys, they must also carry a viable and complete society.

Clearly we're talking about quite a large ship, with a population in the hundreds at least: high enough to prevent genetic drift. Centrifugal force substitutes for gravity. We're going to be doing a lot of that. We spin the ship on its axis, and put all the things that need full gravity at the outside, along the hull. Plant rooms, exercise rooms, et cetera. Things that don't need gravity, like fuel and guidance instruments, we line along the axis. If our motors thrust through the same axis, we will have to build a lot of the machinery on tracks, because the aft wall will be the floor when the ship is under power.

The "Universe" ship is basic to a discussion of life in space. We'll be talking about much larger structures, but they are designed to do the same things on a larger scale: to provide a place to live, with as much security and variety and pleasure as Earth itself offers—or more.

GRAVITY

Gravity is basic to our life style. It may or may not be necessary to life itself, but we'll want it if we can get it, whatever we build.

I know of only four methods of generating gravity aboard spacecraft.

Centrifugal force seems to be most likely. There is a drawback: coriolis effects would force us to relearn how to walk, sit down, pour coffee, throw a baseball. But such effects would decrease with increasing moment arm—that is, with larger structures. On a Ring City, for example, you'd never notice it.

Our second choice is to use actual mass: plate the floor with neutronium, for instance, at a density of fifty quadrillion tons per cubic foot; or build the ship around a quantum black hole, invisibly small and around as massive as, say, Phobos. But this will vastly increase our fuel consumption if we expect the vehicle to go anywhere.

Third choice is to generate gravity waves. This may remain forever beyond our abilities. But it's one of those things that people are going to keep trying to build, forever, because it would be so damn useful. We could put laboratories on the sun, or colonize Jupiter. We could launch ships at a million gravities, and the passengers would feel nothing.

The fourth method is to accelerate all the way, making turnover at the midpoint and decelerating the rest of the way. This works fine. Over interstellar distances it would take an infinite fuel supply—which we may have, in the Bussard ramjet. A Bussard ramjet would use an electromagnetic field to scoop up the interstellar hydrogen ahead of it—with an intake a thousand miles or more in diameter—compress it, and burn it as fuel for a fusion drive. Now the multigeneration ship would become unnecessary as relativity shortens our trip time: four years to the nearest star, twenty-one years to the galactic hub, twenty-eight to Andromeda galaxy—all at one gravity acceleration.

The Bussard ramjet looks unlikely. It's another ultimate, like generated gravity. Is the interstellar medium sufficiently

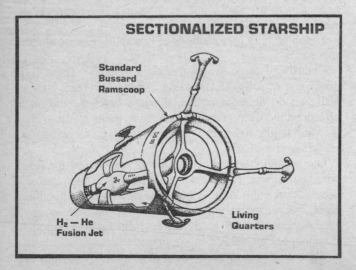

SECTIONALIZED STARSHIP

Standard
Bussard
Ramscoop

H₂ — He
Fusion Jet

Living
Quarters

ionized for such finicky control? Maybe not. But it's worth a try.

Meanwhile, our first step to other worlds is the "Universe" ship—huge, spun for gravity, its population in the hundreds, its travel time in generations.

FLYING CITIES

James Blish used a variant of generated gravity in his tales of the Okie cities.

His "spindizzy" motors used a little-known law of physics (still undiscovered) to create their own gravity and their own motive force. Because the spindizzy motors worked better for higher mass, his vehicles tended to be big. Most of the stories centered around Manhattan Island, which had been bodily uprooted from its present location and flown intact to the stars. Two of the stories involved whole worlds fitted out with spindizzies. They were even harder to land than the flying cities.

But we don't really need spindizzies or generated gravity to build flying cities

In fact, we don't really need to fill out Heinlein's "Universe" ship. The outer hull is all we need. Visualize a ship like this:

1. Cut a strip of Los Angeles, say, ten miles long by a mile wide.

2. Roll it in a hoop. Buildings and streets face inward.

3. Roof it over with glass or something stronger.

4. Transport it to space. (Actually we'll build it in space.)

5. Put reaction motors, air and water recycling systems, and storage areas in the basement, outward from the street level. Also the fuel tanks. Jettisoning an empty fuel tank is easy. We just cut it loose, and it falls into the universe.

6. Use a low-thrust, high-efficiency drive: ion jets, perhaps. The axis of the city can be kept clear. A smaller ship

A FLYING CITY

Fuel Tanks

Buildings on inside.

Ion Motors

Conning Tower at center.

can rise to the axis for sightings before a course change; or we can set the control bridge atop a slender fin. A ten-mile circumference makes the fin a mile and a half tall if the bridge is at the axis; but the strain on the structure would diminish approaching the axis.

What would it be like aboard the Ring City? One gravity everywhere, except in the bridge. We may want to enlarge the bridge to accommodate a schoolroom; teaching physics would be easier in free fall.

Otherwise it would be a lot like the multigeneration ship. The populace would be less likely to forget their destiny, as Heinlein's people did. They can see the sky from anywhere in the city; and the only fixed stars are Sol and the target star.

It would be like living anywhere, except that great attention must be paid to environmental quality. This can be taken for granted throughout this article. The more thoroughly we control our environment, the more dangerous it is to forget it.

INSIDE-OUTSIDE

The next step up in size is the hollow planetoid. I got my designs from a book of scientific speculation, *Islands in Space*, by Dandridge M. Cole and Donald W. Cox.

Step One: Construct a giant solar mirror. Formed under zero gravity conditions, it need be nothing more than an echo balloon sprayed with something to harden it, then cut in half and silvered on the inside. It would be fragile as a butterfly, and *huge*.

Step Two: Pick a planetoid. Ideally, we need an elongated chunk of nickel-iron, perhaps one mile in diameter and two miles long.

Step Three: Bore a hole down the long axis.

Step Four: Charge the hole with tanks of water. Plug the openings, and weld the plugs, using the solar mirror.

Step Five: Set the planetoid spinning slowly on its axis. As it spins, bathe the entire mass in the concentrated sunlight from the solar mirror. Gradually the flying iron mountain would be heated to melting all over its surface. Then the heat would creep inward, until the object is almost entirely molten.

Step Six: The axis would be the last part to reach melting point. At that point the water tanks explode. The pressure blows the planetoid up into an iron balloon some ten miles in diameter and twenty miles long, if everybody has done his job right.

The hollow world is now ready for tenants. Except that certain things have to be moved in: air, water, soil, living things. It should be possible to set up a closed ecology. Cole and Cox suggested setting up the solar mirror at one end and using it to reflect sunlight back and forth along the long axis. We might prefer to use fusion power, if we've got it.

"BLOWING" AN ASTEROID

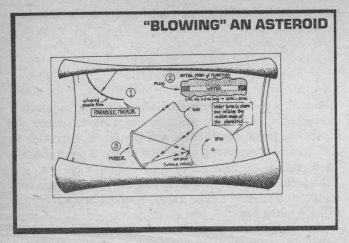

Naturally we spin the thing for gravity.

Living in such an inside-out world would be odd in some respects. The whole landscape is overhead. Our sky contains farms and houses and so forth. If we came to space to see the stars, we'd have to go down into the basement.

We get our choice of gravity and weather. Weather is easy. We give the asteroid a slight equatorial bulge, to get a circular central lake. We shade the endpoints of the asteroid from the sun, so that it's always raining there, and the water runs downhill to the central lake. If we keep the gravity low enough, we should be able to fly with an appropriate set of muscle-powered wings; and the closer we get to the axis, the easier it becomes. (Of course, if we get too close the wax melts and the wings come apart . . .)

MACROLIFE

Let's back up a bit, to the Heinlein "Universe" ship. Why do we want to land it?

If the ship has survived long enough to reach its target

star, it could probably survive indefinitely; and so can the nth-generation society it now carries. Why should their descendants live out their lives on a primitive Earthlike world? Perhaps they were born to better things.

Let the "Universe" ship become their universe, then. They can mine new materials from the asteroids of the new system, and use them to enlarge the ship when necessary, or build new ships. They can loosen the population control laws. Change stars when convenient. Colonize space itself, and let the planets become mere way-stations. See the universe!

The concept is called *Macrolife*: large, powered, self-sufficient environments capable of expanding or reproducing. Put a drive on the Inside-Outside asteroid bubble and it becomes a Macrolife vehicle. The ring-shaped flying city can be extended indefinitely from the forward rim. Blish's spindizzy cities were a step away from being Macrolife; but they were too dependent on planet-based society.

A Macrolife vehicle would have to carry its own mining tools and chemical laboratories, and God knows what else. We'd learn what else accidentally, by losing interstellar colony-ships. At best a Macrolife vehicle would never be as safe as a planet, unless it was as big as a planet, and perhaps not then. But there are values other than safety. An airplane isn't as safe as a house, but a house doesn't go anywhere. Neither does a world.

WORLDS

The terraforming of worlds is the next logical step up in size. For a variety of reasons, I'm going to skip lightly over it. We know both too much and too little to talk coherently about what makes a world habitable.

But we're learning fast, and will learn faster. Our present pollution problems will end by telling us exactly how to keep a habitable environment habitable, how to keep a stable ecology stable, and how to put it all back together again after it falls apart. As usual, the universe will teach us or kill us. If we live long enough to build ships of the "Universe" type, we will know what to put inside them. We may even know how to terraform a hostile world for the convenience of human colonists, having tried our techniques on Earth itself.

Now take a giant step.

DYSON SPHERES

Freeman Dyson's original argument went as follows, approximately.

No industrial society has ever reduced its need for power, except by collapsing. An intelligent optimist will expect his own society's need for power to increase geometrically, and will make his plans accordingly. According to Dyson, it will not be an impossibly long time before our own civilization needs all the power generated by our sun. Every last erg of it. We will then have to enclose the sun so as to control all of its output.

What we use to enclose the sun is problematic. Dyson was speaking of shells in the astronomical sense: solid or liquid, continuous or discontinuous, anything to interrupt the sunlight so that it can be turned into power. One move might be to convert the mass of the solar system into as many little ten-by-twenty-mile hollow iron bubbles as will fit. The smaller we subdivide the mass of a planet, the more useful surface area we get. We put all the little asteroid bubbles in circular orbits at distances of about one Earth orbit from the sun, but differing enough that they won't collide. It's a gradual process. We start by converting the existing asteroids. When we run out, we convert Mars, Jupiter, Saturn, Uranus . . . and eventually, Earth.

DYSON SPHERE (all around sun)

Now, aside from the fact that our need for power increases geometrically, our population also increases geometrically. If we didn't need the power, we'd still need the room in those bubbles. Eventually we've blocked out all of the sunlight. From outside, from another star, such a system would be a great globe radiating enormous energy in the deep infrared.

What some science-fiction writers have been calling a Dyson Sphere is something else: a hollow spherical shell, like a ping pong ball with a star in the middle. Mathematically at least, it is possible to build such a shell without leaving the solar system for materials. The planet Jupiter has a mass of 2×10^{30} grams, which is most of the mass of the solar system excluding the sun. Given massive transmutation of elements, we can convert Jupiter into a spherical shell ninety-three million miles in radius and maybe ten to twenty feet thick. If we don't have transmutation, we can still do it, with a thinner shell. There are at least ten Earth-masses of building material in the solar system, once we throw away the useless gases.

The surface area inside a Dyson Sphere is about a billion times that of the Earth. Very few galactic civilizations in science fiction have included as many as a billion worlds. Here you'd have that much territory within walking distance, assuming you were immortal.

Naturally we would have to set up a biosphere on the inner surface. We'd also need gravity generators. The gravitational attraction inside a uniform spherical shell is zero. The net pull would come from the sun, and everything would gradually drift upward into it.

So. We spot gravity generators all over the shell, to hold down the air and the people and the buildings. "Down" is outward, toward the stars.

We can control the temperature of any locality by varying the heat-retaining properties of the shell. In fact, we may want to enlarge the shell, to give us more room or to make the permanent noonday sun look smaller. All we need do is make the shell a better insulator: foam the material, for instance. If it holds heat too well, we may want to add radiator fins to the outside.

Note that life is not necessarily pleasant in a Dyson Sphere. We can't see the stars. It is always noon. We can't dig mines or basements. And if one of the gravity generators ever went out, the resulting disaster would make the end of the Earth look trivial by comparison.

But if we need a Dyson Sphere, and if it can be built, we'll probably build it.

Now, Dyson's assumptions (expanding population, expanding need for power) may hold for any industrial society, human or not. If an astronomer were looking for inhabited stellar systems, he would be missing the point if he watched only the visible stars. The galaxy's most advanced civilizations may be spherical shells about the size of the Earth's orbit, radiating as much power as a Sol-type sun, but at about 10μ wavelength—in the deep infrared . . .

. . . assuming that the galaxy's most advanced civilizations are protoplasmic. But beings whose chemistry is based on molten copper, say, would want a hotter environment. They might have evolved faster, in temperatures where chemistry, and biochemistry, would move *far* faster. There might be a lot more of them than of us. And their red-hot Dyson Spheres would look deceptively like red giant or supergiant stars. One wonders.

In *The Wanderer*, novelist Fritz Leiber suggested that most of the visible stars have already been surrounded by shells of worlds. We are watching old light, he suggested, light that was on its way to Earth before the industrial expansion of galactic civilization really hit its stride. Already we see part of the result: the opaque dust clouds astronomers find in the direction of the galactic core are not dust clouds, but walls of Dyson Spheres blocking the stars within.

RINGWORLD

I have come up with an intermediate step between Dyson Spheres and planets. Build a ring ninety-three million miles in radius—one Earth orbit—which would make it six hundred million miles long. If we have the mass of Jupiter to work with, and if we make it a million miles wide, we get a thickness of about a thousand meters. The Ringworld would thus be much sturdier than a Dyson Sphere.

There are other advantages. We can spin it for gravity. A rotation on its axis of 770 miles/second would give the

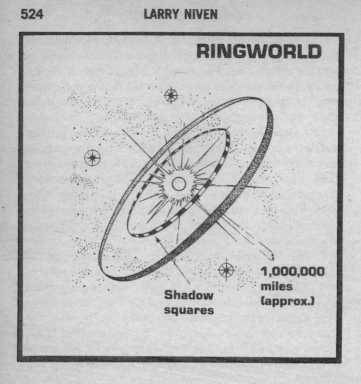

RINGWORLD

Shadow squares

1,000,000 miles (approx.)

Ringworld one gravity outward. We wouldn't even have to roof it over. Put walls a thousand miles high at each rim, aimed inward at the sun, and very little of the air will leak over the edges.

Set up an inner ring of shadow squares—light orbiting structures to block out part of the sunlight—and we can have day-and-night cycles in whatever period we like. And we can see the stars—unlike the inhabitants of a Dyson Sphere.

The thing is roomy enough: three million times the area of the Earth. It will be some time before anyone complains of the crowding.

As with most of these structures, our landscape is optional, a challenge to engineer and artist alike. A look at the outer surface of a Ringworld or Dyson Sphere would be most instructive. Seas would show as bulges, mountains as dents. Riverbeds and river deltas would be sculptured in; there would be no room for erosion on something as thin as a Ringworld or a Dyson Sphere. Seas would be flat-bottomed—as we use only the top of a sea anyway—and small, with convoluted shorelines. Lots of beachfront. Mountains would exist only for scenery and recreation.

A large meteor would be a disaster on such a structure. A hole in the floor of the Ringworld, if not plugged, would eventually let all the air out, and the pressure differential would cause storms the size of a world, making repairs difficult.

The Ringworld concept is flexible. Consider:

1. More than one Ringworld can circle a sun. Imagine many Ringworlds, noncoplanar, of slightly differing radii—or of widely differing radii—inhabited by very different intelligent races.

2. We'd get seasons by bobbing the sun up and down. Actually the Ring would do the bobbing; the sun would stay put (one Ring to a sun for this trick).

3. To build a Ringworld when all the planets in the system are colonized to the hilt (and, baby, we don't *need* a Ringworld until it's gotten that bad!) pro tem structures are needed. A structure the size of a world and the shape of a pie plate, with a huge rocket thruster underneath and a biosphere in the dish, might serve to house a planet's population while the planet in question is being disassembled. It circles the sun at 770 miles/second, firing outward to maintain its orbit. The depopulated planet becomes two more pie plates, and we wire them in an equilateral triangle and turn off the thrusters, evacuate more planets and start building the Ringworld.

MULTIPLE RINGS

DYSON SPHERES II

I pointed out earlier that gravity generators look unlikely. We may never be able to build them at all. Do we really need to assume gravity generators on a Dyson Sphere? There are at least two other solutions.

We can spin the Dyson Sphere. It still picks up all the

energy of the sun, as planned; but the atmosphere collects around the equator, and the rest is in vacuum. We would do better to reshape the structure like a canister of movie film; it gives us greater structural strength. And we wind up with a closed Ringworld.

Or, we can live with the fact that we can't have gravity. According to the suggestion of Dan Alderson, Ph.D., we can build two concentric spherical shells, the inner shell transparent, the outer transparent or opaque, at our whim. The biosphere is between the two shells.

It would be fun. We can build anything we like within the freefall environment. Buildings would be fragile as a butterfly. Left to themselves they would drift up against the inner shell, but a heavy thread would be enough to tether them against the sun's puny gravity. The only question is, can humanity stand long periods of free fall?

HOLD IT A MINUTE

Have you reached the point of vertigo? These structures are hard to hold in your head. They're so flipping *big*. It might help if I tell you that, though we can't *begin* to *build* any of these things, practically anyone can handle them mathematically. Any college freshman can prove that the gravitational attraction inside a spherical shell is zero. The stresses are easy to compute (and generally too strong for anything we can make). The mathematics of a Ringworld are those of a suspension bridge with no endpoints.

OK, go on with whatever you were doing.

THE DISC

What's bigger than a Dyson Sphere? Dan Alderson, designer of the Alderson Double Dyson Sphere, now brings you the

ALDERSON DISC

Gravity perpendicular to plane

Spin

·Alderson Disc. The shape is that of a phonograph record, with a sun situated in the little hole. The radius is about that of the orbit of Mars or Jupiter. Thickness: a few thousand miles.

Gravity is uniformly vertical to the surface (freshman physics again) except for edge effects. Engineers do have to worry about edge effects; so we'll build a thousand-mile wall around the inner well to keep the atmosphere from drifting into the sun. The outer edge will take care of itself.

This thing is massive. It weighs far more than the sun. We ignore problems of structural strength. Please note that we can inhabit *both* sides of the Alderson Disc.

The sun will always be on the horizon—unless we bob it, which we do. (This time it is the sun that does the bobbing.) Now it is always dawn, or dusk, or night.

The Disc would be a wonderful place to stage a Gothic or a sword-and-sorcery novel. The atmosphere is right, and there are real monsters. Consider: we can occupy only a part of the Disc the right distance from the sun. We might as well share the Disc and the cost of its construction with aliens from hotter or colder climes. Mercurians and Venusians nearer the sun, Martians out toward the rim, aliens from other stars living wherever it suits them best. Over the tens of thousands of years, mutations and adaptations would migrate across the sparsely settled borders. If civilization should fall, things could get eerie and interesting.

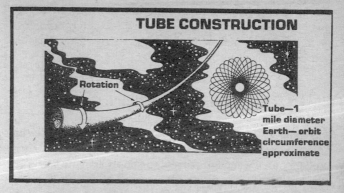

TUBE CONSTRUCTION

Rotation

Tube—1 mile diameter Earth— orbit circumference approximate

COSMIC MACARONI

Pat Gunkel has designed a structure analogous to the Ringworld. Imagine a hollow strand of macaroni six hundred million miles long and not particularly thick--say a mile in diameter. Join it in a loop around the sun.

Pat calls it a *topopolis*. He points out that we could rotate the thing as in the illustration--—getting gravity through centrifugal force—because of the lack of torsion effects. At six hundred million miles long and a mile wide, the curvature of the tube is negligible. We can set up a biosphere on the inner surface, with a sunlight tube down the axis and photoelectric power sources on the outside. So far, we've got something bigger than a world but smaller than a Ringworld.

But we don't have to be satisfied with one loop! We can go round and round the sun, as often as we like, as long as the strands don't touch. Pat visualizes endless loops of rotating tube, shaped like a hell of a lot of spaghetti patted roughly into a hollow sphere with a star at the center (and now we call it an *aegagropilous topopolis*). As the madhouse civilization that built it continued to expand, the coil would reach to other stars. With the interstellar links using power supplied by the inner coils, the tube city would expand through the galaxy. Eventually our *aegagropilous galactotopopolis* would look like all the stars in the heavens had been embedded in hair.

THE MEGASPHERE

Mathematically at least, it is possible to build a really big Dyson Sphere, with the heart of a galaxy at its center. There probably aren't enough planets to supply us with material. We would have to disassemble some of the stars of the galactic arms. But we'll be able to do it by the time we need to.

We put the biosphere on the outside this time. Surface gravity is minute, but the atmospheric gradient is infinitesimal. Once again, we assume that it is possible for human beings to adapt to free fall. We live in free fall, above a

MEGA DYSON SPHERE

surface area of tens of millions of light-years, within an atmosphere that doesn't thin out for scores of light-years.

Temperature control is easy: We vary the heat conductivity of the sphere to pick up and hold enough of the energy from the stars within. Though the radiating surface is great, the volume to hold heat is much greater. Industrial power would come from photoreceptors inside the shell.

Within this limitless universe of air we can build exceptionally large structures, Ringworld-sized and larger. We could even spin them for gravity. They would remain aloft for many times the lifespan of any known civilization before the gravity of the core stars pulled them down to contact the surface.

The Megasphere would be a pleasantly poetic place to live. From a flat Earth hanging in space, one could actually reach a nearby Moon via a chariot drawn by swans, and stand a good chance of finding selenites there. There would be none of this nonsense about carrying bottles of air along.

FINAL SOLUTION

One final step is to join two opposing life styles, the Macrolife tourist types and the sedentary types who prefer to restructure their home worlds.

The Ringworld rotates at 770 miles/second. Given appropriate conducting surfaces, this rotation could set up enormous magnetic effects. These could be used to control the burning of the sun, to cause it to fire off a jet of gas along the Ringworld axis of rotation. The sun becomes its own rocket. The Ringworld follows, tethered by gravity.

By the time we run out of sun, the Ring is moving through space at Bussard ramjet velocities. We continue to use the magnetic effect to pinch the interstellar gas into a fusion flame, which now becomes our sun and our motive power.

The Ringworld makes a problematical vehicle. What's it *for?* You can't land the damn thing anywhere. A traveling

Ringworld is not useful as a tourist vehicle; anything you want to see, you can put on the Ringworld itself . . . unless it's a lovely multiple star system like Beta Lyrae; but you just can't get that *close* on a flying Ringworld.

A Ringworld in flight would be a bird of ill omen. It could only be fleeing some galaxy-wide disaster.

Now, galaxies do explode. We have pictures of it happening. The probable explanation is a chain reaction of novas in the galactic core. Perhaps we should be maintaining a space watch for fleeing Ringworlds . . . except that we couldn't do anything about it.

We live on a world: small, immobile, vulnerable and unprotected. But it will not be so forever.

My first contact with Jim Baen was a phone call at eight A.M.

I'm never awake at eight A.M. Pournelle has learned to tell friends to call *him* if they have a message for *us*. He sounds grouchy at eight A.M., but I sound pleasant and plausible. When you've hung up, you realize that I made no sense. You will presently learn that I remember nothing of the conversation.

By some fluke, I remember this one. "Hello! You don't know me, but I'm Jim Baen and I'm the new editor of *Galaxy* magazine. I've just read your article in *Analog* about huge structures. I'm wondering, could you be talked into doing the same kind of thing for *Galaxy*?"

"Whazza? Bean?"

"I don't quite . . . oh my *God!* I forgot the time change! What time is it there? Oh, I'm so sorry . . ." Click.

GHETTO? BUT I THOUGHT . . .

Ghetto. In the '60s and '70s, every boy and his dog had fallen in love with this private word. Black ghettos, Puerto Rican ghettos, ghettoization, science fiction ghetto . . .

I'd read about ghettos. There were walls around them. You didn't leave because it was illegal. Every so often the goyim would burn you out.

So I listened as various knowledgeable science fiction writers told of the science fiction ghetto. And I learned:

1. A good writer can't get himself taken seriously if he's known as a science fiction writer. This cuts into sales even of his mainstream books. When *The Boys From Brazil*, a fine science fiction novel, was nominated for a Nebula Award, Ira Levin's publisher hastily withdrew the book. The words "kiss of death" were never used, but *it's expensive to join the science fiction community*.

2. Writers of the stature of Kurt Vonnegut and John D. MacDonald have learned their trade writing SF, then migrated to the mainstream. Bob Silverberg sells regularly to *Playboy*. Barry Malzberg and Harlan Ellison saw to it that the "science fiction" labels were taken off their books. *You can leave any time*.

3. Those who stay gain certain advantages:

   Security. A book with the SF label will sell a minimum of copies no matter what.

   The company of our own kind. Which includes some fine original thinkers among readers as well as writers. A few weeks ago I fired a missile up to lunar escape velocity in a Washington University basement. The effort it took to bring that about was considerable, and none of it was mine. It sometimes seems that the brightest people in the world want us to do their talking; they don't have leisure to educate the rest of the species.

Recreation. Autographing isn't the fun part, but autograph tours do have some fun in them. We don't get interviewed as often as the mainstream authors, but we get a more intelligent, better-educated audience. We get a better class of groupies than the rock stars.

Ego-stroking. Writers are naturally arrogant; but arrogance wilts if it isn't fed. We're not movie stars, and our faces aren't known; fans won't spot us in a restaurant. But we can go to the science fiction conventions to be admired.

The conventions are matched in no other branch of literature, and are like nothing else on Earth.

4. *We are picky about outsiders.* If not actively hostile. Writers who wouldn't permit sloppy research in their mainstream or historical or detective novels think they can get away with it in science fiction. They mistake infrared for ultraviolet and break physical laws without noticing. They twist sociology out of all reason to make some dubious point. SF reviewers are merciless toward such mistakes. Arthur Clarke, certainly one of the top dozen SF writers in the world, was roasted when he misunderstood the nature of cloning (in *Imperial Earth*).

A reputable mainstream writer must still demonstrate his talents and his education before we'll let him in. Mainstream critics fare no better. Naturally this contributes to the gap between SF/fantasy and the mainstream: the "Ghettoization."

* * *

Okay, gang. What kind of a place is it that won't let outsiders join unless they meet certain standards; is expensive to belong to; that a member can leave any time, to make a little money, then return to at whim; that people join for the company of their peers, the recreation facilities, the ego boost, and the security; that places a barrier between itself and the outside world?

I know that place. My Dad was a member.

Ghetto? That's the Los Angeles Country Club!

Well, almost. When financial or social pressure forces a member to resign from the L.A. Country Club, he does it quietly. He doesn't brag about it. Maybe he can keep up his contacts; he may even return as somebody's guest.

But I've barely mentioned the grounds!

Acres of rolling greens, scattered trees, a few sand pits . . . sorry, that's the wrong club. The Science Fiction Country Club is mostly the interiors of hotels. But . . . it's magical. Like Ningauble's Cave, its doorways open into every city in the world.

At my first World Science Fiction Convention, in Oakland in 1964, my car was stolen the moment I left it. I didn't realize it until Sunday evening. By then the police already had it. That convention was a weird experience. Fred Pohl had already bought three of my stories, and he was there to introduce me around. I was a neofan and a pro too.

I love science fiction conventions.

Too many of us never get outside to explore the city: "Every science fiction convention takes place in Cleveland." Never mind. There's more variety inside the hotel than you'd ever find out there. Fauns and aliens and fantasy women wander the halls. In the art show you can find better artwork than ever reaches the mundane galleries. Minds that have touched yours through their books, you may meet here. The secrets of the universe are exposed, the problems of human and other sapient species are raised and solved, there are classes for artists and writers and fantasy gamers, all onstage at the panel discussions.

Moreover, conventions generate stories, from wonderful to funny to horrifying.

NUCON, 1981 was held in Sydney, Australia.

Fans were there to pick us up at the airport, but they were waiting at the wrong gate. Nobody appeared to be searching for the Guests of Honor. I guarded the luggage while Marilyn went scouting. I looked up—and a Pierson's puppeteer was coming at me!

Who else would a Pierson's puppeteer be seeking? But the beast was stuffed, being rolled on a triangular wheeled platform by almost a dozen Sydney fans.

We found a borrowed house waiting for us, complete with cats. How thoughtful! We *need* cats. The owners (Texas oil people) were wandering while one of the fans house-sat for them. We used it as a base of operations while we wandered ourselves: to Lightning Ridge (for black opals) and Siding Spring (telescopes) and zoos (alien life forms).

The Nucon, throughout, seemed aimed at the Guest of Honor. We'd been promised that we'd be taken to dinner every night, and it was true. The masquerade featured costumes from the Known Space series. As judge I gave it to the protagonist from "Wait It Out." He was clearly frozen solid, and would go motionless on command. The puppeteer lived at the reception desk until Sunday and "This is your life, Beowulf Shaeffer!" He talked through a curtain. The vengeance-minded Julian Forward presently produced a mini-black-hole, which swallowed up everybody.

OZARKON—1970 was to be in St. Louis, Missouri. We started a week early to visit Marilyn's parents, who live near Chicago.

In St. Louis we took a taxi to the appropriate motel. They had never heard of an Ozarkon.

This is the trip where I learned to take all of the relevant papers with me. We hadn't done that. We wound up calling Boston and getting Tony Lewis to read us a telephone number from *Locus*!

I called it. I got a woman's voice. I explained that we were looking for the Ozarkon. Are we at the right—? Do you know anything—? And finally, "Well, is there an Ozarkon or not?"

She burst into tears.

Ultimately we got an explanation. When two successive teams of convention organizers dropped out entirely, a lady had volunteered/been pressured to run the Ozarkon. A nice woman, but she didn't know conventions. Too few attendees had signed up; the motel naturally canceled; she'd kept trying, and only given up a week ago. When someone tried to phone us, we had already left.

Our contacts took us to dinner, and I got them to organize a party. We damned well showed ourselves having fun. The lady took us to the St. Louis Arch before driving us to the airport. If St. Louis fandom was going to fall apart, it wouldn't be because Larry Niven went into a shrieking fury.

Notice that I've named no names.

NYCON—1967 had all the makings of a disaster. The Hilton was about to automate its elevators, and the operators were on slowdown strike. Sympathy slowdowns were going on in other regions.

Conventions have always suffered from a dearth of elevators. Can you imagine one in which the operators spend twenty minutes on the top floor; in which they deliberately pass floors; in which anyone who enters an elevator is treated as an enemy? I noticed little of this. I was competing for my first Hugo, and I met Marilyn Joyce Wisowaty.

We must have been in the main restaurant when the waiters were having fun with the customers. Did we notice Lester del Rey throwing the wrong salad at a waiter in a desperate attempt to get his attention? No, we heard that later. I don't think Marilyn and I noticed anything except each other.

You make your own convention.

The Banquet *would* have been a disaster. I was up for a Hugo for the first time in my life! There was no place to get a drink on that entire floor. I was out of cigarettes. Bob Tucker gave an uncharacteristically depressing speech. Sam Moskowitz spoke. I'd have gone right up the wall without Marilyn to hold my hand and Adrienne (at that time) Hicks to loan me cigarettes.

Best short story, 1966: "Neutron Star." I *loved* that convention.

NASFIC, 1976: The Tale of Harlan's Hugo.

The Worldcon that year was in Australia. It took place a little earlier than the Nasfic in Los Angeles. Bruce Pelz had already phoned to tell me that I had won the short-story award for "The Hole Man." He was bringing it home for me.

The charter flight would land about the same time as the Banquet.

Harlan Ellison was Guest of Honor. He wasn't at the Banquet itself—gourmet instincts?—but his awards were arrayed around the podium: Hugos, Nebulas, and miscellaneous awards including an Edgar for best detective fiction. I remember that one because I want one.

After dinner, tradition allowed the rest of the attendees to form up along the walls. Harlan took the podium. He explained that he was getting out of the science fiction ghetto. He was getting all the "SF" labels taken off his books. He was going to the mainstream for its greater critical acclaim, higher advances, and other benefits. Barry Malzberg and Bob Silverberg and others had done it successfully . . .

We were halfway through the panel that followed the

Banquet, when Bruce Pelz entered to present me with—a silver rocket ship on a wooden base. When the "Stardrive" panel broke up, I headed for an elevator with my Hugo cradled in my arms.

Four of five young strangers got in behind me. Neofans? One said, "Hey, I like it! What is it?"

Neofans. Keep it simple. "Why, this is a science-fiction achievement award, my child. They're given out every year for—"

"A Hugo! I've heard of Hugos. Is that one of Harlan's?"

Hell, what do you say to that? I said, "That's right. Harlan is getting out of the SF ghetto, as you must have heard. He's making a clean break by giving away his Hugos. He had two left when I left his room. I wish I could give you his room number—"

I waited four months to hear rumors of the neofannish invasion of Harlan Ellison's room. Nothing. I couldn't stand it anymore. I told Harlan the tale, and asked him. They never made it . . . and I was designated a fiend in human form! But what would *you* have said?

LACON, 1972: The Great Duel.

First you must know of a short story. "Cloak of Anarchy" required a character who was capable of knocking out all the monitoring devices in King's Free Park, turning a fake anarchy into a real anarchy, and would do it. What I needed was a combination of Russell Seitz (who lives on the East Coast, and who tends to carry advanced technological toys in his pockets) and Don Simpson (a West Coast fan who uses technology to create his own art forms). I combined them into "Ron Cole."

I must have done it right. All the East Coast fans recognized Russell. All the West Coast fans recognized Don.

Comes the Los Angeles World Science Fiction Convention. We were at a room party. I recognized Russell Seitz, "Hi, Russell!"

''You used me in a story.''

''Yeah!''

''You, er, didn't ask permission.''

I'm spoiled, maybe. I expect such a thing to be taken as flattery. I disengaged myself. A few minutes later I ran across Gordon Dickson.

''Hi, Gordy!''

''Russell Seitz has asked me to speak for him in an affair of honor.''

Oooops! Through the humming in my ears I said, ''I expect I should choose a second to speak for me.''

Gordy agreed.

I looked around and there was Ben Bova. Ben had published ''Cloak of Anarchy'' in *Analog*. Choosing Ben meant that I would have to do less explaining.

Gordy explained that a venerable dueling law set a limit on the bore size of weapons. ''We'll have to settle for magnums.''

Champagne corks?

Ara Pashinian is a world traveler who shows occasionally at world conventions. He kindly offered us his roomy suite ''to test-fire the propellants.''

Gordy and Russell disappeared to get weaponry Russell had brought along. In Ara's suite Ben and I discussed strategy. ''Don't argue about the weaponry,'' Ben said. ''Remember, Russell Seitz is the world's sixth nuclear power!''

Oooops! It was true. As one of the Board of Trustees of a Boston museum, Russell had built a Titan II missile from parts he acquired from junkyards for under a thousand dollars.

''Not to worry,'' Ben said. ''I know some Air Force people. I can promise instant massive retaliation the instant you're dead.''

Marilyn is an admirer of Georgette Heyer's tales of the English Regency period. She knew what to do. She threw her arms around me crying, "Give up this madness! You'll be killed!"

But time was passing, and where were Russell and Gordy?

Here they came, bursting through the door in full 7th century Samurai armor! (Remember the Boston museum?) Ben cried, "No, no, no! No armor during the duel!"

"During the duel, no armor," Gordy said. "During the negotiations we take no chances."

Which raised a question. The badges at that convention were metal disks three inches across. Did they constitute armor? We decided they did not; they would be worn.

Our seconds test-fired the champagne bottles. It was decided that Russell and I would take two paces, turn and fire. And we drank the propellants.

By High Dawn (designated as 1 P.M.) I had bought replacement champagne. I went up to the swimming pool to fight for my honor. I didn't realize that I'd replaced cork corks with more dangerous plastic corks. I wore a bathing suit, thinking I might want a swim too.

I'd forgotten my big metal badge. Marilyn noticed and loaned me hers. I pinned it where it might do me some good. My genitalia were now labelled as the property of Marilyn Niven.

Russell appeared. He noticed the harder plastic corks, but said nothing. "Given the known propensities of my opponent—" he said, and pinned his badge between his shoulder blades.

We squared off, took two paces, faced each other—

I twisted the wire open. Worked it off. Peeled away the foil. Went to work on the cork with my thumbs. Easy does it, don't want to break the cork . . . Looked up, and Russell was ready.

He fired past my shoulder.

I went back to work. Ease the cork loose. Russell was

standing at attention, expressionless. The cork was easing
out . . . faster than I thought. I fired through his hair.

And we drank the propellants.

MIDAMERICON—Kansas City, 1976: The Tale of Walter the Lobster.

This was a wild convention.

It's the one at which Russell Seitz found two very expensive bottles of cognac in a line of cheaper bottles by the same manufacturer, and a clerk who didn't know the difference. He was pouring brandy for friends throughout the convention.

It's the only time Russell ever bought a wine for its name. He brought a case of Inferno, a wine from Italy. INFERNO was also the name of the collaboration novel (a sequel to Dante's *Inferno*) for which Jerry Pournelle and I hoped to win a Hugo. When other sources ran out one night at a room party, Jerry drank half a bottle of the stuff. The next afternoon he looked like he had risen from the grave. And shouldn't have.

I was up for three Hugos: a novelet in competition with Jerry, a novella, and the collaboration novel INFERNO. I feared that I would take Jerry's Hugo award from him, and nothing else. It didn't occur to me that I would then drop and break it.

Russell had plans for that convention. He intended to walk into the Muehlbach Hotel in Kansas City with a giant lobster on a leash. He would arrange for the hotel to cook the thing and serve it to a dozen people that night.

To this end he lodged an order for the biggest lobster caught in a three-day period, with three Boston seafood companies. We'd gamble on a roughly 24-pound lobster. Russell would bring the wines too.

Things began to go awry.

In July, Russell called me to say he was swamped in other work. He had worked out a preferred menu. Would I invite the guests, and deal with the Muehlbach in his stead? Oh, hell, why not?

My phone call got me the catering department and a Miss English. I described what we wanted. Miss English saw no problems at all, except that she wasn't prepared to give me a price yet.

I issued some invitations.

Now, notice the timing: we were to leave Thursday. The lobster was to walk in Friday and be eaten that night (one-day membership). On Wednesday Russell called to say that he'd spoken to the Muehlbach, and I'd better do the same.

Miss English had finally given Russell some prices. $7.00/bottle corkage fee on the wines Russell was to bring. $35.00 per guest, in 1976 dollars, and we bring our own lobster.

It was the timing, as much as the ferocious fees, that convinced me to cancel. Rightly or wrongly, I felt that the Muehlbach was ripping me off.

I called Russell and we arranged new rules. Russell would bring the lobster cooked. We'd figure on a midnight snack situation. On that basis, would I bring pliers and a ball peen hammer?

I phoned the people I'd invited, starting with Jerry Pournelle. I asked him to toss pliers and a ball-peen hammer in his luggage.

Russell appeared on the sidewalk Friday evening. He had an incredible load of luggage, which Marilyn and I stored in our room.

We gathered around midnight.

Some things went wrong, some went right. We couldn't find Poul and Karen Anderson, or Frank and Beverly Herbert. But—Robert Heinlein, as Guest of Honor, had held a press conference that afternoon. The Heinleins still had clean silverware, plates, glasses, a tub of mayonnaise. Wealth!

Walter was only a twelve-pounder. Russell would have

brought two of him if things had gone as planned. He still looked *huge*, big enough that I found it cost-effective to chew the spinnerets. Without Jerry's hammer and pliers Walter would have been quite safe. The wines included a glorious Madeira that doesn't usually get out of Portugal; but there had been a revolution scare . . .

It could have been worse. One night we ate in the restaurant that was to have cooked Walter. Among other problems, Roberta Pournelle's dinner didn't arrive until after Jerry sent back his inedible steak, and then the waiter attempted to serve the same steak to Roberta. Perhaps it's as well that things didn't go as planned.

As it was, Walter was delicious, and a good time was had by all, except for the Andersons and the Herberts, to whom I can only apologize.

Frank and Bev Herbert didn't share Walter, but they grew to know him. He sat in the hall in front of the Herberts' door for two days. Perhaps the Muehlbach was expressing an opinion. I have now expressed mine.

WESTERCON—Vancouver, 1977.

Three times in my life have I amused Robert Silverberg. I have his word for it.

The first time was at a convention party, the most crowded you can imagine. Shoulder to shoulder we stood, throughout the room. No place for a claustrophobe! I made for the door, pushing between bodies. An avenue of freedom played out and left me jammed nose to nose with Robert Silverberg. Neither of us could move. I couldn't think of anything to say.

So I leaned forward and kissed him on the nose.

The third time? The Westercon that year was held at the University in Vancouver. Many attendees used dorm rooms. Others of us stayed at the nearest motel. Craig Miller arranged a shuttle service, buses every hour.

Getting back and forth was a real hassle, and it ate up

time, too. One night an exhausted half-dozen of us staggered off the last bus, wobbled into the motel, boarded the elevator. Bob Silverberg looked around at a cluster of sagging faces and asked, "All right, where's the room party?"

There were groans. I said, "My room, 1034."

He looked at me. "Really?"

"Sure. Drop your coats in your rooms and come on up - Push five for me, willya?"

Bob cracks up very nicely. He comes completely apart, loses all dignity. Neither of us can now remember the second time it happened; but it happened.

CLOSER TO HOME

Until I began writing, my mother had never read any science fiction. Afterward she would read my stuff, but nobody else's. She held out for about ten years.

Then, one morning she was feeling adventurous. She had a book at hand, a Nebula Awards anthology. She'd already read my story. She looked down the Table of Contents for a title that might appeal to her.

My mother has bred the best Keeshonds in the country for going on fifty years. She must have attended around a thousand dog shows.

All she had to do was phone me and ask.

Her eye stopped at "A Boy and His Dog," by Harlan Ellison.

She read every word. She hasn't read any science fiction since, unless my name was on it.

CHICON—Chicago, 1982: the German Translator.

This one's hearsay; but Jerry won't talk about it anymore. He told me about it a few days after the Chicago Worldcon.

Jerry reads a little German. Sometime before the convention he had read through a German copy of *The Mercenary*. Jerry found that the translator had taken out all explanations, all justifications, anything that might express the reasoning behind the violence in that violent, bloody story. There was only the blood.

That's enough to set any writer to thinking of assassination. But there was worse to come. The German translator attended that convention. Jerry confronted him one evening in the Con Suite.

Some of you may recall the shouting match. Jerry quotes only one phrase: "But you *are* a fascist, you *should* sound like a fascist!" But it went on long enough for Jerry—who is an ex-communist—to recognize that the man was a Party member.

Jerry Pournelle likes to describe himself as a 13th century liberal. ("The king is taking too much power to himself! The rights of the nobles are being unjustly eroded—") And Jerry's publisher had hired a communist to translate *The Mercenary*!

I didn't fall out of my chair because I was hanging on to the poker table. I lost all dignity. I could see in Jerry's face that I was near losing a friendship. I was lucky not to lose control of my sphincters! Jerry took it badly; but in ten years, he'll see this as a very funny story.

I think he's coming to realize that now. Why don't you ask him about the German Translator? I'm sure it'll bring a smile.

VIKING CON, 1983, Bellingham, Washington.

Bellingham is small and green and lovely. It also has the partly disused harbor and the scattering of survivalist enclaves that we needed for a massive collaboration novel, *Footfall*. Our need to research Bellingham made it convenient for Jerry and me to attend Viking Con.

"Lovely town! We're going to destroy it," we explained.

Our thanks to the pair of nice young ladies who drove us around. We got exactly what we wanted, even down to the X-shaped house with a tennis court placed to conceal the Enclave's bomb shelter.

Jerry's back was giving him hell that trip. I had to move the luggage, and I could have lived without his portable computer. One morning I watched him trying to put his socks on. He couldn't reach his feet. Presently I said, "Just how close *is* this collaboration?"

He got his socks on. Desperation helps.

At the Banquet Jerry still looked like an integral sign, and he was in pain. A spine is supposed to look like that; but *sideways*? Ed Bryant, as Toastmaster, was introducing people by the "Surprise!" technique: describe the victim, then reveal his name at the last instant. When we heard references to Damon and Pythias and Siamese twins and male pair-bonding, Jerry said, "He's doing it to us."

I said, "Yeah. When he says my name, you stand up."

"—Author of *RINGWORLD*—"

Standing up wasn't easy, but Jerry would have done it if he *knew* it would kill him. It took Ed about thirty seconds (with laughter and whispering to cover the delay) to decide that there was no way out: he'd have to follow his notes.

"—Author of *The Mercenary*—" I stood up.

Next Ed began describing Wendy Fletcher, one of the Guests of Honor. It became clear that he loved Wendy not in the normal fashion, but as Dante Alighieri loved Beatrice, with worship. The audience was getting sugar diabetes. So, evidently, was Wendy.

Ed, already a bit flustered, couldn't imagine why he was being laughed at *now*. Heads were blocking his view of Wendy, who appeared to have her forefinger up her nose to the second knuckle.

WESTERCON 1974, Santa Barbara: the Randall Garrett Story. I can't tell the Randall Garrett story.

ADRIENNE AND IRISH COFFEE

Bergin's House of Irish Coffee was already a favorite with my siblings and cousins. When my first story appeared, it was very natural for me to go home from the LASFS via Bergin's, and drink Irish coffee while reading "The Coldest Place" . . . and wish it had illustrations and my name on the cover . . .

I did it again with "Wrong Way Street." I learned how much better a story looks in print, because I could stop worrying about minute changes.

"World of Ptavvs," the novella, had my name on the cover. Jack Gaughan had done pictures of all the strange life forms I'd dreamed up for the Slaver Empire. This was it! This was what I was after, this was why I had written for a year without selling a damn word. I developed a strong preference for Irish coffee.

Somewhere in there, I started taking Adrienne Martine to Bergin's. She too was a novice writer. She says that Bergin's should have put our names on the wall, for all the Irish coffee we consumed. We may have overdone it. Adrienne developed an allergy to caffeine.

We'd spin stories at each other, then poke holes in the plot lines. Hers were generally fantasy: a heroine in her late teens finds a portal out of an intolerable situation into a world where magic is more powerful. I don't remember what tales I told her. Some reached print, no doubt, and some didn't.

I nagged her from time to time, and so did everyone else, about finishing some novel. She was good at starting them.

She taught me how to use chopsticks.

Not long after we met, she married and moved to New

York. We still met, but not often. I took her to dinner at the New York World Science Fiction convention in 1967, and then followed her into a party, where I met Marilyn "Fuzzy Pink" Wisowaty.

Fuzzy Pink and I wound up married and living in Brentwood, a suburb of Los Angeles.

Thursday nights after the LASFS meetings, several of us would gather at the Niven house for poker. I took to serving Irish coffee at these gatherings. In this limited range I became an expert bartender.

Jerry Pournelle was among the regulars.

The damn trouble was that the games would continue until four or six in the morning.

Hour 25 is a science fiction radio show that runs from ten to midnight Fridays. One evening Jerry and I arrived to promote our books and take phone calls. We were wiped out, exhausted; we could barely talk. It became clear to us that the Thursday poker games were ruining us. They had to stop.

Adrienne Martine-Barnes became an agent. She has always thought of herself as a muse, germinating stories in others. Ultimately she did what a thousand friends had been nagging her to do: she finished a novel and sold it. And now she's published several.

I kept my taste for Irish coffee. On Saturday night at a LosCon (local Los Angeles SF conventions) I generally operate an Irish coffee bar, closing down when the liquor runs out.

IRISH COFFEE BY NIVEN

You wouldn't think it would take much effort would you? Irish coffee has only four ingredients! Serving only Irish coffee is work for an idiot, if others are doing all of the work except pouring.

My first Irish coffee bar opened on Sunday night of the 1985 LosCon. I offered because I thought it might be fun. Emotionally I was prepared for failure. Nobody had tried this before.

Subsequent LosCons have featured an Irish coffee bar on Saturday night. Oddly enough, it changes nothing.

In a pinch you can always go to hotel coffee. We almost did. I brought my Bunn coffeemaker, and remembered to bring all the other stuff: filters and filter cones and pots and all that (though I forgot plates and spoons). Then I cut the cord on the coffeemaker by slamming it in the lid of my trunk! Committee member Bob Null repaired it on the spot.

Quantities were guesswork. I poured by hand, and tasted often, trying to get the proportions right. *Hic*! Excuse me. I had to do that every time, because the Committee keeps changing the size of the cups on me . . . and finally I thought of bringing a measuring cup.

I learned of another problem the first time I tried this outside of a LosCon. Is the kid old enough to drink? Did I offer to bartend in order to tell a reader and fan what he *can't* have? I did not. The woman who helped me out in Dallas and Houston was tough enough to do that part of the job for me. In Los Angeles I've had to refuse two or three customers; but we had to insult scores of them in Texas. Then again, those were comics conventions . . .

What follows is my recipe for Elsewhere-Cons. If I can drive to the convention, I have another list: I can bring some of my own equipment. You should consider doing the same.

The proportions were developed by experiment, *after* I realized that I can mix bigger quantities in a nice stable measuring cup and then pour into whatever cups the committee has bought me. Proportions are a matter of taste. Feel free to fiddle.

I like stable cups that don't tip over when I pour. I never

get them, but that's what I want. The whipped cream should not be too stiff to flow; you want it to melt a little on the coffee. Brandy or rum work as alternatives to Irish, but use less sugar. Don't add sugar if you're using liqueurs instead of Irish, and you won't use much of that until the Irish runs out or the line thins, because you have to keep explaining what it's for.

The two most important rules are these:

1. You should run out of booze first. You'd feel like an idiot running out of whipped cream or ground coffee or sugar *or cups* when there's two bottles of whiskey left. (Once or twice the Committee has had to search a darkened city for whipped cream or cups.)

2. The booze should run out before the bartender collapses. Rather than staggering off to bed after spilling too many drinks in a row, you should be *forced* to quit while there's still time to join a party or a singing group.

Why bother?

Put it this way. You've worked your tale off to become a well-known author. If you came to a convention, you came to be admired, like the rest of us. It gives you back your motivation. You'll work better afterward.

But they make you *scintillate*! They stop you for autographs and pop quizzes on your work, in the halls and at parties and even in the restaurant! Anyone who ever stood in an autograph line thinks you should remember his name. Enough of that can wipe the smile off your face and make you forget how to string words together . . . and they still expect you to be witty.

What can you do at a convention, in public, that will take you off the hook for a while?

This was one of the brightest ideas I ever had. Nobody expects me to scintillate. They expect me to pour; nothing else. When the Irish runs out, then I'm ready to scintillate again.

IRISH COFFEE requirements

Proportions

1/4 cup Irish whiskey.
3/4 cup strong coffee, noticeably stronger than normal.
1 heaping tablespoon brown sugar or to taste.

First time: stir like hell, then taste, then adjust. Keep it sweet.

Pour plastic cups half-full or better, then add glob of whipping cream.

If it tastes too strong, you may want to use less booze; but try making the coffee stronger first!

Filling the plastic cup may be a mistake. If it's big and tall, it may topple over.

Always stir completely. Don't get sloppy with that!

Tools

To serve 200 cups I will need:

A 2-cup or 4-cup measuring cup.

7 or 8 half-liters or fifths Irish whiskey (Jameson's or Bushmills are good).

1 bottle Sambucca or Gran Marnier or almost any liqueur that isn't fruity (interesting variants).

3 pounds Mocha Java coffee, ground appropriately. I use a Bunn coffeemaker, so grind the coffee fine.

5 quarts heavy cream.

4 pounds of brown sugar (or Demerara sugar or white sugar, in order of preference).

A refrigerator or portable icebox for the cream, or just a container of ice; no big deal here.

Working room! A stretch of counter, or a big table.

The more room I have to work in, the better, up to a point.

300 or more cups. (Yes, I said I'd make 200. I could be wrong. Running out of cups has nothing to recommend it.) Use foam plastic. Better: there are plastic cups with handles, and they look more elegant than the foam cups, and they're stable. **Don't** buy thin plastic that will burn a customer's fingers if there's hot stuff in it!

A sink would be nice. Otherwise someone has to keep going for water for the coffee.

A garbage can or wastebasket. It takes either a big one, or many, or one that gets emptied frequently (not by the bartender).

Help! The LosCon event was a dead dog party that started at 8 P.M. I looked up at a line like the autograph line at a WorldCon! I needed a permanent volunteer to make the coffee and whip the cream, continually, and things still didn't slow down until twenty minutes before the Irish ran out.

Mixing bowl and mixer for the cream.

A bowl for sugar (digging into the box slows me down).

Bunn coffeemaker, with all accessories: plastic cone and many paper filters. OR anything that makes coffee.

Containers for coffee. 3 glass and 1 thermos worked out fine.

At least 2 large spoons (tablespoons or thereabouts).
At least 2 plates to put them on.
Measuring spoons for coffee. Use large ones.
A jigger.

I WILL BRING my own mug or buy one at the Convention. (I'm entitled to a perk, and that's it. Also I'm likely to lose track of which drink is mine.)

CLEANING UP IS SOMEBODY ELSE'S JOB.

ONE NIGHT AT THE
DRACO TAVERN

This was the script used for Kathy Sanders's group presentation at the WorldCon Masquerade, Los Angeles, 1984. Steven Barnes played "Rick Schumann." I played "Larry."

Drew and Kathy Sanders generally win major awards in the Masquerades. In 1984 Drew was *running* the Masquerade. Kathy was on her own.

She began making costumes more than a year early. By the time she finished she had duplicated a dozen of the most alien characters from my stories.

I wrote the script. Steven and I recorded the sound background early.

The kzin and thrint costumes were *hot*. I had to fan the occupants through their open mouths. The puppeteer must have been worse yet, though it was designed so that Kathy was half out of it until we were called.

I'd seen previous attempts at a Pierson's puppeteer costume. A puppeteer has three legs and two heads. Kathy in her costume had one leg bound up against her chest; heads empty and propped up (they flopped over the first time she tried it); and her arms for the forelegs, on short stilts because human arms aren't long enough. Muscle structure was quilted in, following the Bonnie Dalzell illustration for Ballantine Books, and it looked amazingly lifelike.

She wasn't exactly agile, though.
We won the Master's Award for "Funniest."

ONSTAGE:

RICK SCHUMANN *behind bar. The bar is vertical to the audience.*
YELLOW BUGS *around a table.*
WUNDERLANDER *and* GROG *at the bar.*
QARASHT *seated alone, sense-cluster retracted.*

ACTION, simultaneously--
RICK *finishes preparing the* BUGS' *order, circles bar and takes them a tray with enough liqueur glasses.*

    RICK: Here you are, gentlemen.
    BUGS: Queepee? [*sound done with whistle or some such*]

LARRY *enters, pulling down zipper or opening buttons and shaking off the cold or the heat (to signal his entry from outside) while he looks around. He heads for the* QARASHT.

    RICK: It's arak. You'll taste licorice and some other—
            Wups!

RICK *moves to intercept* LARRY.

    LARRY: [*to* QARASHT] Hello, I'm--
    RICK: I wouldn't talk to the qarasht if I were you. It
            doesn't want company.
    LARRY: How can you tell?
    RICK: It's got its sense cluster retracted.

LARRY: Now, that's my problem. I don't know any of these aliens. Would you be the bartender?

RICK: I own the Draco Tavern. Rick Schumann, at your service. What can I get you?

LARRY: Irish coffee, and a little advice. [*indicates* WUNDERLANDER] Is he human?

MACHINE PEOPLE GIRL *enters, goes to* QARASHT. QARASHT *extrudes sense cluster as she enters.* RICK *moves behind the bar and goes to work, interrupting himself to talk and gesture expansively. He's showing off, as if he owns the customers too.*

Other aliens are entering—

ENTER:
JINXIAN *and* CRASHLANDER *together*
BELTER (?)

RICK: That's a Wunderlander. Human, but from one of the colonies. Our lady of the beard isn't quite human. She's a Machine People, from the Ringworld. I doubt she can have rishathra with a Qarasht, but she'll probably offer.

LARRY: [*embarrassed*] Hey, can they hear us?

RICK: Naw, they've all got sonic shields. The Jinxian and the Crashlander, they're human too, from Jinx and We Made It. The Belter, the one with the funny haircut, he's from right here in the solar system—

ENTER MOTIE MEDIATOR
ENTER KZIN *and* PUPPETEER, *together*

RICK *continues:* You'll like the Motie Mediator. Hell, she can interpret for the rest of them. Uh oh.

LARRY: What's wrong?

RICK: It's all right. It's a kzin and a puppeteer, but they don't seem to be fighting.

LARRY: [*indicates* GROG] The, uh, hairy cone at the end of the bar looks interesting . . .

RICK: I don't advise talking to a Grog. She can take over your mind. At least if you run she can't chase you. Heh heh.

LARRY *doesn't get the joke*
ENTER THRINT
LARRY *turns to look at Thrint.*

RICK *continues:* Now, that's a rare one. That's a thrint, what you'd call a Slaver. Stay away—

RICK *interrupts himself to circle the bar, rapidly, carrying* LARRY's *drink.*

LARRY: Why? (*Double take.*) Hey! That's my drink!

RICK *gives the drink to* THRINT, *hastily, and bowing low.*
LARRY *moves to intercept, too slow.*
KZIN *is holding a chair for the* THRINT JINXIAN *moves a table for him.*

FREEZE FRAME
EXEUNT [*the hale help the clumsier costumes*]

TRANTORCON REPORT

"TrantorCon in 23,309! Lazarus Long says, 'I'll be there! Will you?' "

It started as a toast. Eventually I got the Heinleins' permission to use it in a larger context.

Trantor is given (by Isaac Asimov in the *Foundation* stories) as the ruling planet of a galaxy-wide Empire, sited in the galactic core, 33,000 light-years away. We started the bidding twenty-one thousand years early, to avoid time pressure.

We didn't intend to stick to the laws of the Foundation universe. Why restrict a daydream? TrantorCon was to be the ultimate convention, attended by every intelligent species anyone ever wrote about, with every technology available to add to the fun. Something like the party at the end of Robert Heinlein's *The Number of the Beast*.

I got Marilyn involved. We designated ourselves the Bidding Committee. Randall Garrett became intrigued. Ultimately we gathered others:

Guest of Honor: HARI SELDON
Fan Guest of Honor: ISAAC ASIMOV
Toastmaster: LIEUTENANT COMMANDER SPOCK*

The Committee

Chairbeings: LARRY NIVEN; FUZZY PINK*
Secretary: FRANK CATALANO
Publications: RANDALL GARRETT
Artwork: MIKE MERENBACH

We wrested promises from several Big Name Writers: they will attend the TrantorCon "barring acts of God." I wrote a hotel report, a restaurant report and a travel guide. We passed out buttons, sold some memberships, published a Progress Report . . .

And then I was busy with other things, Randall got sick, Isaac moved Trantor to a globular cluster, and it all kind of faded. But before that happened I did some work that never appeared in the first Progress Report.

MEMBERSHIPS

You're either a member or you're not. Right? Your Committee didn't see the implications until the Pelzes registered their cat.

Memberships can be passed to heirs and descendants; given the time span, that's reasonable. Bandit is a great cat; it's likely enough that he'll have mutated or gene-tailored sapient descendants. If not, what's lost? In 1976 a Trantor-Con membership costs only three bucks.

But what if Bandit's heir is *not* sapient? Our members include small mammals, big-headed birds of varying sizes, and hives of brightly colored moths. Then there's the machinery. I've let my cat use my typewriter on occasion, and the results were cryptic at best. The thought of a cat wandering over the keys of one of Trantor's superrealistic war games computers is enough to send your Committee diving under the bed.

The membership situation is a bag of snakes (No offense intended to our Kitht and Shssifsir members). We need at least eight classes:

---

* Alien names have been transliterated or translated to the best of our ability

* * *

FULL MEMBERS are sapient at all times and have paid their membership fees.

Fees vary among species according to mass, volume, the volume of room they occupy, nutritional needs, and the cost of protecting them or protecting members *from* them. We've registered no bandersnatchi at all due to their mass and the need for artificial swamp terrain. Our only coeurls are bonded guards. Humans, being roughly equal in size, pay a flat fee.

Badges must be worn at all times. They broadcast their position—an advantage where attendees are expected to number in the low trillions. They identify species, special needs, and membership level. Some project protective forcefields. Without your badge, the kzinti and coeurl guards may consider you prey.

SUPERVISED MEMBERS are not sapient at all times or under all conditions. (For instance, a Vulcan in *pon-farr* is irrational and violent.) These must designate a supervisor, who must be a Full Member and must be capable of controlling his charge. Some guards "moonlight" in this capacity. SM badges carry a stun device.

PETS must be placed in stasis for the duration of the convention.

SYMBIOTES. What one member considers a symbiote may be dangerous or lethal to another. The Committee will attempt to provide protection; the cost will be reflected in membership fees. In many cases there will exist technology to replace a symbiote for the duration.

The Committee will decide what constitutes a symbiote. Human intestinal flora are symbiotes, for instance, though they threaten a good dozen species and can be replaced by diet supplements. Cats are not. Any member may choose to keep his symbiotes, for sentimental or religious reasons; but his membership fee may be affected.

CHILDREN. The Committee has arranged extensive babysitting facilities. Guards may moonlight in the case of really dangerous children. However, the stasis vaults offer a cheaper alternative: children may be registered as pets.

Or as full members, if they can demonstrate intelligence. As with pets and symbiotes, the Committee's decision is final.

HIVES AND HERDS, creatures sapient only in clusters, may register as one entity.

However, any member of a registered hive found wandering loose may be considered an animal, expendable, and prey. For hives that reproduce fast, this is a reasonable assumption. For a commune or a kibbutz, it is probably *not* a good way to save money.

DISCORPORATES—ghosts, espers, Guardians, and wizards capable of leaving their bodies home—may attend the Convention free.

Why not? We can't catch you at it, and you're not bothering the other members. However, discorporates may buy memberships for the material advantages: the badge, calling service, a guided luggage carrier, credit at the huckster tables . . .

If distance is a problem, discorporeals may register as pets and leave their bodies in the stasis vault.

TIME TRAVELERS must pay full membership fees each time they attend!

This ruling is not intended to make your Committee rich. Buy your memberships in 1974 at a dollar each, as many as you need. Our purpose is to prevent confusion. Things could get messy if a message to David Gerrold went to a dozen badges!

Time travel is the only case where a Supervised member may name himself as Supervisor.

WHY MEN FIGHT WARS, AND WHAT *YOU* CAN DO ABOUT IT!

THE SURRENDER REFLEX

Virtually every animal with a backbone has a reflexive surrender signal. It applies only between members of a single species. Dogs do not take surrender from rabbits. But stags fighting for mates do not fight to kill. They fight until one turns tail—a popular surrender reflex. When a Siamese fighting fish has lost his plumage and leaves the fight, the winner will not pursue.

Members of a species will not normally kill each other even to steal food. It is common enough for one male of a group to grab all the females and the lion's share of the food—not only among lions. The rest go hungry and horny, and some die of it. You may consider this reprehensible. But it isn't murder, and it isn't war.

Lions have a problem. Too often, the juvenile male challenges the head of the pride before he is ready. The elder male kills him. It's a bug, not a feature, and a costly one in evolutionary terms.

Man has a problem too.

Man kept his surrender reflex. If you want to see it in action, watch children roughhousing in a playground. A child gets hurt, he cries, and the others stop picking on him. If a bully refuses to obey the surrender signal, the others may turn on him.

The problem with Man is that he can kill faster than his victim can decide to surrender, and from farther away than he can see a surrender signal.

Watch a bar fight. In most cases it continues until one fighter is tired and bloody. The other has proved he can win; he is in a position to kill his opponent. They stop.

But if one knows karate, the other may be dead or maimed in seconds. If one has a heavy glass ashtray at hand, or a knife, it will take less time yet. The surrender reflex becomes useless as tits on a boar if either opponent has a gun.

And we've had weapons for two million years!

WHY MEN FIGHT WARS

You already have a good intuitive grasp of this subject. Read new or old newspapers. Wars start for an insult, or because a bluff failed, or a nation's leaders claimed certain territory, or certain rights within certain territory . . . for economic reasons, or to keep an alliance, or because citizens must be distracted from trouble at home . . .

Scenario: There's a famine going in Nation N. Basic statesmanship says that the army *must* be kept happy. To feed the army, King N could wrest food from the peasants; but King N knows a better answer. A peacetime army is always a problem anyway. He can send the army into Nation N + 1 and let them forage. Maybe they'll come back with loot. Maybe they'll annex some cropland. Maybe they'll all be killed.

Wars aren't always fought for stupid reasons.

The interesting question is, why does *this* species choose *that* solution? Why can't these things be accomplished before people are dead? In any other species, when armies N and N + 1 come together, soldiers would be surrendering one-on-one.

WHY WARS DON'T STOP

Remember the Peace Talks during the Vietnam War? Not once did any diplomat on either side drop to his knees and burst into tears, wailing, "Don't hurt me any more!"

And none ever will. This is clearly the losing ambassador's function, and clearly he will never fulfill it. He doesn't feel like a loser. The bad news of his nation's defeats comes to him on paper. His nose isn't bloody. He may be tired, but only of sitting too long. Tomorrow he won't be tired any more. Nobody's hitting him. If he's breathing hard, it's probably anger, and it's probably fake.

Wars continue because ambassadors are not in a position to prevent them or to end them.

When does a *soldier* surrender? When he's tired and bloody? But he's *always* tired, and a bloody soldier is usually a dead one. His weapons are intended to let out *all* the blood. He can only surrender to a threat.

If he surrenders, or flees, his superior may shoot him. The enemy may shoot him despite his own formalized surrender signal. His white flag has nothing to do with evolved reflexes. There are forebrain functions involved in the decision as to whether to accept an enemy's surrender.

There are *always* forebrain functions. A winner in war can't trust a surrender signal. It can be faked. In wartime a prisoner cannot be turned loose to run away crying and wiping his bloody nose. He'll get another gun and come back. If he cannot be guarded and fed, he may have to be shot.

Then who can end a war? The leaders of embattled nations? They aren't bleeding, except by proxy. It's only their own imaginations that make war different from a complex chess game.

The citizens at home? They are usually assured either that they are winning, or that the enemy are inhuman monsters, or that to lose would be annihilation, or all of the above.

Aside from all this, surrender is dishonorable. This is only partly an ethical judgment. It *feels* dishonorable. Nobody fakes a surrender reflex without cost. Surrender is losing a fight, and we aren't wired to take that lightly. All of evolution is against losing casually, for trout as well as men.

Wars continue because there is nobody who can end them

WHAT *YOU* CAN DO ABOUT IT

You can't do anything about it.

COMICS

To write the bible for the *Green Lantern* comic book was always beyond my ambitions.

There's a forty-year-old oil painting in my mother's living room, commissioned from a family friend, Cleanthe Carr. It's a crowded Hermosa Beach scene showing friends and relatives and some typical beach denizens playing on the sand. Cleanthe showed me ignoring everyone around me while I read the Sunday funnies.

My love affair with comics is almost as old as I am. When other eight-year-olds were supposed to be socializing (yes, it was *that* kind of culture), I was in my host's basement reading through the comics pile.

I found the E.C. titles in Martindale's bookstore in Beverly Hills. Those would not have been on display in any home. What stuck in my head was the tale of an unseen closet-dweller that befriended a butcher's battered child, and presently . . . well, the industrial size meat grinder had been left running, and there on the floor was 200 pounds of fresh hamburger. Scared the liver out of me.

When I hit my mid-teens I supposed I had given up comics.

"Man of Steel, *Woman of Kleenex*" was an analysis of fertility problems in Kryptonians, written in my late twenties. I wasn't reading comic books then, but there were comics fans in the LASFS. I used this stuff for party conversation. One rainy Sunday, Bjo Trimble made me write it up for a one-shot fanzine. It was all done from memory. The only research was a phone call to Harlan Ellison to get Superman's birthdate. (June 1938, *Action Comics*. He's two months younger than I am. Wears it better, though.)

In later years (my thirties) I got regular invitations to the Comic-Con in San Diego. Eventually Marilyn and I went. We didn't expect a lot, but the Sturgeons had enjoyed it . . .

I was pleasantly surprised. The inner circles of the comic book industry regard science fiction as their honored ancestor! I've been back many times, but Marilyn hasn't. I don't think she was ever a comics fan.

I don't know how I got on their mailing list, but it came about that a package of Marvel comic books would reach my mailbox from time to time. Sometimes there would be material from DC. Later I wound up on the First Comics list too.

I was delighted. I've never been a collector; just a reader. Do you know the difference between a comic book and a graphic novel? If you try to read a graphic novel in the sauna, it comes apart. (Glue melts; staples don't.

From time to time one or another of my stories went to comics. "Man of Steel . . ." appeared in an underground comic, dramatized. Julius Schwartz published a wonderful graphic version of THE MAGIC GOES AWAY.

Near the end of 1988, comics entered my life like a conquering army. Several letters arrived at once—

Malibu Comics wanted to buy a lot of Known Space stories. We've started easy: they're publishing all of the "Gil the ARM" stories. They're treating them very well. I expect we'll deal again.

Marvel Comics (Kurt Busiak) invited me into a shared universe. I instead offered him "The Gripping Hand," by me and Jerry Pournelle, the first chunk of a sequel to THE

MOTE IN GOD'S EYE, for a graphic novel. We agreed on terms; we approved Kurt Busiak's editorial changes. Then we waited.

No contract ever appeared, and no check. Our agent ran out of patience and tried to offer it to First Comics, with no joy. I hope something works out. You'll love the "crottled greeps" restaurant scene.

Then there's the Green Lantern.

Larry Niven
Tarzana, CA

February 3

Dear Larry:

Here's what we'd like the Green Lantern deal to be:

You write us a bible for the three-issue History of the Green Lantern Corps (or whatever we end up calling it) which will probably also double as the bible for the forthcoming monthly magazine. This will basically spell out everything that you and I have discussed— everything in your letters. Length is impossible to judge, but these things are usually more than ten and less than 20 pages; however many words you need to do the job is the right number. For this, you'll be paid the amount agreed upon by your agent and our Executive Vice President, Paul Levitz.

Then, we'd like you to either write or plot one of the stories that will go into the limited series. For this, you'll be paid a separate amount and, probably, a pro-rated royalty.

Everything is still fluid at this point, so if you'd like to discuss anything, please call. In any case, I'll be in touch with you next week.

As I told you earlier, I like what you've given us this far. I think you're the perfect writer for the project and I'm looking forward to working with you.

Cordially,
Dennis O'Neil

Green Lantern is a DC Comics character, like Batman and Superman himself. He's been treated as science fiction throughout . . . almost. Over the years some silliness and inconsistency has crept in. It can happen to any series. Assumptions made for individual stories are what clogged up Known Space.

Dan Raspler and Denny O'Neil wrote to several SF authors asking help in working out a new background universe to the Green Lantern.

Every so often I have to do something to prove I'm still versatile. Norman Spinrad once warned me against getting into a mental rut, and I took it to heart. I've written Saturday morning TV, a newspaper comic strip, and a planetarium show; taught science fact and fiction alongside Jerry Pournelle, off campus at UCLA; built worlds alone and as part of teams; collaborated with every description of writer, excluding stupid and illiterate. I'll try anything that improves my education and is fun at the time.

So I ran down their list of the questions they most wanted answered. "Why a ring?" Because it'll stay on almost any shape of alien. "Blue skin on the Guardians? They evolved pink." It's a gene-engineered uniform. "Krona introduced evil into the universe—" No. Entropy! "The oath that recharges the magic rings—" is for timing and to concentrate the will power (as Denny suggested). "Antimatter—" Hopelessly fouled up; drop it entirely.

They liked it. They hired me. I've written the bible that others will refer to for several years' worth of stories. (But they won't let me drop antimatter. Or demons. At least I'm rid of "evil unleashed.")

I submitted a three-issue story too. They're a bit taken aback. The trouble was, I got inspired and sprinted way ahead of the contract. There came a point at which the only way to make myself stop fiddling with GANTHET'S TALE was to print it out and send it to my agent.

I wrote DC a three-issue story when what they really wanted, it seems, was a *little* story to go with other stories in *one* issue.

It's worse than that. I wanted to make the *crazy* Green Lantern, Guy Gardner, into an alien, a Guardian's "cuckoo." I thought I had permission. Then the guy who had the right to give Guy Gardner away came back from vacation!

As I write (November 1990), there's still a chance that GANTHET'S TALE will be published. I hope so. There's a wonderful interstellar fight scene I'd hate to see disappear.

Meanwhile, the stories generated by the GL Bible have been delayed.

There were a lot of givens in the decades-old *Green Lantern* universe, but a lot of empty spaces, too, in that fifteen billion years. The first intelligent species (I've so designated them) evolved on Maltus, eventually settle Oa, presently called themselves Guardians of the universe, and ultimately founded a Green Lantern Corps from more recently evolved species. My task was to fill in the gaps.

From *THE GREEN LANTERN BIBLE*

THE ECOCATASTROPHE ERA

In 9,960,000 AG Maltus was polluted almost to extinction.

It wasn't any of the trite possibilities: injudicious use of nukes, chemicals, spray cans, oil, DDT, sewage. It was those psi powers . . . which by 9,960,000 AG had become very powerful.

Maltusians were long on power and short on control. There was a population boom: four billion Maltusians, very long-lived, so that a mere three percent are immature . . . which is to say, under 1,024 years (that's 2^{10} Maltusian years) and not expected to act responsibly yet. So species kept disappearing!

A tiger killed someone's father; *all* tigers died. Mosquitoes went early. A hummingbird frightened a child; there are no hummingbirds. Lots of people don't like creepy-crawly things in the house; some overreact. Housekeepers don't like mold or termites. (I'm using Earthly life as examples. Of course there is no relation to Maltusian species . . .)

Maltusians developed longevity early. Conscious control of autonomic functions went hand in hand with Guardpower. Every Maltusian developed the Guardpower skill to look within his (her) body for imbalances, invading bacteria, cancers and so forth. Mature Maltusians also learned to cure their own allergies. Immature Maltusians, neurotics and powerful children, wiped out a wide array of plants instead: anything resembling goldenrod, rhododendrons, poison ivy . . .

Disease bacteria went early . . . along with some symbiotic gutbacteria. That caused excitement! For the next eighty years, Maltusians were unable to digest food without exotic techniques. They were at the edge of extinction. Gene engineers were the most admired and least rested beings in the universe. But afterward the lesson was gradually forgotten . . .

Over a billion years, species are forgotten almost as fast as they disappear. Remember the passenger pigeon? How well? That creature is less than two hundred years extinct!

Major Result #1 was a developing reluctance to have children. Children were dangerous; raising them to adults took thousands of years of intense effort.

Wait a million years; has anyone died? Yes, two, tragically, but four couples have had babies. Well, who are they? They should have been stopped. Males can walk away from the problem—and males took the blame, until social pressure had seriously decreased their urge to mate. They were blamed for that too, of course. The split between the genders came much later, on the colony world Oa, but its seeds are here.

(It's no less silly the other way. The Koran warns against women as agents of evil. Eve forced the apple on Adam. Women have generally taken the heat for everything. Maybe some of that went on on Maltus, too.)

Men and women are slightly alien to each other; we don't always communicate well. And we associate anyway . . . but when the Maltusians' reproductive urge dropped far enough, there was not enough motivation.

Major Result #2 was an entire science of creation of species. The Psions had their beginning here: they were a local lizard before Maltusian scientists began playing with their genetic makeup.

When the gene altering experiments stopped, the knowledge remained, and travelled with the subsequent refugee colonies.

Major Result #3 derives from swarms of spacecraft leaving Maltus. Many were officially sanctioned terraforming expeditions. Others were flights of refugees.

Throughout the universe in present time, humanoids predominate. Many are descended from Maltusians who were slapped back to savagery by unexpected planetary conditions or failed terraforming, then re-evolved over billions of years of time. (Terraforming refers to techniques for shaping a world into something men/Maltusians can use.) Others used Maltusian gene-altering techniques to fit their descendants for local conditions. Some did that badly.

How do you lose longevity? You stop taking your vitamins; you lose your doctor's phone number, or your telephone is taken out.

Maltusian refugees generally lost most of their civilization. _Of course_ their lifespans were shortened. Typically, the group would lose its advanced tools to the environment; that would shorten lifespans; survival needs would leave them no leisure time to practice and perfect their psi powers, biorhythm control, breathing, meditation, all of the disciplines that allowed their ancestors to live for up to billions of years; and gradually the disciplines would be forgotten.

Major Result #4 was the Oa expedition.

The group that ultimately chose Oa, and became the Guardians, was financed by a world's resources. Maltusians wanted to repair a planet: their own. Their best shot at getting data was to finance someone else in some risky terraforming.

The Oa group (and scores of others, many of whom became refugee colonies) may have ruined many half-useful worlds before their techniques turned Oa into a paradise

. . . a paradise that is mostly desert even in present time. (We're covering 3,200,000 years here. You don't talk about "generations" when you speak of Oans.) At that point the rest of the Maltusians came too, for a better home, and because Maltus had become drearily barren.

Maltus's ecology was eventually rebuilt (and that held into historic time). Maltus currently is occupied by a human-seeming species lacking longevity.

The current inhabitants of Maltus derive from a Maltusian colony, established in the "ecocatastrophe" era, that gradually failed. The refugees returned to a ruined and deserted world. So they too found some hard answers.

They reshaped themselves genetically to a ruined Maltus. To protect a fragile ecology they suppressed the Guardpower. (Then and now, their Guardpower is latent but available.) They rejected immortality too.

(If you prefer other answers—such as that a tampered animal species has evolved this far and been left alone to evolve further—then tell Denny O'Neil what you want, quick. Do it before the concrete sets.)

Maltus was chewed up during the "Crisis" (around 1985, and DC-universe wide) and subsequently restored.

OA

"Oa is the central planet of the universe . . . or at least it's polite to say so." Arrogant the Guardians are, and they do make that claim; but no species capable of space travel *really* thinks the universe has a center.

But Oa must be the center of *something*. Guardians won't see themselves as silly!

We'll put Oa in the core of a big spiral galaxy (our own type, the most common) with a gaudy blazing sky as seen from the planet's surface, that only becomes more terrific as one moves outward. Artists who want to show Oa may find backgrounds in almost any modern book of astronomical paintings.

The core of a galaxy is uninhabitable. Lethal radiation bathes the surfaces of all the worlds therein, even those very distant from their suns. Orbits are weird; weather must be entirely crazy; collisions are too frequent. (Yes, twice per billion years is too bloody frequent.) Oa must be kept constantly livable by the Guardpower of its inhabitants.

But they chose to settle Oa. Is that arrogant, or what?

Rotation of Oa is the same as the rotation of Maltus at the time Oa was colonized, five billion years ago. Oa's spin was altered for the convenience of the colonists. That rotation period is exactly 24 hours.

Why is Oa a barren desert but for the Citadel? Quote a Guardian: "We tried some gardening, but . . ."

Oa may have been fertile for a time, seeded with Maltusian life after its rotation, temperature, atmosphere, etc. were adjusted. Time passed, worlds evolved; as anticipated so long ago, the Guardians made enemies . . . and those have made Oa a target. Around Oa life grows gradually more exciting. Excitement is bad for a garden.

The Oan desert sand has absorbed Guardpower, has become a sapient entity. Maybe that entity can be enlisted as a gardener? Maybe Oa can be made fertile that way. It's a stunt that would not have worked a few billion years ago, and that's how long it's been since they last tried it.

Guardians don't care. They can imagine a garden, make it with their minds, turn it off when they tire of it. But for the Guardian children to come, a garden would be nice.

Why did the females leave Oa? This is a point where my "chronological ordering" breaks down. Bear with me.

The females are said to have deserted Oa 2.5 billion years

ago, at **12,500,000,000 AG**, and this is a tale only partly told. See *GL* Issue 200 for what's known. What follows is Niven.

A pair of Oans, mates, broke the Origin Story barrier.

This is stranger than it sounds.

Male and female Oans show extreme sexual dimorphism. Dumpy rounded males with a low sex urge; tall slender females interested in mating with other humanoids. It's as if they belonged to different species. They think differently too. The females are attuned to tools, the males to powers of the mind including psi.

Untold story: **Thwarcharchura** (female) and **Whisthend** (male) must have been a little weird. They considered each other to be lover, mate, companion, friend, colleague . . . secretly, of course. (Neither has appeared anywhere, to date.)

They attacked the Origin problem together. They built a time camera, reached the Origin Story and (of course) blew the camera to smithereens. They built another, and went *around* the Origin Story to watch their world and species evolve—as many males had done before them, and no female ever. It takes male Guardpower to feel out the shape of spacetime.

Another thing about Oan females: they live closer to reality. Whisthend was badly shaken. *Animals*. *We were animals*. But Thwarcharchura persuaded him to continue playing with the time machine; Whisthend presently was intrigued.

They watched a crucial time in their species' past: the taking of Oa. (More than a history lesson. They knew elders who had participated! At least one such participant, Dawli-kass*tok*tok, survives *currently*.)

They learned that there had been an intelligent species on Oa. Not natives. See descriptions of Oa, above, for reasons why life couldn't develop. But colonists had set up a local-ized terraforming project.

These **Visitors** were aesthetically ugly, psychotic in temperament, short-lived, and generally not admirable. Their claim to the planet was not strong. They attacked the Oan landers on sight.

(Artists: have fun with these.)

The proto-Oan *males* exterminated them (and their Guardpower told them that there were no more: these Visitors were the last of their race). The first crews in were male only! Females were being protected as child-bearers necessary to a colony *and* engineers needed to maintain the ships.

It should be pointed out that the men would have been killed if they hadn't acted.

They sent a message to the women: "Boil us a sea at these coordinates. We need water vapor." The women used their terraforming equipment. A patch of land reached solar temperatures, with most of the Visitors on it. The men then mopped up.

The women had killed without knowing.

Some of these women survived until, two and a half billion years after the taking of Oa, Thwarcharchura exposed the truth. Their mates had never hinted at this crime.

Note: Genocide is just the kind of crime Green Lanterns and Guardians were formed to prevent.

Rag*tok*gond's rage was no transient thing. Her answer was to lead the emigration of the Oan females . . . who thenceforth called themselves **Zamorans**.

Guardians tell other species (if they tell them anything) that their mates left them because the males had lost interest in reproduction and physical sciences and every other pastime interesting to Oan females. Zamorans say the same. The home life of Guardians is no alien's business.

What human male would claim impotence in order to hide his part, or his ancestors' part, in winning a war? But Guardians do that.

The **Zamorans**' subsequent fate is on record. Their reconciliation with the male Oan Guardians is recent, from issue #200. The Guardians (meaning only the survivors of the Crisis) and their mates are currently absent from the universe. It is expected that they are making babies.

CRITICISM

On a Thursday afternoon the 1970s I read a well-written, convincing review in an amateur press magazine. It chopped one of my books into hamburger.

The Los Angeles Science Fiction and Fantasy Society meets Thursday nights. That night Joe Haldeman was visiting. After the meeting Joe and I went to Jerry Pournelle's house to drink and talk shop.

I was still worried. Not angry: worried. It wasn't my first bad review, but this one sounded too plausible. Maybe I was doing everything wrong. After a few years of writing I was still the new kid on the block, and I knew I had a lot to learn.

So I told my friends of my fears. "Does this guy Richard Lupoff know what he's talking about? He's a writer, isn't he?"

Joe said, "He wrote *Sacred Locomotive Flies*."

I laughed and we changed the subject. But I'll never forget the relief that swept over me.

New writers hear it constantly: *Don't read your own reviews. If you do, don't take them seriously.*

It can't be done.

Critics are self-designated. Nobody licenses critics—it would violate First Amendment rights—and nobody votes for them. Where do they come from? Where do they get the arrogance?

They come from *us*.

A novice writer is a critic before he sells his first words. He must judge his own work before he sends it to some stranger who will decide whether other strangers should see it at all. The critic's arrogance is already there, or else the story never goes out. Every writer is a critic, and every critic has a touch of what it takes to be a writer.

A critic is at his best when analyzing good, imaginative work that is yet a little cryptic, a little murky.

Writers are communicators and translators. Our careers are spent learning how to write more lucidly. This is most difficult with science fiction and fantasy, where the pictures a writer must put in a reader's mind are of things never yet seen, or of things impossible. The most complex ideas need the simplest prose. Kurt Vonnegut writes almost in baby-talk, and he can talk to *anyone*.

Any story that needs a critic to explain it, needs rewriting. A lucidly written, easily understood book is likely to escape critical attention.

Can you say "conflict of interest"?

Many critics avoid science fiction and fantasy as demons avoid holy water. And why not? A science fiction work that needs explaining may or may not be trash, but the standard-issue critic is not likely to know the difference, and not likely to be able to explain it either.

Many teachers of science fiction end up letting the students run the classes; many critics end up ignoring science fiction for fear of looking foolish. They are *right*. They *have* looked foolish:

An author of recognized literary worth tries his hand at SF. He confuses infrared with ultraviolet, or loses all track of basic sociology or economics. Everybody notices except the critics.

A critic praises a brilliant new idea brilliantly handled by an author already honored in literary circles. The core idea turns out to be Heinlein's "Universe" ship, decades old and universally imitated.

The standard-issue critic stands some chance of understanding and appreciating Caroline Cherryh or Ursula Le

Guin, and that can make him cocky. (Always give *The Left Hand of Darkness* to an English teacher who hates science fiction. It's good by his standards as well as our own, and short enough that he'll keep his promise to read it.) But Le Guin and Cherryh tend to step lightly around physical laws while they play with sociological implications.

What chance has the same critic of knowing whether Poul Anderson is any good? Anderson is a poet with a solid grasp of every science a mainstream critic can spell, and many he can't. The standard-issue critic took English lit because physics was too hard for him!

It's modern criticism that has ruined modern poetry. Any budding poet will be attracted by the freedom-plus-discipline of science fiction. Kipling saw no reason not to write science fiction and poetry both. Dante Alighieri wrote science fiction *in* poetry. The *Divine Comedy* was the first hard science fiction trilogy . . . but the critic sees only that Poul Anderson and Chip Delany and Roger Zelazny write sci-fi. Their poetry never gains them recognition.

Then again—

Gene Wolfe's writing has depths that only an English teacher or another writer is likely to probe. It was hours after "The Doctor of Death Island" before I figured out the ending. *The Book of the New Sun* was more lucid than anything Wolfe had written previously, yet it can still benefit from a critic's attention.

Often I've wanted to tell Gene what his multilayered style is costing him . . . and I always decide not to. Writers need something to read too, you know.

At a SFRA gathering—that's *Science Fiction Research Association*—I met Thomas J. Remington, critic, author of *The Niven of Oz*: Ringworld *as Science Fictional Reinterpretation*. He told me that RINGWORLD's story line was based on *The Wizard of Oz*. I listened as he explained—

The Scarecrow is *Speaker-to-Animals* (Fear of fire; searching for intelligence).

The Cowardly Lion is *Nessus* (Fear of everything. More dangerous than he seems).

The Tin Woodman is *Teela* (Looking for a heart, for emotions).

The Wizard is *Halrloprillalar* (Lost wayfarer posing as a goddess).

Tourism in fairyland, with dangers and a lethal puzzle to spice the adventure. Dorothy gapes at the parade of wonders while she tries to find her way home. But the solution is much closer than the illusory goals she's been chasing . . .

Remington must be right. It fits too well. I surmise that RINGWORLD seemed to be plotting itself nicely, all those years ago, because it so resembled a book I had loved as a child and then forgotten.

Algis Budrys praised my early work in the *Galaxy* magazines. Richard E. Geis decided I was good, and sent me his fanzines for twenty years or more. Their praise came when I most needed it.

In this field it's easy to forget how good a critic *can* be. We have too few of these. But Bob Gleason remembers David Schow's critical review of John Farris's *All Heads Turn When the Hunt Goes By*. Schow called it the ultimate horror story—and maybe it is—but what impressed Gleason was the work Schow put into his review. He phoned Farris and anyone else who might have been involved in the building of the book, to get a feel for what had gone into it. Just to put you in perspective, Schow wrote his own best-selling horror novel, *The Kill Riff*. Best-selling authors are *not* self-designated.

I do not want all critics hanged alongside the lawyers and tax collectors. The good ones serve a purpose.

Too many writers tend to wander blindly wherever the crowd is going; too many fan critics don't notice. Readers have seen sudden bookshelves full of after-the-bomb tales,

tales of psi powers, tours of "The Enormous Big Thing," giant meteoroid impacts, easy gender change, 1984-style dictatorships, incredible population densities, slums reshaped by advanced computer technology . . .

Are we wasting the vast space within the Science Fiction Country Club?

Maybe not. Maybe we crowd so close because we like each other's company. Some of these huge, roomy ideas need to be looked at from many angles by many minds. So we explore the missing implications in alternate timelines, the multi-generation starship, gene tampering, the world of parthenogenic women, skyhooks . . .

Then again . . . *Watership Down* is a runaway best seller: the money's in sapient burrowing animals. *Neuromancer* got terrific reviews: let's all write about psychotic cyborg bums. Michael Moorcock and Judith Merril (critics!) support intensive psychological studies, no plots and innovative typesetting: if I set my type in an expanding spiral I'll be just as good as Harlan Ellison.

Nope. Following trends is for second-raters . . . and sometimes it takes an outside critic to see a trend and blow the whistle.

An article by Joanna Russ complained that the Ringworld is unstable. That's true, and I put attitude jets in the sequel. But Joanna implied that this is obvious; that she noticed it herself! Joanna's education doesn't reach that far. The instability was obvious to MIT students, and they talked.

In his review of A WORLD OUT OF TIME, Robert Silverberg wrote that my method for moving the Earth would wreck the biosphere. I asked him about that. He told me that the review was in the mail before he remembered that tidal force varies as the inverse cube. He didn't bother to write or telephone the magazine correcting the error. It didn't seem important.

Ursula Le Guin didn't like my short story "Inconstant Moon." She was appalled by my callous murder of half the Earth's population. Yet it did win a Hugo Award, and I don't have all that many love stories in me. I'm intensely proud of "Inconstant Moon."

None of these traumas caused me to write letters of protest.

I once caught Jerry writing a coldly reasonable answer to a bad review. I lectured him thus: "You're giving the publisher free material of professional quality. You're rewarding him for trashing your book!" (Jerry makes a wonderful audience. He quotes me afterward, and gives credit!)

Then came Richard Delap's *F&SF Review*, with a review of THE MOTE IN GOD'S EYE.

It was an exercise in vandalism. I say that not only because the critic didn't like the book, but because his review was loaded with factual mistakes! James Burk quoted Rod Blaine's full name and titles, *wrong*, and wrote *(sic)* after it. He quoted me as saying that there has not been a new breed of dog in hundreds of years. Species, dammit! *Species!*

We wrote a letter pointing these things out. We were sarcastic, we were cutting, we were brilliant. "If you do write a reply to a bad review," I pontificated, "at least make the publisher regret it!"

Delap had an answer to that. He refused to print our letter!

Delap and his magazine have vanished and I haven't. But there is no defense against bad reviews, even dishonest bad reviews (though they're easier to take). I'm still twitching from that one.

I myself have felt the critic's compulsion.

Sacred Locomotive Flies isn't the book that enraged me most. It's a cheat, of course; the author frequently reminds the reader that this is fiction, that he is not bound by physics or reason or even self-consistence. But worse has been done, by better writers.

Sometimes I feel silly, getting mad because I didn't like a book. These days I don't even pay for them! Books arrive because I might put a cover blurb on one. I read one in five, maybe, and too often I wait for other reviews and choose from the best—which isn't fair.

No point in demanding my money back, then. But who's going to return my *time?*

Gather in the Hall of the Planets, by Barry Malzberg (as K. M. O'Donnell), still has me boiling. It's half of an ancient Ace double. Malzberg may not consider it his best work, so I'm *really* taking it too seriously. But Malzberg believes himself to be a qualified critic of science fiction. That's disturbing

The book opens as a science fiction detective story. An alien species has been exterminating intelligent species for as long as they can remember. They always test a randomly chosen member of the species first; but no species has ever passed their test. Now it's the protagonist's turn.

At the end, we are asked to believe that the aliens have been exterminating whole worlds after testing *not* members of the target species, but *each other!*

Of symbolism and character development and deep psychological exploration within the novella, I will say nothing. Why bother? Malzberg posed us a puzzle story when he didn't have a solution. Regarding matters of symbolism and metaphor, I was told early: Moby-Dick doesn't work as *anything* unless he works as a *whale.*

Brian Aldiss does consider a certain book to be among his best; at least he's said so in print. All I have to judge by is my own awful experience, which was not entirely Aldiss's fault:

There was a World Science Fiction Convention in Heidelberg in 1970. Fans arranged for a charter flight, New York to London, return from Amsterdam. We wanted the company of our own. In practice we got little of that. We were packed like sardines; there was no way to circulate and converse.

In Amsterdam I went looking for a book. There'd be precious little of other entertainment on the flight home! I found one in English, by Brian Aldiss. The critics liked him. I remembered fondly *The Long Afternoon of Earth*.

I walked aboard that plane carrying one book, unopened, and that was *Report on Probability A*.

I found the opening a little slow . . . massively slow . . . I got as far as page 38 or so, pushing myself, desperate, unbelieving, before I could accept the fact that *nothing was going to happen in this book*.

Gradually it came back to me: the reviews by critics who were admiring but a little bewildered. *Report on Probability A* uses techniques developed by French novelists, a sub-genre of stories in which nothing happens. As for me, stumbling wide-eyed into a New York City morning after ten hours of sensory deprivation, I had a fixed opinion as to what had been done to me.

An author is always an egotist. Writers who are not egotists define themselves: they never send out a story to be bought. Only an egotist will believe that he can be paid serious money for writing down his daydreams.

In my paranoia I pictured a brilliant, literate, egotistical Brit with a vicious sense of humor. The critics love him, but he's never loved them. One or another critic may think that he's wonderful, but for superficial reasons. Again, there are critics who *don't* love him. Death is too good for them; he intends worse.

To this imaginary Brit comes a brilliant, literate, vicious idea:

Write a book in which nothing happens at all. Justify it by reference to a French tradition (real or imaginary) of books in which nothing happens at all. One or two critics may guess that it's a jape; they can be brought in on the joke. The rest . . . well, they've never understood the Brit's writings before, and they're leery of admitting it. They'll praise the book, because if they don't, the brilliant Brit will somehow make them look like idiots.

I was not comforted by this notion. I was enraged. We trusted a novelist who had dealt fairly with us before, and with what result? We are readers; we have rights!

Worst case of jet lag I ever had.

Once you know about critics, you know about literature. Literature is whatever survives the critics.

Melville lasted long enough to reach critics willing to research whaling. (The standard-issue critic is not typically lazy. He'll do endless research, though he avoids the difficult subjects.)

Shakespeare survived the critics of Victorian times. Even Bowdler missed some of his best off-color references.

Dante wrote the first hard science fiction. His best-known work was a trilogy set in an artificial structure larger than a Dyson shell. Like the best of the hard science fiction writers to follow, he used extensive knowledge of the sciences of his day: theology, the Greek and Roman classics, early attempts at chemistry and physics, and astrology.

In Dante's age, surviving the critics was more than a matter of bad reviews. Dante survived the wrath of the Church and the passage of centuries, and censors: parts of *Inferno* have been judged obscene in every age. His success may be measured by how often his work has been stolen by writers, newspaper cartoonists, animators, you name it.

The test of time has at least the virtue of being unambiguous.

The final critic is a schoolteacher.

Schoolteachers are not interested in changing the verdict of time. It's safe to talk about H. G. Wells, Jules Verne, or Mary Shelley. Wells didn't use anything too complicated, and a lot of what went into his work was pure fantasy. Verne didn't know the physics of his own time. Old science becomes fantasy.

Therefore classes in science fiction typically start far back in history, with stories unlikely to be interesting to the students. They move toward modern times, losing students all the way, and never quite get there.

From *THE LEGACY OF HEOROT*
(with JERRY POURNELLE and STEVEN BARNES)

Have you noticed that Jerry and I worked mostly in my office? His was too small to be comfortable, and we were constantly interrupted by phone calls. He ultimately lost patience and set about building a bigger one.

For a while there he wasn't too sane. There was no roof on his house, local bureaucrats were giving him static, the architect didn't understand airflow, and Jerry couldn't decide whom to assassinate first. Then suddenly there was an office. It's huge: one great big room and three smaller ones. The airflow is geared to let me smoke and him breathe.

If collaborations are difficult, then triple collaborations are impossible. I know of only one in science fiction, and THE LEGACY OF HEOROT is it. So: *how?*

I think the secret is Steven Barnes.

Jerry and I are too logical, too left-brain, to write in horror mode. We don't become frightened enough.

We would gather in Jerry's recently expanded office space and elaborate the outline. The story changed constantly. Then Steven would come back with first-draft material on a disk. Jerry and I would tear it apart and put it back together different, week after week. It took a Steven Barnes to stand up to that and not feel threatened, and not lose the writer's necessary arrogance either.

Call her Mama.

The taste of the river changed with the seasons. For a time the water would run sluggish and cold. Then the taste of life was scarce; the flying things were scarce; the swimming things were dead.

Later the water would race, carrying the taste of past times. Mama had seen scores of cycles of seasons. She was wise enough to ignore the ancient tastes: bodies or blood or feces of life her kind had long since exterminated, long buried in mountain ice, released as the ice melted.

In the hot season the water would be bland again, carrying only spoor of flyers and swimmers and another of her own race.

Mama's taste was discriminating. One of her kind lived upstream. Another lived even farther upstream, and that one was a weakling. It lived where game was so scarce that Mama could taste starvation in its spoor. Not worth killing, that one, or her nearer rival would have taken her domain.

In winter there was something strange in the water, something she couldn't identify. Not life; not interesting.

The world began to warm again . . . and something new was on the island. Something she had never tasted, something weirdly different, was leaving spoor in the water. It was as yet too faint to identify. Mama began to think about moving.

If she followed that spoor she would have to fight, and that was no step to be taken lightly.

By summer she could taste several varieties of prey! The things weren't merely leaving feces in the water; she tasted strange blood too. Her rival was eating well. Was it time?

Her rival was youthful (Mama could taste that) but large. The faintness of her scent placed her many days' journey upstream. She would be rested and fed when Mama arrived . . . and Mama settled back into her pool. She had not lived two scores of cycles by being reckless.

If her rival sickened, she would taste it.

Days flickered past. The time of cold had come. Ordinarily Mama scarcely noticed passing time, for the taste of swimmer meat was always the same. Nothing attacked. Her curiosity lay dormant . . . but it was active now, for living things were leaving spoor even in dead of winter, and blood ran down the river now and again.

Oh, the variety! Here was blood from something vaguely like a flyer. This one must have been big, a plant-eater; she had to dig far into her memory to find anything similar. That horrible chemical stench was entirely mysterious: hot metal and belly acid and thoroughly rotted grass. This unfamiliar scent, judging by its components, would be the urine of a meat eater not of her own kind. Hunger and curiosity warred with discretion, for Mama had never tasted anything like that, nor seen one either.

Once there was a living thing in the water. She snapped it up and chewed contemplatively, trying to learn of it. A swimming thing, primitive, built a little like a swimmer . . .

The world was warming when the river gifted her with two larger members of the same species. Bottom feeders tasting of mud, they must be breeding despite the presence of her rival upstream.

And *that*, one bright hungry morning, was the burnt blood of her own kind!

Taste of fear and *speed* and killing rage, taste of chemicals, taste of burning. If lightning or a forest fire had killed her rival, then an empty territory lay waiting for her upstream. If another rival, then Mama would face a formidable foe.

The swimmers were startled when Mama came forth in

an eating frenzy. Swimmers were nothing; the taste did not engage her curiosity at all. But Mama's rival would be fat now, and hyperkinetic from impact of sensory stimuli, and Mama dared not come upon her as a desperate starveling. She had not fought a serious rival in many years.

Mama had never toured the island. The others of her kind did not like visitors. The map in Mama's mind was not made up of distances, but of the changing taste of the river.

The pond reeked of samlon blood when Mama departed. She staggered with the fullness of her belly. Three days later she was hungry but hopeful. Four mud-sucking alien fish had fallen foul of her. There would be more.

The water ran clean again. Mama understood *that* lesson. She had tasted the burnt meat of her daughter in the water; but the decaying corpse was gone almost immediately. Whatever killed her daughter had eaten the corpse.

Once she was able to streak off the edge of a low bluff and catch a flyer rising from below. She caught another hovering just above the water. The flyers weren't timid enough here between territories. She fed when she could. If her enemy were to find her half starved, her body might betray her, holding her slow while her enemy boiled with speed. If she did not find enough food she would turn back.

She moved cautiously, in fear of ambush. For long stretches she paralleled the river, moving among rocks or trees or other cover where she could find it, returning to the river only when she must.

None of this was carefully thought out. Mama was not sapient. Emotions ran through her blood like vectors, and she followed the vector sum. Anger against the creature who killed her daughter. Hunger: the richly, interestingly populated territory upstream. Curiosity: the urge to learn and explore. Lust: the urge to mate with a gene pattern other than her own. And fear, always fear.

She moved slowly enough to learn the terrain as she traveled. Rocks, plains, grassland; a waterfall to be circled. She found fish of interesting flavor before she would have had to turn back.

Farther upstream, things began to turn weird. There were intermittent droning sounds. Chemical tastes in the water and smells on the wind: tar and hot metal and burning, unfamiliar plants, pulverized wood. Her progress slowed even farther. She kept to rocky terrain or crawled along the bottom where the river ran deep and fast. Sounds of an alien environment might cover her enemy's approach. Her enemy must come. She would find Mama; she could be watching her now; she would come like a meteor across terrain she knew like the inside of her mouth. Mama's life would depend on also knowing the terrain.

There was a cliff of hard rock, and softer rock below, and caverns the river had chewed below the waterline. One of the caverns became her base. Life was plentiful, foraging was easy; she might wait here for the enemy, for a time.

She found things pecking on dry ground. They tried to run (badly), they tried to fly (badly). She ate them all. There were bones all through the meat, and half of it was indigestible feathery stuff.

On another day she saw something far bigger flying too far away to smell. It veered away before she could study it. If she could catch something like that, the meat would surely sustain her until her quarry *must* come to deal with an invader.

The next day something came at her across the water.

First there was a humming. Mama was a good distance from the water, and her mouth was full of blood and feathers. She looked for insects swarming. If she found the nest she would eat it whole . . .

But the swarm sound was louder now, and too uniform,

and there were no dark clouds that could be insects. Something strange, in unfamiliar terrain. Mama made for the water, not yet *fast* but already wary.

The humming was louder as she reached the water.

It came around a bend upstream. She couldn't see the intruder's shape; it was too distant yet. But it moved *on* the water, not through it. Moved *fast*.

Finally. Mama's eyes were above the water. The snorkel between her eyes drew air; her lungs heaved. There was rage in her, and something else: sphincter muscles relaxed back of her neck, *speed* began dripping into her blood, and her entire body began to fizz. The vulnerable snorkel withdrew into her head. She watched the intruder come—not quite toward her, she hadn't been seen yet—then why was the intruder already *fast*?

But Mama was *fast* now, and she moved.

This was her territory now. She knew it that well, she had been here that long. *Mine*. She too was almost above the water as she reached the intruder. She struck from the side. For a bare instant she knew that she had won.

Skin with a thin taste, a taste like metal but not as strong, ruptured on impact and tore in her jaws. No meaty texture, no taste of blood. Not won: lost! Tricked! And where was her enemy?

The metallic skin filled with water and began to sink. Confusing tastes drifted in its wake. Things thrashed the water in slow motion, beasts caught between fighters. She ignored them. Where was her rival?

Still *fast*, Mama streaked for her cave before she could be blindsided. At the underwater mouth she turned. She couldn't be attacked now except from the front.

Now there was time. Mama lifted her eyes above the water and watched two beasts thrashing. If meat were suddenly snatched beneath the surface, she would know that her enemy was below. But the prey were swept downstream, thrashing, trying to reach the river's edge. They reached shore unmolested, and scrambled from the water unmolested.

Mama had been tricked. She had bitten something, but it wasn't meat, and where was her enemy?

There! Just like the other, it skimmed across the water, almost toward her. It swerved away as Mama streaked toward it. The intruder was fully on speed, and young, Mama thought. She herself had never moved so fast . . . but its turn was too slow. She was on it, and her teeth closed with terrible strength—

On thin, tough, tasteless skin, and flesh that ruptured and bone that broke — fragile bone, prey blood, prey meat, with no taste of *speed*. Not at all the flesh of her own kind, and she'd been tricked again!

She had barely slowed. She kept moving, fleeing the site of her kill, curving toward safety, sliding across the bucking surface of the water. *Where is my enemy? Where?*

Behind her, meat thrashed in the water, then subsided. More prey was climbing the cliff, unmolested, and that was hardly surprising. In the middle of a duel one does not pause to dine.

How may I lure my enemy?

My enemy's territory, my enemy's prey. Challenge!

At the shore was injured prey, dying. Two more prey were climbing the cliff, characteristically clumsy. The enemy *must* regard these as hers. Mama planned her move, and then—

Challenge. Mama charged across the water, straight at the feebly moving prey. Her jaw clamped on its hind leg. She dived beneath the froth, released the meat at once and swam for her life. Three seconds later she surfaced far downstream, to watch her enemy come to reclaim stolen meat.

The corpse tumbled unmolested. Her enemy was too clever, far too clever for one so young.

Of the two other prey, one had disappeared. The last was halfway up the cliff.

Mama studied the cliff. It wasn't sheer, but the thought of being stranded there while something came at her was one she rejected at once . . . and retrieved, and toyed with.

She could see most of the cliff, and no danger showed there. Her enemy might be in the water or at the top of the cliffs. She never doubted it was watching.

There were footholds along the cliff. Take any path too fast and she might be stranded in midair, falling toward waiting jaws. Motionless in white froth, with only her eyes showing, Mama chose her path.

Then she moved. Across the seething water. Up along cracks in the rock, now quick, now slow, *dancing* her route, ready to face death with her footing firm. In seconds she was halfway up the cliff, poised on a ledge above live prey.

Challenge. Come and get what's yours!

Carolyn watched the sun rise below. Noon yesterday she had ridden out of the closing mist, moving southwest, uphill and toward the glacier, riding until nightfall. She'd led the horses all night. It was a mistake. While trudging uphill and trying to report her position she'd dropped the comcard and stepped on it. The horse she led stepped on it as well. Now it didn't work. No one knew where she was. Maybe they'd send a Skeeter to look for her. Maybe they wouldn't. She couldn't go back to the Colony—

Southwest and uphill. He'd said southwest and uphill. They'd look for her there, and it was the safest place she could find.

Again the sun rose in blue brilliance, but today it rose over a sea of mist. Clouds had rolled in from the sea; they covered the Colony like a lid, with a great contoured thunderhead for a handle.

Carolyn and the horses were well to the north and west of Cadmann's feudal stronghold, and that, too, was hidden.

The land had flattened out like a tilted table. A line of horses trotted uphill with White Lightnin' at their head.

The horses were all yearlings or younger. Even White Lightnin' wasn't all that big; but Carolyn was small. The horse carried her easily.

She fumed as she rode. *They didn't want me with them! Cadmann Weyland is off fighting Ragnarok with his picked crew, and I'm not in it. They wanted Phyllis, perfect Phyllis, but not me. Not worth fighting with, not worth fighting for—* Yet she wasn't truly unhappy with Cadmann's decision. Where would she have wanted to be? At the Colony, waiting for the grendels to swarm? Aboard *Geographic* while the air grew stale and the Minervas failed to arrive? She had quite another reason for her anger.

Anger held back the fear.

Carolyn had never been on a horse until long after she reached Avalon. She'd tended the colts, and grown used to them, and learned that they were skittish, balky, untrustworthy. If Carolyn lost control of herself, if she screamed at a colt or swatted it, it remembered; it shied from her next time. She had learned to control herself around horses.

Around people . . . well, people were more complex, and they talked to each other. Word had spread.

Once she had known how to steer people where she wanted them. Once she had been Zack's second in command. Without Ruth behind him, Zack would have been working for Carolyn! Though he would still have been part of *Geographic*'s crew, the best of the best.

Hibernation Instability had merely touched Carolyn, but it had left Zack alone.

And of course, Phyllis. Nothing ever stuck to Phyllis. She had Hendrick, she could have had Cadmann, everybody knew it. Phyllis could fall into a mountain of horse manure and come out with roses in her hair.

I'm still smart. Smarter than she is! But I get scared. And that thought was frightening too. She took deep breaths and looked back—

The mist was coming after her in a cloud like a breaking wave, and there were grendels in the mist. She could see lightning flashes in the tops of the clouds. *Rain. The grendels love it. Maybe they won't come out.*

The Colony might have vanished already in a sea of ravening miniature grendels. For all Carolyn could tell, the only earthly life on Avalon was herself and twenty horses. She found herself hoping with savage fervor that that irresponsible butterfly Carlos had made her pregnant before Sylvia took him.

The Geographic Society sent no woman who doesn't want babies, she thought. *I'm locked into that. Preprogrammed.* Hibernation Instability should have taken that too.

Thus far she had avoided water. She couldn't do that forever. Horses could go a long way without food, but not without water. It shouldn't be a problem. She was taking them toward the glacier that ran down the slope of Mucking Great Mountain. There would be streams and springs.

She looked down toward the edge of cloud . . .

She knew what it was as she reached for the binocular case. She was almost relieved. At this distance it looked like a black tadpole. Through the binoculars there was not much more detail: a mini-grendel, plump and streamlined, moving on quick, stubby legs. A meter long, she thought; not one of the big ones. Eyes watching her. How well could it see? It looked at her—

Binoculars. They're lenses. The lenses in the dead grendels are strange. Distortable. Big. It could be seeing me as well as I see it.

"Charlie," she said, as if naming a thing were the same as understanding it, controlling it. Her lips twitched toward a snarl. She lifted the harpoon gun high in the air. "Charlie, is it too late to negotiate?" The grendel watched.

She decided (working against her own well-understood tendency to hysteria) that there was no point in urging the horses to greater speed. Moving uphill, that trot was all they could manage. They hadn't smelled anything yet.

The grendel seemed in no hurry.

It was out of the rain, with no water immediately ahead. There was every chance that it would give up.

She had been given a harpoon gun and four explosive harpoons. There were boulders on the plain, some huge. Carolyn thought of climbing a rock, sending the horses ahead, waiting for the grendel to pass. Her mind worked well enough unless she was pushed. But . . . to wait and wait, while the grendel watched her and considered . . . she would crack. She knew it.

Keep the horses moving. See what happened.

There were five grendels below Carolyn. Four were just clear of the mist; to the naked eye they were mere specks, wide apart and still separating.

"Charlie, do you know you're being followed?" From left to right, she set names on the intruders: "Ayatollah, Khadafi, Jack, Son of Sam . . ." Too long. "Mareta." Mareta Lupoff was the only single human being ever to set off a hydrogen bomb within a city.

Charlie was much too close: two hundred meters away, plodding along at a speed somewhat greater than the horses could manage.

The horses were holding up well, moving a little slower because they were tired. They hadn't smelled anything yet. Carolyn kept them moving, but she kept watch too.

Twenty horses in a line, linked by rope. Should she free them from the rope? Let them fight their own war?

Grendels. Creatures of mystery and fear, and the more

you learned, the more terrifying they were. Those four at the fog level . . . three? One must have turned back. Was it Jack?

They don't cooperate. That's not what Beowulf, excuse me, Weyland, would call a flanking action. It's just grendels trying to stay away from each other. But that near one—Charlie's almost close enough to shoot, and I bet I can guess what it wants.

Carolyn had listened, she wasn't stupid, but it was hard to think of grendels as *she*. Picture Jack the Ripper or Muammar Khadafi as a woman: it was silly.

Those rock knobs had the look of boulders deposited by a glacier—intruders dropped on land scraped flat. That one a hundred meters ahead, twice her height: that would do.

When White Lightnin' was alongside the boulder (and the near grendel was a hundred and fifty meters downslope), she dismounted. She took all four harpoons and the harpoon gun from the saddlebags. She slapped Lightnin' to get her moving.

Lightnin' didn't move.

Patiently, with no overt sign of panic, Carolyn walked down to the end of the line (toward the grendel, toward Charlie). She shouted and slapped the trailing horse, Gorgeous George. The young stallion glared at her, but he moved. She slapped him again and, jogging ahead of him, repeated the slap on the next horse, who was already moving. The tail of the line moved; the wave moved forward; the grendel was a hundred meters distant and watching curiously. Carolyn reached the rock. The line of horses moved past her as she climbed. The grendel was seventy meters away.

Forty. Twenty. Jesus, it was on speed. The horses screamed. Carolyn smelled it herself, a whiff on the wind, bestial and chemical both. She was halfway up the rock, and the grendel had reached the horses.

She set her back solidly against the rock and lifted the gun while . . .

Gorgeous George reared back on his hind legs, forelegs pawing the air, prepared to stamp holes in an enemy. A black torpedo shot under the forelegs and snapped at one of George's ankles without ever slowing. George was yanked backward hard enough to snap the line that bound him. The grendel was behind the rock before Carolyn could fire. George fell downhill, tumbling, screaming, and his left hind leg was gone below the knee. *Where was the grendel?*

Coming up the rock behind her?

Carolyn jumped. She landed without breaking an ankle. She ran away from the rock, trying to see the rock and the horse both—

The grendel was downhill, dragging Gorgeous George. George was very much alive, screaming, thrashing. Carolyn aimed carefully and fired.

She'd have hit it. She would! Charlie must have seen something coming; she saw it shy. The harpoon exploded against George's chest. It ripped the horse wide open. The grendel looked at her for the barest particle of an instant, then dodged behind the dying horse.

The other horses were on the run. Carolyn was reloading. Wait? Watch the grendel? But the horses couldn't be left alone. She ran after them. If she scared them they'd keep running: fine, she'd catch them eventually.

But death was behind her, and she kept looking back. Where was the grendel? As fast as it moved, it could be anywhere.

The grendel was in no hurry. She was overheated, yes, but not to the point of distress. She was small, and had been on speed for less than half a minute.

The horse was not much fun. The grendel fed, trying to

avoid tearing vitals for the moment; but the beast had stopped moving almost immediately.

The taste was far better than grendel meat.

Three of her siblings were in sight. They came in a line. Vectors of attraction and repulsion held them in position: fear of each other, fear of the one above them, smell of *speed*, mist of horse's blood in the air. Hunger was winning.

Charlie tore into the horse. She ate with some haste now. When her belly was full to the point of pain, she ripped one of the horse's hind legs loose and moved uphill, dragging it with her tail. The other grendels closed in behind.

They would eat and grow strong. Let them. Perhaps they would fight. But they would not catch up. Meanwhile nineteen animals moved upslope with their alien guard to tend them. Well and good.

The horses were thinking about letting her catch up. Carolyn cursed the stupid animals in her mind; she didn't have breath for more. Thirst was a fire in her throat. Her burning legs were ready to collapse, and her ride receded coyly before her.

The horses stumbled from time to time. She'd have to get those ropes off them if they were to have any chance to live.

They wheeled to the left. She followed.

The stream was a sudden surprise. It was small and pretty and it ran in graceful curves. She hadn't seen it lower down. It might curve south and join the Amazon; it might seep into the water table and disappear. She could hear it bubbling now, and the thirst rose up in her like a grendel.

The horses lined up to drink. They didn't flinch as she joined them. She had swallowed two cupped handfuls before she noticed how dirty the water was. She was downstream, and the horses had fouled the water.

She spat out the grit. Thirst was still there, but she took the time to free the horses from the line of ropes. *Do everything slowly and carefully. Fool yourself into being calm.*

She patted their necks, she called them by name, she walked around and among them and knelt to drink clean water upstream. And saved her life thereby.

When her belly was a cold fullness, she stood and looked back.

Far down toward the edge of storm, a cloud of spray rose from the stream.

Something dark came out of it. Came fast. Charlie had gone for water first, but now he was on speed and coming for the horses. Carolyn stepped back behind a rock that was only hip high. Knelt. She concentrated on arming the harpoon gun. She didn't lift her head until she was armed.

Just her eyes peeped over the rock.

The horses were scattering, all but Shank's Mare. Shank's Mare had gone thirty meters before the thing tore into her. Now she thrashed with blood spraying from her ravaged hind leg—Charlie had developed a habit—and the black streak circled back to bite away half of the horse's head. Shank's Mare convulsed, then collapsed like a bag of old laundry. The grendel hooked her with its tail and dragged her back into the stream.

Carolyn stood up and walked forward. There was no running from a grendel. Charlie was occupied and the time was *now*.

The horses had hidden her, and then the rock, but now . . . Charlie must have seen her at once. The grendel came straight at her, pulling the mass of the horse and a mass of water too, moving no faster than a jogger. It realized its problem and stopped to shake the horse free. Carolyn shot it from six meters away.

The harpoon exploded against Charlie's wide face.

The grendel came for Carolyn. It was free of the horse, and it accelerated like the best of motorcycles. Carolyn wouldn't have had time to move even if she'd had the nerve and another weapon. The thing went past her in a wind that twisted her around, and she saw it smash into the hip-high boulder, bounce over it, land tumbling, look about—

Look with what? The blast had torn its face entirely away, leaving cracked red-and-white bone. No eyes, no nose, most of the mouth blown away. A grendel's ears were nearly invisible, but she couldn't believe those weren't gone too.

There was blood in Carolyn's mouth. She had bitten deeply into her lower lip. Blood soaked into her trousers, and a line of pain crossed her leg above the knee: the tail of the thing must have brushed her. She lowered the harpoon gun and felt the pain in her cramped hands. "Stupid," she whispered. "Stupid, Charlie. Pulling a horse! I hope your sisters are that stupid."

Charlie's tail was a blur like the blades on a Skeeter. She charged in a straight line, with no clear target. Only by accident did she intersect the stream. She stopped then, sank underwater, then lifted again. To breathe. The snorkel was gone too.

Carolyn became aware that she was grinning like a grendel.

The rest. Where were they? She couldn't see them; the ground curved wrongly, but they must be at least several hundred meters downslope. Three grendels—and two harpoons left. She remembered a line from Dickens and told herself, "I have every confidence that something will turn up."

She knelt down to drink again, then set off to join the horses.

THE PORTRAIT OF DARYANREE THE KING

Jim Baen talked me into opening a franchise: we invited friends to write stories set in the Warlock's universe.

I had hoped that what became THE MAGIC MAY RETURN and MORE MAGIC would re-inspire me. They did; but it might be more accurate to say that writing notes for the other authors inspired me. Some of the ideas I suggested never got used. I wound up writing them myself.

It was a good game while it lasted. Jovan left the palace that night as a hunted fugitive, ruined by the mannerless sixteen-year-old daughter of a border nobleman; but at noon he had joined His Majesty's Thirty-Eighth Birthday Celebration as one of the most powerful men in Seaclaw.

The parades and games made pleasant cover for the real business of the Birthday, as two hundred local and visiting nobles gathered to meet anyone who could do them good. By sunset all was circles of private conversation; an outsider might as well go home. The guests had eaten well and drunk better. King Daryanree was monopolizing the youthful Lady Silvara, to the discomfiture of many who coveted her attention, or his.

Jovan should have been watching them. But he had made an ill-considered remark to Raskad Mil, and the princes' brass-voiced teacher had backed him against a wall to lecture on ghosts.

Jovan was flattered but wary. Old Mil had taught literature and history to the king as well as to his sons. He was treating Jovan as an equal. That could help Jovan's own reputation . . . unless Mil caught the purported artist-magician in some egregious ignorance.

"I only said that I had never seen one," he protested.

Mil would have none of that. "After all, where do barbarous peoples bury their dead? The ancient battlefields become the graveyards, do they not? And so they remain centuries later. You, Jovan, you hail from a war-torn land. Of course you see no ghosts!"

A young man at Jovan's shoulder asked the question Jovan dared not. "Why would it matter, Raskad Mil? Battlefields—"

"Ancient wars were fought with magic as well as swords. The sites are exhausted of the *mana*, the magical force. Ghosts give no trouble on a battlefield."

"But—"

"But Seaclaw's battles were all at sea, and even that was long ago. Our folk have always buried their dead on Worm's-Head Hill, with a view of land and sea for their comfort."

They were superstitious, the Seaclaw folk. Jovan's smile slipped when peals of laughter suddenly rang through the audience hall. He'd missed something—

Conversation stopped. Lady Silvara was easily the loveliest women in the hall; but she was young and fresh from the border, untrained in courtly ways. In the silence her voice was clear, musical. "Majesty, I would have thought that a man of your age would find interest in less strenuous pursuits!"

The King's fury showed only for an instant. Give him credit, King Daryanree had learned self-control at the negotiation tables. He said, "But unlike many a lovely young lady, Silvara, I grow no older."

And Jovan was already working his way through the crowd, not hurrying, but *moving*. He barely heard Silvara's, "Dyeing one's hair does nothing for crow's-feet, Majesty—"

At the great doors Jovan nodded to the guards and passed outside. A sliver of sun still showed at the northern edge of Worm's-Head Hill. An autumn chill was setting in. While an attendant went for Jovan's cloak, another stepped into the courtyard and waved peremptorily toward the line of coaches. Nothing moved. The attendant said, "Councillor, I don't see your driver."

Jovan knew about luck. Like wine: when luck turns sour, the whole barrel is sour. "Kassily probably went for a drink. Well, it's a nice night for a walk."

"We can provide you with a coachman—"

"No, I'll just go on down to the World-Turtle and send Kassily back for the coach." Jovan waited. Death for the price of a cloak? He could not leave without it. In this cold he would seem freakish.

The man returned with Jovan's cloak, and Jovan wished them both goodnight and strolled off into the growing dark.

Now what?

In any place that knew him, the King's men could find him. The King would be wanting explanations! Jovan had known that this might come. For eight years he had postponed his departure. The King might die, some fool might steal the painting for its powers; at worst he could be clear before the King's hairline began to recede; and meanwhile his wealth accumulated in Rynildissen.

Jovan turned left toward the World-Turtle, toward the sea, toward Seaclaw's ancient hill of the dead.

He dared not go home. He had not married; he had not left hostages for the King to take. His house and lands would be confiscated, of course, and the excellent painting of Jovan himself as a decrepit octogenarian . . .

But there was money to keep him comfortable for the rest of his life if he could reach Rynildissen. He could buy passage on a ship, if he could reach the docks. Had he enough coins? Never mind; he wore rings; that was what rings were for. He would sell the silver buckles on his shoes if need be.

He passed the tavern, walking faster now. He'd painted that sign himself: the turtle whose shell was the world, afloat in a sea of stars. Real stars were emerging, and the World-Turtle was noisy and bright with candlelight. *Kassily, we've lost our professions tonight, but you at least will keep your life.*

There were no houses beyond the World-Turtle, and Jovan felt free to run. He had a good view of the castle. Something was happening there. Mounted men galloping down the torchlit drive? But horses wouldn't come here, nor would the Seaclaw folk. He was passing graves already, though nothing marked them but bare rounded earth or thicker grass: the graves of those who could not afford better.

Jovan was panting now. He passed white stones set upright, with marks chiseled into them. Higher up the stones had been hacked into rectangular shape. He could see small buildings, crypts, a miniature city of the dead lined along the crest of Worm's-Head Hill. Already he was wading through thickening mist. The night fog might help him.

Hide in a crypt? He would need shelter. A man could go hungry for a few days. It might do him good; he had fed too well, perhaps, these eight years. Water would be a problem, but this was wet country. There would be dew to collect in the morning.

The crypt he was passing was shoulder-high, built of stone with a stone door barred on the outside. The next was like it. Children's tales spoke of a time when ghosts were deadly dangerous . . . but an outside bar meant that he could get in.

A miniature castle loomed to his right: the royal crypt, centuries old, with (reputedly) plenty of room left for future generations. No guard would enter there. Jovan circled, making for the great stone door that faced the harbor. The fog was thick, waist-high; it rippled as he moved.

Clothes would be a problem when he reached the harbor. He could hardly walk the docks dressed for a ball! But his cloak would hide him long enough . . . and Jovan had begun to think past the next hour of life. That was all to the good.

He slowed to a walk, and a grin began to form as he pictured King Daryanree dancing with fury. None would dare go near; how would they get their orders? Would the Guard even know what they were hunting?

Just before the door, the fog rose up and faced him.

Elsewhere the mist was rising to take other shapes, but Jovan didn't turn his head. This before him was enough: a burly man with a ravaged, eyeless face, six inches broader of shoulder than Jovan and a head taller, wearing the crown of Seaclaw. He leaned on the haft of a two-handed war-axe. The skin of the right arm flapped loose; it had been flayed away nearly to the shoulder. The left hand looked soft, with every bone broken. Loops of . . . what might have been sausage hung below his torso-armor.

The ghost spoke in a voice that seemed to come from miles away. "I know you. Samal! Usurper! I would kill you slowly, but to what point? Time enough to torment you in the ages after you're *dead*," it shrieked, and the war-axe moved with supernatural speed.

Somehow, Jovan hadn't thought of moving.

The axe swung down, split him from crown to crotch and drove deep into the dirt. Jovan felt no sensation at all. The old King stared, aghast. He swung from the side, a blow that would have severed Jovan at the waist. Then he howled and hurled the axe away.

The axe was a wisp of mist. The King, turning toward the crypt, lost shape and became a whorl in the waist-high fog. And a voice behind Jovan said, "He's mad, of course."

"Is he." Jovan turned.

Ghosts formed an arc around him. They watched him solemnly, like the audience that often formed to watch him paint. Some were only an unevenness in the mist layer, mere suggestions of human shape. Others showed detail: men and women ravaged by disease or age; the heads of children just showing above the mist; a burly man who hung back from the crowd, whose rope-burned neck hung askew and whose fingertips dripped big droplets of fog.

The nearest had the shape of a lean old man with pointed nose and chin, bald scalp, a fringe of long hair blurred at the ends: a very clear, precise image. That apparition said, "Zale the Tenth was tortured to death. He lasted ten days. It would have driven anyone mad."

Jovan got his own throat working, largely to see if he could do it. Could he get the ghosts talking? "I take it you got off easier."

"I think not. The plague is an easier death, but it took my family. Will you be here long?"

"A few days."

"Good. We'd like the company, and we won't harm you. Can't."

"The *mana* level's worn too low." Jovan sighed, perhaps in relief; he wasn't sure himself. "Over most of the world ghosts have no power at all. You're the first I've ever seen."

A child's voice asked, "Are you a magician? You talk like one."

"I am," Jovan said.

The old man's ghost drifted toward him. Jovan held himself from flinching at its immaterial touch. The ghost reached into Jovan's chest. Jovan thought he felt cold fingers wrapped around his heart. The ghost grinned (the teeth were missing all down the right side, and scarce on the left) and said, "You're not."

"Why not?"

"A magician keeps some of the magic that passes through him. A touch of *mana* makes a ghost stronger. You don't have any. We all know about *mana* here, but how did you find out?"

Jovan sat down on a headstone. "The old woman who taught me to paint, *she* was a magician. She'd given it up long before I met her, when all the spells gradually stopped working. But Laneerda made her magic by painting. You know, paint a successful hunt, put hairs of the animal and the hunter in the paint. Or paint your own army winning a battle—"

A distant scream caused Jovan to jump. The scream of a horse? Two horses in chorus, down at the foot of the hill.

The specter didn't appear to have noticed. "Hunters still did that when I was a young man," it said. "So you're a painter. Why did you say you were a magician?"

Jovan wore a guilty grin. "Well, the King thinks so."

"So?"

"Maybe he doesn't by now. But he did, for eight years. I came to Seaclaw just four days ahead of the King's thirtieth birthday. I got into the celebration at the palace by painting my landlady's daughter and bringing it as a present.

"King Daryanree wanted a few words with me. He wanted to meet the girl. She wasn't as pretty as I painted her. But I mentioned my teacher Laneerda, and Daryanree knew the name. Legend has her a lot more powerful than she ever was! We talked some more, and I saw how much Daryanree hated the idea of getting old. So I told him I could keep it from happening."

"That sounds dangerous," the ghost pointed out. "Not to mention dishonest."

"But they did it that way! Paint a portrait, put hair and fingernail clippings and blood and urine from the subject in the paint. Do it right, the painting grows old instead of the subject. Of course you have to guard the painting, because if that gets hurt . . . but the better the painting is, the better the spell works. It's not my fault if the magic isn't good anymore. *I'm* good.''

''Why didn't you just take the money and run?''

It was strange to be talking to a ring of ghosts as if they were any normal audience. Strange, and oddly pleasant, to finally speak his secret where it could not harm him. ''Daryanree isn't a complete fool. He offered me a house and an annual fee. I couldn't see any way to turn that down without making him suspicious, and it was good money. So I told him it was just as well, because the painting would have to be tended—even Daryanree knows that *manna* fades with time—and when I told him about the old spell I added some details.

''I painted him naked, and I made him shave so more of his face would show in the painting, otherwise he'd get old under the whiskers. He wouldn't shave his head. He did agree to keep his face shaved for the rest of his life. It started a court fashion. I made him up a fluid to rinse his hair every few days, to maintain an affinity with the paint—''

''He'll still get old,'' the ghost protested. ''Only the dead don't get old.''

''Well, but I had him washing his hair in berry juice that turns dark, and there's no gray in his beard because he shaves it off, and maybe he's getting wrinkled, but who's going to tell him? Nobody says that to the King! As for the painting, I insisted on absolute privacy while I renewed the spells. Trust me, the King's painting did grow older!

''I did some good, too. Daryanree was due to execute a bunch of farmers for not paying their taxes. The hands in the painting showed bloody. I told the King, made him come see. He freed the farmers. When he was ready to declare war on Rynildissen, the painting sprouted a dripping red line across the neck, and his crown and robes turned transparent. That took days. I had to paint it in my house and smuggle it in. But the King signed a peace treaty, and he made me a councillor.

"Then this afternoon the King made an advance to the wrong girl. Right about now he's staring into a mirror and wondering how he could have been so gullible."

"And you came here."

"I thought I'd be safe. I didn't really believe in ghosts. I was sure they couldn't hurt me."

"And now?"

The murmuring around Jovan didn't sound entirely friendly. Nonetheless Jovan said, "It's still the way to bet."

"Do you believe in a finding-stone?"

"Mmm? For finding a man?" Jovan had never heard of such a thing. "Well, it would be magic, of course. It wouldn't work except in a few places . . . Why?"

The elderly ghost said, "I was second in command of Zale the Tenth's forces when I was alive. A lot of us joined the usurper, and that way a lot of blood wasn't spilled, but the plague that followed . . . maybe we brought that on us too. Killing a king carries a curse, and Samal's veins carried no more than a jigger of royal blood. But the Guard had a finding-stone spelled by the wizard Clubfoot himself. The kings of Seaclaw still have it, even if it's lost some of its power."

Jovan felt a numbing fear flowing through his body. "Will they dare come here?"

A voice cleared its throat and said, "I did." It was clearly human and very close.

Jovan didn't turn. A clean swing of a sword through his neck? When the luck turns sour— "Companion of dogs," Jovan whispered to the old man's ghost. "You kept me here. You made me talk. You're dead! You're not an officer anymore, you didn't have to—I didn't do any real harm—" He couldn't speak further, his tongue was too thick.

Something massive moved through the ring of ghosts,

and their bodies swirled and steadied as it passed. Jovan stood up to face a man of the King's Guard.

Daryanree chose his guards partly for their appearance. The man was tall; he fitted his armor well. He carried a well-polished, well-honed sword in one hand and what might have been a large volcanic-glass arrowhead in the open palm of the other.

But he was alone. No horse would walk among ghosts and no companion had followed, and he must be half out of his mind with fear. Jovan could smell chilled fear-sweat. And Jovan cried piteously, "I can't move! They've got me, but it's not too late for you. Run!"

There was a tremor in the burly guard's voice. "These specters are my own people, barbarian! I heard what you said. The King wants to talk to you. Will you come quietly?"

A king cannot afford to look the fool. Jovan knew too much to live.

He said, "Yes! Yes, if you can pull me loose from this." He let his eyes roll; he stretched his arms toward the guard; he writhed on the headstone, then sagged in defeat.

"Liar!" the guard roared. He moved forward as if through glue. Jovan waited to see if the guard would break.

The mist surged up, and Zale the Tenth stood before the guard. The skin of his arm flapped as he moved. Massive, flayed and blind and tormented, the old king's ghost was a horrid sight. "I know you," it cried. "Samal! Usurper!" The war-axe rose and fell.

The guard tried to riposte. The axe wafted through his sword and smashed his naked shield-arm back across his chest. The guard reeled backward and smacked against the rough stone of a crypt.

Jovan shook his head.

The guard didn't move. And the fog had clumped above him, nearly hiding him. Ghosts surrounded the man like jackals feeding. Jovan remembered other legends, of vampires—

He forced himself to move among them, through them, feeling resistance and chill. He unlaced the guard's leather torso armor and pulled it off and placed his palm on the man's chest.

"His heart's still beating. I don't understand," the artist said, and sudden claustrophobic terror took him. He could see nothing; he was embedded in ghosts.

The finding-stone was shattered in the guard's hand. The magic in it could have made Zale's axe real enough to hurt, real enough to send a man flying backward. But there was no blood, no break in the armor or the tunic beneath or, when Jovan carefully pulled the tunic off, in the skin either. Not real enough to cut, then. A bruise was forming above the sternum, but Jovan found no broken ribs.

"Bumped his head," Jovan mumbled. He found blood on the back of the man's scalp, but no splintered softness beneath. "He'll wake soon. I've got to get moving. They think the stone will find me. They won't look for me at the docks—"

"They'll look," said the old Guard officer's voice.

Jovan stripped hurriedly. The touch of the ghosts was cold, and they clustered close. He donned the guard's clothing as rapidly as he could. The boots were roomy; he tore up his own shirt to pad them. His rings he took off and put in the toes. His cloak wouldn't fit the look of the uniform. He spread it over the guard.

He strode out of the mist of ghosts. The fog ran away from him downhill, to form a pale carpet over the harbor and the sea. The lighthouse on Seaclaw Point showed above. Jovan took it as his target.

The dead general took shape, striding alongside him, clutching something. It said briskly, "They'll look. I'll follow you and point you out."

Jovan stopped. He said, "You can't leave Worm's-Head Hill. You never could before and you can't now."

"Do you believe that?"

With the magic of the finding-stone to give them life, ghosts could harm him now. When the luck turns sour . . . but luck had saved him from the guard. Push it, then!

He snatched at the ghost's clenched fist. The bones of his hand passed with a grating sensation through other bones, and tore away two shards of black glass, two pieces of the broken finding-stone. Jovan flung them far into the dark. The ghost ran after them. Jovan ran the other way, downhill toward the light.

THE WISHING GAME

For two survivors of the Warlock's Era, a final tale.

Crunching and grinding sounds brought him half-awake. He was being pulled upward through gritty sand, in jerks. Then the stopper jerked free, sudden sunlight flamed into his refuge, and the highly compressed substance that was Kreezerast the Frightener exploded into the open air.

Kreezerast attempted to gather his senses and his thoughts. He had slept for a long time . . .

A long time. A human male, an older man not in the best of shape, was standing above the bottle. There was desert all about. Kreezerast, tall as the tallest of trees and still expanding, had a good view of scores of miles of yellow sand blazing with heat and light. Far south he saw a lone pond ringed by stunted trees, the only sign of life. And this had been forest when he entered his refuge!

What of the man? He was looking up at Kreezerast, doubtless perceiving him as a cloud of thinning smoke. His aura was that of a magic user, though much faded from disuse. At his feet, beside Kreezerast's bottle, was a block of gold wrapped in ropes.

Gold?

Gold was wild magic. It would take no spells. It drove some creatures mad. Humans would collect the soft, useless metal, making themselves crazier yet. Was that why the man had carried this heavy thing into a desert? Or had its magic somehow pointed the way to Kreezerast's refuge?

Humans' wishes were often for gold. Once upon a time Kreezerast had given three men too much gold to carry or to hide, and watched them try to move it all, until bandits put the cap to his jest.

Loose white cloth covered most of the man's body. Knobby hands showed, and part of a sun-darkened face. Deep wrinkles surrounded the eyes. The nose was prominent, curved and sharp-edged like an eagle's beak, and sunburnt. The mouth was calm as he watched the cloud grow.

Kreezerast pulled himself together: the cloud congealed into a tremendous man. He shaped a face that was a cartoon of the other's features, wide mouth, nose like a great axe, red-brown skin, disproportionately large eyes and ears. He bellowed genially, "Make yourself known to me, my rescuer!"

"I am Clubfoot," the man said. "And you are an afrit, I think."

"Indeed! I am Kreezerast the Frightener, but you need not fear me, my rescuer. How may I reward you?"

"What I—"

"Three wishes!" Kreezerast boomed. He had always enjoyed the wishing game. "You shall have three wishes if I have the power to grant them."

"I want to be healthy," Clubfoot said.

The answer had come quickly. This was no wandering yokel. Good: brighter minds made for better entertainment. "What disease do you suffer from?"

"Nothing too serious. Nothing you cannot see, Kreezerast, with your senses more powerful than human. I suffer from sunburn, from too little water, and from various symptoms of age. And there's this." The man sat; he took the slipper off his left foot. The foot was twisted inward. Callus was thick along the outer edge and side. "I was born this way."

"You could have healed yourself. There is magic, and you are a magician."

Clubfoot smiled. "There was magic."

Kreezerast nodded. His own kind were creatures of magic. Over tens of thousands of years the world's *mana*, the power that worked spells, had dwindled almost to nothing. The most powerful of magical creatures had gone mythical first. Afrits had outlived gods. They had watched dragons sickening, merpeople becoming handless creatures of the sea; and they had survived that. They had watched men spread across the land, and change.

"There was magic," Kreezerast affirmed. "Why didn't you heal your foot?"

"It would have cost me half my power. That mattered, when I had power. Now I can't heal myself."

"But now you have me. So! What is your wish?"

"I wish to be healthy."

Did this Clubfoot intend to be entirely healed from all the ills of mankind on the strength of one wish? The question answered itself: he did. Kreezerast said, "There are things I can't do for you—"

"Don't do them."

Was there no way to force Clubfoot to make his wish more specific, more detailed? "Total health is impossible for your kind."

"Fortunate it is, that I have not wished for total health."

The wish was well chosen. It was comprehensive. It was unambiguous. The Frightener could not claim that he could not fulfill the conditions; they were too general.

Magic was still relatively strong in this place. Kreezerast knew that he had the power to search Clubfoot's structure and heal every ill he found.

To lose the first wish was no disaster. One did like to play the game to the end. Still Kreezerast preferred that the first wish come out a bit wrong. To give the victim warning was only fair.

Pause a bit. Think. They stood in a barren waste. What was a man doing here? His magic must have led him to Kreezerast's refuge, but—

Footprints led north: parallel lines of sandal-marks and shapeless splotches. They led to the corpse of a starved beast, not long dead, half a mile away. Here was more life: scavengers had set to work.

Saddlebags lay near the dead beast. They held (Kreezerast adjusted his eyes) only water skins. Three were quite dry; the fourth held five or six mouthfuls.

Hoofprints blurred as he followed them further. Dunes, more dunes . . . the prints faded, but Kreezerast's gaze followed the pathless path . . . a fleck of scarlet at the peak of a crescent dune, twelve miles north . . . and beyond that his eyes still saw, but his other senses did not. The *mana* level dropped to nothing, as if cut by a sword. The desert continued for scores of miles.

It tickled Kreezerast's fancy. Clubfoot would be obscenely healthy when he died of thirst. He would suffer no ill save for fatigue and water loss and sunstroke. Of course he still had two wishes—but such was the nature of the game.

"You shall be healthy," Kreezerast roared jovially. "This will hurt."

He looked deep within Clubfoot. Spells had eased some of the stresses that were the human lot, and other stresses due to a twisted walk, but those spells were long gone.

First: brain and nerves had lost some sensitivity. Inert matter had accumulated in the cells. Kreezerast removed that, carefully. The wrinkles deepened around Clubfoot's eyes. The nerves of youth now sensed the aches and pains of an aged half-cripple.

Next: bones. Here were arthritis, swollen joints. Kreezerast reshaped them. He softened the cartilage. The bones of the left foot he straightened. The man howled and flailed aimlessly. He did not beg Kreezerast to stop.

The callus on that foot was now wrong. Kreezerast burned it away.

Age had dimmed the man's eyes. Kreezerast took the opacity from the humor, tightened the irises. He was enjoying himself, for his task challenged his skills. Arteries and veins were half-clogged with goo, particularly around and through the heart. Kreezerast removed it. Digestive organs were losing their function; Kreezerast repaired them, grinning in anticipation.

In a few hours Clubfoot would be as hungry as an adolescent boy. He'd want a banquet and he'd want it *now*. It would be salty. There would be wine, no water.

Reproductive organs had lost function; the prostate gland was ready to clamp shut on the urethra. Kreezerast made repairs. Perhaps the man would ask for an houri too, when glandular juices commenced bubbling within his veins.

A few hours of pain, a few hours of pleasure. For Kreezerast to win the game, his three wishes must leave a man (or an afrit, for they played the game among themselves) with nothing he hadn't started with. To leave him injured or dead was acceptable but inferior.

The man writhed with pain. His face was in the sand and he was choking. His lungs, for that matter, had collected sixty years of dust. Kreezerast swept them clean. He burned four skin tumors away in tiny flashes.

The sunburn would heal itself. Wrinkled skin was not ill health, nor were dead hair follicles.

Anything else?

Nothing that could be done by an afrit working with insufficient *mana*.

Clubfoot sat up gasping. His breathing eased. A slow smile spread across his face. "No pain. Wait—" The smile died.

"You have lost your sense of magic," the afright said. "Of course."

"I expected that. Ugh. It's like going deaf." The man got up.

"Were you powerful?"

"I was in the Guild. I was part of the group that tried to restore magic to the world by bringing down the Moon."

"The Moon!" Kreezerast guffawed; the sand danced to the sound. He had never heard the like. "It was well you didn't succeed!"

"In the end some of us had to die to stop it. Yes, I was powerful. All things end and so will I, but you've given me a little more time, and I thank you." The man picked up his golden cube by two leather straps and settled it on his back. "My next wish is that you take me to Xyloshan Village without leaving the ground."

Kreezerast laughed a booming laugh. "Do you fear that I will drop you on Xyloshan Village from a height?" It would make a neat finale.

"Not anymore," Clubfoot said.

Here the magic was relatively strong, perhaps because the desert would not support men. Men were not powerful in magic, but there were so many! Where men were, magic disappeared rapidly. That would explain the sharp dropoff to the north. Wars did that. Opposing spells burned the *mana* out locally in a few hours, and then it was down to blades and murder.

To east and west and south the level of power dwindled gradually. "Where is this Xyloshan Village?"

"Almost straight north." Clubfoot pointed. "Rise a mile and you'll see it easily. There are low hills around it, a big bell tower and two good roads—"

The man's level of confidence was an irritant. Struck suddenly young again, free of the ever-present pains that came with age in men, he must be feeling like the king of the world. How pleasant it would be, to puncture the man's balloon of conceit!

—Take me to Xyloshan Village without leaving the ground. Very well, Kreezerast would not leave the ground.

The Frightener didn't rise into the air; he *grew*. At a mile tall he could scan everything to the north. Xyloshan was a village of fifteen or sixteen hundred with a tall, crude bell tower, two hundred miles distant. If he hurled Clubfoot through the air in a parabola . . .

He couldn't. It was too far and he didn't have sufficient magic. Just as well. It would have ended the game early.

He still had two choices.

Clubfoot had made the wrong wish. It could not be fulfilled. The afrit could simply say so. Or . . . mmm?

He laughed. He shrank to twenty feet or so. He picked up Clubfoot, tucked him under his arm and ran. He covered twelve miles in ten minutes (weak!) and stopped with a jolt. He set Clubfoot down in the sand. The man lay gasping. His hands had a deathgrip on the ropes that bound the gold cube.

"Here I must stop," Kreezerast said, "I must not venture where there is no *mana*."

The man's breathing gradually eased. He rolled to his knees. In a moment he'd realize that his minuscule water supply lay twelve miles behind him.

Kreezerast needled him. "And your third wish, my rescuer?"

"Whoof! That was quite a ride. Are you sure rescuer is the word you want?" Clubfoot stood and looked about him. He spoke as if to himself. "All right, where's the smoke? Mirandee!"

"Why should I not say *rescuer*?"

"Your kind can't tolerate boredom. You built those little bottles as refuges. When you're highly compressed and there's no light or sound, you go to sleep. You sleep until something wakes you up."

"You know us very well, do you?"

"I've read a great deal."

"What are you looking for?"

"Smoke. It isn't here. Something must have happened to Mirandee. *Mirandee!*"

"You have a companion? I can find her, if such is your wish." He had already found her. There was a patch of scarlet cloth at the top of a dune, and a small canopy pitched on the north side, two hundred paces west. Kreezerast was twice beaten.

Clubfoot played the game well. He had a companion waiting just this side of the border between magic and no magic, on a line between Xyloshan Village and Kreezerast's refuge. The afrit had taken him almost straight to her. And to their camp, where waited two more loadbeasts and their water supply.

A puff of wind could cover that scarlet blanket with sand . . .

An afrit would have gloated. The man merely picked up his gold and walked. In a moment he was jogging, then running flat out, testing his symmetrical feet and newly youthful legs. He bellowed, "Mirandee!" half in the joy of new youth, half in desperation. He ran straight up the side of a tall dune, spraying sand. At the top he looked about him, and favored Kreezerast with a poisonous glare. Then he was running again.

Kreezerast's little whirlwind had buried the scarlet marker. But of course: the man had failed to find it, but he'd seen a dying whirlwind!

Kreezerast followed, taking his time.

The man was in the shade of the canopy, bending over a woman. Kreezerast stopped as his highly sensitive ears picked up Clubfoot's near-whisper. "I came as quick as I could. Oh, Mirandee! Hang on, Mirandee, stay with me, we're almost there."

The Frightener could study her more thoroughly now: a very old woman, tall and still straight. An aura of magic, nearly gone. She was unconscious and days from death. The golden cube lay beside her, pushed up against her ribs. Wild magic might reinforce some old spell.

Once upon a time, a man had wished for a woman who didn't want him. Kreezerast found her and brought her to him, but made no effort to hide where she had gone. He'd watched her relatives take their vengeance. Humans took their lusts seriously—but this woman did not seem a proper object for lust. She'd be thirty or forty years older than the man.

The man must have thought the Frightener was out of earshot. He rubbed her knobby hand. "We got this far. The bottle was there. The afrit was there. The magic was there. The first spell worked. Look at me, can you see? It worked!"

Her eyes opened. She stirred.

"Don't mind the wrinkles. I don't *hurt* anywhere. Here, feel!" He wrapped the woman's fingers around his left foot. "The second spell, he did just as we thought. I don't think we'll even need—" The man looked up. He raised his voice. "Frightener, this is Mirandee."

Kreezerast approached. "Your mate?"

"Close enough. My companion. My final wish is that Mirandee be healthy."

This was too much. "You know we hate boredom. It is discourteous of you to make two wishes that are the same."

Clubfoot picked up the gold, turned his back and walked away. "I'll remain as courteous as possible," he snarled over his shoulder. "I remind you that you carried me facing backward. Was that discourteous, or did you consider it a joke?"

"A joke. Here's another. Your . . . companion must be nearly one hundred years old. A healthy woman of that age would be dead."

"Hah hah. Nobody dead is healthy. I already know that you can fulfill my wish."

Kreezerast wondered if the man would use the gold to

bribe him. *That* would be amusing. "I point out also that you are not truly my rescuer—"

"Am I not? Haven't I rescued you from boredom? Aren't you enjoying the wishing game?" Clubfoot was shouting over his shoulder across a gap of twenty paces. In fact he had walked beyond the region where magic lived, while Kreezerast was still looking for ways to twist his third wish.

That easily, he was beyond Kreezerast's vengeance. "You have bested me. I admit it, but I can limit your satisfaction. One more word from you and I kill the woman."

Clubfoot nodded. He spread a robe from the saddlebags against the side of a dune and made himself comfortable on it.

No curses, no pleading, no bribe? Kreezerast said, "Speak your one word."

"Wait."

What? "I won't hurt her. Speak."

The man's voice now showed no anger. "Our biggest danger was that we would find you to be stupid."

"Well?"

"I think we've been lucky. A stupid afrit would have been very dangerous."

The man spoke riddles. Kreezerast turned to black smoke and drifted south, beaten and humiliated.

Once upon a time a man had wished to be taller. Kreezerast had lengthened his bones and left the muscles and tendons alone. Over time he'd healed. A woman had wished for beauty; Kreezerast had given her an afrit's beauty. Afterward men admired her eerie, abstract loveliness, but never wished her favors—and she was one who had shied from men.

But no man had ever bested him like this!

What did the magician expect? Kreezerast had watched men evolve over the thousands of years. He had watched magicians strip the land of magic, until better species died or changed. He had no reason to love men, nor to keep his promises to a lesser breed.

The bottle beckoned . . . but Kreezerast rose into the air. High, higher: three miles, ten. Was there any sign of his own kind? None at all. Patches where *mana* still glowed strong? None. Here and here were encampments, muffled men and women attended by strange misshapen beasts. Men had taken the world.

The world had changed. It would change again. Kreezerast the Frightener would wait in his refuge until something or someone dug him up. A companion would come . . . and would hear the tale. Afrits didn't lie to each other.

So be it. At least he need not confess to killing the woman out of mere spite. Let her man watch her die over the next few days. Let him tend her while his water dwindled.

The key to survival was to live only through interesting times.

Here was the bottle. Now, where . . .

Where was the stopper?

The stopper bore afrit's magic. Sand could not hide it from him.

Gold would. Wild magic would hide the magic in the stopper. It was a box, a box!

The camp was untouched. The woman had not moved. Her breathing was labored.

Clubfoot lay against the next dune. He had gone for the beasts and the supplies in their saddle bags. He said nothing. The golden cube glowed at his feet.

Kreezerast said, "Very well. You can reach Xyloshan Village and I cannot stop you, if you are willing to abandon the woman. So. You win."

Clubfoot said, "Why do I want to talk to a liar?"

The answer was obvious enough. "For the woman."

"And why will you stoop to bargaining with a mere man?"

"For the stopper. But I can make another."

"Can you? I could never make another Mirandee." The man sat up. "We feared you would twist the third wish somehow. We never dreamed you'd refuse to grant it at all."

He would have to remake stopper *and* bottle, for they were linked. And he could do that, but not here, nor anywhere on this *mana*-poor desert. Perhaps nowhere.

He said, "Give me the stopper and I will grant your third wish, or any other you care to make."

"But I don't trust you."

"Trust this, then. I can repair this Mirandee's nerves. In fact . . . yes." He looked deep into her body, deep into her fine structure. This one had never been crippled. She'd never borne children either. Odd. It was humankind's only form of immortality.

He cleared inert goo out of big blood vessels and myriads of tiny ones. He repaired the heart. Now she would not die inconveniently. Nerves had become inert through the body; he fixed that too.

She stirred, flung out an arm. Her breathing was faster now. He sensed increased blood flow to her brain.

Kreezerast called, "So sensation has returned—"

She whispered, "Clubfoot?" She rolled over, and squeaked with pain. She saw the tremendous man-shape above her; studied it without blinking, then rolled to her knees and faced north. "Clubfoot. Stay there," she croaked. "Well done!" He couldn't have heard her.

"So her sensation has returned and her mind is active too," the Frightener called. "Now she can feel and understand pain. I will give her pain. Do you trust my word?"

"Let us see if you trust mine," the man called. "I will never give the stopper to you. Never. Mirandee must do that for me. You must persuade her to do that."

Persuade? Torture! Until she begged to do him any service he asked. But then she must go and get the stopper, where magic failed . . . fool. Fool!

The Frightener shrank until he stood some seven feet tall. He said, "Woman, your paramour has wished you to be healthy. If I make you healthy, will you give me that which he holds in ransom?"

She blinked. "Yes."

"Will you also keep me company for a day?" Postpone. Delay. Wait. "Tell me stories. The world is not familiar to me anymore."

Her thoughts were slow . . . and careful. "I will do that, if you will give me food and water. As for keeping you company—"

"I speak of social intercourse," he said quickly. To show Clubfoot's woman that an afrit was a better mate would have been entertaining. *If* they were lovers. She was far older than he was . . . but there were spells to keep a woman young. Had been spells. She had been a powerful magician, he saw that. In fact (that unwinking gaze, as if he were being judged by an equal!) this whole plan might have been hers.

He had lost. He was even losing his anger. They had *known* the danger. What a gamble they had taken! And Kreezerast must even be polite to this woman, and persuade her not to break her promise after she had walked beyond his reach.

He said, "Then tell me how you almost brought the Moon to Earth. But first I will heal you. This will hurt." He set to work. She screamed a good deal; and so he kept that promise too.

Bones, joints, tendons: he healed them all. Ovaries were shrunken, but not all eggs were gone; they could be brought to life. Glands. Stomach. Gut. Kreezerast continued until she was a young woman writhing and gasping, new inside and withered outside.

Clubfoot did not run to his lady to help her in her pain.

They might still make a mistake. If nothing else thwarted them, perhaps he had one last joke to play.

She'd feel the wrinkles when she touched her face! But wrinkles do not constitute ill health. But she *must* give him the stopper. Kreezerast pulled her skin smooth, face and hands and forearms (but not where cloth covers her. Hah! She'll never notice until it's too late!) legs, belly, breasts, pectoral muscles too. (She might.)

The sun had gone. He set sand afire for warmth and summoned up a king's banquet. Clubfoot stayed in his place of safety and chewed dried meat. She didn't touch the wine. Mirandee and the Frightener ate together, and talked long, while Clubfoot listened at a distance.

He told her of the tinker and his family who had wished for jewels, once upon a time. He'd given them eighty pounds of jewels. They had one horse and a travois. A hundred curious villagers were swarming to where they had seen the looming, smoky form of an afright.

But the tinker and his wife had thrown handfuls of jewels about the road and into the low bushes, and fled for a day before they stopped to hide what they kept. Forty years later their grandchildren were wealthy merchants.

Mirandee had seen the last god die, and it was a harrowing tale. She spoke of a changed world, where powerless sorcerers were becoming artists and artisans and musicians, where men learned to fish for themselves because the merpeople were gone, where war was fought with bloody blades and no magic at all.

Almost he was tempted to see more of it. But what would he see? If he ventured where the *mana* was gone, he would go mythical.

Presently he watched her sleep. Boring.

They talked the morning and afternoon away. At evening Mirandee folded the canopy and gathered the blankets and bedding and walked away with it all on her shoulders. She had been strong; she was strong again. She crossed the barrier between magic and no magic. Kreezerast could do nothing. She came back to collect food and wine left over from the banquet, and crossed again.

She and her man set up their camp. Kreezerast heard them talking and laughing. He saw Clubfoot's hands wander beneath the woman's robes, and was relieved: he had not fooled *himself*, at least. *What of the stopper?*

Neither had mentioned it at all.

He waited. He would not beg.

Mirandee took Clubfoot's golden cube. She carried it to the margin of magic. Her magical sense was gone; would she cross? No, they'd marked it. She swung the cube by the straps and hurled it several feet.

Kreezerast picked it up. The wild magic hurt his hands. There was no lid. He pulled the soft metal apart and had the stopper.

Time to sleep.

He let himself become smoke, and let the smoke thin. The humans ignored him. Perhaps they thought he had gone away; perhaps they didn't care. He hovered.

The canopy and the darkness hid their lovemaking, but it couldn't hide their surging, flashing auras. Magic was being made in that dead region. They were lovers indeed, if they had not been before. And Kreezerast grinned and turned toward his bottle.

In her youth she had chosen not to bear children.

Kreezerast had given them their health in meticulous detail. The ex-sorceress's natural lust to mate had already set their auras blazing again. She'd have a dozen children before time caught up with her, unless she chose abstinence, and abstinence would be a hardship on her.

Some human cultures considered many children a blessing. Some did not. Certainly their traveling days were over; they'd never get past that little village. And Kreezerast the Frightener crawled into his bottle and pulled the stopper after him.

THE LION IN HIS ATTIC

Mon Grenier, "My Attic," is the Nivens' favorite restaurant. It's the Pournelles' too. I mention that because we gave Mon Grenier a mention in LUCIFER'S HAMMER.

And one day I moved "My Attic" and its proprietor, Andre Lion, 14,000 years into the past, to shortly after the Warlock's era, when magic was disappearing from the land . . .

Before the quake it had been called Castle Minterl, but almost nobody outside Minterl remembered that. Small events drown in large ones. Atlantis itself, an entire continent, had drowned in the tectonic event that sank this small peninsula.

For seventy years the seat of government had been at Beesh, and that place was called Castle Minterl. Outsiders called this drowned place Nihilil's Castle, for its last lord, if they remembered at all. Three and a fraction stories of what had been the south tower still stood above the waves. They bore a third name now: Lion's Attic.

The sea was choppy today. Durily squinted against bright sunlight glinting off waves. Nothing of Nihilil's Castle showed beneath the froth.

The lovely golden-haired woman ceased peering over the side of the boat. She lifted her eyes to watch the south tower come toward them. She murmured into Karskon's ear, "And that's all that's left."

Thone was out of earshot, busy lowering the sails; but he might glance back. The boy was not likely to have seen a lovelier woman in his life, and as far as Thone was concerned, his passengers were seeing this place for the first time. Karskon turned to look at Durily and was relieved. She looked interested, eager, even charmed.

But she *sounded* shaken. "It's all gone! Tapestries and banquet hall and bedrooms and the big ballroom . . . the gardens . . . all down there with the fishes, and not even merpeople to enjoy them . . . that little knob of rock must have been Crown Hill . . . Oh, Karskon, I wish you could have seen it." She shuddered, though her face still wore the mask of eager interest. "Maybe the riding-birds survived. Nihilil kept them on the roof."

"You couldn't have been more than . . . ten? How can you remember so much?"

A shrug. "After the Torovan invasion, after we had to get out . . . Mother talked incessantly about palace life. I think she got lost in the past. I don't blame her much, considering what the present was like. What she told me and what I saw myself, it's all a little mixed up after so long. I saw the traveling eye, though."

"How'd that happen?"

"Mother was there when a messenger passed it to the king. She snatched it out of his hand, playfully, you know, and admired it and showed it to me. Maybe she thought he'd give it to her. He got very angry, and he was trying not to show it, and that was even more frightening. We left the palace the next day. Twelve days before the quake."

Karskon asked, "What about the other—?" But warning pressure from her hand cut him off.

Thone had finished rolling up the sail. As the boat thumped against the stone wall he sprang upward, onto what had been a balcony, and moored the bowline fast. A girl in her teens came from within the tower to fasten the stern line for him. She was big as Thone was big: not yet fat, but hefty, rounded of feature. Thone's sister, Karskon thought, a year or two older.

Durily, seeing no easier way out of the boat, reached hands up to them. They heaved as she jumped. Karskon passed their luggage up and joined them, leaving the cargo for others to move.

Thone made introductions. "Sir Karskon, Lady Durily, this is Estrayle, my sister. Estrayle, they'll be our guests for a month. I'll have to tell Father. We bring red meat in trade."

The girl said, "Oh, very good! Father will love that. How was the trip?"

"Well enough. Sometimes the spells for wind just don't do anything. Then there's no telling where you wind up." To Karskon and Durily he said, "We live on this floor. These outside stairs take you right up past us. You'll be staying on the floor above. The top floor is the restaurant."

Durily asked, "And the roof?"

"It's flat. Very convenient. We raise rabbits and poultry there." Thone didn't see the look that passed across Durily's face. "Shall I show you to your rooms? And then I'll have to speak to Father."

Nihilil's Castle dated from the last days of real magic. The South Tower was a wide cylindrical structure twelve stories tall, with several rooms on each floor. In this age nobody would have tried to build anything so ambitious.

When Lion petitioned for the right to occupy these ruins, he had already done so. Perhaps the idea amused Minterl's new rulers. A restaurant in Nihilil's Castle! Reached only by boats! At any rate, nobody else wanted the probably haunted tower.

The restaurant was on the top floor. The floor below would serve as an inn, but as custom decreed that the main meal was served at noon, it was rare for guests to stay over.

Lion and his wife and eight children lived on the third floor down.

Though "Lion's Attic" was gaining some reputation on the mainland, the majority of Lion's guests were fishermen. They often paid their score in fish or in smuggled wines. So it was that Thone found Lion and Merle hauling in lines through the big kitchen window.

Even Lion looked small next to Merle. Merle was two and a half yards tall, and rounded everywhere, with no corners and no indentations: His chin curved in one graceful sweep down to his wishbone; his torso expanded around him like a tethered balloon. There was just enough solidity, enough muscle in the fat, so that none of it sagged at all.

And that was considerable muscle. The flat-topped fish they were wrestling through the window was as big as a normal man, but Merle and Lion handled it easily. They settled the corpse on its side on the center table, and Merle asked, "Don't you wish you had an oven that size?"

"I do," said Lion. "What is it?"

"Dwarf island-fish. See the frilly spines all over the top of the thing? Meant to be trees. Moor at an island, go ashore. When you're all settled the island dives under you, then snaps the crew up one by one while you're trying to swim. But they're magical, these fish, and with the magic dying away—"

"I'm wondering how to cook the beast."

That really wasn't Merle's department, but he was willing to advise. "Low heat in an oven, for a long time, maybe an eighth of an arc," meaning an eighth of the sun's path from horizon to horizon.

Lion nodded. "Low heat, covered. I'll fillet it first. I can fiddle up a sauce, but I'll have to see how fatty the meat is . . . All right, Merle. Six meals in trade. Anyone else could have a dozen, but you . . ."

Merle nodded placidly. He never argued price. "I'll start

now.'' He went through into the restaurant section, scraping the door on both sides, and Lion turned to greet his son.

''We have guests,'' said Thone, ''and we have red meat, and we have a bigger boat. I thought it proper to bargain for you.''

''Guests, good. Red meat, good. What have you committed me to?''

''Let me tell you the way of it.'' Thone was not used to making business judgments in his father's name. He looked down at his hands and said, ''Most of the gold you gave me, I had spent. I had spices and dried meat and vegetables and pickle and the rest. Then a boat pulled in with sides of ox for sale. I was wondering what I could sell, to buy some of that beef, when these two found me at the dock.''

''Was it you they were looking for?''

''I think so. The lady Durily is of the old Minterl nobility, judging by her accent. Karskon speaks Minterl but he may be of the new nobility, the invaders from Torov. Odd to find them together . . .''

''You didn't trust them. Why did you deal with them?''

Thone smiled. ''Their offer. The fame of Lion's Attic has spread throughout Minterl, so they say. They want a place to honeymoon; they had married that same day. For two weeks' stay they offered . . . well, enough to buy four sides of ox and enough left over to trade *Strandhugger* in on a larger boat, large enough for the beef and two extra passengers.''

''Where are they now? And where's the beef?''

''I told . . . Eep. It's still aboard.''

The Lion roared. *''Arilta!''*

''I meant to tell Estrayle to do something about that, but it—''

''Never mind, you've done well.''

Arilta came hurrying from the restaurant area. Lion's wife resembled her husband to some extent: big-boned, heavy, placid of disposition, carrying her weight well. "What is it?"

"Set the boys to unloading the new boat. Four sides of beef. Get those into the meat box fast; they can take their time with the other goods."

She left, calling loudly for the boys. Lion said, "The guests?"

"I gave them the two leeward rooms as a suite."

"Good. Why don't you tell them dinner is being served? And then you can have your own meal."

The dining hall was a roar of voices, but when Lion's guests appeared the noise dropped markedly. Both were wearing court dress of a style that had not yet reached the provinces. The man was imposing in black and silver, with a figured silver patch over his right eye. The lady was eerily beautiful, dressed in flowing sea-green and a centimeter taller than her escort. They were conversation-stoppers, and they knew it.

And then a man came hurrying to greet them, clapping his hands in delight. "Lady Durily, Lord Karskon? I am Lion. Are your quarters comfortable? Most of the middle floor is empty; we can offer a variety of choices—"

"Quite comfortable, thank you," Karskon said. Lion had taken him by surprise. Rumor said that he was what his name implied, a were-lion. He was large, and his short reddish-blond hair might be the color of a lion's mane; but Lion was balding on top, and smooth-shaven, and well-fed, with a round and happy face. He looked far from ferocious . . .

"Lion! Bring 'em here!"

Lion looked around, disconcerted. "I have an empty table in the corner, but if you would prefer Merle's company . . ."

The man who had called was tremendous. The huge platter before him bore an entire swordfish fillet. Durily stared in what might have been awe or admiration. "Merle, by all means! And can you be persuaded to join us, Lion?"

"I would be delighted." Lion escorted them to the huge man's table and seated them. "The swordfish is good—"

"The swordfish is *wonderful!*" Merle boomed. He'd made amazing progress with the half-swordfish while they were approaching. "It's baked with apricots and slivered nuts and . . . something else, I can't tell. Lion?"

"The nuts are soaked in a liqueur called *brosa*, from Rynildissen, and dried in the oven."

"I'll try it," Karskon said, and Durily nodded. Lion disappeared into the kitchen.

The noise level was rising toward its previous pitch. Durily raised her voice just high enough. "Most of you seem to be fishers. It must have been hard for you after the merpeople went away."

"It was, Lady. They had to learn to catch their own fish instead of trading. All the techniques had to be invented from scratch. They tell me they tried magic at first. To breathe water, you know. Some of them drowned. Then came fishing spears, and special boats, and nets . . ."

"You said *they?*"

"I'm a whale," said Merle. "I came later."

"Oh. There aren't many were-folk around these days. Anywhere."

"We aren't all gone," Merle said, while Karskon smiled at how easily they had broached the subject. "The merpeople went away, all right, but it wasn't just because they're magical creatures. Their life-*styles* include a lot of magic. Whales don't practice much magic."

"Even so," Karskon wondered, "what are you doing on land? Aren't you afraid you might, ah, change? Magic isn't dependable anymore . . ."

"But Lion is. Lion would get me out in time. Anyway, I spend most of my time aboard *Shrimp*. See, if the change comes over me there, it's no problem. A whale's weight would swamp my little boat and leave me floating."

"I still don't see—"

"Sharks."

"Ah."

"Damn brainless toothy wandering weapons! The more you kill, the more the blood draws more till . . ." Merle shifted restlessly. "Anyway, there are no sharks ashore. And there are books, and people to talk to. Out on the sea there's only the singing. Now, I like the singing; who wouldn't? But it's only family gossip, and weather patterns, and shoreline changes, and where are the fish."

"That sounds useful."

"Sure it is. Fisherfolk learn the whale songs to find out where the fish are. But for any kind of intelligent conversation you have to come ashore. Ah, here's Lion."

Lion set three plates in place, bearing generous slabs of swordfish and vegetables cooked in elaborate fashions. "What's under discussion?"

"Were-creatures," Karskon said. "They're having a terrible time of it almost everywhere."

Lion sat down. "Even in Rynildissen? The wolf people sector?"

"Well," Durily said uncomfortably, "they're changing. You know, there are people who can change into animals, but that's because there are were folk among their ancestors. Most were-folk are animals who learned how to take human form. The human shape has magic in it, you know." Lion nodded, and she continued. "In places where the magic's gone, it's terrible. The animals lose their minds. Even human folk with some animal ancestry, they can't make the change, but their minds aren't quite human either. Wolf ancestry makes for good soldiers, but it's hard for them to stop. A touch of hyena or raccoon makes for thieves. A man with a touch of lion makes a good general, but—"

Merle shifted restlessly, as if the subject were painful to him. His platter was quite clean now. "Oh, to hell with the problems of were-folk. Tell me how you lost your eye."

Karskon jumped, but he answered. "Happened in the

baths when I was thirteen. We were having a fight with wet towels and one of my half-brothers flicked my eye out with the corner of a towel. Dull story.''

"You should make up a better one. Want some help?'' Karskon shook his head, smiling despite himself. ''Where are you from?''

"Inland. It's been years since I tasted fresh fish. You were right, it's wonderful.'' He paused, but the silence forced him to continue. ''I'm half Torovan, half Minterl. Duke Chamil of Konth made me his librarian, and I teach his legitimate children. Lady Durily descends from the old Minterl nobility. She's one of Duchess Chamil's ladies-in-waiting. That's how we met.''

"I never understood shoreside politics,'' Merle said. ''There was a war, wasn't there, long ago?''

Karskon answered for fear that Durily would. ''Torov invaded after the quake. It was an obvious power vacuum. I gather the armies never got this far south. What was left of the dukes surrendered first. You'll find a good many of the old Minterls hereabouts. The Torovans have to go in packs.''

Merle was looking disgusted. ''Whales don't play at war.''

"It's not a game,'' Karskon said.

Lion added, ''Or at least the stakes are too high for ordinary people.''

There was murky darkness, black with a hint of green. Blocky shapes. Motion flicked past, drifted back more slowly. Too dark to see, but Karskon sensed something looking back at him. A fish? A ghost?

Karskon opened his good eye.

Durily was at the window, looking out to sea. Leftward, waves washed the spike of island that had been Crown Hill. ''There was grass almost to the top,'' Durily said, ''but the peak was always a bare knob. We picnicked there once, the whole family . . ."

"What else do you remember? Anything we can use?"

"Two flights of stairs," Durily said. "You've seen the one that winds up the outside of the tower, like a snake. Snake-headed, it used to be, but the quake must have knocked off the head."

"Animated?"

"No, just a big carving . . . um. It could have been animated once. The magic was going out of everything. The merpeople were all gone; the mainlanders were trying to learn to catch their own fish, and we had trouble getting food. Nihilil was thinking of moving the whole court to Beesh. Am I rambling too much, darling?"

"No telling what we can use. Keep it up."

"The inside stairs lead down from the kitchen, through the laundry room on this floor and through Thone's room on the lower floor."

"Thone." Karskon's hand strayed to his belt buckle, which was silver and massive—which was in fact the hilt of a concealed dagger. "He's not as big as Lion, but I'd hate to have him angry with me. They're all too big. We'd best not be caught . . . unless we, or *you*, can find a legitimate reason for being in Thone's room?"

Durily scowled. "He's just not interested. He sees me, he knows I'm a woman, but he doesn't seem to care . . . or else he's very stupid about suggestions. That's possible."

"If he's part of a were-lion family—"

"He wouldn't mate with human beings?" Durily laughed, and it sounded like silver coins falling. No, he thought, she wouldn't have had trouble seducing a young man . . . or *anything* male. *I* gave her no trouble. Even now, knowing the truth . . .

"Our host isn't a were-lion," she said. "Lions eat red meat. We've brought red meat to his table, but he was eating fish. Lions don't lust for a varied diet, and they aren't particular about what they eat. Our host has exquisite taste. If I'd known how fine a cook he is, I'd have come for that alone.''

"He shows some other signs. The whole family's big, but he's a lot bigger. Why does he shave his face and clip his hair short? Is it to hide a mane?"

"Does it matter if they're lions? We don't want to be caught,'' Durily said. "Any one of them is big enough to be a threat. Stop fondling that canapé sticker, dear. On this trip we use stealth and magic.''

Oddly reluctant, Karskon said, "Speaking of magic . . .''

"Yes. It's time.''

"You're quite right. They're hiding something,'' Lion said absently. He was carving the meat from a quarter of ox and cutting it into chunks, briskly, apparently risking his fingers at every stroke. "What of it? Don't we all have something to hide? They are my guests. They appreciate my food.''

"Well,'' said his wife, "don't we all have something worth gossiping about? And for a honeymooning couple—''

At which point Estrayle burst into a peal of laughter.

Arilta asked, "Now what brought that on?'' But Estrayle only shook her head and bent over the pale yellow roots she was cutting. Arilta turned back to her husband. "They don't seem loving enough somehow. And she so beautiful, too.''

"It makes a pattern,'' Lion said. "The woman is beautiful, as you noticed. She is the Duchess's lady-in-waiting. The man serves the Duke. Could Lady Durily be the Duke's mistress? Might the Duke have married her to one of his men? It would provide for her if she's pregnant. It might keep the Duchess happy. It happens.''

Arilta said, "Ah.'' She began dumping double handfuls of meat into a pot. Estrayle added the chopped root.

"On the other hand," Lion said, "she is of the old Mint-erl aristocracy. Karskon may be too—half anyway. Perhaps they're not welcome near Beesh because of some failed plot. The people around here are of the old Minterl blood. They'd protect them, if it came to that."

"Well," his wife teased with some irritation, "which is it?"

Lion teased her with a third choice. "They spend money freely. Where does it come from? They could be involved in a theft we will presently hear about."

Estrayle looked up from cutting onions, tears dripping past a mischievous smile. "Listen for word of a large cat's-eye emerald."

"Estrayle, you will explain that!" said her mother.

Estrayle hesitated, but her father's hands had stopped moving and he was looking up. "It was after supper," she said. "I was turning down the beds. Karskon found me. We talked a bit, and then he, well, made advances. Poor little man, he weighs less than I do. I slapped him hard enough to knock that lovely patch right off his face. Then I informed him that if he's interested in marriage he should be talking to my father, and in any case there are problems he should be aware of . . ." Her eyes were dancing. "I must say he took it well. He asked about my dowry! I hinted at undersea treasures. When I said we'd have to live here, he said at least he'd never have to worry about the cooking, but his religion permitted him only one wife, and I said what a pity—"

"The jewel," Lion reminded her.

"Oh, it's beautiful! Deep green, with a blazing vertical line, just like a cat's eye. He wears it in the socket of his right eye."

Arilta considered. "If he thinks that's a safe place to hide it, he should get another patch. Someone might steal that silver thing."

"Whatever their secret, it's unlikely to disturb us," Lion said. "And this is their old seat of royalty. Even the ghost . . . Which reminds me. Jarper?"

He spoke to empty air, and it remained empty. "I haven't seen Jarper since lunch. Has anyone?"

Nobody answered. Lion continued, "He was behind Karskon at lunch. Karskon must have something magical on him. Maybe the jewel? Oh, never mind, Jarper can take care of himself. I was saying he probably won't bother our guests; he's of old Minterl blood himself. If he had blood."

They stuffed wool around the door and windows. They propped a chair under the doorknob. Karskon and Durily had no intention of being disturbed at this point. An inn-keeper who found his guests marking patterns on the floor with powdered bone, and heating almost-fresh blood over a small flame, could rightly be expected to show annoyance.

Durily spoke in a language once common to the Sorcerer's Guild, now common to nobody. The words seemed to hurt her throat, and no wonder, Karskon thought. He had doffed his silver eye patch. He tended the flame and the pot of blood, and stayed near Durily, as instructed.

He closed his good eye and saw green-tinged darkness. Something darker drifted past, slowly, something huge and rounded that suddenly vanished with a flick of finny tail. Now a drifting current of luminescence . . . congealing, somehow, to a vaguely human shape . . .

The night he robbed the jewel merchant's shop, this sight had almost killed him.

The Movement had wealth to buy the emerald, but Durily swore that the Torovan lords must not learn that the jewel existed. She hadn't told him why. It wasn't for the Movement that he had obeyed her. The Movement would destroy the Torovan invaders, would punish his father and his half-brothers for their arrogance, for the way they had treated him . . . for his eye. But he had obeyed *her*. He was her slave in those days, the slave of his lust for the lady Durily, his father's mistress.

He had guessed that it was *glamour* that held him: magic. It hadn't seemed to matter. He had invaded the jeweler's shop expecting to die, and it hadn't mattered.

The merchant had heard some sound and come to investigate. Karskon had already scooped up everything of value he could find, to distract attention from the single missing stone. Waiting for discovery in the dark cellar, he had pushed the jewel into his empty eye socket.

Greenish darkness, drifting motion, a sudden flicker that might be a fish's tail. Karskon was seeing with his missing eye.

The jeweler had found him while he was distracted, but Karskon had killed him after all. Afterward, knowing that much, he had forced Durily to tell the rest. She had lost a good deal of her power over him. He had outgrown his terror of that greenish dark place. He had seen it every night while he waited for sleep, these past two years.

Karskon opened his good eye to find that they had company. The color of fading fog, it took the wavering form of a wiry old man garbed for war, with his helmet tucked under his arm.

"I want to speak to King Nihilil," Durily said. "Fetch him."

"Your pardon, Lady." The voice was less than a whisper, clearer than a memory. "I c-can't leave here."

"Who were you?"

The fog-wisp straightened to attention. "Sergeant Jarper Sleen, serving Minterl and the King. I was on duty in the watchtower when the land th-th-thrashed like an island-fish submerging. The wall broke my arm and some ribs. After things got quiet again there were only these three floors left, and no food anywhere. I s-starved to death."

Durily examined him with a critical eye. "You seem nicely solid after seventy-six years."

The ghost smiled. "That's the Lion's doing. He lets me take the smells of his cooking as offerings. But I can't leave where I d-died."

"Was the King home that day?"

"Lady, I have to say he was. The quake came fast. I don't doubt that he drowned in his throne room."

"Drowned," Durily said thoughtfully. "All right." She poured a small flask of seawater into the blood, which was now bubbling. Something must have been added to keep it from clotting. She spoke high and fast in the Sorcerer's Guild tongue.

The ghost of Jarper Sleen sank to its knees. Karskon saw the draperies wavering as if heated air was moving there, and when he realized what that meant, he knelt too.

An unimaginative man would have seen nothing. This ghost was more imagination than substance; in fact the foggy crown had more definition, more reality, than the head beneath. Its voice was very much like a memory surfacing from the past . . . not even Karskon's past, but Durily's.

"You have dared to waken Minterl's king."

Seventy-six years after the loss of Atlantis and the almost incidental drowning of the seat of government of Minterl, the ghost of Minterl's king seemed harmless enough. But Durily's voice quavered. "You knew me. Durily. Lady Tinylla of Beesh was my mother."

"Durily. You've grown," said the ghost. "Well, what do you want of me?"

"The barbarians of Torov have invaded Minterl."

"Have you ever been tired unto death, when the pain in an old wound keeps you awake nonetheless? Well, tell me of these invaders. If you can lure them here, I and my army will pull them under the water."

Karskon thought that Minterl's ancient king couldn't have drowned a bumblebee. Again he kept silent, while Durily said, "They invaded the year after the great quake. They have ruled Minterl for seventy-four years. The palace is drowned but for these top floors.'' Durily's voice became a whip. ''They are used as an inn! Rabbits and chickens are kept where the fighting-birds roosted!''

The ghost-king's voice grew stronger. ''Why was I not told?''

This time Karskon spoke. ''We can't lure them here, to a drowned island. We must fight them where they rule, in Beesh.''

''And who are you?''

''I am Karskon Lor, Your Majesty. My mother was of Beesh. My father, a Torovan calling himself a lord, Chamil of Konth. Lord Chamil raised me to be his librarian. His legitimate sons he—'' Karskon fell silent.

''You're a bastard?''

''Yes.''

''But you would strike against the Torovan invaders. How?''

Durily seemed minded to let him speak. Karskon lifted the silver eye patch to show the great green gem. ''There were two of these, weren't there?''

''Yes.''

''Durily tells me they were used for spying.''

The King said, ''That was the traveling stone. Usually I had it mounted in a ring. If I thought a lord needed watching, I made him a present of it. If he was innocent, I made him another present and took it back.''

Karskon heaved a shuddering sigh. He had *almost* believed; always he had *almost* believed.

Durily asked, ''Where was the other stone?''

''Did your mother tell you of my secret suite? For times when I wanted company away from the Queen? It was a very badly kept secret. Many ladies could describe that room. Your mother was one.''

''Yes.''

The ghost smiled. ''But it stood empty most of the time, except for the man on watch in the bathing chamber. There is a statue of the one-eyed god in the bathing chamber, and its eye is a cat's-eye emerald.''

Durily nodded. "Can you guide us there?"

"I can. Can you breathe under water?"

Durily smiled. "Yes."

"The gem holds *mana*. If it leaves Minterl Castle, the ghosts will fade."

Durily lost her smile. "King Nihilil—"

"I will show you. Duty runs two ways between a king and his subjects. Now?"

"A day or two. We'll have to reach the stairwell, past the innkeeper's family."

The ghost went where ghosts go. Karskon and Durily pulled the wool loose from the windows and opened them wide. A brisk sea wind whipped away the smell of scorched blood. "I wish we could have done this on the roof," she said viciously. "Among Lion's damned chickens. Used their blood."

It happened the second day after their arrival. Karskon was expecting it.

The dining room was jammed before noon. Lion's huge pot of stew dwindled almost to nothing. He set his older children to frying thick steaks with black pepper and cream and essence of wine, his younger children to serving. Providentially, Merle showed up, and Lion set him to moving tables and chairs to the roof. The younger children set the extra tables.

Karskon and Durily found themselves squeezing through a host of seamen to reach the roof. Lion laughed as he apologized. "But after all, it's your own doing! I have red meat! Usually there is nothing but fish and shellfish. What do you prefer? My stew has evaporated—*poof*—but I can offer—"

Durily asked, "Is there still fish?" Lion nodded happily and vanished.

Cages of rabbits and pigeons and large, bewildered-looking *moas* had been clustered in the center of the roof, to give the diners a sea view. A salvo of torpedoes shot from the sea: bottle-nosed mammals with a laughing expression. They acted like they were trying to get someone's attention. Merle, carrying a table and chairs, said, "Merpeople. They must be lost. Where the magic's been used up they lose their half-human shape, and their sense too. If they're still around when I put out, I'll lead them out to sea."

Lion served them himself but didn't join them. Today he was too busy. Under a brilliant blue sky they ate island-fish baked with slivered nuts and some kind of liqueur, and vegetables treated with respect. They ate quickly. Butterflies fluttered in Karskon's belly, but he was jubilant.

The Lion had red meat. Of *course* the Attic was jammed, of *course* the Lion and his family were busy as a fallen hive. The third floor would be entirely deserted.

Water, black and stagnant, covered the sixth step down. Durily stopped before she reached it. "Come closer," she said. "Stay close to me."

Karskon's protective urge responded to her fear and her beauty. But, he reminded himself, it wasn't *his* nearness she needed; it was the gem . . . He moved down to join Durily and her ally.

She arrayed her equipment on the steps. No blood this time: King Nihilil was already with them, barely, like an intrusive memory at her side.

She began to chant in the Sorcerer's Guild tongue.

The water sank step by step. What had been done seventy-odd years ago could be undone, partially, temporarily.

Durily's voice grew deep and rusty. Karskon watched as her hair faded from golden to white, as the curves of her body drooped. Wrinkles formed on her face, her neck, her arms.

Glamour is a lesser magic, but it takes *mana*. The magic

that was Durily's youth was being used to move seawater now. Karskon had thought he was ready for this. Now he found himself staring, flinching back, until Durily, without interrupting herself, snarled (teeth brown or missing) and gestured him down.

He descended the wet stone stairs. Durily followed, moving stiffly. King Nihilil floated ahead of them like foxfire on the water.

The sea had left the upper floors, but water still sluiced from the landings. Karskon's torch illuminated dripping walls, and once a stranded fish. Within his chest his heart was fighting for its freedom.

On the fifth floor down there were side corridors. Karskon, peering into their darkness, shied violently from a glimpse of motion. It was an eel flopping as it drowned in air.

Eighth floor down.

Behind him, Durily moved as if her joints hurt. Her appearance repelled him. The deep lines in her face weren't smile wrinkles; they were selfishness, sulks, rage. And her voice ran on, and her hands danced in creaky curves.

She can't hurry. She'd fall. Can't leave her behind. Her spells, my jewel: Keep them together, or— But the ghost was drawing ahead of them. *Would he leave us? Here?* Worse, Nihilil was becoming hard to see. Blurring. The whole corridor seemed filled with the restless fog that was the King's ghost . . .

No. The King's ghost had *multiplied*. A horde of irritated or curious ghosts had joined the procession. Karskon shivered from the cold, and wondered how much the cold was due to ghosts rubbing up against him.

Tenth floor down . . . and the procession had become a crowd. Karskon, trailing, could no longer pick out the King. But the ghosts streamed out of the stairwell, flowed away down a corridor, and Karskon followed. A murmuring was in the air, barely audible, a hundred ghosts whispering gibberish in his ear.

The sea had not retreated from the walls and ceiling there. Water surrounded them, ankle-deep as they walked, rounding up the corridor walls and curving over their heads to form a huge, complex bubble. Carpet disintegrated under his boots.

To his right the wall ended. Karskon looked over a stone railing, down into the water, into a drowned ballroom. There were bones at the bottom, and swamp fires forming on the water's surface. More ghosts.

The ghosts had paused. Now they were like a swirling, continuous, glowing fog. Here and there the motion suggested features . . . and Karskon suddenly realized that he was watching a riot, ghost against ghost. They'd realized why he was here. Drowning the intruders would save the jewel, save their fading lives—

Karskon nerved himself and waded into them. Hands tried to clutch him. A broadsword-shape struck his throat and broke into mist . . .

He was through them, standing before a heavy, ornately carved door. The King's ghost was waiting. Silently he showed Karskon how to manipulate a complex lock. Presently he mimed turning a brass knob and threw his weight back. Karskon imitated him. The door swung open.

A bedchamber, and a canopied bed like a throne. If this place was a ruse, Nihilil must have acted his part with verve. The sea was here, pushing in against the bubble. Karskon could see a bewildered school of minnows in a corner of the chamber. The leader took a wrong turn and the whole school whipped around to follow him, through the water interface and suddenly into the air. They flopped as they fell, splashed into more water, and scattered.

A bead of sweat ran down Durily's cheek.

The King's ghost waited patiently at another door.

Terror was swelling in Karskon's throat. Fighting fear with self-directed rage, he strode soggily to the door and threw it open before the King's warning gesture could register.

He was looking at a loaded crossbow aimed throat-high. The string had rotted and snapped. Karskon remembered to breathe, forced himself to breathe . . .

It was a tiled bathroom, sure enough. There was a considerable array of erotic statuary, some quite good. The Roze-Kattee statue would have been better for less detail, Karskon thought. A skeleton in the pool wore a rotting bath-attendant's kilt; that would be Nihilil's spy. The one-eyed god in a corner . . . yes. The eye not covered by a patch gleamed even in this dim, watery light. Gleamed green, with a bright vertical pupil.

Karskon closed his good eye and found himself looking at himself.

Grinning, eye closed, he moved toward the statue, fumbling in his pouch for the chisel. Odd, to see himself coming toward himself like this. And Durily behind him, the triumph beginning to show through the exhaustion. And behind her—

He drew his sword as he spun. Durily froze in shock as he seemed to leap at her. The bubble of water trembled, the sea began to flow down the walls, before she recovered herself. But by then Karskon was past her and trying to skewer the intruder, who danced back, laughing, through the bedroom and through its ornate door, while Karskon—

Karskon checked himself. The emerald in his eye socket was supplying the *mana* to run the spell that held back the water. It had to stay near Durily. She'd drilled him on this, over and over, until he could recite it in his sleep.

Lion stood in the doorway, comfortably out of reach. He threw his arms wide, careless of the big, broad-bladed kitchen knife in one hand, and said, ''But what a place to spend a honeymoon!''

"Tastes differ," Karskon said. "Innkeeper, this is none of your business."

"There is a thing of power down here. I've known that for a long time. You're here for it, aren't you?"

"The spying stone," Karskon said. "You don't even know what it is?"

"Whatever it is, I'm afraid you can't have it," Lion said. "Perhaps you haven't considered the implications—"

"Oh, but I have. We'll sell the traveling stone to the barbarian king in Beesh. From that moment on the Movement will know everything he does."

"Can you think of any reason why I should care?"

Karskon made a sound of disgust. "So you support the Torovans!"

"I support nobody. Am I a lord, or a soldier? No, I feed people. If someone should supplant the Torovans, I will feed the new conquerors. I don't care who is at the top."

"We care."

"Who? You, because you haven't the rank of your half-brothers? The elderly Lady Durily, who wants vengeance on her enemies' grandchildren? Or the ghosts? It was a ghost who told me you were down here."

Beyond Lion, Karskon watched faintly luminous fog swirling in the corridor. The war of ghosts continued. And Durily was tiring. He couldn't stay here, he had to pry out the jewel. "Is it the jewel you want? You couldn't have reached it without Durily's magic. If you distract her now you'll never reach the air, with or without the jewel. We'll all drown." Karskon kept his sword's point at eye level. If Lion was a were-lion . . .

But he didn't eat red meat.

"The jewel has to stay," Lion said. "Why do you think these walls are still standing?"

Karskon didn't answer.

"The quake that sank Atlantis, the quake that put this entire peninsula underwater. Wouldn't it have shaken down stone walls? But this palace dates from the Sorcerer's Guild period. Magic spells were failing, but not always. The masons built this palace of good, solid stone. Then they had the structure blessed by a competent magician.''

''Oh.''

''Yes. The walls would have been shaken down without the blessing and some source of *mana* to power it. You see the problem. Remove the talisman, the castle crumbles.''

He might be right, Karskon thought. But not until both emeralds were gone, and Karskon too.

Lion was still out of reach. He didn't handle that kitchen knife like a swordsman, and in any case it was too short to be effective. At a dead run Karskon thought he could catch the beefy chef . . . but what of Durily, and the spell that held back the water?

Fool! She had the other jewel!

He charged.

Lion whirled and ran down the hall. The ghost-fog swirled apart as he burst through. He was faster than he looked, but Karskon was faster still. His sword was nearly pricking Lion's buttocks when Lion suddenly leapt over the banister.

Karskon leaned over the dark water. The ghosts crowded around him were his only light source now.

Lion surfaced, thirty feet above the ballroom floor and well out into the water, laughing. ''Well, my guest, can you swim? Many mainlanders can't.''

Karskon removed his boots. He might wait, let Lion tire himself treading water; but Durily must be tiring even faster and growing panicky as she wondered where he had gone. He couldn't leave Lion at their backs.

He didn't dive; he lowered himself carefully into the water, then swam toward Lion. Lion backstroked, grinning. Karskon followed. He was a fine swimmer.

Lion was swimming backward into a corner of the ballroom. Trapping himself. The water surface rose behind him, curving up the wall. Could Lion swim uphill?

Lion didn't try. He dove. Karskon dove after him, kicking, peering down. There were patches of luminosity, confusing . . . and a dark shape far below . . . darting away at a speed Karskon couldn't hope to match. Appalled, Karskon lunged to the surface, blinked, and saw Lion clamber over the railing. He threw Karskon's boots at his head and dashed back toward the King's "secret" bedroom.

The old woman was still waiting, with the King's ghost for her companion. Lion tapped her shoulder. He said, "Boo."

She froze, then tottered creakily around to face him. "Where is Karskon?"

"In the ballroom."

Water was flowing down the walls, knee-high and rising. Lion was smiling as at a secret joke, as he'd smiled while watching her savor her first bite of his incredible swordfish. It meant something different now.

Durily said, "Very well, you killed him. Now, if you want to live, get me that jewel and I will resume the spells. If our plans succeed, I can offer Karskon's place in the new nobility, to you or your son. Otherwise we both drown."

"Karskon could tell you why I refuse. I need the magic in the jewel to maintain my inn. With the jewel Karskon brought me, this structure will remain stable for many years." Lion didn't seem to notice that the King's ghost was clawing at his eyes.

The water was chest-high. "Both jewels, or we don't leave," the old woman said, and immediately resumed her spell, hands waving wildly, voice raspy with effort. She felt Lion's hands on her body and squeaked in outrage, then in terror, as she realized he was tickling her. Then she doubled in helpless laughter.

The water walls were collapsing, flowing down. The odd, magical bubble was collapsing around him. Clawing at the stone banister, Karskon heard his air supply roaring back up the stairwell, out through the broken windows, away. A wave threw him over the banister, and he tried to find his footing, but already it was too deep. Then the air was only a few silver patches on the ceiling, and the seawash was turning him over and over.

A big dark shape brushed past him, fantastically agile in the roiling currents, gone before his sword arm could react. Lion had escaped him. He swam toward one of the smashed ballroom windows, knowing he wouldn't make it, trying anyway. The faint glow ahead might be King Nihilil, guiding him. Then it all seemed to fade and he was breathing water, strangling.

Lion pulled himself over the top step, his flippers already altering to hands. He was gasping, blowing. It was a long trip, even for a sea lion.

The returning sea had surged up the steps and sloshed along the halls and into the rooms where Lion and his family dwelt. Lion shook his head. For a few days they must needs occupy the next level up: the inn, which was now empty.

The change to human form was not so great a change for Lion. He became aware of one last wisp of fog standing beside him.

"Well," it said, "how's the King?"

"Furious," Lion said. "But after all, what can he do? I thank you for the warning."

"I'm glad you could stop them. My curse on their crazy rebellion. We'll all f-fade away in time, I guess, with the magic dwindling and dwindling. But not just yet, if you please!"

"War is bad for everyone," said Lion.

From *FOOTFALL*
(with JERRY POURNELLE)

Bob Gleason was back in California, and we had returned to Mon Grenier. We were driving home. Bob, in the back of my car, was saying, "I think it's time to write the Invasion novel. How soon can you do that?"

I worked it out in my head. "We've got a lot of outstanding contracts. Say five years."

I heard a godawful strangling from behind me. Then, "I think I just saw my whole life pass before me!"

Hell, he could have had it years earlier.

We dug out the old outline. (Bob had looked through that and told us, "Forget the invasion. Do the giant meteoroid impact!")

There was some nice stuff, half forgotten. I had written several scenes with aliens. This one changed enough that I miss it sorely—

> Thousands of alien warriors pour out of ships that slow just enough to drop them, then accelerate back to orbit. The aliens come down on hang gliders. They're wearing foam shoes that will collapse when they hit, so that the bones in their feet won't.
>
> What a Kansas farmer sees is a sky full of baby elephants wearing elevator shoes, dropping out of the sky under paper airplanes.

What he tells the sheriff is, "I didn't get a good look."

We let the baby elephants think in terms of stomping an enemy. "Let's stomp them a little and see what they do." We gave them a surrender reflex: they roll over on their backs to surrender, and the victor puts his foot on the loser's belly. They called their asteroid weapon *the Foot*. VISHNU'S FIST became FOOTFALL.

The Herdmaster's Advisor is not even dead until halfway through the book. We took that long to put the reader in touch with the fithp. We take some pride in being able to embed a murder mystery in the larger tale. A reader *should* be able to solve the mystery before the Herdmaster can. It was up to the authors to help the reader understand the alien invaders to that extent, and to give him the clues he needs.

Del Rey Books doesn't participate in auctions; they don't believe in 'em. Fawcett won the auction for FOOTFALL. Then Del Rey bought Fawcett.

Jerry's ambitions often exceed mine. Our intent was that FOOTFALL would cover all of Earth in present time, with characters numbering in the hundreds . . . as LUCIFER'S HAMMER did, but with a complex group of star-traveling aliens added too.

LUCIFER'S HAMMER had taken a year and a half. We'd promised it in a year. We thought we could do the invasion novel in a year and a half.

What stalled us was Russians.

Jerry knew the Soviets. He'd learned about them as a threat estimate; some of the work he did then is still classified. I waited for him to produce text on the USSR's reaction to invasion by aliens.

Time dragged on. Niven's precarious sanity slipped bit by bit. Pournelle was about to start work in a couple of weeks, *every* week, but first he had to do a little more research . . .

It's obvious only in retrospect. Jerry knew the USSR as a threat estimate. This has nothing to do with writing about them as characters! If he'd said, "This is going to take me six months," I might have gone off and done something else. I might even have volunteered to do it myself! I do understand aliens, after all. Then again, I'm lazy, and we're talking about a *lot* of research . . . and he eventually got through it.

Since Jerry and I first began writing together, our tendency has been to meet to plot out the book, assign each other scenes, then go off to write them. Near the end of FOOTFALL we changed our habit. We wrote in my office, taking turns at the typewriter.

The mood became frenetic.

The more we wrote, the more we saw of scenes that needed to be written. Text in the beginning and middle needed rewriting. The end of the book receded before us like a ghost. Spring became summer . . . yet what we were writing was *superb*, it was *needed*, and the end *was* inching near.

Came the day we worked on the penultimate chapter. We planned a wrap-up-the-threads chapter to follow.

Jerry took his turn. *Will the aliens honor a conditional surrender? The Threat Team dithers. The President makes his choice* . . .

My turn, with the aliens. *Surrender, or all will die! But the Herdmaster must have permission of the females* . . . I was typing fast enough to break bones.

. . . *set their feet on the Herdmaster's chest.* I jumped up. "If I don't quit now I'll go into Cheyne-Stokes breathing," I said.

Jerry read it through. "I can improve this," he said, and typed, "30" (The End.)

The Herdmaster had climbed a huge pillar plant. Like the humans themselves, in the minuscule gravity he had become a brachiator. He found the viewpoint odd, amusing. He watched.

In a forward corner of the Garden the human prisoners worked. The Herdmaster admired their agility, newly trained dirtyfeet that they were. They seemed docile enough as they planted alien seeds in alien soil. Yet the Breakers' disturbing reports could not be ignored much longer. It was more than enough to make his head ache.

Yet here were smells to ease his mind: plants in bloom, and a melancholy whiff of funereal scent. The end of life for the Traveler Fithp was the funeral pit, and then the Garden. Twelve fithp warriors, wounded on Winterhome, had gone to the funeral pit after Digit Ship *Six* returned them to *Message Bearer*.

The Garden was in perpetual bloom. Seasons mixed here, created by differing intensities of light, warmth, moisture. The alien growths might require alterations in weather. He hoped otherwise. Winterhome would be hospitable to Garden life, if the humans actually persuaded anything to grow here.

The Herdmaster would have preferred to loll in warm mud, but *Message Bearer*'s mudrooms had been drained while her drive guided the Foot toward its fiery fate. He had sought rest in the Garden; and it was here that the Year Zero Fithp confronted him. In the riot of scents he had not smelled their presence. Suddenly faces were looking at him over the edges of leaf-spiral, below him on the trunk of the pillar plant.

He looked back silently, letting them know that they had disturbed his time of quiet.

Born within a few eight-days of each other in an orgy of reproduction that had not been matched before or since, the Year Zero Fithp all looked much alike: smooth of skin, long-limbed and lean. Why not? But age clusters didn't always think so much alike. These were the inner herd that led the larger herd of dissidents.

One was different. He looked older than the rest. His skin was darkened and roughened, one leg was immobilized with braces, and there was a *look*. This one had seen horrors.

With the Advisor's consent, the Herdmaster had chosen to divide the Year Zero Fithp. Half the males had gone down to Winterhome. They were dead, or alive and circling Winterhome after the natives' counterattack. That injured one must be fresh from the wars.

The Herdmaster's claws gripped the trunk as he faced nine fithp below him. For a moment he thought to summon warriors; then a sense of amusement came over him. Dissidents they might be, but these were not rebels. So. They sought to awe the Herdmaster, did they?

And they had brought a hero fresh from the wars. No, these were no rogues. They wanted only to increase their influence . . .

"You have found me," he said mildly. "Speak."

Still they were silent. Two of the smaller humans wandered toward the group, but were retrieved by Tashayamp. Now the humans worked more slowly. They watched, no doubt, though they must be out of earshot. What passed here might affect all the herds of Winterhome. Still it was an imposition, and the Herdmaster would have asked Tashayamp to remove them if he could have spared the attention.

Finally one spoke. "Advisor Fathisteh-tulk had said that he would gather with us. He said that he had something to tell us. He did not come. We are told that he has not been seen on the bridge in two days."

"He has neglected his duties," Pastempeh-keph said mildly. "He has avoided the bridge, and his mate, nor does he answer calls. I have alerted my senior officers, but no others. Is it your will that I should ask for his arrest?"

They looked at each other, undecided. One said firmly, "No, Herdmaster." He was a massive young fi', posed a bit ahead of the others: Rashinggith, the Defensemaster's son.

"So you do not know where he is either?"

"We had hoped to find him through you, Herdmaster."

"Ha. I have asked his mate. She has not seen him, yet she has a newborn to show." The Herdmaster became serious. "There are matters to decide, and we have no Advisor. What must I do?"

They looked at each other again. "The teqthuktun—"

"Precisely." Pastempeh-keph breathed more easily. They still worried about the Law and their religion. Not rogues, not yet. "I can take no counsel nor make any decisions without advice from the sleepers. It is the teqthuktun, the pact we made with them, and Fistarteh-thuktun insists upon it. Now I have no Advisor, and there are matters to decide. Speak. What must I do?"

"You must find another Advisor," the wounded one said.

"Indeed." This hardly required discussion. The Traveler fithp might continue on their predetermined path, but no new decisions could be made without an Advisor.

Fathisteh-tulk might be dead, or too badly injured to perform his duties. He might have shirked his duty, crippling the herd at a critical moment. He might have been kidnapped . . . and if some herd within the Traveler Herd had been pushed to such an act, it would be stripped of its status. But the Advisor would still lose his post, for arousing such anger, for being so careless, for being *gone*.

The Herdmaster had already decided on his successor. Still, he must be found. "You, the injured one—"

"Herdmaster, I am Eight-Squared Leader Chintithpit-mang."

He had heard that name; but where? Later. "You must come fresh from the digit ship. Do you know anything of this? Or are you only here to add numbers?"

"I know nothing of the Advisor. What I do know—"

"Later. You, Rashinggith. If you knew where the Advisor might be, you would go there."

His digits knotted and flexed. "I assuredly would, Herdmaster."

"But you might not tell me. Is there a place known only to dissidents? A place where he might commune with other dissidents, or only with himself?"

"No. Herdmaster, we fear for him."

There must be such a place, but the dissidents themselves would have searched it by now. "I too fear for Fathisteh-tulk," the Herdmaster admitted. "I went so far as to examine records of use of the airlocks, following which I summoned a list of fithp in charge of *guarding* the airlocks."

"I chance to know that no dissidents guard the airlocks," Rashinggith said.

An interesting admission. "I was looking for more than dissidents. Did it strike any of you that what Fathisteh-tulk was doing was dangerous? Consider the position of the sleepers. In herd rank the Advisor is the only sleeper of any real authority. The sleepers could not ask his removal. Yet he consistently opposed the War for Winterhome. How many sleepers are dissidents? I know only of one: Fathisteh-tulk."

They looked at each other, and the Herdmaster knew at once that other sleepers held dissident views. *Later*. "There are sleepers in charge of guarding the airlocks. The drive is more powerful than the pull of the Foot's mass. A corpse would drop behind, but would not disintegrate. The drive flame is hot but not dense. Our telescopes have searched for traces of a corpse in our wake." Pause. "There is none.

"Shall we consider murder, then? By dissidents seeking a martyr, or conservative sleepers avoiding future embarrassment? Or did Fathisteh-tulk learn something that some fi' wanted hidden? Or is he alive, hiding somewhere for his own purposes? Rashinggith, what did Fathisteh-tulk plan to tell you?" The Herdmaster looked about him. "Do any of you know? Did he leave hints? Did he even have interesting questions when last you saw him?"

"We don't *know* he's dead," Rashinggith said uneasily.

"Enough," the Herdmaster said. "We will find him. I hope to ask him where he has been." That was a half-truth. Fathisteh-tulk would cause minimal embarrassment by being dead. On to other matters. The Herdmaster had remembered a name.

"Chintithpit-mang, you had something to say?"

Nervous but dogged, the injured warrior got his mouth working. "The prey, the humans, they don't know how to surrender."

"They can be taught."

"There was a—a burly one, bigger than most. I whipped his toy weapon from his hand and knocked him down and put my foot on his chest and he clawed at me with his bony digits until I pushed harder. I think I crushed him. Of the prisoners we brought back, only the scarlet-headed exotic would help us select human food! Even after we take their surrender they do not cooperate. Must we teach them to surrender, four billion of them, one at a time? We must abandon the target world. If we kill them all, the stink will make Winterhome like one vast funeral pit!"

Chintithpit-mang was one of six officers under Siplisteph.

Siplisteph was a sleeper; his mate had not survived frozen sleep, and he had not mated since. He had reached Winterhome as eight-cubed leader of the intelligence group. It was an important post, and Siplisteph had risen higher still due to deaths among his superiors. The Herdmaster intended to ask him to become his Advisor, subject to the approval of the females of the sleeper herd—and Fistarteh-thuktun, as keeper of the teqthuktun.

Chintithpit-mang was among those who might have Siplisteph's post.

"Why did you seek me?" the Herdmaster demanded.

The response was unexpected: first one, then others, began a keening wail. The rest joined.

It was the sound made by lost children.

Frightening. Why do I feel the urge to join my voice to theirs?

"We no longer know who we are, Herdmaster," Chintithpit-mang blurted. "Why are we here?"

"We bear the thuktunthp."

"The creatures do not seek the thuktunthp. They have their own way," Chintithpit-mang insisted.

"If they do not know the thuktunthp, how can they know they do not seek them?" *Could this one be worthy of promotion? Are any? Shall I ask him to remain? No. Now is not the time to judge him, fresh from battle and still twitching, injured, and plunged suddenly into the scents of blooming Winter Flower and sleeper females in heat.* "Chintithpit-mang, you need time and rest to recover from your experience. Go now. All of you, go."

For one moment they stood. Then they filed away.

The Herdmaster remained in the Garden, trying to savor its peace.

Chintithpit-mang did not now seem a candidate for high office. Another dissident! Yet he had fought well on Winterhome; his record was exemplary. Give him a few days.

Meanwhile, interview his mate. Then see if she could pull him together. He didn't remember Shreshleemang well . . . though the mang family was a good line. At a Shipmaster's rank the female *must* be suitable and competent.

Where was Fathisteh-tulk? Murdered or kidnapped. He had suspected the Year Zero Fithp, but that now seemed unlikely. They were nervous, disturbed, as well they should be; but not nervous enough. They could not have hidden that from him. Who, then, had caused the Herdmaster's Advisor to vanish? How many? Of what leaning? He might face a herd too large to fear the justice of the Traveler Herd; though the secrecy with which they had acted argued against it.

There were herds within herds within the Traveler Herd. It must have been like this on the Homeworld too, though in greater, deeper, more fantastical variety. Even here: sleepers, spaceborn, dissidents; Fistarteh-thuktun's core of tradition-minded historians, the Breakers' group driving themselves mad while trying to think like alien beings: the Herdmaster must balance them like a pyramid of smooth rocks in varying thrust.

A clump of cars and people was clustered around a big semi ahead. "We're just about to Collinston," Harry shouted. "That looks like trouble."

He slowed, and drove the motorcycle up to the semi. A highway patrol cruiser was parked nearby, and a lieutenant of the highway patrol stood facing a knot of angry farmers and truckers. Most of them held rifles or shotguns.

"Oh, *shit*," Harry muttered.

The lieutenant eyed Harry and Carlotta. Red beard, dirty clothes; middle-aged woman in designer jeans. He watched Carlotta dismount. "Yes, madam?"

"I am Carlotta Dawson. Yes, *Dawson*. My husband was aboard the Soviet Kosmograd. Lieutenant, I gather there is an alien here?"

"Damn straight," one of the truck drivers shouted. "Goddam snout blew George Mathers in half!" He brandished a military rifle. "Now it's our turn!"

"We have to take it alive," Carlotta stated.

"Bullshit!" This one was a farmer. "I come out of Logan, lady. The goddam snouts killed my sister! They're all over the fucking place."

"How'd you get out? Foot on your chest?" Harry asked. The driver looked sheepish.

"Thought so," Harry said. "Look, give us a chance. The military wants to question that thing. We'll go in after it." He pointed to the willow trees a hundred yards from the highway. "Over there, right?"

"Over there and go to hell," someone yelled.

"Let's go," Harry said. He gestured to Carlotta. She climbed on behind. "In there."

"There" was a dirt path leading to the clump of willow trees. As Harry started the motorcycle, he heard one of the truck drivers. "We can blow it away when he gets out."

There were mutters of approval.

When he stopped at the swamp's edge, he could hear something big in the creek.

For Harpanet, things had become very odd. He had gone through terror and out the other side. He was bemused. Perhaps he was mad. Without his herd about him for comparison, how was a fi' to tell?

Try to surrender: fling the gun to the dirt, roll over, belly in the air. The man gapes, turns and lurches away. Chase him down: he screams and gathers speed, falls and runs again, toward lights. Harpanet will seem to be attacking. Cease! Hide and wait.

A human climbs from the cab of a vehicle. Try again? The man scampers into the cab, emerges with something that flames and roars. Harpanet rolls in time to take the cloud of tiny projectiles in his flank instead of his belly. The man fires again.

He has refused surrender. Harpanet trumpets: rage, woe, betrayal. He sweeps up his own weapon and fires back. The enemy's forelimbs and head explode outward from a mist of blood.

In Harpanet's mind his past fades, his future is unreal. His digits stroke his side, feeling for the deathwound.

No deathwound; no hole big enough for a digit to find. What did the human intend? Torture? Harpanet's whole right side is a burning itch covered with a sheen of blood. An eight to the eighth of black dots form a buzzing storm around him. He lurches through the infinite land, away from roads, downhill where he can, within the buzzing storm and the maddening itch. The jaws of his mind close fast on a memory, vivid in all his senses, more real than his surroundings. He moves through an infinite fantasy of planet, seeking the mudroom aboard *Message Bearer*.

Green . . . tall green plants with leaves like knife blades, but they brush away the hungry swarming dots . . . water? Mud!

He rolls through mud and greenery, over and over, freezing from time to time to look, smell, listen.

Harpanet's past fades against the strange and terrible reality. If he has a future, it is beyond imagining, a mist-gray wall. There is only *now*, a moment of alien plants and fiery itch and cool mud, and *here*, mudroom and garden mushed together, nightmarishly changed. He rolls to wash the wounds; he plucks gobs of mud to spread across his tattered flank.

Afraid to leave, afraid to stay. What might taste his blood in the water, and seek its source? The predators of the Homeworld were pictures on a thuktun, ghosts on an old recording tape, but fearsome enough for all their distance. What lurks in these alien waters? But he hears the distant sound of machines passing, and knows that they are not fithp machines.

A machine comes near, louder, louder. Harpanet's ears and eyes project above the water.

The machine balances crazily on two wheels, like men. It slows, wobbles, stops.

Humans approach on foot.

Harpanet's muscles know what to do when he is hurt, exhausted, friendless, desperate, alone. Harpanet's mind finds no other answer. But he sees no future—

He lurches from the water. Alien weapons come to bear. He casts his gun into the weeds. He rolls on his back and splays his limbs and waits.

The man comes at a toppling run. No adult fi' would try to balance so. The man sets a hind foot on Harpanet's chest, with such force that Harpanet can feel it. He swallows the urge to laugh, but such a weight could hardly bend a rib. Nonetheless he lies with limbs splayed, giving his surrender. The man looks down at his captive, breathing as if he has won a race . . .

"We got him!" Harry shouted. "Now what?" He waved uphill, where a score of armed men, hidden, waited with weapons ready.

"I can talk to them—" Carlotta sounded doubtful.

"They won't listen." *And dammit, this is my snout, they can't kill it now.* Harry thought furiously. A guilty grin came, and he lifted the seat of the motorcycle, where he kept his essential tools.

"You've thought of something?"

"Maybe." He dug into the tool roll and found a hank of parachute cord. It was thin, strong enough to hold a man but not much use against one of *those*. He gestured to the captive, using both hands to make "get up" motions.

The alien stood. It looked at them passively.

"Gives me the creeps," Harry said. He clutched his rifle. *One 30-06 in the eye, and we don't have a problem.* "See if it'll carry you," Harry said.

"Carry me?"

"Sheena, Queen of the Jungle. I know they're strong enough."

A dozen truckers and farmers stood with ready weapons.

Harry walked ahead of the invader, leading it on a length of cord. Carlotta rode its back, sidesaddle. She beamed at them. "Hi!" she called.

None of the watchers spoke. Perhaps they were afraid of saying something foolish

"It surrendered," Carlotta shouted. "We'll take it to the government."

There was a loud click as a safety was taken off.

Harry whistled: *Wheep, wheep, wheep!* "Here, Shep! Hey, it's all right, guys. Shep big gray peanut-loving doggie!"

There were sounds of disgust.

Hell, if they'd just sing it straight through and get it over with . . . The red-bearded man seemed intent on his lesson. Roger decided to wait him out. He took out his notebook and idly flipped through the pages. There was a column due at the end of the week. *Somewhere in here is the story I need . . .*

COLORADO SPRINGS: Military intelligence outfit. Interviewing National Guardsmen from the Jayhawk War area. (Goddam, those Kansans think they're tougher than Texans!) Two turned loose two days before. Didn't want to talk to me. Security? Probably. That bottle of I. W. Harper Rosalee found took care of that . . .

RAFAEL ARMANZETTI. Didn't look like a Kansan, "*I was aiming for the head, of course. It was standing broadside to me, and it shot at something and the recoil jerked it back and I though I'd missed. It whipped around and I was looking right into that huge barrel while it pulled the trigger a dozen times in two seconds. I must have shot out the firing mechanism.*

"It must have known I was going to shoot it," Armanzetti had laughed. *"It did the damnedest thing. It fell over and rolled, just like I'd already shot it. Belly up, legs in the air just like a dog that's been trained to play dead."*

"You shot it?"

"Sure. But, my God! How stupid do they think we are?"

JACK CODY. *"When that beam started spiraling in on us, Greg Bannerman just pulled the chopper hard left and started us dropping. 'Jump out,' he said. No special emphasis, but loud. Me, I jumped. I hit water and there was bubbles all around me. Then the lake lit up with this weird blue-green color. I could see the whole lake even through the bubbles. Fish. Weeds. A car on its back. Bubbles like sapphires.*

"Something big splashed in, and then stuff started pattering down, metal, globs of melted helicopter— I've got one here. I caught it while it was sinking.

"The light went out and I came up for air—there was a layer of hot water—and then I looked for the big chunk, and it was Chuck, waving his arms, drowning. I pulled him out. When I saw his back I thought he was a deader. Charred from his heels to his head. I started pushing on his back and he coughed out a lot of water and started breathing. I wasn't sure I'd done right. But the char was just his clothes. It peeled off him and left him, like, naked and sunburned, except his hands. Black. Crisp. He must have put his hands over his neck.

"But we'd be dead like the rest if we didn't just damn well trust Greg Bannerman. Here's to Greg."

LAS ANIMAS, COLORADO: prosperous man, middle-aged, in good shape. Gymnasium-and-massage look. Good shoes, good clothes, all worn out.

He needed a lift. I didn't want to stop, but Rosalee made me do it. Said he looked like somebody I ought to know. Damn, that woman has a good head for a story. Good head—

HARLEY JACKSON GORDON. *"I kept passing dead cars. Then burning cars. I tried to pick up some of the people on foot, but they just shook their heads. It was spooky. Finally I just got out and left my Mercedes sitting in the road. I walked away, and then I went back and put my keys in it. Maybe someone can use it, after this is all over, and I couldn't stand the thought of that Mercedes just rusting in the road. But it felt like bad luck. So I walked. And yes, the snouts came, and yes, I rolled over on my back, but I don't much like talking about that part, if you don't mind."*

COLORADO SPRINGS: GENEVIEVE MARSH. Tall, slender, not skinny. Handsome. Solid bones. No money. Nervous. Sick of talking with military people. Wanted a change. Dinner and candles—

Rosalee left me the money to buy her dinner and bugged out. Goddam. She'd make a hell of a reporter if she could write.

"They had us for two days. We thought they were getting ready to leave, and I guess they were, and they were going to take us with them. We all felt it. But on the last day some of them brought in a steer and some chickens and a duck, or maybe it was a goose. The aliens took us out of the pen, and they

looked us over. Then they pulled me out, and I was hanging on to Gwen and Beatrice so tight I'm afraid I hurt them. And that crazy man from Menninger's who spent all his time curled up with his head in his arms, they pulled on one arm and he had to follow. He never stopped swearing. No sense in it, just a stream of dirty words. They aimed us at the road and one of them s-swatted me on the ass with its—trunk? and I started walking, pulling Gwen along, Beatrice in my arms, and then we ran. Beatrice was like lead. We didn't wait for the crazy man. When the spaceship took off we were far enough away that we only got a hot wind, and that glare. But they took the rest with them, and the animals took our place." (Laughter). *"Maybe, they think the steer will breed!"*

NEAR LOGAN. Whole bunch, all types, digging around in a wrecked Howard Johnson's.

Nobody's too proud to root for garbage now. Shit.

GINO PIETSCH. *"I knew that there'd be a tornado shelter. Every building in Kansas has something, even if it's a brick closet in a motel room. I broke in, and I found the tornado closet, and I hid. The snouts never ever even came looking. I guess they didn't care much, if you were the type to hide. Every so often I came out just long enough to get water. And I was in the closet when the bombs came, and getting pretty hungry, but not hungry enough to come out. How much radiation did I get? Am I going to die?"*

LAUREN, KANSAS:

That page was nearly blank. Roger stared at it. *I have to write it down some day. Damn. Damnation.*
Not just yet . . .

ROGER BROOKS, NATHANIEL REYNOLDS, ROSALEE PI-
NELLI, CAROL NORTH. The snouts were all over the
city. George Bergson came up with the notion of using
Molotov cocktails to wreck a snout tank . . .

When you think you're through, you're not.

Lester Del Rey argued against killing the President.
He made it very plain that he did not insist, but he
felt very strongly about it. We found that we agreed
with him, and we made it work.

We'd been keeping a Cast of Characters throughout. It still needed to be whipped into shape. It covered four pages! We planned to print it on the inside
covers, so that the crowd of names wouldn't scare
readers off. Ultimately it wound up inside *too*. The
best laid plans . . .

The Herdmaster wasn't Herdmaster by the time
that last sentence was written. Yet the phrasing was
so nice! We sweated it through during a long dinner
break, and finally decided. . . . *on the Herdmaster's
Advisor's chest*.

At four dollars a word, the publisher is entitled to
see that every word is perfect.

WORKS IN PROGRESS

It takes me two years to write a book, working alone. Collaborations vary. INFERNO took four months, once Jerry and I started serious writing. Some have taken much longer.

As of October 24, 1990, I'm in the middle of three collaboration novels, and postponing two contracted novels of my own. Older obligations keep popping up: old stories resold for comic books, mail, movie subsidiary rights, read proofs of a collection from an old friend, a novel by a stranger, proofread a finished novella, rewrite biographical material for PLAYGROUNDS OF THE MIND because the facts have changed . . .

Chances are that none of these projects will reach the bookstores ahead of PLAYGROUNDS. So you can't read them yet, but they're all in the chute.

From *THE MOAT AROUND MURCHESON'S EYE*

A sequel to THE MOTE IN GOD'S EYE was always possible. The blockade established at the Murcheson's Eye Jump Point could not hold forever, and I was working out ways to trash it before the book hit print. But Jerry and I don't write sequels just because they're easy.

Then again, there was an option clause.

We thought we'd fulfilled it, twice. I'll never know what really went on during the negotiations between Kirby MacCauley and Ron Busch. Leave it at this: **ten** years ago Jerry and I were persuaded to sign a contract for THE MOAT AROUND MURCHESON'S EYE.

But nobody at Simon & Schuster/Pocket seemed interested in MOAT. The contract blocked us from collaborating on anything until we'd finished MOAT; but not triple collaborations.

So we wrote THE LEGACY OF HEOROT with Steven Barnes. We planned, then dropped a computer game. With Wendy All we wrote a version of A LABOR OF MOLES: returned as too short. We hit a brick wall on FALLEN ANGELS.

Then there was another musical chairs dance at S&S/Pocket. The new guy in charge, Jack Romanos, did his best to get us going again.

So we were at work on MOAT when Jerry dropped out.

Part One went easily. I'd written the first scenes of "The Gripping Hand" years ago. You'll love the "crottled greeps" scene; we based it on a local Indian restaurant.

Part Two was set on Sparta, the seat of government of Jerry's thousand-year-old interstellar empire. He's written several books set in that history—without ever designing a planet Sparta. We did that in his office in a few hours of intensive work.

Then . . . what was happening was this: I'd drive to Jerry's house. We'd spend the whole day gearing up to write. Then he wouldn't have time for a couple of weeks . . . postponed to three . . . then I'd drive to Jerry's house and we'd spend the whole day gearing up to write. It was like being in the government.

It was driving me nuts. I'd pushed the book as far as I could without a collaborator. If I could write the damn thing alone, I'd be doing that. So I waited for Jerry to produce good new text. And I waited three years.

To me it felt like he was in a coma.

He wasn't. Mostly he was working with computers, writing the Users Column for *Byte* magazine (now called *Chaos Manor*), making speeches and so forth. When the Pournelles were imported to the USSR, they learned that Jerry is regarded there as a heavy-duty philosopher. He speaks of computers in language that can be understood and translated across the civilized world and the USSR too.

And he could *generate* stories by taking a collaborator for a brisk walk on the hill that faces his house. That's how he and Steve Stirling wrote their delightful tales of kzinti and thrintun family life for the second and third MAN-KZIN WARS.

(Just kidding. Only a deeply disturbed mind would have used the word *delightful*.)

He just wasn't able to write text.

. . . And then he was.

As I write this, THE MOAT AROUND MURCHESON'S EYE is more than half written (and I'll give up the punning title as soon as I'm offered a better one).

"The Gripping Hand" would make a wonderful graphic novel. You won't see it in print otherwise. Jack Romanos of S&S/Pocket is understandably reluctant to allow that, after waiting so many years for the full novel.

TOURISTS

The bus was supposed to land on the hotel roof at 0830. Kevin and Ruth got there five minutes early. A dozen others waited for the tour to start.

The rooftop was still shadowed by the mountains to the east, but south and west the harbor was in bright sunshine. Even this early the vast harbor bay was lined with the wakes of both big ships and sailing craft. A warren of small boats, power and sail, many of them multi-hulled, jammed much of the docking area nearest the hotel. Most appeared to be yachts, but there were also square-hulled junks covered with laundry and children.

The tops of the mountains to the east and north were hidden in clouds.

Renner pointed. Far to the south they could see where the continent ended in steep mountains. "Blaine Institute is down there. According to the maps it's over a hundred kilometers to the ocean."

"One benefit of Empire," Ruth said. Renner raised an eyebrow. "Clear air. Out in the new provinces they're still burning coal."

"True enough. Bury makes a fortune bringing in fusion plants and power satellites. It helps if your customers have to buy—"

"They don't have to buy from Bury. And even if they did, hey, it's worth it!"

Renner took a deep breath. "Sure."

The bus landed on the hotel roof at exactly 0830. When Kevin and Ruth got on, a small man with a round face and red-veined nose looked at them quizzically. "Sir Kevin Renner?"

"That's me."

"Durk Riley. I'm your guide, sir. And you must be Commander Cohen."

"Did we order a guide?" Ruth asked.

"Nabil," Renner said. "I'm Renner."

"I've reserved you seats, sir." Riley indicated three places near the front of the bus. "Always like to have Navy people with me. I put in nearly forty years. Retired as coxs'n about twenty years ago. I'd have stayed in, but my wife talked me out of it. Civilian life's no good, you know. Nothing to do. Nothing important. Well, I don't mean that the way it sounds—"

Ruth smiled. "We understand."

"Thank you, ma'am. I don't usually talk so much about myself. Sure glad to see Navy people. You Navy, Sir Kevin?"

"Reserve," Kevin said. "Sailing Master. I went inactive about the same time you retired."

Kevin and Ruth took their seats and settled back. Riley produced a hip flask. "Little nip?"

"Thank you, no," Kevin said.

"You're thinking it's a bit early. Guess it is, even for Sparta, but with the short days we tend to do things a little different here."

"Well, why not?" Kevin said. He reached for the flask. "Good stuff. Irish?"

"What they call Irish most places," Riley said. "We just call it whiskey. Better strap in—"

The sky was as crowded as the sea. The bus rose through a swarm of light planes and heavy cargo craft and other airfoil-contoured buses, curved wide away from an empty area a minute before some kind of spacecraft came whistling through it, and went east toward the mountains. It followed the tiers of houses and estates up into the clouds. They broke through cloud cover to see that the black mountain tops went up high above them.

"That's pretty," Ruth said. "What do you call those mountains?"

"Drakenbergs," Riley said. "Run down most of the length of the Serpens. Serpens is the continent."

"Barren up here," Renner said.

The Serpens had a sharp curled spine, black mountain flanks bare of life. Sparta hadn't developed foliage to handle that soil, and it held too much heavy metal for most earthly plants. The tour director told them that and more as they flew along the spine of the continent.

The bus dropped back below the tablecloth of clouds and followed the curve of the mountains to where they dipped into the ocean, dropped to half a kilometer altitude, and headed south across the harbor.

"That's Old Sparta to the left," Riley said. "Parts date back to CoDominium days. See that green patch with tall buildings around it? That's the Palace area."

"Will we go closer?" Ruth asked.

" 'Fraid not. There are Palace tours, though."

Boats of every size moved randomly across the calm water. They continued south. The calm water of the tremendous harbor changed from green to blue, sharply. The sea bottom was visible, still shallow; the boats were fewer, and larger.

"It doesn't show," Ruth said.

"Yeah." Renner had guessed what she meant. "They rule a thousand worlds from here, but . . . It's like the zoo on Mote Prime. *Sure* it's a different world, *sure* there's nothing like it anywhere in the universe, but you get used to that when you travel enough. You expect *major* differences. But it's not fair, Ruth. We look for worlds like Earth because that's where we can live."

Riley was staring. Other heads had turned from windows. *Zoo on Mote Prime?*

"Defenses," Ruth said. "*There's* a difference. Sparta must be the most heavily defended world of all."

"Yeah. And all that means is, there are places the bus won't go. And questions Mr. Riley won't answer."

Riley said, "Well, of course—"

Ruth was smiling. "Don't test that, all right? I *know* you. We're on holiday."

"Okay."

"I don't know anything about Sparta's defenses anyway," Riley said uncomfortably. "Mr. Renner? You were on the Mote expedition?"

"Yup. Riley, I didn't keep any secrets, and it's all been declassified. You can get my testimony under 'What I Did on my Summer Vacation,' by Kevin Renner. Published by Athenaeum in 3021. I get a royalty."

There was a storm to the east. The bus flew west, and dropped even lower (the ride became bumpy) to fly above a huge cargo ship. Big stabilizer fins showed with the roll of the waves, waves the size of small hills. There were pleasure boats too, graceful sailing boats that rolled as they climbed up and down the water mountains; their sails were constantly shifting along the masts.

The bus skimmed over a big island patterned in rectangles of farmland. "That's the Devil Crab," Riley said. "Two sugar cane plantations and maybe a hundred independents. I'd love to be a farmer. They don't pay taxes."

Renner jumped. "Hey?"

"Population's dense on Sparta. The cost of land on Serpens is . . . well, I never tried to buy any, but it's way up there. If the farmers didn't get some kind of break, they'd all sell out to the people who build hotels. Then all the food would have to be shipped in from far away, and where would the Emperor get his fresh fruit?"

"Wow! No taxes. What about these guys below us?"

"They don't pay either. Transport costs are high, and the produce isn't as fresh when it gets to Serpens. The Serpens farmers can still compete. Even so, this is the way I'd go. Lease an island a thousand klicks from Serpens and raise beef. There's no room to raise red meat on Serpens."

They veered away from another rocky island that seemed to be covered with a patchwork of concrete slabs and domes. "There's some of the defense stuff," Renner said. "Battle management radars, and I'd bet there are some pretty hefty lasers in there."

"It's a good guess, but I wouldn't know," Riley said.

Presently the bus turned north and east, and flew toward the narrow hooked spit that enclosed the harbor from the west. "That was the prison colony back in CoDominium days," Riley said. "If you look close you can see where the old wall was. Ran right across the peninsula."

"There? It's mostly parks," Ruth said. "Or—"

"Rose gardens," Riley said. "When Lysander III tore down the old prison walls he gave all that area to the public. There's the rose festival every year. Citizen fraternities compete, and it's a big deal. We do tours every other day, if you're interested."

"Where's Blaine Institute?" Ruth asked.

"Off east. To the right there. See that mountain covered with buildings?"

"Yes—it looks like an old painting I saw once."

"*That's* the Blaine Institute?" Renner said. "Captain Blaine's richer than I suspected. And to think I knew him—"

"Did you, sir?" Riley sounded impressed. "But that's the Biology section of Imperial University. The Institute is the smaller area next to it." He offered his binoculars. "And Blaine Manor sits on the hill just east of that. Would you like a tour of the Institute?"

"Thanks, we'll be there this afternoon," Ruth said.

The bus crossed the narrow spit and then stayed well out over the harbor. The sun had burned off most of the cloud cover over the city. The skyline was a jumble of shapes: in the center and to the south were massive square skyscrapers, thin towers, tall buildings connected by bridges a thousand feet above street level. North of that were lower granite buildings in a classic style. In the center were the green parks of the Palace district.

Renner looked thoughtful. "Ruth, think about it. *The Emperor* is over there. Just lob a big fusion bomb in the general direction of the Palace—"

He stopped because everyone on the bus was looking at him.

"Hey! I'm a Naval Reserve officer!" he said quickly. "I'm trying to figure out how you keep someone else from doing it. With this many people on Sparta, and visitors from everywhere, there're bound to be crazies . . ."

"We get our share, Sir Kevin." Riley emphasized the title so everyone would hear it.

"We do check on people coming to Sparta," Ruth said. Her voice had dropped. "And it's not all that easy to buy an atom bomb."

"That might stop amateurs—"

"Oh, all right," Ruth said. "Drop it, huh? It's a depressing thought."

"It's something we live with," Riley said. "Look, we have ways to spot the crazies. And generally professionals won't try, because it won't do them any good. Everybody knows the Royal Family's never all in the same place. Prince Aeneas doesn't even live on this planet. Blow up Serpens and you'll get the Fleet mad as hell, but you won't kill the Empire. One thing we do not do—sir—is tell everybody on a random tour bus all about the defenses!"

"And one thing I don't do," Renner answered—and his voice had dropped low, "is guard my mouth. It would prevent me from learning things. Even so: sorry."

Riley grunted. "Yes, sir. Look over there. Those are the fish farms." He pointed to a series of brightly colored sea patches divided by low walls. "That's another good racket. Fish from off-planet don't do well out in Sparta's oceans. You want sea bass or ocean cat, it'll come from here or someplace like it."

From *FALLEN ANGELS*

James Patrick Baen, the editor and publisher, once told me that he wanted to write a novel.

Jim is more interested in politics than I am. Otherwise he's pro-technology, pro-space, and perceives a lot of humankind as fools. The way to keep the environment clean is to move the polluting industries into space, strip-mine asteroids instead of real estate . . . and so forth; you've read the sermons.

What the hell: I spent most of that evening carving out a story line with him.

Then I went home and forgot about it until, at a dinner that included the Pournelles, Jim described the story back to me. What he wanted now was a Niven/Pournelle collaboration. He could have had a Niven story years earlier.

FALLEN ANGELS involves a near-future Earth whose space programs have collapsed worldwide after generating a space station or two, maybe a moon base, a handful of ships . . . They're hanging on by the skin of their teeth. They're scoop-diving the Earth's atmosphere for nitrogen. Greens are in power in the USA, and they've cleaned up the environment, shutting down the greenhouse effect. Earth is in an ice age.

A missile wounds a scoop ship and brings it down on the ice cap. The Angels can't move in Earth's savage gravity. They must be rescued, and somehow returned to orbit, by the heroic underground: by organized science fiction fandom.

We didn't see FALLEN ANGELS as a money maker.

This one was a gift for the fans, and for pure fun. We were looking down the barrels of the MOAT contract; so we asked an old friend to act as third collaborator, to buy us some time.

Several years later, after he had produced nothing whatever, we invited him out.

I then spoke to Jim Baen as follows: "We need a third collaborator. Jerry and I tried picking one ourselves, and discovered ourselves to be inept. You seem to be good at that. You want a novel, *find a writer.*"

And he found a quality control specialist named Mike Flynn . . . who knew nothing of organized science fiction fandom.

I've got to tell you, It's been nothing but fun since then.

Flynn lives on the wrong coast, but he came as far as San Francisco for a convention of quality control specialists—he was a speaker—and I flew up to meet him. ("I'm going to tell funny stories." A *quality control specialist*? Yes, he *does* have funny stories. *Very.*) We talked story. I introduced him to Patricia Davis (artist) and Adrienne Martine-Barnes (author). I got him to a Westercon, and he met more of us. He's been attending East Coast conventions. I've been writing and sending him biographical squibs of friends.

Flynn doesn't use the same software *or* hardware we do. He pulled 70,000 words ahead of us, with Jerry and me backseat driving as best we could, before Baen got us a disk Jerry's computers could read.

Then . . . Jerry had shown me good new text for MOAT. Hallelujah! Time to resume work. But first . . . we spent nine days blitzing FALLEN ANGELS.

We hadn't worked together in three years. It was intense. Jerry's huge office, Chaos Manor, is a maze of computers waiting to be critiqued. He set one computer up for me and worked his own simultaneously.

The book changed shape under our hands. A solid block of Flynn's lecturing on the coming Ice Age got integrated into one hell of a party. I wrote a filksong—not my first, but the first I've been proud of—and integrated that too, as sung by anarchist Jenny Trout, daughter of a science fiction writer who vanished on his fiftieth birthday. I've told the real-life Leslie Fish about this scene; she thinks it's hilarious, and she plans to sing the song.

WANTED FAN

Wanted fan in Luna City, wanted fan on Dune and
 Down,
Wanted fan at Ophiuchus, wanted fan in Dydeetown.
All across the sky they want me, am I flattered? Yes I
 am!
If I could just reach orbit, then I'd be a wanted fan.

Wanted fan for mining coal and wanted fan for drilling
 oil,
I went very fast through Portland, hunted hard like
 Gully Foyle.
Built reactors in Seattle against every man's advice,
Couldn't do that in Alaska, Fonda says it isn't nice.

*"Nice touch, Jenny. They'll be expecting you to rhyme it
with 'ice'."*
*"You don't really think the nukes could have saved
Alaska, do you, Jenny?"*
Alaska had been beneath the ice for fifteen years . . .

Wanted fan for plain sedition, like the singing of this
 tune.
If NASA hadn't failed us we'd have cities on the
 Moon.
If it { weren't for fucking NASA   we'd at least have
      { hadn't been for NASA   walked on Mars.
If I never can make orbit, then I'll never reach the stars.

Naders Raiders want my freedom, OSHA wants my
 scalp and hair,

If I'm wanted in Wisconsin, be damned sure I won't
    be there!

If the E-P-A still wants me, I'll avoid them if I can.
They're tearing down the cities, so I'll be a wanted
    fan!

Wanted fan on Jinx and Sparta and the Hub's ten
    million stars,
Wanted fan for singing silly in a thousand spaceport
    bars.
If it's what we really want, we'll build a starship when
    we can;
If I could just make orbit then I'd be a wanted fan.

*Maybe we'll bill this as "unfinished" at its first appear-
ance and complete it during the book, as in "The Green
Hills of Earth." We can show verses later replaced*:

Wanted fan for mining coal and wanted fan for
    building nukes;
Wanted fan by William Proxmire and a maddened
    horde of kooks.
Washington D-C still wants me 'cause I tried to build a
    dam
If they're tearing down the cities I'll help anywhere I
    can.

At least, Jenny Trout would.

Final draft of song describes the Angels, maybe writ by
Gordon himself:

Wanted fan for building spacecraft, wanted fan for
  scooping air,
Using microwaves for power, building habitats up
  there.
Oh the glacier caught us last time; next time we'll try
  to land!
And when the ice is conquered, it'll be by wanted
  fans.
(*quasi-repeat*) And when the stars are conquered, it'll
  be by wanted fans!

THE CALIFORNIA
VOODOO GAME

DREAM PARK was complex, a mystery wrapped in a fantasy embedded in science fiction. THE BARSOOM PROJECT added complications: espionage and a retrospective murder and the terraforming of Mars. THE CALIFORNIA VOODOO GAME . . . well, we're handling it, but that's an awful lot of threads we're trying to weave together. We're running the Game through an abandoned building the size of a small city, as five teams of Gamers compete against each other in a fantasy domain based on voodoo as it might have evolved through centuries of the California environment.

And I worked in a formal puzzle, a Martin Gardner style puzzle, the only such that I've ever invented.

"Look," Acacia said. "We've accumulated 12,300 points. If we can get to 13,000, we can get a tunnel through the mirrors. But we have to risk the same number of points to get it, and on a level four puzzle."

"What categories are left?"

She tapped out a request, and categories began to appear:

        1. Historical Trivia
        2. Famous Battles

   3. Killer Konundrums
   4. Minor Masters.

Corby's rather protruding eyes studied them. Finally he said: "I fear history was always my weakest subject."

"I might be able to handle that—"

"Not at level four. They'll pull out some fourth-century Mesopotamian bullshit, trust me. Minor Masters is probably third-rate composers, painters or actors of the eighteenth century. At fourth level their names won't even be in the Britannica. I like Killer Konundrums."

She rubbed his shoulder affectionately. "I'm gonna trust you."

"With a face like mine, who can blame you?"

It was a face, Acacia decided, that only a mother or a desperate Loremaster could love.

She made her choice. The screen blanked, then cleared. A cool synthesized voice spoke while words crawled across the screen.

"*A hunter leaves home one morning. He walks a mile south and finds nothing. He walks a mile west, sees a bird, runs it down and spears it for his supper. He walks a mile north and is home again. Tell me: what probable color is the bird, and why?*"

Acacia stared, perplexity creasing her lovely face. "I've heard that one," she said. "It's too easy. The bear is white."

"Bird, not bear. So the answer can't be, 'It's white, it's a polar bear, he's at the North Pole.' So."

The maze around them began to throb, and smoke began to pour from beneath the nearest sliding panel.

Captain Cipher's eyes were glazed; his jaw hung slack. He said, "*Spears* it. Runs it down and spears it. That takes . . ."

"Can you solve it?" They could take their loss and scamper, or try to answer the question. Every second cost them another five points.

"I've got half of it already. The bird . . ."

Acacia spun, deciding to let him work. She raised her sword high, set her back against the Captain's and waited, ready for danger.

The mirror behind Captain Cipher flamed red. A mouth had appeared in it now, glowing brightly, a vast, grinning diamond-shape, chock-a-block with needle teeth. Fire blazed within. Laughter rang in her ears.

The demon of the maze. This was the final trump—if Captain Cipher failed, all of their accumulated points might vanish. If he succeeded but she was killed by the materializing demon, the Troglodykes would hunt Cipher down and kill him.

"Have you got an answer?" she hissed.

"Never published. Brand new puzzle. Well—"

And the demon leapt.

Panthesilea screamed her battle cry, and—

The demon froze in mid-leap. Captain Cipher had begun to answer the question. Mutilations were temporarily suspended.

She peered anxiously over Cipher's shoulders.

"Black and White. Penguin," he typed.

The face of the demon appeared on the screen, politely inquisitive. "Why?" he/she/it asked sonorously.

Cipher looked around. "The camp is one plus one over two Pi times N miles north of the South Pole."

Acacia stared. "What?"

"The hunter runs it down, yes? The bird's *flightless*. Do penguins ring a bell? Find the tuxedoed darlings near the *South* Pole." He was typing furiously:

"*1 + ½Pi (N) miles north of the South Pole (N a positive integer.)*"

"Just so the demon knows I mean business," he said arrogantly. "Now, Hunter set his tent just north of the South Pole, right? He walks a mile south, toward the pole, then *circles* the pole. That takes him 'a mile west,' see? If he's closer yet, he can circle the pole two or three or four times. Then he goes a mile north, and he's back at base camp. Only place he can do that is at the South Pole.''

She felt dazed. Captain Cipher waited coolly, matching gazes with the ruby-flame apparition dancing in the glass before him.

''Dinner,'' it said, ''is served.'' Its mouth opened wider, wider. A tunnel to the beyond.

Panthesilea whispered ''Stay here,'' and stepped through the portal.

THE GHOST SHIPS

The Ghost Ships have been hanging around in my head for many years. They're a life form. Think of a ghost ship as a pattern of shock waves in the interstellar medium: a Bussard ramjet with no ship in the middle. Primitive forms may have been born in the shock waves of a supernova explosion. That would have given them their initial velocity too. (Bussard ramjets theoretically can't work below 1000 kilometers/second.)

Okay, I *know* where there was a supernova, a billion years ago.

And I know how ghost ships mate. (I talked this over with Jack Cohen, who knows more about fertility than anyone else on Earth.)

And what if ghost ships come home to mate? The Smoke Ring could be in for a hell of a shock. And Sharls Davis Kendy won't like it either.

The peculiar conditions of the Smoke Ring—microgravity and powerful tides and winds—require new techniques. Robert W. Davis of Millburn, New

Jersey, wrote me a letter describing technology I'd never touched. I've made good use of his suggestions involving sails and kites.

And I'd love to give you an excerpt, but we learned better while working on N-SPACE. *There's no way to partially describe the Smoke Ring.*

DESTINY'S ROAD

I've described this novel before, and everybody in the business goes, "Yeah!" It's a wonderful idea, and a very simple one. Nobody seems to doubt I can make it work, except me.

But I need several months of sensory deprivation, and I don't see a way to get it. I've got to get inside a man's head. I've contracted to tell his life story.

Spiral City grew up around the place where two landers came down. Then one fusion-powered lander rose on its ground-effect skirt, described an expanding spiral, then went off to explore . . . leaving a trail of molten rock behind it all the way. It never came back.

Families have followed the lava road. Other communities grew up, and trading caravans return from time to time. There's the mystery of what happened to *Cavorite*'s crew.

At one time this was the only form for a novel. But I've never tried anything like it before.

Wish me luck.

LETTER

Ralph Vicinanza Ltd.
111 Eighth Avenue #1501
New York, N.Y. 10011

Dear Ralph,

I got a phone call from the Soviet Union, Tuesday evening. What the voice wanted was . . . well, something from another author, until the guy looked at his notes to see who he'd phoned. The connection faded in and out. I sensed some urgency (his and his translator's, not mine). He's offering rubles, wants to publish certain books. Any proper names were sure to get scrambled, and . . . he wanted my power of attorney. That sounded like something not to pass out like peanuts at a party.

So I said I couldn't understand, suggested hard copy, and presently hung up.

This arrived Tuesday.

I had all Wednesday to phone you. I forgot. Now it's Thanksgiving; you'll be out of your office. So I'll do this by mail, *and* phone as soon as I can.

What do I do next? **Over to you, Ralph.**

Best wishes,
Larry Niven

FROM: U.S.S.R. SUVG
TO: NIVEN
POWER ATTORNEY STATEMENT TO IGOR
TOLOCONNICOV BORIS ZAVGORODNY
WITH YOUR APPROVAL CLAUSE ON DEALS

WE CONCLUDE PERMISSION IN LETTER
FOR ONETIME APPEARANCE PROTECTOR
RINGLORLD RINGWORLD INGENEERS
MIRIMUM 35000 RUBLES
VOLGOGRAD 400026